THE LOST CONSTITUTION

The

LOST

CONSTITUTION

WILLIAM MARTIN

A TOM DOHERTY ASSOCIATES BOOK

New York

THE LOST CONSTITUTION

Copyright © 2007 by William Martin

This book is printed on acid-free paper.

Book design by Mary A. Wirth

A Forge Book
Published by Tom Doherty Associates, LLC
175 Fifth Avenue
New York, NY 10010

www.tor-forge.com

Forge® is a registered trademark of Tom Doherty Associates, LLC.

Library of Congress Cataloging-in-Publication Data

Martin, William, 1950–
    The lost constitution / William Martin.
        p. cm.
    "A Tom Doherty Associates Book."
    ISBN-13: 978-0-7653-1538-0
    ISBN-10: 0-7653-1538-6
    1. United States. Constitution—Fiction. 2. United States. Constitution. 1st-10th
Amendments—Fiction. 3. United States—History—Confederation, 1783–1789—Fiction. I.
Title
PS3563.A7297L67   2007
813'.54—dc22

                                                                        2006102850

First Edition: May 2007

Printed in the United States of America

0 9 8 7 6 5 4 3 2 1

For
Louise
and
Kitty,
two wonderful mothers

ACKNOWLEDGMENTS

In a scene early in this novel, Peter Fallon reads the acknowledgments in a book called *The Magnificent Dreamers*. He skims through the names and thinks, "Requisite stuff, polite and thankful."

Well, I hope my acknowledgments have more impact, because they are certainly more than "requisite." Polite? At the very least. Thankful? Absolutely. Throw in appreciative, grateful, indebted, too.

Writing any book is a journey, especially one that spans two hundred and twenty years and touches on the history of all six New England states. If not for the people willing to help along the way, the going would be very lonely. Thanks to all of them.

Start with Peter Drummey, librarian of the Massachusetts Historical Society, whose fictional counterpart in *The Lost Constitution* has "a photographic memory for all the manuscripts, books, and artifacts in the collection, no mean talent at a place that had been gathering historical treasures since the end of the Revolution." It's true of Peter, too. He is a friend to scholars, researchers, historians, and at least one New England novelist. I decided to write this book following an afternoon spent examining one of the society's most treasured documents and discussing it with Peter Drummey.

Others have provided everything from moral support to specific technical information: Jonathan Chu, Thomas Cook, Lou Gorman, Helen Gow, Jeffrey Hollis, Christopher Keane, William Key, William Kuntz, Stephen Martell, Wendell Minor, Ann Rauscher, Martin Weinkle, Robert and Joan Wilson, Sue Zacharias.

And if writing one of these books is a journey, getting there is half the fun, thanks to the librarians, docents, and park rangers who keep history alive across New England.

In Vermont: at the St. Albans Historical Museum.

In New Hampshire: at the American Independence Museum in Exeter; on trails and at shelters maintained by the Appalachian Mountain Club; at natural and historical sites across the White Mountain National Forest, Franconia Notch State Park, and Crawford Notch State Park; at the Mount Washington Hotel, where a bygone era lives on.

In Maine: at the Joshua Lawrence Chamberlain House in Brunswick; at the Maine Historical Society in Portland; at the Portland Observatory; at the Museum at Portland Head Light.

In Massachusetts: at the Charles River Museum of Industry in Waltham; at Fenway Park; at the Lowell National Historical Park and Boott Cotton Mills Museum; at the Quabbin Reservoir; at the Springfield Armory National Historic Site; at River Bend Farm and other sites up and down the Blackstone River Valley National Heritage Corridor, which also rolls south into Rhode Island.

In Rhode Island: at the Slater Mill and Museum in Pawtucket; at the Museum of Newport History; and at the Preservation Society of Newport County, which maintains the mansions.

In Connecticut: at the Mystic Seaport in Mystic; at the Mark Twain House in Hartford; at various sites across the Litchfield Hills.

Beyond New England: at the Independence National Historic Park in Philadelphia, Pennsylvania, and the Fredericksburg Battlefield Park in Fredericksburg, Virginia.

As always, thanks to my agent and friend, Robert Gottlieb, who has represented me for over twenty years; to Bob Gleason, my editor at Forge, and his assistant, Eric Raab; and of course to my wife and family, who are ready to offer insights, opinions, and in the case of this book, companionship on the New England hiking trails that led to the vistas that inspired much of this book.

WILLIAM MARTIN
December 2006

THE LOST CONSTITUTION

PROLOGUE

᠙ "I'M A GOOD AMERICAN."

"Sure you are." Peter Fallon studied the man on the other side of the bulletproof glass.

"Bein' in here is just the cost of doin' business."

In here was the Massachusetts Correctional Institution at Cedar Junction, formerly known as Walpole State Prison, home to the most felonious citizens in the Commonwealth, or at least the ones who'd been caught.

"Why did you want to see me?" Peter Fallon didn't like being *in here* any more than the prisoners did.

"Like I say, I'm a good American, and I don't hold a grudge."

"I appreciate that." Peter also appreciated that they were separated by that glass and talking on telephones.

Bingo had once been the toughest troublemaker in South Boston. If you wanted to fence stolen property, steal the property to fence, or steal a fence, you saw Bingo. If you wanted to sell controlled substances, from absinthe to OxyContin, you asked Bingo. If you wanted to buy a weapon without a background check, forge a driver's license, steal Social Security numbers, or do anything else to make money outside the law, you had to tell Bingo.

People said that even *in here*, Bingo was calling the shots on the street.

Peter Fallon was not so sure. Life on the street followed the laws of physics, starting with the one about nature abhorring a vacuum. So some other thug had probably taken over. Besides, Bingo was in his sixties now, once a threatening man who never needed to threaten, always a small man who never seemed small . . . until they took away his scally cap and cigarettes and gave him a prison suit.

"Don't get me wrong," Bingo said, "I thought about sendin' you some payback. Imagine if the sprinklers went off in that fancy bookshop of yours."

"You're not in here because of me," answered Peter Fallon. "You're in here because you killed two people . . . at least."

"Shit happens."

"So . . . why am *I* here?"

Bingo looked to his right and his left: a black man in his fifties, a young Hispanic, both talking on telephones to women on Peter's side of the glass. Bingo turned back to Peter. "What I have is an address."

"Address?"

"Two fourteen Boston Road."

"Off Columbia Road?"

"Right. Dunkin' Donuts at one end, Dunkin' Donuts at the other, body shops, some nice three-deckers, a few dumps . . . If you keep goin', you go into Southie."

"What's there?"

Bingo's eyes shifted again. "Guns."

"Guns?"

"Automatic weapons. Uzis, M-16s. AK clones."

"What does that have to do with me? If it's antique guns, I'm interested. But if somebody's running guns and you're mad because you're not in on it—"

"Just shut the fuck up and listen."

And for the first time, Peter Fallon saw something other than cold confidence in the eyes of Bingo Keegan.

"I'm a tough guy," said Bingo, "but there's guys in here who'd slice me open like a fuckin' haddock for what I'm gonna tell you."

"So why tell me?"

"Because, like I say, I'm a good American. Anyone sees me talkin' to you, they'll think I'm spillin' the beans about stolen art or somethin'. Nobody in here gives a shit about that."

"So . . . I should pretend you're telling me who robbed the Gardner Museum twenty years ago?"

"Sure. Most people think I did it anyway." Bingo leaned closer to the glass. "Now, there's two kinds of Muslims, right?"

Peter shrugged.

"There's the good ones and the bad ones."

"I suppose."

"The good ones, believe it or not, are the Niggers. The Black Muslims. They tell their people to get off welfare and stay in their own neighborhoods and keep the hell out of Southie."

Peter didn't say anything. He knew this was not a debate.

"The bad Muslims," Bingo went on, "are the ones who fly planes into buildings and kill thousands of Americans."

Peter nodded.

"Well, one of the good ones in here says that his boys on the outside don't like what's been happenin' in their neighborhood."

"How so?"

"There's this florist, see. Has a storefront in Upham's Corner. Name is Vartaby. Mo Vartaby."

"Black?"

"No. A fuckin' Syrian or somethin'. Come to this country about six years ago. Starts a florist business. Everybody likes him. But he goes to this house, this one crummy three-decker in Dorchester, every single day."

"So?"

"All he delivers are roses . . . boxed fuckin' roses."

"So somebody loves somebody in a crummy three-decker. So what?"

"The boxes. That's what. Long and skinny." Bingo brought his hand to his mouth and his fingers played against his lips, as if he would have loved a cigarette, but no smoking at Cedar Junction.

"Am I supposed to think there are guns in the boxes?" asked Peter.

"Start by thinkin' about this florist's first name. *Mo*. Not Larry. Not Curly. *Mo*."

"*Mo* as in *Mohammed*?"

"As in might as well be A-hab the fuckin' A-rab, for Chrissakes."

"And you think he's bringing guns to that apartment? Why?"

"I don't know, but that's the word on the street, and the word's usually good. So maybe the FBI should know. And you know people. Right?"

"Let me get this straight." Peter leaned closer to the glass. "A florist named Mohammed delivers long boxes in Dorchester, and you want me to call the FBI?"

"Two fourteen Boston Road." Bingo hung up and left.

PETER FALLON CONSIDERED himself a good American, too. And he had a client, a retired FBI agent who collected first editions of Ian Fleming. . . .

But maybe a drive to Dorchester first.

He waited until ten thirty at night, when the traffic would be light.

Boston was having its early June heat wave, so he was happy to get in the BMW, open the moonroof, and cruise.

This was his town. He had grown up in Southie. He had gone to B.C. High and Harvard. He was a respected dealer in rare books and documents, a board member of three museums, a quarter owner of Red Sox season tickets, and like most Bostonians, a born skeptic. So he had to see for himself just how crummy this three-decker really was.

He picked up Mass Ave in the Back Bay, went past Symphony Hall, through Roxbury, down to Columbia Road. It was like a ride from the top of Boston's real estate ladder to the bottom, though real estate prices were so crazy that the bottom here was higher than the top in most towns.

At Columbia, he took a left onto Boston Road.

The sodium vapor streetlamps turned everything to hideous orange daylight, so it was easy to see that the mechanic shops and other businesses on the left side of the street were all closed, and strange to see the Clapp house, one of the oldest houses in Boston, sitting on a grassy knoll, just a dark shadow looking out at all the televisions flickering in the three-deckers across the street.

Three-deckers had once been called "Boston weeds" because so many had popped up in the early 1900s. Wood-frame structures with balconies, bay windows, three floors for three families, built at that moment when quality material, cheap skilled labor, and mass construction all intersected. They had once been called castles for the common man. Today, the nice ones were called Boston treasures.

Number 214 was not one of them. The balcony was drooping. The shingles were curling. The windows were dark.

Peter slowed but did not stop.

Across the street, a mongrel dog paced behind the fence of an auto body shop. Two battered cars sat in the lot. Peter thought he noticed someone sitting in one of them. *Strange.*

But there was no sign of life in the three-decker, just an old Plymouth minivan parked outside.

So Peter kept going down to the intersection, pulled into a Dunkin' Donuts, and bought half a dozen jelly crullers and raised glazed.

Then he cruised back up the street. Now there was a light on in the cellar. And the dog across the street was still pacing. And it sure looked like someone was sitting in that trashed car.

Peter decided to keep driving, back to Columbia Road and on to Upham's Corner.

This had once been an Irish neighborhood, dominated by St. Kevin's Parish and St. Margaret's Hospital. Now the hospital was closed and St. Kevin's served a population that was lowercase "catholic" as well as upper.

Peter glanced into the storefronts—a local bank, Sanchez Puerto

Rican grocery, a Vietnamese nail salon, a beauty shop with the sign in the window—"Beaded corn rows $5 each." And *there*—Vartaby's Flowers.

Peter slowed a bit and got a few horn blasts. Columbia Road was four lanes, divided, and people drove fast.

He couldn't tell much from a glance into the shop, except that there were lights on in the back room. At eleven o'clock? Most florists went to bed before nine, so they could get to the Flower Exchange by five in the morning. Was Mo Vartaby up late doing his books?

Then another question dawned on Peter Fallon. *What in hell was* he *doing here?* Sure, he was a treasure hunter, and he did well at it, because he was willing to get himself into trouble. He'd been chased, shot at, and forced to fight for his life more than once. And he didn't like any of it.

So he decided to go home and do what Bingo had suggested: call the FBI.

BUT THE FBI called him first. Or called *on* him.

They were waiting when he arrived at his office the next day.

Two men with short haircuts and government-issue gray suits were standing over his secretary's desk. One of them was asking questions. The other was reading the titles of the rare books in the locked cases.

"Morning, boss," said Bernice. "These gents say they're from the FBI."

As the agents turned, Bernice made a face at Peter. *What in hell is going on?*

She was in her sixties, wore her bleached hair in a beehive that was big in the sixties, and had worked for the Fallon family since the sixties. Her skirt did nothing to flatter her thighs, her pantyhose rubbed like fine-grit sandpaper when she walked, and her accent and attitude were South Boston smart-ass, not Newbury Street chic. But she could run an office, and she carried a Beretta in her purse. She was also Peter's aunt.

He handed her the bag of Dunkin' Donuts and told her to get three cups of coffee. Then he invited Agents George Hause and Will Luzier into his office.

Fallon Antiquaria occupied an L-shaped space on the third floor of an old Boston bowfront, above a gallery that was above a restaurant. The display room, with all the fine volumes in all the locked cases, was in the long section of the L. Peter's office was where the bowfront bowed out.

"So"—Peter seized the initiative—"was it one of your guys sitting in the car with the stove-in front end last night?"

The agents looked at each other. Hause wore glasses and seemed to be in charge. Luzier was taller and took notes.

Hause said, "Why were you casing Boston Street and Vartaby's Flowers last night?"

"I was following a lead."

"A lead?" asked Luzier. "On what? A rare book?"

"I know it sounds crazy. A lead an inmate down at Cedar Junction gave me."

"Inmate?" said Hause, his face expressionless.

And Peter told them everything that Bingo Keegan had told him. Then he described every detail of his trip to Dorchester.

When he was done, Agent Hause said, "Why should we believe you?"

"Because I'm a good American." Peter could think of no other reason, and he liked the sound of that one.

"A good American," said Luzier, "even though you sell Arab books in here?"

"Arab books?" said Peter.

"In the display case. Something by someone called"—Luzier looked in his notebook—"Omar Khayyam."

"*The Rubaiyat of Omar Khayyam?*" Fallon laughed. "It's one of the classics of world literature."

Hause gave his partner a roll of the eyes; then he asked Fallon, "Where did Keegan get his information?"

"He said it was 'word on the street,'" answered Peter.

"Word on the street?" Luzier looked at Hause. "If convicts are hearing about this, and they're telling booksellers, the subjects may know that the secret is out. They may decide to speed things up. Or go underground."

"We should move." Hause tapped a finger against his lip. "This will take an enormous amount of coordination in a very short time."

In the outer office, Bernice picked up the telephone.

Luzier pointed a finger at her. "No calls."

"No calls?" she said. "Why?"

"Never mind why. Just hang up the phone and . . . read a book."

Peter made a small gesture with his hand, as if to tell her it was all right. But he knew now that it wasn't.

Agent Hause took out his cell phone, placed a call, spoke softly.

Meanwhile, Luzier said to Peter Fallon, "Who else knows about this?"

"No one."

"Not even your wife?"

"I'm not married."

"Boyfriend?" Luzier raised an eyebrow and looked around again at the books.

"Girlfriend," said Peter. "She's traveling."

Hause closed his phone and said, "Mr. Fallon, I'm afraid we're going to have to ask you to come with us."

"Come with you? Why?"

"You've stumbled into something. You may have alerted the target in Boston. We have to take him down today. And other teams need to be alerted in other cities. The best way to be sure that you don't reveal anything else, even inadvertently, is for you to . . . ah . . . spend the day with us."

BY EVENING, IT was over, and Peter Fallon was back in his condo on Marlborough Street, sitting slack-jawed before the television, just like everyone else in America.

On the local station, a tape rolled over and over: an FBI SWAT team attacking a house on Boston Road with tear gas, which was answered with semi-automatic weapons fire from every window. A rocket-propelled grenade hit a police car. *Boom.*

Click. Fox News. The anchorman was saying, "Federal and state agencies across the country have averted an Al Qaeda massacre planned for the Fourth of July. We now know that their targets were fireworks celebrations in the East, crowded airport ticket lines in the Midwest, and beaches in California."

Click. CNN: Another anchor speaking over footage of agents entering a storefront. "Before the action in Boston began, agents were moving on this grocery in Brooklyn, believed to be the nerve center of the plan."

Click. MSNBC: A reporter in front of the White House, saying that the FBI, "working on tips from within the American Muslim community, had been watching several locations across the country, preparing to interdict while observing Al Qaeda cells, hoping to learn as much as they could before the Fourth of July. However, an informant today made it plain to authorities in Boston that the cat was out of the bag."

That informant, Peter knew, was himself. He hoped that was all the identification he would ever receive.

Click. ANN, the American News Network: the commissioner of the Los Angeles Police Department holding up an AR-15. "These weapons were bought legally over the last three months across the United States, then moved surreptitiously to central locations by couriers posing as florists, delivery men, even postal workers." A reporter asked why they would not have kept the weapons dispersed until the day of attack. An FBI representative leaned into the microphone: "As with most Al Qaeda strikes, their operatives are kept in the dark until the last moment to protect the mission. Spreading the guns around would have spread the plan."

In a story this big, everyone had plenty of spectacular footage—the fire-fight in Boston; an attack on a Chicago warehouse; an explosion at a U-Haul storage facility in South Central Los Angeles; Middle Eastern men doing the perp walk in Brooklyn, in Boston, in half a dozen other cities.

And in a story this big, everyone had an opinion. So at eight o'clock, the heads started talking and the cable cacophony began to rise. What had happened? Who was to blame? What could be done now to protect Americans?

On Fox, analysts praised the actions of the FBI and called for more funding for police agencies. On MSNBC, a Republican member of the Senate Intelligence Committee defended the Patriot Act while a Democrat argued that the Patriot Act had nothing to do with good police work.

And on ANN, the American News Network, Congresswoman Harriet Holden appeared on *Rapid Fire* with host Harry Hawkins, looked straight at the camera, and said, "I think that, in light of the horror that has been averted, it's time to reconsider our gun laws. The Founding Fathers never imagined the kind of killing power that anyone—honest American or murderous terrorist—can now hold in his hands. Tomorrow, I will begin the legislative process that I hope will lead to the repeal of the Second Amendment."

"The Right to Keep and Bear Arms?" said Hawkins. "You can't be serious."

"You can't be serious," whispered Peter Fallon to himself.

"I am deadly serious," said the congresswoman. "If not for good law enforcement and the good consciences of American Muslims, we would be mourning thousands of our fellow citizens this July. And the massacre would have been perpetrated by weapons bought as legally and in some cases as easily as you or I would buy a dozen roses."

Peter Fallon clicked off the television. He had voted for Harriet Holden. She was his congresswoman. And she was setting off on a journey that, the day before, would have made Don Quixote look like a coldhearted realist.

But now . . . he imagined editorial writers all over America rushing to their keyboards, writing pieces proclaiming that Harriet Holden was bringing Americans to their senses, while as many radio talk hosts were clearing their throats, getting ready to go after one more liberal attack on our freedoms.

Whether Harriet Holden was right or wrong, right or left, the noise had only just begun, because firearms had been part of the American story since the beginning. . . .

ONE

August 1786

∞ "Where's your musket, Will?"

"In the house."

"It should be in your hand."

"But it's the sheriff and his men comin' out of those woods."

"It's an unjust government comin' to take your rights. Go get your musket."

Will Pike stood his ground instead. He studied the woods. He glanced up at a hawk making perfect circles in a perfect blue sky.

And for a moment, he was a boy again, daydreaming that he could see what the hawk saw: the mountains of New Hampshire and Vermont to the north; the flatlands of Connecticut and Rhode Island spreading south; the steeples of Boston, tiny on the eastern horizon, and beyond them, the sharp-etched green islands in the Gulf of Maine.

Then the hawk seemed to stop in midair. Then it swooped, pouncing in a burst of feathers and fur on some hapless field mouse working its way home.

Will wiped his palms on his leather jerkin. He was as rawboned as any seventeen-year-old, but his eyes were already set in the permanent squint of one who studied the world quietly, who thought hard before he spoke and even harder before he acted.

His brother, North, was six years older and, it seemed, twice as big, over six feet tall, over two hundred pounds, big face scarred from fights, big hands scarred from fishhooks, big shoulders callused from the harness he wore when he plowed his father's fields.

North had marched with Washington's army. He had fished on the Grand Banks. He had cut trees in the great woods. Will had not seen much more of the world than the circle of earth beneath the circle of sky drawn by that hawk.

They stood that morning on the sloping ground in front of their father's little house. Rock walls ran everywhere, segmenting the small farm into smaller fields, each of which looked as if it had been sewn with rocks in the hope of growing more rocks.

"Where'd Pa go?" North kept his eyes on the men riding up the road.

"Inside," said Will.

"Went to get his musket, I hope."

Will glanced toward the house. He could not believe that his father was leaving them to face this alone.

The sheriff reined his horse and looked down at North. "Well . . . the prodigal brother. When did you get back?"

"When I heard you was plannin' to arrest my Pa." North held his musket at his hip. "I'm loaded with ball and buck, Chauncey. I'll take down the lot of you with one shot."

Will wanted to slip into the house and coax his father out, but he feared that if he moved, North would start shooting. So he stayed put and hoped that no one would see his knees shaking.

"Now, boys . . ." Sheriff Chauncey Yates had a big belly and a broad face better suited to grins and good spirits than the scowl he wore. "The court says your father's to spend six months in the Hampshire County House of Correction for nonpayment of debts to Mr. Nathan Liggett of Springfield."

"Damn the courts," said North. "And damn Nathan Liggett. Damn you, too, Sheriff. And while we're doin' our damnin', damn the damn state for taxin' us at thirty damn percent, so we don't have the money to pay any other damn bills."

"It's happenin' to farmers all over," said the sheriff. "The state has to tax property to pay war debts. And farmers has more *real* property than most."

"But farmers don't have hard coin," said Will, "and the state won't take barter."

"Nor merchants neither," added North.

"Because merchants is squeezed by Boston creditors," said the sheriff, "and *they're* squeezed by European suppliers."

"So men like our Pa get squeezed by lawyers," said North.

"Yup." The sheriff swung a leg and dismounted. "Makes you wonder why we fought the damn Revolution in the first place."

North gave the sheriff a grin. "Time for another uprisin', I'd say."

"I have a court order"—the sheriff patted his pocket—"all fit and proper-like. It's my job to execute it."

"I'll die first." North raised his musket. "And you before me."

With a sudden clattering of wood, leather, and metal, every deputy leveled a musket at the Pikes. And for a moment, there was quiet.

The breeze rustled in the trees. A horse snorted. Another pawed the ground.

Then North said, "Seems we has a stand-off."

And from the house came a voice: "There'll be no stand-off. You Pike boys stand *down*. Nobody'll do any dyin' on my account."

Will Pike turned to see his father in the doorway, and after relief poured over him, he filled with a son's pride.

George North Pike had chosen to dress that day not in the threadbare smallclothes of a bankrupt farmer but in the uniform of a captain in the Massachusetts Artillery. It did not fit him so well as it had when the war ended, for an ague of the stomach had taken twenty pounds off his frame. But the uniform had its effect. No deputy would point a weapon at the blue-and-buff.

The elder Pike strode out of the house, as if determined to show his best face. He stopped beside his sons and said, "Sheriff, my boys think we've traded bad masters in Britain for worse masters in Boston."

"Damn right," said North, the only man still pointing a musket at anyone.

"But," said George North Pike, "I'll not rebel against the country I fought for."

He lifted the musket from North's hands, blew into the pan, and sent up a little cloud of priming powder. He tossed the gun back to his son.

Then he said, "My boys been raised right, Chauncey. They know that this is a government of laws, and laws are made by men, and men might not always be what God intended them to be, but men like you and me, we're decent, just the same."

"I appreciate the sentiment, Captain," said Chauncey Yates. "Now will you mount the horse we brought for you?"

George North Pike tugged at his waistcoat and looked at his sons. "Boys, the livestock been sold off, but we still have our land. So tend to it while I'm gone."

"We'll go with you," said North.

"We'll help you get settled," added Will.

"No." Their father mounted the horse. "I'll not have you see me in stripes just yet. Let me try them on first."

And the Pike brothers watched their father ride away at the head of that little group, as though he were their leader rather than their prisoner.

Then North spat and said, "Time for an uprisin'."

THERE WAS NOT much to the town of Pelham. On the west were rocky farms, a tavern, a Congregational meetinghouse at the crossroads. Then the east-west road dipped down to a plank bridge that crossed the Swift River, a narrow stream that lived up to its name even in the driest summers. Just beyond, the road rose toward more rocky farms. But right at the bridge was Conkey's Tavern.

That was where the Pike brothers headed come sundown.

"A man shouldn't go to bed dry," said North, "especially on a day like this. So let's wet our throats and dream of wet quims, which be a bit scarce hereabouts."

"Is that why you went wanderin' after the war?" asked Will. "For the quims?"

"Once you've marched with the Continental Army, coaxin' corn out of a rocky hillside don't hold much attraction. And once you've sampled a few of the ladies who follow an army, coaxin' a kiss from a neighbor girl ain't quite enough to slake your thirst for somethin' . . . wet and juicy."

Will thought every night about things wet and juicy, and he envied his brother's knowledge. He had never yet inspired any of the neighbor girls to kiss him, not that there were many.

And for certain there were none at the tavern, which was full of loud voices and strong opinions and the strong smells of men who spent their days sweating hard under a hot sun. But when the Pikes entered, it was as if the stifling air were blown off by a wind, cold and ominous.

One by one, then group by group, men fell silent and turned. None had quarrel with the Pikes. But the Pikes reminded them of what they all faced—heavy taxes, a Boston government more responsive to the needs of merchants than of self-sufficient farmers, and financial ruin.

When the room was dead quiet and all eyes were on the Pikes, North announced, "Time for an uprisin', boys."

In an instant, they were crowding around, offering condolences and congratulations. Word of George North Pike's pride, even in disgrace, had already spread.

Daniel Shays, who farmed a plot as bad as the Pikes', swept two mugs of flip from the bar and gave one to each of them. "Your pa's a good man."

"A good man indeed," said Doc Hines. He set the broken bones of Pelham and, as Town Moderator, set the political discussion as well.

North looked around and asked, "So who's to lead the uprisin'? You, Dan'l?"

"Not me." Shays shook his head.

"We've asked him," said Doc Hines "He's been to debtor's court himself, so he knows how humiliatin' it is. And he went from private to captain in Washington's army, so he knows how to lead—"

"I'll back no rebellion till the state answers our petition," said Shays.

He had always reminded Will of a bull—big-headed, brawny through the chest, with eyes that bespoke more stubbornness than brains. But if Daniel Shays kept to his present line of talk, Will would have to raise his opinion.

Doc Hines said, "We're just back from the convention in Hatfield."

"Aye," added Shays. "Farmers from across the county. Wrote a petition to Boston. Told 'em we need paper money, debt relief, tax relief, and the closin' of the Courts of Common pleas, so we can get out from under the lawyers—"

"You sound like my brother," said North. "He wants to *be* one of them lawyers."

Shays gave Will the once-over. "I'd say your brother's a smart boy, then."

"I'd say this—" North drained his mug and slammed it on the bar. "—we tell the legislature we want no taxation without representation. Then we have an uprisin'."

And that was what they did.

IN THE SMALL hours of August 29, the Pikes rose in the bedroom under the eaves in their father's home, dressed, and headed down the hill.

At the meetinghouse, they joined with twenty or thirty more who had gathered under sputtering torches and lanterns.

"Fine day for an uprisin'," North announced when he spied Daniel Shays.

"State rejects our petition," said Shays, "we need to make 'em listen."

With their torches and lanterns bobbing above them, they headed out the west road toward the Connecticut River. Some carried muskets, others had clubs or axes, and a few, like Daniel Shays and Will Pike, carried nothing at all.

Will had told his brother that he disapproved of mob action, but North had insisted he march, because a boy who dreamed of becoming a barrister should see what happened when lawyers and judges denied the people their rights.

By dawn, they had reached the Connecticut and joined other bands from other towns. A great coming together it was, of angry farmers crossing fields and forests to march with that column from Pelham and protest the injustices heaped upon them since the end of the Revolution.

At full daylight, they took formation behind fifes and drums, and began to parade eight abreast, like a Continental regiment, with muskets in the van, clubs and shovels in support, unarmed men bringing up the rear.

Will admitted that there was something stirring in the sound of the fifes trilling out one marching tune after another—"Yankee Doodle," "Banish Misfortune," "The Road to Boston." He could feel the drums beating in his belly, urging him on. And for a moment, he wished that he had brought his own musket after all.

The music must have moved Daniel Shays, too, because he snatched a post from a split-rail fence, shouldered it, and joined the men marching behind the muskets.

Will stayed at the rear and told himself that he was stronger than the momentary power of the music. A young man who hoped to become an officer of the Massachusetts court should not be seen laying siege to a Massachusetts courthouse.

The farmers had determined to close every courthouse in the state, so that no debt cases would be heard anywhere and no farmer could face foreclosure because he did not have the money to pay his taxes and his bills both.

When three justices arrived in Northampton to convene the Court of Common Pleas for Hampshire County, they were met by fifteen hundred men.

Will heard his brother say to Doc Hines, "Looks like the odds don't favor the justices today, but I'd say they favor justice."

And the justices agreed, at least in part, because they continued all cases and galloped back to Boston as fast as their mounts would carry them.

His brother's uprising, thought Will, had begun.

BUT WILL DID not march home with the Pelhamites. He might not have marched at all had they not been going to Northampton, because the House of Correction was there, too. It sat on a rise looking across the valley toward old Mount Tom.

Will took some comfort in that, for a well-sited jail might also be well-kept. But as he drew closer, the wind shifted, and the smell that rose off the roof and wafted from the windows was worse than a dungpile in July.

He should not have been surprised. The jails were packed in those days of foreclosure and debt crisis. So many farmers had been imprisoned at the behest of creditors who believed that they still could pay, or at the whim of a state that sought to make an example of them, that the practice of separating debtors from criminals had been suspended.

As for the man brought out to see his son, he looked as if he had aged a year in a fortnight. His hair hung around his face and snagged in the stubble on his chin. And his pallor was more than the prisoner's shadow. Sickness and despair had turned him as gray as gravel.

"Don't worry, lad." George North Pike sat at a rough table, under the eye of the jailkeeper. "'Tis the thin gruel we get thrice a day that has me lookin' like an old hag."

"But Pa, you've lost another twenty pounds."

"Don't worry," he said again, then asked, "Where's your brother?"

"He said he couldn't stand to see you like this."

The old man nodded. "I can't stand to see myself."

Will reached into his sack and produced a loaf of bread, sausage, and three apples.

George Pike looked at the food. "Our apples?"

"Aye. One thing Nathan Liggett didn't take."

The prisoner ran his hand over the apples, as if to convince himself that they were real. Then he touched the bread, then the sausage. But he sampled nothing. "You should be sellin' them apples. Not bringin' them to me."

Will ignored that and said, "Would you like a slice of sausage?"

The answer, from a man who looked like he was starving, was a shock to his son: "No, Willie. I . . . I reckon I'm not hungry."

"Not hungry?"

George North Pike laughed. "A place like this can kill a man's appetite."

Or his spirit . . .

An hour later, Will stood to leave in the lowest spirits of his own life. But he would go with one promise. "We'll get you out of this place, Pa."

"I've labored hard all my days, son, because I believe that good things come to good men. And I give this country six years of service, but when I come home, I was loaded with class-rates and lawsuits, saw my livestock sold for half its value, had to pay when no one would pay me, got hauled off by the sheriff, and—" Whatever else he had to say, he could not go on. He simply stopped and buried his head in his hands.

Will Pike touched his father's shoulder. "We'll get you out."

"I'll serve my time. Then we'll pay our bills. That's how I'll get out."

THERE HAD TO be a better way, thought Will.

"There's better ways," said North that night at Conkey's. "Ain't that so, Dan'l?"

"Better ways. Aye." Daniel Shays took a swallow of flip.

North elbowed his brother. "Dan'l's agreed to lead us after all."

"I've set my hand to the plow." Shays sounded more resigned than committed. "Though it be hard ground. Neighbors don't make the best soldiers."

The uprising would soon be called Shays's Rebellion, but there were many leaders in many towns. And while the rebels would be called "Shaysites" by their enemies, they called themselves Regulators, after farmers in England and the American South who had taken the law into their own hands in earlier days.

That fall, they put sprigs of evergreen in their hats, like the men of the Revolution. They marched behind old soldiers like Shays. And they struck fear into the elected officials in Boston.

The governor implored the legislature to take "vigorous measures to vindicate the insulted dignity of the government." So they passed the Riot Act, calling for the Regulators to forfeit "their lands, tenements, goods, and chattels," and to be whipped and imprisoned if convicted.

But in Pelham, men took an oath: "We do each one of us acknowledge ourselves to be enlisted in Shays's Regiment of Regulators for the suppressing of tyrannical government in Massachusetts." And men took oaths in the other towns, too.

They closed the courts in Worcester, then in Taunton and Concord. When the governor sent militia to protect the court in Great Barrington, the Regulators handed out evergreen sprigs and brought the militia to their side. In Springfield, hundreds of merchants surrounded the court to protect it from the Regulators, but no one answered the jury summons, so the court did not open.

While North marched, Will stayed at home, did chores, read what law books he could find, practiced the handwriting that a good legal apprentice needed, and continued to seek a better way to free his father. When he heard that Henry Knox, his father's old commander and the Secretary of War, was visiting Springfield to investigate the uprising, Will saw his better way.

"GOIN' TO SPRINGFIELD are you?" said Shays.

"Goin' to see Henry Knox," said Will.

"You'll be goin' to the arsenal, then," said North.

"I reckon." In truth, Will did not know where in Springfield he would find Henry Knox. He supposed the arsenal would be as good a place as any.

It was early in the day, so the taproom at Conkey's was mostly empty. Sunlight slanted through the front door and the windows. Old Man Conkey was sweeping up. His wife was stirring a pot on the fire. Mugs of tea sat on the table.

North scratched at the stubble on his chin and looked at Shays. "An honest lad, bringin' a petition to Henry Knox at the Springfield arsenal . . ."

Shays looked at Will. "You could do us a service."

"Service?" said Will.

"If you get onto the grounds of the arsenal, keep your eyes open, watch the guards, where they are, when they change, what—"

"I'm goin' to help my father."

Shays leaned closer. "The day may come when the government heeds nothin' we say. Then we'll need guns, new guns, guns to arm every farmer who marches. Nothin' makes a politician concentrate better than the barrel of a gun."

"And they keep the guns in the arsenal," said North.

Will sipped his tea and said, "It's my intention to obey the law."

"Our intention, too," said North, "till we're forced to start shootin'."

Will looked from one face to the other, from those wide-apart eyes of Daniel Shays to the rock-hard gaze of his brother. This was not something he wanted. His family was in trouble enough already, but he told them he would do what he could, because they had taken a stand on principle, and his father always told him that the principles made the man.

Then he left on the family's swaybacked mare to meet Henry Knox.

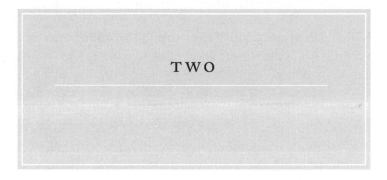

TWO

By fall, the gun debate decibels were drowning out just about every other political discussion in America.

But life went on.

For Peter Fallon that meant a cross-country drive with his son, who was entering law school at Boalt Hall, Berkeley. Peter spent three days in San Francisco, exploring the bookstores and the restaurants. Then he flew home to proof his fall catalogue.

His theme for the season was American history. Some of his offerings: a 1930s pamphlet on the life of Washington, published by an insurance company, for ten bucks; a first edition of U. S. Grant's *Personal Memoirs* for $895; a signed copy of Hawthorne's Campaign Biography of Franklin Pierce for $8,500; and a beautiful three-volume 1815 edition of Lewis and Clark's *Travels to the Source of the Missouri*, a steal at $22,500.

Soon private collectors, dealers, librarians, and museum curators would be poring over the pages, and his phone would be ringing. Peter never worried that one of his catalogues might inspire thefts, forgeries, or frivolous lawsuits. And he never imagined that something in the *Fallon Antiquaria* catalogue might lead to murder.

But on an afternoon in early October, a black Chrysler Sebring stopped in front of an old house in Millbridge, Massachusetts.

The driver watched the house for a time, then smoothed his hair, straightened his tie, and got out.

On the passenger seat was a copy of *Antiquaria*, open to page twenty-five. The item circled: "A letter from Henry Knox to Rufus King RE: William Pike of Pelham, Massachusetts."

Buster McGillis was on the telephone when his murderer came to the door.

He didn't hear the bell. After a life of working in a noisy mill, he didn't hear much of anything. After a life of breathing cigarette smoke whenever he wasn't inhaling the cotton lint floating in the mill, he didn't breathe too well either.

So he wore two hearing aids and took his oxygen through plastic tubes attached to a tank. He coughed all the time and talked too loud on the telephone.

"Yeah," he shouted into the receiver, "a professor from Dartmouth. He came right here to the house. . . . Asked all kinds of questions . . . I told him the same as I told that bookseller. I don't know anything." Buster coughed and spat into the tin can beside his recliner; then he said, "Hey, the Sox are up. . . . See you later."

Buster turned to the television: bottom of the sixth, fifth game of the American League Divisional Series, Red Sox 6, Angels 2. If the score held, there'd be another showdown with the Yankees in the play-offs. Just what every New Englander wanted, whether he lived in a seaside mansion in Maine, a dairy farm in Vermont, or here in tired old Millbridge, Massachusetts.

Buster decided to celebrate . . . with a cigarette.

People with emphysema weren't supposed to smoke. Neither were people on oxygen. But there wasn't enough life left in him to matter, and all his friends were gone, and the mill had been closed for twenty years, and he had lived long enough to see the Red Sox win a World Series already.

So . . . what the hell? He put the Lucky Strike on his lower lip, turned off the tank, scratched a match . . . and heard the pounding at the door.

Who was this, interrupting his ball game on an October afternoon?

He levered himself out of the recliner, grabbed the handle of the oxygen tank, and rolled it ahead of him. He avoided the pile of newspapers in the living room and the one in the foyer. Someday, he was going to have to recycle those. . . .

As soon as he peered through the sidelight, the guy outside straightened his tie and started chirping, "Mr. McGillis? Mr. McGillis?" as though he was afraid Buster might not open the door.

But Buster did; then he rolled his oxygen tank into the way so that the guy couldn't just step into the house. "Yeah?"

"My name is Walter Stanley."

Buster looked him over—hair carefully parted, blue blazer and red tie, big smile, cheery manner—one of those guys in his late thirties who decides to become a real estate agent after he's failed at everything else, then goes looking for old folks and talks them into selling homes they've lived in for decades. Guys like that were always knocking on Buster's door, once they knew that he lived alone in the biggest house in town, a decrepit old place with floor-to-ceiling windows and grand Greek Revival pillars, built by Buster's great-great-grandfather in the 1830s.

Then the man held out a business card. "I'm a book scout."

"A what?"

"A book scout. I look for books."

"To read?"

"To *buy*. Sometimes I buy whole libraries from estates. Sometimes I buy a few boxes from someone like you."

"Then what?" asked Buster.

"Sometimes dealers buy them for a flat fee. Sometimes I get a percentage."

Buster started to close the door. "The Red Sox are up. I got to go."

"There's money in it for you."

Buster held the door. "How much?"

Walter Stanley put his foot on the threshold. "Twenty-five cents for every book I take, hardcover or paperback."

On television, the crowd roared. Buster's eyes shifted toward the living room.

The guy said, "I can see you're a hard bargainer. Fifty cents. I'll take your books home, look them over, and any I sell, I'll share the profits."

"I don't think so." Buster tried to close the door again.

But Walter Stanley's foot was in the way. "I'd love to see the last few innings. I . . . I played in minor leagues, myself."

"You did? Where?"

"Made it to Triple A. Played half a season for Pawtucket."

"The Pawtucket Red Sox? The Pawsox?"

"I got some great stories."

So Buster let Walter Stanley, book scout and ex–minor leaguer, into the house.

But Walter Stanley was not the man's name, and he was no baseball player, and he wasn't looking for a book but a document he had reason to believe Buster knew about. He was also the last person that Buster McGillis ever saw.

The next day, Buster's friend, Morris Bindle, found him.

Buster was dead in his recliner, his oxygen tank empty, his ashtray full of cigarettes, and a rerun of the Red Sox game playing on television.

By then, the man who called himself Walter Stanley was in New Hampshire, observing the habits of a certain history professor from Dartmouth.

THE PROFESSOR'S NAME was Stuart Conrad. And he liked to imagine ice.

Even in the calm October dawn, when his breath was a wisp in the air and winter was just a shadow beyond the northern mountains, he imagined ice, because ice had shaped New England. Ice and ideas.

Professor Conrad knew more about ideas. But each morning, when he and his dog explored the world together, he thought more about ice.

The dog, a yellow Lab with a powerful head and gentle jaws, scampered out of the house ahead of him and leaped onto the backseat of the Volvo.

The professor took a sip from his coffee mug, gave the wipers a quick turn to clear the dew from the windshield, and off he went.

He drove past Fraternity Row and along the edge of the college green, where the mist hovered a few feet above the grass, and he fancied that he could see the ghost of Daniel Webster strolling down from Dartmouth Hall. He did not notice the Chrysler Sebring that slipped out of a parking spot to follow him.

He turned on Wheelock Street and headed for the Connecticut River.

Thirty thousand years earlier, thought the professor, after the mountains had risen and settled, the ice had begun to move south. After ten thousand years, it covered all of New England under a mile-thick sheet that sat for ten thousand years more. Then it began to retreat. It scraped the tops off the mountains and dropped them into the valleys. It left lonely boulders in some places, great veins of gravel in others. It retreated around hillocks of ice so dense that they did not melt for centuries more. And it scoured huge furrows that would become the riverbeds of New England.

The Connecticut was born in far northern New Hampshire, in three lakes that were born of the streams that drained the woods of western Maine. It widened quickly, marking the boundary between New Hampshire and Vermont. It bisected Massachusetts, creating two unofficial states, one that looked toward Boston, the other that paid Boston and its politicians as little mind as possible. Then it flowed through the state that took its name, laying down a rich riparian plain on its way to the sea.

In New England, only Rhode Island was not touched by its waters.

If the professor had been thinking more about the cars on the road and less about ancient ice, he might have noticed that the Sebring behind him had Rhode Island plates, and it followed him north on Interstate 91, then west a few miles on Route 4.

The dog began to shiver when they passed the plastic moose in front of the Queechee Village gift shops. He let out a whimper when they pulled into the parking lot near the bridge.

It was October, so people from all over the world were coming to see the foliage. They came in cars and SUVs and lumbering tour buses from Boston. Most of them were retirees, taking that fall trip they'd always dreamed about. And retirees got up early. But not this early.

The lot was empty, except for that black Chrysler Sebring pulling in. Its driver was a younger man, around thirty-five. He got out, turned on his digital camera, and glanced up at the hills.

Sunlight had just struck the highest branches. Over the next half hour, as the sun rose and the light descended, the golds and reds glimmering in the treetops would flow down until the whole valley burned with color. Then the tour buses would arrive.

For a man who imagined ice and valued solitude, there was no time to waste. So the professor followed the dog toward the sign: QUEECHEE GORGE FOOTPATH.

The ice had done mighty work here, opening a crevasse a mile long, a hundred and seventy feet deep, sixty feet wide. And year by year the Outaqueechee River continued the work, smoothing out little pools and wearing the rock imperceptibly away.

Whenever he descended the gorge, the professor felt as if he were slicing down into time itself. But he taught American history, so slicing into time was his business.

He had written a book, *The Magnificent Dreamers*, about the Constitutional Convention of 1787. It had made him an expert, which got him onto television whenever people argued about the Constitution. And as autumn spilled across New England, people were arguing about the Constitution more and more.

Stuart Conrad looked good on television. He had a strong jaw and a professorial brow. And he knew how to handle himself in front of the cameras. *Hardball*, *The O'Reilly Factor*, *Rapid Fire* . . . he'd done them all. He wouldn't let Chris Matthews interrupt him. He got the last word with Sean Hannity. And when Bill O'Reilly called him a pinhead, he called O'Reilly a pinhead right back, all in the best tradition of rational, cable-televised political discourse.

Thanks to television, his book was appearing on college reading lists across the country. Better yet, he was mentoring a young woman who had a scholar's brains and a showgirl's legs, while he power-tripped on weekends in the bed of a Massachusetts congresswoman. And best of all, he was close to finding the document that some would call the Holy Grail of American history.

But he did not think long about any of that. This was his time for exercise and meditation. He would think later. So he followed his dog into the gorge.

The river, held back by an upstream dam, was a bare trickle near the place where the path reached the bottom.

The dog got there first and ran straight to his favorite pool for a drink. His claws scratched on the rocks.

Time for a clipping, thought the professor.

The dog lapped at the puddle, looked up, and the hackles rose on his back.

The professor followed the dog's gaze up the side of the gorge. The walls were steep, but there were ledges, bushes, trees clinging tenaciously, as if suspended in space.

The dog must have seen something up there, a rabbit or a squirrel. But whatever it was, he lost interest and went back to lapping.

The rest took only an instant.

Something falling . . . the dog's head snapping up again . . . the professor turning . . . four boulders, each the size of a jagged-edged basketball, bouncing and tumbling. . .

The first one missed the professor and shattered on the rocks.

The second one struck him in the face, severed the bridge of his nose, drove into his brain, and killed him instantly.

A WEEK LATER, a young woman with a scholar's brains and a showgirl's legs appeared at the office of Fallon Antiquaria in Boston.

Peter was on the phone, negotiating the purchase of a private library from an estate in Dover. The prize of the collection was a first edition of *Leaves of Grass,* inscribed, "To my friend Ralph Waldo Emerson, Walt Whitman." Peter was saying that he would buy the whole library just to get a presentation copy of Whitman.

He hung up, leaned back in his chair, put his feet on his desk, and saw her.

"This is Jennifer Segal, boss." Bernice was leading her into his office. "She doesn't have an appointment, but . . . she's from Dartmouth College."

The girl looked to be in her late twenties. She was wearing a tweed jacket and a black turtleneck which, along with her black hair, made her skin seem milk-white. To this she added rimless glasses and an expression that young women often affected to discourage even casual conversation, never mind advances.

Still, she had the kind of beauty that could make a man in his late forties feel wistful, or at least inspire him to suck in his stomach when he stood to shake her hand. Not that Peter had much stomach. He was in better shape than men ten years younger. And he looked ten years younger, too, which he attributed to a daily workout, a job he enjoyed, and a commute of a few blocks.

The girl, however, seemed unimpressed with Fallon's appearance. She expressed no interest small talk, coffee, or anything else but business.

She produced a copy of *Antiquaria*, opened it to a page she had bookmarked, and asked, "Is this still for sale?"

Peter looked at the page: "A letter from Henry Knox to Rufus King RE: William Pike of Pelham, Massachusetts."

The catalogue offered dozens of letters. Peter couldn't remember every detail. So he turned to his computer, called up the item, and found that, yes, that letter had been sold to a collector in Litchfield, Connecticut.

"That's too bad," she said. "I was hoping I might get a look at it."

"The text is available." Peter pretended to be helpful as he tried to guess what she was really after. "It's written in 1786. Knox was Washington's artillery commander in the Revolution and later the Secretary of War. In the letter, he recommends a young man named William Pike to the employ Rufus King, who will become—"

"—a Massachusetts delegate to the Constitutional Convention." The girl smiled for the first time. "I'm a PhD candidate in history at Dartmouth. The so-called Critical Period, between the end of the Revolution and the beginning of the Washington administration—that's my area of expertise."

"So, you're not interested in the letter as a collector?"

"I'm a scholar. I'd like to know its provenance and whether the seller had any other material relating to Rufus King and William Pike."

Peter looked at his computer. "It says we sold this for another broker who represented an anonymous seller." Peter tapped in another code and the name of the broker appeared: Morris Bindle of Millbridge, Massachusetts.

The young woman waited quietly, as if expecting him to give up the name.

He didn't. It was none of her business. Instead he asked, "Are you working for someone, Miss Segal?"

"I was . . . until a week ago." And her façade seemed to crack. "I was the graduate student assistant to Professor Stuart Conrad."

"Conrad of Dartmouth? *The Magnificent Dreamers?* I read about the accident."

"That's what they called it."

"You think differently?"

"Rock slides are not that common in Queechee Gorge, or that accurate."

"Accidents happen," said Peter. "And Murphy's Law rules. If you're in a gorge when there's a rock slide—"

"You sound like the Vermont State Police." The girl stood.

"What was he working on?"

"The mindset of the men who wrote the Constitution, men like Rufus King . . . important work, considering what's going on these days. I don't want it to end with him."

Peter sensed that she was telling him what she thought he needed to know but not the whole story. "Why come to me?"

"Professor Conrad enjoyed reading about your hunts for lost tea sets and Shakespeare manuscripts. He said you made the study of history an adventure."

"He made it an art."

"When he saw the King letter in your catalogue, he circled it and made a note to call you. Rufus King was present at the creation, so to speak. Professor Conrad was interested in everything he left behind."

Peter glanced at the catalogue and noticed that the professor had marked the page with a clipping from the *Blackstone Valley Weekly*, a regional paper from Worcester. The clipping was the obituary of Buster McGillis, last floor manager of the defunct Pike-Perkins Mill. That much was interesting, but this sentence stopped Peter cold: "His body was discovered by Morris Bindle, friend and local antique dealer."

Peter closed the catalogue and handed it back to Ms. Segal. "Let me look a little deeper. Maybe there's more information out there on King and William Pike. If I find anything, it might help your dissertation."

As soon as she left, Peter called his assistant into the office.

Antoine Scarborough was twenty-four, son of a laborer who worked for Peter's brother. His friends in the hood called him Twan, the nickname of an NBA player who was also tall, black, and shaved his head. He wanted to go to graduate school in history, while his father wanted him to go to law school. Peter had lived the same conflict with his own father, so he had given Antoine a job and the time to make a decision.

"You did the research on that Rufus King letter, didn't you?"

"Yes."

"What about William Pike? Who was he?"

"William Pike. Born in 1770. Mother died in childbirth. Father served with the Massachusetts Artillery during the Revolution, then he went back to his farm in Pelham, Massachusetts—"

"Pelham? That's the town where Daniel Shays came from, isn't it?"

"Shays of Shays's Rebellion. And the Pikes were right in the middle of it. . . ."

THREE

October 1786

WILL PIKE WATCHED the hawks for twenty miles, until he approached the place where the land dropped away and there seemed a peculiar brightness radiating upward. The power of the Connecticut River was that considerable. Its valley cut a wide furrow through the landscape, and it waters reflected the sunlight, so that the traveler knew, long before he could see the river, that it was there.

Springfield was there, too. Washington himself had chosen it as the safest yet most accessible New England site for an arms depot. A windowless stone warehouse had been built on a rise near the Post Road and stocked with muskets, flints, bullets, and powder. It was surrounded, on what was now called Armory Hill, by storehouses and barracks.

Will positioned himself opposite the entrance, noted the things that Shays had asked him to observe, and waited less than an hour before he saw Henry Knox.

The Secretary of War was arriving on foot, in company with several men of the town, no doubt after a dinner at some local tavern. It was easy to pick him out. He stood six foot three and well fit the description Will's father had drawn: "Imagine two men rolled together and stuffed into a waistcoat, with one man's huge head comin' out the top and the other man's big feet stickin' out the bottom and the bulk of them both fillin' out the breeches."

Will had planned to follow Knox to his lodgings and beg an audience that night. But he might not get a better chance than now. So this polite young man, who seldom spoke unless spoken to, cleared his throat and cried out, "General Knox! A word, sir!"

Knox and the others stopped and looked across the road.

"Who is it?" said one of the gentlemen.

"I'm the son of George North Pike, a captain in the Massachusetts Artillery." Will strode toward them. "You may remember him, General."

"Pike?" said Knox.

"A debtor," said one of the others, whom Will recognized by his height and spider-thin body as Nathan Liggett, the very creditor who had lodged the complaint against Will's father.

"A brave soldier, sir," said Will. "A man hard-used by the state and by certain merchants, too."

"Sir," said Liggett to Knox, "this boy can offer you nothing."

Will kept his eyes on Knox. "I seek a favor, sir, for a veteran, sir." Will knew that he was inserting a few too many "sirs," but he was nervous.

Knox gestured to Liggett and the others. His coarse features and high-crowned tricorne made him seem even more enormous than he was. "These gentlemen have priority on my time, young man—"

"Thank you, sir," said Liggett, as smug as a priest. "That's as it should be."

Knox cocked an eyebrow at Liggett, then went on, "But I'll never turn away the son of one of my captains."

Without so much as a glance at Liggett, which was a smugness of its own, Will followed Knox into the barracks office. Papers covered the table, and a big-seated wing chair, suitable for a man as big-seated as Knox, had been pulled over from the hearth.

Knox dropped into the chair with a great huff, dropped his hat on the table, and gestured Will to the other side.

As he sat, Will's eyes scanned the papers.

And Knox noticed the boy's interest. "A report to General Washington. My impressions of the crisis here in central Massachusetts."

Will closed his mouth, realizing he was slack-jawed before a letter bound for the great Washington.

"What would you have me say to the general?" asked Knox.

"I think that . . . er . . . I would say that—" Will had rehearsed a speech in behalf of his father. He had not expected to offer opinions for George Washington.

So Knox read from the letter: "'It is indeed fact that high taxes are the ostensible cause of the commotions, but that they are the real cause is as far from the truth as light from darkness. The insurgents have never paid any, or but very little taxes—'"

"That's not true!" blurted Will.

Knox stopped. "Oh?"

Will swallowed his awe of Knox and his surprise at own outburst. "My father paid his taxes, and he had nothing left to pay his debts to men like Nathan Liggett, because Liggett and his ilk won't take paper money."

"Paper money loses value too quickly," said Knox.

"Then something should be done, sir."

"What would you suggest?"

Will grew bolder. "I would not allow a man like my father to be imprisoned."

"I remember your father. A good officer. But there are laws—"

"There are God-made laws, sir, and there are man-made laws. We cannot change God's laws, but a wise man should know enough to change an unwise law."

Knox ruminated a moment, as if he liked the young man's answer and perhaps his spirit, too. "Would you agree also that the creed of the rebels—"

"Regulators, sir. They call themselves Regulators."

"Regulators, then . . . would you agree that their creed is"—Knox read from his letter—"'that the property of the United States has been protected from confiscation of Britain by the joint executions of all, and he that attempts opposition to this creed is an enemy to equity and justice and ought to be swept off the face of the earth'?"

Will swallowed. "No, sir. I would not."

"You would not?" Knox leaned across the table, and the effect was as if the moon had passed between the earth and sun, so enormous was the face blocking the light from the window. "Why would you not?"

"Because you include"—Will did not to mention his brother—"men who are neighbors of mine. I know their spirit to be constructive."

Knox worked his lips together. "Would one of these neighbors be Daniel Shays?"

"Yes, sir."

Knox grew angry at the mention of the name. "A leveller. An anarchist. You'd do well to stay away from him. He and his ilk will bring our American experiment to ruin. I'm writing as much to General Washington." Knox picked up his quill and began to scratch out a few more words.

It had been said that the uprisings had greatly disturbed Knox, and his sudden change of mood suggested the depth of his emotion.

But Will had not come to defend Shays. So he held his peace until Knox paused to dip his quill again, then asked, "May I speak of my father, sir?"

"You already have." Knox kept his eyes on the paper. "If your father is allied with Daniel Shays, there's nothing I can do for him."

"My father is allied with the cause of America, sir."

Knox stopped writing. "And your brother? It's known he marches with Shays."

"My brother follows his conscience, sir. I follow mine."

"If yours dictates debate rather than riot, you're the better for it. But desperate factions are at work here, son. Mind that they don't work upon you." Knox went back to writing, as if to set down the thoughts that Will had inspired in him before they fled.

"My father is part of no faction, sir, except your own." Will stood and swept his hat from the table. "He even wore his Continental uniform to prison."

Knox's quill stopped moving. For a moment, he kept his eyes on the paper. Then he sat back, emotion ebbing at last. "These are difficult times, Will Pike. We are threatened on all sides. But your father was a good man. I'll speak for him. On my word."

"Thank you, sir."

"And . . . I take interest in the children of my men. What do you see as a future?"

Will clutched his hat before him. "I hope to make a mark, sir, among men who matter . . . as a barrister, perhaps. But I first must apprentice in the law."

After a moment's thought, Knox took a new sheet of paper, wrote a letter, sealed it with wax. "Do you know Rufus King?"

"I know of him, sir . . . a Massacusetts delegate to the Confederation Congress in New York."

"A fine lawyer, too, in need of a new apprentice at year's end. This letter states how well you hold your own in argument. It goes out in my next post to Congress. When King comes to Boston over Christmas, perhaps you'll hear from him."

"Thank you, sir. I . . . I don't know what to say."

"Know this: There's talk that King will be delegate to a convention in Philadelphia, to strengthen the articles under which we govern. Considering this Massachusetts crisis, such a gathering is now imperative. Work for King, and you may effect real change."

"Thank you, sir."

"One more thing." Knox leaned forward in the chair. "Have you heard talk about the rebels—the *Regulators*—marching on this arsenal?"

After a quick swallow, Will lied. "I've heard nothing, sir."

Knox smiled. "Then I'll sleep well tonight."

WILL PIKE DID not sleep well for many nights, so guilt stricken was he at lying to Knox, so fearful was he of the day when his brother would summon him to march on the arsenal. And denying that summons would bring its own guilt. But he had made it plain that while he might provide observations about the arsenal's defenses (which were few) and its guards (fewer), he would not march against government property.

As October faded, Will's resolve hardened with the freezing earth. Then, on the day of the first snowfall, resolve became conviction, for that was the day that Will's father came home, having served only three months instead of six.

Knox had restored him to freedom, but no one could restore him to health. Whatever afflicted George North Pike, he continued to lose weight, suffered ever more brutal stomach pains, and had little appetite, even at Christmas, when they roasted a fat goose stuffed with brandied apples.

"Look at him," said North one cold January night. "A broken man, sleepin' by the fire, not even interested in a bowl of mush. The government done that to him."

"The government is changing," said Will. "And I may help to change it."

"You'll march with us then? On the arsenal?"

"Arsenal?" Will's stomach turned.

"What do you think this is for?" North pointed to the sheet of paper on the table.

It was a broadside that had been posted across the county. It warned of a four-thousand-man army marching west, financed by Boston merchants. The army's intent: "by point of sword to crush the power of the people and render them unable of ever opposing the cruel hand of tyranny." The petition called for the men of Hampshire County to "assemble in arms to support and maintain not only the rights but the lives and liberties of the people."

North said, "If we're to assemble in arms, we *need* arms."

"When?"

"We march day after tomorrow. Shays wants to know if you'll be with us."

"Day after tomorrow, I'm leavin' for Boston."

"Boston? Why?"

Will pulled a letter from his waistcoat pocket. "This come in today's post."

North took the letter and read it aloud. He always read aloud. He had been a poor reader in the schoolhouse where they had learned their alphabets and their sums, so reading aloud proved his comprehension.

"'Dear Mister Pike'"—North looked up—"*Mister?* Someone calls you *Mister* and you're ready to turn your back on your neighbors and your blood?"

"Read," said Will.

So North read, stopping not at all and stumbling only a little. "'I am in receipt of a letter from Henry Knox, October 26 of last year, which recommends you to my service. As my apprentice moved on at year's end, I shall wait upon you on January 26, while I am in Boston to confer with the legislature. I shall be at Government House the whole day. Should I find myself favorably disposed to a relationship, be prepared to step immediately into my service. Yours, Rufus King.'"

Will gave his brother a moment, then said, "I plan to use my brain."

"You'd desert us? To work for some Boston lawyer?"

"Lawyer and a congressman, too."

"Even worse." North threw the letter back at his brother. "We'll need every able-bodied man in Hampshire County to take that arsenal. Every man needs a weapon. 'Tis the only way to stand against a government set out to oppress the people."

"You don't need me." Will folded the letter and put it back into his pocket.

North stood—the older brother, intimidating by his size, his personality, his simple position in the birth order. "You desert us now, Willie, and you won't be able to hold your head up in this town again . . . or in this family."

And from the hearth came these words: "He's goin' to Boston."

Both brothers were shocked to hear the sudden strength in their father's voice, shocked as well that he was awake and listening.

The old man stood, steadied himself, and shuffled across the room. "Whatever lies ahead, we can't be killin' a boy's dream. Especially when it makes good sense."

"Good sense?" said North. "To join the other side?"

"We're all Americans. We're on the *same* side," said George North Pike. "I got out of jail because Will used his smart brain, not because you closed the courts."

"If not for the closin' of the courts," answered North, "Henry Knox never would've went to Springfield so Will could go there and impress him."

The father sat at the table, thought about that a moment, and said, "True enough . . . I'd have to say you both done good."

Then North dropped into his chair, swept up the petition again, glanced at it, threw it back on the table.

And their father continued to talk more than he had since he came home. "A man with two strong sons is lucky for certain. Especially when they're strong willed, too. So I'll stand by both of you. And if one wants to march on the Springfield arsenal and one wants to go to Boston, I say that each of you is right."

AT DAWN TWO days later, the brothers bade good-bye to their father. Will had stoked the fire and made an extra-large pot of cornmeal mush. North had brought in three days' worth of firewood and promised he would be back before it ran out.

At the meetinghouse, two dozen Pelham Regulators were waiting. A bonfire released waving sheets of warmth into the gray sky and lent a strangely festive air to the scene. But the bundled bodies of men hulked inward against the cold and the tentlike stacks of muskets—fewer muskets than men, to be sure—gave the moment a more appropriate foreshadowing. Will Pike smelled snow and trouble in the wind.

Daniel Shays stood on the meetinghouse steps, motionless under a black wool cape. Doc Hines stood near him, holding a ledger on which he was writing the names of the men as they arrived.

"Hot rebellion in the freezin' cold!" shouted North Pike.

"Mornin' boys," said Shays. "Glad to see the both of you."

"I'll set down both names, then?" asked Doc Hines.

"Not mine," said Will. "I'm only goin' as far as Palmer."

"Palmer?" Hines looked faintly comical with a scarf tied around his ears and his tricorne plunked on top of it. "If it's Palmer and no farther, why go at all?"

"He's gettin' the coach in Palmer," said North. "Goin' to Boston. Goin' to do our politickin'."

"Politickin'?" said Doc Hines. "Who appointed *him*?"

North said, "*I* did," so that it sounded like a threat.

And Shays said, "Good. We need good men doin' our talkin'."

After that, no one said a bad word to Will Pike. They wished him Godspeed in Palmer, and he wished them the same. Any who watched were struck by his farewell to North: a strong handshake and a brotherly embrace. One had inherited his father's analytical calm, the other the fiery nature of a mother they did not remember. One headed east toward politics; the other went west to war.

And the northeast wind gusted across the snowfields.

THE NEXT MORNING, Will Pike awoke to the sound of farting.

He was in a bed with two other men, in a chamber containing another bed and three more men, in the Post Road hostelry known as the Wayside Inn. And someone in his bed was farting. He guessed that the culprit was the clockmaker named Adolf Gefahlz, who had partaken of a bowl of cabbage soup in the taproom before retiring.

Will got up and cracked a window to let in a bit of fresh air. He was glad to see that the snow, which had stopped them the night before, had now stopped falling. They were a day's ride from Boston, a day and a night by foot, but to keep his appointment with Rufus King, Will had resolved that he would walk the whole way if need be.

In the taproom, he downed a mug of tea, declining a larger breakfast so as to save shillings and hasten their departure. When the coachman called for help to clear the wheels, Will grabbed a shovel and went to work, but it was after ten before they dug the coach out of a snowdrift and began to roll.

SOME FORTY MILES away, eleven hundred men under the command of Daniel Shays were tramping west on the Post Road toward Springfield. Their plan was for three columns of Regulators to attack the arsenal at the same time—from West Springfield on the west, from Chicopee on the north, and from Palmer on the east.

By three that afternoon, Shays's column was drawn up before the arsenal. But the column in the west had not marched. The commander had changed the plan on his own, and his message to Shays had been intercepted, then brought to General William Shepard, who defended the arsenal.

AT THE SAME time, Will Pike was getting his first glimpse of the steeples of Boston. The snow was not as deep here, perhaps because the city was surrounded by water and reached by a causeway called the Neck.

As the coach approached the gates, Herr Gefahlz—who was still farting silently, or so Will was certain—explained that the water to the north was the Back Bay, to the south Dorchester Bay, and the snowy hills beyond were Dorchester Heights, where Henry Knox had entrenched the cannon that drove the British from Boston ten years before.

"My father commanded one of the artillery companies," said Will.

And Herr Gefahlz brightened. "*Ja?* So? A man to make a son proud, eh?"

"Yes, sir. Very proud."

WHILE WILL SPOKE of cannon in Boston, his brother faced them in Springfield.

North Pike and several of the other lieutenants stood with Shays, about two hundred yards from the arsenal, and studied the ranks of defenders drawn up on the snowy ground before it.

"This ain't what my brother saw in October," said North. "Two cannon, four hundred men armed with new muskets taken right from the stores. A tall order, Dan'l."

"Yeah," said Doc Hines. "And where are the other columns?"

"Don't know," said Shays. "But we'd best drive this team today, or they'll never pull for us again."

A rider was coming down from the arsenal. He reined up close to Shays and said, "I bring General Shepard's ultimatum: If you put your troops in motion, they will be fired upon."

The wind skittered across the road. It ruffled coattails and hat brims and two American flags, one fluttering over the arsenal, the other at the head of that cold column of farmers.

Then Daniel Shays pulled his sword from his hanger and shouted, as much for his own men as for those before the arsenal, "We are here in defense of the country you've come to destroy."

"Aye!" cried North Pike. "And if we're not in possession of new muskets by sundown, the people of New England will see a day such as they've never seen before." Then he gave Shays a wink, as if to say that yes, they would brazen their way through.

Some of the troops cheered. But it was a halfhearted sound that caught in most throats, because none of these Regulators had yet marched against cannon. Big talk would not protect them from grapeshot.

Then the messenger leaned down and said to Shays: "You see the stakes in the ground on either side of the road? A hundred yards from the arsenal? They form the line of demarcation. Cross it, and General Shepard will give the order to fire."

Shays laughed. He was normally a morose man, not much given to display. It had been shocking enough to see him swinging his sword about. But to hear him laugh . . . perhaps it was more brazening.

Then Shays turned to his lieutenants and said, "Your posts, men."

WHILE NORTH WAS taking his place at the front of the Pelhamite column, Will Pike was walking through Boston with his flatulent new friend.

Herr Gefahlz explained that as a Hessian soldier he had been captured by the Massachusetts Artillery at Trenton. "They treat me better than my own sergeants. So I decide to stay in America and make clocks. And because your father command them, I treat you good now."

The red bricks of the city seemed to glow in the setting sun. The world, Will Pike concluded, was brightening.

BACK IN SPRINGFIELD the light was fading, and North Pike, who had fought on battlefields and in forecastles and in Boston back alleys, was preparing to fight in the cold blue of a January afternoon.

At Shays's command, North shouted, "Forward!"

Few of the men moved, except to shiver.

"Forward!" shouted Shays. "Forward march! March, Goddamn you!"

The other officers from the other towns took up the cry.

And four hundred men—the only ones who were armed—began to advance.

North tried to call out a cadence, as he had when he drilled these men on the Pelham town green. But they were farmers, and they were frightened. Their advance, so slow in starting, quickly became a stampede.

And General Shepard was true to his word.

As the first units crossed the line, his cannon flashed and blasted jets of smoke. The sound echoed off the advancing farmers, then bounced back and echoed off the walls of the arsenal. But the shots went high, a warning.

A few of the Regulators stopped, as if shocked by the sound. But many others pressed forward with even greater momentum, as if they would be safe once they closed with the cannon.

North cried for the Pelham men to keep order, to remember their training, but there was no stopping the column now. Unless . . .

The cannoneers were reloading, lowering their barrels, raising their linstocks. . . .

Another flash ignited the fading light, another blast hammered the attackers, and hundreds of pieces of grapeshot whizzed and sizzled and seared into the flesh of frightened men. A great shout of shock and pain went up from the head of the column, which seemed to stop as if it had run into an invisible wall.

A man beside North Pike was struck in the forehead with a piece of shot the size of—yes—a Concord grape. He staggered, looked at North with wide, unseeing eyes, and fell over dead.

That did it.

If the Regulators had expected that the militia would not fire, would possibly run, and would probably come over to their side, they were wrong.

In an instant, those Hampshire County farmers became the rioters that the Boston moneychangers had always considered them to be. But it was a riot of retreat. They did not stop running until midnight. By then, they had run all the way back to Pelham.

THE NEXT MORNING, Will Pike put on his best deerskin breeches and a green velvet coat that his father had worn on his wedding day. He bade farewell to Gefahlz and his wife and their three plump children, and following Gefahlz's directions, he took himself from the North End to Long Wharf, where Boston's commerce made its way into the world. He looked out to sea, past the schooners and East Indiamen, and his heart filled with a grand sense of possibility.

Then he turned and looked up State Street, past the wagons, the horses, the crowds going about the business of the city, toward the building at the head of the street: the Massachusetts State House, former government house of the British Empire, the place where Will would learn his future. He took a deep breath and started walking.

TWO WEEKS LATER, with the snow deep and the cold air shimmering in the winter sunlight, North Pike and Daniel Shays and a few others crossed the Massachusetts border into Vermont. The remains of their army had been routed, the rebellion was over, and the leaders were now fugitives under sentence of death.

But Vermont was its own little republic. They would be as safe in Vermont as if they had crossed into Canada . . . for the time being.

So they went in snowshoes and heavy blanket coats across the frozen landscape.

But toward evening, North Pike decided to split from the others. He told Shays that he had had his fill of uprising. He would take his chances on his own.

He knew a New Hampshire man who cut logs and floated them down the Connecticut each spring. And he knew a woman in the logging camp, too, a woman with breasts big enough to warm both sides of a man's face at once.

So he turned for the river.

ON THE SAME afternoon, Will Pike sat in a coach bouncing over the frozen ruts on the Middle Post Road. His toes and the tip of his nose were numb with cold, but he and the man beside him shared a bearskin lap blanket that kept them both passably warm.

Some masters would have kept the bearskin for themselves and let the apprentice freeze, but Rufus King had treated Will like a colleague rather than an apprentice.

King had graduated first in his class at Harvard, had established himself as one of Boston's brightest lawyers, and at thirty-three had taken a seat in the Confederation Congress. He dressed well, even for travel, in a suit the color of port wine. And he was considered a handsome man, though to Will his sharp features bespoke sharp intelligence. His aquiline nose seemed like an exclamation mark whenever he made a point, and every point he made was concise.

He cocked an eyebrow at Will and said, "Eight hours out of Boston, and still you've not read a page of contract law?"

"It's just that there's so much to see, sir."

King glanced out the window. "Fields and forests and small crossroads towns. Stare at things worth staring at, like your law books."

"Yes, sir." Will began to dig into the carpet bag at his feet. He had resolved from the start that he would never disappoint Rufus King, because King had given him an opportunity to fulfill his dreams, to soar like one of those Hampshire County hawks.

Then King put a hand on his arm. "We'll be stopping soon. Enjoy the rest of the ride. Read tonight."

"Yes, sir. Thank you, sir."

"You did well in Boston. We move to a larger stage at Congress in New York, and come spring, the convention in Philadelphia, which I expect will work with great urgency, considering the scare that your brother and the Regulators have put into our governments, north and south."

"Do you believe we need a stronger central government, sir?"

"Without it, we're doomed. So work hard, for the better you do, the more I'll ask of you."

"Yes, sir. It's what I hope, sir. Thank you, sir."

"Don't thank me. Thank Henry Knox. I've taken you on ahead of several young men who have bachelor's degrees, all because of this letter." King reached under his cape and drew the letter out. "I think you should keep it. A recommendation from such a great man might be of value to you again someday."

Will took the letter, read it, remembered the day that Knox wrote it.

Then the coach began to slow, and the driver called down to them, "Millbridge comin' up, gents. MacReady's Tavern for the night. Good stew, soft beds, and they buy their cornmeal from the Cousins gristmill, where they grind so fine, the Indian puddin's as smooth as mother's milk."

FOUR

"UP AHEAD IS MACREADY'S, the old coach stop," said Peter Fallon. "It's still a restaurant."

"Maybe we should have lunch there." Evangeline Carrington looked at her watch. "Or dinner, we've been driving so long."

"I'm giving you material for your next article, and you're complaining. Take notes instead. We're on the George Washington Heritage Highway. The sunroof is open. The autumn colors are glorious. Call it, 'Route 16: Washington Passed This Way.'"

"How about, 'Washington Passed Wind This Way'?"

Peter rolled his eyes and kept driving.

They had met in their twenties, when he had been searching her family's history for clues to a lost tea set. They had lived together for a time, when he tried teaching history in a midwestern college. They had found each other again in their forties, when each was recovering from a divorce.

This time, it seemed to be working, despite their differences. He came from the neighborhood and had made good selling rarities to the upper crust. She came from the upper crust and didn't much care. And while they spent more time together than apart, they practiced what experience preached: no sharing of toothpaste or utility bills.

As they went by MacReady's Family Restaurant, Peter said, "Washington really *did* pass this way."

"You don't know when to quit, do you?"

"If I did, you and I might never have gotten together again."

"The road not taken . . . unlike this one." She looked out at a strip mall, which was followed by a wooded lot on which an old farmhouse was falling to ruin, which was followed by a half-acre of used cars arrayed around a little shack. "Where are we, again?"

"On one of the three main roads to New York back in the eighteenth century, known then as Middle Post Road. Coach left Boston at three a.m. Breakfast in Medfield—"

"Read a magazine and then you're in—"

"Millbridge, below Uxbridge, where Massachusetts, Connecticut, and Rhode Island meet."

"New England's very own middle of nowhere," she said.

"Coaches would stop here for the night—"

"You know, Peter—"

She turned to him and a strand of blond hair caught in one of her earrings. She brushed it back, and he thought she looked as good in her forties as she had in her twenties, even when she was about to zing him.

"—sometimes I wonder how you find room in that brain for things like phone numbers and computer passwords, considering all the useless knowledge you've stored."

"Knowledge is never useless. As I always say, history matters. Washington took this route home after his presidential trip to New England—"

"After they gave him the Golden Eagle Tea Set?"

"Which brought us together."

"Proof that history matters," she cracked, "more than it should."

"Washington had come into New England on Upper Post Road," Peter continued. "He wanted to go back by a different route. But he wouldn't take Lower Road because it went through Rhode Island, which hadn't ratified the Constitution—"

"So they were fighting over the Constitution even then," she said.

"The more things change, the more they stay the same. The lesson of history."

"Do you really think we'll be able to repeal this Second Amendment?"

"What do you mean, *we?*"

"Peter . . . we've been over this already. If you're against the repeal, you're against gun control. If you're against gun control, pull over and let me out."

Peter fixed his eyes on the road. "We're looking for the Millbridge Historical Society. It's in the old Pike-Perkins Mill complex."

"Don't change the subject."

"*You* changed the subject. We were talking about George Washington."

"We were talking about the Constitution," she said. "And these days, the only talk is about the repeal movement."

"Can we get back to the business at hand?"

"What? History? We can get guns off the street for good, and you want to talk about history."

"I told you, history matters. Even on this trip."

"I thought we were here to see a guy about a letter you sold for him."

"A letter to Rufus King, who helped write the Constitution that everyone is fighting over." Peter reached into his pocket and handed her a copy. "Read it."

She started to singsong through it: "'October 26, 1786. Dear Mr. King, It is my pleasure to recommend to you a young man of good character and background, his father having served with distinction in one of my regiments. William Pike is sober, serious, and possesses instinctive skills for debate. In discussion with me over the rule of law, he said, "There are God-made laws, and there are man-made laws. We cannot change God's laws, but a wise man should know enough to change an unwise law. . . ."'"

Evangeline looked up. "He could be talking about today."

Peter just nodded.

"Don't look so smug." Then she read on: "'Such well-phrased sentiment alone makes him worthy of consideration. Your Obedient Servant, Henry Knox.'"

"See?" said Peter. "History matters. Why would a professor of constitutional history be so interested in this letter? And in the death of the man who, if my instincts are correct, sold it through Morris Bindle? And why now?"

THE PIKE-PERKINS MILL was set back from the road, behind a stand of sugar maples planted by some enlightened mill manager a century before. The driveway cut a graceful arc under the trees, so that the visitor's first impression was of entering a park.

But this was no park. A pair of buildings flanked the main gate. Beyond them rose the mill itself, a huge utilitarian cathedral of brick and glass—flaking brick and broken glass—four hundred feet long and four stories high, with a five-story clock tower that looked like a steeple grafted onto the front.

Peter pulled in under the trees. There were no other parked cars and hardly a sound, except for the traffic speeding by.

Across the road was a row of little story-and-a-half houses, and another row beyond, and perhaps another beyond that. Worker housing, thought Peter, built back when there was work.

It had rained the night before, so there was a powerful smell of damp wood and decay in the air. Peter realized it was coming off the mill.

"Welcome to the land that time and the Superfund forgot," said Evangeline.

"Welcome to the New England your editors never ask you to write about," said Peter. "Nice trees, though."

The building to the right of the gate was a large Colonial house, dating from the days when the mill was no more than a granite wheel grinding grain for country farmers. What windows weren't boarded up were broken, and the only paint that hadn't peeled was the sign on the door: MAIN OFFICE: VISITORS PLEASE REGISTER.

The building on the left was bigger and in better shape: two stories of brick with a slate roof, an old loading dock by the gate, a millrace running past the foundation at the far end. When belts and looms replaced granite wheels, this building replaced the wooden mill house; then it had given way to the structure now looming behind it. There was a sign at the loading dock door: MILLBRIDGE HISTORICAL SOCIETY. OPEN SUNDAYS AND TUESDAYS, II A.M.–I P.M.

"Historical society," said Evangeline. "Looks like history is all they have left."

A smaller sign said, PLEASE ENTER.

So they did . . . into a jumble. Small town historical societies were often defined by the word. *Jumble.* Jumbles of stuff, usually displayed with little regard for the niceties of museum science but with plenty of enthusiasm and occasionally a bit of artistry.

This was a large room, maybe twenty-five by fifty, perfect for a jumble—an old loom, a cabinet with a collection of tools, two crammed bookcases, a musket, a diorama of the original Cousins Mill, a clothes dummy wearing a union suit—one-piece underwear "made from Millbridge weave." On the walls—a collection of old doorknockers, framed prints from nineteenth-century newspapers, photographs of young men in military uniforms and women in high-necked dresses, all staring severely out of the past. . . .

At the far end, above an ornate desk, a huge photograph hung from a ceiling molding. It showed scores of people standing in front of the mill. "The Men and Women of the Mill, 1861" was carved into the frame and on the matte above the photo was etched the legend, "In America, we get up in the morning, we go to work, and we solve our problems."

The room had a musty smell that suggested mold, which suggested to Peter that he should not handle any of the old books and should change his clothes before he carried any spores back to his office. The smell mingled with the aroma of brewing coffee and the stink of stale cigarettes.

"Mr. Bindle!" shouted Peter.

"Hello?" Morris Bindle popped out the bathroom door, just off the display room. He was holding three coffee cups he had just rinsed. "Mr. Fallon! This is a surprise. I wasn't expecting—" His eye fell on Evangeline, and he went speechless.

She could do that to some men . . . especially when she was wearing the jeans, the leather sportcoat, the cowboy boots, and the blue blouse that brought out the blue of her eyes . . . and especially to men like Bindle— balding, big-bellied, fifties, no wedding band, wearing brown corduroy trousers and a New England Patriots sweatshirt with cigarette ashes down the front.

Peter introduced her, and she offered her hand.

Bindle extended his, even though there were three cups in it.

"I'd love some," she said.

"Oh, yeah." Bindle looked down, seemed surprised at the cups twined into his fingers, gave a little laugh. "Like I say, I wasn't expecting beautiful women and famous booksellers."

Peter pulled an envelope from his jacket pocket. "I've brought your money."

Bindle went behind his desk and filled the three cups. "It sold fast, eh?"

"Not for a Henry Knox letter. Collectors love Knox."

Bindle handed cups to Evangeline and Peter and gestured to the cream and sugar on his desk. "Who bought it?"

Peter said, "He wanted to remain anonymous, like your seller."

"Fair enough. I'm just glad it sold. But you didn't have to drive all the way down here. The mailman knows where Millbridge is."

Peter tapped the envelope against his cup. "I have a few questions."

"About what?" Bindle's eyes shifted to Evangeline, then back to the envelope.

Peter said, "You told me the Knox letter belonged to a Pike descendant."

"Right," said Bindle, a note of suspicion creeping into his voice.

"Can you tell me who the descendant is?"

"Like you said, the seller wanted to remain anonymous. That means—"

"I *know* what that means," snapped Peter.

Evangeline changed the subject. "This is a very interesting location, Mr. Bindle."

Peter took the hint and backed off. "She's right. How did the historical society end up in a defunct mill?"

"Not defunct for long," answered Bindle. "The mill closed down twenty years ago. Now we got a developer—local boy—buying it out of bankruptcy. He's planning condos, restaurants, shops. It's the happy ending for a lot of old mills around here."

"And you just stumbled in?" asked Evangeline.

"Oh, no. The historical society's been here for twenty years. We used to have a corner in the library. But we needed space, and the town wanted a presence here."

"Are you the president of this society?"

"Nobody else wanted the job, and since I dabble in antiques, too, I can give the expert eye to things that people donate."

Peter looked out the back windows at the mill. "An amazing pile of brick."

"A two-acre footprint," said Bindle. "You couldn't build something this big today, not on the Blackstone. You'd need so many easements and permissions, the lawyers would suck you dry."

"Well, they won't suck this." Peter held out the envelope containing the check. "Not unless there's an estate lawyer around."

"Estate lawyer?" Bindle eyed Peter. "Why?"

"The death of a retired mill manager named Buster McGillis."

"I found him. Dead in his easy chair. So?"

"Did he own the letter?"

Bindle pulled himself up. He was not just big-bellied; he was burly, and as tall as Peter, too. "What are you after?"

Peter took a step back. "Relax, Morris. There's fifteen g's in here. A cashier's check. And I'm hoping there are more letters, so there'll be more money. But I can't keep selling material without knowing its source."

Bindle looked at Evangeline, then at the envelope, then at Peter.

"Come on, Bindle," said Peter. "You know my predicament."

"Well, yeah." Bindle seemed to stand down a bit. Then he chuckled. "I wasn't going to offer you more till you proved yourself. The letter was in a scrapbook."

Peter held the envelope over Bindle's hand. "Scrapbook?"

"From McGillis's attic." Bindle snatched the envelope.

"That's all I wanted to know," said Peter.

Bindle opened the envelope and gave the check a quick look. "A nice payday. Would've been a nice one for old Buster, too."

"That means you're just taking a commission?"

"Buster was my friend," said Bindle. "I look out for my friends."

"But now the money goes to the estate," said Evangeline.

Bindle grunted. "Closest living relative, the only one who cared, is

Tommy Farrell. And he's not a blood relative. He lives in Newport, but he's still a local boy. He bought the mill. Bought it at auction. Not sure if I'm glad about that."

"So you're sending him the check?" asked Peter.

"No. It goes to a probate account." Bindle dropped into the chair and put his feet on the desk. "But I get my commission."

"Why did Buster decide to sell now?" asked Evangeline.

"He said he wanted to sit in the EMC Club at Fenway once before he died. He loved the Red Sox. But he didn't have much cash. So I reminded him of the Pike family motto."

"What was that?" asked Evangeline.

Bindle jerked a thumb at the picture on the wall behind him, "'In America, we get up in the morning, we go to work, and we solve our problems.' Buster always liked it. Then I told him what I thought the Knox letter would bring."

Evangeline studied the picture on the wall, then picked up the smaller framed photograph on Bindle's desk. It showed a man with a mustache in a 1930s three-piece suit, standing before the very desk, before the very picture.

Bindle said, "That's Jack Choury. That picture hung in his American Immigrant Bank of Millbridge. His daughter donated the desk and the picture."

Peter wasn't interested. "The Knox letter, Morris. Did Buster say where it came from?"

Bindle shrugged. "An old family thing . . . in the scrapbook. I told him it was the most valuable letter he had, and if he sold it, he'd have enough money to sit in the dugout if he wanted. So he gave it to me on consignment and sold me the rest of the scrapbook outright."

"Where is it?" asked Peter.

"The scrapbook? In a safety deposit box."

"Anything else to sell? Any more letters from famous Americans?"

Morris Bindle smiled. "Maybe."

"HE KNOWS MORE," said Evangeline.

"You think?" Peter started the car. "The president of a historical society sells one letter for an old man who dies mysteriously, then he gets to keep a scrapbook full of letters for himself?"

"Sound fishy?"

"It's a violation of society ethics, at least."

She laughed. "Small society, small violation."

Just down the road a bridge crossed the Blackstone River. Traffic was light and cars were moving across the little span as though it were as nondescript as a thousand other New England bridges.

But Peter slowed as they approached. "Look . . . all stone, a single graceful arch—"

"The river isn't wide enough for more than one arch," she said.

"But it's the fourth most powerful river in North America."

"You're joking."

"It drops two hundred and forty feet in forty-six miles between Worcester and Providence. You're looking at the birth canal of the American industrial revolution."

"I guess I won't go swimming, then."

The mill ran along the north side of the river. On the other side, shielded by trees, was the grand house.

Every nineteenth-century mill town had one. It was the house where the owner lived, proclaiming both his wealth and his commitment to the community. It was also the house where Buster McGillis had died.

"Greek Revival," said Evangeline. "Built some time in the 1830s. Big white pillars supporting a triangular front, so the house looks a little like a Greek temple, and everyone is reminded of the kinship between the first democracy and ours."

"Very observant. Have you also observed that we're heading south?"

"What about lunch at MacReady's?"

They drove under the ancient railroad bridge. Then they came into the town square—a nice bank in the old train depot, a thrift shop, a doughnut shop, a Tru Value hardware, Bindle's Antiques, and of course, a white steeple. The road forked. Left to Rhode Island and Connecticut. Right to Worcester.

"Rhode Island?" she said as Peter turned left.

"Connecticut, if you can wait for lunch. I think we should talk to the buyer."

A few cars behind them, a black Chrysler Sebring made the same turn. Though it had Rhode Island plates, it headed for Connecticut, too.

ON A GEOLOGICAL map, the hills of Litchfield County, Connecticut looked like ripples radiating out from the Taconics and the Berkshires, which themselves were ripples from the big mountains of Vermont, New Hampshire, and Maine. But draw a graphic map that put the emphasis on money, and those rippling hills became the Rockies, taller than anything around them, because there was money in northwestern Connecticut, new money and old money, trust fund money from New England and fast-made money from New York, money sleeping quietly in the forests and fields and money galloping with the horses and grazing with the sheep on the gentleman farms.

Don Cottle represented himself as a gentleman farmer, though Peter Fallon wasn't so sure. Most of New England's gentleman farmers were long and angular and talked as if they had Connecticut Yankee lockjaw, even if they'd grown up in the Bronx. Don Cottle was square and solid, with a crew cut and a broken nose. He had no affectations, except, perhaps, a distaste for small talk.

He met them at the George Washington Tavern in the little town of Washington Depot.

The Father of His Country was everywhere here—in an engraving over the taproom fireplace, in an old inn sign hanging from a beam in the dining room, in prints on the walls, in silhouette on the restroom wallpaper.

Evangeline looked up at one of the great frozen faces and ordered an omelet.

Peter and Don Cottle ordered hamburgers and beers.

Then Peter looked out at the hillside behind the restaurant, at the trees exploding into color. "Now *those* are sugar maples."

"They certainly are," said Cottle. "You have another letter for me to buy?"

"Depends on whether the owner decides to sell. He comes from a place with sugar maples, too."

Cottle looked at Evangeline. "Does he always speak in riddles?"

"Sometimes, it's conundrums," she said.

"There are sugar maples all over New England," said Fallon. "The owner lives somewhere in New England. That's all I can tell you right now."

Cottle took a sip of beer, then said, "Look, Mr. Fallon, I'm enjoying lunch and all, but you said you had a letter."

"I said I *may*. I'd like to offer it to you. But I need to know if it's right for you. Otherwise, I might offer it to one of my more regular customers."

Cottle laughed. "I've heard of adoption agencies for dogs, where the owner has to pass muster, but not for Henry Knox letters."

"Well, that's the thing. Is it just Knox letters you're after?"

"I'm interested in letters that relate to the founding of the country. And it was not founded in 1776 but in 1787."

"You mean, the year the Constitution was written?" said Evangeline.

"That would be 1787," said Cottle.

"Does this relate to the present political fight?" asked Evangeline.

Cottle blinked once. "My interest is in preserving the past for the future. That's why I bought the Knox letter. And I'd love to continue collecting things from that period, with signatures by Knox, King, or even Will Pike."

"Why someone as insignificant as William Pike?" asked Peter.

Cottle shrugged. "Because of his connection to these other people."

And as food arrived, Evangeline came to a conclusion. *He's lying.*

This was ironic, she thought, considering that on the wall behind him was the face of the man who could not tell a lie.

George Washington was staring at Will Pike, and he did not seem pleased.

Will looked into those gray eyes, then diverted his gaze to something a bit closer—the tops of Washington's shoes, because Will was on his hands and knees.

He was not there out of devotion. That would have irritated Washington even more. But an attitude of groveling suited Will Pike at that moment, for he had dropped a sheaf of papers, and among the material fluttering to the Philadelphia cobblestones was a first draft of the document that they had been ruminating over, arguing over, and compromising over through that whole humid Philadelphia summer.

The Committee of Detail had organized the draft into sections and articles. Copies had been printed and distributed that morning. Then the convention had adjourned so that the delegates could read the draft.

Will was charged with handling Rufus King's papers. This meant that as the Massachusetts delegates returned for the afternoon session, Will followed with a leather satchel under his arm and a respectable distance between himself and his superiors so as not to intrude upon their private conversation.

This had brought him to the gates of the state house at the same moment as Washington, who had been walking alone from the opposite direction. The guards had presented arms, and Will had naturally deferred to the general, who acknowledged him with a decorous nod.

And so awestruck was Will by the presence before him—the height, the regal gait, the fine black suit—that he had not noticed the clasps on his satchel opening and the papers slipping out. . . .

Now Will was on all fours, snatching up notes, letters, and a long sheet of paper—the second page of the new-printed draft. As he reached for the first page, Washington's shadow grew and a big hand snatched the page from under Will's nose.

Will stood and looked into those eyes, two nail heads set amidst reddening pockmarks. He had heard of Washington's temper, legendary though rarely displayed. He feared that it was about to explode in his face.

"Instead of dropping our papers on the street," said Washington, "protect them with your life."

"Yes, sir."

Washington held the sheet out. Will looked at it, afraid to move.

"Take it," snapped Washington.

By now, Rufus King had hurried back from the state house steps. He slipped the sheet from Washington's hand and said, "Thank you, sir."

Washington's color returned to gray composure. "We must mind the rule of secrecy. If our private papers should be discovered by those inimical to our interests, it could go badly for us."

"Yes, sir," answered King.

"See that your assistant is more careful. Either that or carry your papers yourself." Washington turned and strode across the garden.

King handed the sheet back to Will, who placed it in the satchel. As he did, he noticed a second folio sheet within the first. Rufus King was actually in possession of *two* copies of the plan.

Will tried to tell him. "Unh . . . sir."

But King was in a rush. "Come along. I have letters for you to transcribe."

"Yes, sir." Will closed the satchel and followed. "I'm . . . I'm sorry, sir. I hope the general doesn't hold it against you, that I dropped the papers."

"He brings us to order in the morning and gavels the end of each day. Otherwise, he has spoken only once in open session—when a packet of papers was discovered on the floor of the chamber."

"Was he angry?"

"He threw the papers on the table and said, 'I must entreat the gentlemen to be more careful, lest our transactions get into the newspapers and disturb the public repose by premature speculations.'" King looked at Will. "He used more direct language with you because our ideas have now been set in print, which makes them all the more volatile in a country where half the people distrust what we're doing and the rest don't think we have a right to be doing it."

WILL WAS NOT privy to the deliberations that day. He never was. He had his tasks and his reading, and he spent the afternoon in the library, making copies of King's letters. But that evening, King invited him to dine with some of the New England delegates—Elbridge Gerry and Samuel Gorham of Massachusetts, Roger Sherman and William Johnson of Connecticut, Arthur Gilman and John Langdon of New Hampshire. As New Englanders, these men considered themselves of like interest, if not like mind, on most issues.

Not all of New England was represented, however. No one came from Vermont, as it was not a state; or from Maine, as it was part of Massachusetts; or from Rhode Island, as it was controlled by the political cousins of the Massachusetts Regulators, who saw no good in a convention of merchants and lawyers determining how power would be shared in a nation where they were the smallest state.

During the meal, the gentlemen said little about the day's business. Instead, they discussed the weather, Will's meeting with Washington, and news from home. But once the table was cleared and the port was brought out, along with walnuts and fruit and a round of cheddar, Elbridge Gerry turned the talk to the plan.

"A moment, sir." Rufus King filled a glass and gave it to Will. "Lest we incur the wrath of General Washington, I'll ask my assistant to step outside and guard the door."

Will was happy to remove himself to the hallway, sip port, and read his law books. He positioned a chair in front of the door, so that the lamp in the wall sconce would cast its light over his left shoulder. Then he sat and considered the day just past.

He had held in his hands the blueprint for a new government. He had looked George Washington in the eye. And he had broken bread with some of the most brilliant men in New England. Even then, their voices were rumbling in the room behind him, while loud voices and laughter reverberated up from the taproom.

It had been a year, almost to the day, since the sheriff had come for Will's father. The young man who had stood in that field watching a Hampshire County hawk could never have imagined how far he would travel or how much he would see in so short a time. But still he thought of home.

So he took out a letter from his father, written four months before:

All is well. I am eating better. And the state has lifted the death sentence on the Regulators, so your brother has visited. He brought news that someone killed Nathan Liggett. I asked him to stay, but he said a man had offered him a job on a Newport East Indiaman. He said he'd had enough of tree-cutting and the sea would be his new home. It will not last. Something else will tempt him . . . a new job, another woman. My guess is there's a woman in Newport. Remember, son, love is for rich men and fools. Ignore women until you gain a reputation. Let your brother blow like the wind. You stick like the rock. Hold to your convictions and remember that your father is proud.

Will had answered the letter immediately, had reread it dozens of times, had prayed for a reply ever since. . . .

The voices of the gentlemen grew louder on the other side of the door.

Will took up his law book, angled it to the lamp, read a paragraph, felt his eyelids droop. After another paragraph, his head dropped, his chin struck his chest, his eyes popped open.

He could hear the high-pitched voice of Elbridge Gerry: "We *must* have a bill of rights. Otherwise, this document is a hollow sham."

Someone said, "A bill of rights is implicit in the plan, because the plan does not supersede any bill of rights in any state constitution." It sounded like Roger Sherman, the simple, square-faced barrister who had signed for independence in '76 and had returned to reshape an independent nation in '87.

"If a right is not granted, that does not rescind it," said one of the others.

"Gentlemen"—the voice of Arthur Gilman—"'tis more important to contend with the material printed here than with things which are not addressed. . . ."

Will recognized Rufus King's voice: "I, for one, would like to see what a bill of rights might look like. What issues would we confront? How would we codify them?"

Someone else said, "We must guarantee that church and state are separate."

"But we *are* a Christian nation," mumbled another.

"Indeed," said John Langdon. "But we need no state religions."

"And what about the right to bear arms?" demanded another voice.

"An interesting issue," said Gerry, who sounded as if he was standing just the other side of the door, "especially given the actions of the so-called Regulators against the Springfield arsenal."

Will imagined Gerry, bald head reflecting lamplight, eyes radiating flinty resolve.

Rufus King said, "If those farmers had had more weaponry, their uprising might have been more destructive."

"You don't suggest men should not have the right to carry weapons?" said Gerry.

"I simply state the obvious," answered King. "There was bloodshed that day. And there might have been more if they had gotten their hands on the guns."

Will yawned, blinked several times, tried to get back to his reading.

There came a sound of shuffling papers and the voice of Rufus King: "It seems, gentlemen, that I have an extra copy of the draft. Each of the four folio pages wraps another. Perhaps we might use the extra pages to set down our thoughts on matters we wish to spell out in the next draft or in an attached bill—"

And Will Pike felt his eyes droop once more. . . .

Some time later, he heard the door opening. He leaped to his feet and turned.

Rufus King was smiling at him. "A noble guard. Come and collect the papers."

"Yes, sir." Will slurred the "s" because he had fallen asleep with his mouth open. He moistened his tongue and said, "Will you be needing them again tonight, sir?"

"No. I'll be spending the rest of the evening at the parlor of Mrs. Powel and her husband. They keep a late salon. Leave the papers in my room."

THE PHILADELPHIA STREETS were lit by whale-oil lamps and paved in cobblestone. Though the hour was late, ladies and gentlemen strolled leisurely along. Carriages clattered through pools of yellow light, into deep shadow, back into light. And the clopping of the horses' hooves of-fered counterpoint to the human music of the night . . . someone playing a spinet in a home on Walnut Street, ladies talking by an open window on Sixth, two men laughing at the witticisms of a third as they walked along Eighth.

The boarding house was on Spruce Street. Will slept in a room over the barn. Though he carried a key to King's room, he did not have one to the main house. And the front door was locked, which meant the master had retired early with his jug.

Will considered him a cranky old sot who would be even crankier should a young man awaken him from a drunken stupor, even to deposit papers in the chamber of Rufus King. Such a young man would receive a torrent of invective sprayed through a mist of foul-smelling breath, then see the door slammed in his face.

Will decided that instead he would sleep with King's papers under his pillow and deliver them in the morning. So he made a stop in the out-house, then went up the stairs at the back of the barn.

The horses were quiet in the stalls.

The smell of hay and manure reminded him of home.

At the top of the stairs a door led into the loft. The hay bales were stored at one end, and a rough room, perfect for servant or apprentice, occupied the other.

Will pushed open the door to the room . . . and froze.

Someone was sitting by the window.

"Who's there?" demanded Will.

The shadow said nothing.

"I'm armed," said Will.

The shadow laughed. "You're never armed."

Will squinted into the darkness. "North?"

A flame flared in a lamp. North's face appeared, as if afloat in the darkness.

"My God . . . it's you." Will rushed across the room, took his brother's hand. "There were times I thought they'd hang you."

North grinned. "Times I thought the same. So did Pa. When I come home, he made me sleep in the root cellar, in case Chauncey Yates—"

"How is he?"

"Chauncey?"

"Pa?"

"Well, I come home to tell him how someone killed Nathan Liggett, with his long nose and his droopin' money bags." North chuckled. "Made Pa laugh . . . laugh out loud."

"So," said Will, "how is he?"

"Liggett? Dead."

"No. Pa!" Will felt an invisible hand close around his throat. "How's Pa?"

North pulled the cork out of the bottle on the table and filled two glasses.

"Pa?"

North pushed a glass toward his brother. "He got no more pain."

And now Will felt a sinking in his chest, as if the hand were suddenly letting go, and the fiber of his torso could not hold his organs in place, so they collapsed into his gut as he collapsed into the chair opposite his brother.

"Doc Hines said it was a cancer. But you know what drove the stake in his heart."

"What?"

"You was there." North drained his glass. "The day they took him to prison was the day they killed him."

After a moment, Will got up and took off his linen coat, buff-colored and cool. He folded it and put it in his pine chest of drawers. Then he undid the lace stock around his neck. Then he came back to the table, sat, and took a sip of the drink.

North said, "Seems you care more for your clothes than for all what's been done to our family."

"Pa's gone. I suppose I expected it. But I can't believe it."

"Gone, all right. Killed by lawyers and politicians."

" 'Twas a cancer took him."

"Don't say that." And from somewhere, North Pike produced his knife, swung it through the air, and drove it into the table. "Do not . . . say . . . that. It was the *government* killed him. The government you come here to make stronger."

Will looked at the knife. It was still quivering. So was his brother.

Without making sudden movements, Will took the Madeira bottle and refilled North's glass. He had learned at Conkey's that one of the quickest ways to calm an angry man was to pour him a drink, and he had never seen it fail at the City Tavern, either.

North took a sip. Then he said, "The government killed him." Then he grabbed the knife and drove it back into the table with enough force to split the board. "As sure as if they stuck this blade into his belly."

"All I can tell you about the government—" Will took a swallow. "—is that Rufus King and the others are doing something extraordinary."

"Big damn word, little brother."

"They're finding a way for every state to get along, so that when something is everyone's business, everyone can have a say in it."

"Everyone? Every state?"

"Every state." Will took another swallow and felt his gums begin to tingle.

North said, "I work for a man named Corliss, out of Newport. . . . Newport, *Rhode Island*, and nobody in Rhode Island—not Corliss, not his pretty daughter, no one—trusts anyone who's come here to see that the big states tell the little states what to do."

"Remember what Pa always said. This is a government of laws, and laws are made by men, and men might not always be what God intended them to be, but most are decent just the same."

"Pa had a good heart. But after what we've seen, you're a fool to believe that."

"I'm a good American."

"A fool!" North pulled the knife from the table again and fired it past Will's right ear, so that stuck in the rafter just beyond. "And that's what happens to fools who do foolish things to their neighbors."

Will sat very still, wondering. How could he calm his brother now? He had tried drink. Perhaps an appeal to reason. So he went over to the dresser, opened the leather satchel, and slipped out the four long folio sheets that carried seven printed pages of text. He brought them into the light and said, "Look here. See what they're thinking about, day and night. The first draft . . . the blueprint of the new government."

"And the writing on it?"

Will saw Rufus King's handwriting in one corner, Elbridge Gerry's neat script in another, both in ink. Someone else had left pencil notes in the margin on another page. Will recognized the hand of Roger Sherman, and those of Gorham and Gilman, and John Langdon, too.

King had written "Rights" and a series of fragmentary ideas. Will read the first: "No law regarding religion; freedoms of press, speech protected; peaceable assembly respected. . . ."

Meanwhile, North read aloud a comment from Gerry: "'A well regulated militia being necessary to the Security of a Free State, the right of the people to keep and bear arms shall not be infringed.'"

North looked at his brother, "Does he mean that only the militia will have arms? Better not show this to the men who tried to take the Springfield arsenal."

Will pointed to King's notes. "The right to keep and bear arms must be discussed and defined."

"What does that mean?" demanded North. "'Discussed and defined'?"

Will shook his head. "It's . . . it's only a small part of the document. These handwritten articles may never even be included."

"If I don't like what's handwritten, why should I like what's printed? Why should any man in Rhode Island? Or any man in New England? Or any who values freedom?"

"Wait and see. These men are well-intentioned."

"These men are *rich* men, fixin' to do what rich men do." North got up and pulled the knife out of the rafter.

"What is it that rich men do?" asked Will, keeping his eyes on the document.

"See to the rich." North drove the knife into the table again.

"Maybe you're right." Will gathered up the pages, knowing that he never should have taken them out in the first place. He slipped them back into the satchel, which he slipped under his pillow. Then he refilled both glasses. "Let's just drink."

And the second time he tried it, drink seemed to work.

They finished the first bottle. Then North pulled the knife out of the table and raised it to eye level. He put his other hand on the table, fingers splayed wide, and dropped the knife. It struck between his thumb and index finger. "Missed. Guess I need more to drink."

So Will pulled a bottle of port from beneath his mattress.

"A bottle under the bed," said North. "My brother's becomin' a man."

Will filled both glasses and raised his. "To Pa." He threw back another long swallow, hot and sweet. And a sob burst out of him. It shocked him, as if an animal had leaped out of a burrow in his belly. Then he surrendered to the grief, and he felt the better for it, as he would have vomiting up bad meat.

North put a big scarred hand on Will's forearm; then he dragged a dirty sleeve across his face, because he was crying, too.

But they did not cry long. They may have been the sons of a dead father. But as their father would have told them, they were men, too, and men did not cry.

So they drank some more and ended the night pissing onto the manure pile from the loft door.

WILL DID NOT awaken until he heard the stable boy mucking the stalls below. The sunlight was on his face . . . and in his eyes. After eight o'clock!

He popped up in bed, and a hammer-on-anvil pain struck him on the top of the skull. He dropped back onto the pillow and groaned because his eyeballs were pressing into his brain . . . or was his brain forcing his eyeballs out of their sockets?

He could not tell, but something was forcing its way up from his stomach, too, something foul and burning. He made it to the loft door in time to drop a long stream of vomit onto the manure pile.

Then he sat back on the rough-board floor, grief once more clutching his chest while port and Madeira throbbed in his head. . . .

His father was gone. And his brother was . . .

He vaguely remembered North cutting into a hay bale, spreading it and . . .

He staggered back to the room. There was the hay on the floor . . . empty bottles on the table . . . his pillow in the sunlight . . . and no North. He snatched the pillow off the bed . . . no leather satchel, either. He almost vomited again.

Then he saw the satchel on the chest of drawers and said, "Thank God."

Had he left it there after all? His mind was still foggy. He opened it and there were letters . . . papers . . . one sheet of the first draft, without annotations . . . another . . . and . . .

He sat on the edge of his bed and tried to force his head clear of grief, anger, and popskull pain, so that he could face the reality: His brother had taken the annotated draft.

What would he tell Rufus King? Or Washington? That his brother had stolen the papers because . . . why? He wished to impress a Rhode Island shipper who had a pretty daughter? In the hands of the Rhode Island opposition, a first draft could be a potent tool when the time came to ratify the new plan.

If Will did not get it back, and soon, his reputation was ruined, and the future of the country might be in jeopardy. Washington had said as much the day before.

Then Will noticed something else on the chest of drawers: a watch, and beneath it, a note: "You say you are a good American. I am too. Americans should see what goes on here. I am sorry if this causes you trouble. I don't do it for money. If I did I would not leave you the watch. It's gold. I give it to Pa. He liked it. His eyes were bad, so he never read the initials."

The letters "N.L." were engraved into the watch. Nathan Liggett.

Rufus King was already at the dining room table, perusing his copy of the *Pennsylvania Packet and Daily Advertiser.* "Ah, Good morning, Will. Slept late. Slept well, I hope?"

Will put the satchel on the table and said that, no, he had not slept well and did not feel well, either. "Something I ate, sir, or perhaps drank."

"Perhaps." King looked at the colorless complexion and bloodshot eyes, nodded as if he had seen such things before, and excused Will from his duties for the morning. "Drink some hot tea. Make it strong. It will make you vomit. By afternoon, you should feel better."

By afternoon, Will Pike felt worse than he ever had in his life.

After strong tea and more vomiting, he had dragged himself down to the dock and discovered that the *Pretty Eve*, registered to Thornton Corliss of Newport, Rhode Island, had sailed at dawn with a load of Pennsylvania pig iron.

Will rushed back to the boarding house, packed his bag, and wrote a note that he placed on Rufus King's pillow.

Dear Sir: It is with extreme humiliation that I inform you of the theft of the annotated draft. I have suspicion as to the thief, so I go in pursuit. I pray that I am able to restore it to you before your private deliberations are made public. I pray as well that I am able to restore my reputation, if not in the eyes of the world, at least in the eyes of a man who has shown me such respect and taught me so much.

Will Pike fled Philadelphia on the afternoon coach.

As it rocked north on the Post Road, he cursed his brother and prayed that he could reach Newport more quickly by land than his brother could reach it by sea. And the motion made him want to vomit again.

SIX

P E T E R A N D E V A N G E L I N E A P P R O A C H E D Newport late in the afternoon.

They were coming from the west, so they crossed Narragansett Bay on two majestic bridges—the Jamestown, then the Pell. They were traveling east, so the sky ahead of them was darkening and the water was cool blue. It was drive time, so the syndicated talker named Kelly Cutter was on the radio. It was Sunday, so the show was on tape.

"Why do you listen to her?" asked Evangeline.

"To see all sides," said Peter. "And sometimes, she's right."

Kelly was saying, "It's simple folks. The liberal elite . . ."

"Elite, my ass," said Evangeline. "She went to Yale, and she's whining about the elites. What a phony."

". . . thinks that their agenda is more important than your freedom. It's always that way. And why? Because they want everyone beholden to the government. It's the only way they can stay in power."

"Now what does that have to do with gun control?" asked Evangeline.

Peter pulled out his cell phone. "Call her. She loves to get some liberal sweetie on the phone and fight with her."

Kelly's cool voice began to rise. "Liberals created the welfare state because once people stand on their own two feet, they don't need welfare, so they don't need liberals, so liberals lose power. We've seen that for seventy-five years. And now the liberals want to take our guns. Why?"

"So the only ones who'll have guns are liberals?" said Evangeline to the radio.

Kelly was answering her own question. "So the only ones who'll have guns are the government."

"Do we have to listen to this?" asked Evangeline.

"Let her finish," said Peter. "She's funny."

"She's full of shit."

"That way, when something bad happens, we have to pick up the phone and call the government. 'Help! Help! There's a robber in my house. Quick! Get me Barney Frank! He's not there? Well, get me another congressman. A Democrat congressman.'"

"It's Demo*cratic*." Evangeline clicked off the radio. "When it modifies a noun, it's Demo*cratic*. It's an adjective. It's in the dictionary. Why do these rightie stooges think they can piss us off by doing that?"

"Because they do," Peter said. "Kelly sits up there in her Vermont studio and talks trash and takes calls and pisses people off all over America."

"Well, I am pissed off. And I have a headache. A carsick headache."

"Cheer up. Lunch in the Litchfield Hills, dinner in Newport, maybe a nice stroll along the Cliff Walk . . . what can be bad?"

"That we have to do it all in a single day."

"I have the sense we're on to something. I don't want the trail to go cold."

"I'm a travel writer. I write about Vermont bed-and-breakfasts and bouillabaisse in Provence. I'm not *on to* anything."

"Famous last words."

She opened the glove compartment. "Do you have any Advil in here?"

He reached into a side pocket on his door and pulled out a tin of aspirin. "Here."

She took the pills with the last swallow of her Evian.

"So aren't you the least bit curious?" Peter asked. "We couldn't meet the seller because he's dead, so we met the seller's agent and the buyer."

"And one knew more than he was telling, and the other was lying," she said.

"Right. You think Bindle has more up his sleeve, and Cottle is after more than documents relating to the birth of the nation. So let's meet someone else who has an interest in the proceeds of that Knox letter—the seller's closest relation—and see what you think about him."

They were coming to the end of the Pell Bridge. They could see the old town and wharves to their right. But they did not notice the black Chrysler Sebring that had followed them from western Connecticut.

In summer or fall, Newport oozed people. It oozed history, too, year round.

Even with the traffic speeding along America's Cup Avenue and the tourist buses and the cruise ships disgorging gawkers in tank tops and Tevas, Peter Fallon felt time itself flowing along the boulevards and side streets, bubbling up through the manhole covers, reacting in the air with molecules of fried food and exhaust, so that every breath of today carried a scent of the past, whether people knew what they were inhaling or not.

And it wasn't just the Gilded Age, when the rich built their monuments in a world with no income tax. There was an earlier Newport, too. You could find it in Colonial House, where Royal governors ruled and George Washington dined; in the handsome homes around Trinity Church, which boasted the oldest steeple in America; at Touro Synagogue, the oldest temple; or at the waterfront, where the Triangle Trade—molasses to rum to slaves—had once set one of its legs.

Now, the offices of Farrell Development were on one of the wharves, overlooking the boat slips and seafood restaurants.

An operator.

That was Peter's Fallon's first impression of Tommy Farrell:

About forty. Green golf shirt showing the simian slope of his shoulders. The slung-forward chest and belly suggesting he had spent plenty of time swinging hammers on his own jobs. Black trousers, no pleats, thin waist. Black hair combed straight back. A young face, skin as tight as a grape and shiny, too, as if he had just shaved. And one of those dog-toothed smiles—all lips and choppers, not a bit of motion around the eyes.

Yes . . . *an operator.*

They made their way through a little reception area to a space that seemed larger than it was because a floor-to-ceiling window overlooked the harbor.

Peter and Evangeline sat on the sofa. On the wall behind them were elevations for what looked like a strip mall. On the opposite wall was a huge aerial photo of the Pike-Perkins Mill complex.

Tommy dropped into the chair behind his desk and picked up the phone. "Can I get you anything?

"No thanks," said Peter.

"You sure? I own the wharf so the Snappin' Scallop—that's the restaurant—they take good care of me. How about some oysters-on-the-half and a few beers?"

"Sounds good," said Peter, "but—"

"Business first." Tommy hung up the phone.

"I'd like a Diet Coke," said Evangeline.

Tommy got up and took a one from the little refrigerator in the corner. "Glass?"

"No thanks," she said. "I'm a can girl, myself."

Peter chuckled to himself. She was a Riedel glass girl. She was also a neat freak. A place for everything, everything in its place. Better a clean can than a dirty glass.

Tommy sat again and glanced out the window, all casual, all cool, a good way to act when you were praising yourself. "Best thing I ever did, buyin' this wharf. Rent on thirty slips, the restaurant, a sail-making shop, and I can look out any time and watch for the nice chicks around the raw bar down there."

Evangeline wiped off the can and popped the top. "Do you see any now?"

"It's a little slow for a Sunday afternoon in October." He leaned back. "But that sofa's had a lot of use after hours, if you know what I mean."

Peter noticed Evangeline eyeing the cushions. Looking for stains?

"Now, what can I do for you?" asked Farrell.

Peter said, "As I told you on the phone, I'm interested in doing business with your late uncle's friend, Morris Bindle."

"Nice guy," said Tommy.

"Did you know that he has a scrapbook that belonged to Buster?"

"Scrapbook?" Tommy showed the dog teeth, pretending to smile, perhaps because he was hearing something for the first time. "Buster had a bunch of scrapbooks. Clippings, letters, old stuff like that. Some old ancestor of his filled them. Buster said he planned to show them to Bindle some time."

"He did. And Bindle sold a letter out of one of them for Buster." Peter paused. He could have offered more but he wanted to see if Farrell bit on anything he had said. "Any objections to that?"

"That he sold something for Buster? Unh . . . no. Why should I? Bindle was a good friend to Buster. And he keeps his eye on that complex for me." Farrell swept his hand toward the photograph of the mill. "Having the historical society in there looks good. Looks like something is happening while I get the financing together. Mixed use, restaurants, retail, condos."

Peter said, "A big headache to develop such an old place."

"Yeah," said Evangeline. "Much easier to build another strip mall."

Tommy Farrell showed her the dog teeth. "Have you ever bought a pizza? Ever needed to get your oil changed? Bought a gallon of milk at Cumberland Farms? Nothing wrong with strip malls."

"I didn't say there was," she answered.

"Strip malls are part of my vision. So are wharves. So's Pike-Perkins."

"You have to have a vision," said Peter.

"Damn right."

"Now, about Uncle Buster," said Peter.

"A good old soul. Married late. Never had kids. I tried to visit him once in a while, tried to get him to make out a will. Never got around to it. Died in his recliner, with the ashtray full of butts and the oxygen tank empty and the ball game on TV."

"What about the Pikes?" asked Peter. "Are you the only one left?"

"I'm not a Pike. Buster married my aunt back in the eighties. But she was good to me, so I made sure I was good to Buster after she passed."

"Are there any Pikes around?" asked Evangeline.

"None with the name, but descendants all over New England. We don't hang out. And Buster had no money to bring out the vultures. I didn't even know who to call when he died. But now, I get this in the mail—" He held up two tickets to the Bishop Media Box at Fenway Park for game eight on the strip of play-off tickets.

Peter let out a whistle. Pure envy. "If they beat the Yanks, that will be the first game of the World Series."

"Charlie Bishop, the media king. He's one of Buster's blood relatives. He wants to bring all the descendants together at the—" Tommy held up the note accompanying the tickets. "—'mecca of New England.'"

"For a kind of memorial to Buster?" asked Evangeline.

"Either that or he wants to put in his dibs on the house in Millbridge. Everyone gets a piece of the house, once the probate court decides."

"Back to our business," said Peter. "Do you think the rest of the family will come after Bindle if we sell a letter for a lot of money out of that scrapbook?"

"If Bindle has a bill of sale, I'll vouch for Buster's sanity. I saw him a few days before he died, and he was sharp as a tack." And he flashed the dog teeth one last time.

"ANY THOUGHTS," SAID Peter when they got outside.

"I need a little ocean air to clear my head," said Evangeline. "Let's take a stroll on the Cliff Walk. Then we can drive back to Boston and I'll cook you dinner."

"Works for me," said Peter. "And while we're strolling, come up with an answer to this: What does a small-time developer from Rhode Island have that someone like Charles Bishop could want so much that he'd waste a World Series ticket trying to get it?"

"Beats me. You're the baseball fan."

Peter turned the BMW toward Bellevue Avenue, away from the harbor, where old Newport had been born as a haven of religious freedom in the seventeenth century, had outstripped New York as a trading port in the eighteenth, and had then died. Resurrection had come in the 1850s, when a local real estate man decided to cut a road along the cliff that faced the Atlantic. The breeze there was steady and cool on hot afternoons, and the view stretched all the way to England. Within a few years, it had become the most valuable real estate in America, where the rich built their grand summer "cottages" and the Gilded Age went to glitter in the sun.

Most of the "cottages" were museums now. But names like the Breakers, Kingscote Mansion, and the Elms still resonated with the sound of money in its most refined forms—the clatter of china and glassware, the harmonies of a string quartet playing an evening waltz or late-night ragtime, the thump of a tennis racket striking a ball, and the laughter of the ones with the money, sometimes gentle, sometimes mirthful, sometimes simply smug.

Along these shaded avenues, behind these high walls, across these broad lawns, a handful of people—just four hundred according to the social register—had balanced themselves for generations atop the pyramid of American capitalism, as secure in their wealth as the mansions were on that granite cliff.

Whenever he parked on Ruggles Avenue, at the public access to the Cliff Walk, Peter glanced up at the windows of the Breakers and expected to see rich ghosts peering out, wondering why this son of a Boston bricklayer was trespassing on their turf. But the rich ghosts were as dead as their servants. And Peter didn't let anyone, living or dead, rich or poor, intimidate him out of any neighborhood.

So he followed Evangeline onto the Cliff Walk.

"Welcome to one of the fifty places of a lifetime," she said. "That's what National Geographic *Traveler* calls this."

"Leave it to you to know that."

"A three-and-a-half-mile path along the rim of the Atlantic, right through the backyards of all those glorious monuments to robber-baron empire building."

"It's really a monument to fishermen," said Peter. "When they saw the houses going up, the locals said no one was going to keep them from fishing on the rocks. So they fought for a path."

"Leave it to you to know *that*," she said.

There weren't many people on the Cliff Walk as the October light faded. A young couple was meandering, stopping every now and then to take in the view and steal a kiss. A mother was hustling along with two squalling kids in a twin stroller, promising in strained but sweet tones that they'd be home soon. A black Chrysler Sebring was pulling up on Ruggles Street and a young man with a digital camera was getting out.

"Come on." Evangeline started to move briskly along the path. "Let's go to the Forty Steps and back."

"Are you power walking? No power walking," said Peter. "Power walking is for people who want to look like they're exercising when they're not. Either walk or run."

"I'm walking fast. And I'm feeling better." She picked up her pace. "The smell of salt air and old money always helps."

"Reminds you of your family." Peter followed after her.

"Tommy Farrell reminds you of yours."

"No one in my family was ever that sleazy," said Peter. "Or that ambitious."

"He doesn't seem too bothered by whatever Buster sold."

"And he doesn't seem to have a clue about Henry Knox and his contemporaries."

"So he's clueless," she said, "like us."

For a while, they didn't say any more. The Cliff Walk was a place to move and think and look. They would have an hour in the car for talking.

In some places, the path was right at the edge of the cliff, with a wall to lean on while you watched the waves crashing on the rocks below. In other places, it was a garden path, flanked by evergreens or expanses of lawn from which to view the big houses, which seemed all the more enormous in the gloaming.

When Peter and Evangeline reached the Forty Steps, he asked her if she wanted to go down onto the rocks.

"No," she said. "I shouldn't have had that Diet Coke. I need to get to a bathroom."

"Too slippery down there anyway," said Peter. "And it's starting to get dark."

Just then, a light flashed nearby.

A young man was photographing the south side of the Breakers in the rose glow of sunset.

"Evening," he said as Peter and Evangeline approached.

He would have been nondescript—bland features, dirty blond hair, T-shirt, Dockers, topsiders—but for the physique. He didn't seem to know what he was doing with a camera, but it looked as if he did in the weight room. He was all shoulders and pectorals, lean muscle, built by lots of reps with light weights.

"Nice night," said Peter.

"Would you folks do me a favor?" asked the man. "Would you take a picture of me in front of Breakers?"

"Sure," said Peter. "But it's getting dark. The flash may not fill past ten feet."

"Let's do two. One with, one without." He handed Peter his Canon Elph digital.

"I have one of these myself." Peter raised the camera.

The man struck a pose. "I've been taking pictures all over New England. I want to do a book."

"Smile," said Evangeline.

The flash fired, and Peter said, "What's the title?"

"*Digital New England*. With themes. I like themes. I'm doing the Cliff Walk at dusk every month."

Peter flipped a switch on the back of the camera to look at the picture. "Pretty good," he said. Then he clicked the "back" button, which showed the Breakers in the last rays of the sun. Then he clicked it again and saw himself and Evangeline on the Cliff Walk.

The man came over and gently took the camera from Peter's hand. "Here." He flipped another switch and turned off the flash. "One more for posterity."

And that was that. The young man headed toward the Forty Steps, Peter and Evangeline toward their car.

But as soon as Peter turned onto Ruggles Street, he sensed that something was wrong. His BMW was tilted to the driver's side.

Two flat tires. Not low. Absolutely flattened.

Evangeline made a crack about the luck needed to hit the same nail with two wheels.

Peter grabbed the jack, cursed a few times, and went to work. Before long he had the car's tail in the air and the lugs off.

"Wow." The guy with the camera came strolling up. "Twin flats. Don't see that too often."

Peter dropped the last lug nut into his hubcap.

Evangeline was standing beside the car, holding the spare up with her fingertips.

"Here, let me help." The guy took the spare from Evangeline, and as Peter lifted the flat off the car, he raised the spare, slid the tire onto the wheel, and screwed the lugs loosely into place.

Peter checked the sidewall, but there were no slash marks. So maybe he really had been unlucky enough to drive over the same nail twice. Then he ran his hands over the treads and felt nothing, no nailheads, no holes, just a few pieces of gravel stuck in the treads.

"That's the damnedest thing," he said.

"Damnedest things always seem to happen at the damnedest times. My name is Stanley, by the way, Stanley Benson."

Peter introduced himself and Evangeline, and she thanked Stanley Benson, too.

Then Stanley Benson said. "Why don't I take the flat up to that gas station in town, get it fixed, and bring it back. Meanwhile, you can jack up the front and have it ready."

Evangeline said, "The station must have a ladies' room."

"Most do." Without waiting for Peter to say yes or no, Stanley Benson picked up the flat rear tire and flung it into his trunk. Then he opened his passenger door for Evangeline.

"Do you want anything?" she asked Peter.

"No. Unh . . . do you really have to—?"

"Yes. I really do," she said, and she got into Benson's black Sebring.

And Peter made a snap decision: This guy is all right. She'll be safe with him. And he watched them drive away.

Then he made one of those after-the-fact justifications to convince himself that he had made a good decision, even if a voice in the back of his head was saying otherwise: If Evangeline is with him, Stanley Benson won't drive off with the tire, and the guy in the gas station will fix it faster, because Evangeline can be very persuasive. Besides, she's traveled the world on her own. She's relied hundreds of times on the kindness of strangers. She has a sixth sense about people.

So Peter tightened the nuts on the rear wheel, then lowered the car and took the jack to the front and fitted it under the frame.

And then a thought struck him: If he believed, even for a moment, that the guy might steal the tire, why would he let Evangeline get into the car with him?

So he went back to convincing himself: They were in Newport. There was no crime in Newport. Crime happened in big cities, not tourist towns in October. But once upon a time, Newport had been home to pirates, slavers, privateers, troublemakers of every kind. . . .

WILL PIKE REACHED Rhode Island in five days.

Through scores of towns and across dozens of rivers, he had prayed that the winds would be contrary, for a schooner making six knots around the clock could surely get to Newport before a coach that stopped each night.

In South Ferry, Will took passage across Narragansett Bay, bound for the ancient capital that was renowned for a fine harbor, for religious tolerance, and since the Revolution, for hard times, too.

Newport had been occupied by the British and then by the French, and while one was enemy and the other ally, neither had done any good for the seafaring economy that once thrived there. As the ferry master said, "Only a few shippers made it through the war, mostly the ones who was good at smugglin' and privateerin'."

Will asked if Thornton Corliss was one of them.

"Was and is. Was and is. One of the last shippers to own a wharf, so he must be makin' money somehow."

It was raining when the ferry docked, and getting dark earlier each night.

Even in August, the New Englander could sense the coming of winter in the shortening of the days. And Will knew that if he did not find his brother, his reputation would face a lifelong winter in the minds of men who mattered.

He had swallowed his trepidations so often recently that they had become a source of sustenance. He swallowed them once more, picked up his bag, and started walking. He made his way along the waterfront, past the taverns and counting houses and working wharves, and the loudest noise he heard was the patter of the rain.

What the ferryman said was true. Newport's day had passed.

Lights burned in a ship chandler's. A few people hurried with their heads down in the deepening darkness. A lone fishing boat unloaded a catch. But it was not until he approached Corliss Wharf that Will sensed any life.

Laughter, fiddle music, and golden lamplight poured from a tavern, along with a staggering of sailors and their doxies. And if sailors were carousing, thought Will, it meant that they had gotten paid, which meant that a ship had come in. He needed to go only a short distance down the wharf to find the name *Pretty Eve* on the transom of a big black-hulled schooner.

And his trepidations rose again, like the bilious puke that woke him that last morning in Philadelphia. His brother had gotten there first.

No lights burned aboard the ship, so Will turned to the tavern.

The sign hanging over the door showed two eyes looking in opposite directions and the words WALL-EYED FRANK's above a frothing tankard. Will wiped his hands down the front of his waistcoat, then stepped into the tobacco smoke and noise.

And every eye turned to him. Some were bleary, others sharp. Some looked him down from hat to boots; others looked first at the burlap bag in his hand. Even the fiddle player glanced up but kept scratching out a jig that kept a pair of sailors dancing.

This was no City Tavern, thought Will. It wasn't even Conkey's. It was the kind of place his brother had told him about, "where a man needed a knife in his belt and a third eye in the back of his head."

Will had hoped that his brother might be among the drinkers. But there was no North Pike to be seen. So he went to the bar, dropped the bag on the floor between his feet, and asked for a pint of ale.

The publican was bullwhip-skinny and seemed to be looking around you when he looked right at you. This, Will surmised, was Frank. He said, "Two shillin's."

Will flipped a coin from his waistcoat and a mug appeared on the bar. As he reached for it, a hand came from behind him and grabbed it.

The hand belonged to a sailor with a chest like a cask, breath like bilge, and a face that looked like three bungholes driven into a hogshead. "It's custom at Wall-Eyed Frank's for strangers to buy everyone a drink."

"I'm afraid I don't have the money to buy but one, sir." As soon as he said it, Will knew it sounded too polite.

"Then this one's for me." The sailor slid the mug toward himself.

"Let the lad alone," said Wall-Eyed Frank, and from beneath the bar, a club appeared and came whistling down on the sailor's wrist.

The hand flew back, Will snatched the mug before it spilled, and the sailor lunged at Frank, who cocked the club again: "Come closer, and your brains'll be on the floor."

And the fiddler kept fiddling, as if this were all in a night beneath the sign of the wall-eyes.

The sailor spat, looked at his two friends in the corner, jerked his head at Will.

"I'm warnin' you, Curly Bill Barton," said Frank, whose wall-eyes seemed to miss nothing. "This stranger paid me coin. Hard money, which be what Old Man Corliss likes."

Curly fixed a false grin on his face and said to Will, "You carryin' more coin?"

Frank snapped the club again, this time right off the top of Curly's knit cap. "I said stand down, you son of a bitch. Leave him alone."

Curly pulled off the cap, revealing a head as shiny bald as a binnacle, and rubbed a knot on the top of his skull. "Wall-Eye, some night I'm gonna kill you."

"If you do, Old Man Corliss won't ever let you sail on one of his ships again, 'cause he likes a clean wharf and clean sailors."

Curly headed back to the corner, but stopped when Will said, "Hey."

"What?"

"Did you sail on the *Pretty Eve?*"

Curly turned. "And if did?"

"I'll buy you that drink." Will handed him the mug and put a coin on the bar.

Curly drained the first mug, plunked it down, and snatched the second before Will could touch it.

No matter. Will's mouth was cotton-dry but not from thirst. Best to ask his questions and get out of there. "Do you know North Pike?" he asked.

And for the first time, the fiddler missed a beat.

Curly brought his face close to Will's again. "What's North Pike to you?"

"My brother." Will knew that was a mistake as soon as it was out of his mouth.

Curly grabbed him, while the two in the corner—one as big, both as ugly—pushed away from their table. "That son of a bitch took my job. And he cheats at cards. And he owes me money—"

And with a loud crack, the barkeep's club landed again on the Curly's head. This time, Curly collapsed. Then Wall-Eyed Frank told Will to get out.

"Just tell me where I can find Corliss," said Will.

"We'll take you." It was one of the other sailors, coming toward him.

Wall-Eyed Frank pulled a musket from behind the bar. "Stand down," he said to the sailors; then he told Will, "In the shadow of the church steeple, yellow house, white fence. And tell Corliss how hard I work to keep a clean wharf."

THE STEEPLE OF Trinity Church poked into the clouds lowering over the town. Will went toward it and was soon climbing a gentle hill. The yellow house with the white fence was easy enough to find, even in the dark. It was a grand house—two full stories, with dormers and six-over-six windows, not a house that a Pelham farm boy would have visited, but Will had been to Boston and New York and Philadelphia, so no Newport house would impress him.

He could hear voices coming out of the window to his left—two men and a woman, arguing. Words like "West Indies molasses," "godless Niggers," and "Rhode Island rum" were flying like fists.

Will shook the rain from his tricorne, brushed it from his shoulders, and dragged the bottoms of his shoes across the boot scraper. As for the mud splattered over his stockings, there was nothing to do. He banged the knocker, and the conversation stopped, followed by footfalls in the foyer, then the front door popping open.

"Yes?" The man was tall and long-faced, with dark hair tied in a queue and side whiskers almost to his chin.

"Good evening, sir. My name is William Pike. I've come a great distance in the . . . in the hopes of seeing Mr. Corliss."

"Pike, did you say?"

Will heard an accent. He had met a Frenchman in Philadelphia who sounded much the same. He said, "Yes, sir. Pike."

The man's eyes narrowed. He looked Will over, looked behind him to see if anyone was hiding in the shadows, then opened the door. "Please to wait here."

Yes, thought Will, a Frenchman who worked for a rich man, if the Turkey carpets, tall-case clock, and flat-glass mirrors in the foyer were any indication.

The Frenchman's voice rumbled in the next room, stopping at the word, "Pike." The female voice said, "Pike?" The older man said, "Good God! Not another one!"

A moment later, Will was in the library, looking into the face of Thornton Corliss. He had expected a big man, but Corliss was small and gray, dressed in breeches and waistcoat of black.

The real presence was the young woman standing by the bookcase. She was slender, not yet twenty, with dark brows that gave her face a kind of proud ferocity, even in repose. And her long neck enhanced the angle of her chin, which she held as if to announce that she thought herself the better of anyone in the room.

"Stop staring at my daughter," Corliss snapped at Will.

"It runs in the family," said the Frenchman.

"Aye," grunted Corliss. "Now, Mr. Pike, what do you want?"

"I'm looking for my brother." Will returned his gaze to Corliss, though he felt the eyes of the girl and the Frenchman boring into him.

"North Pike?" said Corliss. "He was here last night."

"Mr. Corliss, he does not speak to his sailors," said the Frenchman. "But your brother said he had a thing of value for us. And he has done us good turns."

"Good turns?" said the girl. "He stopped a mutiny on your slave ship."

Corliss looked at Will. "We were busy arguing when you knocked."

"I'm sorry to interrupt, sir," said Will, "but my brother has spoken highly of you."

The Frenchman laughed at that.

Will had already decided he did not like the Frenchman's attitude, and he was liking it even less.

"Your brother came here after the *Pretty Eve* docked." Corliss shot a glance at his daughter. "We sent him on his way."

The girl raised her chin. "You were very impolite, Father. He said he had a gift, something that would stand you in good stead throughout Rhode Island."

Will asked the girl, "Did he say what the gift was?"

"Is that any of your business, m'sieur?" asked the Frenchman.

"If it's what I think it is, he stole it from me," said Will. "I want it back."

"He told us it was the new Constitution," said Corliss. "He said that since Rhode Island opposes stronger government, I'd gain favor if I gave it to our lawmakers, so they might study it, find its flaws, and prepare to fight it when it's offered to the nation."

Just as Will had suspected.

"I told him I didn't want any part of his document," Corliss went on. "It'll have no rule over me. Now or ever. And that's how most Americans feel."

"It's my hope that most Americans will change their minds," said Will. "But if their opinions harden before the drafting is complete—"

"Mr. Pike," said Corliss, "your brother doesn't care a fig about most Americans or their opinions. He was trying to ingratiate himself. He's sweet on my daughter."

"Father!" cried the girl. "I have no interest in him, or"—she glanced at the Frenchman—"anyone else in breeches." Then she stalked out of the room.

Corliss watched her go, then shuffled over to his desk and sat. "'Tis a mistake to discuss business with one's daughter, Mr. Pike. We ship rum to Africa, then transport slaves to the plantation owned by M'sieur Danton's family in the West Indies, then carry molasses back to Rhode Island, so our distillers can make more rum. My daughter considers it a crime."

"No crime," said the Frenchman. "Only good business, *n'est-ce pas?*"

Will did not offer his opinion. He did not think they would like it.

"Good business," said Corliss "That's my goal. So *I* don't care a fig for politics, either, and I don't care where your brother has gone, so long as he's gone from here."

"Your brother, he say that if men in the capital of Rhode Island do not want his gift," the Frenchman added, "there are men in the capital of Massachusetts who will."

"So it's to Boston you should go," said Corliss. "But since you seem more cultured than your brother, we'll offer you lodging for the night. And perhaps you'll offer us a few stories. Tell me, have you met Washington?"

"Is he still a—how do you say—bungler?"

"Bungler?" said Will. "General Washington?"

Corliss explained that Robert Danton had been on the staff of General Rochambeau when the French came to Newport. He had met Washington and had been unimpressed.

Another reason, thought Will, to dislike the big Frenchman.

THORNTON CORLISS MADE more noise asleep than awake.

Though Will was in a room at the back of the house and Corliss was in the front, Will could feel the floor vibrate with the sound of snoring.

But even if the house had been silent, Will could not have slept for the questions swirling in his head. How would he find his brother in Boston? What would he do if his brother had sold the document? How would he ever show his face again in the places that mattered?

His ambition had been to leave a mark. Rufus King had given him a chance. And his own brother had ruined it. The only mark he would leave now would be as ephemeral as the circle of a hawk in the sky, or worse, as indelible as a tattoo. He might as well go home to Pelham and forget his dreams . . . or go to sea like his brother . . . or . . .

He tried to clear his mind so that he could sleep. Instead, the face of Washington appeared, telling him to protect the Constitution with his life.

He tried to drive Washington out by ruminating on his father's philosophy that men might not always be what God intended them to be but most were decent just the same. Recent events had called that wisdom into question. So he tried thinking about something a young man thought about often—young women.

And the young woman he conjured was Eve Corliss. He imagined kissing her, pressing his lips to the side of her neck, untying her bodice, touching her breasts. In a moment, she was naked in his mind's eye, as naked as the pictures he had seen in sketchbooks, of voluptuous women with rouged lips and risen nipples and tendrils of dark hair between their legs.

And he was doing in his mind all that he yearned to do with his body. This brought a bodily response that drained every thought from his head and in a few moments led to a physical release that allowed him at last to sleep. . . .

HE DID NOT expect that the girl in his imagination would stay in his bed. Or that she would take on weight and warmth as he slept. Or that she would shake him awake him later in the night. But she did.

He tried to speak "What—"

Her hand, wet with real perspiration, clamped over his mouth. She whispered, "I know where your brother has gone." Then she took the hand away.

Will sat up and looked into the eyes shining in the dark. She was right there, under the covers, in her nightgown.

She leaned toward him, her breast pressing against his arm.

"You . . . you shouldn't be here," he said. "Your father will shoot me."

"If you want to find your brother, get dressed. I'll take you to him."

"Is he here? In Newport?

"He's gone to Boston."

Will lifted himself on his elbow, though at that moment, he could have lifted himself on the member rising between his legs. "Where in Boston?"

"I won't tell you. I'll take you."

"But—"

"I'll take you. Or you can find him yourself."

He rolled toward her, and she twitched away, which was for the best, because he didn't think he could control himself much longer.

He said, "Your father won't let you go to Boston with me."

"Neither will Danton. He wants to marry me and unite my father's company with his family's plantation in the Indies."

"Marry you? He must be ten years older."

"And I don't love him. So I'm going to your brother."

"Then you *are* you sweet on him?"

"Sweet on him? Sweet on him?" She managed to fill her whisper with indignation. "I love him. And he loves me."

And for all the other emotions roiling him, Will Pike let out a burst of laughter. He knew that his brother never loved any woman . . . for long.

But Eve Corliss did not seem a girl who was used to having anyone laugh at her. She rolled back to him and pressed herself against him, so that his hardness met her softness. . . .

That stopped the laughing because Will's breath suddenly caught in his throat. He looked into those glistening eyes and pressed against her. Then he pulled back. And she pressed forward . . . and he pulled back . . . and she pressed . . . and he pressed . . . and—God help him—he let his hands slide down her back and bunch her nightgown and . . .

Her whisper was hot and moist in his ear, "Take me with you or I'll cry rape right now. Say you'll take me, then try to run, and I'll cry rape as soon as you're gone. And who in this house would not believe me, when I told them of your nightshirt, all damp from what you've been doing with yourself? Proof of your depravity."

FLEEING WITH THE daughter of Thornton Corliss was a bad decision that looked even worse in the dawn drizzle. They had put twenty miles between themselves and Newport, crossed the Sakonnet River by ferry, and were moving through the woods north of Fall River, Massachusetts. And Will was wishing he had stayed to face a cry of rape.

Eve was riding her own horse, a dappled gray filly. For Will, she had taken a big black gelding out of the barn. And though the night before she had demonstrated the most feminine of wiles in her ability to manipulate him, daylight made her seem more a girl than a woman, which only heightened Will's resentment.

"You don't think they'll catch up, do you?" she asked.

"How could they catch up? You said the household didn't rise until six."

"What time is it now?"

He pulled out the gold watch that had once belonged to Nathan Liggett. "It's half past six. Ten minutes ago, it was twenty past. Ten minutes before that, ten past."

"So they're on the road now," she said. "So we should be riding faster."

"We're going plenty fast for horses on a long trip," said Will.

Her answer was to kick her filly into a canter.

He reined his horse and watched her. She wore good boots, hiked her skirts, and sat astride like a man. He expected that she could ride rings around a farm boy who knew more about the plow than the bridle.

But she went only a short distance before cantering back. "You're hoping I'll ride too far ahead, so you can slip away, aren't you?"

"And be charged with horse theft in addition to rape?"

She gave him a smile, as if to say that she was proud of her plan and perhaps surprised that it had worked. The expression made her seem even more girlish.

"How old are you?" he asked.

"Seventeen," she said.

"Why, you're younger than I am."

"Old enough for my father to marry me off to Danton. And old enough to run." She kicked her horse closer. "We need each other, Will Pike. We're allies. We can be friends."

"All right. Just promise not to ask what time it is every ten minutes."

"I promise, but we must go faster, because Danton will be coming after us."

"Because he wants to marry you?"

"No. Because you're riding his horse."

IT WAS WELL after dark when they passed through the fields and fens of Roxbury and came at last to Boston Neck.

Up ahead, the lights of the city shimmered in the showery rain, and a string of flaming cressets lit the way along the Neck. Will Pike had never been happier to see journey's end, because Eve Corliss had not stopped talking since morning.

She had talked through her childhood, her adolescence, and was now telling Will about the birth of her conscience. "Would you like to know the date?"

"All I asked was when you met my brother," muttered Will.

"I'm coming to that. But . . . do you know what the Triangle Trade is?"

"Yes."

"And your opinion?"

"An abomination."

"Then you see why I couldn't stay in that house another moment."

"I thought you left because you're in love with my brother."

"I abhorred the Triangle Trade before I loved your brother. So I abhorred him before I loved him, because he shipped on the *Pretty Sarah*. . . . Such an abomination to name a slave ship after my mother. . . . The *Pretty Sarah* left Newport in March. She dropped rum in Africa, took on slaves, and turned back to the Indies."

They were on the Neck now. The smell of low tide rose off the Back Bay.

She made a face. "Boston stinks."

"Most cities do," he said. "Finish your story . . . if you can."

"Halfway home, the crew decided to seize the *Sarah*, kill the captain, and sell the slaves for themselves. They asked your brother to join. He told the captain instead."

"My brother sides with authority?"

"He said the only thing worse than authority was *no* authority."

"Henry Knox would agree with that."

"Who's he?"

"Never mind. Keep talking . . . as if I could stop you."

"Your brother helped the captain put down the mutiny. They locked the mutineers in the fo'c'sle and finished the voyage, which put my father in debt to him."

"So your father made North a first mate?"

"He offered North the job on the *Sarah*. But North said he wouldn't go back to Africa, as he didn't hold with slaving if there was a better way to make a living."

"A man of principle, he is."

"That's when I decided I liked him. Then he asked for the mate's position on the *Pretty Eve*." She laughed. "Later, he told me he wanted it because he wanted to be closer to me . . . because *I* was the Pretty Eve."

"A man of charm, too."

"More charmin' than you know."

"So he charmed his way right into Curly Bill's job?"

"He made Curly Bill mad. He made Danton mad, too."

"He has a skill for that."

They were halfway across the Neck and had not passed a person in either direction. The rain was falling more heavily and the flames in the cressets, fed on piles of pitch-soaked logs, were hissing and sputtering.

Suddenly they heard the sound of riders, coming hard.

"Oh, good Lord," she said, looking over her shoulder. "It could be them."

In the flaming light Will counted, "One . . . two . . ." The riders went back into the darkness, then into the light of the next cresset. "Three . . . four . . ."

"It is them!" she cried.

Will looked at the city gates, and while he was calculating the distance to safety, Eve spurred her horse.

"Wait!" he shouted after her.

But she was already off. An instant later, the four riders were sweeping past. Will's horse reared, leaving him dangling from its mane. And all at once, before his horse dropped back onto four hooves, he heard Eve's horse scream.

Then Eve screamed.

Will came upon them in front of the gates. Two of the men were dismounted, a third was holding their reins.

The fourth sat his horse and gave orders. "See if she's hurt."

"She's hurt," said one of the others, "and the horse is hurt worse." He drew his pistol.

"Don't shoot!" Will reined up in front of them. He saw no familiar faces. Only tradesmen, mechanics of some sort, clustered around Eve. She was on the ground and bleeding at the forehead. He jumped down and ran to her.

"She hit her head," said the man with the gun.

"Knocked cold. Bleedin' good," said another.

"We can bandage her head," said the mounted man, "but we can't help the horse."

Will knew more about horses than women, and while he prayed that Eve's skull was not broken, he could see, even in the dark, that the horse's leg was.

"It's for the best to put her down," said the man with the gun.

"Put her down!" cried Will.

"He means the horse," said one of the others.

There was a single shot, and the filly collapsed where she stood.

"Now then," said the mounted man. "I'm Dr. John Warren. These are my students. We've just come from birthing babies in Roxbury. Twins. I wanted them to see that the process works as well with two as one."

Will stood and looked into each face. They still reminded him of mechanics, and in a way, they were.

Dr. Warren added that it would be good for them to study head injuries, so he would be glad to take the young lady back to the small dispensary he kept in his home.

Will rode with them to Warren's house, watched them bind her bleeding scalp and discuss further treatment, should she not awaken in the morning—"and such things have been known to happen," said Dr. Warren.

They appeared competent and trustworthy men, so Will felt that it was safe to leave her. Then he made for the home of his only friend in Boston.

As he rode through the rain, he prayed that further treatment would not be necessary. The girl simply had to wake up. How else would he find his brother?

A SHORT TIME later, Will Pike—wet, hungry, depressed—pounded on the door of a Hanover Street clock shop and watched candlelight descend from an upper chamber.

The beefy face and curled mustache appeared in a window, the door flew open, and Herr Gefahlz cried, "Will Pike? Will Pike is it? I was in bed, but I was not sleeping. Now I am not sleeping, but I am dreaming."

Will stepped in and was embraced by the sound of clocks, each ticking with its own timbre and rhythm. No sound save his father's voice had ever been so soothing.

And never had he tasted ham as smoky, as salty, as spiced, or as satisfying as the ham that Frau Gefahlz—a buxom Boston woman whose real name was Mary Milton—brought out for her "special boy."

Herr Gefahlz poured a wine that was golden and came from a crock rather than a bottle. Will had never seen such color in wine before.

"You like?" asked Gefahlz. "It comes from Germany. It is called Riesling."

"It's sweet," said Will.

"Sweet like the girls of Boston," said Frau Gefahlz. "Sweet because sweet goes with salt and spice."

"*Ja,*" said Herr Gefahlz, "so take a bite of ham, then a sip of wine."

And though the day had been long, and the week had been longer, and the shock of losing the document had yet to wear off, and the shock of seeing Eve bleeding on the road had yet to sink in, nothing had ever soothed him more than that meal with friends.

And so comforted was he in their presence that he told them the whole story, from the day that the sheriff came to arrest his father.

With each twist in the tale, Herr Gefahlz twisted his mustache and muttered, "*Ja?* So?" And his wife sliced a bit more ham and poured a bit more wine for everyone.

"A big problem, you have," said Herr Gefahlz finally. "But this is America. In America, we get up in the morning and go to work and solve our problems. Tomorrow, you will solve yours."

And Will Pike slept more soundly than he had in a week.

AUGUST IN NEW ENGLAND could bring a fortnight of gloomy rain followed by a single morning so glorious that the dead would wish to live again. On such mornings, the wind backed into the northwest and began to rise, and the sea was roiled, and the sky was swept of clouds, fog, smoke, and the sins of the city, leaving nothing in the atmosphere but color—a blue so intense that every man considered himself royalty robed in golden sunshine, drinking in air so fresh that it might have been distilled from a snowcap.

The day grew even brighter for Will Pike when word arrived that Eve was awake. He hurried to Dr. Warren's house, where he expected to find an invalid perched on pillows. Instead, Eve was dressed and perched on a chair, a bandage wrapping her head and a spot of blood seeping through it like a badge of courage.

"I'm ready," she proclaimed.

"But—"

"She can travel," said the doctor. "And since we caused her accident, her care is free, but I would speak to you in private, Mr. Pike."

Will followed the doctor into the adjoining room.

A chart showing a human's insides hung on one wall; another of a skeleton hung opposite. A third wall was covered in books and a fourth with bottles containing liquids and powders of every color, none more intense than the scarlet that flushed Dr. Warren's face as he turned on Will and demanded, "What do you propose to do with that virginal young woman, sir?"

"Do with her?"

"She asked me this morning to direct her to the home of Nan Dreedle."

"Nan Dreedle?"

"By God, sir, if you've brought her to Boston to make a whore of her, I'll have your testicles in a jar." As proof, the good doctor whipped a scalpel from the leather case on his desk and held it before Will's face.

Will stepped back. "I don't know what you mean."

"Nan Dreedle kept a house until the syphilis drove her mad."

"You have me wrong, sir. We seek my brother. He may have told Miss Corliss that he could be found at Nan Dreedle's."

The doctor lowered the scalpel. "Was he known to frequent whorehouses?"

"It wouldn't surprise me."

"Then you have no interest in ruining this young woman's life?"

"Were it up to me, she'd be back in Newport, ruining someone else's. But she thinks she loves my brother."

"Then perhaps we can find him."

MOUNT WHOREDOM WAS what they called the back side of Beacon Hill, for reasons that became clear as they climbed from Cambridge Street, past rows of stylike storefronts and rotting row houses. Since the end of the Revolution, the whores had been moving out and families of black freedmen had been moving in, so that some now called it Mount Africa. But either way, even this poorest section of Boston looked bright and brilliant that late summer day.

And it did not take long for them to find the information they sought.

The whores trusted Dr. Warren, for he had helped many of them, providing them with ointments for their sores, setting bones broken by rambunctious customers, and counseling them on the dangers of the life they had chosen.

Some of the girls called him Dr. Do-Good behind his back, but it was plain from the way they greeted him that they respected him.

Nan Dreedle's two-story house was shuttered. "Clapped up" someone had written on the door. So they went a short distance up the hill, to where a woman in a low-cut dress and tall feathered hat sat on a stoop. The sign above her door read, RABBIT ANNIE'S HOME FOR MEN.

"Hello, Annie," said the doctor.

Annie squinted in the morning sunlight. Her hair was hennaed red, though gray roots showed. Her teeth were blackened from wine. Her lips and cheeks were reddened from rouge, so too were her breasts where the tops of her nipples showed above her bodice.

"A bit early for you, ain't it, Doc?" she asked.

"How are you feeling, Annie?"

"Fit as a fiddle. Tight as a drum. Wet as a fish—" Annie's eyes fell on Eve, who was listening, wide-eyed. "Hell . . . I feel terrible, Doc. Sore in the . . . in the . . . down there. I was hopin' there'd be no customers today, but a girl has to eat."

"Have you recently had a customer named Pike?" asked the doctor. "North Pike?"

"I remember a name. But my memory is—" Annie rubbed thumb and forefinger, and Will placed a coin in her hand. "He didn't want me. Too old, I guess."

Eve spoke up. "Is he here?"

Rabbit Annie laughed. "He was all over the hill the last two days. Said he'd have every girl in every house, 'fore he headed up Falmouth way, up to Maine."

"Maine?" said Eve. "Why Maine?"

"Well, dearie," Rabbit Annie grinned, "I hate to say bad to such a sweet-lookin' biscuit as you, but he said he was headin' north to settle down with a jealous woman, so he was spendin' big for the last time."

"Jealous woman?" Eve's face lost all color. "*I'm* his jealous woman."

"Be quiet," snapped Will. Then he turned back to Annie. "Did he say where he got the money to spend so free?"

"Said he'd sold 'a fine piece of parchment.' Said he felt richer than a rooster in a fresh-painted henhouse."

Now Will's face lost its color. "Did he say what the parchment was?"

"Dearie, he was more interested in pussy than parchment."

Without another word to Rabbit Annie, Will thanked the doctor, turned, and headed down the hill.

"Where are you going?" demanded Eve.

"Falmouth, Maine," he said.

"They've renamed it." Dr. Warren followed. "They call it Portland, now."

"Why don't you all stay?" shouted Rabbit Annie. "For another five shillings, I'll tell you how I got my name . . . every detail."

A FEW HOURS LATER, Will Pike and Eve Corliss stood at the rail of a Portland-bound packet leaving Boston Harbor.

Will's task had grown infinitely more complicated. If he found his brother, he would then have to find the man to whom his brother had sold the document, then convince the man to sell it back.

And a greater complication was Eve Corliss herself, who had threatened that if Will left her in Boston, she would tell Dr. Warren that he had raped her.

"My brother no longer loves you," Will had said as they stood on the wharf. "He never loved you. That should be obvious."

"And so will my belly be obvious in another month."

"My brother?"

She had looked out to sea. "A man should not ask a lady such questions."

Now, the northwesterlies were pushing the packet over the wave tops, and Eve was already seasick.

Will stood behind her on the pitching deck, steadied her, and said, "Keep your eyes on the horizon. That's how my brother told me to outsmart seasickness."

So she retched over the side, then fixed her eyes on Nantasket Roads, the channel to the south, and after a few moments cried out, "Good God! They're here!"

She pointed to a black-hulled schooner tacking up from the south. The gunwales were painted red and there was a red diamond on each sail, trademarks of the Corliss line.

"That's the *Pretty Eve*," said Eve.

Will borrowed a glass from a passenger and looked, and there on the quarterdeck were Robert Danton and Curly Bill Barton.

"They've found us," cried Eve.

"They've found Boston. They may never find us," said Will, "unless they put their glass on us right now and see you puking over the side. So get below."

And the two vessels passed in the wind.

EIGHT

PETER AND EVANGELINE were jogging his favorite route: from the Back Bay over the Fiedler footbridge to the Esplanade, then along the Charles River and onto Atlantic Avenue, where they could glimpse the harbor glittering in the morning sunlight.

"*This* is exercise," he said. "Not like that silly power walking."

"I don't power walk," she said. "I stride aggressively." And she sped up.

He hung back for a moment to look at her. It was a good angle. She had long legs and—there was no better way to say it—a nice ass, nicely covered in running shorts over spandex. It was all right to think that way about the woman you loved . . . or had once loved and had fallen in love with again. Especially after that business with the flat tires.

"I know what you're looking at," she said. "Stop it and pick up the pace. I want to talk."

Peter's suspicions about the guy on the Cliff Walk had turned out to be just that—bad thoughts about a helpful stranger . . . but modern thoughts, the kind that were planted in the minds of people who watched cable news or read the papers. The message, whether they were talking about terrorists or sex killers, was simple: It's a scary world out there, and bad things can happen. Be afraid. Be very afraid.

Peter liked to believe that neighbors looked out for each other, a man's word was his bond, and, as his mother used to tell him, a stranger was just a friend you hadn't been introduced to. That was the world he remembered from his boyhood, a better world than most Americans lived in now, and probably a better world than they'd lived in back then.

Still, the chances of meeting the serial killer instead of the Good Samaritan were small, no matter what they told you on television. So Peter was glad he had trusted that guy on the Cliff Walk. It meant they had the flat tire fixed quickly and were back on the road to Boston before eight.

And even though Evangeline had promised to cook dinner, Peter had two rib-eyes in his refrigerator. They'd go nicely with the 2005 St. Emilion he wanted to taste before deciding to buy a case. So he cooked the steaks, the wine showed promise, and she stayed the night.

Now he caught up to her. "What do you want to talk about?"

"Pick a topic. If you can talk while doing aerobic exercise, you haven't reached your maximum heart rate. So talk."

"All right," he said over the *thump* of Reeboks on sidewalk. "That guy last night . . . what made you trust him enough to get into his car?"

"Instinct," she said. "People who do photography books aren't dangerous."

Thump-thump-thump.

"And he liked that I was a travel writer," she added.

"Did he want a job with your magazine?"

"Don't know," she said as they turned off Atlantic Avenue and started up Hanover Street. "But he let me see some of the pictures that were still on his—" She took a couple of breaths. "—on his memory card."

They ran past the cafés and Italian bakeries just opening for business.

"How about an espresso and a cannoli?" said Peter.

"No. This was your idea. A run through the city, you said. Good for the circulation, you said. The couple that jogs together scrogs together, you said."

So they kept going through the North End, the oldest neighborhood in Boston, once Puritan, later Irish, now Italian and changing again.

"He had a good eye," she told Peter as they passed Paul Revere Park. His pictures . . . the Cliff Walk, Queechee Gorge—"

"What?" Peter stopped on the sidewalk.

Paul Revere looked down from his bronze horse.

Evangeline kept jogging in place. "Queechee Gorge."

"Queechee Gorge? Taken recently?"

"Taken in foliage season."

"Recently, then. What else did he talk about?"

"The beauty of the Cliff Walk . . . current events."

"Like the repeal of the Second Amendment?"

"If you're photographing New England, you go to Queechee Gorge in October. He didn't have anything to do with that professor." And she set off again.

Maybe she was right, thought Peter. Maybe he was too suspicious. Maybe they needed something sweet for breakfast. So he jogged across the street and ducked into Modern Pastry.

When he caught up to her on State Street, he was carrying a box. "Two almond turnovers, for after we shower."

"The prince of willpower."

They didn't talk much more as they ran toward the Old State House. They went up Tremont, by the Old Granary Burying Ground, over Boston Common.

"I'll race you to your stoop," she said as they came through the Public Garden.

"All right. Let's start from—"

"Go!" And she took off.

"Hey!" He sprinted after her.

She darted across Arlington Street, which was jammed with morning traffic. Horns blared, somebody shouted at them, then she sprinted up Marlborough Street and into a different world, a tree-lined low-traffic tunnel of brownstones and restricted parking, quiet enough that Peter could hear Evangeline's *thump-thump-thump* half a block ahead of him.

He dodged an old woman walking her bichon frise, then he dodged the dog's droppings, then he shouted over his shoulder, "Pick up after your dog!"

"Fuck you!" came the answer, along with a few barks.

Evangeline laughed and crossed Berkeley Street and sprinted to the finish—the steps of his condo.

Peter burst across Berkeley right after her, dodging cars and talking trash. "You can't beat me, baby. I'm right on your ass."

"Don't drop the pastries! And leave my ass out of this!" With a final kick, she grabbed for the newel post in front of his house. "I win."

Peter flopped onto the stoop right after her, they caught their breaths, then they started laughing. The runner's high washed over them, the hit-me-with-a-hammer-because-it-feels-so-good-when-I-stop sensation that some people found exhilarating.

The only thing better: a shower for two, almond turnovers, espresso. . . .

Peter got up to follow her inside, and someone called his name.

A young man was getting out of a Lexus across the street. He had dark hair, blue blazer, golf shirt; he looked like an assistant English professor at a local college.

"I'm Josh Sutherland." He strode toward them. "I work for Harriet Holden."

"Congresswoman Holden?" Evangeline came off the stoop. "Tell her we're big supporters."

"Tell her yourself." The young man gestured over his shoulder.

The shaded back window of the Lexus powered down and a woman peered out. She was wearing sunglasses, blue sweatsuit, and a pink ball cap with the Boston "B". "Is the coast clear, Josh?"

Sutherland looked up the street and down. "No one in this block."

So the woman got out, and before she was halfway across the street, Evangeline was extending her hand.

"Not out here." Harriet Holden barely glanced at Evangeline. She said to Peter, "We need to talk," and climbed the stairs.

WITHOUT MAKEUP, HARRIET Holden looked like any other forty-five-year-old woman who spent too much time in the sun and was damned if she wasn't going to keep doing it, because Botox was the greatest invention since hair coloring. But no injection or face-lift could loosen the lines of tension around her mouth.

Her whole body seemed nervous, jerking and twitching, all elbows and angles, as if it had never worn sweats before and wasn't sure how to move unless wrapped in one of those expensive suits she favored for the C-SPAN cameras.

In the condo, she took off her hat, stuck her sunglasses into it, held it out to Josh Sutherland, said to Peter, "I need your help," said to Evangeline, "Coffee. No sugar. Just a dash of one percent. And Josh will have—"

Evangeline raised her hand. "Representative Holden—"

"I prefer Congresswoman. Or Congress*person*."

Peter chuckled at that, and Sutherland shot him an annoyed look.

"Whatever," said Evangeline. "I'm a visitor here myself. And—"

Before she could finish, the congress*person* shifted her eyes to Peter. "Coffee?"

"Coming right up." Peter left the ladies to look at each other.

Harriet Holden looked around the condo instead.

Peter owned the second and third floors of a five-story building, put up as a single-family town house in 1872. The second floor included the original parlor with the bay window, the original dining room, and a modern kitchen fashioned from the butler's pantry at the rear.

Both rooms had high ceilings, fireplaces, Persian carpets, and wallpaper—green in the living room, light brown in the dining room—that complemented the gold-hued oak woodwork. And of course, books, lots of books, and antique prints on the walls.

"Nice." Harriet Holden dropped onto the sofa. "Very . . . masculine." She gave Evangeline a thin smile. "I should have seen from the décor that there was no woman living here . . . permanently, that is."

Evangeline was beginning to think she didn't like this congress*person* too much.

Then Harriet Holden showed why she was good at her job. As if sensing that she had come on too strong, she put a hand on Evangeline's arm. "If I seem a bit snippy . . . it's just that, with this Second Amendment fight—"

And that was enough for Evangeline. The congresswoman could be forgiven.

Peter carried in a tray of cups and an Italian twin-chambered coffeepot, along with two huge turnovers, each cut in half. He poured a cup and handed it to Harriet Holden.

She took a sip and said, "I was just telling—"

"Evangeline," said Evangeline.

"I was just telling Evangeline that I have a tiger by the tail, Mr. Fallon."

"The Second Amendment business," added Evangeline.

The congresswoman nodded. "It's the reason for all this secrecy. I didn't want to visit you in your office. It might attract attention. No matter what I do these days I attract attention. There are reporters at Logan Airport right now wondering why I'm not on the seven a.m. flight to D.C. But I like to look a man in the eye before I ask him for help."

"So—" Peter pulled over a hard-backed chair. "—how can I help?"

"You've been following our repeal movement?"

"Since the day it began . . . more closely than you could imagine."

Evangeline sipped her coffee and said nothing. She was one of the few who knew about Peter's small part in the FBI action of June, and he had sworn her to secrecy.

"What's your opinion?" asked Harriet Holden.

"I admire your courage," said Peter.

"The NRA has put me on a poster. Nothing but my face and the words, 'An enemy of freedom.'"

"And *they're* the rational ones," said Josh Sutherland, who sat in the bay window like a lookout, with a view up and down Marlborough Street.

Harriet Holden said, "I have a stack of hate mail as tall as you are, Mr. Fallon. I'm excoriated on talk shows all across America. . . ."

"But getting the guns off the street is a noble cause," said Evangeline.

"Thank you." Harriet Holden took a bite of the turnover.

"More quixotic than noble," said Peter.

The congresswoman brushed a fleck of almond from the corner of her mouth. "You disagree with the repeal movement?"

"I think that a musket over the mantelpiece is part of the American heritage."

"What about an Uzi?" asked Harriet Holden. "The Founding Fathers never imagined the firepower of the weapons those terrorists wanted to use on us."

"The NRA thinks that once you ban Uzis," said Peter, "you'll try to ban muskets, shotguns, target pistols. The slippery slope. They'll fight you to the last bullet."

"That's why we chose the nuclear option," said Sutherland. "To hell with ten-day waiting periods and background checks. Go after the amendment itself and get the story out: There are police chiefs who agree with us, district attorneys, even Republicans."

"The repeal would never have made it this far," added Harriet Holden, "unless the Republicans allowed it."

Peter glanced at Evangeline, who was listening and nodding and drinking down all this insider talk like cold beer on a hot day.

He hated to spoil her mood with the truth: "I've read that the Republicans want to give a certain ambitious congress*person* enough rope to hang herself on a national stage."

For a moment, Harriet Holden just looked at Peter Fallon. She had begun her career in the Suffolk County D.A.'s office and had long ago perfected the prosecutor's level stare: cold, piercing, righteously pissed. "The day I started this, Mr. Fallon, I sacrificed my dreams of higher office. But if we repeal the amendment, we can make more rational gun laws."

"Or throw the gun question back to the states," said Peter. "Then you'll be able to buy an Uzi in New Hampshire while you can't buy a BB gun in Massachusetts."

Evangeline said to Harriet Holden, "If you're wondering why we don't live together, there's your answer."

Harriet Holden kept her eyes on Peter. "Have I come to the wrong place?"

"I'm not very political," said Peter.

"But you *did* contribute to our last campaign," said Sutherland.

"You do your homework," said Peter.

"Listen"—Harriet Holden put down her coffee cup—"we didn't start thinking about that Second Amendment repeal on the day of the FBI bust. That was simply the catalyst. We'd been researching awhile . . . doing our homework, as you say."

"We started," said Josh Sutherland, "by reading *The Magnificent Dreamers*, Professor Stuart Conrad's great book."

Peter did not usually tell one client that another was interested in the same item, but since he didn't know what the item was, he might learn something by tossing out a bit of information. So he told them the professor's assistant had come to him a few days before.

"Ms. Segal?" Harriet Holden looked at Sutherland. "We asked her not to go off on her own until we had talked to you."

"Talked to me about what?"

"The professor's work." Sutherland came over from the bay window. "He said he was getting close to something that might affect the course of the Second Amendment hearings, which begin in committee next Monday."

"One week," said Harriet Holden.

"Did he tell you what it was?"

"No," said Harriet Holden. "Only that he was on the trail of a rare document."

"Does Jennifer Segal know what it is?"

"She might," said the congresswoman. "But I think she's playing a game, trying to keep the information for herself."

"Why would she do that?" asked Evangeline.

"Jealousy," said Harriet.

"Jealousy?" asked Evangeline.

"The professor and I were lovers," said Harriet bluntly. "I took Ms. Segal's place."

"Jealousy, then," said Peter. "Or maybe greed. Depending on what this is, it could be worth a lot of money."

"I don't care about the money," said the congresswoman. "But if the Framers were debating gun laws from the beginning, I think the country should know about it. The NRA has owned this issue for too long."

"But what happens," asked Peter, "if this rare document says the NRA is right?"

"You find the document," she said. "I'll deal with the consequences."

Then Sutherland asked, "Is there any reason why you can't work for us instead of Ms. Segal?"

"Well, she didn't tell me what she was looking for, and you did . . . sort of."

Peter explained that in cases like this, he functioned as a detective. He charged $1,000 a day plus expenses, or he took 50 percent of the value of the document when found and sold.

They agreed that he would take 50 percent if he found the document.

"So long as we take possession of it," said Sutherland.

"If you find it," said Harriet Holden, "you may change the course of American history."

On the way out, Sutherland pointed a finger at Fallon. "One week."

As soon as the door closed, Peter turned to Evangeline and gave her a high-pitched voice, "'If you're wondering why we don't live together, there's your answer.'"

"You were very rude to her," she said.

"She's pretty rude herself."

"She has reason. I bet she fears assassination. Maybe in the next week."

"Not much time to find something when we don't even know what it is."

"So, what are you going to do?"

"Take a shower."

"Me first."

He had given up thoughts of a romantic morning. He now had things to do, and she had a column to write about the Cliff Walk, so long as her editor agreed.

While he waited for the shower, he went upstairs and slipped *The Magnificent Dreamers* from the pile of books beside his bed. He thumbed through it, glanced at the pictures of the Framers, looked at the jacket photo of the telegenic professor, read the opening lines:

> There were fifty-five of them. They came from twelve states. Some lived in cities and some lived on farms. Some were already giants. The rest would soon grow tall. And none would ever do anything as important as what they did in the Philadelphia summer of 1787.

Nice, thought Peter. It made you want to read on. It wasn't writing from the *I-have-a-PhD-and-you-don't* school of prose.

He flipped to the acknowledgments.

The introductory paragraph: "Every author sits on the shoulders of those who came before. . . ." Requisite stuff, polite and thankful.

Then came the names of people who had helped in the research: the usual suspects—professors, writers, curators at repositories where historical papers were collected; then the people from outside the "academy"— park rangers in Philadelphia, docents at James Madison's home, and . . . Martin Bloom.

Peter laughed out loud. "Bloom!"

Evangeline was just coming out of the bathroom. She was wrapped in a towel. Her hair was stringy wet. "What's so funny?"

"Call your editor. Tell him you want to write about Portland, Maine, instead of the Cliff Walk."

"Why? What's in Portland? Or should I say *who*?"

"A collector of autographs and documents whose specialty is 1775 to 1800."

Evangeline sat on the edge of the bed and began to towel her hair.

He knew she was thinking this through. Should she go with him? What kind of adventure would this be? How dangerous? But what if they really could change the course of American history by finding a document?

And he was thinking of how good she looked, from that wet blond head to the pedicure . . . and how good she smelled, just soap and warm skin. Her head was tilted to one side as she worked the towel, offering her long neck for . . . a kiss? That might lead to a deft twist of a finger, a towel-knot undone. . . .

She turned to him. "All right. I'll do it."

"I was hoping you'd say that." He leaned closer.

"Not that." She put a finger on his chest. "You got that last night. I'm talking about Portland. Shower and let's go."

INTERSTATE 95 NORTH.

You could start in Miami and go all the way to the Canadian border. And you always paid a toll in New Hampshire. There were other tolls, but usually you got something for your money. In New Hampshire, I-95 crossed one bridge and about twelve miles of turf. And not only did they extract a fee at the infamous Hampton tolls, but on most weekends, they wasted half the surplus gasoline in New England as drivers idled through three-mile traffic jams, steamed at the other drivers, growled at their wives, and yelled at their kids.

It was leaf season, so even on a Monday there was tourist traffic. But New Hampshire had retooled to take EZ Pass, so Peter sailed through, grumbling all the way.

"If you hate the Hampton tolls so much, why didn't you just call this guy?"

"The longer you stay in a business"—Peter accelerated back into traffic—"the more you learn about people. Some guys will talk for hours on the phone, about the Red Sox, the weather, all the rumors they've heard, and all the places they're finding good stuff. And if you ask the right questions, they'll give away sellers and buyers, too."

"But not Bloom?"

"He and his partner have been in business for thirty years. He plays it close. If you want to do business with him, you'll have better luck looking him in the eye."

"And his partner? Will he be there?"

"I hope not. Paul Doherty. Grouchy bastard. He usually scouts. Leaves Bloom to run the store."

As Peter settled into the right lane, he got a chill when he noticed a black Chrysler Sebring a few cars behind. He slowed down to a highway crawl, about fifty, and watched. The Toyota on his tail quickly lost patience and passed, so that the Sebring was directly behind him.

He slowed a bit more, and it inched closer . . . closer. . . .

Evangeline leaned over and looked at the speedometer. "Are you getting sleepy?"

"Wide awake." He kept his eyes on the rearview. "It's just . . . that Sebring behind us . . . it's moving but it has no driver."

Evangeline whipped around, squinted against the glare, then laughed. "An old lady, Peter. And if you don't step on it, she may run you down."

Peter laughed too, but he realized that he was still wondering about that guy from the Cliff Walk.

PORTLAND, MAINE, WAS one of the safest anchorages in America and closer to England than any other American city. So it had once been a gateway for Irish immigrants coming in, for north country lumber, Maine granite, and Grand Banks cod going out. It had been a railhead town, a shipping town, a working town. But after World War II, the old port had fallen on hard times and stayed there until the eighties.

Then vacationers passing through to Cape Elizabeth or Casco Bay or the Nova Scotia ferry began to notice that along with great views and grand Victorian architecture, Portland had lively bars, good restaurants, a growing colony of artists. Word got out. Money came in. And the old port became the *Olde Port.*

"This burg's had more rebirths than a Hindu headed for the last level of enlightenment," said Peter. "It's burned down and been rebuilt four or five times. And look at it now. Jumpin' even at lunchtime."

If Boston was a miniature city when compared with most American megalopoli, Portland was like a miniature of Boston: three blocks of waterfront, three blocks of business district, neighborhoods both rich and poor, hotels, museums, restaurants, a powerful sense of identity all compressed into a peninsula of a few square miles.

The Old Curiosity Bookshop was on the west side of Market Street, two blocks from the waterfront. It may have gotten a shaft of morning sunlight in July, but the front window was usually in shadow.

Peter knew Martin Bloom liked it that way, because it meant he could attract window-shopping tourists by displaying New England treasures without fear of fading sunlight: a photograph of one of Maine's greatest citizens, Civil War hero Joshua Lawrence Chamberlain, framed with one of his letters; an antique map with different colors showing the extent of each Portland fire; the three-volume set that proclaimed Bloom's real interest—the papers of James Madison, including *Notes of Debates in the Federal Convention of 1787.*

A little bell rang over the door. The Schumann piano concerto was playing on the sound system. The shop was empty.

Just inside, a case held more treasures: a first edition of *Uncle Tom's Cabin,* written in Brunswick, Maine; a photo of the steamer *Portland* framed with a letter by Captain Hollis Blanchard, mailed just before he took her on her last voyage; a dirk—wooden handle, shiny sharp blade—that had belonged to Edward Preble, the Maine man who commanded the U.S.S. *Constitution* in the Barbary Wars. Price tags on all of them, all pretty steep.

Peter left Evangeline to browse while he went toward the back. Two leather sofas in the middle of the floor invited visitors to sit. The open cases of secondhand books gave them something to read. The locked cases of rare books gave them something to aspire to.

The door was open to the office at the back. Martin Bloom was writing at his desk, head down, bald spot shining through a film of hairs.

"Peter Fallon," he said without looking up, as though he had a third eye peering through his comb-over. "You must be looking for something."

"Martin, what would ever give you that idea?"

"You only show up here when you're looking for something." Bloom raised his head. He had impeccable taste in coordinating the color of his shirts and bow ties, but he had never learned that a long skinny face should not wear horn-rimmed glasses with round lenses. They became his only feature, making him look happily surprised if he was smiling, sadly shocked the rest of the time.

"Martin," said Peter, "that's an exaggeration."

"This is Maine. We don't exaggerate. Remember when you heard that a collector in Camden had three letters from George Washington to Martha?"

"Would've been worth a fortune."

"Except that she burned their letters after he died."

Peter shrugged. "I was misinformed."

"You could've called." Bloom came around his desk and they shook hands. "Instead it took three hours, dinner, and two expensive bottles of wine."

"I paid the bill."

"So, let's save your money and my time." Bloom smiled, which caused long eyebrows to rise like caterpillars from behind the horn-rims. "What are you looking for, and how can I get a piece of it?"

Peter dove right in. "Tell me about Professor Stuart Conrad."

Bloom's eyebrows dropped. "A friend, a customer, a scholar. A terrible loss." Then Bloom noticed Evangeline. "And who's this?"

After introductions, Evangeline said, "You have a wonderful collection."

Peter said, "He knows where more Federal era bodies are buried than anyone in the business."

That remark seemed to upset Bloom. The eyebrows dropped again. "Bodies? That's not a very nice thing to say." Then he turned to Evangeline. "I wouldn't know one thing about bodies."

Touchy, thought Peter. So he decided to probe a bit more. "The market for Founding Fathers paper is getting hot. I'll bet you've been doing well ever since this Second Amendment business started."

Bloom turned things back onto Peter, as if he would be the player rather than the playee. "You're living proof of the hot market, what with that Henry Knox letter you sold last month."

"It's a living," answered Peter.

Now it was Bloom who probed. "I've heard there are more Knox letters out there, and more from that Will Pike."

And the question alone told Peter he had come to the right place. "Why this sudden interest in a bit player like Pike?"

Bloom's eyebrows dropped, as if he realized he had revealed too much.

Peter kept at it. "What was that professor after, Martin?"

Bloom considered a moment, then said, "I can't tell you, because I'm not really sure. And Paul Doherty wouldn't approve if I told you anything."

"Where is he?"

"At the Mount Washington Hotel, at the New England Rarities Convention."

Peter turned to Evangeline, "Art, books, prints, all relating to New England history. It's a big anniversary, so they're doing it at a fancy venue."

"I'm getting ready to head up there myself," said Bloom.

"I was thinking about going, too, before I got distracted." Peter glanced at his watch. "Through Crawford Notch, we can be there in two and a half hours."

Bloom's eyebrows fluttered. "Paul doesn't like people mixing in our business. He'll want tit-for-tat if we tell you anything."

"You give me something, I'll give you something back."

"Will you tell us what else you know about Will Pike's letters?"

"If that's what you want," said Peter.

"So . . ." Bloom turned to Evangeline. "We'll enjoy cocktail hour at the Mount Washington Hotel. But how about a Portland lobster for lunch?"

NINE

August 1787

❧ WHEN THOMAS JEFFERSON wrote in the Declaration of Independence that King George had "burnt our towns," one of them was Falmouth, Maine. And it was not the first time that it had been burnt. The Indians had done it during King Philip's War in 1675, and they had come back and burnt it again a decade later.

Will Pike thought a name change might bring the town better luck, though nature had already given it many advantages. Cape Elizabeth and the rocky islands of Casco Bay protected the harbor. Two hills—Munjoy and Bramhall's—offered fine heights for defense. And the summer southwesterlies could push a schooner far and fast to the fishing grounds.

People here were called Downeasters, because the rest of America reached them by sailing down wind to the east, and Downeasters got to the Grand Banks and the great ports of Europe by doing the same thing. They were not known for their warmth, even on a summer afternoon. And they were suspicious of strangers, too.

But several fishermen at the wharf had hauled nets with North Pike, and once they reckoned Will's resemblance, they directed him to a rooming house called Cochran's Rest on Bramhall's Hill. It was run by a shipbuilder who had lost everything—including a leg—when the British burnt the town in 1776.

Cochran's was a house befitting a rich man, thought Will, or one who had once been rich. The paint was peeling. Chickens picked over cracked corn in the front yard. A sullen old dog, asleep on the porch, raised its head when Will struck the knocker, then the head dropped of its own weight, and the dog went back to sleep. No one answered the door.

"Lady of the house must be off buying provisions," said Will.

"Let's go around to the back, then," said Eve.

"No." Will pushed the door open. "We'll go in like guests, not sneak thieves."

There was a center hallway, a wide stairwell, rooms on either side.

"Hello?" said Will.

In the sitting room to the right, a one-legged man was sleeping more soundly than the dog. Will took a step toward him, then saw Eve go past the window.

Bad enough that he was in the house uninvited. Now Eve was poking around outside, just as he had told her not to. He hurried through the house to head her off.

There was no one in the dining room to stop him and no one stirring the vat of stew over the kitchen cookfire. But if stew was simmering, it meant the lady of the house couldn't be far.

As Will came out the back door, he saw Eve walking toward the woodshed, drawn by the sounds of a man and a woman and a cord of wood thumping against a wall.

"Eve," said Will, "wait. Don't—" But he was too late.

Eve shrieked, "You filthy whoreson!"

Then came a familiar voice: "Eve? Eve Corliss?"

Will looked over Eve's shoulder into the shed.

North Pike was standing by the stack of wood, his white ass muscles flexed on a forward thrust, bare female legs over his shoulders, a jumble of skirt flowing over the stack of wood.

The woman's head popped up and she screamed, "Who are you?"

"Who are *you*?" demanded Eve.

"Who am I? Who am *I*?" The woman swung a leg and the stack of wood collapsed under her, so that she landed on the ground and her skirt fluttered back to her ankles but her breasts swung loose above the neckline of her blouse.

"This is Mary Cousins," said North. "And Will! Why . . . what a surprise."

"Pull up your breeches," said Will.

North looked down at his aroused and ready self and did as his brother told him, for once. Then he grabbed the woman, who slapped his hands away and came up screaming for them all to leave.

"Not till I get an answer," said Eve. "Who are you?"

"I'm the lady of the house."

"Best put your tits back in your blouse," said North, "or they won't believe you."

Will could not keep his eyes from the woman's breasts. Somewhere in the back of his head, he was thinking that his brother always picked pretty women . . . first Eve, now this "lady of the house" with the blond hair tucked under her mobcap, and the red flush of anger on every bit of skin he could see.

"I'll put my tits back," she shouted. "I'll put 'em back. I'll put 'em back, and you'll never get another taste of 'em." All of this as she pulled up her bodice, straightened her skirt, and snapped at Will. "So what are you staring at?"

Will turned his eyes back to his brother. "Where is it?"

Mary Cousins shouted at North. "Who *are* these people?"

Eve shouted at Mary, "Who are *you*?"

"This is *my* woodshed," answered Mary. "Who are *you*?"

Eve raised her chin, "I'm this man's fiancée."

"Fiancee? You are not! I am."

North took a step back. "Now, girls, let's leave off arguin' and—"

A gunshot quieted all of them.

Instinctively, Will threw an arm around Eve, dropped, and considered how far he had come from the debates in Philadelphia to the chickenshit-covered floor of a woodshed in Portland, Maine.

From the sound of the gun, it was a pistol. From the sound of the voice, it was an old man. "You can let him fuck you in the woodshed if you want, Mary Cousins, but if he's doin' it whilst the stew burns, I'll shoot him dead."

"Comin', boss." Mary shoved past them. "Be gone before supper. All of you."

"Yes, ma'am," said North, sounding as if it were all a great joke.

Mary spun back at him. "If I'm not to marry you, you'll be owin' me one Spanish milled dollar for every favor I give you, includin' just now, even if you didn't finish. And I'll be damned if I don't collect." Then she stomped into the house.

North turned to the others and said, "So . . . what brings you folks to Portland?"

As FAR AS Old Man Cochran was concerned, if the daughter of a New England shipper wanted to stay in his house and could pay in specie, he'd hear no objections out of "a housekeeper from Millbridge, Massachusetts, no matter how good she made stew or how fine her tits bounced in her blouse." Cochran, it seemed, had abandoned dreams of bedding the housekeeper, but he still had dreams of reviving his shipbuilding business, and a commission from Thornton Corliss might be just the thing.

So that night, the new visitors took their places at the house table, along with a husband and wife awaiting passage to Nova Scotia, a lumber cruiser bound for the north woods, and a button salesman out of Portsmouth, New Hampshire. And everyone sensed the tension in the dining room whenever Mary Cousins brought in another tureen of stew or plate of biscuits.

It was not until Eve excused herself and went upstairs that conversation brightened, and it brightened again when Will and his brother excused themselves and went outside.

But Will had nothing bright to say and only one conversation in mind, which his brother had been trying to avoid. Will took North by the armhole of his waistcoat, pulled him across the porch, past the old dog, out to the shadow of a big maple. Then he said, "I won't ask you again. Where is the Constitution?"

"I'm sorry, Will. I truly am. It's"—North gestured to the distant mountains—"out there."

"Out there? Out where?"

"I sold it to a New Hampshirite named Caldwell P. Caldwell. He's in the state legislature. Met him at Rabbit Annie's. Said he didn't trust the Philadelphia convention any more than I did. So I told him what I took and why I took it."

"You took it to impress Eve Corliss's father."

"That's not true, and even if it was, it didn't do me any good. She never let me near her. No matter what she says. And her father didn't want any part of me."

"I don't know who's lying. You or her."

"Would I lie to my own brother?"

"Why not? You sold my reputation and spent it on whores and—"

He was interrupted by the sound of breaking glass in a chamber above, then by Eve's sharp voice. "There's my answer. Get out!"

"I'll get out"—that was the voice of Mary Cousins—"when I know which of us is a damn fool for liftin' our skirts to North Pike."

"We're *both* fools," said Eve.

"Maybe," answered Mary. "But I'm collectin' for every time I let him do me and claimed he loved me. You should do the same."

North said, "Little brother, I know where to buy two horses tonight. If it's the only way to make things straight with you, I'll take you to Caldwell."

"What about—?" Will gestured to the window. The curtains were fluttering in the breeze. The women's voices were dropping to more conversational tones.

"Nothin' but trouble, the both of them," said North. "Rescuin' your reputation in the eyes of Rufus King, and rescuin' mine in the eyes of my brother—those matter more to me than a pair of peeved women."

Will was inclined to agree, although he could not deny that he had come to enjoy Eve's company. "Where do we have to go?" he asked.

North led him out from under the maple, so they could see the distant panoply of mountains against the evening sky. "There's a notch up there. We can get through and be at the Connecticut River in three days. Just you and me, movin' fast. We'll follow the river north to Lancaster, where Caldwell lives. We'll buy back your document—"

"With what?"

"With this." North reached into Will's pocket and pulled out the watch. "Solid gold . . . worth a lot more than some old document."

"That's stolen property," said Will.

"Like hell it is. Nathan Liggett give it to me just before he died. Put it right in my hand."

Will decided not to ask further about Liggett's demise. He had a more pressing question: "When do we leave?"

North looked up at the window, where the women were now talking softly, almost conspiratorially, as if they had come to some understanding. "The sooner the better."

BY NOON THE next day, Will Pike was watching a hawk ride the updrafts west of Lake Sebago, and he imagined that he could see what the hawk could see—hundreds of lakes and ponds reflecting the sunlight, so many that it seemed the land was afloat on a sea of fresh water; the rivers and streams, bringing the water and carrying it away; and the endless green forests rolling back from the coast like a blanket pulled up and over those sleeping mountains.

"Always watchin' the hawks," said North, "ever since you was a boy."

"I'm watching the mountains," said Will. "The closer we get to them, the closer we get to this Caldwell P. Caldwell."

"Do you want to know how he got his name?" asked North.

"I want to know why you did it."

For a time, there was no sound but the horses' hooves on the dusty road.

Then North said, "I did it for America."

"You did it because you're a selfish son of a bitch."

"I did it because people need to know that the government they're makin' in Philadelphia won't be any better than the government they made in Boston, except there'll be more of it . . . more rich men in more places havin' more of a say in how fishermen fish and loggers log and farmers farm. They'll put more taxes on us, too, and more laws . . . they're even thinkin' about who gets to carry a gun and who don't—"

"Everyone gets to carry a gun who wants to."

"Depends on what the fellers in Philadelphia decide."

Presently, they came to a rise in the road, and a rich valley opened before them—cornfields, pastures, a pond, a single mountain jumping abruptly from the landscape.

It was so beautiful that Will reined up to take it all in.

North stopped beside him. "I did it because the only way to settle this fine land is to let free men be about their business. And"—he grinned— "I did it because I'm a selfish son of a bitch. It comes from growin' up without a mother, the one who died birthin' you."

By NIGHTFALL, THEY reached the town of Conway, just over the New Hampshire border, and made for the McMillan House.

For his service in the French and Indian War, Colonel McMillan had been rewarded with a land grant in the Saco River valley. He had built a handsome twin-gabled house in the most northerly village in the township and turned it into a center of business—a store, a registry of deeds, an inn.

It was a fine bit of gentility, thought Will, in a lonely place on the edge of the wilderness. McMillan greeted his guests in satin coat and waistcoat. He ordered a Negro servant to tend to their horses. And he showed them to a table in the taproom, amidst local drinkers and thirsty travelers. There, another Negro served them mutton stew and mugs of ale.

"Now . . . about this Caldwell P. Caldwell," said North, once they were seated and spooning stew, "he got his name because his mother and father were both Caldwells—cousins—one from the New Hampshire side of the river and one from Vermont."

"Cousins aren't supposed to marry," said Will.

"No, but people be few and far between in the back country. If you live in a place where the only girl willin' to wet your dick is your cousin—"

"Pa always said controlling yourself was part of being a man."

"Bein' a man is a complicated matter. Some do better at it than others." North chuckled. "A feller once said that I'd mount a snake if I could hold it down. I said, hell, I'd mount a woodpile if I thought there was a snake hidin' in it."

"You like woodpiles. Wood*sheds*, too."

"I was havin' a fine poke till you and Eve spoiled it. But I never had

Eve. I tried. Even told her I loved her. But—" North's face froze at something beyond Will's shoulder.

In the doorway, two women wearing floppy hats and dusty coats surveyed the room while every man in the room surveyed them.

Colonel McMillan hurried over and greeted them with a bow, then invited them to a private table, "where unescorted ladies might dine at their leisure."

But Mary Cousins gestured to the pair by the fireplace. Then she and Eve Corliss marched among the tables with all the confidence of women who had covered more than fifty miles on horseback in a single day and would let no taproom custom deter them.

North whispered to Will, "I told Mary I loved *her*, too. Looks like they've both come to find out the truth."

Eve reached them first, stood over Will, put her hands on her hips. He was not happy to see her but he was glad she had come. He knew that she would slow them, but her face, even now, covered in grime and etched in anger, was more beautiful than the mountains.

She said, "The *Pretty Eve* sailed into Portland last night. I thought you'd want to know. I won't let Danton take me back to Newport."

"And pregnant women shouldn't travel alone," said Mary Cousins, "nor women who've been lied to."

"Pregnant, eh?" North glanced at Eve's belly, then said, "Women who've been lied to need men who'll tell them the truth."

"Men like that are hard to find." Mary sat at the table, pulled off her hat, and shook out her hair. "Much easier to find men who lie to us and take our money."

Will looked at his brother. "Did you take her money?"

"To buy the horses," said North. "I planned to pay it back."

"Plannin' and doin' are two different things." Mary pulled a flintlock from the folds of her skirt and pointed it at North's midsection. "I'm *plannin'* to shoot your balls off, but I won't *do* it if you give me my money."

Without taking his eyes from hers, North reached into the pocket of his buckskin, withdrew a pouch of coins, and dropped it on the table. "It ain't all there, but once we get where we're goin' and sell the gold watch Will's carryin'—"

"I'll be goin' with you, then." Mary snatched the money. "I'll get every penny owed me, what you took out of this pouch and what you put in my skin pouch. Fifty Spanish dollars. My freedom from Cochran and every other lyin' man I ever met."

Will gestured to the gun. "Can you use that?"

"She sure can," said North. "And if those Newport boys come after us—"

"They'll come," said Mary. "If they could find someone in Boston—"

"Rabbit Annie," said Eve, "the only whore in Boston you didn't—"

"—they'll find Old Man Cochran in Portland." Mary looked at Will. "And he knows plenty. When he's not nappin', he's eavesdroppin'. And he don't like your brother much, since I give him what Cochran wanted . . . what Cochran tried takin' a few times."

"That's why she keeps the gun," said North.

"I keep the gun to protect my money. I *was* plannin' to go back and buy my father's old gristmill in Millbridge. Your brother said he'd marry me and come with me."

"But plannin' and doin' are two different things," said North.

THE WOMEN SLEPT in the room that North had rented because, as Mary said, her money had paid for it. The Pike brothers slept in the barn, and not too well.

Will rose before dawn, took a bucket, and went groggily down to the river.

The air was cool and sweet and full of fresh dampness rising up off the water.

A short distance downstream, at the base of a little bridge, a horse was drinking. Its rider, a man in a brown coat and good boots, stood under the bridge with his back to the world and pissed against a piling.

Will was glad to be upstream. He knelt and dipped his bucket into a pool. The shadow of a trout shot away, and he thought idly that he should come back with a fishing pole some time.

He brought the bucket up brimming, set it down on the stony bank, dipped his hands into the water. Whatever sleep remained in his head was gone in a cold splash.

He went to dip his hands again and saw riding boots appear beside the bucket. Then he heard a flintlock cocking a few inches from his skull.

"Bonjour, m'sieur."

Danton. But where were the others?

"Stand," said Danton.

As he obeyed, Will grabbed the handle of the bucket and came up swinging.

Danton pulled the trigger.

But Will was gambling that the morning damp would wet the powder. And he was right. The flint in the hammer struck with a click and a fizzle.

Before Danton could curse, the bucket slammed into his jaw.

THE PIKES DRAGGED the Frenchman back to the barn, gagged him and trussed him, and hid him beneath a pile of hay.

"It'll be some time before he wakes up," said North, "and some time longer before anyone finds him."

"Where could the others be?" asked Will.

"Curly Bill and his boys? Back a few miles, too sore to ride just yet."

"Sore?"

"A sailor on horseback . . . like a pig in the crow's nest. He uses muscles he didn't know he had." North rubbed his backside.

"And this Frenchman?"

"Scoutin'. Too itchy to wait." North took the Frenchman's pistol and primed it from the little brass powder horn in his pocket.

Will said, "What are you doing?"

"Even if we truss Eve right beside him, Frenchy and the others'll keep comin'."

"We're not leaving Eve," said Will.

"'Course not"—North gave his brother a wink—"seein' as you're sweet on her."

"Seein' as she's carrying your child."

"If she's carryin', it ain't mine. Eve's for you, unless our Frog friend catches up to us. But there's one way to make certain that won't happen. . . ." North aimed the pistol at the Frenchman's head and pulled back the hammer.

"Are you crazy?" Will snatched the pistol from his brother and blew out the prime. "McMillan would come after us with half the town."

"Suit yourself," said North. "But the Frog'll keep comin', him and Curly Bill and the boys, too. . . . Never been chased this far over a woman or a gamblin' debt before."

THE NOTCH OF the Mountains was a twelve-mile-long valley running roughly southeast to northwest. On either side dropped walls of stubborn greenery or bare granite or slagged rock, in some places a mile or more apart, in others so close that if a man shouted in one direction, his voice would echo back to him, then past him, then echo again from the other side.

And it was plain wilderness. They had seen not a single dwelling since entering the Notch, and few enough since leaving North Conway some twenty miles back.

As the rough road rose and twisted through the trees and crossed again and again on teetering plank bridges over the Saco, Will remembered something from a soliloquy he had learned in school, something about "that undiscovered country from whose bourne no traveler returns."

But he planned to come back from this country, with the document, his reputation, and Eve Corliss at his side. So he put Hamlet out his head and breathed the perfume of those New Hampshire mountains—the sweet smell of balsam needles warmed by the sun and wafted on the summer breeze. And he watched a pair of hawks riding the updrafts.

North led the way, followed by Mary, then Eve, with Will bringing up the rear.

At each turn in the trail, Will stopped to give a look at the terrain sloping behind them. In four hours, he had not seen a rider, though from time to time, he had seen trail dust puff above the trees. The dust worried him some, but North seemed unconcerned and said the best thing to do was keep moving.

So they had ridden on, most of the time in silence.

Finally, Eve said, "Do these mountains have names?"

Will liked hearing her talk again. Talk might break the tension.

"They're called the White Mountains," said North, "'cause they're covered in snow nine months of the year."

"But the individual mountains?" Eve said. "Mount Such-and-Such or So-and-So."

"I suppose the Indians have names for them," said Mary.

"Saco is an Injun name," said North, "from the words *Skog Kooe*— 'snake-shaped stream runnin' through pine trees.'"

"That says a lot in two words," suggested Eve.

"*You'd* need *twenty*-two to say the same thing," answered Will.

Eve threw a look over her shoulder and gave him a laugh.

Will liked her looks and her laughs, because they seemed to let him in on her secrets. But he knew there were a few secrets she was keeping. He liked that, too.

"The first white men to see this Notch were a pair of hunters," said North. "About fifteen years ago. Royal governor promised 'em a land grant if they could cut a road . . . make a trade route. Took 'em five years."

Up ahead, it looked as if the wall of mountains closed altogether.

"It narrows up there," said North. "Just a path through the rubble-rock. Folks call it the Gateway of the Notch. Better goin' on the other side."

"Is it hard to get through?" asked Eve.

"It's steep," said North. "But if there's no rock slides . . ."

Will asked Eve if she needed a rest.

"No restin' now," snapped North. "Not till we get through."

"This girl's pregnant," said Mary. "If she needs a rest, she gets a rest."

"No restin'," repeated North, and he peered back down the Notch, toward a puff of trail dust rising a mile or so behind them.

Eve asked North, "Are there places to stay up there?"

"Five farms . . . families brought in to settle the land grant. I stayed with one of them once. But we don't want places to stay, darlin'. We need places to hide."

"Hide?" said Eve. "You think we need to hide?"

North did not answer. Instead, he said to Will, "Watch that dust. Road's gettin' steeper, but the dust's comin' closer."

"Men riding harder?" said Will.

North nodded. "Men always ride harder when they smell their quarry."

"Us?" said Mary.

"Don't worry," said North. "Just keep goin'."

Up and up they rode, with the horses gasping and straining at every turn.

The roar of the river grew louder as the Notch grew narrower and concentrated the sound. The riverbed of boulders and tumbledown rocks to their left resembled a badly built staircase steepening toward the Gateway. And the mountains rose a thousand feet on either flank.

They came to a waterfall on the right side of the road, a long silver cascade, dropping hundreds of feet down the rock face.

The horses tried to stop and drink from the pool at its base, but if they watered now, they might founder and never make it through the Gateway.

So North told them all to dismount and lead the horses, keep them moving, keep them climbing. "Plenty of water on the other side, a pond where the river rises."

They pushed themselves and pulled the tired horses, climbing until they heard the sound of another waterfall. It was spreading water across a smooth granite face and slithering under a little bridge to join the rock-strewn river.

A few hundred feet beyond was the Gateway—a literal notch no more than twenty-five feet wide, a hundred feet long, already in afternoon shadow.

"There it is." North studied the terrain, looked back down the road, then said to Will, "You know . . . sooner or later, we have to face them."

Eve swung toward him. "You said once we're through, we could hide."

"They'll still be after us. Until we stop 'em." North pulled his musket from his saddle. "And there won't be a better spot to do it than here."

"I'll stay," said Will. "You have a baby on the way."

North looked at Eve, first at her belly, then into her eyes.

Eve turned and looked up toward the Gateway.

North said, "I owe you all somethin'. I'll buy you time. Then I'll be along."

Will said, "But North—"

"I fought in Washington's army. I know about delayin' tactics. Hit and run. Stall and retreat. From this pass, I can hold up four riders all day."

"Not with one musket," said Will.

"That's a lesson for you, Willie. Always carry a musket *and* a pistol. Would to God you carried either one."

Mary Cousins slipped her pistol from her skirt. "This has good range, maybe twenty-five feet."

"Darlin'"—North took off his tricorne and wiped the sweat from his forehead—"if they get that close, I'll use my knife."

A shot exploded from down the road. Eve's horse screamed and reared and the bullet ricocheted off a rock above them.

"Damn!" shouted Will. "They're on us!"

North took a pack from his horse and flipped it to Will. "The Frenchman's pistol is in there. Load it."

Another shot cracked. This one hit Will's horse in the ear, about eight inches to the right of Will's face.

The horse collapsed onto its own lifeless legs.

Eve's horse screamed again, but Eve held her down.

At the same time, two more shots exploded from the rocks and trees below. One went high; another struck the road thirty feet in front of them.

"Two muskets and two rifles," said North, his voice growing calmer with each shot. "Four men. We have a minute before they reload the muskets. More with the rifles."

"It's the rifles we have to worry about," said Will.

"'Twas a musket killed your horse," said North. "Lucky shot, or one of them is close enough to make it count."

"What do you want us to do?" asked Mary.

"Mount and ride." North grabbed his shot pouch and powder horn. "Willie, get up to those rocks up in the Gateway. Hunker down. Fire at anything that moves. Keep 'em busy. Maybe they'll think you have more than a hog-leg pistol in your hand. I'm goin' higher. Some good ledges up higher."

Will tried to say something, but his brother was already scampering over the face of the waterfall, rising ten, twenty, thirty feet in the space of a few sure-footed strides. Then he disappeared into the trees above.

So Will turned and ran up the path, stumbling on rocks, leaping over boulders, following after the horses and the women until he reached the shadow of the Gateway.

There he stopped and watched the women ride into the bright sunlight beyond.

The road led through the Gateway, toward a marsh-limned pond. Then it crossed a meadow and disappeared into the distant woods. A true valley, thought Will, framed by mountains set miles apart, mountains that seemed to have been placed on the earth to express the benevolent majesty of nature, a distant country from which a traveler might wish never to return on an August afternoon.

Then another shot struck the rocks just above him.

Will dropped behind a boulder and peered back down the Notch. No more musing on the grandeur of God's landscape. He was in a fight. From behind his boulder, he could see the road to his left, and if he moved, he could look down the slope of the narrow river to his right.

He primed the pistol, rested it on the edge of the rock, listened to the sound of the water rushing down the river, and waited for a target.

It did not take long.

A shot rang out; then Curly Bill and one of the others emerged from opposite sides of the road, not ten feet from the rickety bridge where Will's horse lay.

One of them fired and both of them charged. A frontal assault, plain and simple.

Will took aim. He knew he wouldn't hit anything at this range, but he was following orders.

His shot whined off the rocks twenty feet above Curly Bill, who stopped and pulled himself back out of sight.

The sailor on the other side of the road kept coming, as if he knew that Will was alone and reloading, and a quick charge could take him.

But North was somewhere above, with good cover and a good angle. And he made a good shot. It hit the sailor in the side and send him tumbling onto the wet rocks.

Now there were three.

One of them, maybe the Frenchman, answered North's shot with one of his own from cover down the road.

Will thought he heard North grunt. Was it pain? Or was he stumbling to another ledge up among the greenery?

Reload, thought Will. Whatever had happened up there, reload and quickly.

Curly Bill took that moment to charge.

Will poured powder down the barrel, rammed home ball and wadding, turned the gun over . . . primed it . . .

He could see the bunghole features of Bill's face and the rum-barrel body coming fast, musket held at his hip.

Quickly. *Quickly.* Don't misfire.

Will pulled back the hammer. Then he heard the blast of a gun, not ten feet away. All in an instant, he cursed, ducked, and prepared to be struck.

But someone else was shooting . . . at Bill.

It was Mary. She had found a spot on the other side of the road, gotten behind a rock, and fired.

The shot was enough to stop Bill and send him spinning back for cover, his face three ugly circles of shock.

Mary was already reloading, while Eve stood a short distance away, holding the reins of both horses.

Then North shouted from above. "Willie! On your right!"

Will jumped to the other side of the boulder and saw the third sailor leaping from rock to rock, climbing in the riverbed. He was no more than twenty feet away, had a rifle slung over his shoulder and a musket in his hand.

Will pulled the trigger.

The big pistol kicked, and a fifty-caliber red hole appeared on the sailor's chest.

But there was no time for Will to consider what he had just done, because Eve was screaming his name, screaming for him to look out.

Curly Bill was charging again.

He came first at Mary. She leaped from behind her rock and swung at him with her pistol. He parried, then struck her a single quick blow in the forehead with the butt of his musket. Mary collapsed in the road, her skirt billowing around her.

Will poured powder down the barrel, rammed home ball and wadding, primed . . .

Again, the bunghole features were turning toward him.

Quickly. *Quickly.*

Will stood and pulled back the hammer. This was it. Kill this one and the Frenchman will run.

Bill was twenty feet away. *Close enough.*

Will pulled the trigger and his gun misfired.

But Curly Bill's musket did not.

The ball struck Will in the thigh. It was as if a horse had kicked him, a shod horse kicking hard. Will felt his leg break under him and he collapsed.

Now the Frenchman was galloping up the road.

Will rolled onto his side and cried out in agony, the sound as surprising as the pain itself. He tried to suck it back in, to get onto his feet and fight, because Curly Bill was coming to kill him.

Where was North?

Then Danton's big horse thundered past, clearing the Gateway and galloping out into the meadow beyond.

As soon as Eve saw Danton coming at her, she let go the reins of the two horses and began to run toward the trees.

But Danton galloped around her, herded her back toward the road, then picked her up and threw her over his saddle.

Will heard her screaming, "No! No! I'm not going back."

There came a loud slap, and Eve's shouting ceased.

From where he lay, Will could see a patch of blue sky and the rock face above the road. The rock was sloped like the head of an African elephant. And now North appeared on its brow, fifty feet above.

Will wanted to cheer. His brother would shoot them both and this would be over.

North dropped to one knee, aimed toward the Frenchmen, moved the musket about as if seeking a clear shot. Then he seemed to give up on that target and looked down at Curly Bill. That was when Will saw the blood on his brother's shirt. North tried to aim the musket, but it fell from his hands and came clattering down.

Then North pitched forward.

Will cried "No!"

North seemed to fall straight at him, headfirst, arms outstretched as if he were trying to fly. He turned once in the air and landed on his back with an explosive thud, right in the middle of the road.

Will cried again, "Nooooo." And he tried to get up.

But Curly Bill's face appeared above him, with that tight round mouth and those round ugly eyes. His bald head was covered in sweat that dripped into Will's eyes and stung as bitterly as the pain in the leg.

"Thighbone broke. You're finished." He bent down, and slipped a gold watch from Will's waistcoat. Then he scurried to North's body and fished his pockets. Then he went over to the unconscious Mary Cousins and rifled her clothes, found her purse in her blouse, and muttered something about nice titties.

Danton rode up, with the reins of Eve's horse in his hand and Eve slung over his saddle, unconscious.

"One dead, two finished," said Curly Bill.

"Our story is simple," answered Danton. "They ambushed us as we came through the Notch, on our way to do business on the Connecticut River. We fought them off."

"No one will believe you!" cried Will. "Not when I tell them the truth."

"That is true," said Danton. "Kill them both."

Curly Bill took out his knife.

"No," said Danton. "With the musket, or it will look as if *we* ambushed *them*."

During this, Eve came to, looked around, slid off the saddle, began to run again.

Danton dismounted, loped after her, and grabbed her by the hair. "Do what you're told, or I will kill you, too."

"If you do," she screamed, "you kill your own child."

The Frenchman let her go. He seemed as shocked as if she had shot him. "Child?"

"It's what happens when a man forces himself on a woman," she said.

Danton grasped her shoulders, looked into her eyes. "I took what was promised by your father. If there is a child, I will protect it." He picked her up and put her on her horse. She jumped right down on the other side.

He went around and grabbed her again, slapped her a loud crack across the face, picked her up again, and slammed her down on the horse.

Then he turned to Curly Bill. "Kill them."

Curly Bill stood over Will and put the barrel of the musket against his forehead.

"Kill them and I'll never stop running," said Eve.

"If we spare them?" asked Danton. "Will you be docile? Will you be my wife?"

"I will be docile . . . until we reach Newport."

Danton reached over and stroked her chin. "That will be time enough."

"WILL. WILL . . ."

It was Mary Cousins. She was kneeling over him. There was a bloody bruise on her forehead. Grime and trail dust covered her face.

She brought a wooden canteen to his lips, held his head, gave him a drink.

He could not tell how much time had passed. The sky was barely light. It could have been late afternoon. It might have been early morning.

"I've found someone to help us. He's got a farm in the valley, near the place they call Bretton Woods. His name is Dewlap."

There was a cart nearby. Two big horses were snorting. A farmer with a sun-browned face was peering down at him.

Will smelled horseshit on the farmer's shoes.

"Who did you say done this, miss?"

"I didn't," said Mary.

"And don't." Will groaned.

Horace Dewlap crouched down. His eyes were close together, the spaces in his teeth were wide apart, and he had the nervous look of a crow coming upon an animal carcass in the road. "Son, there's a dead man at the base of the cliff, and another one down in the riverbed and a blood trail windin' off to the west. Who done this?"

"Highwaymen," said Mary.

Will's mind was fogged by pain, but one thing was clear. If the *who* and the *why* of this story were told, more men would know about the stolen Constitution, about the foolishness of the young man who had lost it, about the perfidy of the brother who stole it. And how could any of it be good for the reputation of Will Pike or the future of the nation?

So Will said, "Highwaymen. They rode off. Makin' for the Connecticut."

"Well, the law might wonder about highwaymen," said Farmer Dewlap, "bein' as there ain't exactly rich pickin's hereabout. But the law's a day's ride in either direction. And you got a bigger problem, son."

"What?"

The farmer inspected the wound. "Shot missed the artery. That's good. Hit the bone. That's bad."

"Maybe I can walk," said Will, and he levered himself up onto his elbows.

The farmer put a big sun-browned hand on Will's shoulder. "You ain't walkin' anywhere. That leg has to come off."

TEN

Peter Fallon said there was no better drive in New England than through Crawford Notch, and never better than in October.

Once you cleared the North Conway strip, you left the crowds and the bargain outlets behind. Then Route 302 wound past the Attitash ski area and began to climb.

In October, he said, you could call it "the climb sublime."

"Forgive me if I don't quote you," said Evangeline.

But it *was* sublime. In the lower elevations, where the hardwoods grew, the colors were layered, yellow birch on red American beech on orange sugar maple. As your eye traveled up the sheer slopes, conifers added green to the color bursts, first as accent and then, where the hardwoods gave way, as a theme of their own.

The landscape seemed to warn you: warm days follow cool nights that bring bright foliage, but up high, up where the firs grow dark, winter is awakening, breathing deep, stretching its claws.

In the last three miles, you climbed six hundred feet, and the walls of the Notch drew ever closer. The road was modern and smooth, with gentle curves and bridges so unobtrusive, you hardly noticed that sometimes the Saco River was on one side, sometimes the other. Then, after you passed the Silver Cascade and the Flume Cascade, the Gateway appeared.

It was an almost perfect square, hewn and hewn again over the centuries, first by the river, which rose just beyond; then by the Indians who turned a deer path into a trail; then by a pair of enterprising explorers who widened the trail and won a land grant; by the state that turned it into the tenth New Hampshire Turnpike in 1803; by workers blasting rock and laying rails to bring in tourists and take out lumber; and finally by the men who built Route 302, once automobiles had enough horsepower to make the grade.

"Of course," said Peter, "all that history is just an eyeblink of human time. Ten thousand years ago, these mountains were covered in ice a mile thick. And come to think of it, that was just an eyeblink in the life of the earth."

"No plate tectonics, Peter," said Evangeline. "Let's just enjoy the colors."

"But it makes you wonder about spending your life chasing down books and documents, simply because they're a few centuries old, when the mountains are—"

"You've been driving all day. You need a drink."

Evangeline was right. If anything could rearrange your perspective amid the grandeur of that landscape, it was a drink at the Mount Washington Hotel.

One moment, you were gliding past meadows and hills and thick stands of trees. Then it was there, on a rise about five miles from the Gateway, at the place called Bretton Woods, where the Amonoosuc River dropped out of the mountains and turned toward the west.

It reminded Peter of a ship, something from Theodore Roosevelt's Great White Fleet, cresting a wave of green golf courses. And it seemed to rise from that faraway time, too. It was grandiose, ambitious, aggressive, optimistic, like Roosevelt himself. No coincidence that it had been built during TR's presidency.

Behind it rose the aptly named Presidential Range, including Mount Washington, tallest peak in the Northeast, home to some of the worst weather in the world. But so powerful was the impression that the old hotel made upon the landscape, it seemed that the mountains were oriented toward it and not the other way around.

"Just so you know," said Evangeline as they pulled into the parking lot, "I'm not driving any more today. Two hours to Portland. Two and half to here. That's enough."

"Fine by me. But how do we get a room in the Mount Washington in leaf-peeping season, when the New England Rarities Convention is going on, too?"

"I write travel articles." She led him under the hotel portico. "Leave it to me."

Which he did. Let her go to the desk and talk her way in, while he scouted the exhibitors. They had set up on the great veranda that wrapped the hotel in a railed colonnade: white wicker sofas, red rocking chairs, westerly views of ski slopes, southerly views of Crawford Notch, easterly vistas to the Presidentials.

There were dealers from Bar Harbor to Greenwich, displaying engravings, rare books, ephemera, artifacts. Some were big names, some small-timers, and Peter knew just about all of them. So it took a while for him to work his way down the porch to where Martin Bloom and his partner, Paul Doherty, were in hot conversation.

Peter said hello to Ben Perry of Camden, Maine, who sold nautical prints and first editions devoted to Down East sailing. Peter didn't like buying from Ben, because he smoked, so his books always smelled like ashtrays. But Peter liked talking to him because he had a high-pitched laugh that let loose at the slightest joke.

Then Peter shook hands with the Butterfield twins of Burlington, Vermont, Joseph and John, known for wearing the same color shirts and contrasting ties. Today: blue Oxford button-downs, a yellow tie on John, red on Joseph. Or was it the other way round?

"We have a Second Folio," said John.

"Good condition?" asked Peter.

"Some damage," said Joseph. "That's how we got it. Too rich for our blood otherwise."

"We're cutting it up," said John, "rebinding plays in leather."

"Two plays to the volume," said Joseph, "pricing them right."

"Three thousand for Comedies and Romances, four for Histories, more for Tragedies," said John. "And we remember how much you like Shakespeare."

"I thought this was a convention for *New England* rarities," answered Peter.

"Well, that's what *we* are," said John.

"New England rarities," said Joseph.

From the next booth, Ben Perry gave out with a laugh.

. . . and so it went until Peter reached the Old Curiosity display.

Martin Bloom had managed to disappear, leaving Peter to do his own talking with Paul Doherty. *Thanks a lot.*

Unlike Bloom, who had warmth beneath his crust, Paul Doherty was crust all the way through. He shot Peter an annoyed look but kept his attention on a couple from Chicago, foliage tourists, commonly called leaf-peepers, who were asking for a catalogue.

"Are you collectors?" Doherty was asking them.

"Not yet," said the wife cheerily, "but we're interested."

"Do you know what you're looking for?" Doherty snapped.

"Well," said the husband, more wary than cheerful, "we're not sure."

"Catalogues are expensive," said Doherty. "I try not to waste them."

"Waste them?" said the husband. "Why do you print them then?"

Doherty gestured to the table. "Take a business card. It has the Web site. Read that."

And the couple from Chicago huffed off.

"Way to spread that New England hospitality," said Peter.

"What are *you* after?" Doherty's face was square, solid, red, and the nose was broken. He didn't look like a rare book man, more like one of those hard-drinking bricklayers who used to work for Fallon & Son Construction.

"I'm like that couple," said Peter. "I'm not sure. What do you have?"

"You're on a fishing expedition?" Doherty lowered his voice. "You see Martin's name in the acknowledgments of a book and you think . . . what *do* you think?"

"That I ought to talk to Martin. So I do. And he says we have to talk to you."

"About what?"

"You tell me," said Peter. "Martin told me nothing."

"Neither will I. So go back to Boston, or set up your own booth."

Martin Bloom was coming back. "I ordered three Tuckermans. Let's call it a day and go sit on one of the wicker sofas and—"

"Too late," said Peter. "Paul wants to keep whatever he knows to himself."

Doherty's face got a bit redder.

It was plain that these two were on to something that had to do with that professor. How to tease it out?

A waiter brought three tall glasses of amber beer. Bloom signed for them. Peter offered a toast to see how Doherty would react. "Here's to Will Pike. A great American."

"Here's to minding our own business," said Doherty.

Martin Bloom picked up his glass, shrugged, and toasted both of them.

"How do you stand him?" asked Peter in the lounge a while later.

Bloom said, "Paul and I, we've been partners for over thirty years."

Evangeline came toward them, waving a room key.

"Ah," said Peter, "there's a little good news, anyway."

She stood over them. "What are you doing inside when you could be sitting on the veranda, watching the light change on the mountains?"

"In October," said Martin, "the temperature drops as the light changes."

The lounge was on the east side, the Presidential side. It was crowded. The veranda was crowded. The whole hotel was crowded.

"Better to look out the window than look at that—" Evangeline pointed at the TV.

American News Network with the sound turned down and stock prices sliding by, so that guests could see how Citigroup and GE were doing and spend more in the bar because they had more to spend or drink more to drown their sorrows. The face on the screen: Kelly Cutter. Sharp features, blond hair, strong jaw, toothy smile, a right-wing Carly Simon.

"I don't know what she's doing on this channel," said Evangeline. "Let's go."

But as Peter stood, he saw another face appear on TV: Harriet Holden. She looked better with makeup. He asked the bartender to turn up volume.

"Ah, who wants to listen to her?" said a big guy at another table. He was wearing a black ball cap with the word PING across the front in silver. "All she wants to do is take away our guns."

"Yeah," said one of his friends. "Next thing, she'll want our golf clubs."

A foursome, thought Peter, having a few pops after a round on the Donald Ross course with the great views. Old buddies following the siren of the little dimpled ball. It said so on their clothes. Pebble Beach shirts, Pinehurst sweaters, Augusta National Windbreakers, and of course, hats that advertised the makers of balls and clubs and shoes. Titleist. Ping. Foot Joy. Just like their heroes on the Golf Channel.

One of them said, "Somebody should tell that Harriet Holden that golf clubs don't kill people, golf *courses* do."

Peter couldn't place their accents, but he knew the explosive guffaws of guys ready to laugh at just about anything, including a liberal female politician or the sensitive male who wanted to listen to her. A generally harmless breed. And Peter didn't want to get in their way. Best to let Harriet Holden ramble on in silence.

Then Mr. Ping said to the bartender, "Keep the sound down. Anybody wants to listen to her, they can watch in their room."

This caused Peter to change his mind. He said to Mr. Ping, "By the time I get to my room, she'll be finished."

"Yeah, well—" Mr. Ping waved his glass "—you can thank me later." He was a big guy, an old athlete, probably still formidable, even if he drank a little more beer for every year that he slipped beyond fifty.

In his politest voice, Peter asked the bartender to turn up the volume.

"Let's go, Peter." Evangeline had seen it happen before, when Peter let his stubbornness get in the way of his good sense.

"Yeah, Peter," said Mr. Ping. "Don't go away mad. Just go away."

The golfers laughed. Heads turned.

Peter felt his mouth going dry, a sure sign that his body was waiting for him to make up his mind. Fight or flight. As old as the species.

He glanced at Evangeline and she waved the key at him. He got the message. Not worth staying here and busting his knuckles.

Then the face of Kelly Cutter appeared on the screen again, and Mr. Ping said, "Now *her* I can listen to."

The bartender, no doubt happy to avert a confrontation, turned up the volume.

Talking blond head: ". . . wrong about guns, wrong about Americans, and wrong about the Constitution."

"You're wrong." Harriet Holden's head appeared onscreen.

Mr. Ping's foursome began to boo, all except one, a small guy with a crew cut. He just watched. He was the reserved one, the sober one, the designated driver.

"The Framers wanted the Constitution to evolve as the nation evolved. They could never have conceived of today's weapons."

Cut to split screen: two talking heads.

Blond head: "They could never have conceived of today's liberals, either."

Ping laughed and clapped his hands.

Peter sensed Evangeline getting mad.

Congressperson head: "I would submit to you that the men who conceived of the Constitution were liberals themselves . . . in the best sense."

"A liberal in the best sense is dead," said Mr. Ping.

Blond head: "The Founders were conservatives. Remember what Franklin said: 'That government governs best which governs least.'"

Congressperson head: "They believed in the right of the people to be heard through government. That's the essence of liberalism."

"Ah"—Mr. Ping waved at the screen—"somebody ought to shoot that old bag with one of the guns she wants to ban."

That was enough for Evangeline.

A waitress was coming by with a tray of four Tuckermans in tall glasses. Evangeline stepped aside, then stepped back into the waitress, so that tray, tall glasses, and Tuckermans landed on Mr. Ping, who jumped up swearing, all six feet four of him.

"Oh, excuse me," said Evangeline. "But you got me so upset advocating political assassination."

Mr. Ping was dripping beer, and two of the others were standing, too. Only the designated driver remained seated, scowling.

Peter braced himself to go flying into the grand lobby with two guys in Tiger Woods golf shirts wrapped around his neck. That would leave at least one for Evangeline, because Peter didn't think there would be much help from Martin Bloom. He was just sitting in the corner, watching and listening.

But help was coming from the concierge and the head bellman, a local in crimson vest and bow tie, a big guy who carried bags in the summer and drove a groomer on the ski trails in the winter.

"Is there a problem?" asked the concierge.

Before Mr. Ping could start swearing, Martin Bloom said, "There's been a small accident. No reason to make it more than that, certainly not in the Mount Washington."

Ping looked at Bloom and said, "Who asked you, you little book-selling fairy?"

Peter looked at Bloom. "You know this guy?"

Martin just shrugged, neither yes or no.

"I think the gentleman in the bow tie is right," said the designated driver. A cooler head prevailing.

"Sir—" the concierge snapped his fingers, "—allow us to freshen your drinks." Four more beers appeared, and the concierge placed one in Ping's hands.

Then the bellman magically produced a garment bag.

"For the clothes," the concierge explained. "They'll be cleaned before your next round, sir."

The bellman stood close to Mr. Ping and tugged at his bow tie, almost a threat.

Mr. Ping got out of it by giving Peter a look and a laugh, the bully's best defense when he's backing off. Then he took the beer, toasted Evangeline, turned, and sat.

Things worked smoothly in the old hotel.

But even there, in that luxurious isolation, the national argument was getting ugly.

"Nice room," said Peter.

Evangeline pulled off her beery sweater. "There's always room for a magazine writer who might say good things about the hotel."

"So long as she isn't thrown out for dumping beer on a patron." He walked over to the window.

They had a "Mountain View" across the golf course to the Presidential Range. A puff of smoke smudged the sky. The little coal-burning engine on the Cog Railway was climbing Mount Washington.

"I think Bloom knew that guy," he said.

"Bloom must know a lot of guys up here."

He turned. "Even golfers?"

"So they golf by day and buy rare books by night." She started unbuttoning her blouse. "I'm just glad we didn't have to fight them."

He watched her for a moment, then said, "I think it would be good if you kept your political passions to yourself."

Her hands stopped at the fourth button. "What?"

"Your politics. Too passionate. This is business. Politics and business don't mix."

"*You* wanted to hear what Harriet Holden had to say."

"For business," he said.

"*And* you were ready to fight that guy before I was."

"Bad judgment. Not something you can afford in business."

"When a man publicly advocates shooting someone I've met and admire, I get mad." She popped the rest of her buttons and pulled off her shirt. "So screw business." Then she twitched out of her jeans, which were soaked with beer.

He looked out the window. He knew when not to look at her, even though looking at her was better than looking at the mountains.

"I'm taking a hot bath," she said. "Maybe it will cool me off." And she slammed the bathroom door.

Peter watched the puff of smoke ascend. Then he took his laptop out of its bag.

Wireless Internet, so we're never out of touch. One of the wonders of the age . . . and one of the scourges. He tapped into his e-mail.

Two Viagra ads—DELETE. DELETE. He didn't need Viagra . . . yet.

Spam from Africa about a poor exile who had accidentally left six million dollars in an American bank and just needed an account number to . . . DELETE.

Then he came to an e-mail from Antoine. Subject line: FW: Will Pike Letter.

Peter clicked the e-mail. It had come from Morris Bindle that morning:

"Mr. Fallon: This was in the scrapbook. I think it's worth a lot."

Beneath was the scanned-in text of a letter. The handwriting was shaky, hard to read on the screen. The letter was dated November 12, 1787, and was written to "Mr. King." *Rufus King.*

"I write from a farmhouse some five miles distant from what is called the Gateway of the Notch, in New Hampshire, where the Amonoosuc

River comes down from the mountains and turns west. The area is known as Bretton Woods. . . ."

"Jesus," whispered Peter.

He pushed open the bathroom door, and Evangeline shouted at him. "Dammit, Peter!"

"But—"

"I'm mad. Let me be mad in peace."

"Will Pike was here."

"Here?" She straightened up. "Where?"

"In this valley. Listen. A letter to Rufus King." Peter read the first two sentences and she whistled softly, so that her breath carved a little furrow in the soap bubbles.

He kept reading. "'The cold comes early here. The ground has already frozen. We smell snow in the wind. But I cannot travel. A musket ball splintered my femur in August. I sometimes wish the ball struck my chest, as death might have been preferable to my present feelings. I know that I have lost your trust. I again beg your forgiveness and promise that when my strength returns, I will continue my search.'"

"Search for what?" asked Evangeline.

He read the last sentences very slowly. "'I pray God that my failure in Philadelphia will not impact ratification. Neither you nor the other New Englanders who set their thoughts upon the Committee of Detail draft should spend a day in worry that those thoughts will be made public.'"

"Committee of Detail?" she said.

"They wrote the first draft of the Constitution."

"And New Englanders annotated it." She paused, then said, "Five million?"

"Ten."

"Who else knows about this letter?"

"Morris Bindle. It came from him."

"Do you think he understands what it means?"

"I'm not sure *I* understand what it means—" Peter went to the window and watched the little engine exhale a final burst of steam as it reached the top "—except that a first draft of the Constitution was around in 1788. It doesn't mean it's still around."

"It means we're getting somewhere, though."

He heard a gentle splash and turned. She was standing, her body glistening with bubbles and water and exquisite surface tension.

"Yes." He looked her up and down. "We *are* getting somewhere."

"Just throw me a towel and dress for dinner."

ENTERING THE HOTEL dining room was like walking into a 1930s movie. A slow tracking shot rolled down a corridor, toward a maître d' in a tuxedo. A gracious nod, a whispered comment, a glance at the reservation book. Then the camera was rolling again and the music was rising. A five-piece band played old standards as the room expanded to fill the screen with light and color, grand and intimate at the same time.

The high ceilings and windows and white woodwork gave it the grandeur. The candlelight and the peach-colored walls and table linens conveyed the intimacy. And any dining room where so many people seemed so happy with each other had intimacy built in. Old couples, fall honeymooners, a few May-Decembers, vacationing double-daters at tables for four . . . even the golfers seemed happy.

The band was playing "Dancing in the Dark" and half a dozen couples were on the floor.

Peter and Evangeline had a table by the window, overlooking the illuminated tennis courts. They were starting with a split of Veuve Clicquot.

"Do you think Bindle's all right?" Evangeline was asking.

Peter shrugged. "He's not answering his phone. But I don't always answer mine."

"Do you think he could be in danger?"

"If this is as big as it sounds, a lot of people are in danger, including us."

"Not tonight, though. No one knows we're here."

"Martin Bloom and Paul Doherty know. And who knows what they know? Or *who* they know? They may see us as their chief competition."

"I thought you liked Bloom."

"I said I liked him. I don't trust him."

"Doherty and Bloom look like an old married couple," said Evangeline. "Are they?"

"Doherty likes the ladies," said Peter. "I think Martin likes to follow when he dances."

Paul Doherty and Martin Bloom were sitting at a table across the floor, with several other exhibitors, including the Butterfield twins and two blondes in their late forties—Nancy Lee Dutton and Kara Spellman. Since this was primarily a man's business, the presence of the ladies was (a) exotic, and (b) magnetic. They attracted straight men and gays alike. And since they specialized in the history of Newport and called themselves the Common Cliff Walkers, their presence suggested a little humor, too.

The first course arrived. Duck pâté for Peter. Mussels in white wine for Evangeline.

She tasted the broth. "Just enough garlic . . . So what are you going to do with the letter? Bindle wants you to sell it, doesn't he?"

"We could offer it to Cottle in Litchfield. Or we could see who else wants it."

Evangeline's eyes widened. "You're not going to put it on the Web?"

"If it was a simple sale, I would." He spread pâté on a bit of roll. "That would be due diligence."

"This is no simple sale." She opened a shell with her fork. "And we only have six days."

"Six days to find something that could be anywhere, if it exists at all. We have about as much chance of finding it as—"

She put down her fork with a loud clatter. "Peter, we've signed on to help a woman who has political courage. Physical courage, too. Now that we know what we're looking for, I don't think we should be letting up."

"Usually, you hate yourself when you get into the middle of one of my treasure hunts." He took another sip of champagne. "Why the change?"

"This time, it matters. It could change the future of this country."

"For better or worse?" he asked.

"Better, of course."

He wasn't sure about that, but he kept the opinion to himself. He leaned across the table. "So . . . how do we get Bloom and Doherty to talk?"

"Maybe we show them the latest letter."

"Before I give them anything, Doherty has to give me something."

She ate her last mussel. Then she glanced toward the dance floor, where Doherty and one of the Common Cliff Walkers were stepping into a fox-trot. The tune was "Cheek to Cheek."

"Let's dance," said Evangeline. "After a bit, cut in on Doherty. I'll dance with him and see if I can get him to talk."

"Intrigue. I love intrigue."

It might be intrigue, but Peter and Evangeline enjoyed the moment, too. They danced close and slow. And she seemed to anticipate every move he made.

"This is the only place where you take my lead," he whispered. "Makes me look good."

"I know." She glanced over his shoulder. "And the other blonde is about to make Martin look good. Straight, too. She's getting up to dance with him."

"Gay guys are usually good dancers."

For a few moments, they all danced. "Cheek to Cheek," then "Night and Day."

Then Peter noticed Mr. Ping get up from a table full of golfers in blue blazers—jackets required for gentlemen at dinner—and lurch onto the floor.

Trouble. Peter should have danced away from it. Or toward Doherty, who was on the other side of the floor, but his instinct was to help. So he led Evangeline into Bloom's range just as Mr. Ping tapped Bloom on the shoulder.

Bloom looked at Mr. Ping and kept dancing. Bloom was a graceful fox-trotter, and Kara Spellman of Newport seemed to be enjoying the dance, too.

Mr. Ping, however, had a chip on the shoulder of the sport coat with the Augusta National patch on the breast pocket. He also had a few more beers in his belly.

He tapped Bloom's shoulder again. "Hey, Martin, why don't you step aside so I can dance with the nice blond lady?"

"So he *does* know him," muttered Peter.

"No thank you." With a deft move, Bloom danced in retreat toward his table.

"Peter," whispered Evangeline, "the guy's drunk. Dance the other way before he sees you and tries to cut in on *us*."

"No," said Peter. "If he bothers Bloom, he might come and bother us."

Peter danced Evangeline along, with one gray-haired couple in the way like a moving screen.

Evangeline whispered, "Don't do anything stupid, Peter."

Ping looked at Kara Spellman and said, "How about a dance with a real man?"

"I like dancing with a real *dancer*," said Kara.

Without missing a beat, Peter slipped a leg through the tangle of dancers, and swept it quickly between the legs of the big guy. Peter rowed a shell three times a week. He had strong legs.

Mr. Ping landed on his ass with a thud. But the music kept playing. And the old couple kept dancing. And Ping seemed oblivious, too, or maybe just too drunk.

Kara Spellman looked down at Mr. Ping and said, "Stick to golf, buddy. No fancy footwork required. Not like Martin Astaire, here."

Ping's own companions roared, all but the serious one, the designated driver. He came and put a hand under Mr. Ping's arm, helped him up, and led him back to his table. And that was that.

Peter guided Evangeline away, as if he hadn't even been there.

"Very smooth," she whispered. "Even if we missed a chance with Doherty."

"Funny that he danced away. Wouldn't stick up for Martin."

"I don't think they like each other too much," she said. "But I like you."

"That's because I'm smooth on the dance floor, smooth in other places."

"Not too smooth, I hope."

EVANGELINE ROSE EARLY to watch the sunrise. She got a cup of coffee from the urn in the lobby and went out onto the east veranda, which was deserted at dawn. She sat in a red rocker, wrapped her hands around her cup to feel the warmth, and looked out.

Down by the tennis courts, the sound of the river was strong and soothing at the same time. An enormous moose on spindly legs stopped for a drink, then loped across a fairway and into the woods. Beyond the golf course, the land rose toward the mountains in layer after layer of dark pines silhouetted by morning mist.

Evangeline heard someone coming out the door behind her: Martin Bloom, lost in his own little contemplation, carrying his own coffee and newspaper.

At first, he did not seem to notice her, so she called his name.

"Oh, good morning." Martin spread the pages of the newspaper out on the damp rocking chair beside her and sat. "I wanted to thank Peter for last night."

"I'm sure he was glad to do it. He's an Irish street brawler at heart."

"I'm glad of it. And Kara Spellman treated me well later."

Evangeline laughed. "Why Martin . . . what are you saying?"

"People think I'm gay, but"—he spoke softly, though there was no one else on the veranda to hear him—"Peter gave me a chance to look good next to that big golfer."

"He seemed to know you. Is he a friend of yours?"

"Friend . . . hell, no. An old customer. A collector. He and his friends come up here to play golf and buy books."

"So he's more cultured than he seems."

"He knows a good investment. Rare books. But he drinks too much."

"You know—" She measured a sip of coffee, a little beat before speaking. "—you could give Peter a chance to look good, too."

Martin gazed to the east as the first crescent of sun appeared.

Evangeline said, "This is about more than another lost document, isn't it? It's about ideas that matter today. It's about the difference between what you believe and what . . . what that golfer believes . . . about guns, anyway."

"His name is Marlon Secourt," said Martin. "And Paul thinks we should have nothing to say to you."

"We think someone killed that professor," she said. "We think you know something about it."

Bloom looked out at the mountains again.

Evangeline heard footfalls. Peter stepped out, coffee cup in hand. She caught his eye and shook her head. So he stopped where he was.

Then she whispered to Martin. "In 1788, Will Pike was chasing a first draft of the United States Constitution. That's what we know. And we have evidence."

Martin said nothing. The sun rose higher.

Evangeline said, "I've taken the first step, Martin. Help Peter. Help me. Help Harriet Holden. And even if you don't care about her, help us find the truth."

He turned to her, as if he could not hold it in any longer. "It's the Holy Grail of American documents, a first draft of the Constitution, annotated by the New England delegates. We've been chasing it for thirty years."

In the quiet, even whispered voices echoed along the ceiling of the veranda.

And Peter could no longer restrain himself. He came striding down the porch and said, "Where did you first hear about it?"

Bloom jumped up. "Peter!"

Evangeline made a face. *Way to go.*

"In for a penny, in for a pound, Martin," he said. "Where did you hear about it?"

"From . . . from an old drunk in Portland . . . back in the early seventies. But it's just a legend. It's not worth getting yourselves killed over."

"Killed?" Peter looked at Evangeline.

"Goddamn you, Martin." Paul Doherty stalked out of the solarium. "I told you not to tell these two anything."

Peter turned to him. "We can pool our resources. We can try to find this together."

Doherty put his face close to Peter's. "This is the work of a lifetime, Fallon. I'm not sharing it. And neither is Martin. For your own good, stay out of it."

Then Doherty turned on his heels. About halfway down the long porch, he stopped and said to Martin, "It's me or them. Make your choice."

After a moment, Martin said to Evangeline, "Let me go and talk to him." Then he jumped up and followed his partner.

"So," said Evangeline, "that went well . . . for a while."

Peter watched Martin and Paul retreat along the porch. "People in Portland call them the Old Curiosities. They've certainly piqued mine. Stay out of it? For my own good?"

"Wrong thing to say to you. Even if you don't think we can find it."

"Even if I don't, we'd better make the most of Tuesday, which starts just . . . about—" Peter looked up at the sun, which was appearing full from behind the mountain. "—now."

FROM A PALLET in the great room of Horace Dewlap's cabin, Will Pike watched the sun rise. He could just see it through a tiny window, a sliver of red coming up from behind the biggest mountain.

He had spent the predawn hours writing two letters: to Rufus King and Caldwell P. Caldwell.

He would ask Horace Dewlap to deliver them. . . .

Dewlap had proved to be a man of considerable independence.

"It's why I come here," he had told Mary on the day after he found them, "to live free or die, like they say in New Hampshire."

"Live free or die . . . on *two* legs," Will Pike had said through a haze of pain. "Too much to be doin' to live on one."

"But son," Dewlap had told him, "the leg's already startin' to smell. Wound's putrefyin'. And long bones is hard to heal."

Dewlap had served with a surgical unit in the Continental Army. He had hacked off shattered limbs, dug musket balls out of bloody guts, dosed men with laudanum, but he had never proclaimed himself a doctor, just a "sawbones" who had learned how to tend people by treating livestock.

And he was not one to go running forty miles to tell the sheriff about a small thing like two dead men in the Notch, or an even smaller thing like a man with shot-through leg, especially if the man was traveling with a good-looking woman who proved to be as strong as a horse, as strong-willed as a mule, and a good cook, too.

Dewlap needed a woman like that, he had said, because his own wife had left him.

"Couldn't stand the winter. Got cabin fever somethin' fierce. One night, with the snow bowin' the roof and the cold colder than hell is hot, she said she wanted to boil the kids. I said I didn't expect they'd be good for much of anything after boilin'. So she turned her mind to other things, like sharpenin' knives whilst I et my supper. Worried me till spring.

"But we made it. So I went down to Conway, to fetch supplies and fish the lake at ice-out. Three days later, I come home with a barrel of white perch, and my Bess was gone. Took the kids. Left a note sayin' she couldn't stand it no more. I thought to go after her, but I had livestock and plantin' . . . figured I'd light out after harvest, if I could find someone to tend the place through winter."

Then Dewlap had offered them a deal: If Mary would see to his livestock, she and Will could live off Dewlap's supplies until he returned in the spring.

Mary had told Will that she still planned to pursue the men who stole her money, "But I had true feelin's for your brother. So I'll help you. If you heal, you can help me get back my money."

So Dewlap and Mary had buried North Pike on a rise behind the house.

Then, instead of cutting off Will's leg, Dewlap had cut a certain patch of moss from the north side of a certain tree. He had dressed Will's wound with the moss. Then he had trussed the leg in a three-piece splint fashioned from barrel staves and leather straps and fixed it to a piece of barn board.

"No weight on this for twelve weeks," he had ordered. "Normal bone heals in six, but this ain't a normal break. If it heals at all, it'll take twelve. Leastways, we'll know 'fore I leave if the Injun moss-medicine works."

By late October, the infection had retreated, perhaps because of the moss-medicine, perhaps in spite of it. Dewlap's crops had been harvested. And news had reached even that remote valley in those high mountains: The Philadelphia Convention had presented the states with a new Constitution. To become law, it would need the ratification of nine. In all thirteen, the fighting had begun.

And Will had lain awake a whole night thinking of something other than the pain in his leg. . . .

To Caldwell, Will wrote that the document he had purchased was stolen and should "be returned via my agent, Horace Dewlap." To Rufus King, he wrote another apology and promised to find the document so that "my failure in Philadelphia will not impact ratification."

That morning, he showed both letters to Mary.

She said she doubted that Caldwell would return something he had paid for. And she did not think Will should apologize to Rufus King again. "Once is sufficient. Twice is a sign of weakness."

If Will were not so burdened by pain and the mortification of his own failure, he might have agreed on both counts.

Instead, he asked Dewlap to carry a letter to Caldwell's home in Lancaster, twenty miles away. Dewlap came back the next day still carrying the letter. Caldwell had gone south to the state capital and would not return until after the ratifying convention in the spring. So Will asked Dewlap to post both letters as soon as he reached "civilization."

With a final round of instructions, Horace Dewlap left for the winter.

AND WILL PIKE and Mary Cousins were alone, in a November landscape of bare trees and browning meadows. Three days later, the snow came. It fell for four days. Then it stopped. Then it fell for four days more.

Inexorably the world around the little farmhouse closed in. The views to the mountains and down to the Notch became as illusions. By December, even illusions faded before the reality of blinding white days, bitter black nights, and bone-cracking cold.

Mary worked hard outside and seemed to grow stronger with the work.

Will stayed inside and tried to heal.

To take his mind from his pain, he practiced loading Mary's pistol as quickly as he could and throwing his brother's knife so that it struck, nine times out of ten, in the center of a target he had hung on a wall. But he knew that until he could walk on two legs, neither pistol nor knife would aid him in his purpose. And if he spent much longer on a pallet in his snowbound prison, he might start looking for kids to boil.

So he determined that on New Year's Day, he would walk. By then he had put weight on the leg and could thump about with crutches. But it had come time to test himself. He sat on the edge of his pallet and untied the splint. Then he pulled on his breeches and levered himself to his feet.

Mary stood by the fire, a shaft of sunlight slanting through the little window. "Walk to the square of sun on the floor," she said, "and I'll give you johnnycakes with Dewlap's maple syrup and fresh-churned butter."

He took a first step, then a second, wobbling and hesitating because the muscle was gone and the leg felt like glass. For a moment, he did not think he could take another.

Then Mary lifted the skillet from the hearth and passed it under his nose, and he followed all the way to the table.

That was when he knew: Come spring, he would walk out of those mountains and resume his search. He was filled with such joy that after breakfast he asked Mary to help him back to his pallet.

"Help?" she said. "After what you just did? You can walk."

But he begged her. He told her he was exhausted, that he might fall, and then where would they be? So she slipped a shoulder under him, and together they hobbled back to the pallet. And it was all a ruse, for when they got there, Will wrapped his arms around her, drew her down, and kissed her.

She said she had been wondering what she would do when he finally tried that; then she kissed him back.

And his newfound confidence became euphoria as she let him lower her blouse and caress her breasts, as he felt her flesh rise to his touch, as she wrapped her fingers into his hair and drew his face against her. He kissed one nipple, then other, and that would have been pleasure exquisite enough for a young man who had spent far more time thinking about women than knowing them.

But Mary pushed Will back onto the pallet and told him to slip off his breeches. Then she hiked her skirt above her waist. and hooked a leg over his hip and lowered herself onto him, and Will Pike understood in an instant why his brother had spent his life either chasing women or running away from them.

For the rest of the day, and for many days after, they did not notice the cold.

And in the evenings, after Mary had done hauling firewood and mucking stables, after Will had exercised his leg, practiced with pistol and knife, and finished what small chores he could, they sat by the fire, Mary to spin yarn from Dewlap's wool, Will to read from Dewlap's Bible. And they shared their dreams.

Will's remained simple and grand: to make a mark among men who mattered.

Mary's was simple but realistic: to go back to the town where her father ran the grist mill and prove herself a respectable woman.

At fifteen, she had been betrothed to a Millbridge boy, but he was killed at Yorktown. In her grief, she had allowed herself to be impregnated by the son of an Uxbridge barrister who then denied her, besmirched her character, and did not even offer condolences when the baby was stillborn. After that, she had fled the town gossips and gone to work, first as servant in Boston, then in Falmouth, Maine.

That was where she met a fisherman named North Pike.

"And now, I'm twenty-three, unmarried, destitute, couplin' with a little brother who may love me or may just be happy to have a woman to screw when he's snowed in."

Will said, "I love you. I may be younger but—"

Mary simply smiled, an expression as inscrutable as a smile from Eve Corliss, a smile that told a man she was amused but that perhaps, the joke was on him.

SPRING CAME AT first with a gentle melting, then with a cold rain that poured down on the snowpack. Soon the river began to roar and rise over its banks and spill in great sheets down the hillsides, washing away the last of the snow and flooding the lowland places wherever it went. Then it grew cold and everything froze. Then came a day when the sun gave warmth as well as light. Then it snowed. Then came a day that brought robins listening for worms in the softening ground. Then it snowed.

Then a new season descended, neither winter nor spring. It was called mud. For almost a month, nothing moved, neither shod horses, nor wide-wheeled wagons, nor men with weak legs, for mud was harder to walk through than snow.

If winter did not drive northern New Englanders to boil their kids, said Will, waiting for spring surely would.

It was not until late May, when the buds had leafed out and green tinted the ridges and darkened the valleys, that the roads were firm enough for a man to drive a cart into those mountains. And it was another fortnight before the voracious black flies finished their business.

Then Horace Dewlap returned. He brought two little boys who leaped from the cart and scampered joyously about. He brought a wife who looked as if she had been captured and brought back to prison. He also brought newspapers and a copy of the new Constitution.

Eight states had already ratified it, he said, some unanimously. People north and south wished for a government to maintain good relations among the states and protect against troubles like Shays's Rebellion. But many people, and sometimes the same people, feared that such a government would threaten a man's right to live free or die.

Will asked Dewlap, "Did you ever hear from Caldwell?"

"No. Never."

Will was disappointed but not surprised. He took the newspapers and the Constitution and retreated to the rise behind the cabin, up where North was buried. The wooden cross had fallen. Will straightened it, then sat on a rock and read.

Even in the warm sun, he felt a chill at the first words: "We the People of the United States, in order to form a more perfect union . . ." It was a preamble, a statement of purpose as pointed and exquisite as anything he had ever read. ". . . establish Justice, ensure domestic Tranquillity, provide for the common defence, promote the general Welfare, and secure the Blessings of Liberty to ourselves and our Posterity, do ordain and establish this Constitution for the United States of America."

It prescribed a government of three branches, with two legislative houses to balance the interests of large states and small. It would have the power to levy taxes, make treaties, and mediate interstate disputes. Most important, it contained the mechanism for its own improvement, an amending process to keep it flexible and growing as the nation grew.

It took Will only a few minutes to read. The document was that simple and that pure, a collection of compromises that somehow rose to the level of first principles. And when he was done, relief flowed over him, as clear and cool as the river tumbling over the rocks nearby. The men of Philadelphia had done their work in a way that guaranteed success, no matter that a first draft—covered with the ruminations of a few New Englanders—had been spirited away six weeks before the final draft was signed.

So, in a most positive frame of mind, Will turned to the newspapers.

From the *Boston Gazette*, he learned that ratification had carried in Massachusetts but only by nineteen votes out of three hundred and fifty-five cast. Elbridge Gerry had appeared at the convention, explained his reasons for refusing to sign a constitution that did not have a bill of rights, then left. Rufus King had stayed to do the politicking that made the difference.

And what of New Hampshire?

Will read that the state convention had adjourned before a vote, because it appeared that ratification would go down to defeat. "New Hampshirites want no one put over them. They value their freedom. It will take a bit more time to convince them that a federal structure, properly built, is meant to guarantee rights, not impinge upon them."

The word "federal," Will knew, came from the Latin *foedus*, meaning a league or treaty. Those who supported the Constitution were now called Federalists. Arrayed against them were the anti-Federalists, one of whom was Caldwell P. Caldwell.

Will feared that if Caldwell could find a way to use the first draft, with its unformed jottings on religion, free speech, and the possession of a musket, he might push New Hampshirites toward rejection. And if one state turned, others might follow, and a ninth state might *never* ratify, and all the work of all those men in Philadelphia, all the work of his father across all those years of Revolution, might still go for naught.

So there was reason yet for Will Pike to track down Caldwell P. Caldwell.

A FEW DAYS later, Will prepared to leave.

And Mary prepared to go to with him. But she had begun to question their common purpose. Was it necessary to rescue the document? Would it not be better to turn their minds to a dream of solidity—a house, a home, that mill on the Middle Post Road?

In the barn, where they had taken up residence after the return of the Dewlaps, Mary watched Will wrap her flintlock in an oiled rag and shove it into his canvas satchel. "Are you planning to shoot this Caldwell?"

"No," said Will, "but I must see him."

"It won't do any good for your reputation, or for America, or for us."

Will took his brother's knife and strapped the scabbard to his belt. Then he put on his brother's buckskin jacket. It fitted him loosely but well. "A man once said to me that in America, we get up in the morning and go to work and solve our problems. After I solve mine, we'll see to yours."

"If that's a promise," she said, "I'll go with you."

So they made their good-byes to Dewlap and his sad-eyed wife, then journeyed down from the mountains, south by the New Hampshire lakes, across a landscape embracing the beauty of June. They went by cart, by raft, and by foot, a hundred miles to Exeter, the capital.

"AND WHO IS it that's lookin' for Mr. Caldwell?" asked the sergeant-at-arms outside the Exeter meetinghouse.

"My name is Will Pike. Brother of North Pike. The *late* North Pike."

"Well, the gents on the other side of this door are doin' some big talkin', and lots of it, now that they've reconvened. Not sure Caldwell has time for chitchat. But I'll give him the message."

Caldwell P. Caldwell sent out a note: "Meet in Folsom's Tavern when convention stops for dinner. And order me a pint."

At two o'clock, the delegates poured into Folsom's—gentlemen in suits and lace stocks, farmers in rough coats, backwoodsmen in buckskins, all elbowing for seats at the four groaning boards set up to feed them, all except for one. He stopped in the doorway and scanned the room as if he owned it. His big belly proclaimed him a man of property, especially among skinny New Englanders. His enormous round head proclaimed him a man of republican tastes, one who would wear no aristocrat's wig to cover his baldness.

When he saw the young man and woman seated at the end of a table, he went straight for them . . . or perhaps it was the mug that drew him.

He sat, took a draft of ale, and said, "Will Pike, is it?" After offering condolences on North's death, he called for plates of stew, then asked, "So . . . what can I do for you?"

"You received my letter?" asked Will.

"I did. Fine penmanship. The work of an amanuensis." Caldwell shot a glance at Mary. "You know what that is, young lady?"

"One who writes down the words of others," she said.

"Very good." Caldwell toasted her, drank, licked foam from his lip.

"Then you know why we're here," said Will. "I was Rufus King's amanuensis."

"So *that's* where that draft came from," said Caldwell. "Your brother was never too clear on that."

"I want it back," said Will, as blunt as fist.

Caldwell smiled. He seemed a cheerful sort, not one to stand on ceremony or take offense. "I paid good money for that draft, son. Fifty Spanish dollars. Bought in good faith. I couldn't just give it to anyone who lays claim to it."

"Receiving stolen property is a crime." Will fell back on an argument he had hoped not to use. He said "crime" as harshly he could, trying to unnerve Caldwell.

Caldwell kept smiling, as though Will Pike was not worth a frown. "Can you prove the document is stolen? Can you bring Rufus King up here and have him testify that it's his handwriting on it?"

Will looked down at the foam in his mug.

Caldwell laughed. "There's an old sayin': 'Don't get in a pissin' contest with a skunk.' Well, I'm a lawyer. A *trained* skunk. Don't argue with me, son, till you're a little better . . . equipped."

"I'm not your son," was the best that Will could shoot back.

"Mr. Caldwell," said Mary, "we're worried that the document could fall into the wrong hands and affect the outcome of this convention."

"It could, if I had it," answered Caldwell. "I'd show the delegates that New Englanders were thinkin' on a bill of rights from the start and we should hold out till we get one, or maybe just hold out on general principle. When so many people say somethin's good medicine, I get leery."

Will heard only Caldwell's first sentence. "*If* you had it? You mean you don't?"

"Back last August, a feller from Rhode Island come through Lancaster—"

Will felt pain shoot from his brain to his stomach, which turned, then to his leg, which started to throb.

"—a Frenchman. Had a girl with him, and a big burly sailor, too. They knew your brother. The Frenchman asked after the document, and, well . . . I figured a Rhode Islander might need it more than I did. So I sold it to him. Fifty-*five* Spanish dollars."

Will could not speak. He did not think he could move. And if he tried to stand on that leg, he thought it might snap.

Caldwell, who seemed to like filling silence as well as space, said, "There's a lesson for you, son. If you can't buy cheap and sell dear, make a little profit anyway."

Will managed to stand and dig into his waistcoat pocket for a few coins.

Caldwell put up a hand. "The least I can do its pay for your meal."

As Caldwell dropped coins on the table, Will took Mary's arm. Mary pulled away.

Caldwell noticed this—he seemed a man who noticed things—then he pushed himself from the table and said, "Where will you be headed now?"

"South," said Will.

"I'd head north," said Caldwell. "Vermont. That's the place to go. Good land in Vermont. Cheap and fertile. Vermont's the place."

Will thanked him, still polite, "But—"

Caldwell kept talking, "I own some fine land on Lake Champlain. I'm sellin'—"

"Not interested." Will started for the door.

"What kind of land?" asked Mary.

"The kind where a young family could settle." Caldwell gave her belly an appraising look.

"Is your land expensive?" asked Mary.

"If you couldn't pay, you could work it, pay rent," Caldwell smiled as if to close a deal, "and I'd put it towards the sale."

"I have land in Massachusetts." Will took Mary's arm again.

Caldwell kept smiling. "Sell in Massachusetts. Buy twice as much in Vermont."

Will ignored him and said to Mary. "Come on. Newport's a long way."

Caldwell followed them out into the sunlight. It was market day in Exeter, so the town square was rumbling with carts and wagons, with horses clopping by, with New Englanders trading upon the fruits of their labor.

"Son," said Caldwell, "no matter what folks decide in New Hampshire or Rhode Island, that Constitution will be law soon enough. If I was you, I'd get on with my life."

"Washington told me to protect it *with* my life." Will started walking.

Caldwell looked at Mary. "Stubborn, ain't he?"

"Yes," said Mary, "but so am I."

"Two stubborn people," said Caldwell, "don't always make a good stew."

Mary followed Will.

And Caldwell shouted after them, "Do you know what they're callin' this Constitution? The Gilded Trap. A glitterin' thing that will enslave many a good man—and woman—under the yoke of a government, a ruling class, heavy taxes, monarchy. . . ."

THE NEW HAMPSHIRE convention ratified the Gilded Trap the next day. Nine states were now committed to the new union, and the rest—Virginia, New York, North Carolina, and Rhode Island—were bound to join.

By then, Will and Mary had walked ten miles to Portsmouth and, with their last bit of money, had taken passage on a packet to Boston.

Word of New Hampshire's ratification, carried by express rider, reached the city ahead of them. At Long Wharf, they were greeted by a young boy selling copies of the *Boston Gazette* and shouting the news. They would have bought a paper if they'd had a coin. As it was, they just listened.

"So," said Mary, "no more need to rescue a document to save the country."

"But the men who have the document have your money." Will started up State Street. "And they killed my brother."

"And they've surely concocted a story by now. Rhode Islanders, in Rhode Island, accused by a man from Massachusetts and a woman living in Maine about something that happened in New Hampshire. Who'll believe us?"

"Any who'd believe Rufus King's amanuensis," said Will.

"Did you spend the winter practicing with pistol and blade because you expect to be believed? You disappeared from Philadelphia with papers belonging to Rufus King." Mary stepped over a pile of horse dung. "He may have charged you with theft by now."

"But I wrote to him and explained myself. I wrote to him twice."

"Once," answered Mary.

"Twice . . . a note before I left Philadelphia, a letter that Dewlap mailed."

Mary walked a few paces and stopped. She dropped her bag on the State Street boardwalk and took out the letter he had written to King the previous fall. "I asked Dewlap not to send it. Too much apologizing. A sign of weakness."

Will's confusion was greater than his anger. He simply shoved the letter into his pocket and said, "But we need money. And that document is still worth something."

"How much? Fifty-*six* Spanish dollars? Even if you get it back, you won't sell it. You'll give it to Rufus King." She started walking again. "The only way to get my money is to kill the Frenchman and Curly Bill. And we're no match for them."

As they walked through the city, the truth that had been growing between them grew plain: The mountain cabin had been a cocoon in which they had grown together. Now they had emerged into the world as independent spirits.

Will no longer felt a burst of affection, followed by a surge of desire, every time he looked at her. Mary no longer embraced his dream of retribution as a pathway to her dream of respectability.

At the door of the Gefahlz Clock Shop, as Will pulled the bell rope, Mary forced the issue. "Are we to be man and wife to these people?"

"Married we will be welcome," he said. "Unmarried also."

"Then . . . unmarried," said Mary. "In separate beds."

"Fine, then." Will pulled the bell rope again.

She put a hand on his arm. "I've thought hard on this, Will . . . we don't need to go to Newport. The country is secure. And my money is spent. Going to Newport can only bring trouble."

"Where then, if not Newport?"

"To Millbridge and my father's mill, if it's not sold yet."

"To do what? Grind corn the rest of our lives?"

"Then to Pelham . . . or Vermont. Maybe Caldwell's right. Maybe Vermont's the place."

"I must go to Newport. I must"—he surprised himself with his admission—"see Eve again. That day in the Notch, she bartered herself and my brother's baby for our lives."

"She said the baby was Danton's. Your own brother said it wasn't his."

"I think they both lied. I must see her."

"You *must* see her?" Mary Cousins took her hand from his arm. "Am I a fool, then? As I was with your brother?"

The door swung open, and Herr Gefahlz shouted into their faces, "Will Pike! A miracle comes to our door. And . . . and a greater miracle is a beautiful girl."

Mary looked at the big German clockmaker and managed a smile, though tears were brimming in her eyes.

Will wanted to take her in his arms and promise to do whatever she thought best, but the joyous Hessian was sweeping over them, clapping Will on the back, grabbing the bag from Mary's hands, ushering them into the house, shouting for everyone to come down and "see who has come for the horse that last year he left."

WILL AWOKE BEFORE dawn and found a note slipped under his door:

Dear Will. I have changed since we left the cabin, but you have not. I see the world as it is, but you do not. You want me to be second to another woman, but

I will not. I leave off trying to save you from yourself. Send your apologizing
letters, search for your lost documents, see Eve if you must. I am going home.

Will hurried downstairs, but she was gone.

He saddled the black gelding he had ridden to Boston the year before;
then he cantered across the quiet city and down the Neck, all the while
hoping that he would come upon her. Soon the landscape widened into
fields and farmlands, but he kept up hope for nine miles more.

He overtook other riders and other walkers. He passed carts carrying
food to Boston and wagons bringing goods to the countryside. But he met
no young woman walking alone toward home.

So he stopped in the village of Dedham, where the Lower Post Road
and the Middle diverged. If he went toward Millbridge, he might still find
her. But what would he do then? Settle down, surrender his ambition, and
wonder forever if he had done the right thing? And what if she had gone
in the other direction altogether? What if she had taken Caldwell's advice
and made for Vermont?

There was only one thing for him. He spurred his horse onto the
Lower Road.

In Newport, a thunderstorm was blowing through, a perfect summer
tempest of wind and rain and shafts of gilded sunlight slanting between
the clouds. It drove people off the streets, which was for the best because
Will did not want to be recognized. He left the black gelding tied up at
the White Horse tavern; then he pulled his hat down and walked toward
the waterfront.

At Corliss Wharf, *Pretty Eve* and *Pretty Sarah* were taking on supplies. Curly Bill Barton stood at the head of the wharf, shouting at the
dockhands.

Will thought he saw Nathan Liggett's gold watch fob flash on Bill's
belly, but he didn't see anything else, because he kept moving, past Wall-
Eyed Frank's, past the next wharf, to a warehouse doorway where he
waited for the rain to end and the night to begin.

The air came in cool and fresh after the storm. The clouds caught
the last glow of dusk, so that they glimmered pink that darkened to purple as they blew off easterly. Will watched them and waited until the glow
faded. Then he made his move.

He did not go directly toward the big yellow house. He came up the
other side of the street, paused beneath a maple tree, and noticed black
crepe over the door.

Someone had died. Danton? Eve? The baby? Old Thornton Corliss?

Will moved to the shadow of another tree, from which he could peer directly into the library. The Frenchman was sitting behind Corliss's desk, writing. Was he alone? Where was Eve? Had childbirth taken her? Taken the baby? Taken both?

Then the evening quiet was pierced by a baby's cry.

The Frenchman looked up, made a gesture, said something.

Will felt relief fill his belly, because Eve was rising from a chair, lifting a lamp off the mantel. The light led her into the hallway and up the stairs. It appeared a moment later in the room above the library. It was set down, and the shadow of a mother lifted her child to her breast in the universal gesture of love.

So it was Corliss who was dead, thought Will, dead in his time.

And the child? North's baby? Flesh of his flesh? Will told himself he had made the right decision. He would save mother and child from their imprisonment, and save the Constitution, too.

But how? He stood in the shadows, watched, and wondered.

Eve put the baby back in its crib. The lamplight crossed to the other bedroom and soon went out.

In the library, the Frenchman took down a book and settled into a wing chair. From where he stood, Will could see only the pages, turning, and the Frenchman's pipe smoke, curling.

The tall case clock in the foyer chimed out nine, ten, eleven, the sound echoing muffled through the door. Otherwise, there was silence. A dense fog seemed to settle out of the trees and layer itself on the ground.

TOWARD MIDNIGHT, THE Frenchman's book dropped. A moment later, he got up, poured a glass of port, drank it in a swallow, and went upstairs.

Will watched the bedroom window for ten minutes, twenty minutes. Then he crossed the street, pushing the ground fog ahead of him like smoke. He did not stop to compose himself, as he had a year before. Instead, he pulled his pistol and tried the door.

The Frenchman had forgotten to lock it. Or perhaps he had no fear of invasion.

Will stepped across the foyer to the library and almost tripped on a packing crate. He stopped for a moment so that his eyes could adjust and realized that there were more books in crates than in the bookcases.

But the Constitution?

He went to the desk and tugged the drawers. Locked. All locked.

In the room above, the baby stirred, cried briefly, then quieted.

Will knew little about babies, but he suspected that this one would wake again. So he slipped off his boots and tiptoed upstairs. In the baby's room, he slid down into the shadows and wondered if he should pull his boots back on, for he might need to kick with them or run in them. He decided to keep them off.

It must have been near two when the baby began to fuss again. And the first outright cry drew a sleep-staggered mother into the room. As Eve bent over the crib, a hand closed over her mouth, and a voice whispered into her ear, "It's me. It's Will. I've come back."

Eve's eyes widened in fright.

"I've come back to take you away." With a nod to reassure her, Will removed his hand.

"Take me away?" she whispered. "From what?"

"Why . . . the Frenchman."

"He's my husband. He's the father of my baby."

Will brought his finger to his own lips and tried to shush her.

But her voice grew louder. "My father left him half of the estate, to be sure we would marry and stay married."

"But—"

Eve bolted for the door with the baby screaming in her arms. "Robert!"

"Quiet!" Will ran after her. "Quiet or I'll . . . I'll shoot."

In the bedroom, the Frenchman was already on his feet, a huge shadow in the darkness. He gave an animal cry and leaped at Will, black hair and nightshirt flying.

Will aimed the pistol, and Eve cried, "Don't shoot."

In Will's half-second of hesitation, the Frenchman was on him. So Will swung the pistol, smashing it into the big forehead, collapsing the Frenchman on the carpet.

"Robert!" Eve scuttled over to her husband, while Will pulled back the hammer of his pistol and put it against the Frenchman's unconscious head.

"Will Pike, what are you doing?" Eve pushed the gun away.

Will pointed it again. "He killed my brother. He kidnapped you—"

The baby continued to bawl, a piercing, hysterical cry that Eve calmed by opening her gown and giving the child one of her breasts.

That sight drained Will of whatever fury was in him. He lowered the pistol. He crouched and looked into Eve's eyes. "But I've come to save you."

"What makes you think I want to be saved? I can't take my baby from his father. It would be unnatural."

Will sat back on his haunches. The pain that shot through his leg was almost as sharp as his shock. "Then . . . what you said in the Notch was true? He raped you?"

Eve looked down at her husband, who was beginning to stir. "He took his advantage. So I ran away. To punish him. He said he pursued us because he loved me. He's been kind to me ever since, and he loves the baby."

In all his imaginings of this moment, Will had never expected this. "But—"

"We leave for the Indies on tomorrow's tide, for Robert's estate. Go, Will. Go before he wakes up and knows it was you. Then he won't rest until he kills you."

Will looked at the pistol. "Then I should be killing him, like he killed my brother."

"Please, Will. My baby needs a father. Just go, and I'll never tell."

Will looked into those eyes, glistening in the dark. On a night ten months earlier, they had intoxicated him. Now they were beams of light, burning away his illusions. He stood and shoved the pistol back into his waistband. "I'll go. But not without the Constitution."

"Constitution?"

"You went to see a man named Caldwell after the fight in the Notch."

"Yes. Because of Robert. He said that after all you went through to get that document, it had to be valuable. But Caldwell said he didn't have it."

"Didn't have it?" Will knelt again.

Eve moved the baby to the other breast. After a moment, the infant burrowed.

Will hardly noticed. He simply repeated, "*Didn't* have it?"

"Robert thought he was lying. But . . . afterward, we rode home through the Connecticut Valley, and in every town, they knew Caldwell . . . all the farmers, all the old soldiers. They said that if he couldn't buy their land, he'd try to buy their money."

"Their money?"

"Caldwell's a speculator. He bought Continental money from veterans for pennies on the dollar. A new government may redeem it at face value. A huge profit for him."

"So he *wanted* ratification," said Will. "Even though he pretended to be anti-Federalist. He bought the draft from my brother to keep it off the market, keep it out of the hands of people who might use it against ratification—"

Outside, there was a noise. Two men were laughing in front of the house.

"Curly Bill," said Eve. "He lives back of the kitchen now, in the room that Robert had until he became master. Some nights, he steals a bottle of port from the library and goes to sleep. Tonight he has a sailor with him. The sailor will distract him."

The front door swung open, and two sets of footfalls receded through the house.

"Go now," said Eve. "Go by the front door."

Will looked into those eyes again. "I'll always remember our journey."

"So will I. But I don't love you. And I didn't love your brother. And I don't love Robert. Men are greedy, lustful, murderous creatures. But I love my baby." She pulled Will's face to hers and kissed him. "Now go."

WILL TOOK HIS boots, slipped silently down the stairs, stopped in the foyer, listened for footfalls. Instead, he heard a strange animal groan of pleasure and pain.

He should have sneaked out. But curiosity drew him to the door of the library. The room was lit by a shaft of moonlight. It fell upon a pile of clothes on the floor. And something in the pile was shining—Nathan Liggett's watch.

Beyond the shaft of light were Curly Bill and the sailor, and what they were doing was yet another shock for Will Pike.

The sailor was on his knees, his elbows on the seat of the wing chair, his ass in the air. And Bill was behind him, his breeches off, the port bottle in his hand. And . . .

There came another strange groan from the sailor. And Bill gave out with a deep, gutteral groan of his own.

Will thought to snatch the watch and be gone. Then he considered cutting Bill's throat. Bill should be punished for that day in the Notch, for general thuggery, and by the lights of normal men or Bible readers, for this night of buggery.

But Will had been saved once from murder. He would not submit to hatred now. Men might not always be what God intended them to be, but most were decent nevertheless, and he counted himself in that number. He also counted himself as smarter than most.

So, while Curly Bill pounded himself against the sailor's backside, Will pulled out his brother's knife, reached into the room, and with the tip of the blade snagged Curly Bill's breeches and dragged them across the floor. He slipped Bill's purse from the pocket, but he left the watch.

Then he tiptoed out and disappeared into the ground fog.

In the morning, a note appeared beneath the sheriff's door:

Before the Pretty Sarah *sails, ask First Mate Bill Barton how he came by a certain watch, the initials belonging to a businessman of Springfield, Massachusetts, murdered last year, by the name Nathan Liggett. Signed, A friend.*

Though the note might not convict Curly Bill of a crime he did not commit, it would certainly cause him a share of discomfiture, and that would be small satisfaction for Will Pike.

By the time the sheriff appeared at Corliss Wharf, Will Pike had ferried across Narragansett Bay and was heading back to find Caldwell. But the purse he had taken weighed heavily on his belt. He did not consider that he had stolen it but that he had recovered it and so should return it to its rightful owner. He also wanted to tell the rightful owner that she had been right . . . about many things.

It was a brilliant day, the sun near its apex but the air still fresh and dry, the kind of June day when summer stretched before New England like infinity before a godly man.

Somewhere between Providence and Pawtucket, Will made his decision. He would leave the Post Road and go north along the Blackstone to Millbridge. But the black gelding, ridden farther in two days than in the previous ten months, went lame a short distance later, forcing Will to take to the shank's mare while the horse hobbled behind.

It was not long before the driver of a two-seat chaise stopped beside them. "Good day to thee, sir." The man wore a simple black suit and broad-brimmed hat.

From his manner of dress and address, Will took him for a Quaker. "Good day to . . . *you*, sir."

"May I be of some assistance?" The man had a narrow ascetic face, but there was a sincerity about him that inspired trust. "Where dost thee travel?"

"Millbridge, sir, on the Blackstone."

"I go no farther than Blackstone Falls in Pawtucket, but perhaps one of the Friends there might do a bit of horse-trading with thee, so that thou may be on thy way. Climb aboard."

And that was how Will Pike came to meet Moses Brown, one of the wealthiest merchants in Rhode Island, a man of foresight and judgment who was traveling to Pawtucket, as he explained, "because it has come time for Americans to learn to spin their own thread."

Will thought Brown spoke metaphorically until he elaborated: "A man bound for Millbridge knowest whereof I speak. The Blackstone River is like many of God's gifts, a wondrous thing that needs only the appreciation of men to prove its value."

"Yes, sir," said Will, without much certainty as to what Brown was talking about.

But Moses Brown seemed a most garrulous Quaker. "Water power. God's own muscle. From Lake Quinsigamond to salt water at the Seekonk, the Blackstone flows fast and true, so that honest men may grind their grain and cut their logs and do a hundred other things to lighten their load. Once the load is lightened, men have more time to bear witness. 'Tis a great gift, and one that God intends us to use greatly."

"I have not given much thought to water power, sir. I'm the son of a farmer."

"A noble profession, the tilling of the soil. But"—Brown glanced at Will's knife and pistol—"thou art armed for more than scything wheat."

Will closed the buckskin jacket. "I've seen much of the world, sir, and too much of life."

"Older but wiser, art thou?"

"Older, at least," said Will.

"A wise answer."

That afternoon, Will Pike enjoyed simple hospitality and honest horse-trading on Quaker Lane in Pawtucket.

At sunset Moses Brown brought him down to the river to witness the power of God made manifest, and Will understood why this smart old Quaker would want to build a mill at the mouth of the Blackstone.

Will stayed until dark, listening to the water roar, feeling its power vibrate into the earth, and watching the purple of night spread across the sky. And he thanked God for the mistakes he had not made in Newport. He thanked Him also for the opportunity to get up in the morning, go to Millbridge, and unmake the mistake that he already regretted.

THE NEXT MORNING, he rode north on Great Road, through small villages, across meadows, in and out of woods, always with the river nearby like a great vessel pumping lifeblood through the countryside.

The town of Millbridge shaped itself into a neat square around a town green. A white steeple held the northwest corner in place. At the southeast corner, Great Road from Rhode Island met the Middle Post Road, which led to the single-arch stone bridge. On the other side of the river, stood the Cousins Mill. It looked like a modest house attached to a wheel, but as there was little grain to grind in June, the wheel was still.

An old man was hoeing a garden out front.

Mary was scrubbing clothes on a washboard in a tub by the door. When she noticed the rider, she stopped in midmotion. Then she straightened, brushed the back of her hand through her hair, wiped her palms on her apron.

Will dismounted and tipped his hat to the old man, who stopped hoeing and gave him a squint. Then Will took the purse from his belt and held it out to Mary.

"How much?" asked Mary.

"Forty-two Spanish milled dollars. I owe you eight more."

Before she took it, she asked, "Are you stayin' or goin'?"

"That will be your decision."

She took the bag and flipped it to the old man. "There's rent for a year, Pa. You can't sell this place out from under me now."

The old man was frail and skinny, except for huge hands and head that seemed like husks of a youth long past. He fingered the coins and said, "Who's your friend?"

"A man who'd throw away his life pursuin' a document, when he should honor it by practicin' what it preaches."

"Is that so?" The old man made a face. "How?"

"By enjoyin' life, liberty, and the pursuit of *happiness*," she said.

Will looked at the old man. "Your daughter confuses the Declaration with the Constitution. But the man she describes is a man she knew yesterday. Today, you might call me a man ready to . . . to spin my own thread. I'd also like to marry your daughter."

"Would you? Would you now?" The old man nodded, as though Will had asked the price to grind a bushel of corn. "I suppose I should go in and clean up, then."

Will and Mary waited until the old man had made himself scarce, and then, though they had been apart only a day, they fell together as if it had been a year.

"You were right," said Will. "I'm sorry I didn't see it."

"So am I." She kissed him. "And there's the end of it."

"Too much apologizing," he said. "A sign of weakness."

Somewhere above them, a hawk circled. . . .

THE NEW ENGLANDER was an industrious creature, whether Quaker or Congregationalist, immigrant or native born, Federalist or anti-Federalist, who soon came to be known as a Democratic-Republican. And when New England industry was set into a framework shaped by a Constitution, and God's power flowed from the rain to the rivers to the mills that rose beside them, great things happened.

A year after Will Pike met Moses Brown, an Englishman named John Slater came to work for Brown. Slater carried in his head the plans for the newest British spinning technology and a genius for marketing what he spun. Soon families were leaving their farms to work in the mills at the mouth of the Pawtucket, and a new world was born.

In time, the clatter of spinning machines could be heard up and down the Blackstone. Men learned by watching Brown and Slater. They built machines of their own, or copied Slater's, or bought Slater patents. They invested in land and river rights and built mills to spin yarn, then bigger mills to loom cotton cloth from the yarn.

And one of those men was Will Pike, who boasted to his friends that his wife had a knack for childbirth, a mind for business, and a patch of golden ground by the Blackstone.

Their first mill resembled a great barn grafted to the back of the original Cousins Mill. Then it rose into the sky. And as it grew, a family grew with it. So Will and Mary built a fine house beside it, then an even finer house—with a grand portico and white pillars—across the river.

And every day, Will watched the millwheels turn. And some days, he looked for the circling hawks and wondered what they could see, but he never once regretted the decision he had made.

And the Blackstone ran, and the decades were carried on the current. . . .

ON A SPRING morning some fifty years after ratification, a leather-bound volume arrived at the house with the white pillars. It was called *Notes of Debates in the Federal Convention of 1787*, by James Madison.

Accompanying the book was a letter from Eve Corliss Danton.

> *Dear Will, I thought of you recently. There has been much talk of late regarding those days in '87, because of this volume. Accept it as a gift from someone who remembers you "in your youth." Our youths have long since fled. Our spouses are long since dead. Mine has been gone so long I barely remember him. The passing of your Mary must yet remain a wound unhealed. But know this: At your side she built something that will endure. She was a lucky woman.*

More than that, thought Will, he had been a lucky man.

And the book? He opened it and began to read and in an instant he was carried back to 1787 and his youth. . . .

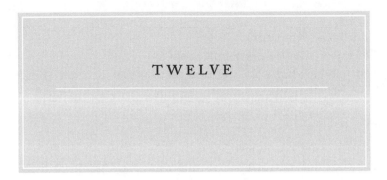

TWELVE

PETER FALLON READ the title page: *Notes of Debates in the Federal Convention of 1787*, by James Madison.

"Very rare," said James Fitzpatrick. "But you knew that."

"First edition." Peter inspected the leather binding, the rough-cut edge, the marbled endpapers. "Published by the Library of Congress, part of the three-volume *Papers of James Madison*."

"Signed?" asked Evangeline.

"Published posthumously," said Fitzpatrick, chief librarian of the Massachusetts Historical Society, a skinny bachelor with a photographic memory for all the manuscripts, books, and artifacts in the collection, no mean talent at a place that had been gathering historical treasures since the end of the Revolution.

Peter often said that, based on the dollar value alone, Fitzpatrick presided over more assets than the CEO of a mid-cap on the New York Stock Exchange.

"I wish they paid me like one," was Fitzpatrick's standard answer.

It was a slow day. There were no scholars working, so there was no need for whispering in the Ellis Hall reading room.

Evangeline slipped the book from Peter's hands. "Published in 1840. Madison died in—"

"—in 1836," said Fitzpatrick. "He kept notes through the whole convention. He sat in front of Washington and wrote down everything that was said in a kind of shorthand, then transcribed it at night and saved it for posterity. He didn't want it published until all the Framers were dead, because he didn't want the public to see how contentiously they argued over the shape of the government, over issues like slave representation, which they were still arguing about fifty years later."

"He took the rule of secrecy seriously," said Evangeline.

"We know there were three drafts of the Constitution." said Peter.

"Right" said Fitzpatrick.

"Do any of the first drafts still exist?"

"Not only do they exist, we *have* one. It's part of a set." Fitzpatrick's grin lit up his librarian's yellow complexion. "*And* it's annotated."

Peter and Evangeline looked at each other, then both said, "Annotated?"

Fitzpatrick raised a finger. "Wait here."

And they did, nervously. Was this what they had been looking for? Had they found it already? Right under their noses in the Back Bay?

Evangeline paged through the Madison book.

Peter looked at the pictures on the paneled walls: ancient New Englanders who had lived long enough to sit for portraits but hadn't gotten around to it until after they'd lost their teeth. In New England portraits, no one seemed to smile. And how puzzled would they have been by the parade outside? Cars crawled along on the Fenway, while a stream of people in Red Sox paraphernalia headed for the park.

Afternoon playoff game . . . against the Yankees, no less. Reason enough not to drive from New Hampshire into the Back Bay traffic, but now that Peter knew what they were looking for, there was no better place to start than at the MHS.

Fitzpatrick came back with three folders. "I don't bring them out often, but for Peter Fallon and my favorite travel writer . . ." He placed them on a table.

Folder One: "August 6, 1787, Committee of Detail draft printed by Dunlap and Claypoole from the proof copy. Sixty printed, sixteen in existence that we know of." *Folder Two*: "September 12, Committee of Style Draft, same printer, sixty copies, fifteen extant. *Folder Three*: "Final copy, the first public printing in the *Pennsylvania Packet and Daily Advertiser,* September 19, 1787."

Fitzpatrick opened the folders:

The first two drafts were printed on long folio sheets, in large type, offset right, with wide left-side margins for annotation. The margins and the text were covered in neat handwritten additions, deletions, and changes in punctuation. The final version of this set, on heavy-duty newsprint, was clean.

"Extraordinary," said Peter. "Who made these notes?"

"Elbridge Gerry of Massachusetts. He refused to sign because he wanted a bill of rights, which they finally got in 1791. One of his descendants gave us these in 1832."

Peter read an article on the first draft. "'The president shall be impeached for high crimes, treason, and bribery.'"

Evangeline said, "What about 'misdemeanors'?"

"That must be in the second draft," said Peter.

Fitzpatrick nodded. "If they'd adopted the first draft, Bill Clinton might not have been impeached. And George Bush would not have appointed two men to the Supreme Court, because in the first draft, that was the Senate's job."

"Amazing that they gave that one to the president," said Peter, "considering how fearful they were of the concentration of executive power."

"During the debate," Fitzpatrick said, "Ben Franklin looked at Washington and remarked that the first chief executive would be a good one, but in time, the concentration of power would tend toward monarchy."

"I think Franklin was right," said Evangeline.

Fitzpatrick picked up a page from the first draft and held it out to Peter. "Go ahead. Wipe your hands, then you can hold it for a second. It helps to hold it."

Peter took it with his fingertips and felt the fine texture of the paper. It was almost soft, like a cushion to receive the type or a bed to receive the wisdom.

"Read the last article," said Fitzpatrick. "Article Nineteen."

"'The members of the Legislatures and the Executives and the Judicial officers of the United States shall be bound by oath to support this Constitution.'"

Fitzpatrick leaned over his shoulder. "Now read Gerry's addition."

Peter angled the sheet toward the window for better light because the handwriting was so small. "'But no religious test shall ever be required as a qualification to any office or public trust under the authority of the United States.'"

"Wow," said Evangeline. "The separation of church and state. Right there."

"The Gerry draft shows history in action," said Fitzpatrick. "It reminds you of what Madison said: 'Every word decides a question between liberty and power.'"

"Where are the other copies of the first draft?" asked Evangeline.

"Spread around the country. George Washington's is at the National Archives. Samuel Gilman's is in Exeter, New Hampshire. . . ."

"What happened to the rest?" asked Peter.

"You mean"—Fitzpatrick grinned—"'Where do I look for one?'"

"You know me too well," said Peter. "Any thoughts?"

"If Gerry's draft survived, others must have, too."

"What do you think a draft would be worth?" asked Evangeline.

"Millions. More millions if it's annotated, especially if it's annotated by someone like Franklin or Washington."

"Has anybody else been nosing around these drafts recently?" asked Peter.

"Let's see." Fitzgerald looked at the record attached to one of the folders. "Professor Conrad, when he was writing *The Magnificent Dreamers* . . . his assistant, Jennifer Segal . . . Martin Bloom, a bookseller from Maine . . ."

"The usual suspects," said Peter to Evangeline.

Fitzpatrick kept reading. "A man named Don Cottle, who identified himself as an independent scholar."

"Ha!" said Evangeline. "I told you he was lying."

Fitzpatrick glanced up at Evangeline; then his eyes flicked back to the list. "About a week after Cottle, a man named Joshua Sutherland."

"Doing his research," said Peter. "Anybody else? Morris Bindle, maybe?"

"Hard to say, because we only keep records back two years, as you know."

"I wouldn't be surprised," said Peter. "I wonder how many other people are stringing us along."

"Are you saying all these people know each other?" said Fitzpatrick.

"I don't know," said Peter. "But I plan to find out."

THEY WALKED BACK to Peter's office against the tide of Red Sox fans.

Peter didn't say anything until they crossed Mass Ave. He was thinking, and he was steaming. Evangeline could tell by the way he strode along, head down and heedless, as if there were no one in his path.

Finally he said, "All those damn people asking me to look for something when they knew what it was all along—Sutherland . . . Cottle . . . Blooms . . . Jennifer Segal."

"Somebody is using you," said Evangeline.

"Time to make some phone calls."

"Time to figure out who's protecting the Constitution and who's for shredding it."

"I think any one of them would shred it if they thought it was in their interests."

"You mean, they're *all* Republicans?" she cracked.

"Not funny."

"But accurate."

Peter stopped in front of the Prudential Center, so that she had to stop, too, or lose him in the crowd of fans streaming up Boylston Street. "This isn't about Republicans and Democrats. It's about finding a document and protecting it, whatever it says."

"Does the government protect it? Or did they answer 9/11 by suspending the law of habeas corpus, which is right in the Constitution?"

"They suspended it for enemy combatants," he said, "not Americans."

"Well, we're next. Just look how they're trying to bend the Fourth Amendment with their invasions of privacy and their snooping and . . . to hell with it." She pivoted on her heels and started down the street, throwing this over her shoulder: "We're in a fight for the soul of the nation, Peter. The least we can do is fight back."

"By repealing the Second Amendment?" Peter went after her, sidestepping half a dozen baseball fans. "If you're worried about the government, you should fight the repeal. The Framers knew that an armed citizenry guarantees our civil liberties against all tyrants, foreign and domestic."

"The Framers expected us to change the Constitution when circumstances demanded it."

"They expected us to be vigilant. Franklin said, 'Any man who surrenders a little freedom for a little safety deserves neither the freedom nor the safety.'"

"You're making my point," she said.

"You're making mine."

"You don't *have* a point. You have a cop-out." She stopped in front of the library. "You have to take a stand, Peter."

"I am. You heard Martin say this wasn't something to get myself killed over. But here I am, taking a stand, still looking, and endangering the both of us in the process."

"I can look out for myself."

"OH, BOY," BERNICE said when they came in. "Looks like you two been fightin'."

"Five blocks of political disagreement," said Evangeline.

Peter pointed at Bernice. "Get me Don Cottle on the phone."

Evangeline went to her right, to the desk at the back of the showroom. Peter went to his left, into his office, and picked up the phone.

"Cottle here," said the voice on the other end. "What do you have for me?"

"A question," said Peter. "Two weeks ago, you were looking at the Gerry drafts of the United States Constitution—"

"The Massachusetts Society Historical drafts?" said Cottle, who didn't seem to like chitchat. "So what?"

"So what were you looking for?"

"It's what I was looking *at*. A national treasure."

Peter let the silence hang, waiting for more.

But Cottle gave up nothing. "Do you have one? If you have one, I'll pay top dollar."

"Do you know about one?"

Now there was a silence on Cottle's end, a pause, and finally, "I've heard stories."

"I'll bet you have." But Peter couldn't get any of them out of Cottle, so his next call went to Jennifer Segal. *No answer. Leave message.*

Third call: Josh Sutherland.

"Do you have it?" asked Sutherland.

"Have what?" said Peter.

"Well . . . whatever the professor was looking for?"

"No, but I have a photocopy of a call slip you filled out at the Massachusetts Historical Society less than a month ago. The Elbridge Gerry drafts of the Constitution. Are you holding out on me?"

"Holding out?" Sutherland sounded indignant. "We hired you, didn't we?"

"Why didn't you tell me you were after a first draft of the Constitution, with annotations?"

"Because we didn't know, but if that's what it is . . . Wow."

Peter tried to gauge Sutherland's tone against his words. Sincere? Or another operator?

Sutherland said, "Just find it. Please. By Monday. Sunday night if you can."

"Sunday night?"

"We're getting air time on the World Series," said Sutherland. "We're fighting this battle on all fronts."

After a moment, Peter spat out a question: "Republican or Democrat?"

"What?"

"Are you a Republican or a Democrat? In private, I mean. Are you a true believer, or a professional doing a job?" Peter didn't know which answer he would respect more.

"I believe what the congresswoman believes. Thirty thousand Americans die in gun violence every year. We have to control guns. And the way to do it is to use all the political skills we have. Now . . . she's being called to a hearing. I have to go." *Click.*

Peter's mind spun until it stopped on "Not Enough Information." True believer or political gun for hire? He still didn't know. But either way, Sutherland was doing his job. And Peter would do his.

So he logged on to his computer. An instant message popped up from E-Traveler, aka Evangeline. "Are we still arguing?"

Rarebooks, aka Peter, typed: "Not arguing. Debating."

"Good, because we need to talk to Bindle again. Let me show you."

Evangeline was working at the two-sided partners desk that Antoine Scarborough and Peter's mentor, Orson Lunt, used when they were in the office. The window at this end of the showroom looked out on the alley behind the building.

Evangeline was at her laptop, reading the Web site for the Millbridge Historical Society. "Webmaster Bindle has posted a series of letters from a woman named Eve Corliss Danton to Will Pike."

Peter pulled up a chair and looked at the screen. "What are the letters about?"

Evangeline pointed to the words just below a photo of one of the letters. "Ranging from 1789 to 1840, these letters describe a long relationship, which apparently had no ill effects on Pike's marriage. They also describe the development of the mill and the town."

Evangeline clicked through them. "In the first one, Eve writes about the heat in Martinique, about her baby, about someone named Curly Bill, arrested and charged with murder before they sailed. 'Later, Bill attacked the marshal who was bringing him back to Massachusetts. The marshal shot and killed him. So you needn't worry about him in the future. And'—here's the important part—'I assure you that Robert knows nothing of your visit here. Did you go back to Caldwell and ask about that document?'"

"'That document,'" said Peter. "Interesting. What else?"

"Letters congratulating Will on the births of his children. Letters about the growth of the gristmill to a yarn mill about 1805, then to a fully integrated cotton mill. Then . . . mmmh . . . Eve's husband dies on a sea journey . . . family fortune wanes . . . bad investments . . . her only son dies of tuberculosis. . . . In the last letter, she sends Will Pike a copy of the Madison book we saw this morning."

"You're right. We need to talk to Bindle again."

WHILE EVANGELINE DROVE, Peter made two more phone calls.

First to Bindle, who said he'd be waiting with a few more letters.

"Good," said Peter. "And I'd like to know why you posted those letters on your Web site."

"The letters from Eve?" said Bindle. "I came across them when I decided to sell the Henry Knox letter. I thought they were pretty interesting, so I posted them. Maybe they'll up the ante on the letters I hold. Why?"

"One of them mentions a document. Do you know what it is?"

Bindle's answer: the sound of a cigarette lighter flicking open, a couple of fast puffs, then, "I've heard legends. Hell, I've read them. So have you, in that letter I sent you yesterday. But I never believed them. Buster didn't either, even when people came sniffin' around."

"People? What people?"

"Well, that Dartmouth professor, and . . . somebody just came in. It's Tuesday. So the Society's open for visitors. I'll talk to you when you get here."

After he clicked off, Peter said to Evangeline, "I don't know if Bindle's innocent, ignorant, or the biggest operator of the bunch."

Then he called his brother, Danny, at Fallon Salvage and Restoration, which occupied a warehouse in South Boston. Peter heard the echo of the ball game in the background. "Who's winning?"

"No score. Yanks just batted in the first. Commercial's on. I wouldn't have picked up otherwise."

From the time they were kids, the Fallon brothers had been opposites. Danny liked street hockey, the South Boston sport, so Peter played basketball. Danny liked beer, so Peter drank wine. Danny wore Sears work-suits. Peter went for Joseph Abboud. Danny looked like a power lifter who'd let his paunch pop out. Peter still had the long, stringy muscles of a rower. But they both liked baseball. And they were business partners.

"What's up?" asked Danny.

"Ever heard of a rehab development called the Pike-Perkins Mill?"

"I went through it before they auctioned it. Don't you remember?"

"I don't remember everything. I'm supposed to be your silent partner."

"Silent until you get into trouble with some guy like Bingo Keegan. Then it's, 'Wah wah wah. I need backup. Come and save me.'"

"Hey, Dan—" Peter glanced at Evangeline. "—I have enough smart-asses around here. I don't need another one."

"Oh, you got your girlfriend with you?"

"I heard that," she said.

Danny chuckled. He was a needler, always happy when the needle hit home. But all business, too. He said, "The last owner bought the mill at auction after it closed in the seventies. He got loans from the state to buy new equipment, worked awhile, went bankrupt. The place was empty for about twenty years, a big white elephant. Finally auctioned for back taxes. A developer from Rhode Island picked it up for a song, a guy by the name of Farrell."

"What do you know about him?"

"A small-timer thinkin' big. All he's done is fix the holes in the roof and upgrade the sprinkler system so the kids can't set it on fire."

"Does he have a chance?" asked Peter.

"I thought he was throwin' his money away," said Danny, "but even with a downturn, Boston real estate prices keep pushin' people west. Mill-bridge is growin'. Median income's goin' up. And people like the idea of livin' in an old mill with a nice view of a famous river, so . . . Sox are up. Anything else?"

"Not now," said Peter. "Maybe later."

"I can't wait."

ALL WAS AS before at the Pike-Perkins Mill—the same sign, the same sugar maples, the same smell of decay.

The door to the historical society was open, but Bindle wasn't there.

They called. *No answer.* Peter put his hand on the coffeepot behind the desk. *Still warm.*

Evangeline looked out at the mill. "Maybe he's—did you hear that?"

"What?"

"Breaking glass. A bottle or something."

"Where?"

"In the mill." She looked out one of the back windows. "I think there's someone up there. I saw a shadow. *There.*" It flicked past one of the windows in the staircase tower.

Peter started for the door. "Wait here."

"Like hell."

As they went out, he grabbed an old blackthorn cane from an exhibit. It had a handle as thick as an Indian root club.

"What's that for?" asked Evangeline.

"A conversation starter . . . or finisher."

They crossed the broken glass and cracking tarmac in the mill yard and approached the entrance in the stairwell steeple.

The door was half off its hinge. The one-by-four boards that usually blocked it had been pulled away.

As they stepped inside, cold air and the smell of dead pigeons hit them like fetid air-conditioning. To the left was the stairway, winding tight up the tower. Straight ahead was the door that led to the mill floor. On the wall to the right hung a rack for holding time cards and next to it was a punch clock, glass face broken, rust covering the works.

Water was running somewhere, not a trickle but a steady flow.

Evangeline took a few steps, listened, looked at Peter. "Do you hear that?"

"The old millrace," said Peter. "It must run into a pit under the building, where the millwheels would have been. Then it empties through a culvert and back to the river."

She took a few steps more.

Peter raised his hand for her to stop, then shouted up the stairs. "Hello?"

No answer. No sound except for the water and the twittering of a few birds caught inside the mill.

"Maybe it was a ghost I saw before," whispered Evangeline.

"Ghosts come back to places where they were sad. How sad were all those clock punchers? Sad people walking through here for thousands of mornings. *Hello!*"

No answer.

Then, a creak, something moving in the stairwell above them.

"Hello, Bindle!" shouted Peter.

Another bit of movement. Then nothing.

Peter whispered, "The breaking glass . . . first floor or higher? Could you tell?"

"Higher," said Evangeline.

"Ghosts don't break glass."

One full turn up the steep risers took them to the second floor. There were windows on either side of the tower, and a door in the middle that opened so that big things like bales and machinery could be hoisted up or down.

Peter listened, heard nothing.

He gave Evangeline a nudge and they walked out onto the mill floor. It was like walking through a tunnel at Fenway and emerging into the grandstand. Everything opened up—two acres of floor space, defined by three dimensions of gridwork: a pattern of metal pillars holding up the floor, another of sprinkler pipes running across the ceiling, one of windowpanes, another of blackened floorboards. And paint—dung brown? vomit green?—peeled from every surface, including the tongue-and-groove paneling on the walls of the old glassed-in office, where generations of managers had watched generations of workers spin their fabric and spin out their days.

At the far end of the floor, there was a door, a big metal slider, leading to another segment of the mill. There was a stairway at that end, too, and someone was moving on it. They could hear him.

Peter shouted in that direction, "Hey! Bindle!" Then he started walking.

The footfalls stopped, then began to move faster. Up or down? Peter couldn't tell.

"Stay close," said Peter, then they went back into the tower staircase. More footfalls. Above or below? *Above.*

"Hey!" shouted Peter, and he started up again.

"Peter," said Evangeline. "Let's go."

"One more flight," he said.

"Peter!" she said. "Let's get out of here and get help."

He ignored her and took another turn of the staircase. She followed him.

On the next landing Peter went to the window and looked down at the millyard. Then he cocked his head and listened.

What he heard was the sound of Evangeline's footfalls on the old floor, then her voice: "Oh, God. Peter, look."

Morris Bindle was hanging by a leather strap from one of the sprinkler lines. His face was already blue, a large wet stain had spread across his trousers as his bladder purged. A small stool had been turned over beneath his feet. And a bottle of whiskey was broken on the floor beneath him.

"Oh, Jesus." Peter followed Evangeline.

At the same moment, they heard those footfalls . . . coming closer . . . on the staircase and at the far end of the floor.

"Peter," whispered Evangeline. "We're trapped."

"Do you have your cell phone?"

She pulled it out and punched nine-one-one.

The steel door at the far end of the floor slid open. At the same time, the footfalls grew louder in the staircase.

A figure was appearing through the metal sliders. A big man in a black leather jacket, stopping a moment in a shaft of sunlight.

"Hello, police," said Evangeline.

"She's callin' the cops," said the one in the black leather, the one they could see, but he said it calmly, as if he were calling for coffee.

"We have time," said the other one, who was emerging from the staircase tower. He had on a black ball cap pulled low, sunglasses.

They were coming, cops or not.

Peter raised the blackthorn, hoped that neither of them went for a gun.

Think quick. Act quicker.

"Yes, police," said Evangeline, "I want to report an assault. . . . Who? Me!"

Peter noticed Bindle's cigarettes and lighter on the floor beside the broken whiskey bottle, part of the stage managing: make it look like he had a last butt, a last drink, and then—

Peter grabbed the lighter. Then he lifted the stool that they'd stood Bindle on to hang him, stepped up, and flicked the lighter under one of the sprinkler heads.

"Don't do that," said the one in the ball cap and shades. "We just want to talk."

Evangeline pointed the phone at him. "Talk to the police."

A few seconds later, water exploded from every sprinkler in the mill. A second after that, the fire alarm rang in the station on the other side of the river. A long time ago, someone had had the good sense to put the fire station close to the mill.

Peter grabbed Evangeline by the elbow and pulled her back to the little office and slammed the door. It was all glass and would protect them for only a few moments, but it was all they needed because the engine sirens were screaming.

Unless these guys started shooting . . .

Then the one in black leather took a look out the window as a siren arrived right below. "Beat it," he said to the other guy.

The one in the ball cap took another step toward the office; then he turned and disappeared into the staircase tower.

"WILL YOU BE available for further questioning, Mr. Fallon?" said State Police Detective Patrick Mee. He was a big man. All the Staties were. They handled jobs like this in small towns that had four squad cars and tiny budgets.

"You have my cell phone," answered Peter.

"You have any plans for travel?" asked Mee.

"Not beyond New England."

"And you, miss?" he asked Evangeline.

She shook her head. Her hair had dried with a Chia Pet frizz.

"Good. We don't know what we'll be looking for, but—any idea why someone might kill the president of this historical society?"

"I don't know," said Peter. "It could have something to do with the death of Buster McGillis. After all, Mr. Bindle found McGillis. Didn't he?"

Detective Mee considered this a moment. "We know about you, Fallon. This isn't the first time that someone has ended up dead after they've done business with you."

"It's a dangerous business," said Peter.

"Dangerous? Rare books? Historical treasures?" Detective Mee looked up at the mill. "Were you looking for a treasure in that dump?"

Peter was glad the question was phrased like that. Answering "No" would not come back to bite him later on.

"We expect you to cooperate," said the detective.

"I always cooperate with the police," he said. "Call Detective Scavullo of the Harvard police force. He and I worked to find the Shakespeare Manuscript."

"Did you find it?"

"No, but we know where it is, safe and sound."

PETER STARTED THE BMW.

"Those guys were stalking us, Peter."

"One of them has been stalking us since the Cliff Walk. Maybe before."

"Who is he?"

"I don't know, but we are now officially on the run."

"On the run?"

"No going home. No going to the office. The usual."

"So . . . where do we go?"

"Vermont, Maine, New Hampshire . . . while we keep in touch with the office. We have a lot to learn about these Pikes and their descendants and all the visitors to the Massachusetts Historical Society."

"Why do we have to go on the run?"

"Because it's that or stand still, and if we stand still, one of the bastards might get us."

"Yeah," she said, "but who are the bastards?"

"I don't know . . . yet."

One of the bastards was still in the mill, hidden in the rafters of the cupola at the top of the staircase. He dropped down and watched the green BMW go over the old bridge.

He might have been the most dangerous man ever to gaze upon the world from that perch, but he was not the first. . . .

THEY WERE BORN COUSINS and born to be rivals.

One climbed each dawn to the cupola above the mill and looked out at all that the Pikes had wrought on the Blackstone Valley.

The other began his day before first light, in the office on the spinning room floor, where he invented new ways to get more work out of the girls . . .

. . . until one day their grandfather told them that climbing to the cupola each dawn seemed like "a kind of prayer."

The next morning, the cousin named George Amory was in his usual place at the usual time, watching the mist rise from valleys and rooftops, when the cousin named Bartlett Pike popped up through the trapdoor and announced, "I've come to join you in prayer."

"I'm a Unitarian," said George. "We pray by living."

"A Unitarian in a family of Congregationalists—" Bartlett hauled himself into the cupola. "—an anomaly that Grandfather overlooks."

"Let's enjoy the sunrise," said George. "And leave religion to Sunday."

George was twenty-one, Bartlett twenty-two. During their summers, they learned the textile business, from the basic jobs to the boardroom, because one of them would carry Pike fortunes into a third generation.

And though they shared a set of grandparents, they shared little else.

George had inherited his height and angles from his father, but people said that he had inherited his warmth from his grandmother, the beloved Mary Pike. He enhanced a natural brightness of personality with light-colored suits, pastel cravats, and a facility for quoting from whatever poetry he had recently been reading. Some called him a dandy and he did nothing to discourage them. He even nurtured a rakish Vandyke with mustache points like rapiers.

Bartlett was not so tall but presented more bulk. His side whiskers resembled weeds sprouting in a new-mown field, and he dressed in the dark suits favored by most men of business, which meant most men in the family. He also favored the reading of history over poetry. As he told those men in the dark suits, the family's history was too illustrious to forget. Even in his reading, what workers said about him was true: He knew just when to toady up, just when to bully down.

Bartlett hated returning to Harvard College at the end of the summer, because he believed that his destiny lay in Millbridge.

George hated coming from Bowdoin College at the start of the summer, because he dreamed of things far beyond Millbridge, or Bowdoin, or New England itself. He dreamed them every morning in the cupola atop the staircase tower, which reminded him of a steeple. And its bell called workers to worship as surely as the one that rang each Sunday in the steeple across the river. Honest labor, it seemed to say, brought rewards as real as faith.

Bartlett seldom saw the symbolism of such things. He looked to their utility. If the staircase rose in a tower at the front of the mill, there would be space for more machines on each floor. If there was a fire, the staircase could be closed off to control the draft. If there was labor trouble, the staircase would make it easier to control the workers, too.

The cousins watched the workers coming through the fresh morning light, flowing as steady and reliable as the river itself. They poured out of the long tenements that housed single workers and out of the small duplexes built for families. Some of them had grown up in Millbridge but many had traveled far, from the farm counties to the west and the seacoast cities filling fast with immigrants. And the trains brought more of them all the time, because the trains brought everything now—raw material, machines, replacement parts, and people, too.

There was a train off to the north just then, a smudge of smoke rising above the river, a shrill whistle proclaiming a future that crossed the fields eight times a day. Passengers and freight. Hopes and dreams. Iron sinews binding New England and the nation together, like the document that had bound Americans to an idea until war tore it asunder.

George glanced at his watch. "Almost time."

In a few minutes, the bell would ring. Then the headrace would open. The water would flow. The wheel would turn. A gear would engage the vertical drive shaft that pierced the mill like a giant spindle. Gears on the drive shaft would engage gears that turned line shafts that ran across the ceilings, spinning flywheels geared to smaller wheels, which turned leather belts, which engaged carders and throstles and looms that would thump and spin and clatter and clack, and the whole building would begin to vibrate, all four floors of machinery, men, women, and nimble-fingered children, too, coming to life as a single sentient creature.

And out in the countryside, where corn grew green in spring and ripened in August and stubbled the fields come fall, farmers would stop to wipe their brows. And they would hear, beneath the rustle of the wind, a sound no New Englander had ever heard in the quiet before the nineteenth century, the distant rumble of a mighty mill turning . . . turning. . . .

"So," said Bartlett. "To our posts."

"To our posts." George gave him a mock salute. "To do our duty."

"And remember . . . meeting in the boardroom at ten o'clock."

Another meeting, thought George. He hated meetings as much as Bartlett liked them. This one would be interesting, though, the first since the debacle at Bull Run.

THE MILL OFFICES occupied the Colonial-style house that Will and Mary Pike had built in the early years, when they were expanding the mill again and again to meet the demands of their business. When they moved to the Greek Revival house across the river, and the mill moved into the mighty edifice now looming behind the original buildings, the men who ran the mill moved their board meetings to the mahogany table in Will Pike's first dining room.

They were the Blackstone Investors: graying heads, dark suits, sober demeanors, forests of facial hair shrouded in a fog of cigar smoke in an atmosphere growing tenser with every dispatch from the Virginia battlefront.

Bartlett's father, Charles Pike, sat with his belly pressing against the table.

George's father, the cadaverous Reverend Mr. Jacob Amory, had traveled from Portland to see to interests that had been his since he'd married George's mother "and rescued a thirty-eight-year-old woman from the misery of old maid-hood."

George gave his father a polite nod. Deeper affection was seldom expressed between them, perhaps because Reverend Jacob was a distant man growing more distant as he aged, a late-in-life father growing old before his son had grown to maturity.

As the boys took their seats along the wall, Uncle William glanced at them over his spectacles, then squinted at the clock: 10:04. He was the oldest of Will and Mary's children, a bachelor who had given his life—sixty-nine years of it—to the Pike Mill. He sat at the head of the table, though he seemed to hunch rather than sit, as if bowed by the weight of his position.

"Sorry we're late," said Bartlett.

"Yes," said George. "Sorry."

"Don't apologize twice," said Grandfather Will, the grayest éminence grise in the room. "It's a sign of weakness."

"As I was saying"—Bartlett's father had the floor—"Bull Run changes everything. This will not be a ninety-day war. So where are we to get our cotton?"

"Stockpiling has protected us against bad harvests," said Uncle William. "It shall protect us against the decisions of whimsical voters, too."

George, without a shred of whimsy, had cast the first ballot of his life for Lincoln, but he did not speak up. He enjoyed these meetings only because they rescued him from the incessant *click-cla-clack-cla-click-cla-clack* of two hundred shuttles slamming bobbins back and forth in as many looms. So he nodded occasionally to appear attentive and tried to recall lines from a poem, "Self-Dependence," by Matthew Arnold. "Weary of myself, and sick of asking/What I am and what I ought to be. . . ." He remained in his reverie until he heard his grandfather's voice:

"Horace Greeley is a fool!" Most of the time, the old man sat on a wing chair in the corner and stared out the window. But when he spoke, he commanded attention. "A New York *fool*!"

"Horace Greeley's right." Charles Pike read from a newspaper: "'If it is best for the country and for mankind that we make peace with the rebels, and on their own terms, do not shrink even from that.' That's in a Greeley editorial, and I say he's right."

"I say it's time we stopped making money from cotton picked by slaves," answered the old man.

"*You* started by making Negro cloth," said Arthur Perkins, who always seemed to speak through his nose, which he always seemed to point at the ceiling. "Cheap sacking to clothe the poor darky."

"Then we invested in better machinery to make better cloth," said Will Pike.

"And you did so well that you attracted Boston money," said Perkins. "*Ours*."

"We're more than pleased with a Perkins partnership," said Uncle William, "and with our strategy on cotton. We'll leave wool to the Stanleys in Uxbridge. Let them make uniforms."

"Uniforms?" Reverend Amory raised an eyebrow. "Do you think there's money to be made from uniforms?"

"No," said Charles Pike. "Before this goes too far, brighter men than

Lincoln will recognize that if the South wants to leave the Union, there's nothing in the Constitution that compels them to stay."

"Not true," said Will Pike.

"I've read the Constitution, Father," said Charles, "and—"

"I *lived* the Constitution." Will Pike stood and drove his cane into the floor. "And I tell you that once a state joins the union, it has no right to leave. No right! And . . . and . . ." As if overcome by emotion, he took a fit of coughing that turned his face red, dropped a shock of white hair down over his forehead, and left him wheezing in his chair.

The meeting went on, as though there were not a distressed old man sitting in the corner trying to catch his breath.

It was at last agreed that they had enough raw cotton to keep the mill running another two years, by which time the war would surely be over. Then the gentlemen rose to leave, all except Will and his grandsons. After each meeting, Will talked with them about all that had been said. They always came away realizing that he heard everything and was distracted by nothing.

"I've lived too long," he said, as soon as the room was clear. "My own son advocating the legality of secession . . ."

"But Grandfather," said Bartlett, "the Constitution—"

"Don't quote the Constitution to me, boy." The old man's voice rose, but he remained seated. "I know more about its genesis than . . . than any man living."

They had heard stories of the Philadelphia convention, but the most he would ever say was that he had gone there, had met great men, had heard great talk. Then he would urge them to read Madison's book.

"Grandfather," said George, "why is it that you never say more of those days?"

"What is there to say, now that the document is torn in half?"

"Two sections clash over a philosophy of governance." Bartlett always sought the grandest way to state himself. "The Framers anticipated such things, did they not?"

"They did not anticipate armed rebellion. And enslaving twenty percent of your own population is not a philosophy of governance. It's an . . . an . . ." The old man stopped speaking, his eyes went to the window, to the blue sky above the road.

George and Bartlett waited through one of their grandfather's little "blank spots." They could not have known that his mind was drifting back to a road on a misty evening, a young woman asking his opinion of the Triangle Trade . . . *What was her name?*

"Grandfather?" said George. "You were saying . . . slavery is—"

"Oh . . . oh . . . yes . . . an abomination."

"Didn't they compromise over slavery at the convention?" asked George.

"They compromised over many things. They had to. But *we've* plain forgot the ideals that brought us to Philadelphia." Then he looked down and began tapping his cane on the floorboards.

George prodded him, "You knew Rufus King, didn't you?"

The old man nodded, eyes still on the floor. "Knew him. Served him. Knew the other New Englanders, too."

"Did they voice opinions about slavery?" asked Bartlett.

The old man looked up. "What does it matter?"

"If we knew what they thought," said Bartlett, "we might know how to think."

"People should think for themselves," said George.

"But an intelligent man looks to his ancestors for guidance." Bartlett gave his grandfather a fawning smile. "Isn't that so, sir?"

Old Will Pike studied the young men, sucked on his cheek, and said, "I don't speak much about Philadelphia because I didn't stay through the whole business."

"You didn't?" said Bartlett. "Why?"

"Can you boys keep a secret?"

George and Bartlett looked at each other. A secret? Of course.

So Will said, "I lost a first draft of the Constitution. Worse than that, Rufus King and the other New Englanders wrote on it, wrote their ideas on the Bill of Rights."

"*Lost* it?" said George.

"What happened to it?" asked Bartlett.

"Couldn't say. It's been more than seventy years. Last I knew, it was in the hands of a land grabber from New Hampshire named Caldwell P. Caldwell."

Bartlett Pike had a capacity for making a range of noises that involuntarily proclaimed his opinions, moods, and appetites. Just then, his stomach rumbled. He looked down, pressing a hand against his midsection.

The old man snarled, "I'm about to tell you boys things I've told no man in a generation, and *you're* worried about your belly. Well, the chowder will stay hot awhile longer. So listen. The both of you."

THE NEXT DAY, George climbed to the cupola, and there was Bartlett, staring out as the sun rose above the trees.

Without turning, Bartlett said, "Do you believe what Grandfather told us yesterday?"

"Why not? At his age, it's time for his *Apologia pro vita sua.*"

Bartlett gave a whoosh of awe. "Imagine . . . he looked Washington in the eye."

"Washington looked *him* in the eye. I expect he was blinded by the light."

"I would be, too, but . . . do you think it's out there? A draft of the Constitution, annotated by the New England delegates?"

"Maybe, but as Grandfather says, it's been seventy years." They stood together in silence for a time. Then George offered Bartlett his hand. "So long, cousin. My last day."

"Until next summer, then."

"I'm not coming back."

"Not coming back?" Bartlett's face brightened, as though this was something he had long been hoping to hear.

George looked into Bartlett's eyes. "'At this vessel's prow I stand, which bears me / Forwards, forwards o'er the starlit sea'—Matthew Arnold."

"What? What do you mean?" Bartlett might be confused, but he was still smiling.

"Our talk with Grandfather," said George. "It convinced me. I don't want my adventures kept secret until I'm old. I want to live them and re-live them when I talk about them. So you get to run the mill when the time comes. You're made for it. Grandfather knows that."

Bartlett snorted: "He thinks I'm fat. Like my father. Fat and officious and good for nothing but adding columns and keeping scrapbooks about the history of the mill."

"Prove him wrong," said George.

Down below, a black wagon rattled up. On the side were the words, JOSIAH JOHNSON HAWES, PHOTOGRAPHER. That day all the executives and workers of the mill, from the venerable Will Pike to the lowliest bobbin boy, an immigrant named Khouri from someplace called Lebanon, were assembling for a photograph, "The Men and Women of the Mill, 1861." It was Bartlett's idea.

"I'll stay for the picture"—George looked toward a train steaming out of town—"then I'll follow the smoke."

GEORGE AND HIS father followed the smoke home to Portland. Along the way, they concluded that if the soldiers of the North did not defeat the South, the rivers of New England surely would, because the rivers ran the factories, and the factories would overwhelm the South with guns, uniforms, shoes, belts, buckles, cannonballs, nails, rivets, tin cans, and a thousand other products of the modern world.

Father and son discussed the industry they saw in riverside towns like Whitinsville, in riverhead cities like Worcester, and at simple mill crossings like Newton Lower Falls. But as they came into Boston, Reverend Jacob changed the direction of their talk: "You know, son, across the river is the Harvard Divnity School."

George lifted his gaze from a volume of poems by Whitman. "Yes, Father."

"Could you see your way to studying there? It's the seat of Unitarianism."

"After I graduate, I'll have had my fill of study."

"Perhaps, but I sense that the mill is more for Bartlett than you. So what about settlement in a solid congregation?"

"Settlement is not on my mind. Not in the mill, certainly not in the pulpit."

"I see." Reverend Jacob looked out the window and spoke hardly a word for the rest of the journey.

It was a relief for George to reach Portland that evening and replace his father's angry silence with the chatter of his mother.

Amanda Pike Amory, fifty-nine, was the youngest child of Will and Mary. She had not been a beauty. That explained why she had made it to the age of thirty-eight before she married a widowed minister passing through Millbridge.

As the reverend, in one of his less charitable moments (which were many) said of their courtship, "Even an ugly woman looks good to a man over fifty, if she knows how to cook."

Amanda also knew how to talk, and she and her son talked for days. They talked in the parsonage. They talked as they strolled past schooners and steamers at the waterfront. They talked as they climbed the Munjoy Hill tower, from which observers had signaled the arrival of ships in the days before telegraph. On a brilliant September morning, the tower offered views of the infinite Atlantic, the embracing Casco Bay, and the White Mountains, too.

But their attention was drawn to a Maine regiment training on the hillside below. Perhaps it was the sight of the columns parading, or the sound of drums beating and sergeants shouting that caused George's mother to say, "Your father fears that you are going to go to war."

"Is that why he prefers divinity school for me?"

"He has your best interests at heart."

"There'll be no war for me, mother," he said. "But no divinity school, either."

"That's what I hoped you'd say." She took his hands in both of hers. "Go to Europe after you graduate. Study languages and literature. Bring a bit of culture back to the dollar-mad mill barons of New England."

And however distant George felt from his father was how close he felt to his mother's love.

BOWDOIN COLLEGE WAS thirty miles up the coast, far enough that George's father would not bother him, close enough that he could visit his mother on occasion. It was a campus almost as old as the Constitution, with quadrangles of ancient red brick and squares of modern gray granite. But the spiritual center of college and town was the Congregational Church, which some said was the also spiritual center of the anti-slavery movement itself.

On a Sunday ten years earlier, the wife of Calvin Stowe, professor of Natural and Revealed Religion, had experienced a "vision" during a service there. She had seen an old slave, after a life of suffering, rise over the pulpit and up to heaven. And right then, she had determined to write a book she would call *Uncle Tom's Cabin*. The Stowes had moved on, but they still cast a long shadow in Brunswick and the book cast an even longer one across America.

As George ambled up from the town, however, he was lost in a vision of his own: Her name was Cordelia Edwards.

She was the daughter of Professor Aaron Edwards, who lectured in English literature and was known for classroom evocations of Shakespearean characters, from gloomy Hamlet to ebullient Falstaff. George had met her in the spring, and they had exchanged letters during his summer of mill imprisonment. In her last, she had promised him a kiss when he returned to school.

But Professor Edwards kept a close eye on his daughter, and he had already warned George, "Her name may be Cordelia, but she is my Miranda, my magical child, and you, my young Unitarian friend, are no Ferdinand."

As the semester unfolded, George and Cordelia saw each other when they could, but Bowdoin was a demanding place, and Professor Edwards a jealous father. So George was surprised to receive an invitation to dine at the Edwards house on the first Sunday of November.

THE DAY WAS cold but clear. The sun sent flat rays through the branches, illuminating everything in what George's father had once called the "fool's-gold brightness of November." By four o'clock, darkness would fall and Maine's long winter night would begin. And so would it be, his father had preached, for those who did not heed God's word but preferred the "fool's-gold brightness of gaudy sin."

Before George struck the knocker, the door opened and Cordelia appeared in a blue dress with a wide hoop and a velvet jacket a shade darker. The color brought out the blue in her eyes. The sunlight dazzled her smile.

"Mr. Amory"—she said—"how kind of you to come."

He took her hand and brought it to his lips, maintaining the air of elaborate formality. "The pleasure is all mine, miss."

"You save me from a ghastly afternoon," she whispered, then nodded toward the parlor: several conversations under way, several groups of people, several of them holding glasses of sherry. "My father said I could invite a friend. He did not specify gender."

George's eyes widened. "But he knows I'm coming?"

"When I told him, he said, 'Now we'll see if he can hold up his end of a conversation.' So"—she poked a finger into his upper arm, a gesture he found surprisingly intimate—"be fascinating."

That, he thought, was like the charge to be witty, or intelligent, or any other quality that came easily when unbidden but might not be raised by all the muses when most needed.

"Ah, my boy, welcome." The broad-beamed Aaron Edwards approached, his attitude professorial and paternal, that is to say, condescending and lordly. He ushered George into the parlor, introducing him to President Woods, Professor Smithson, and the ostensible guest of honor, Calvin Stowe, who had returned to preach that Sunday.

But the real guest of honor in any room in the North, and a pariah in any Southern parlor, was Reverend Stowe's wife. She was a small woman with a receding chin and ringlets of hair woven down around her face, no great presence at all.

But before her, George was struck all but dumb, "I . . . I like your book, ma'am."

"Thank you." Harriet Beecher Stowe's smile revealed protruding upper teeth that somehow balanced her chin and gave her face a happy symmetry.

"I . . . I . . . ." George fumbled for something fascinating.

And George's rhetoric professor, Joshua Lawrence Chamberlain, arrived to rescue him. "George has memorized passages from your work, ma'am."

"Well, Lawrence," she said, "you heard the work as I wrote it. I hope you memorized a few of the *ideas*, at least."

"Those of us who attended your Saturday night readings shall never forget them."

"So long ago, Lawrence," she said. "You've gone a bit gray since then."

Chamberlain smoothed a hand over his hair. And yes, several gray strands marched east and west from his part, but still he had an aura of youthful seriousness, as if he had not yet grown the shell that accretes around men after a bit of experience in the world. He was thirty-three, near six feet, with a sharp-featured face, side whiskers, rimless spectacles, and a high collar that held his head in alignment, giving him the air of a stiff-necked north woods preacher. But he had humor in him, too, and he joked with Mrs. Stowe that it was students like George who made him gray. . . .

Just then, the dinner bell rang and the guests turned for the dining room.

In his best sotto voce, George thanked Chamberlain for rescuing him.

"You've studied rhetoric with me," whispered Chamberlain, as he offered his arm to his wife. "You should have more to say to America's most famous author."

"I'll try, sir." George turned to Cordelia and crooked his elbow in her direction.

She took it and whispered, "Remember, George, 'fascinating' does not mean 'frightened into speechlessness.' Redeem yourself at dinner."

All through the meal, George waited for his moment.

Neither oyster stew nor a second-course tureen of duck liver pâté stimulated his eloquence. The baked haddock inspired no more than a comment on the bravery of Grand Banks fishermen who caught it. As for a foul course of wild turkey, its best attribute was stuffing.

Mostly George listened and spoke when spoken to. Yes, he worked summers at the Pike Mill. . . . Yes, they were worried about cotton supplies from the South. . . . Yes, he had taken Professor Chamberlain's rhetoric course, and now that the professor was teaching the modern languages of Europe, George was taking German.

"Are you planning to use the German someday?" asked Professor Stowe.

"I'm hoping to travel to Europe after graduation."

"Europe?" Cordelia sounded surprised, as if this was something he should have told her before sharing with the world.

Again Chamberlain rescued him: "Perhaps military service might postpone that trip? I've seen you watching the Bowdoin Guard drilling on campus."

"The Bowdoin Guard"—Professor Edwards made a dismissive wave of his fork—"college boys with guns, marching about, playing at soldiers."

"Perhaps, but"—President Woods looked at Chamberlain—"I've seen our new chairman of European Languages watching them, too."

Chamberlain said, "I'm spending my sabbatical in Europe, sir, to study those languages."

"Good," said Professor Edwards. "Bowdoin needs you more than Lincoln does. If you were to leave, you might be replaced by a Unitarian instead of a Congregationalist. Can't have that, can we, George?"

George knew this old Congregationalist was putting him on the spot. In certain corners of New England, hostility between the sects ran high. Traditional Congregationalists, who descended directly from the Puritans, resented the rise of what they called the Boston religion, with its emphasis on free will and free thought and the free interpretation of Christ's message.

George's response to the professor was to stammer.

That seemed to satisfy Edwards, who pressed ahead. "Another Unitarian would throw off the balance in the faculty altogether. Leave the Unitarians at Harvard."

"Yes," said President Woods. "We struggle for the soul of the college,"

"We struggle for the soul of the nation, too," said Harriet Beecher Stowe.

"The South will be finished by fall," said President Woods.

"Rather than finishing them," said Professor Edwards, "we should let them go. See how long their 'peculiar institution' lasts without New England mills to buy their cotton, eh, George?"

Again, George stammered, felt himself redden at a reference to the family business. He glanced at Cordelia, who frowned.

Professor Edwards kept talking, "Less blood will be spilled and the pain in Southern pocketbooks will be just as acute."

"But they've challenged the Constitution," said Chamberlain, with sudden vehemence. "They've defied the honor and authority of the Union."

"Some in the South see it as a voluntary union," said Edwards, "and the Constitution as merely a guideline."

George was looking at Cordelia, who was glaring at him, as if he had betrayed her by ineloquence.

Something fascinating, he was thinking. Say something fascinating. So he cleared his throat, lowered his voice, and offered this: "Speaking of the

Constitution, did you know that there exists a first draft, annotated by all the New England delegates?"

"Indeed?" said Professor Edwards.

"Indeed," said George. "I've heard that it may contain their thoughts on slavery."

"How . . . fascinating." Cordelia's expression softened.

"Yes . . . fascinating," said Professor Edwards. "Though, of course, we know that nothing was meant to leave Independence Hall, nothing meant to circulate until the work was completed and agreed upon."

"According to my grandfather, the New England delegates—what's the word?—*caucused* after the draft was distributed. It was there that they set down their thoughts on the Bill of Rights."

"Wouldn't it be wonderful to find such a thing," said Mrs. Stowe, "as our country struggles over the meaning of that Constitution once again?"

"Indeed," said George, "wonderful to know the Framers' thoughts on slavery."

"They saw slavery as an existing fact," snapped Chamberlain, "and they decided that a relative wrong would be done by its immediate abolition."

"They were men of wisdom, then," said Professor Edwards.

"But," said Chamberlain, "there's no doubt that their intent was to limit slavery, not extend it. They hoped that in time, we would wipe the blot off the shield. The time has come."

Professor Edwards gave a laugh, as if emotions were running too high at his table. "Perhaps young Amory can find the annotated draft and write a theme on it."

"YOU REDEEMED YOURSELF," said Cordelia as she walked George to the door.

"Your father thinks I made it all up," said George.

She put a hand on his arm. "We should find it together and prove him wrong."

"It might just confuse people."

"Confuse them?" She took her hand away.

"I've sat in Millbridge boardrooms and Bowdoin dining rooms, and I've seen how people of good faith contend over the Constitution we *have*. Showing them an early draft might just cause more contention."

"Or bring greater certainty as to the thoughts of the New Englanders who are the conscience of the nation," she said. "We should be very great heroes if we uncovered it."

"A lark," he said. "That's all it would be."

She laughed. "A lark to entertain us and save the nation."

He kissed her hand again and stepped out into the cold dark. And he realized, as he hurried back to his chamber in Massachusetts Hall, that he had seldom been happier.

HAPPINESS LASTED A week, until he saw Cordelia after Sunday service.

They talked while her father stopped in the doorway to compliment the minister. And Cordelia informed George that her father had enrolled her in Mrs. Finley's Finishing School for Young Ladies in Boston.

George, who was seldom so direct, snapped, "Defy him."

"My father is a formidable man." She kept smiling, for they were standing in the sunlight, in as public a place as could be found in a small college town, and all who passed offered them a glance, a nod, a smile.

"Is he more formidable than our—" George hesitated to say *love.* "—affection?"

"Affection?" She looked into his eyes, her smile still in place. "I have known my father all my life, George. I have known you barely half a year."

This was not an answer to satisfy a romantic young man.

"What about finding the lost Constitution together?" he asked.

"As you said, a lark." Seeing the anger in his expression, she added, "If our *affection* is strong, separation can strengthen it further. If not, we'll know."

They were not the first young people to be pulled apart by a parent or two, nor the first to find other pursuits once they were.

BY SPRING, GEORGE was thinking less of Cordelia and more of his future.

Several of his mates were enlisting, but he was planning to enter the University of Heidelberg, there to read for a masters in philosophy. When he was informed by the Heidelberg administration that he needed a letter of recommendation from a professor, he could think of only one.

So he found Chamberlain striding across the campus on a hot July afternoon. Two more weeks of classes remained.

"Recommendation?" said Chamberlain. "What about a commission, instead?"

"Commission?"

"Lincoln is calling for three hundred thousand volunteers. I've been to Augusta to see Governor Washburn and offer my services."

"But sir," said George, "I thought you were heading for Europe, too."

"Europe was there before Caesar invaded Gaul. It can wait. The future of our country cannot."

"But the faculty expects—"

"I'm to be made lieutenant colonel of a new regiment, Maine's twentieth." Chamberlain spoke as calmly as if he were discussing new textbooks. "Ten companies, a hundred men to the company."

"But President Woods expects you—"

"The petty struggles between Unitarians and Congregationalists at a New England college are nothing as compared to the struggles of the nation. The governor agrees. He thinks it would be good to have a Unitarian minister's son among the officers. So do I. You should be able to raise a company from your father's congregation alone."

"But—"

"You say your grandfather lost a first draft of the Constitution. Here's your chance to save the *final* draft." Chamberlain went with eyes front, as if he were on a mission rather than just walking home. "You can impress that girl, too."

George quick-stepped to keep up. "I know nothing of soldiering, sir."

"Neither do I. But I've always been interested in military matters, and what I don't know, I'll learn." Chamberlain reached the edge of the campus and stopped.

A few horses and carts were clopping by on Maine Street. A lazy breeze made the maple leaves turn a time or two.

Chamberlain looked across at his little house. His children were playing in the yard. His wife was stepping out the door with a tray in her hands. He watched them a moment, then fixed George with a gaze as resolute as a Maine rock. "This war must be ended, George, ended with a swift and strong hand. Every man ought to come forward."

Just then, Chamberlain's wife spied them and called out, "Tea, Lawrence, tea and ginger nuts, for you and George, too."

And Chamberlain whispered, "*Every* man, no matter what he gives up."

And his intensity struck something in George Amory that his own father had not touched in a lifetime of Sunday sermons.

George had always been expected to follow the family path, but he had never been challenged to find his own truth. The dutiful son might fulfill a destiny preordained in divinity school or textile mill. But a young man answering the call to do what was right might achieve something great.

George heard lines from Arnold: "Resolve to be thyself; and know that he / Who finds himself loses his misery." And he was taken by the belief that he, too, had been called.

That would be better reason to go to war than a talk with Cordelia Edwards.

SHE HAD RETURNED from Boston for the summer.

George had left a calling card at her home, and she had responded with a note inviting him for tea but warning him that she had "met a young Harvard man in Boston" and could only promise George her "sisterly affection."

Though he had not seen her in more than six months and had corresponded with her only occasionally, George had been struck by a bolt of jealousy.

The day that he called on her, Brunswick was covered in humid clouds and the kind of salt-tinged stickiness that afflicted even the most northerly New England coast in the doldrums of summer. But Cordelia seemed cool and perfectly calm. She had been taught well at her finishing school.

She received his news with polite enthusiasm. "A second lieutenant? You'll wear a blue coat with brass buttons and shoulder bars. How stylish."

"Is that what your father would say?" George could not resist a dig at the man he blamed for sending her to Boston, where she had met her "young Harvard man."

"Now, George, Father and I don't agree on everything. But—"

"I suppose my uniform will make me more *fascinating* the next time I'm invited to dinner." That, he knew, sounded too petulant.

She seemed to ignore it. "Did you ever find that lost Constitution?"

"As you told me, a lark. Besides, I've been too busy."

"You shall be even busier saving the Constitution. You shall have my prayers."

He finished his tea. "Hard to imagine the South standing for long against another three hundred thousand men."

"And you certainly wouldn't want to miss the excitement. This will be your chance to do something extraordinary."

Again he fell back on petulance, feeling more angry than he had a right to. "Say something fascinating. Do something extraordinary. Will any of it earn your—?"

"Affection?" She tried to keep the hurt from her voice, but it was there.

"I shall always have affection for you, no matter how far I travel with Edward Atkinson of Harvard."

He thought he saw a tear in her eye. It would give him hope through all the horrors ahead.

IN PORTLAND, GEORGE's father proclaimed himself proud, a rare occurrence. His mother put on a brave face when her son stepped into the pulpit the following Sunday and called for recruits.

George told the congregation that he brought not only a call to arms but a call to faith as well. He did not sound especially inspiring to himself or the audience, but he promised a federal bounty of eighty-five dollars to every enlistee. This attracted a dozen young men, who came into the parish office to sign up after the services.

First in line were the Hoyts, two gangly brothers in their twenties who preferred fighting, even with each other, to keeping shop for their uncle.

After them came Jonathan Corley, a sullen, weather-scarred fisherman who said he was enlisting because he had nothing to do since putting a hook through his hand on his last trip to the Grand Banks.

George looked at the bandaged hand. "Can you hold a gun?"

"Damn clumsy haulin' a line just now." Corley inspected the hand as if for the first time. "Easier pullin' a trigger, I guess."

George had practiced puffing out his chest in the mirror. It seemed like something a lieutenant would do. He did it and sighed. "On that basis you'd go to war?"

"On that basis, when Lincoln calls for three hundred thousand more next year, I'll have a year behind me."

George laughed. "Next year, this war will be over."

"Right," said one of the Hoyts. "We'll *see* to it."

The old fisherman—old to the rest of them at thirty-five—simply smiled, as if time spent on the rolling sea had given him knowledge that other men lacked. George looked at the leathered face, at the gaps in the teeth, and thought of a death's head.

Then Corley asked, "What about you, Lieutenant? You got city hands. Rich boy's hands. What's your basis for goin' to war?"

George puffed his buttons again. "As Colonel Chamberlain says, 'I've always been interested in military matters, and what I don't know, I'll learn.'"

"Just so long as you don't learn over my dead body."

George knew that every eye was on him and that his next words would color him for the whole regiment. He dipped his pen and held it out. "Sign your name or make your mark, if you're man enough. But once you do, remember that you've had your last bit of insubordination."

"I'm man enough." Jonathan Corley took the pen. "The question is, are you?"

GEORGE BROUGHT FIFTEEN men into the regiment, and the Twentieth mustered at Camp Mason, outside Portland.

There were shopkeeps and fishermen, loggers and boatwrights, one lawyer and two grade-school teachers. Some were down-on-their-luckers who joined because their towns added a hundred dollars to the federal bounty. Others joined because their neighbors had and they could not look like slackers. And some joined because, like Chamberlain, they believed it was time for every man to step forward and defend the Union, though men of that class grew harder to find as the war ground into a second year.

New uniforms and three weeks of drilling did little to make them a fighting force or a pretty picture for the parade ground. They marched with sticks on their shoulders because new muskets were sent to the front. Their band could not play in tune, but it did not matter because they could not keep in step. And if they could not master a simple *left-right-left,* how much harder would it be to learn the commands that might save them in battle?

"Some soldiers, eh, Lieutenant?" said Sergeant Enos Turlock.

"Some soldiers." George found that after a few weeks his speech was assuming the cadence of those he commanded. He had always sought to speak like a college man. But in listening to these laconic men, he had come to appreciate the impact of three words instead of four, two instead of three.

"Glad there's no fightin' today, sir."

"Glad. Yes."

"Gladder 'n hell." Turlock was no military man, but he had been a boss in the logging camps, so he had the habit of command and the presence. One look at the short legs supporting that ax-strengthened torso, or one dose of his red-faced invective, and no soldier would consider anything but obedience.

George said, "Plenty of fighting in Virginia."

"Fightin' but not much winnin', sir."

"We'll change that."

"Not without guns." Turlock kept his eyes on the company scuffling past until he could take no more if it. "O'Rourke! You march like a three-legged dog. Mind your feet."

"Mindin' the feet ain't hard," said the soldier. "It's mindin' where to put 'em."

"No back talk," shouted Turlock.

"No, sir." Corley looked at them as he paraded past. "Can't have back talk. Can't even have guns. Just have to keep marchin'."

"I need to flog that Corley," Turlock said to George. "But he's right. We need to get some guns."

"Just get them ready to march." Colonel Chamberlain came up behind them. He had shaved his side whiskers and grown a mustache that drooped down around his mouth. The mustache, the forage cap and uniform, the rank and responsibilities had given the grave Chamberlain an air of even deeper gravity.

"Doin' our best, Colonel," said the sergeant. "Give 'em another week—"

"Tomorrow," said Chamberlain. "We march tomorrow . . . to the depot. Train to Boston, steamer down to the Chesapeake."

THREE MONTHS LATER, George Amory wondered how Americans could do this to each other.

He shook his head to drive the thought away and held his cloak close to his body so that the sweat running down his flanks would not chill him. He could not close his eyes, for his men might notice, but if he kept them open, he could only conclude that he would be dead before dark.

The Twentieth had stood for hours in the December sunshine, watching other divisions carry the attack. And what a glorious sight it had been . . . at the beginning.

The troops marched through the town of Fredericksburg and onto the sloping plain. They went in columns of four that slithered like blue-clad serpents until they crossed a millrace in the middle of the field. Then they split right and left into brigade front—attack formation—etching a quarter-mile line across the landscape.

From the far bank of the Rappahannock, where George and his regiment waited, the bursting of the Confederate shells in the air looked almost festive, as if the troops beneath them were part of a grand celebration. And a hundred yards behind the first brigade came a second, executing the same maneuvers, flags fluttering, muskets shouldered.

Their objective was the road to Richmond, which ran beyond the top of the slope. But the road was protected by a stone wall, behind which waited thousands of Confederate infantry. On the steeper slopes behind the infantry was enough artillery to cover every inch of the field in exploding iron three times over.

And yet the Federal troops climbed steadily, as if oblivious to the shell bursts tearing holes in their ranks. With each stride, with the traversing of each little bump and hillock in the field, their shouldered bayonets rose and fell like the teeth of a huge loom weaving the air with courage and folly both. Their courage, the general's folly.

By the time they came to within a hundred yards of the wall, enemy fire had cut their force by a quarter, but the ranks were still dressed and the colors still fluttered. They dropped down into a defile that offered a last bit of cover, then crested the last fold in the landscape, then stopped to volley.

And a sheet of flame unfurled in their faces.

That was how it looked from a mile away, like a literal sheet, so tight-woven were the Confederates behind the wall—shoulder to shoulder, musket by musket, rank upon rank, like the warp and weft of a well-made fabric.

That first brigade all but disappeared, then the next, then the one after that.

But the generals had their plan, and another division was already going in, already forming brigade front, already etching itself, regiment by regiment, across the plain.

For an hour, George watched . . . or tried not to.

Lines from Tennyson stumbled through his head. "Theirs not to reason why. . . ."

Chamberlain stood with the regimental commander, Colonel Ames. Like their soldiers, they said little. But from time to time, Chamberlain pulled out a small notebook and wrote something down—a detail, perhaps, an observation, an emotion.

George could not understand why. What was there of this worth remembering? And if their regiment went in, who among them would have consciousness for any memory when it was over? Surely St. Peter would not wish to hear this story.

So George stood and waited and willed himself to keep his eyes open, though he feared that his men might see his tears welling at the sight of the slaughter. Then he thought he saw Chamberlain brush away a tear, and somehow it made him feel less alone.

AFTER ANOTHER HOUR, the dead lay in clumps and bunches on the slope and in a growing heap before the wall. Whoever lived on that field seemed to be hugging the ground as if to keep from spinning off.

Now they were calling for Griffin's Division, Fifth Corps.

George smoothed his Vandyke, tugged at his gauntlets, and looked over his shoulder. "Serg—" The word caught in his throat. He coughed it clear, but his voice was still strained: "Sergeant Turlock, form the company."

"Yes, sir," shouted Turlock. "Company B! Fall in!"

George gave Turlock a little nod of thanks and resolved to find his voice. And again he heard his favorite poem in his head. "Resolve to be thyself; and know that he / Who finds himself loses his misery."

Turlock gave George a firm salute, big enough so that every man in the company could see it and know who commanded.

By God, thought George, but there was a man.

In the town, they waited another hour, hunkered behind the ruins of bombed-out buildings, sheltered from the rain of Confederate shells. When any man mustered courage to raise his head, he saw the First Brigade being smashed, then the Second. Then came the call: "Third Brigade to the front!"

Chamberlain would write that his men felt at that moment a "tremulous expectation. Not in fear, for that has little place in manhood when love and duty summon; but in eagerness to do their best and make a finish."

For his part, George Amory felt fear, deep and cold. He had no choice but to go up that hill. Coming down was now in God's hands.

The brigade went forward to the millrace and moved into attack formation on a field that now resembled a scene from Dante. Across eight hundred yards, there were dead men and wounded men, dead horses and dead riders under them, living horses rearing riderless and terrified before explosions that sent great clots of dirt into the air like exclamation marks, and above it all, the fast-falling dusk, a sky almost as red as the puddles of blood and rivulets of blood and swamps of blood that now covered the field.

The soldiers of the Twentieth had left their haversacks and heavy cloaks with the quartermaster. The officers had dismounted and drawn their sabers.

But George had pulled his pistol, a big Navy Colt, heavy as a sashweight. He was a line-closer. His job was to move back and forth behind his company, and as men fell in the front rank, he would push others forward to fill the spaces. Most line-closers used their sabers—swinging them, or prodding with them, or holding them with both hands and pushing the men from the back. George, however, planned to go in shooting.

He noticed Colonel Ames say something to Chamberlain. He could not hear above the din of battle, but he was sure that the last words were, "God help us now."

Chamberlain moved to the right of the line, while Ames stepped to the front, giving example to officers and men both. The bugle sounded, and Ames shouted, "Forward the Twentieth!" The lieutenants called to the sergeants. The sergeants shouted at their companies. And into the inferno they went.

George Amory forgot his fear. Bullets were whizzing around him, explosions were bursting in front of him, human debris spread under his feet—blood and blasted flesh and bodies. But he put them from his mind and kept his part of the line advancing in step with the regiment, which linked with the Seventeenth New York on the right and the Eighty-third Michigan on the left.

Wounded soldiers looked up at them as they came. Some shouted encouragement, waved them on, even cheered. A few cried for them to go back, that the wall could not be taken, that they would all be dead before they reached the top.

But the men of the Third Brigade ignored them, as they had been trained to do, and as all those men on the ground had done earlier.

George raced back and forth behind his men, urging the company ahead. "Hold the line, men! Hold the line! Straight and steady!"

Across rills and streams and dips and defiles they went, tight-disciplined despite the explosions and musket fire tearing gaps in their lines.

By God but they were *all* men.

George saw both of the Hoyt brothers disappear in a flash.

He ignored the splatter of Hoyt blood and brains that sprayed out over the company and shouted, "Keep on, boys! Keep steady!" Then he pushed Corley and O'Rourke forward to fill the hole where the Hoyts had been.

"Steady on, boys! Steady on!" cried Sergeant Turlock. "We've not far. Not far."

"Keep on, lads! Keep on!" shouted George.

Then Colonel Ames called, "The double quick!" And the regiment began moving faster toward its fate, but never running, for that would have broken the line before the fight began, and never stopping to volley, for that would have been worse than useless until they were in range.

Then Turlock was down, tearing at his clothes to see where he had been hit.

And the line moved on as if Turlock had never been with them.

Down into that last defile they went, protected for a few moments from musket fire, close enough now that they were under the artillery.

It seemed a miracle to George that so many were still standing. Enough, he thought, to carry the fight. The Twentieth were green and untested, but they were as disciplined as any unit of veterans, and they crested the last rise as if it were no different than any other undulation in the Virginia earth, and not piled high with the bodies of the twelve brigades already shattered against that wall.

And there, in prime musket range, they answered the orders of their officers, to stop, present, take aim, and . . . *Fire!*

At the same moment, another sheet of flame lashed out from the wall.

Fifty-caliber plugs of lead whizzed and thumped, shattering bone and spraying blood.

O'Rourke spun about, hands at his throat, as if trying to hold his voice in place.

George tried to sidestep him, tripped on a body, slipped on the bloody ground, and fell. He landed on his elbow, and his pistol discharged at the same moment that his right leg flew upward. The bullet took off the tip of his boot and three of his toes. He did not feel the pain, because he was sliding down the blood-slicked defile, landing among a dozen bodies, including Jonathan Corley, who had taken a bullet in the thigh and was cinching his belt above the wound to stop the bleeding.

George tried to stand and cried out, then dropped to one knee.

"A bullet in the foot," Corley said. "A ticket home."

"My gun. It . . . it went off in my hand."

And for a second time, George saw the death's head grin. He did not have time to consider its meaning, because he was standing again, limping back up the little grade.

He got to the top as the regiment delivered another volley. The flame of their fire ignited the dusk for an instant, before another burst of flame knocked the whole regiment back down the slope, some down to death, some down to safety, all down among the bodies of the dying and dead.

THEY STAYED THAT night on the cold field.

Men who had sweated hard during the attack shivered now so miserably that they pulled the bodies of their dead comrades around them to stay warm. And those bodies protected them, too, from the Confederate sharpshooters.

But nothing could protect them from the sound of thousands of men, wounded and dying, spread across that black plain, a sound as insistent as the wailing of the wind, a deep murmur of pain that from time to time separated itself into its component parts—cries for mother, for water, for doctor, for merciful death.

Chamberlain would write of his own men, who were noticeably quiet despite their wounds: "That old New England habit, so reluctant of emotional expression, so prompt to speak conviction, so reticent as to the sensibilities—held perhaps as something intimate and sacred—that habit of the blood had its corollary in this reticence of complaint under the fearful suffering and mortal anguish of the battle field."

George Amory suffered his own misery with barely a sound. He sliced pieces of wool from the uniforms of the dead men around him and used them to pack the boot and stanch the flow of blood.

Late in the night, the ambulance wagons rattled up the hill with their lanterns masked. Their drivers moved cautiously, crouching among the dead and the dying, lighting matches to peer into faces, to ask questions, to ascertain chances.

By then, George was unbearably cold. Though his teeth were chattering, he managed to call to one matchlit shadow.

"Where are you hurt, Lieutenant?"

"In the foot," said George.

"Minie ball?" asked the driver.

"No," came the bitter voice of Jonathan Corley. "His own pistol."

And a murmur finally ran through those reticent Mainers.

"You shot yourself in the foot?" asked one of the faceless forms leaning over him.

"Not on purpose," said George.

"Well how did you come by that wound?" asked another.

"None of that talk," came a familiar voice from the shadows.

"Turlock?" said George. "But you were gut shot."

"Hit in the hip," said Turlock. "Dragged myself up. And from what I seen, I say Lieutenant Amory done his duty."

"Thank you, Sergeant," said George. Then he told the ambulance driver. "See to those who need more help. I can last here."

The driver stood with a lit match in his hand, and some sharpshooter fired at him.

"Keep down!" said Chamberlain from the darkness. "Keep down and take care. There's brave men to save off this hill. You can't save them unless you save yourselves."

The Twentieth stayed there another day, bleeding, bitter cold, empty-bellied, hunkered behind that barricade of dead bodies, answering fire if they could, ducking it the rest of the time. When they were finally ordered to withdraw, they crawled, their way lit by the rare, bluish glow of the northern lights, glimmering above them like a sign from God.

But what God was saying, no one could tell.

AFTER THE REMNANTS of the Twentieth returned to their miserable winter quarters, George was summoned to Chamberlain's tent and presented with resignation papers.

Chamberlain explained that Colonel Ames had lumped George with several lieutenants whose performance at Fredericksburg had disappointed him. Those men were being discharged, and so was George.

"The Colonel says that a man who's blown off his own toes can't be . . . can't be—" Chamberlain looked at the papers, out the open flap of his tent, anywhere but in George's eye. "—such a man can't be trusted to lead, whether he did it on purpose or not."

"Can't be trusted?" said George.

"It's not my opinion. But . . . well, you can't walk right, George. You never will."

"But—"

"Ames is West Point," said Chamberlain. "He thought little enough of us before the fight. He thinks some better now, but he's making a clean sweep of the junior officers."

George pulled himself up straight. "I must protest, sir."

"It's an honorable discharge, George." Chamberlain held out a pen. "Do it. Do it for the regiment."

George Amory felt an anger rising higher than any he had felt for the Confederates. This was simply not fair.

But Chamberlain had a minister's skill at putting the best face on something. He said, "Combat makes bad men worse and good men better. I'll tell any man that George Amory is better for what he's been through."

Later, George wished that Chamberlain had committed those words to writing, because by the time he returned to Portland, the whispering had begun.

A letter had reached Hannah Corley, wife of a fisherman who lay one-legged and embittered in the military hospital at Annapolis. It described the bravery of the men, the folly of the generals who wasted them, and the actions of the regimental officers, including Reverend Amory's son, "who went and shot himself in the foot."

"FATHER, I'M HOME."

Reverend Amory was propped on pillows, coughing. It was winter, when a cold could turn to a grippe, which might become pneumonia, especially in a man past seventy.

Before looking at his son's face, the reverend looked at the bandage wrapping his son's foot. "I knew that war would not be to your liking."

"My liking?"

"You liked it little enough that you shot yourself in the foot."

George looked at his mother, who made a small gesture with her hands, saying that he should remain calm.

So George said to his father. "I did my duty. Ask Colonel Chamberlain."

Reverend Amory nodded, as if it was something he would think about. Then his eyes fluttered and closed.

George's mother gestured for them to go downstairs.

To sit again in his mother's kitchen, while she made tea and busied herself about the woodstove, seemed strangely unreal to him now, something from someone else's experience. His world was a muddy, cold place where men lived in canvas tents and survived on hardtack and beans.

"Your father took to his bed as soon as news about Fredericksburg started arriving. He was worried sick."

"Worried that I'd shoot myself in the foot?" asked George bitterly.

"Worried that you'd be killed. He loves you very much." While the tea steeped, his mother put a hand on his arm. "You should know that there is gossip, George."

"Gossip?"

"Hannah Corley blames you for recruiting her husband. She spreads rumors. And Mrs. Hoyt says her sons would be alive if not for you."

George watched his mother pour tea.

"A congregation is made up of people," she continued. "Sometimes they are more mean than charitable. Perhaps if you stand before them and—"

"Grandfather always said never to apologize twice. I won't apologize *once* to a congregation of busybodies."

"Your grandfather is a wise man." His mother pulled a letter from the pocket of her apron and handed it to him.

It was written in a shaky hand, but the ideas were still strong: "Our George put his convictions to the test. He is the best kind of American. I will welcome him like a hero."

George had no wish to be called hero and he had never imagined returning to Millbridge, but there was nothing for him in Portland. So he lingered a few weeks at his father's bedside until the reverend finally faded away.

By then, the grief of the congregation had spread in ever-widening circles, because each week brought more bad news.

Jonathan Corley survived an infection and came home on one leg. But many others did not. Nurtured by cold and cramped quarters, the sicknesses of winter grew together into a single scourge called camp fever. By spring, it would kill more men of the Twentieth than all the Confederate rifles at Fredericksburg. And every time one of his recruits passed away, George felt the angry stares of mothers in the street.

He left on the first of March, a bright blustery day when the air still stung of winter but the angle of the sun filled New Englanders with the sure knowledge of spring's salvation.

HE STAYED THAT night at the Parker House in Boston.

He might have pushed on to Millbridge, but he wanted to attend services at the Park Street Church because the young ladies of Mrs. Finley's Finishing School worshiped there.

Being a Unitarian visitor without a regular pew, he sat in the back and waited.

Soon enough, a group of young ladies came in, their chatter fading as they were embraced by the austere beauty of the building. They took their places, lowered their heads to their books, and that was when she saw him.

Immediately her eyes went to his foot.

She knew. He wondered what her father had told her. He wondered all through the service and out onto Tremont Street.

"George, this is a surprise," she said, angling her head so that the brim of her bonnet would block the sun.

"I had to see you."

Now, she seemed to make every effort not to look at his foot, as though it were a port-wine birthmark or some other deformity. "I heard that you were wounded. I trust not too painfully."

"I lost half my foot, but it's the damage to my reputation that hurts."

"Undeservedly, I'm sure."

And relief poured over him for the first time since they saw those northern lights. "Your words are a great comfort."

"My young man is with the Twentieth Massachusetts. The Harvard Regiment, they call it. I know how brave you all must be."

He knew what she was telling him. He was not even sure that he was disappointed. He simply felt that he had to explain himself to her.

An omnibus rattled up to the corner. Two snorting draft horses clopped their hooves on the cobblestones.

"Come along, girls," said Mrs. Finley.

"I must go," Cordelia told him.

"May I correspond with you?" he asked.

"I have always promised you my sisterly affections, George."

He looked down.

"George, I'm sorry. But someday you'll do something extraordinary, and some other young woman will notice. And then you'll forget about me."

"I *did* something extraordinary. I went up the hill at Fredericksburg"—he looked along Tremont Street, at the coaches and horses and ladies hurrying arm-in-arm with their gentlemen—"while all these people were warm by their fires."

"Cordelia!" said Mrs. Finley. "It's not polite for ladies to stand talking in the street."

"Yes, ma'am." She met his eyes once more, put a hand on his arm, said, "Do something else extraordinary."

"What?"

"Find your Constitution." She pulled away and headed for the omnibus. "Make the world a better place."

"I'll make the world a better place," he said, "by making cotton cloth for Union suits at Millbridge."

"Oh, George." Cordelia turned back to him, a look of concern—sisterly concern—on her face. "But you hate Millbridge."

"I hate it. I hated war, too."

Her expression softened. He saw real sympathy in her eyes. "Don't waste your life there, George. Dream your dreams."

"Dream them with me," he blurted.

For a moment, he thought she might say yes.

Instead, she pecked him on the cheek.

The girls on the omnibus gasped. And Mrs. Finley cried, "Cordelia! Unless that young man is your brother or father, it is absolutely improper—"

She left George standing on Tremont Street, touching his cheek.

"So, how's your foot?" asked Grandfather Will.

"It hurts," said George.

By evening, George had settled into his grandfather's house on the Blackstone and taken a place at the old man's dinner table.

The bill of fare: ground beef in gravy, peas with butter, mashed potatoes, prepared by Mrs. Murphy, the burly housekeeper who had come from the mill to make herself an indispensable caregiver to a ninety-three-year-old man. She bustled in from the kitchen, poked her round face over the old man's shoulder, and inspected his plate. "Make sure you eat them peas. Steer 'em into the potatoes to pick 'em up."

Grandfather Will wearily raised a hand and waved her away.

George smiled at Mrs. Murphy. The sound of her accent brought him back to his regiment, and Irish faces flashed past him, the last one being Private O'Rourke, his eyes widening as blood welled from his neck.

Grandfather Will lifted the tablecloth to look at the foot. "I got shot in the leg once. Soon as I could walk, I went after the men who did it."

"The fight in Crawford Notch."

"They should call it *Pike* Notch. . . . Did I ever tell you about the Constitution?"

Just then the front door opened and Uncle William came in, sweeping cold air with him. He threw another scoopful of coal into the stove, then hunched into a seat opposite George.

"You're late," said Grandfather Will. "No man should work on the Sabbath."

Uncle William ignored his father and squinted over his spectacles at George. "They say you were an officer."

"A lieutenant."

"You can be a lieutenant on the warping floor, then. If you do well with the second shift, and there's no whispering—"

"Whispering?" asked George.

"Why . . . the wound. The limp. A man back from war, shot in the foot . . . people whisper." Uncle William spoke without malice. For him, business was always business.

But not for George. He glared across the table and changed the subject. "Grandfather was just telling me about the lost Constitution."

"That again?" Uncle William rolled his eyes and mouthed the word, "Senile."

"I'm not senile." Grandfather Will kept his head down, looking at his plate, forking his food to his face, sticking out his tongue to receive it, taking it in, all as slowly as if he were doing it for the first time.

Mrs. Murphy came in and put a plate in front of Uncle William. "Anything else?"

"Yes," said Grandfather, and he directed her to go to his closet and fetch down a box from the top shelf.

"What is that?" asked Uncle William.

"Proof," said the old man. "Proof that I'm not senile."

THE NEXT DAY, George Amory climbed to the top of mill tower.

It had been green August the last time that he stood there. Now it was March in a cold rain. A layer of smoke enhanced the gloom. Many mills now ran on steam. And there were more trains all the time, puffing smoke day and night.

Down below, the workers heeded the first bell, moving as they always had, like draft animals accepting their fate, patiently, ploddingly, no matter the weather. Like draft animals . . . or soldiers.

Then someone was huffing up the little ladder: Cousin Bartlett levered himself through the trapdoor. His beard had thickened, though not nearly so much as his waist. "So, you followed the smoke. And it led to the Confederate guns. How's your foot?"

"It hurts."

"What about your pride?"

"What does that mean?"

"It means ignore the gossips, because none of them had the courage to do what you did. Be proud"—Bartlett took his hand in both of his—"and I'll be proud of you."

George's hot anger melted. He had yearned for the handshake of a friend.

Bartlett gripped tighter and grinned. "So, what are your plans? Europe after all?"

"Europe was there before Caesar invaded Gaul. It will be there when this war is over. Grandfather is giving me a chance to prove myself." George noticed Bartlett's grip loosen. "I mean to take it."

"You have nothing to prove," said Bartlett. "And after all you've seen, Millbridge will be a boring place."

"Don't worry," said George, "I won't usurp you. I won't even quote poetry."

And for a time, they were silent in the cupola, watching the day begin. But Bartlett was thinking about something. George could feel the energy of thought coming off of him. Finally he said, "How would you like me to ease the pain in your foot?"

"Ease it? How?"

Something devilish came into Bartlett's expression, something that George had never seen before. "I'll introduce you to the new Irish girls.

Some'll fuck for pennies, others for a chance to work a loom instead of a warp beam. Others—"

"Fuck?" George said the word with awe. "Fuck?"

He had learned a great deal about life. In a world where men met unimaginable violence with superhuman discipline, the standards of polite society were sometimes lowered. He had seen prostitutes in the camps. He had heard men complain of "the itch" after the prostitutes had gone. He had listened to their stories of fanny-fucks and suck-offs. But he was still a minister's son, raised to believe that sex before marriage was a sin.

"Fuck," Bartlett repeated. "Once you do it, it's all you can think of."

In truth, it was all that most young men could think of, even minister's sons, even if they *hadn't* done it. So George was not lying when he said, "I'll think about it."

"But it'll cost you," said Bartlett. "Uncle William told me Grandfather gave you his old letters last night."

"A few from Rufus King. One that he wrote to Rufus King but didn't send. A letter that Henry Knox wrote to Rufus King about him—"

"Henry Knox?" Bartlett's eyes widened.

George shrugged, as if he didn't get the significance.

"I knew there were King letters, but . . . Henry Knox?" said Bartlett. "A giant. And Grandfather gave *you* a Knox letter? Why you?"

"He said I sacrificed my foot to defend the Constitution."

Above them, the bell began to move. The timekeeper downstairs was getting ready to ring it. Second bell, last chance to get to work. Bartlett reached out and grabbed the rope, stopping the movement.

Then he pointed down into the yard. "The Murphy sisters."

Two young women, hands to their heads to hold their hats, woolen capes aflutter, were rushing toward the entrance. One was a little taller, a little younger, with redder hair.

George said, "Have you . . . ?"

"Not yet," said Bartlett. "Try the tall one, Sheila. Stay away from the sister. Spoken for. One of the smash piecers. A big Mick named McGillis."

Just then, the building began to vibrate. The wheel had been engaged. The drive shaft was turning.

"Remember," said Bartlett, "there's no finer feeling than a good fuck. I'll see that you get a few if you get me those letters."

George gave the girls one more look; then he and Bartlett descended, before the bell made them deaf.

FOURTEEN

෨ "DEAD? BINDLE? Who killed him, boss?" asked Bernice.

"Don't know. Do you have your Beretta?"

"It's one of those, hunh?" Nothing rattled Bernice too much.

Peter said, "Tell Antoine to be careful. Orson will know enough."

"Antoine is out," said Bernice, "but he left something for you."

"What?"

"It's from an old newspaper, the *Blackstone Weekly*. Date is August 3, 1862. 'William Pike, the founder of the mill from which so many in this valley derive their income, yesterday expressed pride that his grandson, George Amory, has joined the Twentieth Maine Regiment of Infantry.' He wants to know if he should read more about George Amory."

"That's the drill," said Peter. "Time he learned. When we're tracking something, we look at major figures in every generation. It's how we establish the chain of ownership."

"So, what should I tell him?"

"Tell him to get the *Regimental History of the Twentieth Maine* and read about Amory."

"Right," said Bernice. "Where are you?"

"On the move. We're going to stay on the move, too. You have the cell. We'll find wireless Internet when you have something for us to read."

"Be careful," said Bernice.

"We will."

Evangeline was staring straight ahead, as if the weight of what she had been through that afternoon had been too much. She finally spoke: "We will *what*?"

"Be careful. But keep going."

"Do we have another choice?"

"We can quit." He didn't say it like a challenge.

But she took it as one. "No. This is too important."

So he kept driving. Half an hour later, he pulled into the parking lot at MCI Cedar Junction.

"I'll do this alone," he said. "Are you all right?"

She flipped down the driver's-side visor and pulled out her compact and comb. "I will be in a bit. Seeing Bindle like that—"

"I guess he wasn't the biggest operator in the bunch after all."

"But was he innocent?" she asked, "Or ignorant?"

"Maybe Bingo Keegan knows. He knows everything."

PETER WENT INTO the gray prison, signed in, passed through the metal detectors. When Bingo was brought down, Peter was waiting in a cubicle on the other side of the glass.

Bingo sat and picked up the receiver. "Crimson turtleneck, tweed sportcoat, jeans, black loafers. A walkin' Harvard cliché."

"Cliché. A big word," said Peter.

"I looked it up after they used it on me in the *Globe*: 'The Irish thug dealing drugs and enforcement in South Boston, relying on the neighborhood code of silence for protection, has become a walking cliché.'"

"So . . . did you send the author an angry letter?"

"I thought about whackin' him. Instead I had one of the boys slash his tires." Bingo opened a stick of gum. "Now, to what do I owe this pleasure?"

"Are you still a good American?"

"Got everyone in here pledgin' allegiance to the flag."

"That's good." Peter was proceeding carefully but not too slowly. He still hated being here. "Any of them talk about anything interesting?"

Bingo popped the gum in his mouth and dropped the wrapping on the floor. "What are you after?"

"Information. Three deaths. All suspicious."

"No. What are you *after?* What's the treasure?"

"If I told you, you might go after it yourself. Even from in here."

"Who says I'm not after it anyway? I got plenty of contacts."

Cat and mouse. Peter had played with this cat before, when he had claws. "It wouldn't surprise me, no matter what you were into."

"So why would I tell you anything?"

Peter shrugged. "Because you'll want a friendly face at a parole hearing some day, because you'd like the personal satisfaction that comes with doing the right thing . . ."

"Personal satisfaction. Like a fuckin' drug once you get a taste." Bingo looked around. "Of course, in here a nickel bag will get you further."

"If I find what I'm after, I can call myself a good American, too."

"So, this is for patriotism, not money?"

"Like last time."

Bingo worked on the gum. "We did help to stop a terrorist attack. *And* we sent a whole country into a fuckin' uproar over guns. Personal satisfaction."

"So . . . three deaths. Two in the town of Millbridge. One up in Queechee Gorge."

"That Dartmouth professor?"

"You know about him?" Peter should not have been surprised.

"I read his book," said Bingo. "Now you want to know why somebody killed him? Maybe somebody didn't like what he had to say about the Second Amendment."

Maybe Bingo knew something already. But maybe not, because he had to ask who the other two were.

"A retired manager at the Pike-Perkins Mill," said Peter, "and the president of a historical society."

Bingo brought his face close to the plate glass. "What are you after?"

Peter looked into Bingo's eyes, as gray and lifeless as two bullets. "I'm after knowledge. Once I know who murdered these guys, I'll know what's next."

"You think someone's whackin' these people on contract?"

"The old mill manager died with his oxygen tank empty. The professor was—"

"—hit by a rock slide. Yeah. I heard."

"They tried to make it look like the last guy hanged himself, but we spoiled that."

"Good work."

"Thanks."

"Not you. The one doin' the whackin'. The boys in here like to talk about good work and guys who do it." Bingo leaned back again. "I'll listen a bit more."

Peter pushed away from the table. "If you find anything, call my cell."

"Which block?"

"Cell *phone*." Peter stood, "I just have one more question."

"Yeah?"

"You can't see my feet. How do you know I'm wearing black loafers?"

"Because that's what a walkin' cliché would wear."

PETER HAD NEW golf shoes and old sneakers in the trunk. He put on the sneakers.

"Did our friend tell you anything?" Evangeline seemed better. She had combed out her hair and put on a touch of lipstick.

"He has nothing to do in there but keep his ear to the ground. Knowing who's whackin' who—"

"Whom."

"—and why—for him that's like knowing who's pitching for the Red Sox."

The cell phone rang.

It was Bernice: "Hey, boss. You got mail here. From Charles Bishop."

"Charles Bishop?" Peter looked at Evangeline.

Another voice came on the phone—intimate, modulated, perfectly accented with the Boston Brahmin long *a*. Orson Lunt, Peter's mentor and partner, retired but still a fixture at Fallon Antiquaria. Peter could almost *hear* Orson's bow tie and clipped gray mustache: "What's all this about Bernice keeping her Beretta in her handbag? I thought we were trying to get guns off the street."

"We're trying to figure out the truth," said Peter. "Let the politicians worry about the rest. If you don't want to hang around the office, get out of town."

"Out of the line of fire, you mean?" said Orson.

"Don't go down any dark alleys. Keep your doors locked. The usual."

"Maybe I'll go down to the hood and hang with Antoine and his homebodies."

"That's home*boys*," said Peter. "Tell me more about Charles Bishop."

"Bishop Media. American News Network, the liberal answer to Fox News. Runs his media operation out of New York, spends most of his time in Litchfield County."

"Litchfield? That's where the Henry Knox buyer came from. Don Cottle. What does the letter say?"

"It's not what it says. It's what's in the envelope: two tickets to the Bishop Media box at Fenway for the first game of the World Series on Sunday night."

"So the Sox beat the Yankees this afternoon?"

"Three to two. Now for the Dodgers and Mets to decide their business—"

"Did Bishop say why he sent me the tickets?"

Orson Lunt read: " 'We have been doing business through a proxy. It is time to do it in person. I am convening interested parties at Fenway on Sunday night, assuming of course that the Red Sox beat the Yankees. There is no better place in New England to bring together people of differing opinions. Come, enjoy the game, and if you have uncovered a certain document by then, bring it. Maybe we'll put it on television.'"

Peter looked at Evangeline. "Put a certain document on television?"

"A man who thinks big," said Evangeline.

IT WAS LATE afternoon when they turned off Route 6 and headed west across Litchfield County. The orange sugar maples reflected the fading light. The old houses and white-steepled towns looked as if they had been dabbed into place by an itinerant artist paid by the gallon to spread his paint.

Evangeline was reading something she'd downloaded from a Web site called Quickbio.com:

"Charles Bishop, b. Hartford, Connecticut, May 8, 1930. Married twice, once widowed, once divorced. Education: Phillips Exeter, 1948. Yale, 1952, Harvard Business School, 1958. He married Julia Elida Morgan, 1962, with whom he had two children, Kate Bishop (b. 1964) and Charles David Bishop (b. 1966). Two generations of Bishops before him built a fortune, first in newspapers, then in radio. Charles Bishop took the next logical step. In 1967, he bought a UHF television station in western Connecticut. Soon he had built a New England empire of small market stations. Out of that grew Bishop Media. Its flagship: American News Network, surrounded by entertainment and sports channels . . . and . . . Blah, blah, blah. . . ."

She skipped to the bottom. "In a *Wall Street Journal* story about him, one of his competitors said, 'He's the definition of an iron fist in a velvet glove.'"

"Now we know what to expect," said Peter.

"Iron fist . . . are we're safe, going to see him?"

"I don't think we have anything to worry about."

"Famous last words."

In a countryside of long driveways, Bishop's stretched half a mile, from a mechanized gate with intercom past surveillance cameras tucked in tree branches all the way to a big white Colonial with a fieldstone front. It looked like something from a 1940s movie starring Cary Grant and Myrna Loy. *Mr. Bishop Builds His Horse Farm,* maybe. There was a barn behind the house, a neat paddock beside it, long runs of white fence dividing the landscape. And a man on a horse was riding across the top of a hill, in the last rays of sunshine.

Peter and Evangeline watched him come down across the darkening fields, past the paddock. He wore brown tweed, brown turtleneck, lighter brown jodhpurs, brown leather boots. The horse was brown, too.

"Mr. Fallon?" He dismounted and offered his hand. "I'm Charles Bishop."

Peter shook his hand and felt a chill presence behind him, like a cold breeze blowing up the legs of his jeans.

Bishop looked past them and said, "Ah . . . Cottle."

Peter and Evangeline turned and there were the square shoulders shaping the tweed sportcoat, the square crew cut shaping the head.

"He's in charge of corporate security," said Bishop.

Peter said, "I guess I'm not surprised."

"Surprised the hell out of me," said Evangeline. "Sneaking up on us without making a sound. On a gravel driveway, no less."

Cottle smiled, but only his mouth moved. "Part of the job description."

Bishop turned it into a joke. "The first thing I ask when I hire a man: Can you sneak up on someone? A good skill to have in corporate security. Now, Sara and I are expecting you to stay for dinner."

Bishop led them into the house, into the study, where three plasma HDTVs were tuned to three different channels. While he poured drinks, he kept up a line of chatter that seemed to reveal everything about him while revealing almost nothing.

Among his tidbits: He was only semi-retired because there was just too much going on for a man with his power to withdraw from the world. He liked Litchfield because it was rural, but he could get to New York in two hours for meetings, get to Fenway in two hours for ball games. He let his son run the company, while he worked on repealing the Second Amendment. And he still got to ride his horses. This combination of political purpose and activity in the saddle, he said, had given him renewed vigor.

As if on cue, in came Sara Wyeth.

Peter caught Evangeline's eye, and he knew that she knew what he was thinking—any old man would have renewed vigor if he spent it in the saddle with this one.

Sara looked about thirty years younger than Bishop, and apparently a natural blonde. Whether her other assets were natural or man-made, they proclaimed that here was a woman who took care of herself and could take care of herself, too, man or no man.

She offered her hand to Peter and Evangeline.

"We met online," said Charles Bishop.

"One of Charles's silly jokes," she said. "I have a PR firm in Boston. Charles is a client."

"I was trying to buy the Red Sox network," said Charles. "I was looking for some local presence in Boston."

"I provide presence," said Sara. "If Fallon Antiquaria is looking for a little more ink in the Boston papers . . ."

"My work requires discretion," said Fallon. "The less attention the better."

"That's why we're happy that—" Bishop was suddenly distracted by something on one of the TV screens. He grabbed the remote and turned up the sound.

". . . absolutely convinced that the American people are ready for this repeal." It was Harriet Holden. "So we're pressing forward. And no amount of opposition from men in funny hats will change that."

Cut to a golf course at dusk, a man in a visored cap with the word PING on the crown.

Evangeline said, "It's—"

Peter gave her an elbow. Subtle, but she got the point: Don't say anything. Listen and learn.

The face on the screen grinned. "Men wear hats like this when they play golf. And in some households, golf supports the Constitution by assuring domestic tranquillity. . . ."

Bishop turned down the sound. "Much better."

"Yes," said Sara.

"We put Harriet on yesterday with Kelly Cutter," said Bishop.

"We saw it." Evangeline sipped her wine.

"Kelly's a pro," said Bishop. "She gave a rational voice to the opposition. Tore the congresswoman to pieces."

"Who's the guy in the Ping hat?" asked Peter.

"The founder of a PAC called the Morning in America Foundation," said Sara.

"Morning in America," said Evangeline. "Wasn't that in a Reagan speech?"

"A very *good* Reagan speech," said Peter.

"No such thing," said Bishop.

Peter gave Evangeline the eye: *Don't tell them that I voted for Reagan in '84.*

Evangeline looked at Bishop. "Who are they?"

"Men with money," said Bishop. "And they put it into right-wing causes that they want to support. You'll find Morning in America money in the coffers of right-to-life organizations, anti-tax groups, the NRA—"

"Don't forget the pro-aerosol gang," said Sara Wyeth.

"What's that?" asked Evangeline.

"The guys who think that every scientist who dares to suggest that our lifestyle is endangering the earth is a Communist."

"Oh," said Evangeline. "The ones who think the glaciers aren't melting."

Peter could tell that Evangeline was relaxing. The wine was helping. It was a very good chardonnay, served in a nice glass. And she was in a roomful of people who thought a lot like her.

Except, perhaps, for Don Cottle, who leaned against a bookcase with his arms folded, and listened. Peter studied him for reactions, but Cottle showed nothing. Not happy with this conversation, not upset. Just there.

"Morning in America got started about twenty-five years ago," said Bishop. "During the fight over the Equal Rights Amendment. The guy in the golf hat was one of the founders."

"What's his name?" asked Peter.

"Marlon Secourt. Has homes in Florida, Newport, and Bar Harbor," said Bishop. "And not a bad guy."

"He's a buffoon," said Sara.

"He believes what he believes. He's happy to be the opposition voice whenever we call him. I might even invite him to the ball game on Sunday."

Peter noticed Cottle look up, as if that was news he had not heard.

Bishop kept talking. "Once in a while we put him on *Rapid Fire* to make the opposition look like . . . well like the lunatic fringe in a funny hat."

"A bit manipulative, isn't it?" said Peter.

"Of course it's manipulative," said Bishop. "The righties do it, too. Rush Limbaugh has the biggest radio audience in America, and every day, he whines about liberal bias in the media."

"There's liberal bias on ANN," said Peter. "You're trying to make Harriet and her cause look good."

"We call it opinion molding," said Bishop.

Sara said, "I consider Harriet Holden a client, even though I'm not on her payroll. That's how firmly I believe in her."

Bishop said to Peter, "She's a client of yours, too, isn't she?"

"I can't say," answered Peter.

"Discretion again," said Bishop. "I like that. It means I can trust you."

OVER GRILLED VEAL chops and California pinot noir, they talked about the Red Sox. Once they got past the pitching match-ups for the

World Series, Bishop explained that he had a soft spot for the Sox because of his first television station. He bought it in 1967, the year that they went from the bottom of the American League to the pennant. "The station held the license for the Red Sox in western Connecticut."

"That's Yankee territory, isn't it?" said Evangeline.

"Not that year. Advertising rates went through the roof. Gave me the cash to buy another station. Bishop Media was born."

"Charles loves his own little creation myth," said Sara.

"It's no myth," growled Charles. "I had family money, brains, and ambition. It's a hard combination to beat."

Then he waved for the butler to take the plates. He ordered coffees and dessert. "A marvelous Normandie tarte de pomme." And he kept talking with the confidence of a man who expected attention whenever he spoke: "If the New England universe has a center, where people can come together in agreement, it's Fenway Park."

"Is that why you invited us to the game on Sunday night?" asked Peter.

"I've invited a lot of people, even Harriet Holden. It's time to reason together over a certain document we call the lost Constitution."

"But if Harriet Holden is so important to you," said Peter, "how is it that she didn't know anything about this lost Constitution when she came to me?"

Bishop laughed. "Here's a life lesson: Never reveal anything to a politician unless you have to."

Cottle said to Fallon, "We didn't expect her to go to you."

"I'm curious," said Bishop. "Did you know what we were looking for when you came down here the other day and had lunch with Don?"

Peter shook his head.

"See that," said Bishop to Cottle. "I told you we should have gotten him on the case sooner. In just a few days, he's gotten as close to this as we have in years."

"I have a good assistant," said Peter.

Evangeline had been watching Sara, studying her reactions. Peter's remark snapped her attention. "What do you mean, assistant?"

"Sorry," said Peter. "Partner."

"On this case, at least," said Evangeline. "It matters that much to me, too."

"Good," said Bishop "I'm prepared to answer any questions. Give you any information. I have an electronic file with all sorts of papers I can send you."

"But remember," said Cottle, "the use of Mr. Bishop's knowledge must be for his benefit."

"Are you a corporate security chief or a lawyer?" aked Peter.

"He has both kinds of muscle, so to speak," said Bishop. "But everything is negotiable. We should at least agree upon a price for your services."

"I'm not offering my services," said Peter. "They're already committed."

Bishop kept talking. "If you find it, what's your price?"

"Already committed," said Peter again. "And yes. It's to Harriet Holden."

"Doesn't matter," said Cottle. "Do business with Mr. Bishop, or he'll lay prima facie claim to the document."

"Prima facie," said Evangeline. "He really *is* a lawyer."

Peter said to Bishop, "Prima facie because—"

"Because my maternal grandmother was the goddamned daughter of Bartlett Pike. He ran the Pike Mill and some say ran it into the ground."

Peter said, "That makes you a cousin of Buster McGillis."

"Second cousin, once removed, I think. We didn't have much in common."

"Did you know that his closest friend was murdered today?" asked Evangeline.

"Murdered?" Bishop shot a glance at Cottle.

Cottle didn't blink. "What does that have to do with us?"

"He was the broker of the Henry Knox letter you bought." Peter watched for a reaction but got nothing. If they were hiding their emotions, they were good at it.

Then Peter said, "You don't know where the document is, and you can't prove that you've ever held it in your hands. This might be one of those cases where—"

"Possession is nine tenths of the law?" said Bishop. "So, what's the document worth?"

"As much as ten million dollars."

"To say nothing of its historical or political value," added Evangeline.

"Ten million." Bishop looked at Sara. "A small price if we can get guns off the streets for good."

Sara said, "Bishop Media is doing the pre-game show on Sunday night. We plan to have a camera in the luxury box interviewing New Englanders who love the game and love America. If you have the document, we'll put it on television. I call that thinking *outside* the luxury box."

"But what if it says nothing?" asked Peter.

"We'll think of something," Bishop leaned back in his chair.

"What if it's negative?" asked Evangeline.

"We'll think of something," repeated Bishop. "As I said, it's all about opinion molding."

"I thought it was all about truth," said Peter.

"Just find it and bring it," snapped Bishop.

"Unless we find it first." Cottle finished his drink.

"We'll be there Sunday night," said Peter. "With the document or without."

THEY FINISHED DINNER around ten. Bishop invited them to stay the night.

Evangeline looked at Peter, and a small flick of her eyes suggested they take what they knew and get out of there.

Soon, they were speeding along the dark roads of Litchfield County.

Peter checked the rearview. No lights.

After a few miles, Evangeline said, "I told you that Cottle was lying after we had lunch with him."

"Where are we going?" he asked.

"You're the one who says we're on the run."

"You're the one who didn't want to stay at Bishop's."

"They were giving me the creeps. The media giant, the PR queen, the corporate security thug—"

"And *they're* on your side," he said.

"Are we bickering? We'd better not be bickering. If we start sounding like an old married couple, you can drop me in Hartford and I'll get a train back to New York."

"We're not going to Hartford."

"Then where?"

"North. My instinct is that we'll find more answers north," said Peter.

"When we get to someplace safe, we should e-mail these names to Antoine and Orson. Check Bartlett Pike of the Pike-Perkins Mill and Marlon Secourt of the Morning in America Foundation. Secourt wasn't up at the Mount Washington just to play golf," said Evangeline.

"And not so much of a yahoo as we thought."

"Well, he *was* a yahoo."

Peter laughed. "A yahoo looking for something at the New England rarities convention. That was why Paul Doherty danced away from him when he started pushing Bloom around on the dance floor."

They didn't drive far. The Litchfield Inn had a room with four hundred-line cotton sheets, down comforters, wireless Internet, and a full breakfast.

They slipped into bed and read their e-mails.

Nothing had come in from Charles Bishop.

But Antoine had sent them biographical facts on George Amory: Date of graduation from Bowdoin, date of mustering out of the Twentieth, and several news stories from the *Blackstone Weekly*. One told of Amory's return to the mill. Another, about fourteen months later: "Comings and Goings at the Pike Mill: Mr. George Amory has left the employ of the mill, it was announced today by Bartlett Pike. No reason was given. Mr. Pike says that Mr. Amory plans to travel in Europe. Also leaving at the same time was a young loomer, Sheila Murphy. . . ."

"Maybe they left together," said Evangeline after she read it.

"Maybe," said Peter, who was drifting off to sleep.

FIFTEEN

August 1863

In the north woods, men were cutting timber.

But in the mill, workers were summoned by the bell each day.

In Europe, young people were exploring the ruins of the Colosseum and the corridors of the Louvre.

But in the mill, two hundred shuttles flew in two hundred looms, causing a roar more deafening than all the cannon at Fredericksburg.

In Pennsylvania, the Twentieth Maine was marching to glory.

But in the mill, George Amory saw that the workers were working and the shuttles were flying, and nothing else mattered to a young man of business . . . or so he told himself.

What he learned of the wider world now came to him in what he read, and if he was envious, he did not admit it to himself.

Enos Turlock wrote and invited him to "come a-cuttin'": "You've no need to prove yourself to any man. But a season in the Maine woods will toughen you more than war or mill work. It'll give you a skin so thick, nothing any man says or does will ever hurt you."

Cordelia wrote to him of the Grand Tour, which she was taking in company with three friends from school. Her letters were full of "sisterly" chitchat and not a hint of passion. "We have seen many churches, Notre Dame, Sainte-Chapelle, Chartres . . . For a country where the senses are well-served, France is certainly a spiritual country, too. . . ."

And the newspapers reported on the Twentieth at Gettysburg and the defense of a place called Little Round Top: "Imagine, if you can, nine small companies of infantry, numbering perhaps three hundred men, in the form of a right angle, on the extreme flank of an army of eighty thousand, put there to hold the key of the entire position against a force at least ten times their number. Stand firm, ye boys from Maine."

George Amory had stood firm, too, in the mill on the banks of the Blackstone.

He had worked so hard and so well that he sensed Cousin Bartlett now considered him a threat. On the whole, he would have been happy to turn it all over and head for Europe, to find that gaggle of girls and go traveling with them. But his late grandfather had given him a chance to prove himself, and he would not betray the memory of the only man who had shown any faith in him after Fredericksburg.

Once, George had believed that the path to self-dependence led away from places like the mill. But he had learned that sticking fast was the way to become a man.

And he had a girl . . . of sorts.

He could see her through the windows of his office. She was crossing the weave room, pretending to look for something she had dropped, so that if anyone asked her why she was there after hours, she would have an excuse.

A lingering July dusk lit the room, but no one was working. The cotton supply had dwindled, so the mill no longer ran double shifts. The belts were still, the looms silent. Without the incessant *click-cla-clack-cla-click-cla-clack*, the quiet was like the surface of a pond disturbed by a few pebbles, a few footfalls made by a girl from Galway.

George closed his ledger and slipped it into a bookcase. Then he pulled out a greenback dollar and put it on the desk.

It was hot in the little office. The mill windows were kept closed because heat and humidity made cotton thread supple so that it would not break during the weave. In July the mills became steaming kilns along the riverbanks. Had it been practical to run with the windows open in winter, the mill managers would have done that, too.

Her name was Sheila. She was still wearing an apron over her work dress. Rings of perspiration expanded on the gray fabric under her arms. Strands of hair dropped down around her cheeks. Her eyes seemed colorless when she looked at him.

The first time she had come to him she had pinned her hair and worn her Sunday dress and smelled of soap. He had been disconcerted by her nervousness because it matched his own. Now she treated their visits as one more job of work.

She stepped into the office and closed the door, then she pulled the shade, so that the office was almost dark.

George would not have minded the light. He liked looking at her. She had symmetrical features, long limbs, auburn hair. In better clothes, in a better place, she might have looked regal.

He pushed back his chair and stood. Her scent was woman-sweet and hard-work sour at the same time. It filled the little space and intoxicated his brain.

She stuffed the dollar into the apron pocket with her tools. Her scissors jangled. Then she turned her eyes away from him, slipped her hands under her dress, pulled down her bloomers, bunched them up and put them into another pocket. Then she hiked her dress to her thighs and sat on the desk.

"Thank you for coming," he whispered.

"We'd best be quick," she said. "I seen Mr. William down in the mill yard."

George listened a moment, heard nothing, then ran his hands under her dress. She was not wearing stockings. Her thighs felt cool and smooth until he reached the tangle of hair where they met.

She made a sound and twitched herself—toward him? Away? He could not tell.

Then she unsnapped the top button of his trousers. The rest of the buttons popped under growing pressure.

He leaned forward to kiss her but before he could, she brought her hand to her lips and wet her fingers. "Like I say, we'd best be quick. But that ain't any problem for you, now, is it?" She reached down and moistened him with her fingertips.

The feeling of her touch and the promise of what was about to happen were almost too much. He controlled himself with this thought: She had grown practiced and impersonal at this. Perhaps she was selling her wares on a wider basis.

Still he let her draw him toward her and guide him into her. He thrust once, twice, then stopped, simply to enjoy the exquisite sensations that flowed from her loins into his, up his spine, into his brain.

And she chose that moment to whisper into his ear, "Tell me one thing."

"What?"

"Have you any feelin's for me, George Amory?"

"Feelings? Of course." He tried to pull back and thrust again.

But she held him, digging her nails into his back. "*Real* feelin's. More than just the feelin's of a man with a hoor, which is what you've made of me."

A man who had no feelings would simply have told her that she had made a hoor of herself. But George was still a minister's son, and though he had fallen into the thrall of fucking, as his cousin so bluntly put it, he tried to think of something gentle to say.

Instead, he heard the key in the door.

Uncle William appeared, shoulders hunched, head down, eyes point-ing like knives over his spectacles. "George! What . . . what would your father say?"

The girl jumped up.

George pulled back, turned away, grabbed his trousers.

Uncle William glared at the girl. "And what would *your* sister say?"

Sheila brought her hand to her mouth, covering a chin that began to quiver.

"Never mind that," said Uncle William. "I want you both gone by to-morrow. I'll not have one of my company officers soiling the morals of the girls we claim to protect. And I won't have one immoral girl soiling the rep-utation of the rest."

Sheila tried to speak, "But—"

"Get out, girl. Be on the train tomorrow."

Without bothering to put her bloomers back on, she left.

Then Uncle William turned to George. "As for you—"

George said, "Uncle, I can explain."

"You can't explain this any more than you can explain how you shot yourself in the foot on the battlefield."

"Goddamn you, sir."

"Goddamn you! Your grandfather trusted you, but I don't. I favor Bartlett. I always have." He turned and started across the mill floor. "Bartlett gets my interest in the mill when the time comes. Not you. You're a coward with a wandering mind, and a sneak. We give you a chance to redeem yourself, and this is how you repay us."

"You led him right to us," George told Bartlett the next morning in the cupola. "You've planned it for months, from that first morning you pointed out Sheila, right here."

"Nothing personal, George," said Bartlett. "It's business. And business is business. I was born for business, and you weren't. You said it yourself."

"I said it a long time ago. I'm going to tell Uncle William it was you who put me onto that girl, you who led me to start fucking her."

Bartlett laughed in George's face. "I work at his side in the office house. You work in the mill. Tell him what you want. I'll tell him you're lying."

George said, "You betrayed me. I want the letters back."

"A deal's a deal." Bartlett shook his head. "I gave you the girls, you gave me the letters. The Henry Knox letter is the gem of my collection. It's right in my scrapbook."

Just then, they heard a distant whistle. Off to the north, the smoke of an engine was cutting across the landscape.

"The train for Providence," said Bartlett. "Worcester Express will be here soon. You should go."

"I have business to clear up before I leave."

"Uncle William said that if you're here after second bell, I should summon the Micks from security." Bartlett shrugged, as if he were only the messenger.

"Are you lying about that, too?"

Bartlett shook his head. "I have it all sewn up, George. The family shares in the mill, the Irish muscle. And I have you right where I want you." Bartlett made the mistake of sliding a hand lightly under George's lapel.

The condescension of the gesture infuriated George Amory. He drove his hands into Bartlett's soft belly and slammed him against the railing, which cracked and began to let go. Bartlett cried out, eyes widening, and he grabbed one of the pillars that supported the roof of the cupola.

George grabbed Bartlett's belt, but he did not pull Bartlett to safety. Instead, he undid the belt and snapped it open.

"Wha . . . what are you doing?" said Bartlett.

There was just enough leather for George to wrap the belt around the pillar and notch it.

"Some day, I'll ask you if you're sorry you betrayed me. You'll say yes, if you can hear the question."

By the time George reached the first floor, the bell was clanging and a man, somewhere above, was crying in pain with every strike of the clapper.

The workers in the yard were all looking up toward the noise. George went past them, neither looking at their faces nor looking back. He hurried out of the yard, crossed the stone bridge, and reached the depot as the last passengers were boarding for Providence.

At the conductor's call, the train began to roll.

George looked up at a window, and there was the face of Sheila Murphy—sad, angry, fearful, brave. Her eyes met his. He wanted to say something, but no word came. Her lips moved, but with the engine noise and the closed window, he could not tell what she said. *I'm pretty? I'm promised?*

Limping along beside the train, he thought to give her some money and fumbled in his pocket.

But the train was moving faster, puffing steam against the wall of the depot.

He cried. "Open the window!"

She did and leaned out and shouted something, but the roar of the engine drowned out her words.

DROPPED FROM HIS regiment because of a wound that damaged his foot and besmirched his reputation. Driven from his community by gossip and angry glares. Cast from the family business by an uncle who forgave no indiscretion except, perhaps, his own intolerance. Betrayed by a cousin far less trustworthy than he seemed.

It had been a bad year.

Would George become a wanderer? Would he go to Europe and live as an expatriate, reading war dispatches from a distance? Would he study philosophy at Heidelburg? Have a romance with a beautiful French girl? Sit for a week in the Sistine Chapel? And do it all with . . . what?

His mother promised to pay his passage to Europe by digging into her savings. But how would he live after that?

The only asset he had, other than his mother's interest in the mill, was a tract of land at the base of Crawford Notch, where his Amory grandfather had obtained a grant on a thousand acres of prime timber in 1800.

Grandpa Amory had planned to cut trees and run them down the Saco. But in its upper reaches, the Saco was a typical White Mountain river, nothing but a boulder-studded slope where big logs hung up every fifty feet. An impossible sluiceway. So the Amory tract had been left standing, growing taller and more valuable by the year.

Now there was talk of running railroads into the White Mountains. And while George still dreamed of wandering the Tuileries Gardens or the Roman Forum, war had made him practical. It might be time to learn how to exploit his New Hampshire tract. What better way would there be than to learn the timber business from the ground up?

And he had another reason for heading to Turlock's camp in the Penobscot wilderness: its name. *John C. Caldwell Camp # 6.*

AT THE END of September, George hitched a ride on an ox-drawn tote-wagon that was part of a supply train heading out of Bangor.

They followed roads north across marshes where the swamp maple flared red and went bare all in a day. They climbed hills still covered in color and evergreen. They crossed logged-out expanses where the stumps stretched to the horizon and not a weed grew tall enough to wave in the breeze.

But always they moved along rivers that led deeper into the wilderness. Some said that the story of New England was the story of the sea. But rivers told the tale, too, in the south, where New Englanders made things, and in the north, where they cut things.

George got to Camp #6 on a day so warm and bright that only the gloomiest of men would think about winter. Boss Enos Turlock was not among that species, but he stood in the middle of a clearing carved from those endless woods and shouted at everyone about everything. He kept a dozen men working their axes, notching logs, stacking them, and building shelters, because they all knew that winter would come, no matter the kindness of September, and it would come first to the north country.

"So," said Enos, when he spied George, "decided to do man's work, eh?"

If George had been a braggart, he might have said that he had come to see what there was that could toughen him more than war. Instead, he climbed down, shook his old sergeant's hand, and looked around. "I thought you cut trees."

"Put roofs over our heads first. *Then* we cut trees." Enos swung a hand toward the hills. "Come spring, all this timber'll be stacked by the streams, stacked on the rivers, stacked every damn place we can get it to water. Then we'll sluice it all down to Bangor, make lumber for houses, paper for books, staves for beer barrels, too. How's the foot?"

"Hurts like hell. How's the hip."

Enos lowered his voice. "If it hurts, I ain't sayin'."

So began George Amory's education in the great north woods: *Don't complain. Don't explain. Just do.*

"Once the cuttin' starts, you'll be sled-tender to them fellers"—Enos gestured to two men notching logs—"Hec Burns and Frenchy LaPointe."

Hec and Frenchy, first chopper and second: wiry, leathered, close-eyed little men who swung their axes with a rhythm that seemed almost musical.

"They've worked together so long, they look alike. Only way to tell 'em apart, Hec wears a red flannel shirt. Frenchy wears whatever his Frenchy wife packed."

"Oui," said Frenchy. "You will see many colors on me, so you know I change my shirt, eh? Hec, he don't change nothin' all winter long."

Hec spat tobacco juice and kept swinging his ax.

Enos said, "Frenchy's from Quebec. Talks a lot."

"I talk a lot," said Frenchy. "Hec, he don't talk at all."

As if to give Frenchy the lie, Hec grunted. "Feller's got city hands. Can he swing an ax?"

"He swung a sword at Fredericksburg," said Enos.

"Swingin' a sword don't mean he can swing anything else." Hec glanced at George from under his hat brim. "You know the first rule of loggin'?"

"Never touch another man's ax," said George.

Hec nodded and kept chopping. "You got an ax?"

George shook his head.

"Give him a hammer," Hec told Frenchy. "Put him to work on the plank floor."

> *Dear Cordelia:*
>
> *I am in receipt of your letter of 17th last. I envy your stay in France, a nation that, as you wrote, "has a democracy born after our own, and yet has had several constitutions to our one." I can agree, for I know more about the genesis of our Constitution than most men.*
>
> *Your letters may reach me here, at Caldwell Camp #6, until spring. Bad foot and all, I am now a logger. By day, I work in the big woods, rain or snow, unseasonably warm or cold enough to freeze your breath. By night, I sleep on a board-bunk with forty other men in a log bunkhouse called, for reasons that escape me, a ram pasture. I arrived earlier than most so my bunk is closer to the stove, and it is on the bottom. That is good because our diet consists mainly of pork and beans. My friend Frenchy warned me to seek a lower bunk "because the air is better there."*
>
> *How I got here from the Pike Mill need not trouble you. However, were this not Caldwell Camp #6, I would have found something less strenuous to do. Caldwell is a common enough name, but the people of northern New England are a close-bred lot, so these Caldwells might be related to the land grabber of my grandfather's tall tales.*
>
> *I have come to agree with you that finding a certain document, with the thoughts of certain New Englanders set down upon it, might be a boon to the country in our present Constitutional crisis, a boon to my reputation as well. More important, if finding it is a way to earn back your love . . .*

He scratched out that last sentence, found another piece of paper, and rewrote the letter, ending with no more than best wishes.

THE MONTHS WENT by, the snow fell as fast as the temperature, and the trees fell, too. Camp #6 ran so well under Enos Turlock that Big Jack

Caldwell never came near. But whenever George and Enos talked about Big Jack, Enos always said—or threatened—that Big Jack would come round eventually.

"When?" asked George one bitter night, after the pork and beans had settled and the loggers had clustered near the stove to play cards and fart and dry their damp socks. "When do you think we'll see him?"

"If he don't come ridin' in someday on a tote-sled, he'll be here for certain when we run the logs come spring."

"Is he a logger or a riverman?" asked George.

Frenchy looked up from the sock he was darning. "Some men is loggers and some is river rats. But that Big Jack, he been both since his Gran'père buy these woods. He drop a tree faster than Hec, and he break up logjams with his bare hands."

"He uses a peavey." Hec was sitting on the other side of the stove, spitting tobacco against the hot iron, making it sizzle. "Like any man."

"Bare hands or peavey," said Enos, "there's none better in the woods or on the river."

"What was his Gran'père's name?" asked George.

"Same name, front and back," said Enos. "Caldwell."

"Big Jack's a man I'd like to talk to," said George.

Enos chuckled. "Big Jack ain't much for talkin' to the men, 'less he's goddamnin' 'em."

"Oui," said Frenchy. "He shout so loud, he give out so many goddamns, he make Boss Turlock here sound like an ol' woman."

"Eh-yeh," said Turlock. "Need to do somethin' stand-out for him to talk to you."

EVERY DAY, EIGHT cutting crews left Caldwell Camp #6 and went to work.

Under their axes, anything with a trunk and a ten-inch diameter came down, spruce mostly, white pine too, more valuable but growing scarce, and white birch that was taken for those two marvels of modern invention, the clothespin and the match. They did not cut other hardwood, because it did not float. So maple and beech were safe, yellow birch too, unless they got in the way.

In woods where no man-made sound had ever been heard, the axes bit bark and rang and echoed like churchbells through the shocked silence.

By the middle of winter, the landscape in that small fiefdom in the realm of the Caldwell Grant had become a patchwork of cut over acres and untouched remnants, overlain by a filigree of ice-covered tote roads that followed the contours of the land like lines on a topographical map, winding their way downhill—always downhill—to the places where water waited, water in the form of ice, water sleeping in the streams that would soon begin to run toward the rivers that always ran to the sea.

Every crew had two choppers, a sled-tender, and a set of teamsters. The choppers cut the trees. The tenders cleared the brush and snubbed the logs down to the two-sleds. The teamsters loaded the sleds and hauled the logs down the drag roads.

It was hard work, and it was dangerous. Just how dangerous came clear to George Amory on an afternoon in early February.

The snow was deep, the air so cold that the snot would freeze on the tip of a man's nose if he didn't wipe it off with his sleeve.

Still, the choppers wore no more than their woolen shirts and gloves. Too much clothing just slowed them down. And what the choppers did, George did. He also did whatever he was told and didn't say more than he had to. He knew the men talked about him some, but he gave none of them reason to say a bad word about his work.

The crew had moved down from a stripped-off height of land, down into a grove of white pine on the south side of a granite outcropping. Here the trees had been so well protected from the wind that they had grown to two hundred feet.

"Good lumber here," said Hec.

"Seems a shame." George looked up into the high canopy.

"It's what we do," said Hec.

"But these are the biggest trees yet," said George. "Like a roof of pines."

"A cathedral of pines, eh?" said Frenchy. "Like Sainte-Anne de Beaupré, maybe."

"It's what we do," said Hec again. Then he walked over to the biggest tree, inspected the trunk, the trees around it, the lay of the land, and said, "We'll start here."

As soon as Hec and Frenchy were swinging in the peculiar rhythm that was so familiar now to George, he began to clear some of the understory. He had worked with these two long enough to know that the first tree dropped would mark the sled path. So he began to envision a route down the hillside to the dragging road.

He turned to say something and a curse caught in his throat.

They called them widow-makers, those limbs that dropped silently from somewhere in the canopy. This one was covered in green needles but as rotten as a mummy inside. With a whoosh that none of them heard above the ringing of the axes, it plummeted through the branches, struck Hec Burns, and killed him where he stood.

THAT NIGHT, THEY passed the hat and told stories of old Hec, while he froze solid beneath a canvas out by the cook shed.

The contents of the hat would go to Hec's widow, a stern-faced woman who peered out from a *carte de visite* tacked to a log beside Hec's bunk. The crew would go back to work the next day with a new first chopper.

"Bad luck, eh?" said Pierre LeBrun, dropping money into the hat.

"Mal chance, oui." Frenchy sniffled and drew a sleeve across his face.

"Bad luck? Mal chance?" growled a big teamster named Beale. "Ain't no such thing. I say there's a Jonah in this here camp."

"A Jonah?" said Enos. "In a loggin' camp? Jonah's are on boats."

"I *been* on boats," said the teamster. "I fished the Grand Banks out of Portland. I know fellers who used to fish, who stump 'round now on one leg they got at Fredericksburg, fellers who tell stories about a officer who shot himself in his own foot. And I say—"

Enos got to his feet, "Listen, you big son of a bitch—"

"Stand down, Sergeant," said George in a low voice, and Enos fell silent.

George fixed his eyes on the teamster, put his foot on the bench between them, and pulled off his boot, then his outer sock—heavy gray wool with a red stripe around the top. Beneath was another wool sock, gray, and finally a white cotton sock that he had changed two weeks before, which made it one of the cleanest socks in the camp.

As he drew it down, the men drew closer, like doctors in an operating theater, fascinated to see how a gunshot foot might heal. They were hard men, those loggers. They stitched their own chilblains together with needles and thread. They dosed themselves with swallows of kerosene to keep away the grippe. None of them would flinch if an ax glanced off a frozen log and cut clean through a boot and into a leg. No surprise that the most any of them said about the mangled foot was that he'd seen worse.

But a deeper sound ran through them, almost as if they could not control it, a murmur . . . of something? Awe? Contempt for a coward? George could not tell.

He wiggled the big toe and the little one. Everything in between was gone, and the flesh where the toes had once connected was scar-tissue white.

George stood—one shoe on, one shoe off—and fixed his gaze on that big teamster. "I slipped in a puddle of blood. My gun went off in my hand.

That's the truth. So . . . if you want to call me a coward, go ahead, but it means you're callin' me a liar, too. I might stand for one or the other, but not both."

The teamster started to say something but he stopped because—

George pulled two new-hewn ax handles from a box in the corner and held them out. "We can fight with these, in here or out in the snow."

The teamster looked at the handles, but he did not move to take one.

George said, "You're big enough to pound me to pieces, but I'll make sure I break your hands, so you can't grip the reins. You want that?"

And a voice growled, "There'll be no heft-fightin' in any camp of mine."

Heads turned toward the dingle, the little door to the cookhouse.

And there stood Big Jack Caldwell. He could be no one else, since "big" was the only adjective that applied. Big frame, big belly, big head, and big bearskin hat. His weight made the boards creak as he came across the floor.

The icicles dripped from his mustache. His eyes traveled from George's knit cap to his mangled foot. He said, "I heard about you."

George lowered the ax handles. "I heard about you, too."

"Well if you heard that I'm the best man in these woods with ax or peavey, you heard right." Big Jack stepped closer to George. "I ain't heard so good about you."

Enos said, "Now, boss—"

"Quiet." Big Jack swung his head around at the circle of men. "You all know me. You know I don't believe anything 'bout a man till he give me reason. If there's any here who say this young feller shirked his work or done bad to 'em, speak up. I'll take him with me in the mornin'. He can ride the tote wagon out with Hec's body."

Big Jack allowed his challenge to sit in the air for a moment. Then he looked at George. "Put your boot on, son." Then he turned to Enos. "I didn't come all the goddamn way up here to haul beans and break up fights. Show me your books."

Enos, who had acted with generals as if he were their equal in all but shoulder bars, hopped to like a greenhorn. He led Big Jack to the end of the bunkhouse, where a curtain separated his space from the rest of the crew, and they disappeared.

After a moment, the big teamster pulled a pint from his pocket and offered it to George. "I was wrong, I reckon. Like Enos says, can't be no Jonahs in a loggin' camp. Jonahs ride in boats and get swallowed by whales."

THE NEXT MORNING, as a light snow fell, they put Hec's body onto the
tote wagon, and Big Jack ordered them all to take off their hats and bow
their heads. Then he led them in the Lord's Prayer.

"All right," he said after the amens. "There's trees to cut. Get to
work."

But George stayed at the side of the wagon. "Mr. Caldwell."

Big Jack looked down, long jets of steam shooting from his nostrils.
"You try me, son. And I'm in a hurry. Got another camp to inspect."

"Could I talk with you?"

"About what?"

"Well . . . a story from your family's past."

"My family? I don't talk about my family with goddamn choppers nor
sled tenders, neither. And I don't talk about nothin' when there's snow
comin' down."

"But—"

Big Jack gave a nod to his teamster, who snapped the reins and the
horses kicked forward. Then he said over his shoulder. "Be here come
spring. Prove yourself. Then ask your questions."

SO GEORGE AMORY stayed, and he became second chopper to Frenchy.

And they cut trees. They cut through March, after the calendar and the
angle of the sun pronounced it spring but the snow lay deep and the nights
stayed old. They cut into April, until just before Easter, when there came an
afternoon that not only looked warm but felt warm, too. And the snow began to melt, and the streams began to rise, and the ringing of the axes was
replaced by thunder, the sound of log pyramids collapsing when the ice
beneath them melted into the rivers.

The cutting was done. Time for the drive to begin.

Soon enough, the Bangor Tigers strode into camp in their red shirts
and sashes and studded boots. There were other log-driving gangs, but
none so famous, and if you asked one of them, they would tell you that
there were none so good.

The loggers were paid off, but Big Jack Caldwell kept a small crew—
the cook and cookie and a few choppers who would clear space for the
wangan, the camp that would now move downstream with the drive.
Since Turlock chose the choppers, George and Frenchy stayed on.

For days, the logs came tumbling and rumbling and thundering down
the little streams. At some places, they were held back by rough sluice
dams and delivered one by one into the bigger waterways. At other places

they were let loose all at once and left to speed their way in an unstoppable wave to the next tributary. The rivers up here were narrow and twisting, but by May, they were all covered with floating logs, moving as fast as the current would carry them. And because the rivers did not stop when night fell, there were drivers who stayed with them, riding them by cold starlight, keeping them headed for the hungry sawmills of Bangor.

George did as he was told and waited for the moment that he could catch Big Jack at the wangan, drinking coffee or taking a bowl of beans.

But Big Jack seemed to be everywhere on the drive except at his ease. He could be heard bellowing his goddamns above the roar of the river. He could be seen leaping across the water with a peavey in his hands, moving as nimbly as a man half his age when the logs began to hang up on some underwater junk or a bend in the river.

"You see a jam," said Frenchy as they rode ahead on a warm morning, "don't do nothin'. Just watch Big Jack and them Tigers. Cause that river, it kill you fast."

So George watched. Sometimes, the Tigers balanced themselves on the spinning logs to do their work. Sometimes they rowed their light-weight bateaux into the middle of the churning, log-choked current to break up the jams. Sometimes, they just got themselves to the front, stood on one of the boom logs, and rode the river the way an engineer rode the rails.

A week into the drive, they approached a place called Dead Man's Bank.

Every river had a Dead Man's Bank, what the rivermen called a dirty spot, where the logs always hung up and often enough killed the man trying to unhang them.

Frenchy stopped the tote wagon beside a pair of studded boots nailed to a tree. Then he took off his hat and blessed himself.

"What's that?" asked George.

"Riverman drowns, they nail his boots to the nearest tree where he went under. Sometime, if you no find the body, them boots his only grave marker, eh."

The river here ran wide, straight, and fast, so logs were thundering mightily along, but as they hit the bend about a hundred yards down-stream, they were slowing, groaning, piling up on themselves.

"This gonna be a bad one." Frenchy snapped the reins and drove his team ahead to the place where the road curved and dropped down to the riverbank. And there was Big Jack, with two of the other Tigers, fighting to find the single log that had twisted itself out of alignment and caused this giant mess.

"You watch," said Frenchy. "A thousand logs, they know just which one to grab."

George jumped down and went to the edge of the water.

Big Jack was booming out his "goddamns" and "son-of-a-bitches" while he and the others dug their peaveys into the logs. Meanwhile a mountain of upstream wood was growing, like a volcano rising from some ancient landscape, driven by forces just as relentless.

"See that," said Frenchy, coming up beside him. "They found the key log, what I call the fucker log."

George watched them work like surgeons in the rising jumble. Big Jack was screaming, "You two pull the top! I'll pull the bottom."

They moved, they pushed, they pulled and tugged, until a single, log twisted up and out of the pile.

There then came a deep, resonating groan that seemed to catch the men by surprise, as if they had expected it, but not so soon. The groan rose into a thunderous roar and one of the Tigers screamed, "Look out!"

Another log broke loose and rocketed down at them, like a falling ice shelf that precedes an avalanche.

An instant later, that mountain of wood collapsed.

Big Jack Caldwell fell backward. One of the Tigers disappeared while the other was knocked over and sent rolling with a log under him and another on top of him.

Big Jack boomed out another "goddamn!"—his word for curses and prayers and praise, too—because the logs were moving underneath him, and he was rolling and floundering, unable to get back to his feet.

And that was the moment when George Amory became a riverman. He did not think. He did not study. He simply acted, leaping, then jumping, then running, then stumbling, then leaping again, log to log across thirty feet in a few seconds that unfolded as slowly as the four-hour wait at Fredericksburg.

He grabbed Big Jack's collar. And by some miracle of balance, ax-built strength, and luck, he pulled Big Jack from between two logs that were about to crush him. Then the log beneath George rolled and he fell back.

He smashed down on his side but held tight to Big Jack's collar.

The log was turning both of them, pulling them under, and another was rising up over the top of them. But he could hear someone shouting "Take it! Grab it!"

Frenchy was holding out a peavey to him, while Enos Turlock was snatching his collar on the hook-end of another. They both roared up all their strength, and the river suddenly heaved a great sigh of wood toward the bank, and George and Big Jack were saved.

"Goddamn!" Big Jack got to his feet with barely a flinch, though his left leg was bent above the boot. "My Tigers!"

"One got saved to the other bank," said Frenchy. "The other, he gone under."

"Goddamn!" Big Jack brought his hands to his hair. Then he turned to George. "Son, you done a goddamn fool thing. Could've been killed."'

"You, too," said George.

"I'm alive. But I broke my goddamn ankle."

BIG JACK SAID that if he couldn't ride the river, he'd go home and do a harder job: comforting a widow. And he'd see to his sawmills, too. So George was delegated to bring him back to Bangor, the "city that lumber built."

What a sight those Bangor sawmills were, scores of them cutting millions of board feet, sending clouds of sawdust swirling into the air above the river, which itself seemed to be made of wood for a miles, all the way back to the falls of the Penobscot.

"Now, then," said Big Jack once he had ensconced himself in his mill office a few days later. "You asked me about my family. I told you to ask me again in the spring." The floor vibrated from the rolling of the millwheel, and they talked with raised voices to be heard over the screaming of the saw blades in the room below.

"I don't mean your wife or children," said George. "Your grandfather."

"Why would you want to know about Caldwell P. Caldwell?"

George pulled up a chair next to the stool where Big Jack had his foot propped. And he told the story as his grandfather had told it to him, finishing with this: "I'd like to find that Constitution, and I think you might know about it, considering your ancestry."

Big Jack Caldwell gave out with a laugh that made his belly and beard shake and his bad leg, too. "You put yourself through a winter in my camp, just to ask me that?"

"I went to your camp to learn a lot of things and prove a few, too."

"Well, I learned that you might be a goddamn fool, but you're a bearcat for courage. No man who run out on that river would shoot himself in the foot. And no man who went up that Fredericksburg hill can be anything but a good goddamn Union man"—Big Jack gestured to a photo of Lincoln on the wall—"like me."

"So . . . do you have the Constitution?"

"'Fraid not. If any Caldwell does, it's my cousin Dawson." Big Jack almost spat the word. "One of the Vermont Caldwells."

"Vermont?"

"Eh-yeh. Plenty of good Union men in Vermont. But not my Caldwell cousins. Goddamn Copperheads. You know Copperheads?"

"A few." George thought of Professor Edwards, and of the Blackstone investors, worrying about their cotton supply. Copperheads would make peace with the South and get back to business rather than continue the war and pay its costs.

"A first draft of the Constitution, you say?" Big Jack stroked his beard. "With writin' on it about the birth of the government, you say?"

"That's what I've been told."

"Be a damn shame if it said things that put the lie to what we're fightin' for, to what Lincoln says about the Union bein' . . . what's the word?"

"Indissoluble," said George.

"Right," said Big Jack. "And what if it said that slavery was just fine?"

"A damn shame," said George.

"Goddamn Copperhead bastards might use that against Lincoln in the election."

"Where does your cousin live?" asked George.

"A town called St. Albans, last town in Vermont before you get to Canada. They say it's grown into a big railhead since the war started. Never liked the Vermont Caldwells. Not good dairy-farmin' Vermonters, nor quarrymen, nor men who actually *do* anything. Just money men. Speculators. Like Grandpa Caldwell."

"Would you write me a letter of introduction?"

Big Jack gave another laugh. "Wouldn't do no good. Just go, tell him you're lookin' to buy land in Vermont. Tell him you want to harvest timber and run it south on the railroad. He'll smell money. He'll talk."

BUT BEFORE ST. ALBANS . . .

George stayed another month to finish the drive, because he kept his promises.

Had Reverend Amory lived long enough to know of his son's dalliances in the mill, he might have found a lesson in George's brutal days at Camp #6: His time in the woods had been his atonement for sin, cleansing him and preparing him for whatever was coming next. His father had found many lessons in human suffering, but few to explain human joy. Perhaps because suffering was always waiting at the end.

In the last week of the log run, George received a letter from his mother. It mentioned that she had not been feeling well of late and had had a "bit of surgical work." He returned to Portland to find her propped in a chair, her head down, her graying hair askew, her whole attitude one of deflation, as if her essence were emptying out and her corporeal being were collapsing in on itself.

But when she looked at him, her eyes brightened. "Georgie! I thought you were going to Vermont."

"I got your letter. I decided to come home." George knelt and took her hand.

She said, "How's that nice girl? That Ophelia, from Brunswick?"

"Cordelia. She's in Europe. But, what's—"

"A cancer. In the breast. Doc Withers says he got all the lumps."

"Does it hurt?"

"Not more than I can bear." She reached out to touch his hair, but the pain on that side seemed too much for her. She lowered her hand and said, "It's grand to see you."

George lowered his head to her lap and let her stroke his curls.

On an October afternoon, Cordelia Edwards wrote a letter:

Dear George: Thank you for your letter of the 3d instant. I am back from Europe near a month, first visiting the Massachusetts troops near Washington, now at my father's Brunswick house. I send my condolences at your mother's death. Had we but known, my father and I would have come with all speed to Portland to comfort you in your time of bereavement.

It is well that you have found something to occupy yourself, now that your mother has passed. The search for your personal grail would seem just the thing. I applaud you and urge you on, for it is the nation's grail, too.

I wait avidly for news of your success. And yes, you may bring it to show us when you find it. Visit even if you do not find it. Perhaps my husband will be here to meet you.

She scratched out that last sentence, then rewrote the letter without it. Some things were better said in person.

Just then, Professor Aaron came into the room, the newspaper in his hand and a solemn look on his face. "My dear, news from the South . . . the Twentieth Massachusetts—"

Cordelia's thoughts left the young man who had always loved her and went to the young man she had married in a burst of wartime passion.

SIXTEEN

⁊ "PLEASE, WILL YOU TELL YOUR DAUGHTER of my quest. I go in search of my personal grail, as I promised her. And in this election year, it may become the national grail. . . ."

"Wow," said Evangeline. "In a letter from George Amory to Aaron Edwards?"

"That's what it says," answered Antoine.

"'The national grail,'" said Peter. "The *Holy* Grail."

"Holy shit," said Evangeline.

It was seven o'clock in the morning. They were driving north along the Housatonic River, which flowed from the Berkshires of Massachusetts into the Litchfield Hills. And they were talking to the office with the cell phone on walkie-talkie.

"Where did you find the letter?" Evangeline asked.

Antoine was on the other end. "Bowdoin College Web site. A link to their rare book department. They're promoting a digitizing project. They use the letter as an example."

"Or as bait," said Peter.

"Bait?" said Evangeline. "It's a college library."

"I don't think it's a coincidence," asked Peter.

"If it's bait, are you biting?" asked Antoine.

"What else is on the Web site?"

"It says the letter is from the Edwards papers. Aaron Edwards was a professor who graduated in the famous Class of 1825, along with Hawthorne and Longfellow. He knew a lot of the big names who passed through Bowdoin in the era—Franklin Pierce, Harriet Beecher Stowe, Joshua Lawrence Chamberlain. . . ."

"Quite a bunch," said Peter. "What else does it say?"

"'The digitizing of the Edwards papers—letters, diaries, and ephemera—will provide insight into college life during the mid-nineteenth century. For the time being, however, this extraordinary trove of information must be viewed in person, except for a diary page, reproduced here below."

"And?" said Peter. "The diary page. What does it say?"

" 'Sunday, November 14, 1861: Dinner this afternoon: President Woods, Professor Smithson, the Chamberlains, and the Stowes, which was an honor. Cordelia invited George Amory, who proved amiable enough when keeping to mundane conversation. Then he sought attention with a fantastical tale of his grandfather, demonstrative of his flighty personality. . . .' Then the page ends."

Peter and Evangeline looked at each other and said, "Bowdoin."

THEY DROVE OVER four hours that morning, from the inland hills to the cold water coast, through a dozen microclimates, and they barely saw a cloud. When the October weather was good, it was very good: cool nights, low humidity, and bright blue days warming into the seventies. High pressure spread its wings across all six states.

By eleven o'clock, they were in Brunswick, Maine, where the Androscoggin River reached Casco Bay.

Once men had built ships in the river and run mills at the powerful falls. Now Brunswick was a commuter town for Portland. And it had been a college town since the founding of Bowdoin in 1799. The working part of the town was joined to the college by a tree-lined stretch called Park Row, which rose toward a statue of Joshua Lawrence Chamberlain, who stood like a sentinel at the entrance to the campus.

"One of the giants." Peter gazed up at the Union hero.

"He looks like he's staring off toward Freeport," cracked Evangeline, "to see if there are any sales at L.L. Bean."

"Don't be irreverent."

"I hear a lecture coming on."

"When you stand on this spot, in this out-of-the-way Maine town, you stand between the alpha and omega of the Civil War."

"If this is good, it's going into an article."

He pointed to the north side of the street. "There's the First Parish Church, a handsome example of Carpenter's Gothic—"

"—which means they didn't have stone so they called in the carpenters and built it of wood."

Then he pointed to the south side. "There's a Cape Cod–style house expanded into a Victorian with arched windows and high ceilings—"

"Carpenter's Gothic on one side, American Gothic on the other. So?"

"In that church, Harriet Beecher Stowe was inspired to write *Uncle Tom's Cabin*. When Lincoln met her later, he said, 'So you're the little woman who wrote the book that started this big war.'"

"And the house?"

"After service at Fredericksburg, Gettysburg, Petersburg, and a lot of other burgs, Chamberlain had the honor of carrying the flag at the end of the last parade of the Grand Army of the Republic. He was the last man to march past the reviewing stand in Washington. Then he came home and moved back into that house."

She thought a moment and said, "That is the most interesting bit of useless information you've ever told me."

"In this line of work, nothing is useless. You stand in places like this and try to hear the ghosts. Sometimes they tell you about their friends. And sometimes their friends lead you to what you're looking for."

"And why would you wish to see the Edwards papers?" asked the librarian, a slight woman in owlish glasses and pageboy haircut. The name tag on her sweater said REBECCA SOLOMONT.

The archives were in the Hawthorne-Longfellow Library, a modern building on the east edge of the campus, a discreet distance from Bowdoin's ancient brick and granite.

Peter said, "I'm researching the relationship of Professor Edwards and Joshua Lawrence Chamberlain."

"Are you a writer?" Mrs. Solomont smiled, as though she were making conversation.

Peter knew that her question was meant to be more pointed. "No."

"A genealogist, then."

"Sort of."

"Well, Mr.—" She looked down at the call slip. "—Fallon. These papers are very fragile. If you have some scholarly purpose, we're happy to let you see them, but—"

"I don't need to see the originals. Are they on microfilm?"

"No. We hope to digitize them after our next fund-raising drive."

"I'll contribute"—Peter tried to keep the impatience out of his voice—"if you'll just go and get them."

"This is a library," said Mrs. Solomont, still smiling. "Please keep your voice down. Just tell me what you're looking for, and I might be able to help you."

"He's sorry," said Evangeline. "Are the documents indexed?"

"What names would you be looking for?"

"Aaron Edwards, Cordelia Edwards, Joshua Lawrence Chamberlain, George Amory."

Mrs. Solomont's expression did not change as Evangeline spoke. "Edwards." *Smile.* "Cordelia." *Smile.* "Chamberlain." *Still a smile.* But "George Amory" made the smile flicker. The face powder at the corners of the mouth cracked. The eyes narrowed behind the glasses. Mrs. Solomont said, "You saw the material on our Web site?"

"We're very interested," said Peter innocently.

Mrs. Solomont excused herself, retreated to her office, and picked up the phone. A moment later, she was back. "Mr. Fallon, phone call for you."

"For me?" Peter looked at Evangeline and mouthed the word. "Bait." Then he stepped into the inner office, took the receiver. "Hello."

A deep voice rumbled. "Mr. Fallon?"

"Who is this?" asked Peter.

"An admirer."

"Another one?"

The voice laughed, low and easy. "They *said* you were a smart-ass."

"Whoever *they* are. I'm busy here at the Bowdoin Library, but . . . you knew that, whoever *you* are." Fallon gave Mrs. Solomont a glance.

She was sitting down at her desk, pretending to check her e-mails.

"We need to talk," said the voice.

"So talk."

"Face-to-face. About Professor Edwards. I asked Mrs. Solomont to post a bit from his diary, just to see who might be looking. Draw you out of the woodwork, so to speak."

"Bait," said Peter.

"Perhaps. So nibble on this: 'Saturday, September 12, 1861: George Amory seems altogether too interested in Cordelia, too much the bright-eyed boy in a world where a man of stature guarantees a young woman's future. Young love is fine, but a life of reliable solidity is what she needs. Pity that Chamberlain is married.'"

"Are you reading this, or making it up?" asked Peter.

"I've memorized it. Here's more from Sunday, November 14, 1861. The page reproduced on the Web site, about the dinner. It goes on: 'Imagine, a first draft of the Constitution, annotated with insights into the Bill of Rights and the meaning of slavery, as if it were something to answer our questions in a vexatious time.'" After a long pause, the voice said, "Now do I have your attention?"

"Who *are* you?"

Mrs. Solomont looked up from her computer. "He's Carter Trask,

Bowdoin alumnus, retired judge, member of the Federalist Society, the NRA, and a man of principle."

The voice on the phone said, "Mrs. Solomont will give you directions."

ABOUT TWO HOURS later, the BMW bounced to a stop on a rutted road in the deep pine woods northwest of Bangor. A small sign—hand-carved, brown with golden letters—hung by the side of the road: ALGON-QUIN ROD AND GUN CLUB. MEMBERS ONLY.

"Not too friendly," said Evangeline.

"Relax. We'll meet the judge, squeeze off a few rounds, bond over buckshot."

"Then what?"

"He tells us where the Constitution is or threatens to kill us if we *don't* tell *him*."

"And I was thinking this might be dangerous."

The gravel road soon turned to dirt and the ruts deepened into pot-holes. The woods pressed in on either side—thick, piney, second growth, logged-over land that had been recovering for a century or more.

"Peter, it feels like we've been going forever."

"Two miles. That's what the directions said."

She flipped open her phone. "At least we've got cell coverage."

After about a mile and a half, they saw the American flag fluttering above the trees and just beneath it, a black MIA flag from the Vietnam era.

An all-terrain four-wheeler burst from the streambed on the right side of the road and screeched to a stop in front of the BMW.

A big guy in camo was riding. He had a tattoo on his neck, an AR-15 strapped to the back of the ATV, a .44 Magnum at his hip. "This is private property."

Peter powered down the window. "We're here to see Judge Trask."

"He invite you?"

"Yes, he did."

"What's your name?"

Peter resisted the impulse to ask, "What business it of yours?" That was not something you said to a heavily armed man wearing camo.

The guy gave a jerk of his head, then shot up the road.

They ate his ATV dust until they pulled into a clearing. In the center was a big log cabin beneath those fluttering flags.

There were a few cars, Jeeps, and pickups parked out front.

Three guys in combat fatigues were walking off into the woods to the left. Naturally, they checked out the newcomers.

The guy on the ATV said, "The judge is probably inside. If he isn't, don't go wanderin' off. You're liable to get yourself shot."

"Thanks." Peter pulled on his Red Sox cap.

"Nice touch," whispered Evangeline. "But the letters NRA would get you further than the Boston B."

"The Red Sox open doors in all six states."

The sound of gunfire played in the woods like a strange symphony. Off to the left, a steady *bupbupbupbup* of a semiautomatic rifle. Closer by, at another target range, the counterpointing *pop-pop-pop-pop* of pistols. And every so often, like percussion, the blast of a shotgun.

"What are they all shooting at?" asked Evangeline.

"Paper targets, clay pigeons, Democrats."

"Mr. Fallon!" The big voice boomed out of the cabin, and the judge emerged. He was short, stocky, with a fringe of gray hair, and more presence than a movie star. He also carried a flintlock rifle. "I'm Carter A. Trask, Aroostook County District Court, Retired. He strode down the flagstone walk and offered his hand. "Thank you for coming."

"Nice weapon." Peter gestured to the flintlock.

The judge held it out. "I was showing it to one of the other members. One of the most important guns in American history."

"Pennsylvania long rifle, isn't it?" asked Peter.

"Very good. Hard weapon to load, but accurate to five hundred yards. Scourge of the king bird in 1775. We might not have won our independence without it."

"And you intend to preserve our independence with it?" asked Evangeline.

"Some people think we're just gun nuts, but we're historians, too. This is a reproduction. I built this weapon myself. And I believe in the principles behind it."

Somewhere in the woods, a tremendous volley of semi-automatic fire shattered the air and sent birds skittering. Evangeline jumped along with the birds.

"Sorry," said the judge. "Truth is, it's quiet here right now. A lot of members are out hunting. It's bear season. Silly season, too, when some politician declares open season on the Constitution."

Then he led them up the walk and into the clubhouse.

A woodstove sat in the middle of the room, as if this were an old-time logger's bunkhouse. But this place had a cathedral ceiling, skylights, polished log walls, and a long bar.

"We built it ourselves," said the judge. "Water from a well, electricity from a generator, ball games from a satellite."

"Sunday night, first game of the World Series," said Peter.

"I'll be in Boston," said the judge. "The Bishop Media box."

"You, too?" said Peter.

"Charlie Bishop's a distant cousin," said the judge. "He wants us to reason together."

"The liberal from Connecticut and the rock-ribbed Republican from Maine," said Peter.

"And the document detective from Boston." Judge Trask gave Fallon a wink.

A few heads turned as they crossed the room. Three guys were playing cards at a table beneath a skylight. Two more in camo were drinking at the bar.

The judge said to Peter. "Club rule: No alcohol till you're done shooting. Would you like a beer?"

"I have a long drive."

"Then some coffee." The judge held up three fingers to the bartender.

There was a bulletin board by the door: announcements of target contests and tournaments, bake sales for the local church, game nights, the NRA poster of Harriet Holden an enemy of freedom, and a flyer from some gun-owners' pressure group, showing Ted Kennedy, John Kerry, Chuck Schumer, and Nancy Pelosi at a cocktail party, all having a fine old laugh. The caption: "These people want your guns."

Evangeline stopped to study it all; then she followed Peter and the judge to a table in the corner and slapped a flyer down. "Is this how you see the loyal opposition?"

Peter gestured to her. *Cool it.*

The bartender brought over three cups of coffee in heavy mugs. The judge kept his eyes on Evangeline. "When people think about gun owners, they remember Charlton Heston holding up a rifle and shouting, 'From my cold dead hands.'"

"How can we forget?" asked Evangeline.

"But do we remember that the next head of the NRA was a woman?" he went on. "A *Jewish* woman?"

Evangeline shrugged. "There are plenty of deluded women out there, too."

"So, Judge"—Peter tried to get back to business before they got thrown out—"why did you want us to come all the way up here?"

"To show you the grass roots, some right-thinking Americans"—the judge shot a glance at Evangeline—"by which I mean *correct* thinking Americans, who believe that the Constitution and the Bill of Rights mean what they say."

"I believe that, too," said Peter.

"So why are you nosing around?" It was ATV man, coming toward them.

"Private conversation here, Mercer," snapped the judge.

Peter noticed that the tattoo on Mercer's neck matched the logo on the MIA flag—a man with a bowed head, barbed wire behind him. The wire wound all the way around his neck. He looked about thirty-five, too young for Vietnam, just old enough for Gulf I. He had a two-day stubble on his face, stringy hair, the bulk of a guy who spent his days lifting heavy objects and his nights lifting beer cans.

"Get over here and ante," growled one of the card players, who did not turn around but let his voice make all the impression.

Mercer ignored him and looked down at Peter. A drop of sweat plopped onto the flyer from somewhere on his face. "No politician takes my guns."

A poker chip clattered. "There," came that voice. "I ante'd for you."

Mercer glanced at the other table, then said to the judge, "I don't know why you're invitin' media snoops up here. Keep them in Massachusetts. Let them leave us the fuck alone."

"Mercer!" The man at the other table stood now, turned, walked toward them. He was as tall as Mercer but rail thin, in his forties, wearing shirt and tie as if he had just come from a desk job. A shaft from the skylight lit his face, revealing the wrinkled white flesh of an old burn, a scar running from his collar to his hairline. His "Afternoon, folks" was only a bit warmer than his appearance.

"This is Jack Batter," said the judge. "Damn fine lawyer and a crack shot."

"Forgive Mercer here," said Batter, "but this Second Amendment business has us all a bit jumpy. We're in for a fight."

"We're going to win," said Mercer. "No matter what they write in Boston."

"If the repeal amendment makes it out of committee," said Batter, "we'll fight it in Congress. If it gets out of Washington, we'll fight it in the Maine legislature and every other state house in the country."

"These people may be here to help," said the judge.

"Help?" Batter's smile lifted the right side of his face but not the scarred left.

"With Massachusetts plates?" said Mercer. "I don't believe it."

One of the other guys shouted across the room, "These cards are gettin' cold."

Batter turned to Mercer. "If they're here to help, let them be."

The judge watched them go back to their game.

"So," said Peter. "What do they play? Texas Hold 'Em?"

"Mainiac Bluff," said the judge.

"Never heard of it," said Peter.

Evangeline said, "It's what we've been getting since we got here."

"Good bluffers in Maine," said the judge. "Straight-faced. Laconic. Like they write about." He leaned a little closer, lowered his voice. "So don't try to bluff me when I ask a simple question: What do you know?"

"About what?"

"They say you're the best document sleuth around. And you're the first one to find his way to the Aaron Edwards papers, which tells me a lot. What drew you to them?"

Peter looked around, as if to say that the walls might not have ears but the guys at the bar certainly did.

So the judge stood and said, "Come with me."

"PULL!"

A clay disc shot into the air and slashed across the sky. There was a blast from the judge's Savage 12-gauge and the clay pigeon evaporated.

"Nice shot," said Peter. He was wearing orange safety glasses and ear protection.

"No one will listen to us out here." The judge handed him the gun. "Let's see what you can do."

Peter took it, aimed, called, and *blast*. A spray of buckshot flew, but the clay disc kept spinning off into the trees.

"It's been a while." Peter handed the judge back the gun.

"Don't apologize," said Evangeline.

"Would you like to try?' asked the judge.

"Try what?" she said. "Shoot?"

The judge smiled. "The best way to achieve empathy with a man is to walk a mile in his shoes or in this case, sight down his barrel."

"Why judge . . . sight down your barrel? What's a girl to say?"

And Peter noticed a change in her. She took the gun from the judge, slipped three shells from his shooting vest and loaded them as though she had done it a hundred times. Then she said, "You know what we're looking for, Judge. You know more about it than we do."

The judge said, "Pull!"

The clay disc shot into the air.

Evangeline blew it to powder. She flicked her hair, gave Peter a look, then asked the judge. "So? Am I right?"

"My middle name is Amory," he said. "I had a great-uncle who knew the story. Gilbert Amory. Of course, no one listened to him. No one cared back when. *Pull!*"

Another disc. Another shot. Another hit.

Peter whistled softly.

"My ex-husband liked to shoot," she said. "He taught me."

"Not a good move, teaching your wife how to handle a shotgun," said Peter, "even if you're as faithful as a swan."

"Which he wasn't," she said.

"Pull!" shouted the judge.

Blast.

A third shell ejected and lay smoking on the ground. A third hit. Evangeline flipped the gun back to the judge. "I believe that the first clause of the Second Amendment—'A well-regulated militia, being necessary to the security of a free state'—gives us the right to make rational adjustments to the second clause—'the right of the people to keep and bear arms, shall not be infringed.'"

The judge shouldered the shotgun. "I've spent years upholding the most rational collection of laws ever devised, the Constitution and the Bill of Rights. And I've been trying to find this document since I first found hard evidence of the family legends."

"When was that?"

"When I retired from the bench, two years ago. I took up a sedentary hobby, for when it's too cold to be outside shooting. Genealogy. I was researching my great-grandfather. He'd been mustered out of the Twentieth Maine after being shot in the foot. There was always a hint that he did it to himself. Studying him led me to the Edwards diary."

"And you've been digging ever since?"

"No . . . only since the repeal movement began. We can argue over that 'militia' clause forever. But an annotated first draft may tell us something we should know."

"For starters," said Peter, "*you* should know that I've been hired by Harriet Holden."

"Can we hire you away?"

"What makes you think we'll find it if you haven't in two years?" asked Peter.

"You're a professional. Most lawyers—and judges are just lawyers who knew politicians—most lawyers pretend to know everything about everything, and even if they don't, they always have an opinion."

"Often wrong but never in doubt," said Evangeline. "I've dated lawyers."

"But one of the merits of getting older is coming to understand how little you know," the judge went on. "You're the best document hunter around, and you're looking for that Constitution. I'm willing to give you my research."

"Why?"

"If the men who left their scratchings on the draft say that the Second Amendment means something less than I think it does, I'll reconsider. But I'm willing to gamble that they were on my side."

"On your side or not, their handiwork will be worth a fortune," said Peter.

"True." The judge opened his gun case—foam lining inside, shiny aluminum outside. He pulled out a manila envelope bursting with papers— copies of handwritten letters, diary pages, newspaper articles. "My research. If you find the draft, I'll expect you to make an assessment of how this material has helped you and what it's worth to you. If you cheat me, I'll sue you. And trust me. *I'm* a professional at that."

"But a real lawyer would insist on a contract," said Peter.

The judge put out his hand. "There's my contract. See you in Boston."

"*THAT WAS A* New Englander." Peter started down the road. "Salt of the earth."

"Don't look now," said Evangeline, "but here comes 'salt in the wounds.'"

Two ATVs were popping up from a gully to their right.

Two more were emerging from the stream bed to their left.

Mercer was driving one. The guys driving the others looked like him, just a bit scrawnier, a bit dirtier.

"How far are we from the main road?" asked Evangeline.

"Not far enough."

Evangeline pulled out her phone. "Did you write down the judge's cell number?"

Peter flipped her a little spiral notebook. "It's in the back."

The ATVs were bouncing over fallen logs, closing on the BMW like wolves around a moose.

"Peter, there are numbers here, but no names. Which is the judge's?"

"Uh . . . bottom one." He swerved to avoid a big pothole and bounced into a bigger one.

The phone flew out of Evangeline's hands. It almost flew out the open sunroof.

"Jesus, Peter. Watch it." She picked up the phone, switched it to walkie-talkie, punched in a series of numbers.

The ATVs on the right had now burst over a little embankment. The ones on the left were growling over the stream bed and rising up from below.

The phone rang, a voice crackled: "Bowdoin College. Rare books."

"Goddamn it." Evangeline disconnected. "Peter, when you write down a phone number, write down a name."

"Try the next Maine area code."

Mercer pulled in front of them and began to slow. The other ATVs closed in on either side. One of them dropped to the rear, boxing him in. A perfect takedown.

"Judge Trask," said the voice on phone.

"Judge," said Evangeline, "we're down the road. We need help. It's Mercer."

"I'll be right there," said the judge.

Mercer waved his arm for Peter to stop. Then he got off his ATV and walked over to the driver's side.

Peter didn't roll down the window, but Mercer was big enough that he could lean his face in the sunroof.

"The judge is coming down the road right now." Evangeline began to fumble in her purse. "And I have Mace."

"Oh yeah?" Mercer laughed and blew hot beery air down on their heads, then he slapped his hip. "I have a .44 Magnum, most powerful handgun in the world—"

Peter looked at Evangeline. "Now he thinks he's Dirty Harry."

"He's half right," she said.

"What does she mean?" said Mercer.

"Half of Dirty Harry means you're just . . . dirty."

As if he were smacking a little sister, Mercer reached in and whacked Evangeline on the top of the head. "You shut the fuck up, lady, or you'll—"

And Peter had enough. Fight or flight. No room for flight. And the Magnum was not yet out of the holster, so fight. Plain and simple.

He shot his fist straight up, right into Mercer's nose.

Then he opened his door, slamming it into Mercer's belly and throwing him over one of the ATVs.

But the other two on that side were coming at him.

They were both street brawlers. So was Peter. Every kid who grew up in Southie was a brawler, even if he ended up at Harvard.

So Peter ducked the first punch from the left, and drove his hand straight into the guy's beer gut, knocking the air out of him for moment and the fight out of him for a few moments more.

The other guy had his fists high, so Peter slammed an elbow up under his chin and sent him staggering.

And now the fourth was scrambling over the hood. Peter turned to face him and heard a snort from behind. The beer gut had sucked in some air and some fight, too.

Peter decided he should have stayed in the car. He had hit three of them with his best shots, and they were still coming. So . . . *hold on till the cavalry arrives.*

He turned and drove his fist into the big guy's nose.

At the same moment, he was struck from the side and slammed against the car. One guy hit him. Then the other. Then Mercer shouted, "Grab his arms. Pin him."

The one on Peter's right tried to do that, and Peter pushed him away.

The one on the other side swung at him, and Peter ducked him. At the same moment, Evangeline popped up through the roof and fired a jet of Mace into the guy's face. Then she turned it on Mercer and Maced him.

Both men screamed and went stumbling.

Mercer tripped over one of the ATVs and fell down into the stream.

And a burst of AR-15 fire tore into the sky. Then Batter was out of his Jeep.

And the judge was jumping out from the other side.

"You goddamned fools!" shouted Batter at the ATV boys. "You'll get us sued."

Mercer staggered up from the gully. "But you told us to—"

"I told you to see them off the property. That's all."

"Well, shit," said Mercer. "That's—"

"Mr. Fallon, we're sorry about this," said the judge. "Some of our members are more rambunctious than others. And—"

"He punched me first," said Mercer.

"That true?" Batter looked at Fallon.

Peter's lip was bleeding and his eyes were burning from the Mace. Friendly fire.

"Why don't you drive?" the judge said to Evangeline, and then in a lower voice, "Get going now, because these boys are bad tempered."

Evangeline kept her wisecracks to herself, pushed Peter into the passenger side, swung around the ATV, and sped down the road. In the rearview, she could see the judge shouting at the others. But none of them were following. That was good.

Once she reached the main road, she said, "Peter Fallon, you are a lot of trouble."

"When I get older, they'll call me feisty."

"*If* you get older." She drove for a mile or so and then said, "Remember what you told me the other day. This is business. Don't let your passions get in the way."

"It wasn't my passion. It was my temper. And it was stupid."

THEY DIDN'T DRIVE back to Boston.

They thought about heading to Portland to see Martin Bloom again, but they decided that could wait till morning.

Evangeline made for a guest house in Greenville, overlooking Moosehead Lake. The innkeepers—John and Mary Duggan, a retired New York stockbroker and his wife—greeted her like their daughter. She had written a piece about them in *New England Travel Magazine* and it had put them put them on the map.

Peter had only question: "Do you have an ice maker?"

"For your drinks?" asked John.

"For my fists."

Evangeline gave the Duggans a smile. "It's a long story."

The ice helped Peter's knuckles.

So did dinner overlooking the lake. The first course—a freshwater soupe de poisson, whitefish from the lake simmered in a light broth. Then, braised short ribs and root vegetables for him. Local sausage sauteed with kale and tossed with pasta for her. Chardonnay to start, a '96 Burgundy for the second course.

They were able to relax a bit, their location unknown to anyone. Of course, the beauty of the sunset reminded them that time was running out.

"Wednesday night," said Evangeline. "Four days left."

"Three, if we're aiming for the World Series. But what difference would it be if it was three weeks? Or three months?"

"Harriet Holden wants a big splash when the committee does its work."

"Big splash or small one," he said, "it won't make any difference."

"Then why drag us up to that armed camp?" she asked angrily. "Why make agreements with Charles Bishop, Judge Trask, and Harriet Holden, all for the same thing, so that all of them end up mad at you?"

"Because they're after their special interests. I'm after the truth." He knew that sounded too windy, but it *was* the truth. "All of them want to use this document for their own purposes. And if the wrong side gets hold of it—"

"Which side is that?" She gave him one of those looks

"The side that doesn't like what it says. I don't want Sara Wyeth the PR queen deciding if the world should see it. I don't want Harriet Holden's assistant reading it and tearing it up. I don't want the judge and his minions making the decision, either."

"The ATV gang, you mean? I don't think he trusts them."

"He sent them after us," said Peter.

"What makes you think that?"

"A smart guy like the judge doesn't let you see anything he doesn't want you to see. He wants us to know that those boys are dangerous."

"Then why do you suppose he wants us to do his bidding?"

"He's run out of ideas. And frankly—" Peter flipped open the folder the judge had given them. "—so had I."

"*Had?* You mean you found something in there?"

"While you were in the shower."

"I was wondering why you didn't try to get in with me."

"That judge did a lot of research into George Amory. Soldier, logger, town builder, letter writer."

The waitress took their dessert order. Evangeline had the crème brûlée. Peter had a cheese plate and—a large miracle in a small place—a by-the-glass pour of Chateau Montrose 2005, young but already deep in the layered complexities of a great Bordeaux.

While they waited, Peter flipped open the folder that the judge had given them. "The longer I've done this work, the more convinced I am that we'll never know the half of it. We can read about them, think about them, stand where they stood and try to feel them. But it's hard enough figuring out a *living* human being, never mind people who've been dead for decades . . . centuries."

"We don't have to figure *them* out, just what they did."

"This morning, we knew from the Bowdoin Web site that George

Amory was going after something he called the national grail. By this afternoon, we knew that it was the lost draft. And now we know that he found something."

"What?"

Peter flipped to the last page copied from the Edwards diary: "October 25, 1864: GA appeared at my door today, as I grieve. He has grown more rawboned. Sharper. More confident in his demeanor. He might have made a decent match for Cordelia after all, Unitarian or no. But we put aside might-have-beens. He said he had come to tell us that he had found his grail, in a Vermont village named for an English saint. . . ."

Evangeline looked out at the Maine forest surrounding the lake. "So . . . Vermont next? Where in Vermont?"

THE ENDLESS PINE FORESTS of Maine could challenge a man. The stern mountains of New Hampshire ignored him. But Vermont wrapped a man in gentle pastures and verdant hillsides, and those Green Mountains beckoned him like a lover toward the bed of Champlain.

George Amory had studied the Romantic poets. He had read of the English lakes that inspired Wordsworth and his friends. But what English lake could equal the beauty of Champlain, stretching serenely to the west while the Vermont Central steamed north?

And what English town could surpass St. Albans? George glimpsed it from a distance as the train rounded a bend, and he decided that if the Lord had planned a New England village, he would have put it there, on that gentle slope a few miles up from the lake. He would have made it a place with neat businesses and solid banks and churches of the several Christian denominations. And he would have arrayed it all around a village green where elm leaves fluttered like hammered gold in October.

But the Lord in his wisdom had not reckoned with the works of man, which sometimes resembled the efforts of the more infernal spirits. That was George's thought as the train pulled into the St. Albans depot. Since the war, this had become an important railhead: acres of iron and brick carved out of the farmland, sidings lined with freight cars, a giant brick engine house, all of it blanketed in the smoke and steaming breath of locomotives being turned or sidetracked or sent on their way.

George rearranged the contents of his leather satchel—a clean shirt, a nightshirt, a crimson cravat, toothbrush and powder, razor—so that they would conceal his Navy Colt revolver. Then he put on his long canvas duster and slung the satchel over his shoulder.

Six others got off the train: a pair of farmers; two young men, one carrying a side valise, the other a leather satchel like George's; and two women—a mother and daughter perhaps, each carrying stacks of hat-boxes bound together with twine.

The young men glanced at George's limp, then at his satchel.

On the platform, another young man sat on a bench, reading a paper. He studied George's satchel, then gave nod.

George nodded, thinking it a friendly town, then he approached the two women. They wore shawls, dresses without hoops (train travel in a hoop skirt was near impossible), and stylish hats.

Yes, mother and daughter: the same bone structure, the same coloring, the same direct gaze, and—further proof—the mother frowned at the young man who might be no more than a common masher, while the daughter gave him a smile, as if to say that life in St. Albans could use a handsome stranger to enliven it.

George tipped his hat. "Might you ladies direct me to the American Hotel?"

"Up Lake Street." The mother gestured toward a street sign, hatboxes swinging.

"And would you allow me to carry a bit of your load?" he asked.

"We can handle it," said the mother.

"Mine *are* heavy, Mummy." The girl offered George the boxes in her right hand.

After a moment, the mother relented and handed one of her stacks to George as well, so that he now had hatboxes in both hands and his satchel over his shoulder.

He introduced himself: Joshua Burns of Bangor, Maine. They were the Widow Mills and daughter Annie.

The mother said, "You didn't get that limp from walkin' with a stone in your shoe. What regiment?"

"Twentieth Maine."

"Fredericksburg. Gettysburg. Now in the trenches of Petersburg," said Annie.

"You know a lot about them," said George.

"Her brother is Tenth Vermont."

In the short walk from depot to hotel, George learned that they ran a millinery shop and had just returned from a buying trip to Burlington, so they would have a selection of hats for the country ladies who came on market day. More important, they not only knew Dawson Caldwell, the Widow Mills was his first cousin, which made her a granddaughter of Caldwell P. Caldwell. These were small towns, after all.

"Are you a friend of Dawson's?" asked the Widow Mills.

George explained that he was a timber man, looking to buy land in Vermont.

"Dawson's the man to meet," she said as they came up to the town green.

Farm families had arrived from every direction with dairy, poultry, the autumn squashes, the last of the tomatoes. They had set up their stalls beneath the elms on the green, while the stores all around—apothecary, dry goods, hardware—bustled with business.

Widow Mills pointed out the American Hotel—four solid stories of brick, a corniced roof, railed balconies overlooking the green. But George insisted that he carry the hats all the way to their shop. He wanted to appear the gentleman, and the widow's tone expressed a degree of animosity toward her cousin that he wanted to explore.

Annie's Millinery was in the block between Bank Street and Congress, in a row of two-and-a-half story buildings with plate-glass windows for first-floor shops, living space above, and triangular gabled fronts that gave even the simplest of them a bit of the grandeur of the Greek Revival, the architectural style that had spread across New England a few decades before, proclaiming every home and every small emporium a temple to the rewards of Democracy.

These Vermonters knew how to build a town, he thought. Two blocks from that seething railyard, all seemed orderly, friendly, and quietly prosperous.

The shop smelled of lavender. There were hats displayed on wooden stands, gloves and purses and other gewgaws in the cases, a ledger open on the countertop.

The Widow Mills thanked George. "We'll put the hats in the window. Once the ladies are done marketing, they'll come by, just for a look. We'll be sold out by dark."

"A pleasure to meet you both." George tipped his hat once more. "And it would be a great honor, Mrs. Mills, if I might call upon your daughter."

"I thought you were here for business," said the mother.

"I am, but—"

"Call tomorrow," said Annie.

Again the Widow Mills relented. "We've seen our share of young men comin' through town lately. Travelers, hunters, Bible students. You're the first who's gentleman enough to ask permission to visit. Two o'clock."

George turned to leave, then asked, "Where does Mr. Caldwell keep his office?"

"Right there." The mother pointed across the street. There was a shingle on another little building: CALDWELL BROTHERS, LAND BROKERS.

"With the McClellan for President poster in the window?" said George.

"My cousin is a Democrat. A Copperhead, if you ask me, goin' back and forth to Canada all the time. Who knows what he does up there?" The widow grew more open as she talked, while the daughter, who had seemed so bright at first, furrowed her brow and shifted her eyes, as if the conversation was going too fast for her.

Finally Annie chimed in, "I think Uncle Dawson takes art lessons in Canada."

"Darlin'," said her mother, "he couldn't draw a mustache on Lincoln's picture."

The girl fixed an exaggerated frown on her face. "I heard him tell Uncle Porter that he went to Canada because of Clay. Clay is what you sculpt things from. It's art."

George was beginning to sense that for all her beauty, Annie was a bit backward.

"I think Clay is a man, dear, a man in Canada," said the mother.

Clay. George would remember the name.

Widow Mills turned back to George, "My cousin would see Lincoln lose, so that the war will end and we can get back to 'business as usual.'"

"Then his opposition is not principled?" asked George.

"Principled?" The widow gave a hoot.

"The rebels claim they fight for the principle of State's Rights," said George, "which they say is derived from the Constitution."

"My cousin's only principle is the one that appreciates, compounded annually. He wants to end the war so soldiers will come home and start buying land again."

"A man like that can't love the Constitution too well." George kept tossing out the word, fishing waters he did not know. He caught no reaction, so he said, "I think I'll go over and introduce myself."

"Don't forget to come tomorrow," said Annie. "Two o'clock."

IN THE LAND broker's office, there were file cabinets, a woodstove, a stand-up desk. A skinny man hunched over the desk, writing in a ledger. Ink stained his fingers and the side of his hand, but sleeve protectors covered his arms. He barely glanced up. "Help you?"

"I'm looking for Mr. Dawson Caldwell. Are you he?"

"No, I am not he," said the man. "*He* will not be here until this evening. You're early. You aren't expected until dinner."

"Dinner?" George realized he had been mistaken for someone else. But he decided to play along.

The man wrote down an address and gave it to George. "What's your name? They never told us your name."

"My name is Joshua Burns."

The man wrote that down.

George thanked him and turned to leave.

"Just one thing," said the man. "They said that you'd limp. Is the limp real?"

"It's real."

THE LOBBY OF the American Hotel: a clerk snoozing behind a counter, French doors leading to the dining room, burgundy carpet wearing in the places where people walked but still bright under the furniture, chairs and sofa circling a woodstove.

Four older women sat around the stove and discussed Scripture with a young man. A minister, thought George, and a handsome one at that, with a strong jaw and a face so smooth-shaven he looked like a boy. No wonder the ladies were enraptured.

The minister glanced at George's limp, then at George's satchel, then he held George's gaze, and held it, and held it a bit more, while one of the ladies was saying, "Isn't that right, Mr. Young? Don't you think this war is a fulfillment of the Book of Revelations?"

Finally the minister turned back to the ladies. "Yes. Indeed. Absolutely."

Serious young men seemed to abound in St. Albans, thought George, and none of them had learned from their mothers that it was impolite to stare.

IN HIS ROOM, George stripped off his shirt, looked into the glass above the basin, and wondered what he had stumbled into. He could run now, or he could take another step and have dinner with Dawson Caldwell. And if a question arose that he could not answer, he would simply fall back on his story, which was half-truth anyway: He was a timber man come to do business.

He stayed in his room the rest of the afternoon. He did not wish for another lingering gaze from another young man, because he plainly did not know what the gazes meant. So he paced for a while, and watched out the window for a while. Then he picked up the Burlington newspaper. And he read this:

CONFEDERATE COMMISSIONER HOPES FOR RECOGNITION
(*reprinted from the* Montreal Star)

Mr. C. C. Clay, Confederate Commissioner in Canada, spoke yesterday regarding the impending American election. "It is my sincere hope that if McClellan wins the presidency, Britain will forthwith recognize the Confederate States of America as a sovereign nation. This can only accelerate the process of ending this war and bringing an amicable peace between two great nations that began as one."

Clay. Mr. Clay. If the widow and her daughter were correct, Dawson Caldwell had recently been in contact with the Confederacy's spokesman north of the border, which had become a haven for blockade runners, escaped prisoners, and infiltrators.

Did Dawson Caldwell hold the same beliefs as Clay? Did he hold the Constitution? Or had he already passed it to Clay?

And did George have it in him to pull off a masquerade, when he did not even know who he was supposed to be?

But he had come too far to turn back. And he carried a letter from Cordelia. It urged him to bring the Constitution to Brunswick, almost as proof that he could do something extraordinary. And there were others in Brunswick who had doubted him, too, others who should see what he could accomplish. And then there were the hypocrites in Millbridge. . . .

So he loaded his Navy Colt and lay down for a nap, with lines from Tennyson singing him to sleep: "All-armed I ride, whate'er betide/Until I find the Holy Grail."

THAT EVENING, AT the appointed hour, he followed Bank Street up from the town green into a neighborhood of big houses, enormous elms, and picket fences. The smell of wood smoke and the crunch of fallen leaves reminded him of happier days.

But up ahead, he noticed the two young men from the train, lurking in the shadows near a spruce hedge. They seemed to be peering from the street into a barn behind one of the houses.

Then he heard the voice of the Widow Mills from her porch. "Is there something I can do for you gentlemen?"

"No, ma'am," said one of them. "Just wonderin' if you might have horses to rent."

"No, I don't," answered the Widow Mills. "So quit sneakin' around."

"Very sorry, ma'am. But we ain't sneakin'. Jest lookin'. Enjoy the evenin'."

The men went on their way, giving George a glance and a smile as they passed.

George watched them go on down the street; then he called, "Evening, Mrs. Mills. It's Joshua Burns. Would you know which house is Caldwell's?"

"Third up on the other side," said the widow from behind her screen door.

"And come for dinner tomorrow," called Annie from behind her mother.

DAWSON CALDWELL ANSWERED his front door himself. He was burly and tall, like the Big Jack branch of the family, and his bushy beard had a single streak of gray running down from the corner of his mouth.

He led George into the front parlor, a room with stuffed chairs, heavy drapes, a red-and-blue Turkey carpet, and a portrait of a burly ancestor on the wall.

"That's the patriarch," said Dawson. "Caldwell P. Caldwell himself. And you've met my brother, Porter."

Porter was the scrawny man from the land office. Without a word, he poured three tumblers of whiskey, handed them out, and they got directly to business.

Dawson said, "So, did you bring the money?"

"The money?" said George.

"Clay said to watch the trains. A man would bring the money, a limpin' man."

So, thought George, the wound that had done so much damage to his public character might at last be working to his benefit.

Dawson repeated, "So, did you bring the money?"

George sipped the whiskey and made a show of admiring the glass, while he looked for a way to draw the Caldwells along without revealing himself.

"Good Canadian rye," said Dawson.

"Smooth," said George, "like Champlain in August."

"A poet," said Porter, "in addition to a rebel."

George said, "Back to the money. Is the merchandise here?"

"It's in the Franklin County Bank," said Caldwell. "In the safe."

"Why sell it?" asked George.

"Because we're good Americans." Dawson Caldwell refilled his glass. "The war's been good to our pocketbooks. We've made good money on freight. But it's time for peace. Time for Lincoln to lose."

"Can you help defeat him?" asked George.

"That's for others to decide. I've read the draft, and there don't seem to be much that's different from the draft they ratified."

Draft. Ratified. George swallowed more whiskey, hoping that it would calm him and sharpen his wits at the same time. "How will this defeat Lincoln?"

"It shows that there was never certainty about things Lincoln claims to be certain about," said Dawson. "There was never a clause sayin' that the South *can't* leave. And the writing on the draft shows how hard the Founders were arguin' over everything . . . even the Bill of Rights."

He had found it. There could be no doubt. Now he had to get it. He said, "Before I pay, I need to see its condition."

"Condition?" said Dawson. "You ain't buyin' a collector's item. You're buyin' a political tool, somethin' to publish in the *New York Tribune* to sway the election."

"Clay said I should read it before buying it."

Dawson looked at his brother. "They're negotiatin'. These rebel bastards are—"

George said, "So send a telegram to Clay. Tell him you can't hand it over."

"Mr. Burns, if folks in St. Albans found me communicatin' with the head Confederate in Canada, they'd string me up. Why do you think we've been so secretive?"

"Then I can't help you," said George.

After a moment's thought, Caldwell downed his whiskey, "All right. Tomorrow. Three o'clock, when the bank closes. Bring the five thousand dollars."

"Just one question," said George. "Will you accept Confederate money?"

"I'm a Copperhead," said Dawson Caldwell. "Not a fool."

GEORGE BEGGED ILLNESS so that he would not have to stay for dinner. This was not easy, because somewhere in the house someone was cooking beef stew, and the smell had set his stomach to rumbling. But the more he talked to the Caldwells, the more likely George Amory was to reveal himself.

So he was glad to get out into the October chill and start walking, until he was startled by a shadow emerging from behind a tree.

"Mr. Burns. It's me. Annie." Her eyes reflected the glow of the street-lamp. "I was waitin' for you . . . to warn you. Those two ain't to be trusted. That's what Mummy says."

"Thank you." George gave her a smile.

And she kissed him.

It happened so quickly that before he could pull back or wrap his arms around her, she stepped away and wiped the back of her hand across her mouth. "Mummy says I'm slow. She says men will do bad things to a slow girl. But I can add my figures and do my letters. I ain't slow."

"No. Not at all." George looked around. If someone found him here with the girl, nothing good would follow.

"Mummy says that I'm slow on account of her granddad. He had two names the same, because his ma and pa was first cousins."

"I don't know about that," said George. "Seems like a long time ago."

From her house came the sound of her mother's voice, calling.

"I better go. But I ain't slow. And my Mummy don't trust those men. So sometimes, I go under their window and listen to their talk. That's how I heard of Clay."

The October chill turned cold against his flanks. "You weren't listen-ing now?"

"Oh, no. I trust you . . . so long as you promise to come tomorrow at two o'clock."

"I promise."

At the American Hotel, the minister was in the dining room with four young men.

George could see them shoveling food and talking. Whoever they were, he did not need their scrutiny. So, despite the words "baked ham" scrawled on the chalkboard outside the dining room, he and his empty stomach headed up the stairs.

Not long after, there was a knock on his door.

It was the minister himself. "May I come in?"

George opened the door.

The minister glanced up the hallway and down, then they were alone together in the room. He looked George over, looked across the room to where the satchel lay. "Forgive me, but I'm curious as to your occupa-tion."

"You first," said George, retreating to Maine monosyllables.

"I'm Bennett Young, a Bible student stopped for a time to discuss the Word with the good ladies of St. Albans." He offered his hand.

George took it and looked down at Young's boots—knee-high, shiny leather, made for holding a horse in line rather than a congregation.

"I like to ride," said Young,

"A horseman of the Apocalypse?"

Young ignored the joke. "You know my name. What's yours?"

"Joshua Burns of Portland, Maine. I'm in timber."

"How did you come by the limp, if I may ask?"

"Loggin' is dangerous work. Axes are sharp."

"The halfwit girl said you're from the Twentieth Maine. She said you hurt your foot in a battle."

"If she's a halfwit, she might be wrong."

"I hope your intentions toward her are honorable, sir."

And that was a remark no man should brook without offense. George opened the door. "Our conversation is over."

"My apologies," said Young, "but I would be remiss—as a man of God—if I did not protect the weaker—and weaker-minded—among us."

"Is that why townsfolk stare at me? They fear for the honor of a halfwit girl?"

"I wouldn't know." Bennett Young stepped into the hallway. "Good evening. Perhaps we can dine together some time and discuss Revelations."

"You don't talk like you're from here," said Will.

"Nor do you."

"We sound different in Maine."

"As we do in Maryland," said Young. "The western hills. Good Union folks there. Not a slaveholder among 'em."

George Amory did not believe a word of it. So he resolved to sleep with one eye open and his gun in his lap.

HE READ *A Tale of Two Cities* until his chin dropped finally onto his chest.

The church bell awoke him. *Bong . . . Bong . . .* Two in the morning. His lamp had sputtered out. The room was lit faintly by a streetlight. He cracked the window to let in a bit of air. He made sure the door was locked, slipped the Navy Colt under his pillow, got into bed. . . .

Just after dawn, the cocking of a pistol awoke him, followed by the press of metal against his face and a whisper in his ear: "Say a word and you're dead."

It was one of the young men from the train. His hair was combed, his Vandyke trimmed, his shirt clean. He could have been dressed for church.

George raised his head, and the pistol slammed down. When he came to, it was full daylight. His head was throbbing. And two figures were sitting in the room.

He tried to speak, but a gag was choking him. He tried to move, but he was trussed to the bed. One of the men was Bennett Young, sitting so close that George could smell the polish on the leather boots.

"Never leave a window open next to a balcony. Makes it easy for nimble fellows to climb in. Now"—Young held up George's revolver—"we're all carryin' these in our satchels."

George spoke into the gag. *I don't know what you're talking about.*

Young gave the other one a nod, and a knife was pressed against George's neck. Then Young said, "Make a noise and it will be your last. Understand?"

George nodded, and the pressure around his mouth was released.

"Why are you carryin' a Navy six?" demanded Young. "The Yankee officer's sidearm?"

"I was a Yankee officer."

"What were you doin' on Bank Street last night, speakin' to the mother of the halfwit girl?"

The one with the knife whispered, "She sure is pretty for a halfwit."

Bennett Young glanced at him, as if annoyed to be interrupted, then he looked back at George. "What were you doin' up there?"

"Visiting Dawson Caldwell."

"Caldwell's a man with strong opinions," said Young. "I've heard he's crossed into Canada to talk with C. C. Clay."

"I don't know anything about that," said George.

"Was Caldwell supposed to tell you somethin'? Somethin' I should know?"

"I told you. I'm a timberman . . . come to do business with a landowner."

"I could have Teavis here strop a knife on your leg. Would that bring a new story? Like, you're a Yankee agent from Canada who thinks he's onto somethin'?"

George shook his head.

Bennett Young sat back. "I believe him, Teavis. We know somethin's goin' on with Caldwell and Clay. I'd telegraph Clay direct, but we agreed, once we crossed the border, no communicatin'. We can't raise suspicion before we make our move."

"My knife needs stroppin' just the same." Teavis thumbed the blade.

"We're soldiers, not murderers. After three o'clock, there's nothin' this Yankee officer knows that can hurt us." Bennett Young replaced the gag and left.

Three o'clock. What was happening at three o'clock? How could he get loose and stop it? George put his head back on the pillow and stared up at the cracked ceiling.

A face appeared above him, the breath sour. "My name is Squire Turner Teavis. Rode with Morgan in Ohio, till we got ourselves captured. Bennett and me and some others, we escaped from a prison camp outside Chicago and made it to Canada."

So that was it. They were raiders.

"You see this?" Teavis fingered his lapel and the square of gray cloth pinned to the brown fabric. "A bit of Confederate uniform. Today, we're bringin' the war to a town full of smug Vermont Yankees."

George tried to ask a question: *How many?*

"We got men here, more filterin' in on the trains. We know most of them. But Clay said he might send more. So we watch. Every one of us carries a leather satchel or a side valise with a Navy Colt. And every man got this"—Teavis pulled out a bottle of clear liquid—"Greek fire. Liquid phosphorus. Throw it and—boom!"

Teavis sat and propped his feet on the bed. "Now, I'm takin' a nap. I got a lot to do today. Twitch around tryin' to get loose, and you might wake me up and I'm liable to geld you right in the bed." Then he slid his hat down over his face and slept.

Nine chimes, ten, eleven.

Three hours, and George Amory lay there, trussed, cramped, trying to think his way out of this predicament.

The sun came out and flooded the room. Then the clouds rolled back, and the drizzle came down.

When Teavis awoke, George asked through the gag for water, and Teavis said no. George asked if he could take a piss, and Teavis said, "Go ahead," but George held it. George asked if his mouth could be untied, if his legs could be loosened, if his hands could be released so that he could scratch his nose. *No. No.* And *no.*

As the clock struck twelve, Teavis stood and put the knife to George's neck. "It's eatin' time. If I hear any noise, I'll come up and cut off your Yankee nose."

And George was alone. For an hour, he tried to get loose, but quietly, as he valued his nose. Left leg . . . right leg . . . left hand . . . right hand. . . . Finally, he gave up and stared at the ceiling and let his mind spin.

It was plain that while Bennett Young might have known of Caldwell's loyalties, Caldwell was like everybody else in town—ignorant of what was coming. Did Young know about the document in the Franklin

County Bank? It sounded as if Caldwell and Clay had had separate dealings, and Clay was trying to get word to Young so that when Young made his move, he would know what was in the bank.

If George could get loose, perhaps he could get to the bank first.

At about two thirty, Bennett Young came back. He was wearing a gray suit with a shirt of butternut and a red neck cloth—almost a Confederate uniform. Teavis was with him.

"What you want to do with him?" asked Teavis.

"Leave him," said Young.

"If we put Greek fire to the hotel, he won't get out," said Teavis.

"The fortunes of war. Isn't that so, Lieutenant Burns?" Young patted George's shoulder, one soldier to another. "Anything else to tell me?"

George shook his head.

"Then good luck to you, sir."

Except for the footfalls of the Confederates going downstairs, the hotel was quiet.

And there seemed to be little noise outside. Most towns went quiet on the day after market day, and many of the men of St. Albans had gone to meetings in Burlington that morning. It was the perfect day to stage a raid.

After a time, George heard Young's voice in the street: "I hereby take possession of this town in the name of the Confederate States of America!"

This was followed by rebel yells . . . the sounds of men running . . . a gunshot . . . horses galloping . . . more rebel yells . . . shattering glass . . . screams in the street. . . .

Then the door swung open. There stood Annie Mills, in a blue gingham dress and a gray apron.

"I *knew* it," she said. "I knew you didn't not come 'cause you didn't like me."

He swung his head. *Get over here and untie me.*

"I *was* comin' to yell at you," she said, "but Mr. Young come out of the hotel and looked at me and said 'Best get out of the way, girl' . . . This is a tight knot."

He felt her hands trembling against the sides of his face. But she got the gag off.

"How many?" he said.

"I was worried." She leaned forward and kissed him. Then she stepped back. "We spent all mornin' cookin' fried chicken."

"How many? How many men are with Bennett Young?"

She started untying one of his feet.

"The *wrists*. Do the wrists first. And how many men?"

"Twenty, maybe? Mr. Young, he shouted about takin' the town, then in a soft voice he told the men, 'You know what to do.'"

"What? What are they doing?"

"Four went to the St. Albans Bank, and four went to the First National, and four went to the Franklin County Bank. Then Mr. Young, he told four to go down Lake Street and keep people from comin' up from the rail yards. And—"

"That's sixteen," said George.

"The rest are out in the street, shootin', yellin' . . . I don't like yellin'."

The right wrist came loose.

"Now the *legs*," he said. "Untie my legs!"

"Don't you yell at me, either. I cooked all mornin' and you never came."

"I'm sorry." George untied his own left wrist.

"I *hate* gettin' yelled at." She untied the left leg. "And they're throwin' bottles of fire. I'm not goin' out there again, and if you yell at me again, I'll tie you up again."

Finally free, he sprang to the window.

Down in the street, two mounted men were swinging pistols, herding people onto the town green, where two others kept them under guard.

George dressed quickly, threw on his hat, then his duster.

Right below the window, one of the other rebels was speaking politely to an old man: "The town's closed, sir. Please go over to the green."

"Closed?" said the old man. "Closed? You can't close a town."

Annie peered out over George's shoulder. "Why, that's Mr. Huntington." And she reached out the window, "Hello—"

George put his hand to her mouth and shook his head. No. No noise.

Down below, old Mr. Huntington sniffed the air. "You're drunk, mister."

"If you don't do what I say," shouted the rebel, "I'll shoot you."

"Oh, no, you won't," came the old man's voice. "I guess you won't shoot me."

George heard the *bang* of a big Navy Colt and the sound of a body falling.

Annie screamed.

George told her to be quiet or he'd gag her.

Her eyes widened, and she brought her hand to her mouth.

"Now, dear," he said more gently, "can you read?"

"Well . . . yeah . . . I can even read chapter books."

He snatch a book from the table. "Here's one, all about the best of times and the worst of times. Like now. Sit here and read it and whatever's goin' on down there, you won't notice. It'll take you away, like a . . . a magic carpet."

He led her to the chair in the corner. Then something occurred to him. He slipped the book from her hands and tore out a page: *Ex Libris, George Amory.* Then he kissed her, on the lips. "Don't make a sound, and I'll come back to kiss you again real soon. But if you come out in the street and get in the way, I'll be awful mad."

He reached up and removed a pin from her hair. And her smile caused his insides to wither. She drew a deep breath, as if she expected to be seduced and hoped for it to happen. Instead, he fingered the light material of her apron, pulled out his knife, and cut off a piece. Using the hairpin, he fixed the gray cloth to the lapel of his duster.

Her smile faded. Her brow lowered. "Why . . . you're one of them."

"I'm going to fool them . . . make them *think* I'm one of them. So . . . just read the book. And I'll be back to rescue you." He locked the door behind him.

THE CLERK HAD disappeared from the lobby. Two of the Bible ladies were watching out the window. Another was reading the Twenty-third Psalm, while in the street, Bennett Young was reining his horse in front of the hotel.

"You son of a bitch!" Old Man Huntington was back on his feet. "You shot me."

"Get across the street," said Young, "or we'll shoot you again."

Someone shouted from a store. "What's all the noise? What are you celebratin'?"

"I'll show you!" Young fired his gun, and a door slammed.

One of the ladies whispered to George, "Sir, what are we to do?"

George brought his finger to his lips. The lady nodded and turned again to the window.

Bennett Young was shouting, "You there! Caldwell! Dawson Caldwell!"

George saw Caldwell running across Main Street.

Young galloped after him. "Caldwell! You have something for me?"

"I don't know what you're talking about!" Caldwell kept running.

"Stop, or I'll shoot," said Young.

Caldwell pulled a pistol from his pocket, spun about, and Bennett Young fired.

"Good God," Caldwell staggered and looked down at the blood spreading across his shirt. He raised a hand to touch it as if he did not believe it was his, then he dropped to his knees in the middle of the street, and after a moment, he fell facedown.

George cursed. He had hoped to use Caldwell, but . . . He heard someone behind him. It was the clerk, rushing toward the door with a pistol in his hand.

George grabbed a walking stick from the umbrella stand and with a deft swing sent the clerk sprawling across the carpet into the spittoon.

One of the ladies cried the clerk's name and scurried over to him. "You've killed him, sir."

"Stunned him. Saved him from himself." Then George grabbed the clerk's pistol—a little Colt Wells Fargo—and went out the back.

HE MOVED DOWN the alley behind the hotel, leaped a fence, and came up beside the Franklin County Bank.

He crouched behind a stack of cordwood piled at the side door and peered in the window: Two Confederates were stuffing bills into the satchels.

"Is this it?" demanded one of them.

"That's all the greenbacks."

"All right, then," said the big one to the tellers. "Into the vault with you."

"You can't do that!" said a teller in a green eyeshade.

"You Vermont Yankees are too damned stubborn. Do what you're told." The big rebel kicked the teller in the stomach and sent him flying into the vault. Then he pushed the other one in and slammed the door.

Out on the street, Bennett Young was galloping back and forth, like a good officer, controlling the battle. He shouted into the bank. "You boys done?"

"Done and comin'!"

Young pulled a bottle of Greek fire from his coat and flung it against the bank. It shattered, hissed, sizzled, and went out.

From the looks of things, their efforts to burn the town weren't working. But if their plan was to sow terror in sleepy New England, they were doing a fine job.

Now there was gunfire from across the street. Young wheeled his horse and went galloping toward it. Meanwhile, the robbers came out of the

Franklin County Bank, shooting their pistols into the air and giving out with rebel yells. They leaped onto two horses tethered out front and galloped after Young.

George took his chance. He slipped into the bank by the side door, and went up to the vault. "Hey! Hey in there! We're burning the bank. But we'll let you out if you find one thing."

"What?" came a voice from within.

"Dawson Caldwell's safety desposit box."

There was a moment or two of silence, then, "It's here."

"Tell me the combination."

"You promise you'll let us out?"

"Not without the combination."

"All right," came the muffled voice. "Turn twice, counterclockwise, past zero. Now, three right. . . ." And so forth until the tumblers clicked.

George pulled open the safe and poked the gun inside. "Hand me the box first."

"What's to say that you'll let us out after we give it to you?" demanded the teller.

"My word . . . as a Confederate officer."

So the box appeared, George snatched it and slammed the door. "Never trust a rebel."

"God damn you!" came the voice from inside. "God damn you all."

Out in the street, Bennett Young was shouting at someone in the livery stable.

And the Widow Mills was running down the street, frantically calling her daughter's name.

George wanted to tell her that the girl was safe, that her moments of anguish would be short, but she would know soon enough.

He put the deposit box on the floor and fired into the lock. Another gunshot, barely noticed in the storm of gunshots outside. The box popped open, and there it was, a cylindrical leather map case. A quick look confirmed that it contained papers. Old papers. The first draft.

George pulled off his duster and put on a teller's stovepipe and black frock, which were hanging on a rack in the corner. He tucked the map case under his arm and sneaked out the side door.

As the shouts and gunfire moved north, George went west, along an alley, though back yards, past laundry fluttering on clotheslines, and finally out onto Foundry Street, which paralleled the train yard. A freight was pulling in. An engine was steaming out. The platform was empty.

George slipped between two cars on a siding, crossed a few tracks, hopped onto the platform. The message board said that the next Burlington train was due in two hours, too long to wait, because men were now running up Lake Street toward the sound of the firing. Soon any stranger would become a suspicious stranger.

So George took a printed timetable from the little pocket on the board, walked across the yard, cut through a nearby wood lot, and came back onto Lake Street a quarter mile beyond the train yard.

He whistled as he went, a gentleman in a tall hat strolling to the lake without a care in the world. But soon he was stopped by a group of men galloping toward the town. In his best Maine accent, he told them that he was a cousin of the Caldwells, and no, he hadn't seen anything strange in town because he'd been out exploring all day. They believed him, or perhaps it was his accent they believed, and they rode on.

And George walked on, to the end of the street and a little inlet called St. Albans Bay. He spied a pram on the beach, flipped it over, and found oars to row out to one of the little sloops riding at anchor.

AN HOUR LATER, a man got off the Montreal train in St. Albans. He carried a leather satchel and favored his left foot. He had orders from C. C. Clay to present himself as "a buyer" to Dawson Caldwell, then to present himself to Bennett Young as a fellow agent and tell him exactly where Caldwell's map case could be found, so that it could be stolen along with all the money in the banks. He was a day late, and since he brought no cash, much more than a dollar short.

By then the banks in Burlington were under guard, and five hundred volunteers were in the cars, speeding north for the defense of St. Albans. Meanwhile a posse of fifty men, armed with pistols, bird guns, and old muskets had lit out after the raiders.

But Bennett Young and his men made their escape into Canada by burning the covered bridge at Sheldon.

It was best blaze they started all day, because the Greek fire had done no more than scorch the sides of a few buildings and one St. Albans outhouse. However, the rebels had gotten away with over two hundred thousand dollars and shot three people. One, a contractor named Morrissey, died of his wounds. Some would comment on the irony of this, since he was a vociferous supporter of McClellan. Along those same lines, townspeople were soon speculating on the contents of a safety deposit box belonging to another McClellan supporter, Dawson Caldwell.

Caldwell told a reporter for the *Burlington Times* that the box contained important family documents, deeds, and old letters. Had he revealed more, his meetings with the Confederate Commissioner for Canada might have come to light and cast suspicion on him for the raid itself. But Caldwell would tell no more, because the next day he succumbed to his wounds.

GEORGE AMORY SPENT the night piloting the little sloop south, putting as much distance as he could between himself and St. Albans.

With the sky silvering toward dawn, he sank the sloop in Mallet's Bay, then rowed ashore in the pram, which he pushed back onto the water. A rising easterly wind caught the little boat and, with any luck, would push it all the way to the New York shore. Then his tracks would be covered completely.

As the morning sun poured over his shoulder, he sat on a driftwood log on the deserted shoreline and slipped the top off the map case.

He was a rational young man. He did not expect that light would burst from the case when he opened it or that the document would generate its own heat when struck by the rays of the morning sun. But he would not have been surprised.

He wiped his hands down the front of his jacket and slipped his fingers into the cylinder lined with red baize. He felt the soft paper and the hard letters imprinted upon it. And then the four long folio sheets slid out, the literal handiwork of men imagining a nation into existence.

Yes, he thought, the document really did generate heat.

But as he read, he realized that it shed no new light. Nothing in it clarified the positions of Lincoln or the Secessionists. Nor did the scratchings left by any of the New Englanders. They wrote about free speech, religious freedom, the right to bear arms, all of which had been codified in the Bill of Rights. Only one of them had confronted slavery on the document, and all he wrote was "What about slaves? Ban importation by 1808?"

So . . . could George say that he had saved the Union by this theft? That he had rescued his reputation? Or that he had simply endangered himself and a backward girl?

There was nothing here to stop the war, nothing to guarantee Lincoln's victory or defeat, nothing to illuminate the thinking of the Founders on the great issue of the day.

It was all as Caldwell had said it would be.

At least George had the document, and there were still people in

Brunswick who would be impressed, people in other places, too. Maybe that was all that mattered. . . .

HE THOUGHT IT best to stay off the trains, where they might be look-ing for a young man with a limp, so he bought a horse at the livery stable in Mallet's Bay and headed east.

He crossed the Connecticut River the next morning and followed the Tenth New Hampshire Turnpike into the mountains. By late afternoon he came to a crossroads village called Twin Mountain. From there, the road undulated into the Amonoosuc Valley, with the rockbound riverbed, mostly dry in autumn, undulating beside it.

The high-country hardwoods had dropped their foliage, leaving be-hind the deep greens of spruce and pine. They darkened the mountains that crowded the river on the west, and they covered the hills that spread east toward the Presidential Range. It was the first time that George had come through the valley, and nothing—not Casco Bay in a storm, not the Maine wilderness, not even the Northern Lights above Fredericksburg— had ever seemed more majestic or primeval.

Small wonder that city people were finding their way here in summer to drink in the vistas, fish in the streams, walk in the woods.

THE WHITE MOUNTAIN House was white, a four-story hotel facing Mount Rosebrook and the setting sun. A man was sitting in a rocking chair, watching.

"Evening," said George. "I'm in need of lodging."

"You've come to the right place, and just in time." The man stood. He had a fringe of white beard and the proprietary air of ownership. "Usually closed by now, and we'll be closed for certain come the first of November."

"Thank you, Mr.—"

"—White. Colonel John White of the White Mountain House, late of the U.S. Army. Been runnin' this place since I mustered out after the Mexican War."

"I suppose you've seen a lot of changes since then."

Colonel White slipped his thumbs into his galluses. "Seen some. More comin'." He jerked his head toward the windows behind him, to-ward three men sitting in the dining room. "Timber cruisers. They're the reason we've stayed open."

George stepped into the hotel, signed the register, and heard a famil-iar voice roar from the dining room, "I don't believe it."

Enos Turlock came limping out to greet George as old friends did when they met outside the framework of their friendship—with shouts of recognition, handshakes, and a burst of conversation that began as if it had stopped just the day before.

What was George doing here? Passing through after cruising timber in Vermont.

Why wasn't Enos in Maine, opening Caldwell Camp #7 or #8? Because he had finally found a wife to keep him warm through the winter, so he had hired out as a timber cruiser himself, surveying woodlands after the leaves fell but before the deep snow.

"You gents can have old home week in the dinin' room," said Colonel White. "We got a nice roast chicken comin' out, last one of the season."

Enos ushered George to the table by the fireplace, beneath a menagerie of stuffed New Hampshire animal heads, and introduced him to two men who would have a greater impact on his fortunes than any he had ever met: Daniel Saunders and son Charles, members of the logging aristocracy and the New England aristocracy, too.

Daniel Saunders was a gaunt, balding Bostonian with a pointed beard and the watchful eyes of an owl or a lawyer, which was his stock in trade. He was related by marriage to the late Nicholas Norcross, New England Timber King, and by ancestry and business to the Perkins family of Boston, New England investment royalty, so he also had money in the Pike Mill.

He seemed a gentleman, too. Not the pasteboard kind who believed that all men were created equal except for those who—through dumb luck or lineage—were just a little more equal. Saunders was the genuine article—polite and forthright, with the good sense to treat Turlock as respectfully as he would have treated General Grant.

The father's lessons were not lost on the son. Young Charles, equally tall and gaunt, listened attentively, spoke politely, and asked smart questions.

Once their mutual interests in timber and the Pike Mill became clear, they talked far into the night.

The next morning, Saunders stood on the veranda of the hotel and offered George his hand. "It's been a pleasure, Mr. Amory. I look forward to doing business with you some day."

"It's my hope," said George.

"You own a thousand acres below the Notch"—Saunders walked to his horse—"and it's surrounded by thirty thousand acres of land we've bought."

"He's tellin' you to come up with a price," said Turlock.

Saunders swung a leg over his saddle. "I plan to harvest the timber when the railroad comes, so . . . a fair price."

"I'd prefer partnership to a price," said George. "A man needs to make something of himself more than he needs money."

"A fine philosophy," said Saunders. "But a fair price is what I'm after."

As George watched them ride off, old Colonel White came up beside him. "Someday soon, the state'll sell the timber rights in this valley, and men like Saunders will build their railroads, and this world will change."

"Change is inevitable," said George.

"Some of us come here because we don't like change." Colonel White looked at the old man bringing George's horse around. "Live free or die is what we always say. Ain't that so, Dewlap?"

"Live free or die," said the old man. "My pap done that here eighty years ago."

"Live free or die," mused George. "The New England motto."

"Don't know about New England," White answered, "but it's what we say in New Hampshire."

George rode out that morning, past the place where the Amonoosuc dropped down out of the mountains and made its turn for the Connecticut. He noticed a little farmhouse set back from the road. He wondered if that was where his grandfather had spent a winter, if it was in those woods beyond that his great-uncle was buried.

As he passed the high rocks that formed the Gateway of the Notch, he tried to imagine the fight his grandfather had described. One of his ancestors had died right there, because of the document that he now carried. North Pike had died trying to live free. And men were still dying so that others could live free. They were dying for the North and for the South, and all because of the different ways that men read the same document.

The turnpike road carried him down, over the Saco River, then over it again, then past the Willey House, destroyed by a landslide, immortalized in a story by Hawthorne. Another few miles brought him past the mansion called Notchland and the old Mount Crawford house, run by the family who had given their name to the Notch. Finally, about twelve miles from the Gateway, he came to the place were the Sawyer River dropped out of the mountains and joined the Saco. This was his land.

He left his horse to water in the river while he walked a short distance up the grade and gazed at the tall trees that defined permanence. His permanence, his future, no matter what happened when he got back to Brunswick.

ON THE LAST day of October, George stood at the edge of the Bowdoin campus and looked across the street at a Cape Cod–style house where a man was looking at a horse.

Though the day was gentle and warm, in the melancholy way that only an October day can be when November threatens, the man wore a heavy blue cape, as if he feared taking a chill. His hair, beneath the blue forage cap, had gone gray. With slow and careful motions, he gripped the pommel of the saddle and tried to raise a leg into a stirrup. But pain and weakness seemed too much for him and he lowered the leg again. He put his hands on his hips and contemplated the animal.

George crossed the street. "Can I give you a boost?"

Joshua Lawrence Chamberlain turned, as if he had been discovered at something he should not have been doing. Then his face brightened. "Why, Amory!" Then his expression darkened. "How's the foot?"

"It's healed." George offered his hand.

Chamberlain took it a bit tentatively, but after a moment, he pumped it like an old friend. "It's good . . . good to see you, George."

"I hear that you've been wounded a few times, too."

"In the foot, believe it or not, at Gettysburg. I always told people how easy it was to be wounded in the foot."

"A hard day."

"Not as hard as Petersburg." Chamberlain looked down at his body, as thought it were someone else's. "Bullet went in just below the right hip, exited just above the left. They thought I was going to die, so they breveted me on the field."

"Brigadier general now?"

"Yes, but it doesn't ease the pain. Doctors say it's a miracle I'm alive and can stand on my own two feet and pass my own water."

"It would be a miracle for you to ride a horse, too, I'd say."

"I'd best be able to do it, for when I go back."

"You're going back?"

That knowledge made the document that he carried, and whatever triumph it represented, seem much smaller to George Amory. There was nothing he could do, nothing he had found, to equal such service. So he left the map case on his saddle when Chamberlain's wife invited him in for tea.

They sat by the fireplace, and George felt an embrace of domesticity so warm and comforting that he could not comprehend why Chamberlain would leave it a second time.

"It's not out of selfish ambition." Chamberlain rocked and looked at the fire. "What it is, I can't tell you . . . a sort of fatalism, perhaps. I believe in destiny, George, divinely appointed. So . . ."

They talked for an hour. Chamberlain assured him that Lincoln would win the election. George said he prayed that it would be so.

Then George stood to leave. And once more, he thought of showing the draft to Chamberlain.

But Chamberlain took his hand and said, "Remember what I told you once. Combat makes good men better and bad men worse. For you, it did the former. And now that I am a brigadier general, I can tell you that you would be welcomed back to the Corps."

And George Amory was tempted to accept the invitation. But he knew that he would never go back. He had given all that he could to the uniform. He knew as well, that the lost Constitution could prove nothing about him that he hadn't proved about himself. In the eyes of men whose opinion mattered, George had value. No more needed to be said.

As he left, the poet whispered again, "He who finds himself loses his misery."

ON THE WAY to Cordelia's house, George began to wonder if he would even bother to show her the draft, or simply present himself, as himself, no more and no less. Matthew Arnold would approve.

But when he struck the brass knocker, he had the map case under his arm.

The maid led him into the study, where the broad-beamed professor was writing in his diary.

He had aged. His great belly, which he once carried so pridefully beneath his waistcoat, seemed now to weigh him down like rocks in a sack. His eyes were bloodshot, his hair disheveled, his emotion deep enough that he could not muster a greeting that was either welcoming or sarcastic. He simply said, "George Amory . . . how's your foot?"

"Healed," said George. "Healed well enough that General Chamberlain has asked me to rejoin his brigade." He could not resist.

Edwards simply nodded, distracted.

"Is . . . is Cordelia here?" asked George. "She invited me to come."

"She's in Annapolis, at the hospital. Her husband . . . she has gone to him. . . ."

"Husband?" George tried not to stagger. But before he even opened the map case, he knew he had lost what he wanted most, what he had always hoped this treasure would win for him.

"They married when she came back from Europe. He said he could not go into another battle without her complete love. Now . . ." Edwards waved a letter. "Her young man has . . . has lost his legs, perhaps his manhood. . . . She cannot be certain if he survives."

George had to get out. Twice in a day, his personal victory was overshadowed, first by the sacrifice of Chamberlain, now by this bitter news. So he withdrew a calling card from his pocket and left it with the professor.

"Tell Cordelia that she has my sympathies. Tell her that I did something extraordinary. I found my grail in St. Albans, Vermont. Tell her that I will pray for her . . . her husband."

"Pray?"

"We all pray, sir, in our way. Unitarians, Congregationalists, even Catholics."

LINCOLN WAS REELECTED without the help of the lost draft. The forces of history prevailed. The North would win the war.

So George Amory went to Boston and put the map case in a safety deposit box in the Shawmut Bank. Then he bought a steamer ticket for London.

Then he found his way over to the New Lands on the Back Bay. The city had built out four blocks of landfill and fine houses were rising. He waited outside one of them—which the city directory stated belonged to the Stansfield family—until he saw a footman leave. He followed the man back to a North End tenement.

The next morning, after the man had gone to work, George went up the stairs of the tenement and knocked on the door. It opened, revealing the auburn hair and the physical presence that, in a different place and a different dress, would have seemed regal.

"Mother of Jesus," said Sheila.

George tried to smile. "You once said that your first love had been a footman who worked for the Stansfields of Boston."

"What do you want?" she demanded.

"I want to say I'm sorry, and I want to ask a question."

"I accept your apology. What's your question?"

"That day at the depot you said you were . . . something . . . it never came through."

From somewhere in the little two-room tenement, a baby began to cry

Sheila went back inside, and George followed her.

A table, a stove piped into a wall, a bed, a crib, a single window—the world of a woman who was poor but proud. Sheila came back holding the baby.

He asked her, "Did you say, 'I'm pregnant'?"

"To you? By you? I'd never say such a thing."

He sensed the lie. "Is the child my—" He peered at the baby. "—my daughter?"

"Maureen is the child of John Flaherty." She spoke with sudden ferocity, almost spitting the words in George's face. "He married me after I lost me job in the mill, after me aunt in Providence wouldn't take me in."

George pulled a roll of cash from his pocket. "Take this. My gift for the baby."

She did. She was not that proud, or that fierce.

"When she grows up, tell her you know a man who owns a first draft of the U.S. Constitution, annotated by the New England framers. It's my secret. If she ever needs help, she can come to me, and help is hers."

EIGHTEEN

THE RISING SUN WOKE EVANGELINE FIRST.

Frost gathered at the corners of the window. Mist rose off the lake.

In late October, in northern Maine, cool mornings were just plain cold.

But Peter and Evangeline were buried beneath a mountain of down in a queen-sized bed.

Peter rolled toward her and swung an arm over her. His naked chest against her bare back was warm and cool at the same time. He slipped a leg between hers.

This was the way it was supposed to be, she thought. Then she said his name.

His voice rose from sleep. "Mmm-hm."

"What are we doing?"

"Waking up." He stretched against her. "Waking up naked. Together."

"One of the benefits of being on the run," she said.

"No pajamas in the trunk when you go on the run."

"So . . . why don't we just stay here all day? Do it again, maybe." She twitched herself against him.

"Do it again. Yeah," he said. "Then we have to go. We have things to do."

She rolled toward him and nestled into the crook in his arm. "Why?"

"Because we're good Americans," he said.

"I wish we were just a normal couple again."

"We've never been a normal couple."

"No?" She lifted her head.

"Normal couples in their forties don't do it early in the morning, not after doing it late last night." He kissed her neck; then he trailed the kisses down. . . .

His unshaven face felt scratchy against her breast, scratchy and good. She twined her fingers into his hair and turned herself toward him.

And then . . . his lips were caressing, his fingers teasing, and a current was shooting from the tips of her breasts, down, down from there, down right through her, as it always did when she felt the most . . . alive.

She threw a leg over his hips, pressed him down onto his back, and lowered herself onto him. The comforter draped over her shoulders like a tent. She began to move.

He tried to meet her movement with his own, and she said, "No. Let me do it."

And she moved steady but not too fast, lifting and lowering, lifting and lowering, focusing on herself, knowing that her enjoyment would be his, too. . . .

And when he moved, she squeezed her legs against his sides. "Stay still."

He tried, but she was moving faster, and he felt himself rising higher.

She dropped her face onto the pillow and cried out against it. This was a small guest house, after all.

And he put his hands on her bottom and squeezed, and he held his own sound in his throat, but he couldn't hold anything else. . . .

And when they were done and she was still on top of him, she turned her head to his ear and said, "We have to live through this, Peter."

"We will."

"I'm frightened," she said. "More than I let on. Seeing Bindle—"

"It would frighten anyone." He pulled the comforter over their bodies. And they lay like that for a long time.

Then Peter said, "You don't want to quit, do you?"

She shook her head against his shoulder.

"And if we find it and it doesn't say what you want it to say? No second guessing?"

There was a long pause, then she shook her head again.

"Good. I smell bacon." He slid his hands down her back and gave her bottom a smack. "C'mon. We can't do America's work if we don't have a good breakfast."

"You're late." Martin Bloom was standing behind the display case when Peter and Evangeline arrived in the Old Curiosity.

"We started in Greenville. It's a long drive."

"What were you doing in Greenville?"

"What we've been doing all week."

"Treasure hunting?"

"Tracking the movements of people who've touched the Holy Grail of American history. By the way, you're not the first to use that term."

Doherty came out of the office, as red-faced as if he had just had a three-Guinness lunch at Bull Feeney's. "Who did you track to Greenville?"

"Not who. What," said Peter. And he dropped a page from the diary onto the countertop. "Ever heard of Professor Aaron Edwards?"

"From Bowdoin? Wrote books on Congregationalist history?" said Martin Bloom. "Taught Chamberlain?"

"Taught George Amory, too," said Peter.

Bloom picked it up and read the highlight: "'October 25, 1864: GA appeared at my door . . . Blah blah . . . decent match for Cordelia . . . Blah blah . . . I asked him why he came and he said to tell her he had found his grail. . . . '" Bloom looked up. "In Vermont?"

"We were thinking of picking up Route 2 and heading west," said Peter. "Right across the top of New England, from Maine to St. Albans."

"It would take you all day to get there on Route 2," said Doherty.

"And the Constitution hasn't been there since 1864," said Peter. "We think, if George Amory of Portland had it, it must have passed through Portland."

Doherty turned to Martin. "You're the one who's supposed to be watching the Internet. Once a day, go to a search engine and run all the usual suspects. How did you miss this?"

"Searching the names of every Bowdoin professor between 1858 and 1862 wasn't something I considered," said Bloom. "And no search engine in the world is going to translate GA to George Amory."

"Stop arguing, boys." Peter went over and plunked himself down on the leather sofa. "It makes you look like an old married couple."

Doherty jerked a thumb at Evangeline: "If she wasn't here, Fallon, I'd tell you to go and fuck yourself."

"Tell him anyway," she said. "I've told him the same thing a few times."

"That's right," said Peter. "It makes us *feel* like an old married couple."

"Then go and fuck yourselves," said Doherty.

"Not a constructive attitude," said Peter. "We came here because we promised to share things that we'd learned with you."

"I appreciate that," said Martin Bloom.

"You would." Doherty looked at him as though he had just given away a signed first edition of *Catcher in the Rye*. "They're looking for more."

"Of course we are." Peter enjoyed baiting Doherty, even if it was counterproductive. "We've brought a bit of intelligence. Just as we agreed."

"We agreed to nothing," said Doherty. "Martin gave up more than he should have the other day at the Mount Washington."

Martin's eyebrows rose and fell behind his glasses, but he didn't say anything.

Doherty stalked to the window and stared out.

Peter said, "If the Constitution passed through Portland in 1864, and you heard about it in the 1970s, we're narrowing things. Give us a name and we can narrow a bit more."

"We give you nothing. We're not—" Doherty stopped in midsentence and turned. "You have to get out of here."

"What?" Peter went toward the window. "Who's out there?"

Doherty pushed him back.

"Who is it?" demanded Peter. "What are you afraid of?"

Doherty told Martin, "Get them out the back. For their own good—"

Peter pushed Doherty aside to get a look: a few pedestrians hurrying along, someone getting out of a car.

But Doherty had seen something that caused his color to rise from red to purple. "They're in the sandwich shop."

"Watching us?" asked Peter.

"Buying lunch," said Doherty.

"Lunch?" said Evangeline. "Who are they? Food critics?"

"They like the clam rolls," said Martin. "Now, please—"

Peter looked through the plate glass toward the sandwich shop. Yes. There were people there. A crowd of bodies around the counter. Good clam rolls.

"Who are they?" demanded Peter.

"Two bad guys," growled Doherty. "Now get out of here."

Before turning away, Peter noticed a black Chrysler Sebring parked down the block. He reached for the door, to step out and get a look at the plates.

Doherty grabbed him, "Listen, I don't care if those guys kill you, but if they see us with you, they may kill us. So—"

Then Peter saw the big guy in the black leather jacket. He had been at the mill two days before. Now he was standing on a Portland street picking pieces of fried clam out of a toasted roll.

Had Doherty and Martin tipped them off? Had this guy shown up now to finish the job? You couldn't trust anyone anymore.

Another guy stepped out of the shop. He was wearing a blue blazer. He said something to the guy in the black leather.

"Peter," said Evangeline, "the one from the Cliff Walk. *Digital New England.*"

"The same one who was wearing the baseball cap in the mill."

The two guys stepped off the curb and started across the street.

Doherty said to Martin, "Get them out. Tell them whatever you want, but get them out."

Martin pulled Peter and Evangeline back through the shop, past the sofas, into the stockroom.

"Who are they, Martin?" said Peter.

"Just go." Martin pushed them out the back door and into the alley.

"Martin! Doherty said you'd tell us. Who are they? Partners?"

"No."

"Then who?"

"Suckers. We're playing them," snapped Martin and those eyebrows closed down to a single line. "Just like we're playing *you.*"

Peter looked at Evangeline. "See what I told you. Talk face-to-face with some guys, you learn more."

The doorbell jangled at the front of the shop. The two guys had just come in.

Martin looked over his shoulder.

Peter put out his foot so Martin couldn't close the door. "A name, Martin. Give us a name. Who told you about the draft?"

"Ryan," said Martin Bloom. "Mike Ryan. He worked for the B and M Railroad. He's been dead since 1974."

Clunk. Thunk. The door closed in their faces and the bolt was thrown.

Peter waited a moment, put his head against the door to try to hear something.

Evangeline was tugging at him. "Let's go."

THEY HURRIED UP the alley to Middle Street.

Peter turned right, back to Exchange, and peered around the corner. The row of bookstores was on the right side, the sandwich shop and the black Chrysler on the left. The street sloped from here three blocks to the waterfront.

He asked Evangeline, "How good is your memory?"

"I remember what the guy in the black jacket did to Bindle."

He said, "I need to get the plate off that Chrysler. Can you remember it?"

"I can't believe you didn't get it when I drove off in it the other day."

"I couldn't believe you got into it. Now . . . you can wait here or meet me at the other end of the block."

"I think we should stay together."

So they fell in with a clump of young women—office workers—who were gossiping about a wedding as they walked down the street. Good cover, thought Peter.

They passed Books, Etc. on the right, then Emerson's, then—

"Rhode Island plate." Evangeline said the numbers.

Peter glanced over his shoulder at Old Curiosity. He could see a face in the window, not red, not owlish . . . a flash of white in the shadowed light.

"Keep walking," he said. "Just faster."

"Should I run?"

"Not yet."

The door to the Old Curiosity Bookshop was opening.

"When?" she said.

"Just . . . about—" At the corner, he glanced over his shoulder and saw the black jacket moving toward them, the blue blazer appearing. "—now!"

They turned the corner and were running . . . past restaurants and plate glass storefronts, in and out of gangs of tourists and office workers hurrying along or reading menus or stopping to photograph the restored Victorian architecture, all gray granite and gleaming silver in the sunlight.

Peter and Evangeline turned onto Market Street just as the black leather jacket appeared at the corner of Exchange. The guy look right, then left, then came after them.

"Hurry!" said Peter.

"I'm in cowboy boots," said Evangeline.

"My favorite. Don't scuff them. Just run. And don't trip on the cobblestones."

Another block, and they were at Commercial Street.

An enormous white ship rose behind the waterfront buildings like an iceberg that had drifted into Casco Bay. A mob of tourists was melting out of it, filling the street, flooding up the hill.

"Looks like the leaf-peeper cruise just pulled in," said Peter.

"Maybe we could grab a ride to Boston."

"Next trip." He turned her to the left and they ran for half a block along Commercial Street, then he said, "Jaywalk!"

Horns blared. A refrigerator truck almost hit them. A car almost hit the truck. Not the best way *not* to attract attention, but they made it across four lanes with the container of the big truck blocking them from view.

"Are they still behind us?" asked Evangeline.

"Doesn't matter," said Peter. "We'll lose them now."

He pointed her onto the Portland Pier. They ran a short distance out over the water, then turned and went along the backs of the buildings on Commercial Street.

This was lobster country. There were lobster boats tied up and lobster traps stacked up and orange lobster bodies piled up in trash cans outside lobster restaurants where tourists were lined up to eat lobster all day long. And everything smelled of lobster—the steam pouring from the restaurant vents, the barrels, the boards of the pier, even the seagull shit.

From the air, a working waterfront looked like a logical thing, a series of piers at right angles to main street. But from ground level, it was a maze of buildings and alleys and pathways, a good place to get lost or to lose someone else. So Peter and Evangeline ran down an alley between two restaurants, then along the back of another restaurant. Then they crossed to the Custom House Wharf and kept going.

When they finally popped out at the corner of Franklin and Commercial, they saw no black leather jacket, no blue blazer.

"Either a good sign or a bad one," said Evangeline.

"Let's assume it's bad and keep moving away from the downtown."

A train whistle squealed.

At the end of the waterfront was the museum of the Maine Narrow Gauge Railroad. The train was preparing for its hourly mile-and-a-half tour along the Eastern Promenade, "with views of Casco Bay and all the railroading excitement of yesteryear."

Peter bought two tickets and they jumped onto the last car, an open-air gondola carrying a crowd of tourists, field-tripping schoolkids, and babysitting grandparents.

"Welcome aboard!" shouted the engineer on the PA. "Once, there were trains like this all over Maine, small engines and small cars, running on tracks just two feet apart, taking the sharp turns and riding the long straightaways as far as the Canadian border. . . ."

Peter kept looking back to see if they were being followed.

Just as the little train rounded the bend at Fort Allen Park, he saw the blue blazer approach the end of Commercial Street. The guy looked left, right, back, forth, confused . . . then the train swung round the bend.

"I think we just lost them," said Peter. "Kick back and enjoy the view."

"I've seen all of Portland I want to," she said. "And my feet are killing me."

"We need to buy you some running shoes."

"We need to go back and smack Martin Bloom and Paul Doherty a bit." She took a tissue from her purse and wiped the perspiration from her upper lip.

"I don't think we want to go back there," he said, "not with those two guys running around."

"So what now?"

"We find what we can about a guy named Ryan of the B and M Railroad. We stay after George Amory. We track his movements after the Civil War, pinpoint the place where the story passes from Amory to Ryan."

"But we're trying to pinpoint where the draft is *now*," said Evangeline.

"Trust the process," said Peter. "We're getting closer."

"So long as no one kills us."

The little train chugged through East End Park, with a walking path and beach to the right, a long, gentle slope of grass to the left, and the Eastern Promenade Park above. At a little crossing, the train slowed for a car towing a boat down to the public landing.

That's where Peter and Evangeline jumped off.

"You paid for a round trip, folks," called the conductor.

"Thanks," said Peter, "but we'll catch the Freedom Trolley from here."

They were halfway to the top of the grassy slope when Peter stopped to look out toward the water.

And there he was, rounding the bend on the walking path. He had the blazer under his arm and was moving with a slow and steady lope, like a hunter certain of running his quarry to earth.

Peter cursed.

Evangeline said, "Where's his partner?"

"I don't know. Come on. But don't run. He hasn't seen us yet. Fast movement will only attract his eye."

They made it to the top of the slope and crossed the promenade, so that they were in the shadow of the trees. A row of big houses looked north from here—Victorians with turrets and porches, two-families built in the twenties, newer Colonials from the thirties, with fine views of the bay.

If Peter had been thinking about it, the neighborhood would have reminded him of South Boston. Same kind of housing stock, same changing demographic as you moved back from the water and into the neighbor-hood, where there were more three-deckers, fewer single-families.

But Peter was thinking of putting distance between himself and the guy in the blue blazer.

They went a few blocks up Congress to the top of Munjoy Hill, the highest spot in Portland, atop which sat a giant wooden tower that looked like a lighthouse. A tour bus was parked in front of it.

"What's that?" asked Evangeline.

"The Portland Observatory. Used to be where they watched for ships."

"Maybe we should go up," she said.

"And trap ourselves? Why?"

She stopped and pointed down the street, a steep slope toward down-town.

There was the black leather jacket, five blocks away, jogging up the hill.

Peter looked around. There were no open storefronts and the side streets were too far. "I don't think he's seen us yet." Then he took her elbow and turned her into the tower.

Inside, a volunteer took their money and told them they could join the tour that had just gone up. They found the group on the third level. A do-cent was lecturing about the construction of the tower.

Peter positioned himself by a window and tried to see out. Nothing.

As the group moved up another level, Evangeline whispered to Peter. "Maybe this was stupid."

"No," he whispered. "If we have to, we'll get right onto the bus with this bunch when we come out."

They followed the group to the top, and with admonitions from the docent to mind their heads and watch their steps, they went out onto the wooden deck. One of the most beautiful views in New England opened before them.

Most of the group turned first to see the water, off to the north and east.

Peter and Evangeline went to the other side, where they had a distant view of the White Mountains and a much nearer view of the street below.

There they were: Blue Blazer loping up from the promenade, Black Leather climbing the hill from downtown. Both were talking on cell phones, probably to each other. Whoever they were, they had figured out Fallon's moves and made all the right moves to counter it.

Then Evangeline pointed to a big blue Chevy pickup with a double cab. It was cruising slowly up the hill.

While it was still rolling, a guy got out. He was wearing a camo jacket and a Red Sox cap.

The guy in black leather glanced at him but kept moving.

And the pick-up kept rolling.

The guy in camo took three quick steps, then put something against Black Leather's back, causing him to hunch up in sudden shock. Before he hit the sidewalk, another guy jumped out of the pickup. They swept Black Leather up and stuffed him into the cab.

The pickup never stopped rolling.

"What the hell?" Peter looked toward Blue Blazer, but he was gone. Whatever he had seen, he had known enough to get out of the way.

"What just happened?" asked Evangeline.

"Someone who was after us isn't after us any more."

"Is he dead?"

"Hard to tell from up here."

"So . . . are we in more danger or less?"

"Hard to tell from up here."

THEY DID NOT go back to the Old Curiosity. They got to the car and headed out of town instead.

"What now?" she asked.

"Back to the White Mountains."

"The White Mountains? Why?"

"Trust the process, and trust me."

Once they were on Route 302 going west, Peter placed a call to the Old Curiosity, but there was no answer. Not surprising.

Then he called his office and left instructions for Antoine. He also left messages with two of his "clients": Jennifer Segal of Dartmouth, and Josh Sutherland, Harriet Holden's secretary. "Just touching bases. Nothing to report," he told them both on their voice mails, then clicked off.

"Shouldn't we talk to that girl again?" asked Evangeline.

"We should talk to both of them," he said. "They must know more."

A few hours later, he and Evangeline reached North Conway, eastern gateway to the White Mountains, a strip of outlets, malls, hotels, and motels where the Saco River turned south and meandered down the intervale.

They took a table in the back of a franchise restaurant, Mexican variety.

"Mexican food in New Hampshire," said Evangeline, "like lobster in Nebraska."

"Order the Granite State rellenos," said Peter. "They'll taste like scrambled eggs."

Evangeline looked out the window, across the wide riverbed. The mountains leaped from the earth a few miles beyond. They made everything in North Conway, from the newest mall to the most venerable guest house, seem puny and insignificant.

"I don't know why we have to go back," she said.

"We're following pathways through time. There's one up there."

She looked up at the mountains.

"Once that was the forest primeval," he said. "Then the loggers came. They cut rail lines. Trains from Boston came up on the west, spurred off and came in this direction. Trains from Portland came right through this town, then they followed the Saco up through Crawford Notch.

"The names of the men who logged out those mountains are like a who's who of New England robber barons. Van Dyke, J. E. Henry, Saunders. Most loggers only hauled out pine and spruce. They cut down the hardwood and left it. Left little stuff, too, used it for matting to roll the big trees, then left it to dry to tinder. So you had huge forest fires, fed by the slash, then massive erosion."

He paused, as if he was trying to see something not only from the perspective of a hundred and fifty years away, but from high in the sky, looking down on those White Mountains the way he might look down on a relief map.

"They wrought so much destruction that in 1918, the government funded the White Mountain National Forest to save what was left, otherwise they might have stripped everything, including the roof of the Mount Washington Hotel."

"And George Amory was one of them?"

"It's in the judge's notes." Peter read from a sheet he had dog-eared in the manila folder. "An agreement between D and C Saunders Company and George Amory, from the Carroll County Registry of Deeds, conveying one thousand acres for certain considerations. . . ."

"Leave it to a judge to know where to go to follow a guy's tracks," she said.

"I wonder what 'certain considerations' were. No money changed hands."

Just then, Antoine Scarborough walked into the restaurant. He came straight for them and plunked down an armful of books.

"Did you bring clothes?" asked Evangeline.

"Found everything, right where you told me."

"Did you cover your eyes when you went through my underwear?"

He sat at the table. "Best job all day."

Peter was more serious. "Did anyone follow you?"

"I don't think so. But people have been looking at me. They don't call these the *White* Mountains for nothin'."

"Where's Orson?"

"Hiding out in Newport. Said he'd stay in touch."

"Bernice?"

"Gone to the Cape. With her Beretta."

"What about you?"

"Like Orson said, I'll hang with my homebodies . . . on Newbury Street. Watch the front door and back. Make sure no one messes with the inventory."

Peter picked up one of the books: *Maps of the Logging Towns of the White Mountains, 1895.*

Antoine said, "Rare's not the word for this one, boss."

"Thanks for bringing these up. I couldn't have worked with them over the phone."

"Where you going?" asked Antoine.

"Up into the Notch again."

"You want me to go with you?"

"No. You go back to Boston. Do what you can to find out about a conductor on the B and M named Mike Ryan. He died in 1974."

Antoine gave Peter a long look. "That's all you have on him?"

"At the moment. If I find any more, I'll tell you."

NINETEEN

August 1874

ON A BRILLIANT SUMMER AFTERNOON, a big Baldwin 4-4-2 steamed into the new North Conway depot. It was hauling four cars full of guests bound for the grand opening of the Fabyan House, in the high valley beyond the Gateway.

The ride from Portland had been a great lark. There was much visiting from car to car. Children scampered about. Jugs of lemonade and boxes of cookies were passed. A few flasks made the rounds, too. And once someone noticed that the click of the rails provided a perfect rhythm for songs like "Old Dan Tucker" and the ever-popular "Marching Through Georgia," there was singing in the second car.

Even a dour New Englander might shed his reputation and give out with a tune on a day when the developers of the Fabyan House were paying for the fun.

George Amory was riding on the last car.

He was now a timber man, a small operator but well respected by the Portland businessmen who had built the new hotel. Any doubt about his reputation had been erased when Joshua Lawrence Chamberlain was inaugurated as governor of Maine and invited George to the ceremony. And an unmarried man of thirty-four, with a good reputation, always caused a stir among the husband-hunters and their mothers.

But George had not mingled during the ride. He sat by a window and let his assistant, Edouard "Frenchy" LaPointe spread charm enough for both of them. George's mind was elsewhere—on business and family business.

Business: At the White Mountain House, the Saunders—father and son—were waiting to discuss the purchase of his Sawyer River property.

Family business: In his pocket was a letter from his cousin Bartlett:

Dear George, I will not mince words. I write because I need your help. The post-war downturn has badly hurt our business. The Blackstone Investors are using it as a pretext to replace me at the board meeting in October. But I refuse to let the Pikes go from "shirtsleeves to shirtsleeves in three generations." You should refuse also. If we can combine family shares and gain the support of another board member, we can fend off Arthur Perkins and his gang.

We know of the Saunders ambitions "below the Notch." We know of yours, too. Might we all do business? Or might you and I come to a private arrangement over our shared knowledge of a certain document?

I offer an excerpt from the Boston Post regarding the St. Albans Raid: "Dawson Caldwell was shot in the street and the contents of his safe deposit box stolen from the Franklin County Bank. . . . Annie Mills, a halfwit, claimed that 'a man with a limp,' who represented himself as a Maine timber man, had masqueraded as one of the rebels. Others corroborated part of her story. . . ."

A dead man named Caldwell? A safety deposit box, just right for holding a few sheets of precious paper? A limping timber man from Maine? My cousin, perhaps?

I do not know the value of a first draft of the Constitution, but I know that Grandfather would approve if we used a bit of the nation's history to save a mill that is a part of the nation's history, too.

George had read the letter several times. Each time, his blood had boiled, gone cold, and boiled again. His cousin, who had betrayed him so blithely, hoped now for help. And if help were not offered, his cousin would try to extort it.

George had composed his answer as the train rocked along:

Dear Bartlett, I now divide my time between the natural wonders of the New England north country and the man-made wonders of Europe. I make money from one so that I may enjoy the other. I buy woodlots and bigger tracts where I can, log them as I can. Your thoughts on my involvement with the Saunders family are as speculative as my plans for the tract below the Notch, but not so fantastical as your speculations on an article that appeared in a newspaper ten years ago.

I will educate myself before the board meeting. If I feel that it is in the best interests of my investment to bring the Saunders family to your side, I will make an effort. I leave you to hunt for a limping Maine timber man and the lost Constitution of our grandfather's fantasies. And whatever decision I make, remember: business is business.

FRENCHY POSTED THE letter at the new depot in North Conway, then he stopped at the men's two-holer, and just before the conductor shouted "All Aboard!" he got back to his seat and elbowed George in the ribs. "Pretty lady out there, boss."

"Oh?" George had his head buried in *Harper's Weekly*.

Frenchy pointed out the window. "Take a look."

George raised his head briefly. Then he looked again, and before his brain quite recognized her, his stomach jumped. She was beside the outhouse, helping a man into a wheelchair. He had not seen her in years, but he had never stopped thinking about her.

"Pretty good lookin', eh?"

"Her name is Cordelia Edwards Atkinson." George enunciated each syllable as though he had rolled it over his tongue a hundred times.

"You know her?" Frenchy wagged his brows. "You know women everywhere."

George watched her roll the wheelchair to the front car; then he turned to his paper and tried to put her out of his mind. He had more important things to worry about. But if had been thinking about her for years, how could he stop now that he'd seen her? Perhaps it was time to meet her invalid husband. Whenever he found himself thinking too much about a woman, meeting her husband always cooled his ardor.

So he got up, steadied himself as the train lurched, tugged the wrinkles from his vest, and went forward, in and out of the puffing smoke that swirled between the cars, all the way to the front.

"Excuse me." He stood over her and tipped his hat.

Cordelia looked up. Her face no longer had the adolescent fullness that had lingered into her twenties. Lines had furrowed around her eyes. Her cheekbones seemed sharper. But her smile was as brilliant in the sunlight flickering through the windows as it had been on that November Sunday so long ago. "George! What a pleasant surprise. I . . . I heard that you'd been included. I didn't see you get on."

The man beside her was not her war-ravaged husband but her age-ravaged father, drained of size and, it seemed, personality, staring straight ahead, oblivious.

George dropped into the seat across the aisle. "It's wonderful to see you."

"Father, look," said Cordelia. "It's George Amory."

"Who?" Edwards looked about, as if angry to be brought from wherever his mind had taken him. "George Atkinson? He's dead."

"Dead," said George. "I didn't know."

As if awakening, the old man looked around, then looked at George. "Your Unitarian prayers didn't do a damn bit of good."

Cordelia mouthed the words "I'm sorry" to George.

As the old man came out of his reverie he became more like his old sarcastic self. Best not to contribute to any outbursts.

So George stood, tipped his hat, and said, "I'm sorry for *you*."

"It's been a year," she said. "I'll wear no more black."

"You're going to the opening of Fabyan House, then?"

"My father's middle initial, F, is for Fabyan. He was cousin to Horace Fabyan of Portland, who built the first hotel on that site."

"Then we'll have time over the next few days," he said. "Time to talk."

"That would make me very happy."

GEORGE WENT BACK to his seat, looked out the window, and thought of nothing but Cordelia until the train stopped in Bartlett at the base of the Notch, the end of the line.

Four red stagecoaches, one for each car, were waiting to take the guests the rest of the way. The passengers from the fourth car rode in the fourth coach. George and Frenchy sat in the extra seats on the coach roof. Soon they were moving as steady and confident on the Tenth New Hampshire Turnpike as the train had been on its rails.

"Best coach there is, eh, boss?" said Frenchy.

"Built by Abbott and Downing of Concord, New Hampshire. Sold all over America."

"You invest in the company?"

"I invest in railroads . . . coaches . . . lumber. Investment is the way to build things."

Frenchy laughed. "What you buildin' for? You ain't got no wife, no family."

That question would have infuriated George if it had come from someone else. But Frenchy had a naïve way of saying things that always cut to the simple truth.

"I build for the future," said George. "Like Hec used to say, it's what we do."

The coach went over a bridge where the Sawyer River dropped down from the mountains and met the Saco.

"Your land up there, boss." Frenchy pointed at the wall of trees rising to the left. Then he blessed himself.

"Don't be cursing it with your superstition," said George.

"I'm prayin' . . . prayin' that you and Saunders be on the same side when Saunders try to run track up there."

After a moment, George blessed himself, too, and Frenchy's laugh echoed off the treetops.

From the road they could hear rail gangs, and sometimes they could see them, working on the roadbed or the trestles that teetered above the

Notch. The tracks extended six miles from Bartlett, but it would be another year before trains got through the Gateway and into the high valley. So George had time to negotiate, because there would be no spurs until the main line was finished.

As the road steepened, the horses strained, and the passengers unconsciously leaned forward, willing the coach up the hill. They passed the Silver Cascade, the Flume Cascade. Then a wall of white seemed to rise beyond the Gateway: the Crawford House Hotel, a glorious confection of gables, pillars, and porches proclaiming to all who passed that they were entering a world of natural beauty and man-made wonder.

Five miles farther was the Fabyan House, and when George looked at it for the first time, he thought of a mill. It was as square and as big— three stories high, four hundred feet wide, with a tower and cupola in the middle, just like a mill, but the Fabyan House was grand and white, with a porch festooned in patriotic bunting and a view east toward mighty Mount Washington. What they manufactured here was summertime enjoyment for ladies and gentlemen.

As he went in, Frenchy tipped his hat to two young women in rocking chairs and whispered, "I think we gonna like it here, boss."

"Business first," said George.

BUSINESS FIRST: SUPPER with the Saunderses, *père et fils*, as Frenchy called them.

George left Frenchy with the ladies and set out on foot for the White Mountain House, less than a mile up the road.

Old Colonel White was sitting in a rocker with a few guests. "Why, Mr. Amory . . . here to cut down the trees?"

George gave a theatrical bow. "I've come to live free or die, sir."

"A noble sentiment," said a guest, raising his libation.

White got up, shook George's hand, and lowered his voice. "Truth is, some of my best customers cut trees nowadays. One of them is even tryin' to buy a share of the business, so he'll have a nice place to stay when the cuttin' starts."

"Saunders?" asked George.

"Nope. J. E. Henry. Sittin' at the big table by the south window. Brung his whole brood up to see his new store at Fabyan's."

The same dead New Hampshire animals stared down from the walls of Colonel White's dining room, but now the scene brimmed with summer life, with the din of conversation, with waitresses hustling trays of chicken and dumplings and creamed corn, with raucous families at some tables, chattering couples at others, even a table of nurses caring for half a dozen wartime amputees.

George located the Henry table; then he headed for Saunders and son. As always, the Saunders were gentlemen. Before business, there was friendly talk. They toasted Enos Turlock, who now managed George's office in Portland. They talked about the cog railway, the mechanical wonder that twice a day carried tourists into the clouds on Mount Washington. They praised the beauty of the new Fabyan House. Finally, as plates of blueberry pie and ice cream appeared, they came round to J. E. Henry, who had been logging small tracts all over New Hampshire.

"Unlike Henry, we have a single large tract," said Daniel. "The old Elkins Grant."

"You mean the Elkins-Amory Grant?" said George.

"Your grandfather must have commanded great respect among the New Hampshire legislators," said Charles, "that they would grant him the land on the Sawyer River."

"The lumber barons of New Hampshire must have commanded more than respect," said George, "considering that the state liquidated the logging rights to most of the White Mountains for . . . what? Twenty-six thousand dollars?"

"Twenty-seven." Daniel Saunders swirled blueberries onto his fork. "Governor Harriman hoped to help the schools and fire the state economy after the war."

"Hundreds of thousands of acres of public land sold off for a 'school literary fund,'" said George. "A good deal for the big operators."

"Not us," said Charles. "We secured our grant before the war ended, just before we met you at this very table."

"So," said Daniel, "if you harbor resentment over the size of your own holdings, don't blame us. *Sell* to us instead. You'll get a fair price, just as I promised ten years ago, a better price than the state got."

"Plain speaking," said George. "I appreciate plain speaking."

"Plain speaking is the New England way." Daniel Saunders nodded as if receiving a compliment.

"Then you'll appreciate plain speaking," said George. "The land is not for sale."

Daniel Saunders dabbed blueberry juice from his lips. "We can wait you out."

"You've waited ten years," George answered. "Might be better to join forces."

"You know that's not our way," said Charles, who had grown taller than his father and, if anything, skinnier, though he had consumed his meal and dessert in half the time of the others. "We prefer to command our own destiny."

"If it's your destiny to get the logs out," said George, "your destiny is joined to mine, because you must run your tracks over my land."

"We can claim right of way," said Charles.

"A claim must go to court," said George. "It would cost time and money. I might be forced to find a new partner." George had expected it would come to this. He had planned a dramatic pause before he said, "The man in the corner, perhaps."

The elder Saunders's face, which usually expressed a sort of natural benevolence, lost all warmth. "J. E. Henry? You're joking."

"Henry is a pirate," said Charles. "He strips the land and moves on."

"That's the nature of logging," said George.

"Not for us," said Charles.

"Selective cutting," said his father. "It will take longer each time we go into the woods. We'll only take the largest third of the trees the first time. Leave the rest to grow. In time, we'll make three cuts over our thirty thousand acres, so they'll be like ninety."

"Waste not, want not." Charles cast a look at George's untouched dessert. "There's a lesson in that."

George picked up his spoon and took a mouthful of ice cream. Then he slid the dish to Charles. "I only need a small portion. There's a lesson in that, too."

Charles picked up his fork. "Share and share alike?"

Daniel Saunders watched his son go to work on the second dessert. Then he said to George, "And so . . . what's your opinion of the Grant administration?"

George knew that their negotiations were at an end for the evening. They spent the rest of the meal chatting about politics and trout pools on the Amonoosuc. There would be more time for business.

But George had one more point to make. He bade good evening to the Saunderses, then walked over to the big table in the corner.

"Mr. Henry," he said. "Excuse me, I'm George Amory. I—"

"I know who you are." J. E. Henry had a face shaped like a spade, a face for making a point and getting on with business, an effect heightened by the fringe of beard that trimmed his jawline from ear to ear.

"I wanted to say hello to you and your family." George bowed to the sons, who looked like the father, and to the wife. "Since we're in the same line of work."

"A pleasure to meet you," said Mrs. Henry.

"Yes," said Henry, tucking into his dessert, "but not so pleasurable as pie."

George backed away, glanced over his shoulder, and saw that the Saunderses were watching. It was what he had hoped.

THE NEXT DAY, George had lunch with Cordelia, who listened in rapt fascination as he described—sentence by sentence—the evening before.

And he realized that no one had listened to him in this way in years . . . certainly not the women he bedded in Paris or London . . . not Frenchy or Turlock. . . . His duplicitous cousin had listened for duplicitous reasons. . . . Big Jack Caldwell had listened like a father, but the river had taken him in '69. . . . George's mother had listened, of course. . . .

When George took a breath, Cordelia asked, "Are you really in a position to hold up the Saunders family?"

He laughed. "I'm a mouse under an elephant. If the elephant rolls over, I'll be crushed. If I'm smart, I can live a long time in his shadow."

Her expression lost something of its brightness then, and she said, "I live in shadows. . . . First my husband, who never forgot the blast that took his lower half . . . now my father, who doesn't remember what he did in a life that touched so many young men."

George left his opinion on that matter unspoken.

Then, as if to shake off her emotion, she said, "I should love to see your land."

"I'd love to show you."

So they rented mounts at the hotel stable and down the Turnpike they went, past railroad surveyors shooting lines in the Gateway, past the cascades, past a crew hammering the high trestle across the Frankenstein Cliffs, past Notchland and the old Mount Crawford House, now a barracks for railroad workers . . . all the way back to the confluence of the Sawyer and Saco Rivers.

The winter snows had been heavy, the spring rains plentiful, so even in late summer the rivers ran high, spreading a silver sheen over the rocks and swirling into the black pools where the trout stayed cool.

The distant thump of an explosion startled the horses and Cordelia, too. Somewhere above, railroad workers were blasting rock.

George looked up as if he might see the echo reverberating from one side of the Notch to the other. "Progress," he said.

He nudged his horse ahead, leading Cordelia across the new tracks and under the canopy of leaves. The foliage was dark, embracing, all but impenetrable. It crowded the sides of the trail more like a tropical jungle than an eastern forest.

They rode for about two miles, to a place where the narrow trail split. One fork led up; the other dropped down toward the flatland beside the river.

"There's a pond," said George, "up on Saunders land. My cabin's down on the bank."

It was a small place, and rude—logs notched and fitted, chinks daubed with mud, roof covered in tar paper. George dismounted and said, "I built it myself."

She slid off the sidesaddle as if she had learned that at finishing school, too. She looked around at the river and the pine-covered hillsides. "It's beautiful."

"Built for rough living. I spent the winter of sixty-five here, after I found the—"

"You called it your grail."

"That's what it became, but finding it didn't change my life." George looked at the little cabin. "I came here to feel something permanent."

"Permanent," she said, "until you start cutting it down."

"One things dies to make room for another," he answered. "It's nature."

She tapped the riding crop against her palm, as if the remark brought a spasm of grief. "We spend our lives denying nature, both the good and the bad, but it is insistent."

He wondered what she would say if she knew how he had answered nature's insistence—his visits to foreign prostitutes, his dabblings with married women. Better to say only this: "I'm thirty-four now."

She laughed. "We're both getting old."

He kicked open the cabin door, took off his hat, and used it to wipe away a cobweb. Then, with a flourish of the hat and a deep bow that masked the tightness in his chest, he stepped aside so that she could enter.

It was a single room, with a table and two chairs, a stove, a rocking chair, a bed. Sunlight poured through the front windows and baked into the tar paper roof.

"I come here for the solitude," he said.

"I've had quite the opposite," she said. "The constant company of two men who couldn't care for themselves. My father now, my husband for nine years."

"Solitude helped me," he said. "Living helped, too. Perhaps you should live."

"I'm trying." She laughed nervously. "I'm here with you."

He threw his hat on the bed.

She took off her hat and threw it next to his.

The sound of the river filled the sudden silence between them.

Their eyes played the ancient pas de deux—meeting and flickering, like hands touching and feet spinning, from lips to eyes to lips to eyes and then . . . she laughed.

"What?" he asked.

"You have gray hairs in your Vandyke."

He brought a hand to his face, as if to cover evidence of time's advance, but time gave them reason to be there and reason to go further, because there was less time now than there had been, and there would be even less tomorrow.

She must have understood this, for she said, "I am glad you never married."

He put an arm around her, and in the warmth of the cabin, they kissed.

She molded herself against him. He could feel her breasts pressing softly and her lower half, unprotected by crinoline or hoop, yearning as if she had not felt a man in many years. In truth it had been a decade since her husband was unmanned.

So he grew bolder. He slid his hands between her buttons and felt a silk chemise beneath her blouse. He popped one of the buttons, then another.

And she stepped back.

Had he gone too far?

She reached behind her neck and popped the top two buttons, then extended her arms so that he could help her slip off the blouse. Then she let her hands drop to her sides, so that the outline of her breasts was clear through her chemise.

"If we have little time," she said, "we must make the best of it, before we become our parents. It's something these ageless mountains tell us."

"The mountains are eloquent." He pulled her to him again and unbuttoned her skirt. It dropped to the floor, so that she was in his arms now, wearing only a chemise and cotton pantaloons and riding boots.

Should he proceed slowly, as he would with a Boston virgin in her father's parlor? Or forge ahead, as he would with another man's wife in a New York hotel? Or act as directly as he would with a Parisian courtesan? Part of him urged the last, but a grown man had to show wisdom with a woman.

Cordelia had known the joys of conjugality and sought them again. She would let him know what to do. He kissed her, and she made no protest when he untied the drawstring of her pantaloons, so that they slipped to her hips and gave him room to slide a hand down the front.

He brushed his fingertips across the bare flesh of her stomach.

He told himself that if she withdrew from his touch, he would go no farther. Instead, she made a sweet sound and swept her tongue across his lips and pressed against his hand as if she had not known a lover's touch in . . . well . . . a decade. . . .

She whispered, "This is very improper." But she made no suggestion that he stop, so he moistened his finger against her, then slipped it gently down and slowly in.

She arched her hips to help him and pressed her head against his shoulder.

Her hair smelled of mountain air. Her sighs mingled with the sound of the river.

THE NEXT FEW days for George were as wonderful as any he had ever spent in any European capital, and better than any month he had ever passed in those mountains.

Though they did not travel again to his cabin, he and Cordelia rode out each afternoon to search for quiet bowers in the woods and cool rocks along the streams. Up on the Zealand River, they found a pool and swam in it, as naked together as if they had found Eden. And neither her stern Congregationalist God nor the more forgiving spirit of his Unitarianism cast them from the garden.

But they made sure to be back at the hotel by four o'clock, so that they could take tea with Professor Edwards. Cordelia, as always, was true to her name.

Sometimes the old man engaged them; sometimes he stared off at the mountains. It did not matter.

"It just makes me feel better," said Cordelia, "to know that he feels me near him."

GEORGE AMORY SAW the Saunderses, *père et fils*, twice more, and each time they edged closer to a partnership. But they were hard bargainers, and so was George.

At their second meeting, which was conducted on the veranda of the Fabyan House, he raised the specter of turning instead to J. E. Henry.

"We think you're bluffing," Daniel told him.

"Think what you will," he said. "I'll be cruising Zealand Notch. I hear Henry's interested in it. If I collect a bit of knowledge about it, maybe I'll do business with him."

This caused father and son to stand as one.

"Do business with Henry," said Charles, "and you'll never do business with us."

George stood and offered his hand. "If so, I trust we'll part friends. As my cousin Bartlett is fond of saying, business is business."

"Your cousin Bartlett," said Daniel Saunders, "may not have much more business to do according to Arthur Perkins."

"A pity," said Charles. "He showed true ambition at the mill. But his taste for—"

Daniel made a gesture, as if to quiet his son.

"George must know." Then Charles turned to George. "Bartlett dabbles. The company has paid off more than one girl to keep down the scandal."

George had always suspected. "Some men are weak. But—"

Daniel said, "If you're fond of him, or value your family's control of the mill, you might bring us to his side with a simple stroke of the pen."

"In the mountains of New Hampshire or the river valleys of Massachusetts," said George, "we should not let sentiment interfere with business."

He did not tell them that the more he thought about their philosophy of selective logging, the better he liked it. A good philosophy for life in New England: Don't use all your resources at once. Husband them. Preserve them. Respect them. Because you never knew what lay ahead, only that another winter was a certainty.

However, a man so suddenly in love might be fooled into thinking that summer would last forever.

A THUNDERSTORM BLEW through that evening. It signaled the arrival of cool air from Canada, a crisp northwesterly breeze, a blue-skied clarity that made every tree stand out in sharp relief on the mountainside across from the hotel.

So George decided that he and Cordelia should ride the cog railway.

When a New Hampshirite named Sylvester Marsh had proposed a train to the top of Mount Washington, people called him Crazy Marsh and said he might as well try to build a railroad to the moon.

But he designed an open-cab engine, called "Old Peppersass" because it resembled a bottle of pepper sauce. It was set on a wheelbed canted to match the slope of the track so that the boiler would remain upright. It pushed cars up the mountain, but not with rail-on-rail traction. A revolving cog beneath the engine engaged the greased cog teeth in the middle of the track. And the whole contraption rose toward the clouds.

And why would Crazy Marsh want to climb a mountain with a train? Not simply because it was there, though it most certainly was, but to take people to the top and make money doing it. There was no better motivation for an inventive New Englander.

The train had become one of the most famous attractions in America, the first cog railway in the world, one of the wonders of the age. And Marsh made enough money from it to invest in the Fabyan House, so that all the tourists who came to ride it would have a place to stay, so that his money made money from his money, like the cycle of evaporation to condensation to rain that made New England so green.

George and Cordelia paid their money and rode at the very front of the front car.

It was a dizzying ascent, up from the hardwood forest, up through pine and spruce, past the treeline, across chasms on the teetering trestle known as Jacob's Ladder, then over fields of lichen-covered rock to the bare summit, where a ramshackle meteorological station was literally chained to the rocks so it would not blow away, and a small hotel called the Tip-Top House was built into them for the same reason.

Here, summer was forgotten. The August breeze became a hard-blowing wind. But it scrubbed the air clear for a hundred miles in every direction.

Most of the passengers made for the Tip-Top, to enjoy the view from behind glass. But George and Cordelia braved the wind, going arm in arm across the top to a cairn, a six-foot pile of stones built by visitors on a calmer day. It offered a bit of protection from the ceaseless wind, a good place for them to enjoy the view.

In the far distance, above the mountains, below the light blue of the sky, they could see the dark blue of the Atlantic.

"What a beautiful world," said Cordelia.

"More beautiful than it's looked in many years," George said.

As if she understood where he was headed, and feared the direction, she changed the subject. "Do the Indians have a name for this mountain?"

"*Agiocochook*, home of the great storm spirit. White men call it the big rockpile."

The wind gusted. Instinctively, she leaned into him for protection.

And he told her he loved her. "I always have. Even when you didn't love me."

"I always loved you, George."

"So . . . the gray has only just begun to fill my beard. It won't stop."

"What are you saying?"

"That you should consider marrying me."

She slipped her hand into his.

The train whistle blew. The stay on top of the mountain was a short one.

"I can't leave my father," she said.

"I once asked you to defy him. I won't ask you again."

"I did what a daughter must do, what we all must do for our parents. And I cared for my husband past all hope of recovery, because the vow was for better or worse."

And in the clarity of that thin air, George saw his own life with a clarity he had never known before: Even when he did not realize it, he had been waiting for her, and he would wait longer, if need be, because she was a woman with character.

By afternoon, they were back in the warmth of the valley.

Cordelia went to check on her father. George took a seat on the veranda, with a glass of lemonade and the newspaper and a sense that now, when Frenchy asked him what he was building for, he would have an answer.

Puffy clouds jumped from peak to peak, painting a tableau of shadow and light on the landscape. A group of ladies and gentlemen were playing croquet on the green in front of the hotel. The stagecoach was clattering to a stop in the roundabout.

The driver pulled on the reins, "Welcome to the Fabyan House, folks."

The hotel staff came hurrying. A bundle of newspapers dropped from the driver's seat, followed by a bag of mail. The doors flew open, and the first people off were two chubby little boys.

George watched them for a moment; then he heard their father's voice. And his blood congealed in his throat.

"Now boys, stay still and don't go runnin' off until we find Uncle George."

Uncle George? Was that what they called him?

A heavyset woman emerged first, fanning herself with one hand and dabbing perspiration from her forehead with the other: Mary Watson Pike.

Then a broad ass appeared in the doorway of the coach, beneath gray swallow tails and green plaid—yes, plaid—trousers. Its owner, dressed in what he took to be the colors of recreation, was so large that he had to back out.

The springs groaned, the coach listed, so that the rest of the impatient passengers could not even pile out on the other side.

Then Bartlett Pike turned, his thumbs hooked into the pockets of a vest that was as yellow as his pants were plaid. He surveyed the hotel and said, in the voice of a man who liked to attract attention, "More beautiful than I'd heard." Then he called to one of the hotel boys, flipped him a coin, told him to see to the family luggage. "Every bag is marked with the name Pike."

Mary Watson Pike herded the boys up the stairs. "Come along. We'll see our accommodations before you go running off."

Running off was exactly what George wanted to do.

But Bartlett's eyes had already found him. "Why, George! As I live and breathe." With the thick-thighed waddle of a man twice his age, Bartlett mounted the steps.

"As you live and breathe?" said George. "Or as you live and *wheeze*?"

Bartlett dropped into a rocker next to George. "It's good to see you."

"How did you find me?"

"Your letter. The North Conway postmark. I telegraphed your man Turlock and asked if you were here. He reckoned we were in contact."

George looked out at Mount Washington. "I should fire Turlock."

Bartlett leaned closer, lowered his voice. "I'm here to fight for my life, George. Don't make me grovel."

"Business is business. You taught me that. I've made my way in business ever since I was thrown out of the mill."

Bartlett began to rock. "It's a long time ago."

"You spoiled my reputation," said George. "Now you're spoiling my holiday."

Just then, Cordelia emerged from the hotel.

George got up. "Are you ready?"

"Who's this?" Bartlett pushed himself up from the rocking chair.

George wanted to rush her right past him, but Bartlett was too big to ignore, and Cordelia was too polite to ignore him, so George surrendered to an introduction.

Bartlett took her hand in both of his. "I belong to two wild Indians who are probably terrorizing the upstairs hallways at this very moment."

"Indians?" said Cordelia.

"My boys. Nine and eight." Then Bartlett looked into her face and said, "She's beautiful, Georgie. Plain to see that *she's* no halfwit."

"Halfwit?" Cordelia's cordial expression faded. "What do you mean, halfwit?"

Bartlett tipped his hat. "Perhaps my cousin will explain."

AND HE DID.

As they rode along the Amonoosuc, George told her the story of St. Albans—the halfwit girl, the strange evening with Dawson Caldwell, pistol-whipping, masquerade as a rebel, his theft of the lost Constitution.

"I did it to help the country, but—"

"You *stole* it?" She sounded shocked at first, then she was silent as the horses clopped along, then she laughed. "I suppose you couldn't have just asked for it."

"Now my cousin would blackmail me because of it."

"What does he want?"

"He wants my help, so that the family can keep control of the mill."

"Is that so bad? To help your family?"

"No, but—" He decided not to tell her about his own expulsion from the mill. Some secrets were better left unshared. "He's done a better job than they credit him for."

"Then perhaps you should help him."

"But—"

She pulled hard on her horse's reins. "A man who won't help his cousin might not be trusted to help any who are his flesh and blood. *Perhaps* you should help him."

PERHAPS. BUT PERHAPS not.

Perhaps he might shoot the fat bastard. That was what he was thinking at dawn the next day when he went to the stable and found Bartlett, dressed in a buckskin jacket, neckerchief, riding boots, and broad-brimmed hat.

George looked him over. "You've been reading dime novels, I see."

"Can I ride with you?"

George went over to the mount already saddled for him. "You'll need a horse."

"I reserved one last night," said Bartlett. "I thought we might talk. Man to man."

The stable boy came out with a butterscotch mare. "This should do for you, sir."

Bartlett flipped him a coin.

George swung a leg and mounted. Then he looked down at his cousin. "Well, come on, if you're comin'."

Bartlett lifted himself with surprising grace into the saddle. "Where are we going?"

"Timber cruising."

"What's that?"

"We go to a promontory, look over a tract, estimate the stumpage—"

"Stumps?"

"*Stumpage.* Standing timber. We look at survey lines, find corner trees, estimate how much spruce, pine, and birch, which tells us how many board feet we can take, which tells us how much money we can make, which tells us how much we should offer for the land."

"Sounds complicated."

"I've been in these woods ten years, thanks to you. I've learned plenty," said George. "But first, there's a man I have to see."

He led his cousin across the road to a clump of stores in the village called Fabyan's. Above one of them was the sign, J. E. HENRY, DRYGOODS, NOTIONS.

The sun's disc was just appearing from behind Mount Washington. Somewhere a rooster crowed. Somewhere a coffeepot burbled its aroma into the air.

"Why are we stopping here?" asked Bartlett.

"Just wait." George dismounted and followed the coffee smell inside. As he hoped, J. E. Henry was at the counter, looking over the books while a nervous shopkeep swept the immaculate floor.

"Good morning." George approached the counter.

Henry raised his head. The wide face and lidded eyes offered not a glimmer of recognition.

"They said you were an early riser," offered George.

"Early to bed, early to rise," said Henry without inflection.

George joked, "Early bird catches the worm, too."

"If I'm the bird, what might you be?"

George let his smile drop. No sense grinning like a fool when someone was insulting you. "I'm another timber man."

"Competition?"

"Or a potential partner."

"I have partners. You've heard of Henry, Baldwin, and Joy?"

"I have. And you've heard of the Saunders family? I have land in the middle of their grant, but I might be convinced to join forces with—"

"If I log here, I'll work my way down the valley. They're working their way up. It's a long valley. With luck, we'll never meet."

"Colonel White says you're buyin' into his hotel," George went on.

"And you've opened this fine store. Looks to me like you're plannin' to stay."

Henry looked over George's shoulder. "There's a fat man in buckskins sittin' out there on skinny mare. If she don't move soon, she may go sway-backed all in a mornin'."

George got the message: Henry wasn't interested. But George had taken the measure of J. E. Henry and concluded that Turlock's advice was accurate. You couldn't do business with a man who lived by the maxim, "Do unto others as they would do unto you, only do it first." While Saunders was a hard bargainer but fair, Henry seemed like the sort who wouldn't so much negotiate as try to swallow you whole.

George, of course, had no real desire to negotiate. He was simply trying to use Henry's ambitions to gain an advantage. So he stopped in the doorway. "I'm cruisin' today, up the Zealand River."

Henry said, "Cruise away," as if it were a threat.

WORKING FROM A map and ignoring most of his cousin's efforts at conversation, George headed up the road to the confluence of the Zealand River and the Amonoosuc.

He followed the riverbank for a time, then turned onto a trail no wider than a deer path. He kept the map pinned to the pommel of his saddle and his compass on a lanyard around his neck. From time to time he stopped, wrote notes, checked the map, looked for surveyor's marks on corner trees, checked the compass.

"Do we know where we're going?" asked Bartlett after a while.

"*I* know," grunted George.

"When do we stop?"

"We won't, unless you stop complainin'."

"I've been looking at your horse's ass for an hour."

"Has he shit any?"

"No," answered Bartlett, "but *you* might, once you hear what I have to say."

George pulled up on the reins and cast a long look over his shoulder.

Bartlett smiled now, as if he had just taken the upper hand. "Keep riding."

Maybe that's what George would do. Keep riding, draw Bartlett on, draw him deep into the wilderness, draw him on and leave him. Then the problem would be solved.

Instead, he urged his horse up Middle Sugarloaf until they came to a spot where the trail grew so steep that horses could not negotiate the switchbacks. They were still deep in the foliage, but up above the morning sun was warming the granite ledges.

George dismounted and tethered his horse. "We go the rest of the way on foot. Stay on the trail and stay close." Then he started to climb, moving quickly over the rocky, uneven surface, forcing fat Bartlett to keep up or get lost.

In the next fifteen minutes, Bartlett made every sound of exasperation, exhaustion, and desperation in his repertoire, along with a few that sounded like asphyxiation.

Let him grunt. Let him groan. Let him fall and fracture his skull. George just kept climbing, until he came to a kind of staircase of rocks and boulders, a trail scoured out by rainfall that had eroded the surrounding soil. It led him to the top and a stupendous view northeast to Mount Washington, southeast toward an isolated pass called Zealand Notch.

When Bartlett finally came crashing into the sunlight, the sweat had darkened his hatband and his face had turned the color of raw beefsteak. He stopped, leaned against a rock, gasped a few more times, then stumbled over to where George was sitting on his haunches, studying the valley through binoculars.

With another groan, Bartlett lowered his bulk onto the rock. "It's beautiful."

George kept his eyes to the glasses. "Lookin' down on the world together, like we used to do when we climbed the cupola."

"Every mornin'," said Bartlett. "Good talk. Man to man."

"You lied to me then. What lies do you have for me now?"

"No lies, George. I'm beggin' you. Work with Saunders. Bring him to my side."

"I can't even bring him to *my* side." George got up and walked to the edge of the rocks. It was not a sheer drop, but a forty-five-degree slope smoothed by thousands of years of rain, snow, and wind, curling twenty-five feet down to the next ledge.

Bartlett said, "It's what Grandpa Will would have wanted."

"Did he tell you that before he died?"

"No, but Daniel Saunders told me that if you sign over your Sawyer River land—"

George whipped around. "You *talked* to them?"

"Last night. I dined with them at the White Mountain House."

George strode back and stood over Bartlett, felt the weight of the binoculars in his hand, and fought the impulse to beat Bartlett's skull in with them.

Bartlett pushed himself back to his feet and said, "I told you you'd shit."

"Shit? I ought to kill you."

Bartlett put up his hands in a gesture of conciliation. "George, this can benefit all of us."

"All? Or just you?"

Bartlett walked to the edge. "A long way down."

George said, "It could be a long way down for you, too."

Batlett raised a hand to his ear. "What's that? I don't hear so well, not since someone strapped me in the cupola while the work bell clanged. You might not remember that. But maybe you remember this." Bartlett reached into his pocket and pulled out an envelope, which he held out.

George came over, took it, and opened it: a *carte de visite* of himself, twelve years younger, wearing a lieutenant's uniform.

"Your mother sent it to me," said Bartlett. "She was so proud."

"Mothers always are," said George.

"Yours had so much to be proud of." Bartlett looked over his shoulder. "A reputation damaged at Fredericksburg, damaged again when you couldn't keep your prick in your pants at Millbridge, rebuilt in logging camps, on river drives, in forests all across New England . . . but then there was that Vermont town, and that poor little halfwit girl."

Bartlett made a gesture with his hand. "Turn it over."

On the back of the *carte de visite*, in childish scrawl, were these words: "Joshua Burns. He came to St. Albans the day before the raid. I swear. Annie Mills."

George swallowed the bile that rose in his throat. "Never heard of her."

"Have you heard of private investigators?"

"Like the Pinkertons?"

"They're the most famous. I hired one named Milton Wigg, sent him to St. Albans. He found the halfwit girl. Showed her a dozen *cartes* of members of the Twentieth Maine, even Chamberlain. She picked you out."

George said nothing. So much of his life had come near to fulfillment in the last few days . . . in love, in business . . . he would have been happy to forget the revenge he had long dreamed of extracting from his cousin. And now it might all be lost, even the revenge.

Bartlett smiled and looked into George's eyes. "Make the deal with Saunders. Sign Sawyer River to him and have him commit his mill shares to me. Or give me the Constitution. I'll sell it and put the money into the mill."

"Do you think I'd allow you to use that document as no more than a bargaining chip?"

"It's business, George. Business is business. The American way." Then Bartlett gave a shrug. "Of course, I could ride to the telegraph office in Bethlehem. Send a wire. Wigg can have the girl here tomorrow. We'll introduce her to Saunders, tell him how you used her, how you joined the rebels for a day, how you stole one of the most famous documents in America for . . . what again? To line your own pocket?"

"You know that's not true."

"But people will whisper, as Uncle William used to say. . . . They'll whisper that Chamberlain was wrong about you. You really *were* a coward and a traitor. Even Copperhead sympathizers like me look like better Americans because we took a stand."

"You never took a stand in your life." George clenched his fists at his sides.

Bartlett continued, oblivious to George's rising anger. "And that fine woman back at the Fabyan House might like to know what it was got you thrown out of the mill, when everyone agreed you were smarter than I was. . . ."

George growled, "This won't work."

"I deserve a piece of that Constitution. It's part of my inheritance. I—"

"You deserve shit!" George slammed both fists into the fat belly.

Bartlett stumbled back. Then he tripped on a protruding slice of ledge. His eyes and mouth made three perfect circles of shock, and with no more than a grunt, the man who had a sound for every mood and emotion disappeared.

George ran to the lip of the rock and looked down to the next ledge.

Bartlett lay motionless. His left leg twisted out from under his bulk like a broken sawhorse under a cask of beer.

And George saw his chance. Revenge on his cousin . . . freedom forever from his cousin's claim to the Constitution. The document would stay where it was, undisturbed. And the fate of the Pike Mill would be passed to smarter men. . . .

It would have spoken well of George if these thoughts did not go through his head, but they did. It spoke better of him that he rejected them, took the rope from his saddle, tied it to a tree, and used it to lower himself.

Bartlett was moaning now, "My leg is broken."

George took off his hat, wiped the sweat from his forehead. "I'll rig a splint."

Bartlett managed a smile. "Looks like I have you right where I want you, George . . . again."

IT WAS RAINING on October 15. It had been raining for three days.

But rain did not stop New Englanders from their business.

On State Street, black umbrellas bobbed along from the Old State House to Long Wharf, while the Blackstone Investors gathered at the offices of D. & C. Saunders for their annual meeting.

Arthur Perkins—still forcing his voice through his nose, still pointing his nose at the ceiling—sat at the head of the table. He looked at Daniel Saunders and said, "Giving your vote to Bartlett Pike will cost you money. It will cost all of us money."

"But," answered Saunders, "if we believe in heredity, we must give Bartlett more time to prove his worth. It's what men of breeding always do. We owe it to Will Pike."

This was an argument difficult to resist among the men at that table. None of them could be accused of sentimentality, but many of them descended from hereditary fortunes themselves and sought to pass the same to their own sons.

Bartlett sat at the far end, his leg encased in plaster and an attitude of supreme indifference on his face. He knew already that he was going to win.

For his part, George Amory paid little attention. He sat by the window and watched the tops of the umbrellas bobbing by, while in his head, he framed the phrases he would put into a letter to Cordelia that afternoon:

It is done. Yesterday I completed transfer of my land to Saunders. Today Bartlett retained control of the Pike Mill, though the name was changed to the Pike-Perkins Mill.

  The best way to keep Bartlett at bay is to align myself with Saunders. Should Bartlett come sniffing for more help, I can say that I have extracted all that I can from Saunders, that I have been forced to use the Constitution as collateral.

  To that end, I have accepted the Saunders offer to manage their operations. It is an equity position, only slightly less than I had hoped for when we began negotiations. I will now help them build a town in the wilderness.

  As for the Constitution, you are the only other person who knows the truth. Like the trees that Saunders plans to cut, then cut, then cut again, the document will become our resource, secreted with us in the home we make together.

  All of this means that for a good portion of the year, I must live in the mountains. Might we not marry now and live apart—you in Portland, I on the Sawyer River—until the day when your father no longer needs your care? As in all things, I will abide by your decision. . . .

On a bright September afternoon four years later, Cordelia Edwards Atkinson Amory stepped off the train at the depot house at Sawyer River and felt the baby kick in her belly. Perhaps it kicked at the emotion that gripped its mother, because Cordelia was shocked.

Where she and George had once looked up into the forest primeval, a long spur of railroad track reached into the hills. On a siding by the section house, an engine steamed. And somewhere upstream, a town rumbled and roared and chewed into the woods.

She swallowed her shock and told herself that it was progress, which would bring a bright future for the babe kicking inside her and for the one clutching at her skirts.

And then George rushed up, swept little Gilbert into his arms, kissed Cordelia, and said, "Welcome home."

They took the company buckboard up the right of way to the town, which was called Livermore, maiden name of Daniel Saunders's wife.

Its steeple was a brick smokestack rising above the steam-powered sawmill. Its center was a rail crossing, surrounded by a store, an office, a schoolhouse, various barracks for the workers. And perched on a road overlooking the town were the houses of the managers: substantial two-story dwellings with broad porches, painted shutters, and outhouses built close to the back doors.

It would not be so bad, thought Cordelia. Here she would raise her children and send them to school, and in summers, when the tourists rode up in the trains, she and her family would leave for Casco Bay.

Cordelia felt better once they got to their new home. She had sent many of her things ahead, and they looked now as if they had been chosen just for this house—the settee and upright in the parlor, the Governor Winthrop desk in the foyer, the mahogany table in the dining room. She could live here.

They left little Gilbert on the carpet, playing with his new set of tin soldiers, and George led her down to a safe at the foot of the stairs. He had built it right into the granite foundation. He opened it and pulled out a leather map case. He took the lid off the case and slid the papers out.

She took them and felt a chill.

And the baby kicked, which gave her another chill.

She knew that she carried the future of America inside her, and she now believed she held it in her hands.

TWENTY

It was three thirty on Thursday and the October shadows were already crossing Route 302. The cooling afternoon promised a cold night in the mountains.

Peter and Evangeline had changed into the clothes that Antoine had brought—blue jeans, long-sleeved shirts—khaki for him, denim for her. Peter had put on his hiking boots. Evangeline was still shoeless because her feet were killing her after the foot race through Portland.

"What makes you think Judge Trask's men didn't already look around on the banks of the Sawyer River? After all"—Evangeline held up the letter from George to Cordelia, written a hundred and thirty years before—"they found this mixed in with the papers of Aaron Edwards."

"But do they have the draft?"

"Well, no, but the letter says that the Constitution"—she read—"'will become our resource, secreted with us in the home we make together.'"

"So we should see that home," he said.

"No. We should be in a library, doing more research—"

"Other people have done that—the judge, Bishop's people. Antoine is doing it for us."

"Then we should be interviewing someone, trying to look through their eyes."

"That's what we're doing. That's what we always do. That's why we're going to stand in the place where George Amory hid the Constitution and see if we can see through *his* eyes. See through time to the place where he left it."

She gave him a long look and pulled on her Reeboks.

There was a sign on Route 302: Sawyer River Road, a left turn in the woods, a dirt road.

Peter started up. Pebbles clattered in the wheel wells. Dust puffed out behind the car. Yellow birch and Norway maples bent their branches over the road, forming a canopy of fall color that, a month before, would have been impenetrable green.

Evangeline was looking at Belcher's *Logging Railroads of the White Mountains.* "It says we're on the bed of the old railroad. There's a pond in further. Good fishing."

"I didn't bring my rod," said Peter.

She looked at the pictures. "There was a sawmill and an engine house. There were houses along the road, built into the embankment so that they'd have a nice view."

"Of what?"

"The sawmill and the engine house. Now it's—"

"Nothing but trees."

After about two miles, Peter made a U-turn, careful not to slip into the drainage ditch on one side of the road or over the embankment on the other. He parked on the shoulder, pointed back toward 302.

The river was down to the right, down through the trees, down across a stretch of flat ground.

"Is this the pathway though time?" asked Evangeline.

"Humor me." He took the book of maps and got out.

"Peter"—she got out and almost slid down the embankment—"it's a forest."

He brought a finger to his lips. "So be quiet and listen."

"To what?"

Leaves were falling everywhere, catching the last sunlight, covering the ground like snow. Their flutter and the faint trickle of the river were the only sounds.

She cocked her head. "What am I supposed to hear?"

He leaned close to her. "Hear the quiet. And maybe you'll hear the voices of people who've been dead for a hundred years. Listen and see."

"You're getting way too mystical for me, Peter."

He went to the trunk, where he kept a bucket of tools, including one of his father's old trowels. He pulled it out.

Evangeline looked down the slope, at the slender birch and maple saplings, at the white pines and spruce. And the longer she looked, the more revealed itself.

Halfway down the embankment lay a pile of brick entwined with autumn-red poison ivy. In a shaft of sunlight, a rusted old boiler sprouted goldenrod. Concrete pilings supporting nothing stood among the rocks in the river. There were indentations everywhere in the earth—foundation holes, some lined with stone, others concrete, and all overflowing with trees, brush, weeds.

"It's as if nature is gathering this place back to itself," she said, "or trying to figure out what to do with it."

"When the logging died, so did the town." Peter started down the embankment. "Imagine the trains, the sawmills, the people. . . ."

At the bottom, he opened the old book to the map he had marked. It showed the location of each of the homes and the names of the owners, as they appeared in 1882.

Evangeline looked over his shoulder. "They had a school here, too?"

"They had kids. They had to educate them."

"Can you tell where the sawmill was?"

"Right there." He pointed to a rectangle of concrete, about fifty feet by two hundred, revealing itself from the underbrush as they drew closer.

Peter jumped up on top of the wall and looked around. No trace of the rail sidings remained. No remnant of George Amory's world. But from there, Peter could look again at the map and gauge exactly where the Amory house had been.

"Peter," said Evangeline. "Listen."

A pickup was groaning up the road in low gear, tires thumping in the potholes, dust and leaves swirling in the wake.

"It's blue." Evangeline started to hunker down behind the wall.

"Coincidence," said Peter. "Fishermen or hunters most likely."

They watched the truck thunder on up the road, not even slowing at the BMW.

Peter was glad of that. He didn't tell her that the truck scared him a bit. Even if the camo guys had followed them from Moosehead Lake to Portland, he didn't think they could follow them all the way to the ruins of Livermore. But he had seen *Deliverance.* He knew that bad things happened in the woods . . . for no reason at all.

The sound of the truck faded, so he turned again to the map. He determined that Amory's house must have been along the embankment. They climbed again and found three foundations, each about thirty by twenty. Peter pointed to the middle one—granite stones lining a dirt-filled hole that had given birth to half a dozen trees and a tangle of underbrush.

"Where do you think he'd keep a safe?" asked Peter.

"Oh, I don't know, in one of the corners with the poison ivy." She watched his mind turning things over. "Sometimes, I just don't understand you."

Peter pushed aside a few vines and jumped down into the hole.

Evangeline stood on the wall above him. "You don't think he buried the Constitution in his cellar, do you, and then just forgot it?"

"Hard to say." He pulled the trowel out of his back pocket and probed the crumbling mortar. A big granite foundation stone rolled loose and tumbled against a tree. Then he worked his way around, poking, prodding, looking for . . . something. Then he came to a place where the remnant of a staircase stringer was still affixed to the foundation, driven into the mortar with concrete nails. Right at the bottom was an empty space, as if something had once been there that was gone now.

"A hole for a safe?" she asked.

"Could have been." Peter ran his hand around inside and came away with bits of rust on his fingers. He held them up to show her.

"So, there was a safe here. Was the Constitution in it?" she asked.

"Yes." He levered himself out of the hole and looked around, as if there might be clues that he was just not seeing. "The Constitution was here."

She kept talking. "You said the judge's papers gave you a new idea. Is this it?"

"I always believe that if you can see where it's been, you might be able to figure out where it's gone," said Peter. "I guess it's more a hunch than an idea."

"A hunch?" she shouted. "It's Thursday. On Sunday, you want to put it on TV."

"Evangeline." He grabbed the cuff of her jeans and tried to pull her down next to him. "I honestly don't think we're going to find this thing by Sunday. Maybe not in a month of Sundays."

She pulled away from him. "We promised Harriet Holden."

"I don't care about her—"

"I'm tired of hearing you say that." She strode away.

"—or any of them. Just so long as we find it." He jumped up and followed her.

"But where's your political conscience?"

"Two or three slots down the list from my sense of right and wrong."

"*Right* is controlling guns. *Wrong* is not caring."

"Well, I guess I don't care," he shouted after her. "That's why I'm here in Middle-of-Fucking-Nowhere, New Hampshire, up to my knees in poison ivy, looking for a strand of information that might lead to another one."

"But you're doing it for all the wrong reasons," she said.

"I'm doing it because it's what I do. It's what I'm good at."

"You're doing it because it could be worth millions."

"If find it, I'll have four different groups fighting me for it in court."

She shouted over her shoulder, "We've wasted an afternoon. We've wasted a whole day. We promised Harriet Holden that she'd have the document to present when the committee hearing starts, and her assistant asked you to have it the night before."

"We told them we'd try. The real fight will come if it gets out of committee."

"Making a big splash may be the only way it *gets* out of committee. So I'm officially pissed at you." She got into the car and slammed the door.

He went around to the other side, grabbed the handle, and saw stars. At the same moment, he heard a crunching sound inside his head. At least it seemed to be inside his head in the half-second of consciousness that remained to him.

RINGING. NOT INSIDE his head but nearby.

Where was it? Where was the phone?

Where was he? In the driver's seat of his own car, but where?

And the phone? He fumbled in the pocket beside the driver's seat, found the phone, flipped it open.

"Hello?"

"Peter?" It was Evangeline. "Peter. Are you all right?"

"I think so . . . where are you?" He looked out the window. "Where am *I*?"

He was parked in the lot of a little general store next to the Connecticut River, in a perfect little white square of a town.

"You're in Guildhall, Vermont," she said. "And I'm all right."

"Evangeline, what's—?"

"Listen, Fallon"—a male voice came on the line—"it's time to get serious."

"What? Who is this?"

"Find that Constitution."

"Who hit me?"

"I did."

"Is this Mercer?"

"No. But you can thank him for saving you in Portland. You've made deals with a lot of other so-called good Americans. But we come first. We have insurance."

"Is this Batter? You're the brains, and Mercer's the muscle, right?"

"Find that Constitution, then call your girlfriend's cell." *Click.*

Peter jumped out of his car, crouched down, slid his hand around, feeling . . . feeling, under the fenders, along the rocker panels . . . and *there*, under the rear bumper: a global positioning tracker.

Just the kind of gadget that a well-armed woodsman would like. Had they planted it in the gun club parking lot? Or during that little dustup on the road?

It had given them the eyes to watch him go from the gun camp to Portland to the Sawyer River. Then what? Had they had run out of patience because he went to a site they'd already mined? Did they think he was just touring with his girlfriend and calling it work? Did they think that kidnapping Evangeline would make him work harder?

At least they had been in Portland to take care of one Rhode Island thug.

And that gave him a thought.

He called his old friend Detective Scavullo of the Harvard police force and asked him to run that Rhode Island plate number he had gotten that morning.

EVANGELINE WAS CRANING her neck to see under her blindfold. She had worked through terror to anger at how tightly her hands were bound and finally she'd found her way to some good honest sarcasm.

"You know," she said toward the front seat, "kidnapping is a federal crime."

"You're not kidnapped," said the voice from the passenger seat, the one that had been doing all the talking. "You can get out right here if you want."

"Like hell she can." That was Mercer's voice, coming from behind the wheel.

"The Constitution says something about unlawful seizures, too," she said.

"Shut the fuck up," snapped Mercer, "or we'll gag you."

"There go my rights of free speech."

A backhand struck her in the face.

"No hittin'," said the other one.

"Fuck it, Scrawny. She pisses me off," said Mercer. "Let's just throw her out on her head."

Evangeline swallowed her own blood and said, "If you do that, you'll never get the Constitution."

"She's right," said the other one.

The blow had knocked the blindfold loose. Evangeline angled her head so that she could see under the edge. She recognized one of the other ATV riders. He was about half the size of Mercer—hence the nickname—and had the tattoo of a bullet on his cheek. There was a rank man-smell about both of them—cigarettes and sweat and beer farts that hadn't quite cleared the air.

"Your driver's license says you're from New York." Scrawny was pawing through her purse. "We'll only kill you if you answer wrong: Empire or Nation?"

"What are you talking about?"

"Evil Empire or Red Sox Nation? You're one or the other."

They both laughed.

"Oh, shit," she said, "just shoot me now."

Mercer growled, "I might, lady. You Maced me yesterday. I didn't sleep too good. I'm in a bad fuckin' mood. So shut the fuck up."

This, she decided, was not going well.

She peered out at the road. They passed a sign: Route 2. It ran across the top of Vermont and New Hampshire and into the Maine woods. The sun was behind them.

"So . . . we're going back to Maine then?" she said.

Mercer slammed on the brakes. "What did I tell you?"

"Sorry," she said. "You'd better keep going or you might get a ticket."

PETER WAS STILL in Guildhall.

Under different circumstances he might have noticed how beautiful it was, how tiny, how *New England*—two churches, a library, a general store, and a building that served as town office, town hall, and post office. The library was a yellow Victorian house. The rest were Colonial—neat, white, perfect.

Peter punched in the numbers for Judge Trask, and while the phone rang he walked onto the bridge looking for better cell reception. The Connecticut River widened quickly here, and white water riffled over the rocks.

A car drove by and some smart-ass yelled, "Don't jump."

Small chance of that. This thing had just gotten very personal.

Peter still didn't think there was a way to straighten it out in three days, but he wouldn't rest until Evangeline was safe and he had the Constitution and the world knew about it, in that order.

Judge Trask listened to Peter's story and said, "That son of a bitch."

"Batter?"

"Mercer. He was supposed to follow you, protect you if you got into trouble."

"The way he did in Portland?"

"Precisely. Now let me counsel you against calling the police. Mercer and his pals . . . they're armed like a modern militia. I think your girlfriend will be safe, unless you double-cross them."

"Are you part of this?"

"I influence them less than you think. Now, do you have a pen and paper?"

"Yeah."

"Write down an address in Peacham, Vermont. I want you to go there now. Ask for Kate Morgan. She might put your mind at ease."

"Who is she?"

"A friend, and she has some pretty interesting friends of her own."

"Will they help get Evangeline back?" Peter tried to keep the anger out of his voice, but he couldn't.

"I'm trying to help you, Mr. Fallon" said the judge. "I want this to end well. So go there. Kate will help, too, however she can. And tune to Kelly Cutter's radio show while you drive. She reads e-mails at five thirty. Listen. You might understand me a little more."

PETER PICKED UP Route 2 heading west, clicked on the radio, pressed the SEEK function and let it run until he found Kelly Cutter, beating the rightie drum on a hundred and fifty stations from Maine to Florida.

"It shames me that this repeal movement began in New England," she was saying. "I'm from New England. And we like to think that we have what they call character. So how did we let some Democrat Congresswoman push this? We should know better."

Nothing wrong with trying new ideas, thought Peter. Then he said to the radio: "It's how we get at the goddamn truth."

Kelly kept talking: "We live through seven lousy months, just to get five good ones and call ourselves lucky. We take pride in our historical roots, but we elect Democrats like Ted Kennedy and RINOs like Olympia Snow while people in the rest of the country decide that the only New England patriots are the ones playing football. . . ."

Toxic, thought Peter. The woman was absolutely toxic. She went on like this every day, on every subject, doing her best to poison every well of public discourse.

"But you know, folks," she said, "there *are* patriots in New England. There's a judge in Maine, who sent me an e-mail yesterday . . . and that brings me to 'E-Mails from America.' You won't want to miss this one. Right after the news. So stay tuned."

Peter's cell phone rang. He turned down the radio.

It was Scavullo. "I hear that you were at a murder scene day before yesterday."

"It seems like years ago, but, yeah."

"What are you after this time."

"The usual . . . pearls of wisdom from the past."

"So you can put a few more around your girlfriend's neck?"

Peter thought about telling him everything, but Scavullo was too much the cop, a Massachusetts Statie who retired to join Harvard's criminal investigation unit. Peter had met him on the Shakespeare manuscript case and trusted him, liked the no-nonsense attitude and the smile that never quite happened, respected the strength compacted into the middleweight's body. Still, Peter kept his mouth shut about Evangeline but told him everything about the draft.

"Sounds valuable," said Scavullo. "Worth more than just money these days."

"Every time they try to change the Constitution, somebody starts wondering what the Founding Fathers would say, including the guy in the black Chrysler Sebring."

"It's a company car," said Scavullo.

"Company car? What company?"

"Registered to Jarvis Real Estate Industries, of Newport, Rhode Island. And it's not a stolen plate."

"Is there a Mr. Jarvis?"

"Clinton C. Jarvis owns the company."

"Maybe I should start with Jarvis. Anything else?" asked Peter.

"Not only is he a national real estate developer, he's a writer, too. He's coming out with something called *The Rebirth of a Nation*. I looked it up on Amazon. It's scheduled to ship at the end of the month."

"Are there reviews? *PW*? *Kirkus*?"

"No."

"Publisher?"

"Revelation Press."

"Vanity," said Peter. "That explains the lack of trade reviews."

"Here's the blurb: 'Do you believe that America has lost her way? Do you believe that the Judeo-Christian foundation on which she was built is crumbling? Do you believe that we need to destroy the temple in order to rebuild it in three days? Here, in straight talk, is the vision of Clinton

C. Jarvis. Follow it and take back your children's education, your legal system, your country itself. This is the book for all right-thinking Americans, from Main Line to Born Again, from the lovers of the Latin Mass to those who like guitars at consecration, from the Orthodox to the Reform.'"

"Right-thinking?" said Peter. "Or far-right?"

"Well, there's one of those promo quotes on the site, too, from Kelly Cutter."

"Our favorite rightie," said Peter. "What does she say?"

"A lot of blah blah about a good American writing a great book. She's probably a friend of his," said Scavullo. "She makes it sound pretty good. I might buy it."

"You do that. I might try to find Clinton Jarvis."

"Be careful," said Scavullo. "And call me if you need help."

Ten minutes of news, weather, and commercials carried Peter past St. Johnsbury, Vermont, and up the hill toward Danville.

Meanwhile, he tried to factor the religious right into the equation. Had Clinton Jarvis sent his minions to kill the people who were after the Constitution? But why? Wouldn't he want it, too, just like everyone else?

"AND, WE'RE BACK," said Kelly Cutter. "As I was saying before the break, there's a judge in Maine. He e-mails me regularly. Here's his latest."

Peter turned up the volume.

Kelly read: "'We're six states, jammed into the upper right corner of the American map. We're a small place compared to the rest of the country, but we boast an identity so powerful that it seems to rise from the landscape itself.'"

Ain't that the truth, thought Peter.

"'Our mountains are worn down by time, yet the tallest of them harbors the harshest climate in the world. Our foothills and forests close off the long vistas, but the seaside and the mountain notches offer views to infinity. Most of our rivers are twisty and narrow, but so powerful that they gave birth to America's industrial revolution.

"'It's a landscape of contradictions, which reflects the people who live here. New Englanders can be stubborn, aloof, distant, but they are always reliable. We made America's first journey from agriculture to manufacture to high tech, but we're not known for adapting to new ways. We organized our governments around the town meeting, the heart of true conservatism, and in many ways, we remain a conservative people, but we've advanced some of the most liberal political ideas in history. We have sunk stubborn roots in rocky soil, but history is filled with tales of New Englanders settling other parts of the country and ranging the globe in pursuit of wealth.

"'A real New Englander will tell you that our Constitution is not a tool for politicians hoping to make points, whether it's a cynical Republican pushing flag-burning amendments because his poll numbers are down or a do-gooding Democrat who decides to protect us from ourselves by banning guns.

"'The Founding Fathers knew what they were doing when they made that Constitution difficult to amend, so let's think hard before we mess with it.'

"Now, folks," said Kelly in a sultry voice, "I might not agree with him on everything—he did imply that liberals had a few good ideas—but I know a good man when I hear one, and I wanted you to hear him, too. So I've just read for two minutes and ten seconds. But, Judge, honey, about that flag-burning amendment . . ."

Peter dialed up some music and kept driving.

IN THE HILLSIDE strip of town called West Danville, he turned off the main road and headed south. He was driving away from Evangeline. He did not like it, but it's what the judge had told him to do, and Kelly Cutter was right—you know a good man when you hear him, no matter which side he's on.

So Peter headed deeper into what he called the Vermont dream.

There were locals in Vermont, natives, hardworking paycheck-to-paycheckers whose grandfathers had been there a hundred years before. They worked the dairy farms and the granite quarries and kept the place running. But there were a lot of flatlanders, too, refugees from every variety of urban rat race who thought it would be just great to own a small business in a beautiful place. Some of them would leave when their first Vermont winter turned to mud season. Some would go when they found out that running a B & B was harder than managing a stock portfolio. But many stayed and kept dreaming.

You could feel the dream in the roads that waved and curved through pastures and woodlots and ran by antique shops and along the white fences of gentlemen's farms. And every road seemed to run beside a stream, and all the streams ran toward the Connecticut on the east or Champlain on the west. Nature created the logic of everything in Vermont, and man, if he was smart, conformed to it.

Peter drove ten miles without seeing a traffic light. Then, just south of the hamlet of Peacham, he came to a big red barn. Faded letters—in the style of the early 1900s—covered the side: FULLER'S FARRIER AND BLACK-SMITH. A much newer sign above the door: MORGAN'S ANTIQUES AND FIREARMS.

The BMW crunched across the gravel drive. Peter got out and cocked his head. Nothing. Exquisite. Silence at sunset. There was a fresh, pungent scent in the air: a cord of new-cut firewood stacked near the barn. It mingled with the scent of something sweeter, someone's evening fire, curling smoke into the sky.

Beside the door a cork bulletin board was splattered with thumbtacks and papers, leaflets and circulars. There were the smiling senators again, and that caption: "These people want your guns." There was a bake sale at the Congregational Church in Danville, a slide lecture at the Grafton Library, a meeting of the 4-H in Peacham.

What the hell was he doing here? *Trusting the judge.*

He pushed open the door. And he was greeted by a big brown bear staring straight at him.

Then he heard the metal *clang* of a stove door.

He looked toward the sound and saw more stuffed animals—an owl, a deer's head on the wall, next to a moose.

And guns. Cases and racks and walls of guns. All kinds—flintlocks, cap and ball, what looked like a Spencer carbine. Old guns. New guns. And not just guns. There were lithographs, engravings, old leather chairs, a mahogany chest of drawers . . . half an acre of stuff.

"Beer?" The voice came from somewhere near the woodstove.

Peter said, "Yeah. Sure."

He heard the soft thump of a little refrigerator door, and then a woman stood with two longnecks twined in her fingers.

She was big but not burly, solid but not butch: a starched white shirt and jeans, short hair, lots of jewelry—rings on most of her fingers, a nice belt buckle, and turquoise pendants dangling from her lobes.

She ambled over and held out a beer. "Did you get tickets to the ball game?"

"Hunh?"

"Game eight on the play-off strip, first game of the World Series on Sunday. My father brings all the interested parties together at Fenway, mecca of New England, over the one thing he thinks we can all agree on."

"Who *are* you?"

"Kate Morgan, daughter of Charles Bishop. I use my mother's name, so as not to be confused with my father, who's using you to find the lost

Constitution and using his television empire to repeal the Second Amendment."

Peter looked around at the guns. "I take it you don't agree."

"When Charles Bishop found out he had a gay daughter who liked guns, it blew his mind."

"What part? The gay or the guns?"

She gave a laugh. "They say a conservative is a liberal who's been mugged. Sometimes I think I should hire someone to mug my father, the king of the anti-gun crusaders."

"You know the king. I know the queen. She's just been kidnapped."

"Don't worry about her. She'll be all right." Kate raised her bottle. "Cheers."

Peter took a swallow. It was ice cold and felt as good as it tasted. Her large presence felt good, too. She gave off an aura. *Relax. Come to Mama. It will be all right.*

She led him over to the sofa in front of the woodstove.

"It heats the whole barn till Christmas," she said. "But come New Years's we make for Florida. Much easier to carry concealed in Florida. Just ask those militia types who scooped your girl."

"You know them?"

"I know they read my catalogue. I know they're collectors in addition to shooters. I know that by nine o'clock, they'll be so far into the Maine woods a squadron of Blackhawk helicopters couldn't find them."

"You know a lot. Do you know why the judge wanted me to come here?"

She gave him a grin. "I'm just a target-shootin' dyke come to Vermont to mind my own business and live my own private marriage."

Peter took another swallow of beer. "Are you looking for the Constitution, too?"

"I'm looking to protect it. If people get in the habit of changing the amendments we have, they might start writing new ones, too, against people like me."

Just then there was a crunch of tires on the gravel.

Peter half rose from the sofa.

"Relax," said Kate. "It's a friend."

Footfalls followed, the door swung open, a woman called, "Katie? Are you here?"

That voice. Peter recognized it instantly. Deep, seductive, with a prep-school accent so upper-crusty, it was a wonder that all those simple folk out in radio land could stand listening.

And in she walked, a blonde with strong jaw and long legs, the right-wing Carly Simon. Kelly Cutter herself.

She seemed much less formidable in person than the harridan on television, especially as she smiled and offered her hand. "Peter Fallon? The famous antiquarian? I'm speechless."

"I doubt that," said Peter.

EVANGELINE COULD TELL nothing except that they were moving. Her captors said little enough to each other and nothing to her. And every time she thought about saying something, she let the bruise on the side of her face be her guide.

After an hour, the road turned into a roller coaster, up and down, down and up, bend to the right, twist to the left. After another hour, the pickup slowed, turned onto a dirt road. They went a mile . . . two miles . . . turned, went another ten miles, with the high beams bouncing and flashing ahead.

Finally, they jerked to a stop.

Evangeline stepped out.

Then a shaft of light struck her. A tent flap had just been pulled back. A big man was walking toward her. In the darkness, she could see only shadows.

The man removed her blindfold. It was Jack Batter. He looked at her a moment, as though waiting for her to react. Then he said, "You're our insurance policy. We get the draft, we drive you back. Or you can go right now."

"Go?" she said. "Go where?"

"Out there. We're not kidnappers. Good night, Miss Carrington."

But they were so far from civilization that the sky seemed brighter than the pine forest around them, a luminous arc of stars in the blackness.

PETER HAD DINNER with the Kate and Kelly in their farmhouse.

It was two centuries old and filled with oak antiques, a shrine to the hardworking history of the place, except for the kitchen, which was tricked out like a twenty-first-century hobby cook's funhouse, with granite countertops and stainless steel appliances and a big blue Aga stove in the corner.

Peter felt guilty to be sipping a Zaca Mesa Chardonnay when he should have been doing something to save Evangeline. He also felt guilty to be sitting there with Kelly, who would get Evangeline's vote for Princess of Darkness.

But as Kate set the table, she told him again that Evangeline would be safe.

And as Kelly cooked—chicken breasts sauteed in shallots, garlic, and capers, with a finish of white wine and lemon—she described the details of her life. She said she had tried to go straight but had married an abusive man, the kind who "could turn a nymphomaniac into a nun." After her divorce, she went into radio, first as a disc jockey on an FM station, then as a weekend fill-in on a local talk show. That was in '92, the year Bill Clinton was elected president. So she followed the principle set out by the rising stars of rightie radio, that no Democrat could ever have the best interests of the republic at heart, then she started beating it and beating it and beating it to death.

"Do you believe it?" asked Peter as they sat to dinner.

"It doesn't matter if I believe it," she said. "Look at the ratings. Look at the growth of the Cutter network from one station in New Hampshire to three in northern New England to a hundred and thirty in twenty-eight states."

"And she does it all," said Kate, "from her own studio in St. Johnsbury."

"That way," said Kelly, "we get to live the Vermont dream."

"Do your listeners know"—Peter cut into his chicken—"about your unorthodox relationship?"

"I'm a right-wing lesbian living in the state where civil unions were born," said Kelly. "So what?"

"It's just that—"

"Don't forget," said Kate, "the classiest radio talker of them all was a Boston libertarian named Brudnoy, who also happened to be gay."

"But he always brought civility to the debate," said Peter.

"We can't afford civility anymore," said Kelly.

Peter sipped his wine, measured his words. "No ratings in it?"

"My listeners don't want this." Kelly poked her fork into her chicken and held it up. "They want red meat."

"You weren't feeding them when you read the judge's letter over the air."

"I read it because he asked me. And I respect him. He knows we're all Americans. And we don't always come in pretty packages."

"Right," said Kate. "Just look at us."

He did. From face to face, two handsome women, but he still wasn't sure what they had to tell him. "Your listeners don't know about you. What about your friends and financial supporters. What about—" And here he paused to gauge their expressions. "—someone like Clinton Jarvis?"

Kelly said, "Jarvis is a sophisticated man. He knows how the world works."

"What does he want with a first draft of the Constitution?"

Kelly looked at Peter, as if trying to decide how much to tell him, then said, "I don't think he wants it."

"Everybody who knows about it wants it," said Peter.

"I don't think he wants it," she said, "because he has it."

"Has it?" Peter stopped cutting, stopped chewing, almost stopped breathing.

Kelly looked at Kate, then got up and went to the computer table in the corner. A pile of books sat beside it, as if Kelly used them for reference. She dropped an advanced reader's copy of Jarvis's book on the table. "Read the introduction."

As he reached for the book, Peter's cell phone rang and they all jumped.

It was Antoine: "I have info on a B and M conductor named Michael Ryan . . . and his sister, a maid in Newport. . . ."

TWENTY-ONE

June 1919

ℜ ROSEMARY RYAN AWOKE in the maid's quarters of the Perkins cottage, kicked off the wet sheets clinging to her legs, and wiped the perspiration from her upper lip. A June heat wave was baking New England, so the little room under the eaves felt as stuffy as a nun's cubicle in a convent.

Rosemary had been taught by the nuns at Notre Dame Academy in Roxbury. They had taught her to diagram sentences so that she could express herself. They had taught her to do equations so that she could calculate what portion of the world's weight she would carry. And they had taught her the faith so that she could understand her existence.

What more did a girl need? A husband, a child, a home . . . perhaps a convent. . . .

When Rosemary's father fell drunk from a Boston dock, the nuns promised to pray for his soul. When the influenza swept through her South End tenement, took her pregnant sister-in-law, and left her brother a drunken wreck, the nuns promised to pray for their souls. And when she sat for weeks at the bedside of her dying grandmother, reading to the old woman and listening to her stories, the nuns promised to pray for her soul, too.

The serenity that the nuns derived from their confidence in Christ's love inspired many a young girl to join them in their world of prayer.

But Rosemary preferred women who made their way. It was a habit she inherited from her grandmother, who had begun as a loom girl in the Pike-Perkins Mill and ended as a union organizer in Boston. Rosemary kept a photograph of her on the wall in the tiny bedroom, next to a photo of the famous suffragist, Maud Wood Park.

As Rosemary put on the maid's uniform, she recalled the day that she saw Mrs. Park, the most memorable day of her life.

It was a snowy February afternoon. Rosemary was coming up from the subway, bound for her part-time job at Filene's. As she emerged into the chilly air, she heard chanting, saw crowds and American flags and bobbing placards proclaiming VOTING RIGHTS FOR ALL! and AMEND THE CONSTITUTION! and GIVE US OUR DUE!

Hundreds of women were gathered at the intersection of Summer and Washington, and Maud Wood Park was shouting through a megaphone, urging them to march on the State House: "Senator Lodge visits the governor today. Senator Lodge voted against us once. We must make him hear our voices every day until Congress sends the Suffrage Amendment to the states!"

Someone gave Rosemary a sash with the letters N.W.S.A, National Woman Suffrage Association. She put it over her topcoat. Someone else gave her a placard. And she was swept up in the wave of women marching up Winter Street to the State House, where they continued their chants: "Voting Rights Now!" "Give Us Our Due," and one that probably struck fear into men everywhere, "No More Housework Until We Get the Vote!"

And a nineteen-year-old girl became a suffragist.

But to make her way in the world, a girl needed an income. So Rosemary had heeded the advice of her mother. When a position opened on the Perkins household staff, she took it, and it brought her to Newport.

She peered out the window and saw a biplane puttering through a pure blue sky.

It had already passed over the old town . . . over the waterfront, over the redbrick buildings where the great Washington had dined and danced and done business with the French, over the narrow streets of wooden houses and well-kept storefronts, over the houses of worship, too—Catholic, Quaker, Jewish, Protestant—because old Newport had been born in tolerance.

But there was another Newport now, a town of outsiders. They were likely to attend one of the Protestant churches, but they worshipped at the altar of money. And the life they lived at the southern tip of the Aquidneck peninsula was one to show "the footstools" what heaven would be like.

"The footstools" were the locals.

The outsiders were the summer folk. Also known as the rich. Or the Filthy Rich. Or the Four Hundred, the sacred number determined by Mrs. Astor after she saw that her ballroom could hold no more.

Their Newport had been born in the 1850s, in a meadow overlooking the Atlantic, where four wealthy Boston families and eight from the south had built summer homes to catch the ocean zephyrs. And the great money migration had begun.

Now, a plane circling Newport passed over a playground as opulent as any on earth, over houses that looked like French castles, over a tennis club called the Casino, over beaches where only the rich—ladies in the morning, gentlemen in the afternoon—could cool their toes (the footstools had their own beach), and over a golf course where the rich could while away their five-hour rounds while the footstools caddied and cadged tips.

Rosemary's employers had been among those first Boston families.

Arthur Perkins had made his fortune in New England mills. He put up a Victorian "cottage"—gray and Gothic, twenty rooms and a turret—in 1854. In time it had been dwarfed by the mighty stone "cottages" of the Belmonts and the Astors and their ilk. It was said that Newport was the only place where Arthur Perkins had not seemed to be pointing his nose in the air, because so many others could point theirs so much higher.

Arthur and his nose had passed on, as had his son, but his grandson, Magnus, had mortared the family fortune into a foundation of investment trusts, bonds, and securities, and had done it so well that now, on summer mornings, he could sit in knickers, argyle stockings, and matching sweater vest, in the breakfast room off the kitchen, in the bay window with the view of the Cliff Walk, read the paper, and complain.

Magnus Perkins was forty-eight. He had rowed with the Harvard crew and had stepped from school straight into the family firm. He still had a rower's build and a jaw that sailed before the rest of his face like a bowsprit catching the business wind and bending it to his will. But the wider world did not bend so easily, which was why he complained so regularly.

Usually his wife ignored him.

Florence Perkins was five years younger, with translucent skin and a taste for summer taffeta well satisfied in the dress shops of Newport. She saw that the family social life—afternoon teas, lawn parties, dinners—proceeded according to plan. She saw that her children—a ten-year-old boy and a girl a year younger—were occupied every second of the summer day. And she saw that each morning one of the servants met the first ferry, which carried the early editions of the papers.

That morning, the *Boston Globe* proclaimed that President Wilson was returning from France. It also reported on the heat wave that had sent families like the Perkinses to their summer retreats several weeks early.

But it was neither the heat nor the League of Nations that had Mr. Perkins complaining. He read the front page and shouted, "Good God, they finally did it."

"Who, dear?" Mrs. Perkins glanced up from the *Herald*. "What did they do?"

"The Senate. They went and passed the Women's Suffrage Amendment."

At that moment, Rosemary was carrying in two plates of scrambled eggs. At those words, she almost dropped them.

"Fifty-six to twenty-five, I believe," said Mrs. Perkins.

Rosemary set down the eggs and read over Mr. Perkins's shoulder.

"At least Henry Cabot Lodge voted against it." Magnus Perkins shook the paper as if to shake the words off it; then he gave it a noisy fold.

"Read about the Red Sox, dear. It's better for the health." Florence slid the sports page across the table. "They always win."

"I don't care about the Red Sox and that lout Babe Ruth." Magnus raised his coffee cup, saw that it was empty, and simply held it in the air.

Rosemary heard her mother cough discreetly from the pantry. Their eyes met, and mother gestured toward the cup.

Maureen Ryan was a naturally nervous woman whose mouth was always drawn into a tight line of tension and whose slender body belied her skill as a cook.

"What do *you* think, Rosemary?" asked Mrs. Perkins.

"About what, ma'am?" The girl filled the master's cup, glided around the table as soundlessly as her mother had taught her, and poured for Mrs. Perkins.

"About women getting the vote."

Rosemary glanced again toward the pantry. She knew what her mother was thinking: *Not politics. Mother of God, not politics.* Then Rosemary said to Mrs. Perkins, "I think women should have the vote. It's only right."

Magnus Perkins looked over the corner of his paper. "And why do women need the vote? Look at what you've accomplished without it."

"What's that, sir?" asked Rosemary.

Mother Maureen bustled in with the coffee cake. "Here we go. Hot from the oven. Still gooey, just the way you like it, sir."

Mr. Perkins ignored the cake and kept his eyes on Rosemary: "Soon men won't be able to get an honest drink, thanks to the Eighteenth Amendment, which never would have passed without the Women's Christian Temperance Union. When women get the vote, what else will they do to us?"

Mrs. Perkins smiled. "Just thinking about it is enough to drive a man to drink."

"Nor funny, Florence."

"Perhaps not, but whatever we do, it will be good for you."

"Like the income tax amendment?"

"That wasn't women's work." Mrs. Perkins dropped her eyes back to the paper.

"Not women's work?" cried Magnus Perkins. "With all their talk about social justice? Women and Bolsheviks and *Democrats*. Newport isn't anywhere near as much fun as it used to be. Smaller parties, fewer yacht races . . . Why? Because the government takes our money."

"I thought it was the war that changed things." Mrs. Perkins sounded calm and quietly amused.

"War . . . women . . . taxes . . ." Magnus Perkins leaned across the table. "Once we saw to the rights of the freed slaves, we didn't amend the Constitution again for forty years. Now we get a tax amendment in '13, prohibition in '19, and next year—"

"Women will vote." Mrs. Perkins looked at her servants. "Won't we, girls?"

"Oh, I don't know, ma'am," said Maureen. "These things is way above me." She gave her daughter a jerk of the head: *Follow me and get out of the line of fire.*

Mrs. Perkins looked at her husband. "The amendment will be ratified."

"*Amendment.* Assault, you mean." Mr. Perkins went back to the paper, muttering, "What I wouldn't give to know what the Founding Fathers would have thought about all this change."

MAUREEN KICKED THE stopper from the pantry door so that it swung shut and all but hit Rosemary in the seat. Then she whispered through clenched teeth. "What's the matter with you, sayin' all that? Never tell them what you think."

" 'I don't know, ma'am.' " Rosemary made a face. " 'These things is way above me.' "

"Don't be talkin' about all this votin' business . . . you see how mad it makes Mr. Magnus. I should never have let you go to them suffragist meetings."

"At least I got some education there," said Rosemary.

"Education? Education is for . . . for . . . educated folks."

"I'd be in college now, but for you tellin' me to take this job."

"I wanted you to get a good position is all," said Maureen.

Rosemary stood next to the six-burner that pumped heat, even on a hot June morning. This was her mother's domain, warm and safe but structured and demanding, like a convent. "There's a big world out there, Mama, with big folks and big ideas, and I mean to be part of it."

The bell rang in the breakfast room.

"See what they want," said Maureen, "and keep your mouth shut."

Rosemary looked toward the breakfast room, then pulled off her little white crest and headed for the door.

"Rosemary! Where are you goin'?"

"To find a document. It might tell what the Founding Fathers thought about votin' women. Maybe it'll shut up Mr. Magnus."

Maureen followed her. "What do you know about such a document?"

The girl stopped in the doorway. "Grandma told me."

"Grandma? When?"

"When she was dyin'. When I'd go to read to her from the papers. I read to her about Maud Wood Park and the N.W.S.A. tryin' to get the suffragist amendment through Congress. It got her to talkin' about the Constitution, and a man with a limp. . . ."

"Man with a limp. You *know* about him?" Maureen's hands began to shake.

The bell rang again, more insistently.

But mother and daughter stood where they were, the daughter's defiance an anchor set in her mother's fears.

After a moment, Maureen picked up the maid's crest. "Do your job, dear, please."

Rosemary wanted to run right then, run and disappear into that big world she dreamed about. But her mother had sacrificed her own freedom to send Rosemary to school. She had dragged herself every day, winter, spring, and fall, from their South End tenement to the Perkins home in the Back Bay. She had worked even harder during her summers in the Newport kitchen. So if it took a bit longer to educate her mother, Rosemary would take the time.

She put her little crest back on and returned to the dining room. "Yes, sir?"

"Mrs. Perkins and I are very pleased with your service." Mr. Magnus smiled.

"Thank you, sir." Rosemary did not smile back. She did not like the smiles of Mr. Magnus. They expressed many things, but never goodwill.

"However," he said, "don't be getting too big for your britches." He glanced at her apron, as though trying to see the britches.

Mrs. Perkins looked up from the obituaries. "Bartlett Pike has died."

Bartlett Pike . . . a name that Rosemary had heard before, from her grandmother.

"So," said Magnus, "we finally get him off the Pike-Perkins board. He probably died when he realized that the end of the war means the end of the mill."

Mrs. Perkins angled the paper into the sunshine, "It says here—" She made a little shooing gesture with her fingers to excuse Rosemary.

But Rosemary lingered to listen.

"It says here that his memorial service is Wednesday in Millbridge."

And Rosemary had Wednesday off.

GILBERT AMORY HATED Livermore.

He stood on his father's little porch, waved at the black flies, and looked out at the river, the sawmill, the ramshackle buildings, the old *C. W. Saunders* chugging down from the latest cuttings, and he decided that the days of logging in the Sawyer River Valley were numbered.

He and his brother, Aaron, had grown up here and learned the three R's in the little schoolhouse by the sawmill. They had wandered the hillsides and ridden the log trains with Frenchy. And they had rejoiced when their parents sent them to Phillips Exeter for the seventh grade.

Aaron had become a doctor, Gilbert a lawyer. Both now made their homes in Portland, but since Aaron had a family, it fell to Gilbert to spend time with their father and bring him bad news like Bartlett's death.

"The giants are dead," said George Amory, "and now the midgets are following."

In 1914, Chamberlain's ancient wounds had finally killed him.

In 1917, Daniel Saunders had passed, and Charles a year later. Their house, the largest in Livermore, was now occupied by their widows. Since there were no other heirs, the company had passed from timber men to estate managers who cared only about the last figure on the last line.

The Henrys were gone, too, so the passage of time had been good for something.

Old J. E. had died in 1912. The man who said, "I never seen a tree yet that didn't mean a damn sight more to me goin' under the saw than it did standin' on a mountain," had lived by his motto. Once he had stripped the primeval Zealand Valley, he had moved south and gone to work on the Pemigawasset.

One of his sons had put it as starkly as the landscape: "There's no secret to this business of ours. We own the land and the timber and we're making every dollar out of it we can." When they sold in 1917, they walked away with $3 million.

The Saunders had cut less and made less for themselves and their partners, but it was a source of pride to George Amory that they had cut three times on their tract, while anything the Henrys touched was stripped for a generation.

George was seventy-nine now, and as Frenchy said, he was still white-pine straight, ax-heft strong, and as smart as a jaybird. He credited his longevity to hard work, to friends who were loyal, to sons who respected him, to a wife who loved him.

Gilbert knew that when his father spoke of the death of giants, Cordelia led the list. As they passed the little graveyard on their way to the depot, they left flowers. Then they boarded a train that would take them through the Gateway to meet a southbound connection for Millbridge.

The Crawford House, the Fabyan House, and the White Mountain House glittered in the June sunlight, and two new hotels had risen to join them. The Mount Pleasant perched on a rise looking east toward the grandest of them all: the Mount Washington Hotel, which held its rocky eminence like Camelot, a great gray castle with a green roof, surrounded by fairways instead of moats.

As the train steamed past the Fabyan House, George admitted that no matter how much he and Bartlett had contended, he felt a sense of loss at his cousin's death. "We grew up together. Now I'm alone at the top of the mountain, waiting to be called."

As if to mirror George's darkening mood, the train left the grand hotels behind, rounded a bend, crested a rise, and rumbled into the Zealand wasteland—miles of stumps, stripped hillsides, wasted trunks bleached white by time or burned black by fires, and dead in the middle of it, the remains of the logging town that J. E. Henry had left two decades before. But here and there, new trees were growing, and grasses carpeted the eroded hillsides.

"Look up in the valley," said Gilbert. "It's coming back to life."

The forest was reclaiming the denuded slopes and the ridges, too.

"One thing dies to make way for another," Gilbert said.

THE NEXT MORNING, mourners filled the Congregational Church in Millbridge.

George and Gilbert took family seats in the fourth row.

In front of them sat Bartlett's immediate family, which had not been especially fruitful. Bartlett's sons had each had a daughter, and each daughter had married, so the Pike line would continue though the Pike name would not.

Sarah Pike, a heavyset, good-natured girl, had married a heavyset, good-natured son of Irish millworkers named Bill McGillis. They had inherited the big house and the responsibility of running the mill.

Bartlett's other granddaughter, Audrey Pike, had gone to Connecticut College, where she met Samuel Bishop, son of a Connecticut newspaper publisher. Samuel edited his father's little paper in Litchfield, but he had big dreams. He had spent the night before telling George and Gilbert about something called broadcasting.

The heat wave had not yet broken. All across the church, programs and hats fanned the air. Light colors prevailed among the ladies, though black should have predominated. A few gentlemen had gone to shirt-sleeves with black armbands.

George whispered to Gilbert that Cousin Bartlett had earned many friends in spite of himself.

Just as Bartlett had schemed to take control of the mill in the 1860s, and retain control in the 1870s, he had fought to keep it open when competition from the south had begun to siphon business in the 1900s and when Magnus Perkins had mandated layoffs after the Armistice.

Waves of immigrants had found work in Millbridge. The Irish had been followed by the French Canadians, then the Italians and the Eastern Europeans. There had even been a few from the Middle East. And those who were willing to work had found something to work for in the mill by the Blackstone.

So George thought it strange that no representative from Perkins Holdings had come to pay the company's respects. What he did not know was that there were two women in the church who were Perkins employees, a cook and a maid.

The cook was looking for her daughter.

The daughter was looking for a man she did not know. He would be in his late seventies by now. He might still be handsome, because that was how her grandmother had described him. He most certainly would have a limp.

A hymn began the service . . . "A Mighty Fortress is Our God."

Maureen was sitting in the last pew, her eyes scanning the crowd for Rosemary.

A reading, the Twenty-Third Psalm, followed the hymn.

Rosemary was sitting in the far corner, behind a pillar, well hidden from her mother, who had come in and stopped in the doorway as if expecting to be struck by lightning for entering a Protestant church.

"Bartlett Pike was a man who cared about his fellow men. . . . About his friends and neighbors . . ." That from the minister, eulogizing.

Rosemary had left her mother a note, saying that she was going to Boston, to a meeting of the N.W.S.A. But mothers have a sixth sense.

A eulogy from Bartlett's older son about a man who loved his family.

Maureen twisted her hands around her handkerchief and scanned the crowd.

She had told Rosemary the whole story: One day she had admitted to her mother that she feared her children would inherit the family weakness for whiskey, since both her father and her stevedore husband had "had a taste for the creature." Her mother had agreed that a hard-drinking father sometimes meant hard-drinking children, but that Maureen need not worry. *Why?* Because her real father was not the man who raised her.

"Our Father, who Art in heaven . . ." Recited by the whole congregation.

Sheila Murphy had begged Maureen never to contact the man who had impregnated her in the summer of 1863 . . . for a dollar. No good could come from it, only embarrassment, heartache, and shame. And Maureen had begged her daughter. But . . .

"Onward Christian Soldiers," the exit hymn.

The crowd was standing. The principal mourners were filing out. An old man was limping down the aisle now. He had proud posture and a gray Vandyke. And the young man beside him could only be his son, who stood as straight but substituted a black mustache for a Vandyke.

And Maureen saw it . . . in the firm jaws, in the strong brows. Until this moment, she had not been certain that her mother had been telling the truth. But now she knew.

George Amory noticed a woman looking at him . . . first at his foot, then at his face. . . . For a second, he felt as if he were back in St. Albans in 1864.

Gilbert noticed, too. He thought to stop and help the woman, who looked as if she might faint from the heat, but the crush of people was carrying them out of the church, through the foyer, into the sunlight.

Rosemary was already outside. She had slipped out by a side door and was watching for the man with the limp.

She did not want to confront him like this. But what other chance would she have? There were only a few days left before the Boston rally. And how quickly could a girl gain attention, if she could impress the ladies of the N.W.S.A with her special knowledge of the document they were seeking to amend?

So she went up to the man and said, "Excuse me, sir."

George Amory looked at the young woman . . . and looked . . . and looked . . . auburn hair, a tall, regal demeanor, a face from his youth. . . . First St. Albans had flashed before his eyes, now this strange echo of the first woman he had ever . . .

Were these rising memories some harbinger of an affliction about to strike his brain? Or was it just the heat? Gilbert Amory stepped between his father and the young woman, doffed his straw boater, bowed. "Good morning, Miss . . ."

"Ryan. Rosemary Ryan." So taken was she by Gilbert's manner that she curtsied.

"And did you work in the mill?" asked Gilbert.

"No, sir. I work for Mr. Magnus Perkins."

George stepped closer to her. "Are you his representative at the services?"

"No. I'm . . . I'm a member of the N.W.S.A."

"Well, look here," said Gilbert, "if you're soliciting contributions at a funeral—"

"Oh, no, sir. It's not that." Rosemary noticed her mother at the top of the church steps. Their eyes met, but Maureen seemed too paralyzed to move.

"Then what can we do for you?" Gilbert Amory continued to speak politely.

Rosemary knew she had to get this business over quickly, so she turned again to the old man. "I bring greetings from my grandmother."

"Grandmother?" said George.

"Yes, sir." Rosemary swallowed and said, "Sheila Murphy."

George's memory came to life before him. This girl's grandmother had hiked her dress for him in an office in the huge brick building just across the river. A black spot began to float before his eyes, as though it had risen from the deepest recesses of his memory. For a moment, he thought he might faint.

Gilbert said, "Is she in the N.W.S.A., too?"

"Well . . . no, sir," said Rosemary. "She's, ah . . . dead."

Even in the choking heat, George suddenly felt a chill.

While there might have been more sophisticated ways to approach this subject, Rosemary simply pressed ahead. "My grandmother told me about a draft of the Constitution, sir. She said you had it, and—"

"What?" said Gilbert. "A draft of the—"

George put his hand on his son's arm. "We should join the family."

"Sir," said the girl with sudden vehemence, "I *am* your family."

George's legs buckled. He squeezed his son's forearm.

Rosemary realized that she had pushed too far. She wished that she had listened to her mother. She glanced back at the church steps. But her mother was gone.

Gilbert Amory said, "If this is some kind of joke, miss, let me assure you—"

"Excuse me." Maureen Ryan appeared from the crowd. "I'm sorry if my Rosie has interrupted your mourning. But she's a headstrong—"

And George asked with almost preternatural calm, "Are you Maureen?"

Gilbert turned to his father. "You know this woman?"

George Amory's voice was as clear as his memory of a Boston tenement, a baby girl, a promise. "I haven't seen her in fifty-five years. But . . . yes."

"Then you know why we're here," said Rosemary. "You said you'd help if we came to you and told you who we were."

"Help? What kind of help?" asked Gilbert.

"I want the world to know about the Constitution," said Rosemary.

"Constitution?" Gilbert looked at his father. "What is this?"

George swayed, wiped perspiration from his forehead.

Maureen said, "I'm sorry, sir. I never meant to bother you. I never wanted to know you."

Gilbert took control. "I'm not going to stand in the broiling sun while I'm told by total strangers that they're part of my family." He pulled a business card from his pocket and put it in the mother's hand. "Any further contact should be through my office in Portland. Now, good day."

"A FIRST DRAFT OF the Constitution?" whispered Gilbert to his father. "Annotated by the New England delegates? In the safe at Livermore? Why haven't you told me about this before? Why haven't you told Aaron?"

"Because it wasn't your place to know, or your brother's."

The family had set up a receiving line and refreshment table under the maples that Bartlett had planted. People were offering condolences, then stopping by the table, then seeking out cool spots on the mill grounds or down by the river. For a single day, this place of hard labor seemed almost festive, but the celebration came at the end of a life that foretold the end of a way of life.

George and Gilbert had found a quiet corner in the old boardroom.

Gilbert drank down a glass of lemonade and said, "I'm your legal advisor in addition to your son. I should know if you're holding national treasures as keepsakes, or if I have half sisters in service to rich Bostonians."

George pointed out the window to Maureen and Rosemary, who were shaking hands with Bill McGillis. "There's your half sister out there, talking to her first cousin."

"McGillis? The millworker who married into the family? Talk about ambition."

"His Aunt Sheila had ambition, too. She took money to get out of the mill in exchange for . . . for . . . it was all before your mother consented to marry me."

Sons seldom consider their fathers as sexual beings, and Gilbert was a conventional sort of man, so he simply waved his hands and said, "Back to this Constitution. Did you promise it to that girl, that Rosemary?"

"I promised it to no one. It's a resource to be managed, protected, like the forest."

"It could be worth a substantial lot of money."

"But who owns it?" said the old man. "Do the descendants of Rufus King? Do the Caldwells of Vermont? They bought it. Do I? I *stole* it."

"You possess it," snapped Gilbert with the confidence of one quoting something he knew well. "And possession is nine tenths of the law."

"I've never known what that means." George ran his hands over the polished mahogany table. "It was right here that I first heard the story, from my grandfather."

"I need to see it, Pa, have it appraised," Gilbert said. "And now that Mother is gone, we need to revisit the will, check the language, see that these Irish are kept at bay."

ROSEMARY LIKED THE way men looked at her when they were men her own age. And she liked the way old men's eyes would follow her across a room or a street in Boston, as if she were a spirit, emerging from their lost youth to revive memories of desire.

But she hated the way that Magnus Perkins looked at her.

She took care never to make eye contact with him unless she was speaking to him. She held her head at an aloof angle and always moved with studied silence.

"Like a nun." That was how her mother had described it.

But "like a nun" was not how Mr. Magnus looked at her. Unless he leered at nuns.

"So, Rosemary"—he was reading the paper on the morning after the Pike funeral—"it says here that there's a Women's Suffrage rally in Boston on Sunday."

"Yes, sir," she said. "I'm going."

Rosemary heard her mother clear her throat. *Do not make another scene.*

At the funeral, they had gone through the receiving line, with her mother whispering the same thing in her ear. *Do not make another scene.* And they had argued all the way back to Newport.

The arguing had ended with Rosemary's promise that she would not contact the old Amory man again. She promised nothing about the son. He was a lawyer. He might see some benefit in talking to her, if only to frighten her away. And that might lead to something. So she had already contacted him.

Mr. Perkins said, "Don't you women realize that the best way for you to influence the life of this nation is to hold yourself above the daily warfare of business and politics? It's the reason the Founding Fathers didn't give you the vote."

"They didn't give us the vote because it was a different era," said Mrs. Perkins. "They didn't give the vote to *men* who didn't have property."

"A wise decision," said Magnus.

Mrs. Perkins raised her chin and said to Rosemary, "When is the meeting?"

"Sunday at the Tremont Theater in Boston. Mrs. Maud Wood Park will be there to speak on how she convinced the Senate to vote the Amendment through at last."

"I should like to hear her myself," said Mrs. Perkins.

"Good God," said Magnus, "you can't be serious."

"I can, and I am."

"You're not going," he said, "and that's final."

Rosemary returned to the kitchen, wondering what the ladies of the N.W.S.A. would think if she brought a woman like Mrs. Florence Perkins into the fold.

"Did you cause a scene?" asked her mother.

"I'd say Mr. Magnus caused the scene. I just . . . I just set the stage."

ROSEMARY'S MIDMORNING JOB was to see to the cleaning of the table linens and silver. So she was in a small room off the kitchen with a tub of polish and silver utensils around ten o'clock. The house was empty. Mrs. Perkins had joined her lady friends at the beach. Maureen was off buying groceries with the butler, Mr. Bunson. The maids were upstairs preparing the bedrooms that had not been used since last fall.

Rosemary was humming softly to herself. "Come Josephine, in my Flying Machine." The words promised adventure, a trip in one of those biplanes always puttering over Newport, a young girl aloft with a Navy flier.

And . . . the shine of the polished silver pleased her, and the salt-air tarnish on the candelabra challenged her, and the smell of the polish stung her nostrils, and . . .

So completely was she wrapped up in her work that she did not hear someone come up behind her. Then a Liberty-head dollar appeared on the table.

"Since you're polishing silver, perhaps you'd like to polish that."

"Polish a dollar?" she looked up past the bowsprit chin of Magnus Perkins.

He leaned closer. "I often give servants the chance to polish my money for me."

"And what beyond your money?" She swallowed a mingling of fear and disgust, because she knew the answer without asking.

"Whatever I have that needs polishing." He put his hands on her shoulders, slid them onto the bare flesh of her upper arms. "If a girl does her job well, and doesn't upset the household with silly political notions, I let her keep whatever money she polishes."

Rosemary had been working on the butter knife. She wished she were holding a better blade. She pretended not to notice the hands kneading her upper arms. She kept her voice neutral. "Does Mrs. Perkins know about your polishing projects?"

His hands stopped. His face appeared beside hers, his mouth close to her ear. "Any girl who doesn't like to polish gets another job . . . or finds one on her own."

How to answer? How to gain an advantage? She said, "I'd . . . I'd best see to my polishing, then."

"You're very wise." His hands started moving again, from her arms toward her breasts. Then he was touching them through her uniform and something was rising against her back. She had never felt one before, but she knew what it was.

And what should she do? Sit there in frozen fear and let him do what he would? Or drive him away . . . and lose her job. That might not be so bad . . . but not just yet.

She swept her arm suddenly, knocking the silver clattering to the floor. "Oh, good Lord!" As she turned to pick things up, she crooked one of her elbows toward that thing tenting the Perkin's trousers, and she "accidentally" gave it a good shot.

He let out a yelp and turned away.

"Oh, sir!" she shouted, "are you all right? Are you hurt? I'm so sorry."

He waved her off. And from somewhere came the sound of feet scurrying. In a house with fifteen-foot ceilings, voices echoed and carried.

Mr. Perkins said, "You'll have another chance. But no matter what my wife says, don't go to Boston on Sunday. Or you will lose your job."

THE NEXT AFTERNOON, Rosemary answered a bell from the solarium. The doors were open, so a breeze was blowing through. Palm fronds and giant ferns waved in the heavy moist air. But Mrs. Perkins looked glacially cool and graciously pleased to have a gentleman visitor. "Could you bring us lemonade, please, Rosemary?"

"Yes, ma'am. Sweetened or sour?"

"I'll have sour, and the gentleman—"

He turned toward Rosemary: a tan linen suit, a white celluloid collar, hair shimmering with Macassar oil, mustache neatly trimmed . . . Gilbert Amory. He smiled and said, "Sweetened."

Rosemary's knees went weak, but she managed an "As you wish."

Then Gilbert turned back to Mrs. Perkins. "I have several papers for your husband to sign regarding the sale of his mill in Brunswick, Maine. He had said that he would be here."

"You can't leave them?" she asked.

"They need notarization," said Gilbert. "I'm a notary public in six New England states, admitted to the bar in Maine, New Hampshire, and Massachusetts."

"I'm afraid that my husband has run into slow play on the course."

"If he's as good at golf as business"—Gilbert knew how to flatter, so he flattered—"I'm sure he's having a fine round."

"I'm sure." Mrs. Perkins inclined her head, as if to change the subject. "Tell me, you've been through Boston. What's the mood as regards the Women's Suffrage Amendment?"

"Massachusetts is a hidebound place," said Gilbert. "But I think that women should have the right to vote."

"A liberal opinion," said Mrs. Perkins, "for a man who wears no wedding band."

"Some would say I have such opinions *because* I'm not married." Gilbert waved the finger in front of his face. "The law has been my mistress and my lover."

As if unaware of the meanness of her words, Mrs. Perkins said, "How sad."

Gilbert did not respond. He attributed her remark to the offhand bad manners of the rich. He knew that people talked about him. They speculated behind his back that he was afraid of women, that he was a misogynist, that he liked boys, that he was doomed to loneliness. But seldom did they comment so openly. And if they were business associates, seldom did they speculate long, because he did his work too well for any foible to color him or any opponent to rattle him.

But he was rattled now, quietly. Perhaps he should not have come like this, pretending to hand-deliver documents that might just as easily have been mailed, all so that he could confront the girl now carrying a tray of lemonade. . . . *No.* It was another girl.

"Where's Rosemary?" asked Mrs. Perkins.

"She took ill, ma'am," said the other girl. "Begged that she needed a bit of air."

From where Gilbert sat on a wicker sofa, he could see her leaving by the kitchen door on the other end of the house, hurrying across the lawn to the Cliff Walk.

Mrs. Perkins looked at Gilbert. "My husband thinks that I'm too easy on the girls, especially when they go wandering off, but I try to be understanding."

"A marvelous trait, understanding." Gilbert gulped the lemonade. "I hope you'll understand if I go out for a look at your marvelous Cliff Walk." He plunked down the glass. "I've never seen it, and it's such a marvelous afternoon."

"Marvelous, yes," said Mrs. Perkins. "But Mr. Amory, does it occur to you that perhaps it's your manners that keep women at bay?"

"Perhaps it's the women." Gilbert stood and bowed. "With your permission, I'll leave the papers for your husband's perusal and return in half an hour or so."

He had just committed a serious faux pas, leaving his hostess like that. But he was also giving her something else to talk about, which he knew would please her.

It did not take him long to catch sight of the girl in the gray dress— she had removed her apron and her little crest. He called after her, but she did not look up.

A butler was coming toward him with two Irish wolfhounds on a leash. The dogs were huge but looked benign. The butler was small but scowled at Gilbert, who was so ungentlemanly as to be running along the

Cliff Walk in late afternoon, when the breezes were cool and the best folk came out to enjoy them.

Gilbert ignored glares and gazes and caught up with Rosemary near the Breakers.

She said, "I told you not to come here. I said I'd contact you."

Gilbert pulled out a telegram. "The paper may be yellow, but this is blackmail, plain and simple, and I won't be blackmailed, nor will my father."

"It's not blackmail. I wouldn't know how to blackmail. . . ."

He read as he walked beside her. "'We need to speak of your family treasure. I do not claim it as a birthright. But I claim the right to ask my grandfather for help. Or I will reveal its existence without your consent.'"

Up ahead, Mrs. Hiram Sumner was bustling along with two lady friends. She was self-appointed Queen of the Cliff Walk and took it upon herself to shoo household staff back to work when she found them meandering here. Any staff, any household.

To avoid her, Rosemary went down the Forty Steps, which were set into the rocks on the side of the cliff. She went halfway down, then turned and looked up at Gilbert Amory. "If you want to argue with me, come down here."

Gilbert wrapped his hand around the iron railing at the top and told her that he was a gentleman and he did not conduct business in the open air.

"Excuse me, sir." It was Mrs. Sumner. "But we don't appreciate shouting on the Cliff Walk when we are taking our afternoon constitutionals."

Gilbert glanced at her. He didn't know her. He said, "So don't listen."

Mrs. Sumner gave an indignant huff and paraded on.

And from the other direction came another of the maids, who looked down the steps and shouted, "Rosemary! Hurry. Mr Bunson is calling for you."

Rosemary came back up the steps and looked Gilbert in the eye. "I'll be in Boston on Sunday morning. I'll go to the nine o'clock Mass at the Cathedral. If you bring the Constitution, meet me outside the church afterward."

"You must be crazy."

"I'll only look at it is all, know what's in it, and tell Mrs. Park." Then she went running off, and heads turned.

Running on the Cliff Walk was . . . well . . . never done.

"DID YOU FIND the Cliff Walk satisfying?" asked Mrs. Perkins.

"A spectacular view," said Gilbert.

She looked at her husband, who had finally returned. "Our guest gulped down his lemonade and went running off. I thought it was something I said."

Magnus Perkins grunted, as if he didn't really care what his wife thought, then asked Gilbert, "Do you have your notary stamp?"

The signing went quickly. Perkins treated Gilbert not as a legal representative but as an employee worthy of no more time or attention than he gave to one of his servants.

When Rosemary carried in a tray with more lemonade, Mr. Perkins waved her away. He seemed in a bad mood, as if he had missed a putt that cost him a lot of money. "I don't want more goddamn lemonade. I want a gin and tonic. Bunson!"

The long-faced butler appeared in the doorway. "Sir?"

"G-and-t's for me and Amory."

Mrs. Perkins said, "Would you like to stay for dinner, Mr. Amory?"

"If I can still catch the last ferry to Providence." Gilbert had no great desire to stay. He thought it best to avoid further contact with the girl. And he did not particularly like Magnus, but he sensed that Magnus was warming to him, which might be good for business. With any luck, he could still make it to Boston in time for the midnight train to Portland.

"Amory, you've done an excellent job with our affairs in Maine," said Magnus Perkins.

"Thank you," said Gilbert. "Progress can be painful, but it's all for the best."

"Right answer."

Then Bunson appeared in the door carrying a bottle of Tanqueray, a tonic dispenser, and two glasses with ice.

Mrs. Perkins stood. "We shall set another place, Mr. Amory, and dine presently." Then she left, her linen dress sweeping coolly across the stone floor of the solarium.

Gilbert sensed that Perkins's drinking was an issue with his wife, and that Perkins might be warming to him simply because he was a drinking companion.

Bunson poured generous shots of Tanqeueray, followed by squirts from the bottle. "A slice of lime, sir?" he asked Gilbert.

"Yes. Thank you." Gilbert took a long, satisfied sip.

"Enjoy that," said Perkins, "because there are places where it's already illegal. A year from now no one will be able to have a drink anywhere in these United States. Another assault on the Constitution. Do you study the Constitution, Amory?"

"I'm a lawyer. I must study it."

"Is there anyplace in it that says a man cannot dispose of property as he sees fit?"

"Not if it's his own property."

"Right answer again."

Gilbert did not like the condescension. In Maine, he was seen as an educated man, not one who went about seeking the approbation of the rich. "What's your point?"

"It's time to liquidate the Pike-Perkins Mill."

"Liquidate?"

"The business is dying in New England. The mill is losing money." Magnus Perkins swirled his glass, studied the ice cubes.

"But the people . . . we've already put too many out of work in Maine as it is. I . . ."

"Convince the other members of the family to sell—your father, the McGillis faction, the Bishops. It will make things go more smoothly. But Perkins Holdings is majority owner and we intend to move. We have a buyer who'll meet our price. If we wait, the price will only go down." He gulped the rest of his drink then called, "Bunson!"

"Sir?"

"Mix two more."

Rosemary came in and whispered something to Bunson, who, according to the hierarchy of the household, conveyed the information: "Gentlemen, dinner is served!"

"Dinner? Already?" said Magnus. "But another drink."

And his wife's voice came from somewhere within the house. "Dinner, Magnus. We have wine decanted."

Magnus shot a dirty look toward the dining room, then gestured for Bunson to refill the glasses.

Rosemary turned and went off silently.

Gilbert noticed the way Magnus watched her round young bottom. It was as if he could consume her. And Gilbert realized that he was looking at her in the same way. He averted his eyes, because the girl *was* his niece.

When she was gone, Magnus said, "Do you know that little Irish piece fancies herself a Suffragist. She's even corrupting my wife with her ideas."

"I suspect that your wife has a mind of her own," said Gilbert.

Magnus Perkins laughed without mirth. "Right answer."

OVER DINNER, MRS. PERKINS asked Gilbert his opinion of prohibition, which somehow led to a conversation about the Boston Suffragist Rally.

Mrs. Perkins announced that she would be attending with "young Rosemary."

Magnus slammed his hand on the table. "You are not!"

So Mrs. Perkins offered a polite good evening and excused herself.

"If you go to Boston, I'll fire that girl," shouted Perkins. "And her mother, too!"

"You'll fire no one without my permission. If you try to, I'll—"

"You'll *what?*" he demanded. "Refuse my bed? Bunson! Another g-and-t!"

Then Magnus Perkins turned to Gilbert and turned the talk once more to the closing of the mill. His prescription: "Once you've protected your bedrock in trusts, get out of bad businesses, like New England textiles. Go into new things."

"Such as?" Gilbert poured himself more wine.

"The tube wireless," said Perkins. "Marconi was the Gutenburg of the modern age. It should be for smart men like us to see the genius of broadcasting through the air, just as other men saw the genius of linotype. Everyone reads now. Someday, everyone will listen—to music, to information, to advertising. . . ."

Gilbert had visions for the future, too. And he knew that Perkins was right about the mill. There were better places to put capital. But could he help Perkins kill the business that his own great-grandfather had built from a single-wheel gristmill to two-hundred-loom behemoth? Another gin and tonic did not provide the answer.

Afterward, Bunson drove him to the ferry landing, but they arrived too late.

Bunson said there were ten guest rooms at the Perkins Cottage, but Gilbert preferred to be dropped at the Newport Hotel. Though he did not offer a reason, he sensed that Bunson understood. There was too much tension in that big house, and it would surely hang like a residue on the morning. A quiet night with a book and a soft bed would be just the thing.

ROSEMARY RYAN HAD the late shift, so she sat in the kitchen, turning the pages of the *Saturday Evening Post*, waiting to be summoned by one of the bells. There was a pull cord in each bedroom, each cord strung through the walls to a row of bells in the kitchen, each bell labeled with the name of a bedroom.

She hoped that Mr. Perkins would satisfy himself with the large glass of port and chunk of Stilton that he had Bunson carry up around ten. If a bell rang, let it be the missus. Better yet would be no bells, no running to answer a summons, no yes ma'am, be right back with a slice of cake and a glass of warm milk to help you sleep. . . .

Rosemary thought of her grandmother, fighting to raise a child with a hard-drinking husband, organizing mill girls in places like Lawrence and Lowell, places where people fought for a few extra pennies in their paychecks, for a few more shreds of dignity. And here was Rosemary, waiting on people who expected to be pampered, praised, and presented, even late at night, with the best face a girl could offer.

Around ten thirty, there were loud voices and doors slamming somewhere above. Rosemary ignored them. The bells were strung for a reason. It was not her job to investigate sounds that came from the private parts of the house.

When a bell rang soon after, she thanked the Lord that it was Mrs. Perkins.

A few moments later, Rosemary knocked softly: "You sent for me, ma'am?"

Mrs. Perkins was sitting in a boudoir chair. She wore a robe. She had taken her hair out of its roll and let it drop down over her shoulders. "I want to meet Maud Wood Park. So I'm going with you."

Rosemary was thrilled. "I was hoping you would. But Mr. Magnus—"

"—is a tyrant. The women of this house will rise up against him, all classes . . . you and I and . . . we'll invite your mother, too." And the smile that she offered was as genuine as her hair was luxuriant.

"Yes, ma'am. It will be a day to remember."

How could a girl sleep?

Rosemary had managed, in just a few weeks of service, to upset the balance of the great house, foment rebellion, and make her presence felt. If that was not enough to keep her awake, her room was breathless and stiflingly hot.

She sat on the edge of the bed and took off her shoes.

She did not think that her nightly ablutions, followed by five Our Fathers and ten pages of Willa Cather, would relax her. Had she been in Boston, she might have sneaked out to see her friends. The girls gathered at the all-night restaurant under the el. The boys played craps on the corners. There were stories to hear, cigarettes to smoke, and places where kids could find something strong to drink or perhaps shadows where they could find each other.

But here . . . the wall vibrated with the sound of her mother's snoring in the next room, and the other maids resented Rosemary because she was a favorite not only of Mrs. Perkins but of Bunson, too, and the butler's favorite could find life quite easy, because the butler ran the house. So Rosemary decided to go for a walk by herself.

She took off her apron and crest. Then she unclipped her stockings and rolled them down and pulled them off. Her whole being felt cooler, and she was tempted to take off her bloomers, too. Why not? No one would see her. No one would know. And it would be . . . delicious.

As she went quietly down the back staircase, she heard more raised voices in the family quarters, more slamming doors, angry footfalls on the main staircase.

The kitchen was silent, except for the drip-drip-drip in the icebox and the ticking of the clock, the tyrannical clock by which Rosemary's mother lived her life. But no more of those thoughts. Just a brisk walk, then peaceful sleep.

A breeze rustled the trees and rolled over the lawn, cooling her bare legs, caressing them, filling her with . . . something.

She could not help but wonder what the nuns would say if they knew she was enjoying something so . . . sensually.

The night was intimate and enormous at the same time, an enveloping darkness arced over with an infinity of stars.

She felt something stir in her stomach and lower, in her loins, a yearning in her spirit that made her tingle and—she could not deny it—made her wet.

She opened the gate and stepped onto the Cliff Walk. The breeze embraced her and the darkness was like a drug pouring into her.

Several of the great houses were illuminated. But most of the lights were burning in upstairs rooms. Somewhere someone was playing a piano. She could not recognize the piece but it was beautiful. Was it coming from the Breakers?

No matter. Those who were awake would not be for long. Only she would be awake, she and the wind and the lover she imagined walking with her, for only a lover could make more of this moment.

The ocean rolled against the cliff below.

Up ahead, shadows were hurrying toward her. She stopped, pulled herself against the parapet wall that kept people from falling onto the rocks. What was it? Who?

A man and two huge beasts.

That strange warm feeling in her loins went cold. Yearning turned to fear.

But it was only the butler John Snitterfield, walking the wolfhounds.

He stopped, as startled by her shadow as she was by his. He squinted at the gray Perkins uniform. "Does Bunson give permission for his girls to leave the house at all hours?"

"Ah . . . yes, sir.

He grunted, shook his head, moved on into the darkness.

And on she went in the other direction, rapt again in the wonder of the night. Even the lights of the great mansions seemed feeble and insignificant as the blackness of sky and sea absorbed them.

When she came to the Forty Steps, she stopped and looked east into the night. Then she looked down at the white foaming waves below. Each time one of them rolled against the rocks, it pushed a breeze up the steps, up the cliff, up her legs, so that her dress billowed and she felt the beat of some life source pulsing out there in the dark.

She was drawn down the steps, down in the starlight that glistened on the sea spume coating each step, down closer to that life source.

And when she was halfway down, alone in the deep darkness, she hiked up her dress, up past her calves, up over her knees, up until she felt naked, exposed to nature, to the dark, in her lover's hands.

"That's what I like to see."

She was so startled by the voice behind her that she almost fell.

She dropped her dress and turned. Above her was a shape, a black silhouette against the star-silvered sky.

"Who is it?"

The figure came toward her. "I've been watching that pretty bum of yours. Not just tonight. No. I've been watching it day and night for weeks."

"Mr. Magnus, you shouldn't say such things." Even in the salt air, she could smell gin. "You shouldn't be following a girl when she takes a walk."

He came closer and smiled, his teeth and the whites of his eyes shining. "I wasn't following, but we're well met."

She tried to step around him and get back up to the Cliff Walk. "Excuse me, sir. I must be up early."

But he was a step above her and towered over her. "I'll give you the morning off." Then he leaned forward to kiss her.

She pulled away and almost stumbled.

He took a step down.

"Please, Mr. Magnus, please don't." Her eyes searched beyond him for the shadow of someone else.

"There's no one up there," he said. "Scream and the waves will just swallow it."

He grabbed her arm with one hand and with the other, he grabbed a fistful of her dress and bunched it up, up, up, lifting it as she had just done, up past her calves, over her knees, up toward her crotch. "Just give me a look. Let me see your sweet little—"

"Mr. Magnus, I'll tell your wife."

And the one hand stopped moving, but the other squeezed harder on her arm to hold her in place. "You think my wife is your ally?"

"Please, sir. You're hurting me."

"You think you can go to Boston and bring her along to your suffragist rally."

Rosemary pulled back, but he was strong and held her fast, and he had placed a forearm in such a way as to protect the growth in his trousers.

"She has the right," said Rosemary defiantly, "and so do I."

"You have no rights unless I say so. Nor does your mother. If you go to Boston, I might decide she hasn't raised you properly. I might have to fire her."

"No."

"But—" He grabbed her face and turned it toward him and pressed his lips against hers and jammed his tongue into her mouth.

She thought about biting it, but fighting back now would only enrage him. If she could only get up the steps . . .

"There. That's better." Now he stepped down so that they were both on the same level.

With her shoulder she tried to wipe the spittle of him from her mouth.

Then his hand was at the front of her dress again, bunching it up. And his fingers were probing at her, tugging at her hairs, pushing against her tenderness.

The blackness of night, which had felt so sensuous, so embracing, which had made her feel so much at one with the universe, had turned terrifying.

"I'll let you go to Boston," he said, "and take my wife, too, and infect her with all your suffragist ideas, on one condition." And he pushed his middle finger into her.

She cried out in pain and tried to pull away, so he clamped a hand at her bottom and jammed his finger even harder, and the force of it, on those steps, caused them both to stumble.

He let her go. She felt a ripping pain as his finger pulled out of her.

She lost her footing and was suddenly falling, her body banging, rock riser after riser, first striking her nose, then the back of her skull, then the back of her neck, which took all sensation and an instant later, all consciousness, so that she did not know that she struck the rocks at the bottom, then kept falling toward those waves below.

As for Magnus Perkins, he fell with the luck of a drunk. He landed on his ass. The bruise at the base of his spine, which would keep him from sitting comfortably for days, was well hidden.

A WEEK LATER, AN old man made his way down from the White Mountains, down by train to Portland, down by ferry to Boston, down into the Boston subway.

He did not doubt that he lived in an age of wonders. Since his boyhood, men had learned to fly, to move along roads in carriages powered by liquid pumped from the ground, to talk through wires strung across the landscape, to send signals through the air from ship to shore or from one transmitter to hundreds of homes. But nothing amazed him more than a rattling, roaring subway train that ran on electricity, that picked him up at North Station and whisked him through a tunnel, then up, out of the darkness, up into the bright July daylight, up onto tracks that seemed to teeter two stories in the air.

He got off at Dover Street and found his way to Gloucester Place, a dead end of five-story wooden tenements.

The kids on the corner looked at him suspiciously. Then they looked at the leather map case in his hands. He clutched it tighter.

He knew that the influenza had hit hard on these streets. There were shuttered storefronts, families without breadwinners, too many kids without mothers to watch over them. The epidemic had entered the country through Boston the previous fall and had killed more people than all the bullets in the Great War.

He climbed the steps of number 9 to the top floor and knocked.

Maureen Ryan opened the door. She was wearing a house dress that hung on her as if on a wooden peg. Perspiration plastered her hair in little ringlets to the sides of her head. But he could see it in her bone structure. She was his. She was his daughter.

"You got my wire?" asked George.

Her eyes went to the table. There was the yellow Western Union envelope. "I almost wrote you and told you not to come."

"I'm so sorry for your loss," he said.

"It's your loss, too," she said without recrimination. "She was a beautiful girl."

"I wish I'd known her. I liked her spirit."

Maureen asked if he wanted tea or water. "I keep nothin' stronger. It don't agree with some who live here." She gestured to a picture on the table: a man in a conductor's uniform and a young woman. "Now that his pregnant wife been taken by the flu, my son don't have much to come home for. So he stays out, drinkin'."

"I'm sorry for that loss, too."

"My daughter-in-law took sick. Poor Mrs. Tracy from next door, she come to help, got sick and died the very same night. My daughter-in-law died next mornin'."

"God's ways are past knowing," said George.

"God's are, but man's ain't. A man killed my baby. A man who followed her along the Cliff Walk and smelled of gin, and—"

"—my son was seen following her along the Cliff Walk and stopping at the Forty Steps that very day. That's what I've come to speak to you about."

"What is there to speak of?"

George handed her the map case. "This was what your daughter wanted to see."

Maureen looked at it, as if it had no meaning for her.

"I should have showed it to her. My son should have. After all . . . you're family."

"My family is my hard-drinkin' train conductor, who just about now"—she looked at the clock—"is punchin' tickets on the Portland to Boston express."

"Well, this might help somehow." He gestured to the map case. "It's my most prized possession, and I want you to have it. In memory of your daughter. In memory of what she believed in."

"I'm a cook. I'll go back to work soon as I'm up to it. What will I do with this?"

"Put it in a safety deposit box. Sell it so your son can start a new life. But—" George hesitated, looked down at the case, then looked Maureen in the eye. "—I'm hoping that you'll not sell it for a time, at least until the police stop askin' questions about Gilbert and that night in Newport. They think he did it."

"Do you?"

"He was in his hotel when it happened. So . . . I'm giving you his greatest birthright, giving it to you as your inheritance. In exchange, I'm asking you to say nothing bad about my son."

Maureen looked at the map case. "So you're buyin' me off?"

"In a manner of speaking."

"Well, I don't believe it was him. And I'll say as much when I go back to Newport. The Perkinses done the decent thing and give me a week off. But I expect I'll talk to the police again. And I'll speak the truth." She offered the map case to him. "So you can keep this."

"No," he said. "You grew up without me. I owe you somethin'. Let it be this."

TWENTY-TWO

"THE NEWPORT NEWSPAPER followed Rosemary Ryan's death for a while, but she was just a maid, so they ran out of energy," said Antoine. "Too many polo matches to cover."

"How did you get the old Newport papers?" asked Peter Fallon.

"Orson's staying in Newport with some lady booksellers, the Common Cliffwalkers. I called him."

"Good boy."

"Hey, boss. Don't call me boy. Hurts my image with the homebodies."

"Noted. What else do you have?"

"Get this: Orson says the only suspect the Newport paper ever identified was Gilbert Amory."

"That's it." Peter would have shouted, but he didn't want the girls to hear. He was drinking port by the woodstove while Kate and Kelly cleaned up in the kitchen. He could see them from where he sat, so he knew they weren't listening on the land line, but there was no reason to trust them yet.

"What?" said Antoine. "What's *it*?"

"The place where the story crosses the bridge. There's always a bridge," said Peter. "Always somebody who carries you into the twentieth century."

"Gilbert Amory?"

"Yeah. He must carry it to Michael Ryan. Ryan carries it to us."

"Or at least to Portland," said Antoine. "Why do you think Bloom told you Ryan's name?"

"Beats me," said Peter. "He could have told us anything. Maybe he thinks we'll lead him to it. Or maybe he's sick of his partner browbeating him."

"It could be politics," said Antoine. "He thinks one way. Doherty thinks another."

"Could be, but whatever it is, it's about Evangeline now." Peter took a sip of port to wash down his emotion. No time for emotion. Time for focus.

"So . . . ," said Antoine after a bit.

Peter cleared his throat. "Any e-mails from Charles Bishop this afternoon?"

"Not the last time I checked."

"Shoot him this, under my name: 'It's Thursday night. World Series Sunday. You promised material two days ago. Are you in or out?'"

"Why not call him?"

"He may not field his own phone calls. But I bet he reads his own e-mails. So send it. I don't want to be leaving electronic footprints on any computers around here."

"Where are you leaving your footprints in the morning?"

"Newport."

"Newport? They didn't take Evangeline to Newport."

"There's a man there named Clinton Jarvis—"

"He knows where Evangeline is?"

"No, but he may know where the Constitution is."

By then, Peter had read the introduction of Jarvis's book. It began boldly:

> The United States of America is a Christian country. The men who wrote the Constitution were Christians, plain and simple. They believed in God, and if you asked any of them, they would say that they believed in Jesus Christ. I can say this with confidence, because I have read the Constitution. I have read opinions about it in the very handwriting of one of the Framers. . . .

That was why they were going to Newport.

MAYBE IT HAD to do with the lumpy camp cot, the single blanket, and the temperature below freezing, but Evangeline didn't sleep too well.

Now, as the sky brightened, someone brought her coffee. It was the one from the car, the one called Scrawny.

"Can I go to the bathroom?" she asked.

"No plumbing around here, lady."

"Just an expression," she said. "Where can I take a leak?"

"You mean, like an outhouse?"

"That would do."

"Ain't got one of those, either. We got a hole up back of the tents. And they told me I had to keep my eyes on you at all times so you don't get lost."

"Whatever turns you on."

In the dim light, she saw six tents in camo canvas and six ATVs, along with a couple of pickups parked under the white pines, all but invisible from above.

Scrawny pointed to a little rise. "Up there."

She was a big girl. She'd been camping. She'd used holes in the ground before. And she was a travel writer, so she'd used the facilities in some pretty skeevy places. She remembered that open pipe in the floor of a dive in Marseilles. . . . So she went up to the top of the hill and down the little gully, turned her back, unsnapped her jeans, and saw Scrawny leaning against a tree.

"This isn't going to be pretty," she said.

Scrawny grinned. "Just doin' my job, ma'am."

So she undid her jeans and slid them down. Then she squatted and . . . well . . . she just couldn't. It wasn't that she imagined him smacking his lips at the sight of her white ass glowing in the predawn light. Guys could imagine stuff like that if they wanted. It was just that he was . . . well . . . watching. *Too weird.*

After a few moments, she stood quickly—so as to give him as little show as possible—and pulled up her underpants. She was bending to grab her jeans when she heard someone coming through the woods.

"Goddamn you!" It was Jack Batter.

He gave Scrawny a kick that sent him sprawling toward the shit hole. "Get up and give the lady some privacy."

Batter tossed Evangeline a roll of toilet tissue. "I told you last night, you're our insurance. But you're our guest, too. We don' have much up here, but—"

"Thanks. What time is brunch?"

"Don't be a smart-ass, lady. This is serious business. We're in a fight for something that should matter to every American. It's not a game."

"Guns off the street." She pulled up her jeans. "No game to me."

"No game?" He came closer to her. The scar glistened in the rising light as if this guy were iridescent, maybe, or burning from within. "Then don't play."

"You're playing with me, telling me I'm free to go."

"You are."

She looked around: impenetrable walls of pine and spruce, broken here and there by a skinny oak or beech that had already dropped its leaves.

This was logging country. The only roads were dirt, and all the land was owned by the Great Northern or some other paper company. And somewhere out there was the Golden Road, a true dirt highway that ran a hundred miles across northwestern Maine.

All night, Evangeline had listened for the distant roar of big rigs powering along. If she could get loose, she might follow the sound to the road and flag a trucker. . . . But the woods were all silence . . . and trackless . . . and these guys knew it.

Still, Batter told her to go. "Do Scrawny a favor. Get his mind back on business instead of on your pretty ass."

"What happens when I get back to civilization and tell them I was kidnapped?"

"You haven't been kidnapped. But you won't get back without us."

"Then what happens when you take me back? Assuming that's your plan."

"You worried that we'll kill you if we don't get the Constitution?"

Evangeline nodded. She didn't think she could speak just then, and she did not want any of these guys to see her fear, or hear it.

Batter took a few steps toward her. "If this goes bad, we'll drop you at the side of the road and point you in the right direction."

She didn't say anything. For a moment, she couldn't. At least she didn't swallow down some lump in her throat.

"Of course," he said, "if you have us arrested for kidnapping, remember . . . there's a lot of guys who like what we do, and I can't vouch for all of them. Seeing members of Algonquin Rod and Gun in jail might send them round the bend."

"Are you really just a rod and gun club, or some kind of right-wing militia?"

"You wouldn't see this lack of discipline in a real military force. But we come out here every week and train."

"For what?"

"For whatever is coming. Communists, Al Qaedas, the government trying to take away our guns."

She was tempted to laugh in his face, but it was not a face to laugh at.

He said, "They wrote the Second Amendment because they knew what we know: An armed citizenry is the best protection against an unjust government."

"I'll take an *educated* citizenry. Less bloodshed."

"When Shays's Rebellion started, Jefferson said, 'What country ever before existed without a rebellion? The tree of liberty must be refreshed from time to time with the blood of patriots and tyrants. It is the natural manure.' *He* was educated."

"One man's patriot is another man's tyrant," she said.

Jack Batter looked at her for a long time.

She thought there was another speech coming. But no.

He said, "If I were you, I'd take my piss, then get back to my tent."

PETER FALLON AND the girls took off at dawn from an airstrip in Vermont.

Kate Morgan was at the controls of the single-engine Beechcraft. Peter was in the copilot seat, Kelly in the back. They all wore headsets, so Kate's voice sounded clear and modulated when she spoke above the sound of the engine:

"We're headed to an altitude of five thousand feet. Keep us above the traffic."

"This is how we met." Kelly leaned forward. "I hired Kate to fly me to a speech in Buffalo."

"Ironic, isn't it?" said Kate.

"What?" asked Peter.

"That the two of us should meet in a *cock*pit," said Kelly.

Peter considered a few wisecracks but kept them to himself. Lesbians could joke about each other, but smart-ass straight guys did not have an invitation to join the fun.

Kate put the conversation back on beam. "The flight plan takes us down the Connecticut Valley, so we don't have to worry about updrafts and such."

"From the mountains to the sea," said Kelly, "from the top of New England to the bottom in—what?—an hour and half."

Peter wished Evangeline was with him, to see this and describe it for her readers: *Flying Down the Spine of New England.* Could there be a more beautiful vision anywhere, with the White Mountains on the east and the Vermont hills rolling away to the west? How would she capture the way the colors shimmered, the way the mountains cut long shadows across the earth, the way it felt to look out on that ancient landscape on a perfect October morning?

"We'll be in Clinton Jarvis's condo by nine o'clock," said Kate.

"And you really think that he has the annotated draft?" asked Peter.

"I've seen it," said Kelly.

Peter had already told her he did not believe her. That was why they were in the airplane. If there was a another draft out there, Peter had to see it and see if he could use it to save Evangeline. And if the guy who owned the black Sebring owned this draft . . .

That was an issue that Peter had not raised with Kelly or Kate.

"Jarvis collects Founding Fathers documents," said Kelly. "To build a case that the country's roots are as religious as the Vatican's."

"Why haven't I ever heard of him?" asked Peter.

"You might have done business with him and not even known it. He protects his identity and lets his money do his talking."

"Through people like you?"

"Jarvis invested in my little radio show at the very beginning, when I was one woman crying in the wilderness," said Kelly. "He has money in the Heritage Foundation, the Christian Coalition, the Morning in America Foundation—"

"Morning in America?" Peter felt a circle closing. "Marlon Secourt?"

Kate's voice clicked on. "If you think Jarvis and Kelly are strange bedfellows, imagine Jarvis and Secourt. The quiet guy and big mouth."

"Is Jarvis a minister?" asked Peter.

"No. Real estate. Grew up in New Hampshire, served in Vietnam, came back through California and decided to stay for a while. Orange County real estate. Now he owns shopping malls all across America."

"Where did he find Jesus?"

Kelly said, "He'll tell you Jesus has always been with him, and taken good care of him, too, in 'Nam and at the real estate auctions. Now he spends his money to thank God for his good fortune."

"And save America from moral decay," said Kate.

"You mean, save it from women like you?" asked Peter.

Kelly sat back. "Like Kate says, politics makes strange bedfellows. Business, too."

After about an hour, Kate banked to the southeast, away from the river and out over a massive body of water that seemed to cover most of central Massachusetts.

"The Quabbin Reservoir," said Kate. "Boston's water supply. In the 1930s, they bulldozed eight or nine towns, moved everyone out, and dammed the Swift River. Took three years to fill. Now it holds more water than Lake Erie."

Kate tilted a wing to give Peter a better look. The rays of morning sun slanted in to the cockpit like beams of gold.

"Makes you feel like an angel, doesn't it?" said Kelly.

Peter had to admit it. For a few moments, he almost forgot why he was in that plane. He just let the sensations of flight and light wash over him.

Then he saw a steeple piercing the foliage southwest of the reservoir, and it focused him again. "That's where the real angels are."

"A church," cracked Kate. "That's the last place I'd look."

"What started at that church started us on this quest," said Peter.

"How do you mean?" asked Kelly.

"That's the Pelham meetinghouse," said Peter, "where Daniel Shays and his Regulators worshipped, where the Pikes worshipped, too."

"Angels?"

"Freedom's angels," said Peter. "They rose up against the lawyers and businessmen and convinced the country it was time to go to Philadelphia and a write a new Constitution."

"Freedom's angels," said Kelly. "I like that."

"Of course," Peter looked back at her, "those farmers would have been considered leftists if the term was in use back then. You'd be dead set against them."

"They were populists," said Kelly, "fighting for the people, like me."

Peter backed off. Don't alienate the only people who were helping you.

"Kelly thinks she fights for the people," said Kate. "But most people just want to do the right thing and live their lives and be left alone. The people are like gravity pulling the pendulum to the center."

"Thank God for gravity," said Peter.

Kelly said, "The guys who marched across this landscape weren't interested in gravity. As you say, they were angels."

Peter looked down at the meetinghouse: a little front lawn, a driveway, a graveyard where the body of George North Pike probably lay. A car was turning at the corner. Once the meetinghouse had marked a crossroads, but the eastbound road now ended at the chain-link fence that surrounded the reservoir. Conkey's Tavern, the Pike farm, and the Daniel Shays farm were all under water.

"They dreamed what we all dream," said Peter. "They wanted to live their lives. But they knew that sometimes you have to act, or time washes over you."

When he walked into Jarvis's condo, Peter Fallon thought that perhaps, time had washed over him.

Clinton Jarvis kept a printing of the Constitution in full view, in a locked stainless steel case with UV filtering glass, which was a good idea because the condo itself was mostly glass, with floor-to-ceiling windows that looked out over Newport harbor.

Jarvis was waiting by one of the windows. He stood around five-eight, with a gray brushcut and a good build under his golf shirt, the sort of guy who looked as if he had seen action somewhere and carried it buried deep within.

Then Peter recognized him. *The designated driver.*

"I'm Clint Jarvis," he extended his hand.

Peter took it and said, "The Mount Washington Hotel. You were with—"

"Marlon Secourt. One of our annual trips. Golf and rare books. Pleasure and pleasure." He looked at his watch. "As a matter of fact, Secourt and I have a tee time at the Newport Country Club in a half an hour. But if Kelly wants to talk to me, I'm available."

Kelly looked at Peter. "See, strange bedfellows."

"It's one of my goals in life to straighten Miss Cutter out. Her friend, too."

Kate answered with a laugh, flopped onto the sofa, began flipping through a magazine.

Peter walked over to the glass case and peered down at a full sheet of newsprint, two columns of small, tight type. "Where did you get that?"

"It's a finished draft," said Jarvis. "The first public printing, which appeared in the *Pennsylvania Packet and Daily Advertiser*, September 19, 1787."

So it wasn't the *first* draft. That made Peter feel a bit better. But it was annotated, too, covered with scrawled handwriting, carets, edits, marginalia. He said, "Whose writing?"

Jarvis looked over his shoulder. "John Langdon, New Hampshire delegate. It came to me through channels even a brilliant dealer like you wouldn't have heard of."

"A Langdon descendant?"

"Let's just say someone who knew of my interest in the Christian foundations of our American story."

If Peter had been expecting a religious nut, he was disappointed. Jarvis spoke softly and economically and moved the same way. He seemed a reasonable man, one who understood his place and needed to impress no one.

Peter asked, "Do you know for certain that John Langdon was a Christian?"

"All the men at the Constitutional Convention were Christians," said Jarvis.

"Benjamin Franklin was Deist," said Peter.

"So he claimed," said Jarvis.

"Near the end of his life he said that he admired Jesus but had some doubts as to his divinity. He said he saw no need to worry himself over it, 'when I expect soon an opportunity of knowing the truth with less trouble. . . .' Funny guy, that Franklin."

Jarvis nodded, as though he knew all that. "Still, born and raised Episcopalian, and a pew holder at his church. You can look it up at Adherents.com. Ever visited it?"

"Can't say as I have," said Peter.

"All sorts of statistics, links to religious biographies of famous people—"

"I don't really care about a man's religion," said Peter.

"You should," said Jarvis. "Starting with your own. Until you accept Jesus as your personal savior, you're bound for damnation." He spoke calmly, as though telling a child why it was good not to go swimming right after eating. *Why . . . you could get a cramp.*

"When this crisis is over," said Peter, "I'll give it some thought."

"What better moment for considering your faith than in crisis?"

Peter looked at Kelly. "This guy is a friend of yours?"

"Friend would be too strong," said Kelly. "Business associate."

"Hate the sin but love the sinner," said Clinton Jarvis. "Espeially when she has six million listeners every afternoon. But back to you. If you're in crisis, have you considered what would happen if you were not to survive it?"

Peter didn't like the sound of that. "Are you threatening me?"

Jarvis laughed. "Why would I threaten you? If not for a chance meeting at the Mount Washington Hotel, I would never have laid eyes on you before."

Kelly said, "Mr. Fallon thinks there's another draft out there, a first draft annotated by all the New England Framers."

"I've heard these rumors," said Jarvis, "and done my quiet best to quash them."

"Because—" Peter rolled his eyes, pretending to look for a reason. "—the more annotated drafts there are, the less valuable yours will be?"

Jarvis laughed. "My document cost two million. I have garages that cost more than that."

"We're not talking about a garage here," said Peter. "We're talking about the birth certificate of the nation."

"True. But I suspect my version is the one in question. It's just that the story was garbled as it passed from hand to hand. Instead of first *printing* it became first *draft*."

That was plausible, thought Peter.

Jarvis unlocked the case. "Moreover, when I bought it, I also obtained a letter from Rufus King to Langdon." Jarvis slipped a letter out from under the Constitution. It looked ancient and authentic. "This is Rufus King: 'You should know that I have destroyed the notes we made during our discussions of a bill of rights, as they are outside the purview of our present task, which is to deliberate on the Committee of Detail draft.'"

Here was something Peter hadn't expected, and bad news if it was true, not only for Harriet Holden and Judge Carter Trask, but for Evangeline, too. He gave Jarvis a long look, trying to see behind that low-key exterior.

But Jarvis knew how to protect himself. He smiled and said, "So, you see, all this brouhaha over an annotated first draft is just . . . noise."

"You're a supporter of the Second Amendment, then?" said Peter.

"Of course," said Jarvis. "The right to keep and bear arms is God-given, as are all our rights, delivered by a Christian God to Christian men at a Christian convention. If you read the annotations, you'll see it on my draft."

Jarvis pointed to one of Langdon's handwritten notes. "A state preacher? A decree as to our roles as Christian men? Religion may remain separate, so as to protect the interests of Methodist versus Presbyterians, et cetera, but it must be encouraged."

"I've never seen that before," said Peter. "'Religion must be encouraged.'"

"Strong words," said Jarvis. "But true."

"The other day," said Peter, "I was reading something Elbridge Gerry wrote on his first draft, about no religious test being required of an office holder."

Jarvis nodded again, as if he had heard all that, too. "And in the Massachusetts ratifying convention, his compatriots spoke out. One man proclaimed that he wanted no politicians who did not believe in Christ because, as he put it, 'a person cannot be a good man without being a good Christian.'"

"Couldn't have said it better yourself," said Peter.

"You'll read it all in my new book. I build on Langdon and the faith of the Framers, who could never have imagined the attacks we see today upon their ideas."

Peter looked at Kelly. "This means he'll go after gay marriage."

Kate glanced up from her magazine. "That's why I keep guns."

"We're just fine with a civil union," said Kelly.

Jarvis closed the case and locked it. "People will try to tell you that the Founders were not religious men, but all of them agreed that religion must be encouraged, even Franklin. The first thing that Washington did when he took over at Cambridge was to mandate that the men attend religious services. And they try to tell us that he was not a churchgoer."

Peter was running through his American history, coming up with more than his share of objections, but he didn't think that such a gimlet-eyed student of his own truth would be moved by anything else that Peter said.

"So . . ." Peter asked Kelly, "what should I take from all this?"

"Realization that you've been wasting your time," said Jarvis. "There's no annotated draft, other than this one. It passed through the hands of Will Pike, Caldwell P. Caldwell, and George Amory. It somehow fell to an Irish family—"

Peter took breath. Here was the test. If he had one more name . . . it was . . .

"—the Ryans."

. . . *over*. Jarvis had the right name. This had to be the right version.

And if it was over, could Peter convince those nutbags in the Maine woods to let Evangeline go without a Constitution to show them?

Jarvis kept talking. "It went from the Ryans to the owners of the Pike Mill. Then it found its way to us. I can't tell you how, but you understand."

"So, that's that," said Kelly.

But Peter wasn't giving up quite that easily. He couldn't. There was too much unanswered to leave it all in the hands of this guy. And the biggest question still needed an answer.

"If that's that," said Peter to Jarvis, "how do you explain that someone driving a Chrysler Sebring registered to your real estate company has been following me?"

Jarvis looked puzzled. "I don't know what you're talking about."

"He followed me through Newport. He parked in front of the Old Curiosity Book Store in Portland just before he and his pal chased me through town." Peter left out the murder at the mill. He was only talking here about the car.

Jarvis shook his head. "My company is large. We hire a fleet from Chrysler. But if you'd give me the information, I'll look into it." Then Jarvis looked at his watch. "Tee time with Secourt."

"WHAT NOW?"

They were back in the plane, heading toward the Quabbin.

"I make a call to those boys in Maine, see if they'll let Evangeline go," said Peter.

"So you're convinced," said Kelly.

"Not really. But I can still use the story." Peter was thinking out loud, but not too loudly, because he still didn't trust these women entirely, even if Kelly had taken him to what seemed to be the end of the road.

"If my father is still looking for something," said Kate, "it's still out there."

"We're trying to straighten him out," said Kelly. "Don't keep him hunting for something that doesn't exist."

Peter's phone rang. He saw that it was Antoine, so he slipped his ear bud under the headset and took the call.

"Boss, I got some good stuff on Gilbert Amory."

"Like what?"

"You say you're in Peacham?"

"Heading back now." Peter glanced down. "We're over the Quabbin Reservoir."

"Well, Gilbert bought some land near Peacham in 1927. The year of the Great Flood."

"I didn't know there was a great flood in 1927."

"That's where this story begins. Gilbert did some business up there and—"

Peter didn't notice the engine begin to sputter. But he thought he heard Kate say, "Oh, shit."

"What is it?" asked Kelly.

Peter said, "Unh . . . Antoine, we got a little problem here. Hang on." He pulled the headset over his head. "What is it?

"Oil pressure is dropping," said Kate.

"Did you check it before we took off?" asked Kelly.

"Doesn't matter if I checked it then. It's falling now." Kate sounded dead calm, like a test pilot in a movie.

But Peter saw her hands shaking as she reached out and tapped the gauge.

The sputtering grew louder.

"Oh, Jesus," said Kelly.

"Calm down," said Kate.

Peter said to Antoine, "If you don't hear from me in fifteen minutes, call the State Police and tell them a small plane has gone down in the Quabbin Reservoir."

"Oh, shit," said Antoine.

Peter clicked off.

There was nothing he could do to help, so he followed some of the steps he took when he boarded a commercial airliner. He looked around for the exit door and tried to plan his escape. He told himself that the best thing to do was to stay calm. He might get out of this alive if he did. Which was probably a lie.

The engine sputtered a few more times; then it stopped.

Kate tried to restart. It whirred. It coughed. The prop didn't move.

"Oh, no," whispered Kelly.

Kate said, "Decent wind from the west. It will hold us up for a bit. We might be able to glide straight over the trees. Aim for the steeple. There's a road there, right?"

"Right," said Peter.

"How close are the trees on either side?"

"I can't remember, but the area in front of the meetinghouse gives you room to touch down. You might tear the wings off when you're taxiing but—"

"That's our play."

"But what if you hit a car?" said Kelly.

"Then we die," said Kate. "If we hit the ground at the wrong angle, we die, too."

"What about a water landing?" asked Peter.

"Hitting water is like hitting concrete. Our only hope is to avoid the trees, drop right in front of the church, and taxi to a stop before we kill ourselves."

Then they were quiet. The only sound was the rush of the wind over the wings. It was . . . beautiful. The sound of the angels, thought Peter. But they weren't playing their harps . . . yet.

The plane dropped down . . . down . . . almost clipping the tops of the trees on the west side of the reservoir. Then there was the meeting-house and the road and two cars and a patch of grass.

Peter was making plans for every contingency he could think of: What would he do if the plane clipped a power line and flipped? If the plane lost a wing as it glided? If it hit a car? If it missed the road and hit the meeting-house? The answer to every question: *Stay calm and you'll find your way out. Panic and die.*

Not once did he imagine himself flying through the windshield. Or spinning about the cabin. Or feeling the aluminum skin of the plane crush in around him like a collapsing beer can.

Stay calm. Stay quiet. And. . .

"Wheels down!" said Kate, her voice as cool as Chuck Yeager's.

But it wasn't over yet.

Time slowed. Reality reduced itself to a series of sounds and images, each of them entirely discreet. They were all unfolding at the same moment, but the mind could lift each strand and study it as though it were separate.

Tires squealed . . . horns blared . . . two cars collided.

The meetinghouse was on the right . . . and a tree on the left.

The left wing hit the tree and ripped off with a metallic scream.

At the same instant, the right wing struck the message board in front of the meetinghouse. The board went flying, along with half the wing.

Kate threw over the wheel. The plane spun into the lot in front of the meetinghouse and stopped just feet from the front door.

All three passengers pitched forward and snapped back. Automatic whiplash.

"We're on the ground," said Kate.

Kelly let out with a laugh.

And Peter looked down at the shattered message board. Looking back up at him was the face of Daniel Shays. The historical society occupied the meetinghouse. The message board told the story of the obscure farmers' rebellion that some people called the last campaign of the American Revolution.

Then Peter's cell phone rang. It would be Antoine.

Peter hoped that he had more about Gilbert Amory and the Great Flood, because this story was not over yet, no matter what Clinton Jarvis had told them . . . because who else but Jarvis had just tried to kill them?

TWENTY-THREE

November 1927

❧ OCTOBER HAD BEEN WARM, so warm that by late in the month, people were talking about having no winter.

In Boston, the magnolia blossoms swelled. On Connecticut hillsides, forsythias pushed out yellow blossoms to compete with fall colors. In the mountains, bluejays that should have migrated weeks earlier still screeched in the branches.

A headline in late editions of the *Boston Globe*: "Warmest November 2 in Fifty-two Years; Weatherman Declares Showers Coming." The National Weather Service was predicting "a southwesterly storm from New York to Eastport, Connecticut."

What was coming would be far worse.

THAT AFTERNOON, GILBERT Amory and a timber man by the name of Eustis Morton shook hands on a mountaintop in Vermont. Gilbert had just given this old Yankee a thousand dollars in cash as a deposit on the purchase of Mount Morton.

"Hate to sell my keepsake," said Morton.

"Namesake," said Gilbert.

Morton spat a shot of tobacco at Gilbert's feet. "It's been in my family two hundred years. I'll call it a keepsake if I want."

"Suit yourself," said Gilbert.

Eustis Morton was a small man with false teeth that whistled when he spoke. "Can't figure why you want a mountain that's mostly clear-cut."

"For the slopes."

"Slopes?" The word whistled bow and stern in Morton's mouth.

At twenty-five hundred feet, Mount Morton was not high, even for Vermont. But large swaths had been cleared of trees and subjected to lightning fires that conveniently removed the slash. When it snowed, a man would be able to strap skis onto his feet and glide all the way down. And he would be so exhilarated that he'd want to go right back up again. Gilbert had already imagined the ways in which to get that skier to the top of the slope—T-bars, chairlifts, even a horse-and-pung working the old tote roads.

Ever since he oversaw the Perkins withdrawal from the mill—and pulled out his own money at the same time—Gilbert had been looking for an investment. But he wasn't following the path suggested by Magnus Perkins—trusts, bonds, equities.

Gilbert was now forty-eight. Life was flying fast, like the clouds he could see on the southern horizon. He had enjoyed the company of a few women, but he had missed the pleasures of conjugality. He had loved skiing and travel, but many a year he had stayed in Portland, handling his title and estate work, when he yearned to be elsewhere. His answer to any busybody who asked was always the same: The law had been his mistress and his lover.

But no longer. He was still ramrod straight, but there was gray in his mustache. So he would feed his passions before he turned fifty. New Englanders, who had always endured winter, were learning to enjoy it. Gilbert, who had always endured life, was determined to enjoy it, too.

And he would enjoy it in a big way. He had gone to Chamonix, in France, for the 1924 Winter Olympics. He had dreamed ever since of buying a mountain like this one: it was steep, so the slopes would be challenging, and clear, so preparation would be minimal, and near a rail line, so skiers would have transportation. And there was room enough for a cottage colony at the base. But it would cost more money than he had.

So it was time to sell the Constitution, which meant it was time to visit his father.

AT THAT MOMENT, his father was deciding where the crew should move next on the east-facing slope of Mount Kancamangus.

"Hate to clear-cut," he said, "but that's what the managers want, so . . ."

"Yes, Pa," said Aaron Amory.

"At least we stopped those damn Henrys." The old man popped up in bed. "They were cutting on our land and saying it was theirs. The gall of them."

"Yes, Pa." Doc Aaron Amory gently pushed his father back and placed a stethoscope to the old man's bony chest. "Lie still."

"Could've armed our boys with rifles and gone right up like Fredericksburg," muttered George. "They called me coward, said I went and shot myself in the foot but I went up that hill, brave as any man."

"Shhhh."

"Your mother believes me. Where is she?" He popped up again. "Cordelia!"

Then he dropped back and was quiet.

Frenchy LaPointe leaned over Aaron's shoulder. "He was swingin' his ax. Cuttin' firewood. But the ax slip, hit his leg. He don't send for you till the leg, it start to swell—"

George cried out, "Cordelia . . . Cordelia!"

"Ain't right for husbands to lose wives," said Frenchy. "Wives supposed to live longer."

"God's ways are past knowing." Aaron patted Frenchy's back.

Where Gilbert was distant, formal, fastidious, Aaron was a bit slovenly, built like his grandfather and namesake, though far more forgiving of human weakness. People felt relaxed around Aaron, tense around Gilbert. But Gilbert was a lawyer; it was his job to make people tense. Aaron was a country doctor, and his manner came naturally.

Frenchy brought a red handkerchief to his nose and blew. "Will he be all right?"

Aaron looked down at his father. "He's met the old man's friend."

"Who's that?"

"Pneumonia."

George Amory spent most of his time in Livermore, watching his logging town die a bit more every year. In 1922, the sawmill had burned in a conflagration that lit the sky all the way to Bretton Woods. Operations had stopped for six months. But they had built another sawmill and kept going. Then the ancient *Charles W. Saunders* jumped the tracks and was wrecked, but still they kept on, gasping toward the end.

Aaron pulled out his tobacco pouch and said to Frenchy, "Time for a pipe."

They stepped onto the porch. Down below, the sawmill was whining, and the new Baldwin engine breathed on a siding.

"Mighty warm for November," said Aaron.

"It's changin', though," said Frenchy. "It always does."

IT WAS ALREADY cloudy in Massachusetts.

But Sarah Pike McGillis and her husband, Bill, did not notice the weather. They were doing a final walk-through of the Pike-Perkins Mill with the representatives of the bank that held the mortgage.

Eight years before, Perkins Holdings and members of the Pike family had sold their interest to Manchaug Mills of Sutton, a failing company trying to save itself by expanding. Total collapse was the result.

But the granddaughter of Bartlett Pike and her husband had refused to stand by and see a great legacy sucked down by someone else' failure.

They had made deals with the bank. They had raised capital as they could. They had worked with the unions. If no bidder met the reserve, the mill and looms would go to them. But the outbuildings, the worker housing, the company vehicles, the mountains of finished goods on sidings awaiting shipment—all the ancillaries—would be sold to the highest bidder no matter what.

"The looms alone are equal to the reserve," said Raymond Dunne of the First National Bank.

"Not if they have to be moved," said Sara. "They're worth nothin' 'less you run them."

"And we intend to run them," said Bill McGillis.

IN NEWPORT, MAGNUS Perkins was taking a final sail before pulling his boat for the winter. The thirty-five-foot sloop was sleek and seaworthy, so he wasn't worried about thickening clouds or rising wind. There was a southeasterly blow coming, but the radio said it would head inland over Connecticut and die out once it hit the hills.

Magnus took any chance to sneak away from work and wife.

He was sailing with Bunson, who would never tell tales to Mrs. Perkins about their first stop, at the steamer called the *Brunswick Belle*, Canadian registry, anchored three miles and one foot off the Rhode Island coast.

The Coast Guard now enforced an amendment to the Constitution that had inspired more illegal activity than any law ever written: the Eighteenth, Prohibition. But they could not touch a ship flagged to another country outside territorial waters, so booze-laden rust buckets like the *Brunswick Belle* anchored just beyond the limit and did business with inbound rumrunners and outbound sailors like Magnus Perkins.

By morning, Perkins planned to be at Block Island, with cases of Haig & Haig Pinch Bottle, Stolichnaya Vodka, and Burgundy wine in the hold, and he planned to drink as much of it as he could. What he could not drink, he would smuggle home, where he would continue to drink, just to irritate his wife.

Once they had pushed away from the *Brunswick* and found a comfortable point of sail, Perkins secured the wheel and Bunson broke out the Scotch. They took their spots in the cockpit, with tumblers in hand and the rhythm of the hull on the waves regular and relaxing beneath them. And Perkins toasted, "To our last sail of the year."

Bunson toasted back, then said, "May I ask you something, sir?"

"Certainly."

"You used to drink Tanqueray g-and-t's and nothing else from June twenty-first to the end of boating season. Then, one day, you poured your gin down the sink and switched to Scotch. Why?"

Magnus said, "The juniper."

"Juniper?"

"It makes some people mean. I can drink anything else and I'm always a prince."

"Of course you are, sir."

"But the juniper in the gin . . ." His voice trailed off and he looked out at the sea.

Bunson said, "It was around then that Rosemary Ryan had her fall, wasn't it?"

The boat rocked with the motion that calmed some men and made others seasick.

Magnus snapped his attention back to his butler. "That was eight years ago. That's when I did it. That's when she died. I don't see the correlation."

After a moment, Bunson said. "Snitterfield has died, you know."

"Stansfield's butler? The one who used to walk the wolfhounds?"

"I sat with him at his deathbed. He spoke of that night. The shadow that passed him—a man, tall and skinny, smelling of alcohol."

"Suspicion fell on Amory. But we vouched for him. It went a long way toward exonerating him."

"He did have his share of g-and-t's that night. And Snitterfield told me that what he smelled was gin. Juniper berries. Juniper, which, as you say, makes you mean."

There was a moment of silence between Magnus Perkins and his butler.

Then the wind gusted out of the southeast. The sloop heeled hard and the bottle of Scotch went tumbling over the side.

AT EIGHT O'CLOCK, the train from Boston pulled into Portland.

The conductor, Michael Ryan, punched out.

He didn't mind the routine. He knew where a man could get a bottle in Portland. Then he would curl up on a passenger seat in the front car, drink himself to sleep, and be ready when the morning crew came aboard at five A.M.

BY MIDNIGHT, THE wind was gusting to fifty knots at Providence.

Soon after, it began to rain. But not just to rain. It was as if the wide Sargasso Sea had been sucked up into the clouds and carried north to inundate New England. It poured and roared and fell so thick that it seemed like a fog on the land. It fell through the night and into the morning, and in some places it fell at two inches an hour.

And the storm did not lose power as it rolled toward the higher ground. Instead, it was stopped by cooler air to the north, so the rain-filled clouds kept coming and coming, throwing themselves against the wall of New England mountains like Union soldiers throwing themselves against that wall on the road to Richmond.

But along the Maine coast, the rain was not so heavy.

When Aaron Amory left his house on Bramhall Hill in Portland, it was barely sprinkling. He planned to make his rounds at the hospital, then hop a train back to Livermore and get to his father's bedside by noon.

He crossed to the West Promenade, which overlooked the approaches to the city. There was not a hint of brightening yet. But he could see the lights of the 5:25 to Boston, pushing out of the railyard and heading south, the steam engine moving like a big bull, unbothered by a little rain.

MICHAEL RYAN PUNCHED tickets on the 5:25.

The early businessmen were in their usual places, doing the usual things. The paper-readers were reading the papers, the coffee drinkers were blowing on their cardboard cups of coffee, the Boston-bound lawyers were pulling out their briefs.

Michael Ryan kept up his stream of "good morning, sirs, tickets please, sirs, thank you, sirs," and wouldn't I love just a hair of the dog.

BY SEVEN O'CLOCK, Gilbert Amory was ready to leave his hotel in Barre, Vermont.

The rain was coming in sheets, in curtains, in thick heavy drapes of water, but the most that the man behind the desk could muster was, "Sure is comin' down."

"What about the roads?" asked Gilbert.

"Depends."

"On what?"

"On where you're goin'. Rainin' so hard west of here, you can't walk, never mind drive."

"I'm headed east. New Hampshire."

"Can't speak for New Hampshire. Never been there."

Yes, thought Gilbert, New Englanders could be provincial people.

He stepped onto the veranda. Barre was a gray city even on the brightest day, because almost everything was built of the granite quarried in the surrounding hills. But today it was raining so hard that all other color was obscured. Everything was gray. And the water was roaring down Route 302, pushing stones and dirt like a mountain river in spring. That was the way he had to go.

Most of the roads between Barre and New Hampshire were dirt, but they were solid, well graded, with high crowns in the middle for drainage. They would get him to Livermore despite the downpour. Besides, the rain would have to let up. It simply couldn't rain any harder.

And Gilbert had to get to his father's bedside. He had to say goodbye, and once the old man's eyes were closed, Gilbert would find the combination of the safe and go down and open it. When Gilbert had tried to convince the old man to rewrite his will, the best that Gilbert could get from his father had been a promise to divide the contents of the safe in half. George had stubbornly, resolutely refused to show his sons the Constitution or sign anything that mentioned it. Gilbert had begun to wonder if the old man even owned it, if it hadn't all been a legend. But according to a telegram that had arrived from Aaron the night before, the Amory brothers were about to find out the truth. So Gilbert was hand-cranking the Model T while the rain soaked through his slicker and water swirled around his shoes.

GEORGE AMORY SPENT the night in dreamless slumber and awoke to all the days of his life. They flowed through his brain without order or logic, in slices and shards . . . Forward the Twentieth . . . Why is your father so much older than the other dads? Because your mother is so ugly . . . Do you have feelin's for me, George Amory? . . . Forward the Twentieth . . . There's gray in your Vandyke. . . . You'll not choose the ministry, then? . . . It's an honorable discharge. . . . Business is business. . . . You're big enough to pound me to pieces, but I'll break your hands. . . . Come at two o'clock. Promise? . . . To the wall! Take the wall! . . . Cordelia is there, Cordelia and your two little boys. . . .

The thunder of the rain was like artillery. It roared down on Livermore. It softened the ground under the train tracks. It ran in torrents that no tree-covered watershed could have held, nor any cut-over hillside.

Cordelia! She's under the thunder of the guns. Cordelia!

George Amory tried to get out of bed.

A HUNDRED AND forty miles south, a pocket of torrential rain had settled over the hills of central Massachusetts.

It had already knocked down the tent that the auctioneers had set up under the maples, so Bill and Sarah McGillis stood in the old boardroom, watching it fall and listening to it roar like the mill running balls to the wall.

At eleven o'clock, the auctioneer came in. "Grade crossings washed out from Boston and Worcester. No one knows about the line from Providence. Best that we postpone."

Bill McGillis looked out at the river. "We got bigger problems than that."

"Oh?" said Raymond Dunne, the bank representative.

"We got a mill dam about a hundred yards upstream, and the way the rain's comin' down, it might be topped. It might even break."

"What will happen then?" asked Dunne, whose big belly spread the buttons on his gray vest and whose forehead spread perspiration.

"Why, we'll flood. And—"

"—the bank still owns the building." Dunne looked out at the brown water roaring down the river and rushing through the headrace.

"It's going to be a long day or two," said Sarah. "But this is America. In America, we get up in the morning and go to work and solve our problems."

GILBERT AMORY HUNCHED over the wheel and peered through the rain covering his windshield. He had given up using the wiper. He couldn't drive and work the hand lever fast enough to make any difference. Uphill and down, past his ski slope, through the village of Orange, he puttered along at twenty miles an hour.

The Wells River ran near the road, sometimes hard beside it, sometimes behind a hill and out of sight, and whenever Gilbert was able to take his eyes from the road and glance down into the gorge, the river had risen even more.

Finally, he came down toward the town of Groton. A row of worker's houses lined the rising ground left of the road. To the right, three houses sat on the edge of a wide plain that sloped gently to the river. Except that the river had risen out of its channel, up over the plain, and was now lapping the roadbed.

Gilbert slowed as he came to a group of people standing in the road, dumbly, helplessly, looking out across this boiling brown torrent toward one of the houses.

Gilbert dropped his window and shouted, "You folks need help?"

"Not unless that car can float," answered someone.

A line of rope unspooled toward one of the houses, and Gilbert realized that it was not a single-story house, but two stories, and one was completely underwater.

Then, over the roar of the river, he heard a baby crying and saw a woman waving frantically from one of the windows.

"Oh, Good Lord," shouted someone in the crowd by the road. "We're losin' 'em!"

And the house began to move. It twisted in the torrent like a cardboard box crushed in a child's hands. And with a groan of wood and nails that struck a chord just high enough to be heard over the roar of the river, it lifted off its foundation.

The woman in the window screamed again. So did several on the road.

"Maybe we can get her at the bridge!" shouted someone.

"Bridge is out!" shouted someone else. "There's washouts all the way to Ticklenaked Pond."

The house revolved twice, then broke apart in a burst of furniture and stove pots and bed linens.

The people on the side of the road began to run toward the center of town, following the wreckage that carried the woman and her baby.

Gilbert called after them, but it was as if this was a local tragedy, something personal, and they wanted no stranger to be part of it.

So he drove a short distance more until the came to the Peacham Road. He decided to take it, because he would never get through Groton. Twelve miles of rough road would take him to West Danville. And further north, the Connecticut might not be so swollen. He might still be able to get across and make it to his father's bedside.

He went about seven miles, through farmland and woodlots, on undulating roads that took every bit of concentration. Then he came to a dip, and at the bottom, where there should have been a little bridge, there was water: Peacham Brook had overflowed its banks.

Gilbert stood on the brake. The Model T skidded and began to slide on the muddy road, slide sideways, slowly, inexorably and completely into the brown roaring water.

Gilbert tried to push open the door, but the force of the water held it

shut, then picked up the car and rolled it over, and he thought, how foolish to die in Peacham Brook.

THE 5:25 FROM Portland pulled into North Station at 9:30, an hour late.
Michael Ryan's schedule had him returning to Portland on the 2:10.
Time enough to get over to the South End to buy a couple of bottles of
bathtub gin at the bootlegger's. From North Station to Dover Street, fif-
teen minutes on the subway. Then back with enough booze to get him to
Portland and back one more time.

DR. AARON AMORY'S train made it as far as the Victorian station at
North Conway. Even its gay yellow paint seemed gray in the rain.
The conductor came through the car shouting, "End of the line.
Everybody off!"
"Everybody off?" said Aaron. "What for?"
"The track's washed out below Bartlett, and there's a landslide in
Crawford Notch. Took out a freight train, or so they say."
The passengers muttered and looked at each other, as if for encour-
agement, or perhaps leadership. Wasn't there something that could be
done?
Aaron said, "Is there a place we can hire a car?"
"Hirin' a car ain't the problem," said the conductor. "The hard part'll
be findin' a road."
Aaron was still twenty miles from Livermore. And his father was dying.

THE OLD MAN had not rescued his wife that morning.
He had wobbled to his feet, then fallen back into a stupor. Later
Frenchy had looked in on him, swung his feet back, and covered him so
that he could sleep again.
Now, around three in the afternoon, George Amory awoke.
The guns were still thundering. Would they ever run out of ammuni-
tion? And why were the generals still sending soldiers up that hill?
But Cordelia was up there, held captive behind the wall. Cordelia!
This time, the old man made it to his feet.
He looked down at the bony white toes, all seven of them, and . . . he
had proved it before and he would prove it again. He was no coward. He
was a good American. He had saved the Constitution. He had used it to
save his son. Now he would save his wife.
He smoothed his Vandyke, and Cordelia laughed at his gray hairs.
The roar of the guns was so loud that Frenchy did not hear him go

down the stairs, step out onto the porch, and call to his men. "Theirs not to reason why . . ." Forward the Twentieth!

Then he came off the porch and felt the enemy fire pouring down from the sky. Enemy rain, falling so hard that it hurt his face. He could not appear frightened to his men, so he took a confident step down the embankment, slipped, and went skittering to the bottom, where he stopped a few feet from the foundation of the steam house.

Get up . . . Don't let your men see you down . . . They'll never follow you. . . .

The boiler in the steam house was roaring, so the saws were screaming, like asylum inmates oblivious to the world outside.

No one seemed to notice that the roar of the river was almost as loud. And no one seemed to notice George. It was as if he were invisible, a gray old man in a gray nightshirt stumbling through the gray rain.

So he moved like a ghost between the ramshackle buildings, until something made him stop about thirty yards from the river.

She had been here, on this spot, when the hillsides were covered in virgin timber, when his little cottage was here. She had been here, where the railroad tracks now crossed in the middle of Livermore. She had been here, and she was near again.

He called her name and heard the roar

It was not artillery. It was not the Baldwin coming down from the cuttings. It was a wall of water, roaring down the gorge, rising over the banks, knocking down toolsheds and workhouses, splashing against the sides of flatcars, and striking George knee-deep, knocking him over, bouncing him along, slamming him once, then twice. . . .

It seems, as dark approaches, that most of New England is under water. Nine inches have fallen in some places, and it is estimated that as much as fifteen may fall, but no one knows for certain because rain gauges have been overflowing for hours.

All across the six states, men are piling sandbags against the rising onslaught.

Here in the hills of northwestern Connecticut, we have seen roads washed out, rail crossings destroyed, homes flooded.

New England railways have lost hundreds of miles of track, and hundreds of miles of road have been ruined as well, and millions of dollars in property have been lost. And by dawn, it will be worse.

But we must remember the words of Will Pike, a man who built a fine mill in Massachusetts. This is America. In America, we get up in the morning, we go to work, and we solve our problems. And tomorrow, we will solve ours.

With that, Samuel Bishop finished an editorial on the storm. He called his assistant and ordered him to take it to composition. He congratulated himself on the last line. It would please his wife to read the oft-used family saying, passed down from her great-great-grandfather.

Samuel Bishop did not think it very accurate. Had the McGillises the foresight to solve their problems, they would have followed other investors and sold out of the mill.

GILBERT AMORY DID not know how he got out of the car or made it to the bank. But he did remember a blow on the head. The car door? The car itself? Whatever it was, it was enough to knock him cold.

He did not awaken until he heard voices:

"His card says he's a lawyer, Pa."

"We shoot lawyers around here."

"Maybe he can help us."

"Help us? It's lawyers causin' us problems."

Gilbert realized he was looking into the barrels of a shotgun and the curious gaze of a woman whose face was shaded by a big sou'wester.

The woman pushed the shotgun out of the way and smiled, and her whole face seemed to glow. That was how Gilbert Amory met Mary Beth Meek, a schoolteacher in her forties who had a problem.

Soon he was in their kitchen, a blanket around his shoulders, his wet clothes drying on the stove, a mug of tea in his hands. "An estate problem?"

"My brother got three kids," said Farmer Meek. "So he's suin' for four shares of my mother's land and money, now that she's dead, against two for me and Mary Beth."

Gilbert said, "Your mother died intestate?"

"My mother didn't have testates," growled Farmer Meek. "She was woman."

"He's talking about a will," said Mary Beth. "She died without a will."

"Oh . . . well why didn't he say so, instead of usin' highfalutin lawyer talk?"

"This should be a simple matter." Gilbert told them how he would settle it. "The estate should pass equally to each brother. What they do with it is their own business." It was exactly what he planned to tell Aaron the moment he opened the safe.

"What would it take for you to take our case?" asked Mary Beth.

Gilbert could have given her an estimate of his hours and costs. Instead, he said, "A ride to Livermore . . . and the pleasure of your company."

MAUREEN RYAN WORKED a twelve-hour shift at the Perkins home in the Back Bay.

Mrs. Perkins had not seemed especially bothered that her husband had not contacted her from Block Island to say that he had weathered the storm. And Maureen had worried more about Bunson, who had sailed off saying that no one in his right mind went for a pleasure cruise to Block Island after Columbus Day. It was good that Mrs. Perkins had sent her home early. Otherwise Maureen would have been there for the arrival of a telegram: "Great storm. Bunson lost. Details to follow. MP."

As she climbed her stairs at Gloucester Place, Maureen heard music. The Victrola was playing Al Jolson, "Toot Toot Tootsie." And someone was singing drunkenly.

"Michael!" shouted Maureen. "You're supposed to be working."

Her son looked up through bloodshot eyes, as if he had been crying. He cried sometimes when he drank. And he smelled of work-sweat, alcohol, and urine. He wet himself sometimes, too.

"It's rainin'," he said by way of explanation.

"The trains run in the rain."

"Not this rain." He pulled open his little pint bottle of gin and downed a swallow.

His mother stalked across the room and snatched it away. "Where did you get it?"

He looked stupidly at her. "Sadie Ferguson's. Where else?"

"I'm tellin' her never to sell to you again."

Maureen went into the kitchen, poured the gin down the sink. Then she added a scoopful of coal to the stove to bring up the heat, then she poked at it, all the while trying to keep down her anger . . . at her son, at the local bootlegger, and at herself because somehow she could have stopped this, if only she had raised him better. She could have stopped a lot of things, if only, if only . . .

As she put two chicken breasts into a baking pan and shoved them into the oven, she shouted through the door at her son, "Whatever them women from the W.C.T.U did for America when they got Prohibition, they did nothin' for you."

"Prohibition!" shouted Michael. "They got any sense, they'll repeal it."

Maureen came back into the parlor. Though he was drunk, Michael was the only person she had to talk to, and when she sensed that he was saying something rational, conversational, intelligent, she tried to make something of it, to "have a chat" with him.

"What does that mean, repeal it?"

"They make a law, they can change it. Says so in the Constitution. Then a man'll be able to get an honest drink instead of sneakin' around." He pulled another bottle from between the seat cushions and pulled out the stopper.

"Mikey, I wish you wouldn't do that."

"Well, Ma, don't be wishin' your life away, because I like to drink. It's all I got."

THE RAIN STOPPED around midnight. By then, the rivers had flash flooded in the mountains. But as the skies brightened on Friday morning, the water was moving into the flatlands, where the rivers rose more slowly, more predictably, and more powerfully.

And no river caused more damage the next day than the Blackstone— the little Blackstone, the mighty Blackstone—because one of the most intense pockets of rain had settled the day before above the lake that fed it.

In the early morning, a mill dam in Sutton gave way and swept a mother and daughter to their death. In Uxbridge, citizens were called out to help with rescues as the river rose ten feet above flood. It sent plains of water deep into the surrounding farmland, stranding families, destroying businesses, weakening levees that held water to run the mills. Then the flood moved on toward Millbridge.

Sarah and Bill McGillis knew the crest was coming, so they put out the call for help. They sent four managers to the homes of four workers, each of whom went to see four more, who sent for four more . . . so that soon, every worker had arrived to help.

They stood on the levee upstream from the mill and began to fill sandbags, pass sandbags, and pile sandbags faster and faster while the river rose and the water roared through the open millraces. Maybe the levee would hold.

But the water kept rising. And they kept piling. The higher they piled, the higher the water rose.

Then someone shouted, "Run for it. She's toppin'!"

Without malice or urgency, the water spilled over the wall of sandbags, then caved it in, then began to swirl toward the mill.

Sarah and Bill and the others made it into the building. They scram-

bled up to the second floor and listened as it rushed across the ground between the mill and the headrace, then through the cellar windows and
through the openings in the wheel house.

It filled the cellar, destroying raw cotton and flooding the dyeing tubs.
Then it rose halfway up the first floor and destroyed cotton yarn ready to
be loomed into cloth, then it poured out the first floor windows and ran
across the rail sidings and destroyed pallets of finished cloth that lay under tarps, awaiting shipment.

Mr. Raymond Dunne of the First National Bank of Boston watched
it all in shock. When the water had stopped rising, and the McGillises and
Dunne and half the mill staff were trapped on the second floor, watching
the water pour through the lower levels, Dunne turned to Sarah and Bill
and said, "Jesus, who'll buy this place now?"

BY SUNDAY, THE *Boston Globe* reported, "The mad torrents of New
England's worst flood swept on to the sea last night, spending their fury in
the lower reaches of the Connecticut and the Merrimack."

And while the Connecticut River ran through the streets of Hartford, snow fell on Vermont. The first cold of winter finally got over the
mountains. It coated St. Albans with an inch of white in places that
weren't flooded; then it sent flurries skittering toward the Connecticut
River.

Gilbert Amory was wearing Farmer Meek's barn coat when he and
Mary Beth puttered off to see if there were roads left that could get them
to New Hampshire.

They arrived at Livermore late that afternoon. They had missed the
graveside service. But Gilbert stopped and looked at the mounded earth
next to his mother's grave.

"We had to plant him." Aaron walked down from the house. "The
preacher had to leave before it got dark. I'm sorry."

"It's all right," said Gilbert. "We'll have a memorial service for him in
Portland." Then he introduced Mary Beth Meek. "My new friend, client,
and chauffeur."

Aaron shook her hand. "It's about time that my brother was driven
around by a beautiful woman. Come in and have a drink."

Everyone left in Livermore had gathered in the Amorys' house—the
tough, callused ax men and their tough, callused wives, the teamsters, the
boiler mechanics who kept the Baldwin and the sawmill running, two
dozen people in all, a small, sad family. They had gathered to mourn the
loss of George Amory, but they were mourning the end of Livermore,

too. The flash flood had not destroyed the town, but it had ruined track far back in the valley, and the cost to relay it would be too great.

After a respectable few minutes of conversation, Gilbert found old Frenchy, who could not stop crying and somehow blamed himself for George's death. Gilbert embraced him and whispered in his ear, "My father left an envelope for me in his desk. It's locked."

Frenchy dragged a sleeve across his face. "He said you'd ask . . . before he was cold in the ground." Frenchy unbuttoned his shirt and pulled out a key suspended on a string around his neck. With a penknife, he cut the string and handed the key over.

It opened George's desk, where there was an envelope containing the combination. Soon, Gilbert and Aaron were at the safe, at the foot of the cellar stairs.

"Remember," said Gilbert. "Whatever is in here, we split. It's in the will."

"The Constitution?" Aaron knew the story.

"He never wanted to put it into the will, as if he never wanted to admit he owned it. Or had stolen it." Gilbert pulled open the safe and looked inside.

And there was . . . nothing but an envelope. It contained a letter.

Sons: I am gone, and so is the Constitution. It has been put to good use. If a person should come to you for help and mention it, help them. It will satisfy your heart and give you purpose, and in this life there is no better feeling. But get on with your lives. That was what I did when I realized that this document would not change the world, because its final draft already had. Getting up every day to solve your problems, working hard, dreaming your dreams— that is the best way to be good Americans.

Gilbert Amory looked at his brother and cursed.

A FEW LOGS were cut at Livermore the following year; then everyone left. The last time Gilbert and Aaron visited, Frenchy said to Gilbert, "You want to open a ski hill. Do it here. . . ."

Sarah and Bill McGillis bought the mill from the bank, because no one else wanted it after the flood. Soon the *click-cla-clack-cla-click-cla-clack* was heard again on the banks of the Blackstone, but for how long? Unionization and competition from southern mills were sure to change things. . . .

Maureen Ryan read about their efforts in the paper and wondered what she could do to help. She and Bill McGillis were cousins. And in the hard days after her own father's death, the McGillis family had helped Sheila Murphy Flaherty and her daughter. So someday, perhaps, Maureen would do something for the McGillis family. But first she had to do for her son . . .

. . . who was reprimanded for leaving his shift on the day of the storm and warned that if he ever did such a thing again, he would lose his job. So he took the pledge and gave up the drink. While he liked his whiskey, he loved the sense of purpose that came each day when he put on his heavy brogans and conductor's hat. . . .

In Litchfield County, Samuel Bishop told his wife, Will Pike's other great-great-granddaughter, that if there had been more radio stations people would have listened day and night to news of the storm. He convinced his father that they should purchase a license from the government and put a transmitter on the top of the highest hill they owned. . . .

Gilbert Amory tried to raise money for his ski area, but people said that he had chosen the wrong part of Vermont, that the mountains to the west got the most snow and had the best rail lines. Not even his brother Aaron, who had two children bound for college, could contribute much.

But Gilbert thanked God that fate had forced him into the Peacham Brook, because otherwise, he would not have married Mary Beth Meek. When her father died in September of 1929, she inherited his land. And George wondered if they might sell the orchard and put the money into the ski slope. . . .

BUT BEFORE LONG, some people had no money to buy an apple, never mind an orchard. Like the storm before it, the Crash changed lives irrevocably.

First, it brought a bit of retribution. . . .

On a mild November weekend, Magnus Perkins and his wife went to Newport to close up the house.

The staff worked. Mrs. Perkins sat in the solarium and read *The Sun Also Rises.*

When Magnus told her that he was going for an end-of-the-season sail, she barely looked up. She simply raised her hand and gave him a little finger wave.

That afternoon, Magnus Perkins pointed his boat east, tied down the helm, and opened his last bottle of Scotch. Though it was only two thirty, the eastern sky was already purpling. The November days were short.

Let other men jump from windows on Wall Street. Magnus Perkins would sail away with a bit of elegance, and who could prove that it was suicide?

If he contemplated his sins that day, perhaps he repented of them. . . .

A week later, Florence Perkins brought her staff together in the Back Bay house and said, with the implacable calm that was her hallmark, "I have two bits of news: Mr. Perkins has been officially declared lost at sea. And Perkins Holdings has been wiped out."

The Newport house was to be sold, she told them, "If we can find a buyer."

She then gave each of them a small check; "From Mr. Perkins's life insurance."

Maureen Ryan cried on her walk home. She cried for her children, the living and the dead. She cried for the father she had hardly known and for the man who had raised her. She cried for the mother who had begged her to forget the one and embrace the other. And she cried for Florence Perkins, who had always treated her with respect.

She did not cry for Mr. Magnus. She'd never liked him anyway.

GILBERT AMORY TURNED fifty-one the following November.

Aaron and his family came to celebrate the birthday on a sunny Sunday afternoon. Aaron brought champagne. After ten years of Prohibition, even the most law-abiding citizen could find a bottle of Mumm's when the occasion called for it.

Aaron toasted, "To my brother, a man with a dream."

Gilbert raised his glass to Aaron's family: Adele, his wife of twenty-four years, a daughter named Dorothy, a son named Tristram. These were the people who would carry on the Amory name and remember the works of Dr. Aaron long after he was gone. And while their presence warmed Gilbert, it saddened him, too.

Gilbert would have to mark his own footsteps boldly on the landscape, because he would have no children to widen them and keep them from filling in. He mustered a smile and said, "Some men slow down as they pass fifty, but thanks to Mary Beth and all of you, I feel ten years younger. I'm just warming up."

So Mary Beth offered a toast. "To a man warming up as the weather gets cold."

Aaron said, "A toast to cold, to snow, and a ski trail in Vermont!"

While the women cooked the birthday dinner and Tristram listened to a radio serial, Gilbert and Aaron went outside and packed their pipes. From the porch of Gilbert's Victorian on the East Promenade, the islands of Casco Bay seemed like jewels.

Gilbert took a long suck on his pipe, inhaled, blew out his nose.

"I only puff," said Aaron. "It slows the burn and saves tobacco, and these days, saving anything is good."

For a time, the brothers smoked together in silence and watched a freighter working its way toward the docks.

Then Aaron asked, "Can you meet the taxes on the Vermont land, at least?"

"So far," said Gilbert. "And once this downturn ends, people will have money. They'll want to go to places in the winter as well as the summer and not break the bank."

"The bank's already broken. You'll need money to build your little colony."

"Maybe I'll find that Constitution. Sell it and put the profits into Vermont."

Aaron puffed his pipe. "Do you ever wonder if Pa gave it to that woman? The one who claimed she was his illegitimate daughter?"

"I've written her. She wrote back that she didn't know what I was talking about. She could be lying."

"I'd believe her. Simple folk don't lie well." Aaron tapped his pipe on a porch pillar. "You'll just have to do an honest day's work for an honest day's pay. That's the New England way."

"I want to make money from money. That's the New England way, too."

Soon, only the most optimistic of men were calling it a downturn. Others called it what it was: a depression. The Depression. The Great Depression.

WITHIN A YEAR, the Pike-Perkins Mill was in trouble again. Within two years, they were laying off workers, shutting down looms, failing again to meet payments.

Maureen Ryan read of their travails in the paper and wondered how she could help them. She decided to pray for them at Mass.

One Sunday, she came home from the cathedral to find Michael, who had stumbled in after a night spent . . . somewhere. She looked at him, snoring, stinking of bootleg, a hand hanging over the side of the couch, and she decided that he was never going to change, no matter how many times he sobered up, put on his uniform, promised that he would never touch another drop, and headed off to work.

No woman would ever marry him. No grandchildren would ever warm Maureen's knee. And if he received an inheritance, he would only drink it away. Maureen made a decision that she prayed she would not regret.

On her next day off, she went to the First National Bank, where she kept a safety deposit box, and removed a map case.

She then boarded a train for Millbridge.

A few hours later, she knocked on the door of the old house that looked like a Greek temple with peeling pillars and broken shutters.

Sarah Pike McGillis herself answered the door. There were no servants in Millbridge, not even in the home of the mill owner.

Sarah seemed thrilled to see Aunt Maureen, whom she had met only a few times. She brought out tea and cake. They talked in the parlor, which had a view of the single-arch bridge and, across the river, the great brick mill that had been the focus of Sarah's family for more than a hundred years.

They talked of little Buster, who was sitting on a blanket, gurgling with his mouth around a rattle. And of course, they discussed the challenges to keeping the mill open.

Then, without ceremony, Maureen Ryan reached into her shopping sack and took out the cylindrical black map case. "This might help your business."

Sarah opened it, pulled out four sheets of printed words and handwritten notes.

"George Amory give it to me. He was a grandson of Will Pike."

"And my great-uncle. But . . . he gave it to you?" said Sarah. "Why?"

"A long story. But I think that it would be good if the Pike Mill was saved, and what better way than to use something Will Pike left behind? Maybe you can sell this and it will help you to keep folks workin', keep the mill open."

Sarah Pike McGillis was a girl better known for her gumption than her intellect. She examined the draft and asked, "Can these sheets of paper do that?"

"That's what George Amory told me. He said they were worth somethin'. Might be a lot, might be a little."

"Well, thank you," said Sarah. "We appreciate it. Buster will appreciate it, too."

In Portland, the fall tax bills arrived all at once for Mount Morton, the Meek orchard, and the Portland house.

Gilbert wrote checks on all of them and worried that he could not do it again.

He told Mary Beth about his ancestor, Revolutionary War veteran George North Pike, who was hauled off to debtor's prison because he could not pay his taxes. In time, there had been a farmer's rebellion, which had led to the new Constitution. If things did not change, he said, there might be another rebellion.

"The country will get by," Mary Beth told him. "So will we."

So they traveled regularly to Vermont and tended the old orchard. They sprayed and pruned in spring. They hired French Canadians to help them harvest in fall. Most of the apples went to a farmer's cooperative, except for the bushels they used to make cider. They made it hard and told no one, because some busybody in Portland, some lawyer who had lost a case to Gilbert, would just love to catch him violating the Volstead Act.

But November of 1932 brought the hope that a man might soon be able to get an honest drink again and better yet, a job.

The old saying was "As Maine goes, so goes the nation." It did not hold true, because Maine went for Hoover, along with Vermont, New Hampshire, and Connecticut. Most New England states had voted Republican since Lincoln, so they were not about to change because of a Depression. Massachusetts, Rhode Island, and the rest of the country, however, went for Franklin Roosevelt.

But there was still no money to invest in a ski slope, certainly not for a lawyer who administered estates when estates were shrinking and did real estate work when no one was buying land. So Gilbert did not consider it a lowering of his stature to appear each morning in the courthouse prepared to offer a defense, for short money, to the row of troublemakers and miscreants brought before the magistrate after a night of drunkenness, brawling, or general mischief.

Since the election of Roosevelt and the legalization of 3.2 percent beer, business had been good. It would get even better when Prohibition was repealed altogether.

Gilbert usually found his clients in the hallway outside the courtroom. He would offer his card to some hangover victim and ask if the man could pay a small fee—ten dollars for a pleading to a verdict of ACD, adjournment of proceeding in contemplation of dismissal. Once, such lawyering had been beneath him. But no longer.

So Gilbert was at the courthouse on a chilly April morning in 1933.

The corridors were full of men taken at a fight in a "restaurant" well known for serving legal beer and stronger stuff in the back room.

He stopped in front of a bench and offered his card to a man nursing a shiner.

The man shook his head. "Gilbert Amory . . . No thanks. I got a lawyer."

A big guy at the far end of the bench looked up. He was wearing a blue suit and holding a squashed blue hat with a peaked brim. On the crown of the hat was a badge that read CONDUCTOR. He said, "Gilbert Amory?"

"Can I help you, Mr. . . . ."

"Ryan. Mike Ryan." He stood and offered a big paw. "That makes me—"

Gilbert hustled him around the corner and out of earshot of the rest of the bench-sitters before he said, "My nephew . . . yes."

A few hours later, they sat over bowls of fish chowder at a waterfront lunch counter. Wagons rattled by outside. Stevedores and fishermen dug their way through the midday specials—meatloaf, pie à la mode, bottomless cups of coffee. On the wall beneath the menu chalkboard was a metal sign in orange, black, and white: a man in a lab coat, holding a bottle and pointing. DRINK MOXIE!

Ryan had been released. Gilbert had not charged a fee.

Ryan had also sobered up, but he still exuded a sweet cloud of alcohol vapor.

Gilbert watched him dig into his chowder and said, "How's your mother?"

"Gettin' old." Mike Ryan turned his big moon face to Gilbert and lowered his voice. "So . . . did you kill my sister?"

Gilbert sat back as if he had been struck. "That's absurd."

"There was talk."

"The police ask a lot of questions in an investigation."

"But you were there. On the Cliff Walk, botherin' her that afternoon. People saw you. And you were in Newport that night, drunk in a hotel. That's what the cops told my mother."

"The night clerk vouched for me. Besides, that was fourteen years ago."

"So . . . why did your father come to our house a week later, and give my mother somethin' to buy her off?"

"He gave her something?" said Gilbert.

Mike dropped a fistful of oyster crackers into his chowder. "He called it his most prized possession."

"The Constitution," said Gilbert, almost to himself.

"Yeah. That's what it was." Mike got back to scooping chowder into his mouth.

"Have you seen it?"

"Yeah. She showed it to me once. Had writin' on it." Mike picked up the bowl and drained the last of the chowder. "Is it worth money?"

"My father called it his most prized possession, didn't he?"

Mike drained his coffee, then pulled out a watch as big as a pie plate. "If I show up, they might let me work the two forty-five. I missed the five twenty-five. So my job's in trouble."

Gilbert dropped a bill and several coins on the counter. "Do you think your mother would talk to me sometime about the document?"

Mike Ryan was a big man, and when he stood, he didn't just stand. He loomed. Then he leaned close to Gilbert's ear. "You wouldn't help my sister when she asked. Two days after she sent you a telegram, she was dead. Stay away from my mother."

But Gilbert could not do that. He sent Maureen a telegram that afternoon.

Mike Ryan wrote back, "Stay away from my Mother."

THE BIG SONG that year was "Happy Days Are Here Again."

But they weren't. Not in Millbridge, anyway.

Sarah and Bill McGillis had kept going since they took the mill over in 1927. They had cut production, laid off workers, bought cheaper cotton, and by 1932, they had been able to meet the balloon payment on their loan.

And then the debt cycle had begun again.

They would have turned for help to their board of directors, but the board that might have bailed them out had sold out when Magnus Perkins left.

So Sarah and Bill, the granddaughter of the mill owner and the son of mill workers, had soldiered on alone. And while one was Protestant and the other Catholic, a mixed marriage in the parlance of the Papists, they both had what could only be called blind faith in the mill that so many of their ancestors had loved.

On a cold December night in 1933, they sat in the kitchen of the mansion that Sarah's great-great-grandfather had built nearly a century before. Neither of them could have imagined that it had ever looked bleaker.

The radio was playing "A Connecticut Yankee Christmas." Carols in the Rudy Vallee style.

Little Buster sat on the floor, close by the stove where it was warm, and played with his tin soldiers.

Sarah and Bill studied the books and wondered. Where was the money to buy raw materials? And the money to meet payrolls for a hundred people? And the money to eat?

"We need another loan." Bill rubbed his big hands together and cracked his knuckles. "I guess we'll have to gamble the mill to save it."

"What do you mean?" asked Sarah.

"Put the property up as collateral again."

"What about personal collateral?"

"Darlin', we don't have a pot to piss in."

She leaned across the table and gave him a kiss. Then she went to the front hall closet and pulled down the long cylindrical map case.

"This belonged to George Amory. They tell me it's worth a lot of money."

The following Monday, they appeared at the American Immigrant Bank of Millbridge and asked to see Mr. Chory, the president.

Jack Chory's grandfather had arrived from Lebanon in 1860, with the name Khouri, and had gone to work in the mill. His father had attended college, anglicized the name, and come back to open a bank in Millbridge. The name of the bank was only natural: a place for immigrants to save their hard-earned dollars and a place to celebrate the country that had taken them in and given them opportunity.

The Chorys might have decorated their bank with images from Ireland, Italy, or the Middle East, the lands from which most of their customers had come. They chose instead portraits of Washington and Lincoln over the teller's cage, quotes from great Americans above the customer's table: "A Penny Saved Is a Penny Earned," "The Business of America Is Business," "We Hold These Truths Self-Evident . . . ," and a new one, "The Only Thing We Have to Fear Is Fear Itself."

But the place of honor, behind the president's desk, was reserved for a large photograph, eighteen inches by thirty-six. It showed the mill with people arrayed in front of it. Men in long frock coats were seated. They were the managers and board of directors. Behind them were the workers—men, women, and children. And dead center was Will Pike, white-haired and rheumy-eyed, staring straight at the camera, as if trying to send his gaze as far into the future as possible.

The legend on the bottom of the frame read: "The Men and Woman of the Mill, 1861." And printed in the matting above, the words, "This is America. In America we get up in the morning, we go to work, and we solve our problems."

Mr. Chory, an amiable man with a bald head and a thick black mustache, took pride in pointing out his grandfather: "Two rows behind Mr. Will Pike himself. He was the first Lebanese in the mill."

That day, Chory pledged that he would do whatever he could to save the mill that had helped his grandfather and so many others in the Blackstone Valley. And when he looked at what they had brought for collateral, this student of American history was more than interested.

Two days later, Chory visited Sarah and Bill in Will Pike's old house.

His proposal was direct. Instead of lending them fifty thousand dollars against the first draft of the Constitution, he would buy the document outright for forty thousand.

"Buy it?" said Bill McGillis.

"I'm not sure," said Sarah.

"But consider," said Mr. Chory. "By selling it, you will not have to meet debt service. We will not be in a position to issue a call note should your business turn down again. I'm offering you control of your fate in exchange for this document."

"Is it a fair price?" said Bill.

"I've had an appraiser look at it," said Chory. "He feels that it would be in a range of thirty-five to forty-five thousand. So . . . to me, it looks like a victory all around."

And it was.

The McGillises kept the mill running.

Jack Chory was able to sink forty thousand dollars into an asset that could be moved or hidden, because his bank was one of thousands in America that was failing.

A few weeks after he bought the Constitution, the 1861 photograph was replaced by a portrait of the first Chory.

A few weeks after that, the state bank examiners appeared at his door.

ON THE DAY that the spring tax bills arrived, Gilbert knew that he did not have the money to meet them. There were not enough drunks in all of Portland to help him, and they had drained the inheritance from Farmer Meek.

So . . . where was he going to come up with five hundred dollars for his mountain and two hundred dollars for the Meek orchard?

He sat in his parlor on a Sunday afternoon and seethed. He listened to the radio, which was broadcasting from the Bishop System, "New England's own radio network."

Bishop. There was a man with foresight, and one who had weathered the present difficulties well. Gilbert had always remembered his talk about radio. Might he also be interested in other investments?

In the kitchen, Mary Beth washed dishes, slowly and steadily, as if it were a task that soothed her and would be done well. She was a methodical woman, not given to extravagance or outsized expectations. If plans failed, she had told him many times, they could retreat to the farm, cut wood, grow apples, milk cows, and survive.

She sensed him behind her and looked up. "No matter what, we've been lucky."

"Lucky? How?"

"We found each other when the time had past for most people."

"I'm thinking of selling this house," he said.

"No. This is your home, and the farm is my home. If you must sell something, sell the mountain. The mountain is just a dream."

"But it's the dreams that keep us going," he said.

"It's the little things that keep us going," she said. "Dreams are like mountains. Sometimes, you never reach them, but each day, you do the little things, and in the doing you sometimes get there."

He kissed her. He loved her wisdom, but he had to see to this dream, and in times when there was no money, he had to come up with better ideas.

So the next morning, he went to Boston.

He found his way to Gloucester Place. He climbed the steps of number 9 to the top floor and knocked. He was hoping that Mike would not be home.

Maureen Ryan opened the door. She may have tried *not* to frown at the sight of him, but every year of her life was etched into her face.

"I need to speak to you," said Gilbert. "Please."

Maureen Ryan was almost seventy. Her hair had gone white. She hunched as if there were a weight on her shoulders.

"You have something that I want," he said, "something that belongs to me."

"I don't think so."

"You're saying you don't have it, or that it doesn't belong to me?"

"I'm not sayin' nothin', Mr. Gilbert Amory. I might have it. I might be savin' it for my son. I might have given it to relatives."

"Relatives?"

"I'm not sayin'."

Gilbert tried a little charm. "Maureen, *I'm* a relative. I'm your half brother."

She gave a disgusted laugh. "Fat lot of good that ever done me."

Normally, before a deposition or cross examination, he prepared every question and analyzed every possible answer. He had not expected this witness to be so hostile. So he asked her, "It's the Constitution? Why did my father give it to you?"

She shrugged. "He felt guilty, I guess. He never spent a minute with me. Maybe he was plannin' to give it to my daughter because she asked for it. And he wanted me to have it to shut me up. He thought I'd finger you for the murder if he didn't shut me up."

"Did he say that?"

"He asked me not to sell the Constitution till you was off the hook, so no one would wonder where I got it."

Gilbert could not believe this. He had come to browbeat her into giving it back, or perhaps to negotiate a portion of it. It had to be worth thirty thousand dollars. He said, "Do you have a bill of sale? Did you give my father a receipt? Do you have anything proving that he gave it to you and you did not steal it?"

Maureen Ryan stood and slapped Gilbert Amory in the face. "That's my answer. Everybody knew you were there, chasin' my daughter along the Cliff Walk."

He stood. "I did not kill your daughter. And the police knew that."

"Your father hoped that was true, and he tried to buy my silence with that Constitution thing. I told him he didn't need to, but he insisted."

"Why won't you let me see it? It could make us both a lot of money. It could help you move out of—" He looked around, made a gesture.

"Mr. Gilbert," she said, "this may be nothin' to you, but it's mine. Now get out."

Gilbert tried to think of some way to calm her. But he could not, so he stood, went to the door, turned. "I do estate work, Mrs. Ryan. I know the law."

"I bet you do."

"If you try to sell that document, or give it away, or do anything to profit from something a confused old man gave you, I'll sue you on the grounds of undue influence."

Just then, the downstairs door swung open and a heavy footfall struck the steps.

"Mother of Jesus," said Maureen. "First you, now Michael. At eleven o'clock in the morning. They must've sent him home drunk."

"Maybe I should go out the back way," said Gilbert.

"No," she said. "You'll go out the way you come in if you're a gentleman."

"Gentleman!" boomed Mike Ryan up the stairs. "Is somebody botherin' my mother?"

Gilbert turned. The door slammed behind him.

"You!" Ryan pivoted round the banister. "I told you not to bother my mother. And here you are—"

Gilbert put up his hands. "I can explain."

"Bullshit!" Mike Ryan grabbed Gilbert and threw him down the stairs.

GILBERT AMORY DID not stay to argue. He never argued with drunks. And he had learned a long time ago that if he could not go over the top of the mountain, there might be a way to get around it, so by late that afternoon he was in Hartford, Connecticut.

This was a small city with a big reputation. Once one insurance company had thrived here, others had come as if carried on the currents of the Great River. Now it was called the insurance capital of America. So the streets were full of men with small eyes and tired faces, men in three-piece suits and felt hats—homburgs, derbys, and snap-brim fedoras—hurrying for the evening train or the local saloon.

Gilbert went against their flow to the offices of Samuel Bishop's *Hartford Sun*.

"I'm afraid Mr. Bishop's gone home early," said the receptionist. "Is there something I can help you with?"

"No thanks." Gilbert had Bishop's address, so he hired a taxi to take him to Farmington Avenue.

"Up where the rich folks live," said the cabbie.

The houses were huge Gothic Victorians with broad lawns, turrets, slate roofs, porticos, like wooden castles or, in the case of the house that Mark Twain had built, like a wooden riverboat with balconies and railings to make an old river pilot feel at home. Harriet Beecher Stowe had lived around the corner from Twain.

They were long gone, but the Bishops had lived in their house on Farmington Avenue for three decades.

It was six thirty. Gilbert feared that he might be interrupting dinner. But he rang the bell, took off his hat, smoothed his hair.

It seemed that Gilbert had arrived on a night when Mrs. Bishop was at her ladies' league meeting, so, as Samuel Bishop joked, "Even newspaper editors have to babysit now and then." His five-year-old was riding around in the foyer on a red fire truck. "That's Charlie," he said.

Gilbert said, "I was just passing through and I thought I'd say hello."

Bishop chuckled. "Passing through? We're sort of off the beaten path up here."

Gilbert played with his hat in his hands.

"You'll stay for dinner? I'll have the maid set another place." Bishop had a likable smile and a devilish Clark Gable mustache that matched his personality.

While little Charlie picked at his ground beef, Samuel Bishop warmed to conversation with an adult. They talked about the newspaper business, Hartford and the growth of the insurance business, and Bishop offered his vision of New England's cities as places where men would come to work more with their minds than with their hands.

"The day of industry is coming to an end in New England," said Bishop. "You see the men who work in Hartford. They add columns, they analyze, they think rather than labor. I'm expanding to serve them. They read my papers, they listen to classical music and entertainment—"

"Precisely," said Gilbert. "They will also need places for recreation, because we're physical creatures, too. That's why I'm building a ski resort in Vermont. Do you ski?"

"We ride the train up to Stowe. Little Charlie has taken to it like a fish to water."

When the gentlemen retired to the study, little Charlie went to the fireplace, sat down with his picture book, and started turning pages.

Gilbert took a glass of port and said how well-behaved the boy seemed.

Charlie looked up. He didn't miss a trick.

Samuel said, "He enjoys listening to gentlemanly dealings. It's how a boy learns."

"Well, then," said Gilbert, swallowing port, pride, and trepidation, "let him listen to this: I wasn't just in the neighborhood. I've come looking for a loan."

"A loan?" Bishop laughed. "For what?"

"For my ski resort." Gilbert thought he would have to launch into a sales pitch, but Bishop interrupted him with—

"What can you offer as collateral?"

Gilbert could not believe it was that easy. "Why, a piece of the business."

Bishop said nothing.

Little Charlie flipped the pages of his book.

So Gilbert said, "What would you say to a first draft of the United States Constitution, with annotations from the Founding Fathers?"

"Founding Fathers?" said Bishop. "You mean like George Washington?"

Little Charles looked up. "George Washington?"

Bishop flicked his eyes at his son and smiled. "The boy learns fast and early."

"I may have a line on such document, if—"

"Ah, to hell with it." Samuel Bishop waved his hand.

"To hell with it?" Gilbert thought he was cooked.

"I like skiing. I'll be a silent partner. I'll take the hill as collateral. This Constitution you're talking about, show it to Charlie if you ever get your hands on it."

THE LOAN MADE the difference.

Gilbert and Mary Beth moved to Vermont in June of 1934. By September, they had built fifty one-room cottages, each with its own wood-stove and bathroom. They bought a depot hack to carry people from the station at Barre. They spent hundreds advertising Amory's at Mount Morton. And it didn't snow.

The next winter, it snowed like hell. But nobody came.

Why get off the train after six or seven hours and ride the depot hack for another hour to a small resort that no one knew about, when the train went all the way to Stowe?

So Gilbert and Mary decided to begin their third season by inviting everyone they knew for a free weekend of skiing. They printed invitations and sent them across New England, to the Bishops in Hartford, to the Amorys in Portland, even to the McGillises in Millbridge, though Gilbert knew that they would never come, not with a dying mill to nurse.

And on the day before the guests were to arrive, a blizzard blew into Vermont.

Ordinarily Gilbert would have been thrilled. Snow. White gold. But a bearing in the bull wheel had gone, and the bull wheel ran the T-bar tow, one of the prime features of Mount Morton. Gilbert, who had learned to do his own maintenance to save money, took his tools and climbed the top of the slope to repair the bearing.

It was early afternoon when he started, but by dark he still had not finished. And he saw failure looming on the day that he hoped would inaugurate the do-or-die season at Mount Morton. So he brought up lanterns and kept at it.

The wind was tearing out of the northeast. The snow whipped against his face. He could not feel his fingertips. But still he kept at it.

Sometime around seven o'clock, a gust of wind bit through his jacket and sweater and into his chest. Once it was there, it stayed, and it grew, and grew, until a simple pain became a crushing weight.

Mary Beth, looking out from the family quarters in the big house, saw the lantern suddenly fall. She threw on her coat and boots and scrambled to the top of the slope.

When she got to him, his flesh was cold.

She tried to haul him down, in hopes that a warm house would warm his heart back into motion.

The snow whipped at her face and the wind cut into her flesh, and after she had dragged him a short distance, she knew it was hopeless.

This tough Vermont woman, who had lived so independently for so long, sat down in the snow beside the body of her husband and began to cry.

And that was how they found them the next morning. The New England weather, which had brought them together, would keep them together for eternity on their mountainside.

TWENTY-FOUR

WHEN PETER FALLON DECIDED to stop running, he usually ended up at Fallon Salvage and Restoration. It was no fortress, but it was as close as you could get in Boston. The chain-link fence was topped with razor wire. The warehouse sat in the middle of a half acre lot at the edge of a South Boston neighborhood. The sodium vapor lighting turned night into day, and during the day the neighbors in the three-deckers could be counted on to watch for strangers.

Peter Fallon had gone to ground. Considering what had happened in the air that morning, the ground looked pretty good.

"Small planes are deathtraps," Danny Fallon was saying.

"Unless you have a good pilot," said Peter.

"A good pilot might have noticed that the oil pressure was dropping before she went to *aw-shit* mode."

"I suspect it was rigged," said Peter. "So did the girls I was flying with."

"Pretty?"

"Yeah, but not your type," said Peter. "They stayed behind to answer questions. I rented a car and got back here as fast as I could."

"That means you're in *aw-shit* mode yourself." Danny cracked a beer and handed Peter a can, too. "Time to call in your big brother. Wah wah wah. Save me. Save me."

"They have Evangeline," said Peter bluntly.

"Shit." The beer can stopped just south of Danny's lips. This meant he was shocked, because no beer can lasted long that close to Danny's lips. "Who's *they?*"

"Gun nuts. Militia. Survivalists. She gets loose when they get the first draft of the Constitution."

"Shit." Danny took a swallow of beer. "Gun nuts. Scary. Especially these days."

"At least I know what they want. Then there's the other one. He killed Bindle, chased us through Portland."

Danny's son Bobby came into the office. He was carrying the twelve-gauge shotgun that he hauled out whenever Uncle Peter suggested that he should watch the front gate.

"I wish you'd put that thing away," said Peter.

"You said you needed protection," Bobby answered.

"Then get a bigger gun," said Peter. "Because the other guys have AR-15s."

"Guns," cracked Danny. "About time we got them off the street for good."

"We might need a few," answered Bobby, "because a nigger just pulled up at the gate."

"Nice talk," said Peter. "Did you bother to see if it was Antoine?"

"Antoine? Eddie Scarborough's kid?" said Danny. "Oh, shit. I just saw—sorry."

EVANGELINE CARRINGTON SPENT a few hours wandering, but there was no place to go, so she wandered back to the camp, made herself a peanut butter and jelly sandwich for lunch, and sat in the sun. Working on her tan seemed like the best way to stay out of trouble.

Her guards were the four guys who had been in that dustup at the gun camp. But they seemed to have stopped worrying about her. No one watched her. No one followed her a second time up to the latrine pit.

Scrawny and Mercer were more interested in cleaning their weapons. The one they called Hotshot sat in his tent and read a Tom Clancy novel. The fourth, called Butcher Bob, sharpened a knife and butchered the bodies of half a dozen squirrels he had shot.

Evangeline took a nap, an even better way to stay out of trouble. She was snapped awake by the sound of small-arms fire. Before she knew where she was, she leaped to her feet and ran outside.

Then she heard male laughter, coming from the little rise that shielded the latrine pit. Then *bup-bup-bup-bup*. They were target shooting.

By then, she was bored enough to go and watch. She followed the sound up to where the boys where having their afternoon squeeze-a-few session. When one of them noticed her, he nudged the shooter, and all four turned.

"Hey, it's Lady Mace," said Mercer.

"These are big mean guns," said one of the others. "Hope they don't scare you."

They all snickered, which was a bad idea. Nothing annoyed her more than snickering . . . at her.

Mercer held out the .44 Magnum. "Want to squeeze one off?"

They all snickered again.

She took the gun, raised it with both hands, and pointed it at the target, which happened to be a picture of Harriet Holden. This gave her a moment's pause. Then she squeezed the trigger. *Boom.* The huge handgun recoiled like a cannon.

Boom. A hit beside Harriet's ear. *Boom.* Above her head. *Boom. Boom. Boom.* A perfect semicircle.

Before the sound stopped echoing, Evangeline handed the gun back to Mercer. "There. I just gave her a halo."

"We thought you was against guns," said Scrawny.

"I'm against stupid gun laws." She decided not to stay and talk. Walking away would leave a better impression. She went back to her tent and flopped down on the cot.

After a while, she heard the boys building a fire. The sun was dropping. It was getting chilly. Time to eat.

Then she heard someone outside her tent. She could see the toes of Mercer's boots below the flap. He cleared his throat.

She got up and pushed back the canvas.

Mercer was scowling. He always scowled. "Nobody said you could shoot."

"Nobody asked."

He was holding two bottles of beer. "You want one?"

She hesitated. This might be his first move when he was seducing some biker chick, but she could use a beer. What the hell.

"You ever eat squirrel? Soaked in a little vinegar and pepper sauce?"

She took a swallow of beer. "Squirrel. Yum."

He gestured to follow him. "You better hope your boyfriend comes up with something soon, or you'll be eatin' a lot of it."

"Where's Batter?" she asked.

"Gone down to Bangor," said Mercer.

Down. There was a clue, if she did decide to sneak off. They were north of the most northerly city in the state. So they were *way* north.

"He don't want people to think he's doing anything different."

"Does the judge know about this—?"

"Don't say 'kidnappin'.'"

"I'm your guest. Why else would you give me a beer and . . . squirrel?"

Mercer also gave her his scowl. The fat-crease at the back of his neck made him look like a bull, pumped full of testosterone, nothing but trouble, even when he seemed in a good mood. "Woman can shoot like that, she gets a beer. But she don't get to make fun of us."

"I'll never learn."

"The judge is old school," said Mercer. "Too much of a gentleman. No . . . this is our play."

There were no songs around this campfire.

Butcher Bob skewered the squirrel bodies.

The one called Hotshot was still turning pages in his Tom Clancy.

Scrawny kept sneaking glances at Evangeline, as though he couldn't get the image of her ass out of his mind.

Finally, Evangeline smiled at him, and he took that as a sign to start talking. "You know, we're sorry for what we done."

"Like hell." Mercer drained a beer and pulled another from the cooler by the picnic table. "We have to do what we have to do. We're fightin' for a way of life."

"Damn right," said Butcher Bob.

"That's why we come up here on weekends," said Hotshot. "To practice livin' in the wild."

Butcher Bob rested the skewered squirrels on a rack above the flames. "The day may come when we have to do it for real."

"Why?" She thought she knew the answer.

"Because of you or some other do-gooder takin' our guns," said Mercer. "Or because the rest of the world has blown up and the survivors are headin' this way. We aim to be the ones who last. Us and our families. So we'll have our guns. It's our right."

"Is it your right to kill a man on a Portland street?" She knew as soon as she said it that she should have kept her mouth shut.

But Mercer and the others laughed.

Scrawny said, "We fooled you, hunh?"

"We didn't kill that guy," said Mercer. "We hit him with a Taser, then we put him out with a big syringe full of Demerol. Drove him down to the high-speed ferry and loaded him on."

"Probably woke up halfway to Nova Scotia," said Hotshot.

That made her feel better.

"Yeah," said Scrawny. "If he had any money, he lost it at the craps table once the ferry went into international waters."

"We ain't murderers. But, we'll fight for our rights and for this. It's the last wilderness in the east," Mercer went on. "The loggers leave us alone. But flatlanders are comin', plannin' their big developments because the loggin' companies are sellin' out. And we don't have the money to fight them." Mercer took a long swallow of beer. "Sure would like to get my hands on some money and buy all this."

"Yeah," said Scrawny. "A lot of money."

"Right." Butcher Bob lifted one of the skewers and tested the meat. "Times are tough. . . . Squirrel?"

She gave it a look, tore off a piece, took a bite. It tasted like . . . chicken. "Pretty soon, there won't be anyone can cook squirrel like that any more."

"That's what we're fightin' for," said Hotshot.

"To cook squirrel?" she asked.

"No!" Mercer jumped up, and he was so big that he blocked the heat from the fire. "Don't you get it, lady? We're the last real Americans."

Just then, they heard the sound of an engine somewhere to the south. Mercer's cell phone rang. It was Batter, on his way in. "Maybe he's got some news."

IN SOUTH BOSTON, Peter Fallon sat with Antoine Scarborough and studied the material from Charles Bishop. It included a note from Bishop: "This should have been forwarded to you three days ago. My instructions were not followed. My apologies. See you on Sunday."

Orson Lunt had arrived from Newport, too. He said that he was tired of parties, and he hated to "miss a meeting of the brain trust." Peter was glad to have him, because Orson always gave good advice.

They clustered around the computer in Danny Fallon's office to read the e-mailed files: letters, newspaper articles, an editorial about the great flood of 1927 with a note, written by Samuel Bishop to his wife. "Do you notice how I've quoted your ancestor?" The line that he had underlined was, "This is America. In America, we get up in the morning, we go to work, and we solve our problems."

"I like that," said Peter. "In America we solve our problems."

"But look at this one." Antoine took them to another document. It was an invitation to Samuel Bishop to attend the "seasonal opening" of the Amory ski slope.

"So?" asked Peter.

"There's a note on the back of the invitation."

Antoine hit another button and another scanned image appeared, handwritten: "Dear Samuel: I hope you can come. Accommodations await. I admit that the first two years have been difficult, so you have not seen a return on your investment. I have put heart, soul, and all but a few resources into the project. Those few I have secreted behind fireplace bricks or under the floorboards because—ha, ha—no matter what FDR tells us, we have more to fear than fear itself."

Antoine looked at Peter and Orson. "Didn't someone find the log of the *Mayflower* behind a few fireplace bricks about fifteen years ago?"

"Yeah," said Peter. "I wish it had been me."

Orson stroked his mustache, sat back, crossed his legs. "I think this Gilbert Amory is speaking metaphorically. *Ha ha.*"

"Have you ever been in a deposition, Orson?" asked Peter.

"I've had the displeasure. Yes."

"Then you know that lawyers jump all over metaphorical talk. They pretend they don't understand it. Gilbert was a lawyer. I think he was telling Bishop exactly where he was going to put his prize possession."

"A metaphor." Orson sat there certainly in his gray slacks and blue blazer and turtleneck, looking utterly cool and completely out of place in the office of a construction firm. But Orson never acted out of place, no matter where he was. That was one of the reasons Peter had modeled himself after Orson.

"What if it's not a metaphor?" said Peter. "What if he really did 'secrete it behind some fireplace bricks,' just like those people who hid the log of the *Mayflower*?"

"I suppose that you have to find out." Orson recrossed his legs. "And it may give you the chance to draw Evangeline's captors out into the open."

"That's what I want to do," said Peter, "once I know where this ski slope is."

"I think I know." Antoine tapped in a Web site on the computer. NELSAP: New England's Lost Ski Area Project. With a few more clicks, he navigated right to the hillside in question.

"The Internet," said Orson. "Like the library at Alexandria or Shakespeare's brain. An endlessly fascinating universe."

There was a brief history of the Amory Cabins at Mount Morton: "After the death of Gilbert and Mary in a blizzard, the ski slope was sold by its creditor, the Bishop Company, but subsequent owners could not make it work. It went out of business in the early seventies. Now the slopes are grown over with grasses and cedars, the first trees to reclaim open land, and hardwood saplings sprout everywhere. Only a few rusted wheels remain of the chair lift and T-bar. The cottages and the little lodge stand open to the weather as stark reminders of nature's power to reclaim what is taken from it."

There was an overhead photograph, showing small cottages flanking a big house at the base of the slope.

"Is there a zoom feature?" asked Peter.

Antoine tapped out a few more keys and the house enlarged.

"That's where we're going." Peter pointed to the house. "That's where it is. We find it, tell the Maine militia to bring Evangeline down, and we make the switch."

"*If* we find it," said Antoine.

"Whether we find it or not," said Peter. "We'll give them an empty map case if we have to."

"And then we'll all be shot," said Orson.

"Maybe," said Peter. "But I'm not leaving Vermont tomorrow without her."

AROUND NINE O'CLOCK that night, Danny Fallon's minivan pulled into the driveway in front of Morgan's Antiques and Firearms. The girls were back from Rhode Island, and they were waiting. They had a refrigerator loaded with beers and burgers ready to cook on the grill.

Peter was worried that he had brought along a bit too much muscle. He liked to work alone. But Danny and Bobby had Vermont hunting licenses, and it was duck season in that part of the state, so they could both carry shotguns. Antoine was too smart to leave behind. Orson was the voice of experience.

So there they were, piling out of the van in the crisp air beneath the shimmering Milky Way, a high-country wonder to city folk who seldom saw it.

"Howdy, boys." Kate came out first, looking pretty relaxed for a woman who had survived a plane crash that morning. Of course, thought Peter, once you've survived a plane crash, there can't be much to make you nervous.

Then another shadow came out. "Hello, boys."

"That voice." Danny peered toward the house. "I know that voice."

"Do you listen to the radio?" asked Kelly.

Peter said, "I didn't tell you their names. I thought I'd surprise you."

"My God," said Orson. "That's Kelly Cutter's voice."

Danny stepped into the light and looked at her face. "You're as beautiful as I hoped you'd be. It's an honor to meet you."

Antoine said to Danny, "You actually listen to her?"

"Beautiful on the outside," said Orson Lunt. "Bilious on the inside."

She turned to Orson. "So we have a conservative and a liberal."

"Working together," said Peter. "Like good Americans."

Kelly offered a hand to Orson. "I have a picture in the attic. It shows the real me, all covered in bile."

"I have one like that, too," Orson said. "It puts another wrinkle on my forehead every time I say something bad about someone. I'm about thirty years older than you are, but I'd bet that our pictures make us look the same age."

"Orson, be good," said Peter. "The girls are helping. Kate has a reputation with these militia types. And Kelly is their voice. The antique barn will be neutral ground. Once we have the draft, we'll come back here and make the swap."

"I'll go along with this," said Kelly, "even though I think the draft you're looking for has already been found."

"An opinion I don't share," said Peter.

"Me neither," said Kate. "Not after this morning."

"Clinton Jarvis did not send someone to kill us," said Kelly.

Kate looked at Peter. "We've been arguing."

Maybe they weren't as relaxed as they appeared.

Kelly said, "Clinton Jarvis has too much money tied up in me to kill me. Just because he believes that the separation of church and state has been misinterpreted all these years, and he has the Constitution to prove it—"

"Church and state?" said Danny. "I thought this was about guns."

"It all goes together," said Peter. "How about those burgers?"

THEY DROVE OUT in the autumn dawn, bound for a little hillside where a man once dreamed. The girls knew where it was, so they led the way in their Volvo, south across Peacham Creek. They picked up Route 302 in Groton, an old mill town built along the gentle Wells River.

The Boston boys followed. They took Peter's BMW because the heater was broken in the van. Danny drove. Peter sipped coffee. The others sat in the back, Antoine and Bobby quietly, Orson chattering away about the sights passing by.

Peter told Orson to pay more attention to what was behind them. "If you see a black Chrysler Sebring, or any other car, or even a bicycle that looks like it's following us, sing out."

"Don't tell him to sing," said Bobby. "It's too early for Cole Porter."

They turned west toward Barre, and the road began to rise in a series of sine curves that grew ever steeper. This was not the Vermont of postcards.

It was a land of small houses and double-wides sitting on lots hacked from the woods. The unifying features were dish antennas and metalbestos chimneys puffing wood smoke in the chill morning. Some were neatly kept; others looked like they were competing for the *most-junkers-on-blocks-in-the-front-yard* award.

After about half an hour the girls turned up a dirt driveway. There was no billboard announcing the turn, no sign, no pavement, just a break in the wall of scrawny trees along the road. It dumped them into an old parking lot decorated with a one-way DO NOT ENTER sign and a rusting old snowcat sprouting weeds.

Whatever had gone on here, time had passed it by.

The Volvo bounced ahead of them up the rutted driveway, past a big sign: NO TRESPASSING, NO HUNTING, NO TRAPPING, into a sloping meadow that once had been the lawn of the little resort. Now apple trees dropped leaves and deformed fruit across the meadow, because the last business had been an orchard. An old sign directed all traffic to the right, up the gentle hill, to the large house at the apex of the circular drive: the one that Peter had pointed out on the NELSAP Web site.

Little one-bedroom cottages followed the curve of the drive, flanking the big house like schoolchildren around the teacher, aged schoolchildren—porches collapsing, chimneys collapsed, windows broken, weeds and saplings rising and twining and poking.

They pulled up in front of the big house. It was built in the same style as the cottages, New England vernacular, which meant nothing special, just a two-and-a-half-story woodframe house with a peaked roof and dormers on either side. But there had been additions. Every new owner had brought a new dream: an office wing here, a breakfast room there, a ski shop with floor-to-ceiling windows, all shattered now and boarded up.

The shadows were long and cool. The autumn dew covered the ground. The deep silence of the place swallowed up the slamming of the car doors and the low sound of conversation.

"Welcome to Bates Motel East." Orson was the last to climb out of the van.

"Let's hope we don't meet Mom," said Antoine.

"She's not home," said Kelly. "*No one* is home."

"No one home since 1975," said Kate.

Danny went around to the back of the BMW and pulled out two shotguns.

"No guns," said Peter. "We don't need guns."

"So what the hell did you drag us all the way up here for?" asked Danny.

"Moral support. Advice."

"Who did you say owned this place?" asked Orson.

"Last owner was some New York firm," said Kate. "They thought they could revive the old ski area. But, there's not enough of a mountain here, even if they tore everything down and started over."

"Seems a waste," said Orson.

"You'd be surprised how many places there are like this," said Kelly. "Dreams that never came true. Last I heard, the state had repossessed it for nonpayment of taxes."

"So," said Orson, "if we find the Constitution here, we'll have the state of Vermont on our backs, too."

Antoine said, "Do you really think it's here?"

"We didn't find it at Livermore," said Peter, "which was the last place we could trace it. Now there's documentary evidence that it was here, so we have to look."

They sent Bobby down to the trees near the road to watch the driveway.

Then the bucket of tools was out, and the Fallon brothers took pinch bars to the plywood nailed across the entrance to the house. A dozen shrieks of metal and wood, the sheeting came off, and a wave of cold air hit them in the face.

Danny peered in, then looked at his brother. "You first."

Peter had a big flashlight. He aimed it inside. Cracking plaster, broken glass, rags on the floor, a chair in a corner with the stuffing torn out.

He took a breath and stepped inside. The clamminess grabbed him by the neck. The air smelled of small animals living in leaf and chair-stuffing nests, a mulchy, funky smell, the definition of "entropy." Everything wanted to get back to its simplest state. This old house was well on the way.

Peter turned to his brother. "Maybe you better get the shotgun after all."

"I was hoping you'd say that," said Antoine, who was right behind Danny.

"I'll get it." Kelly took the opportunity to go running back to the car.

Kate and Antoine stepped in and swept their flashlights around.

There was a registration desk straight ahead, a big living room to the left with a fireplace, an entrance to a large, pine-paneled breakfast room on the right.

Kelly was back with the shotgun. She handed it to Danny but said that she'd keep watch out front. Orson said he'd go around and watch the back.

"Sissies," said Kate, then she headed for the stairs.

As soon as she stepped on the first tread, something skittered across a floor upstairs.

Danny let fly into the ceiling *Boom!*

Peter jumped. "Jesus Christ, Dan. That was just a squirrel or something."

"Yeah, well," said Danny, "it's a dead fuckin' squirrel."

Kelly was peering in from the porch. "Is everything all right?"

"Yeah. Fine." Peter shook his head two or three times to stop the ringing in his ears. "One guy is trigger happy, one girl is frightened."

"One boy, too," said Antoine.

"This is why I work alone," said Peter. "Now, here's what we do. We find the family apartment. Probably in the back. We test every floorboard. We go over every bit of exposed brick. We cut into the wall and check the brickwork around the flue."

"Why?" said Danny. "In the flue, you have one course of brick, then a tile liner. There's no room for a map case in a chimney, for Chrissakes."

"What do you suggest?"

"We inspect the fireplaces. That's where they might have bricked something in. We go down in the cellar and see if the floor joists are boxed in. If they are, we tear 'em out. We go upstairs and stomp around, listen for changes in the subflooring."

"If we don't find it?" asked Kate. "What do we do when the militia boys show up?"

"We have another plan," said Peter. "I brought an 1887 repro of the Constitution in a map case, with some scrawling on it. It might work."

In a few minutes, the whole house was vibrating with the sound of stamping, hammering, pinch-barring, and shouting.

Raccoons climbed out of the main chimney. Squirrels came skittering from under the eaves on the second floor. Terrified mice braved the daylight to escape.

Danny and Antoine worked together on the fireboxes with hammers and chisels.

Kate suggested to Peter that they split up—Peter in the cellar, Kate on the second floor.

But Peter said, "If we work together and find something, we'll have another opinion nearby." He still didn't trust her. He trusted Kelly less. Kate could be on the side of the Maine militia. Kelly still trusted that Clinton Jarvis a bit too much. If Kate came across the document before Peter saw her, she might hide it for herself.

None of that.

So they worked quickly through the cellar. They found no evidence of boxed floor joists, nor any sign of a wall safe built into the granite foundation.

They went up the back stairs, to the bedrooms in the rear, the separate apartment, the owner's residence. This would be the most likely place for a man to hide something beneath floorboards.

They pounded and banged, and the whole house shook. When Peter stomped his foot under a window that had been leaking for years, he put it through the oak flooring, through the subflooring, and through the ceiling plaster in the kitchen below.

"Excellent," said Kate. "Now we can rip out the whole kitchen ceiling."

Good idea, thought Peter.

Back in the kitchen, they went to work with the pinch bar. One or two pulls and the ceiling fell down. But the plaster was so wet that there was barely any dust.

Peter shot the flashlight up into the spaces between the newly exposed lathes and joists. "Nothing. What about you, Dan? Anything?"

"Nothing. The fireplace in the front room is fieldstone, and the mortar was never tampered with. The one in the back is brick. Falling apart. And no sign of anything."

"Nothing in the floors either," said Kate.

Peter looked around at the mess they had made. "It was a long shot anyway."

"What next?" asked Kate.

"Time to improvise." Peter shouted through the broken back window at Orson, who was sitting in the sun on an overturned barrel, staring up at the slope, keeping watch.

Orson turned to speak and suddenly he was jumping into the air, and the barrel was rolling over.

"Did you hear that?" said Peter to the others.

"What?" asked Kate.

"A gunshot."

Orson looked around. Puzzled? Shocked? Then another shot rang out, more a *bup* than a blast, a silenced sniper's rifle. The barrel jumped again. So did Orson.

"Good Christ!" Orson ran around to the front of the house.

Peter and the others were out already. "Get into the cars!" shouted Peter. "Let's get out of here."

"What about Bobby?" cried Danny.

"We'll pick him up on the way out."

"*Bup. Bup.* Two more shots. The first lifted a rusted beer can off the driveway. The second hit it again while it was in the air.

"Wow!" said Kate. "Nice shooting."

Two more shots whizzed. And a tire on the BMW blew out.

They could see the shooter now. He was at the top of what looked like the old bunny slope. Hiding behind the big rusted bull wheel.

Danny raised his shotgun and Peter pulled it out of his hands, because he heard the growl of ATVs coming down the hill and up from the parking lot.

Before the ATVs had stopped, Danny was shouting, "Where is my son?"

Jack Batter got off one of the ATVs. "He's fine. He's down there, tied to a tree."

"We were supposed to meet at Morgan's Antiques and Firearms," said Peter.

"Never follow the other guy's plan." Batter flipped Bobby's shotgun to Danny. "That's rule number one of fighting a good guerrilla war."

"Where's Evangeline?" demanded Peter.

Batter pointed up the ski slope, up to the bull wheel, up where the shooter was. She was there, too, wearing the same clothes she had put on two days before. Mercer was beside her, holding an AR-15. She waved.

"She's all right," said Batter.

Peter turned and began to walk toward the hill.

"Not so fast," said Batter. "Don't you have something for me?"

"How did you know we'd be here?" asked Peter.

"We're smart. Now, where is it?"

"It's back at Kelly's house." Peter gestured to Kelly Cutter, whose eyes were wide with the shock of another brush with real life rather than radio world.

Batter didn't seem to recognize Kelly. He snapped at her, "If it's at your house, what are you all doing here?"

Kelly looked at Peter. "I think he just busted you, Peter."

"Oh, thanks, Kelly," said Peter.

She took a few steps toward Batter, who turned his head, as if the scar on the left side of his face afflicted his eyesight.

He looked through his right eye so that he could see better. "Kelly . . . I know that voice."

Kelly smiled. "A lot of people know the voice. I'm a friend of Peter Fallon and his Boston crew."

"Boston crew." Batter looked around at Danny in his camos, Antoine in his Red Sox hoody. Then his eyes fell on Orson. "Did you like the ride on the barrel, old man?"

Orson twitched his mustache. "If you're going to call me *old*, call me *old boy*. And no, I didn't like it. If I didn't have a balky prostate, I would have wet myself."

Scrawny snickered at that.

Batter almost smiled. Then he turned back to Kelly. "I listen to you every day. You're on our side, right?"

"I believe the Second Amendment means what it says," she answered.

"We're all on your side," said Peter. "We've just proved it. We have Kelly working with us. We believe what you believe. So let Evangeline go."

Batter stood there, thinking it over for a moment; then his eye fell on Kate Morgan. "One of the other rules of good guerrilla warfare is to know your enemy."

"Enemy?" Kate pointed to herself. "Me?"

"Your father." Batter climbed aboard the ATV. He revved it once or twice and it whined like a lawn mower. "You dragged us all the way down here from Maine, and you don't have the draft. I'm pissed."

"We're not done looking here," said Peter.

"Looks to me like you are." Batter aimed a finger at Fallon. "Tomorrow night."

"Tomorrow night . . . what?" asked Peter.

"The draft. In my hands."

"People have been looking for years," answered Peter. "What makes you think I'll find it by tomorrow night?"

"Her father thinks so." Batter jabbed his finger at Kate Morgan. "He's promising to reveal something special to America tomorrow night, before the first game of the World Series. I've seen promos on all his stations. The Baseball channel, ANN . . ."

"Bet that's really going to boost the ratings," said Kate.

Batter looked at Peter. "If he puts that draft on television, and it goes against the Second Amendment, you won't see your girlfriend again."

Peter said, "Doesn't it bother you that we know who you are and we'll have you all arrested if anything happens to her?"

Batter simply said, "No." Then he gunned his engine and shot up onto the ski slope. The other ATVs followed, screaming like a pack of coyotes.

BACK AT THE antique shop: Peter was holding the second GPS tracker. They had fixed two to his BMW. He had found only one.

"Batter is a dangerous man," said Peter, "to think that he can frighten us like that and then just show his face."

"Brazen," said Kate.

"No," said Orson. "Shooting a man's seat out from under him. That's brazen. Jack Batter and his friends are so committed that their fate doesn't matter. That's dangerous."

"Did anyone get a good look at Evangeline? Did she look all right?" asked Peter.

"She looked fine," said Kelly. "From what I could see."

"A lot of good you did," he answered. "Miss Right Wing, can't convince your own constituency to do the right thing. And you tell them we're—what was the word—oh, yeah. *Busted*. Blew my backup plan right out of the water."

"Probably saved your girlfriend, too," said Kelly.

Kate said, "Maybe you should backtrack. Try to think this through from the time it began—when?"

"Last Friday. When that Jennifer Segal visited me," said Peter.

"Which one was she?" asked Orson.

"Professor Conrad's graduate student at Dartmouth."

"In what?" asked Kelly.

"History, of course,"

"History? At Dartmouth?"

"She's a Ph.D. candidate."

"Dartmouth has a graduate school of arts and sciences," said Kelly. "I know. I applied once. But they don't offer a degree program in history. Someone is lying to you."

"And she's avoiding me, too," said Peter.

"Where is she?" asked Orson.

"She gave me an address in Hanover, right down the street from the college."

PETER WENT TO Hanover alone. He'd had enough of group efforts, so he took the BMW and sent the rest of the Boston boys back in the van.

But before he left, he called a friend on the Dartmouth faculty, an English professor named Harrington Smithies, who taught Poetry and Prose of the Romantic era and collected first editions of the Lake District gang, as he called them—Wordsworth, Coleridge, and so on.

Peter asked him for a favor: visit an address on Main Street and present himself at the door, pretending to be looking for someone else. "And be careful."

Smithies played the dotty old college professor, as innocent as the bindings on his books and as smart as what was in them. Half an hour later, he called back and said that yes, the young woman was there, and a young man was with her. Lover or associate, he could not tell.

"Did they seem suspicious?"

"Of an old man? Old men are invisible, especially to young women."

"You didn't happen to notice a black Chrysler Sebring with Rhode Island plates parked anywhere nearby, did you?"

"You didn't ask, so I didn't look."

"Just a hunch," said Peter. "I owe you one early edition of Wordsworth."

PETER CROSSED THE Connecticut River from Vermont and came into town on Wheelock Street. He loved Hanover. It had all the vitality that made college towns mythic places in the American imagination. It thrived because of the college. Some said it existed because of the college. Town and college seemed to blend together, meeting in a lover's embrace on the college green.

Parking was always tight on a football Saturday, so Peter had to cruise the town twice before he found a spot in the municipal lot behind the business area.

Then he made for Main Street and the crowd bustling along in the cool October sunshine. There were lots of orange scarves, so Princeton was in town. But Dartmouth green was the dominant color—on old alums and their wives, on young alums and their families, on gangs of raucous sophomores, frat boys with their girlfriends, girls with their boyfriends. The smell of wood smoke and sizzling burgers floated in the air, and . . . he cursed.

He didn't need this. He had a good business without all the danger, without getting his girlfriend into trouble, without having killers stalking him across New England, without feeling as if he was the only man in America protecting the truth simply because it was the right thing to do.

But better him than somebody else.

The address that Jennifer Segal had given him was a few doors down from Molly Malone's Pub, half a block up from the Dartmouth Co-op: a nondescript doorway, a doorbell, three mailboxes. He peered through the door: no foyer, just a steep stairway leading up to three apartments above the local businesses.

Peter took out his cell phone. Her machine answered on the first ring. "This is Peter Fallon. I have news about the item I have been looking for. If you're there, I'd appreciate it if you'd pick up."

Pause. Wait. No pickup. Pete clicked off, stepped back, looked up at the windows of her apartment.

"She's still in there."

Peter turned: "Professor Smithies. I didn't notice you."

"I told you old men are invisible." He had a ruddy face and wore a brown tweed suit and a green tweed hat. "That's why I've been able to stay out here for most of the morning, keeping an eye on the place. I want to earn that Wordsworth."

"And you're sure she's up there?"

"Positive."

"What about the young man?"

"I haven't seen him leave, either."

"What did he look like?"

"Thirties. Dirty blond hair. Very fit. Looked like a weight lifter, perhaps."

"Thanks. I'll be back next Saturday for the Harvard game. How about dinner with me and Evangeline afterward?" At the moment, that sounded ridiculously optimistic.

"So long as you bring Wordsworth. Anything else I can do for you?"

As a matter of fact . . . Peter asked him to wait outside. "If I don't come down in ten minutes, call the police."

The old man's cheery expression froze. "Police. What's this about?"

"Professor Stuart Conrad—"

"Do these people have something to do with his accident?"

Peter didn't want this old man getting in the way. He pointed to a park bench on the sidewalk. "Just sit there and wait for me. If I don't come down in ten minutes—"

"Do you want backup? I'll give you backup. I know how to handle myself."

Peter thanked him but no, he didn't want backup.

At the same moment, the apartment door swung open. The black turtleneck set off the pallid complexion. The gold rims flashed. The girl made eye contact with Peter Fallon, then walked past him and began to heel-toe along, as if she wanted to put some distance between herself and her front door.

Peter said to Professor Smithies, "If the guy comes out, call my cell."

He caught up to her in front of the Dartmouth Co-op. "What's going on?"

"He's in my apartment."

"Who?"

"Walter Stanley. Stanley Benson. Benson Burton. Burton Walters."

"That's four."

"Four pseudonyms."

"What's his real name?"

"Walter Stanley. You've seen him all over New England. He wears a blue blazer most of the time and carries a digital camera."

Peter stopped and looked back at the door.

When he turned to Jennifer, she was walking up one of the alleys that led off Main Street along a little row of businesses: the window of an ice cream shop, the kitchen window of a restaurant.

"He was in the shower," she said. "I got your message. I erased it."

"Who is he? What are you doing with him?" Peter realized he was raising his voice. He saw eyes peering out at him from a kitchen window, a cook working over the Frialator. He lowered his voice, clenched his teeth: "Why did you drag me into this?"

She kept walking. Her pinched face behind the wire-rims, her arms folded in front of her chest—everything about her said fear.

But Peter's circuits were so overloaded by his own emotions that he wasn't reading hers, or the signals of the other people using the alley. This wasn't some bleak passage between two old skyscrapers. The buildings were brightly painted, there was a pennant fluttering over the ice cream shop. People were coming and going, laughing, even singing fight songs.

But Peter grabbed her by the elbow and turned her toward him. "Last week, you asked me to find something. Since then, I've been stalked in Newport, cornered and almost killed in Millbridge, chased through Portland, and yesterday I crashed in a plane to that took off in Vermont, sat on the ground in Rhode Island, and almost hit the goddamn Quabbin Reservoir in Massachusetts!"

"And you will be killed if he catches up with you."

"Who is he? Your boyfriend?"

"We're working together." She pulled away, began to walk again.

He grabbed her again. "Who are you working *for*? You're no student."

"Let me go."

"Stop!" Peter grabbed her by the shoulders, spun her toward him, and pinned her against the wall.

"Who are you working for?" demanded Peter.

"Paul Doherty."

"Doherty? Who is *he* working for?"

"Let me go." She pulled away.

He grabbed her again.

The next two things that Peter Fallon heard were "Hey!" and the *thwang* of a frying pan, thwanging off his forehead.

It knocked him back, bounced him off the wall on the other side of the alley, and by the time he had his bearings, Jennifer Segal was hurrying back toward Main Street, while the fry cook and two frat boys were surrounding Peter.

"Don't let him follow me, please!" she shouted.

Peter went to make a move and one of the frat boys blocked him with two hundred and twenty pounds of bulk. "Let her go, old man."

"Yeah," said the other one. "She's too young for you."

The fry cook just waved his frying pan.

And Peter's cell phone rang. He pulled it out, saw the caller ID, and said, "Professor Smithies."

One frat boy said to the other, "I'm in that guy's class. Let's go."

In a flash, they were gone, but the fry cook held his ground.

Professor Smithies said, "He's out. He's walking toward the campus. No. Now he's turning. I think he just saw her. She just came out of an alley, just beyond the Dartmouth Co-op. . . . But where are you?"

"On my way. See you next week . . . I hope." Peter closed his phone.

The fry cook said, "This ain't the big city. You can't push women around here."

Peter gave him a smile. The frying pan had brought him to his senses. He could go after the girl. But better to go after Paul Doherty. Right now.

So he headed back up the alley to the parking lot.

Go fast, he told himself, before Walter Stanley figured out what was going on.

The parking lot was full of cars cruising for spots. And they all locked on to him at the same moment. A pedestrian meant a space might be opening. He began to run, knowing that they would all converge and cause a traffic jam in the little lot.

But as he went, he passed a car he hadn't seen on his way in, the Chrysler Sebring. Walter Stanley's car. And that gave him an idea.

While the cruisers followed him, he went to his trunk, took out the GPS tracker, turned it on. Then he climbed into the BMW and started to leave.

Immediately, three cars made for his spot, and two tried to get in at the same time. Horns blared, people shouted: parking lot rage, right there in peaceful Hanover. Perfect cover.

He drove around the row of cars, stopped, and jumped out.

In an instant, the GPS tracker was fixed under the bumper of the Sebring.

The cat was belled.

Now to confront the cat's master in Portland.

A TELEVISION IN A BOOKSHOP. A travesty.

That's what some of Martin Bloom's customers said when he set up a black-and-white portable beside the sofa. They preferred classical music with their browsing.

But Martin Bloom was adamant. It would have been unpatriotic not to be watching television around the clock that summer.

If it bothered his customers, too bad. He expected to lose them anyway, because he saw no future in selling trade books. He was turning Old Curiosity into an antiquarian bookshop. If customers wanted Jackie Susann or John Jakes, they could go down the street.

But Martin did not consider himself a snob. Anyone who wanted to sit on the sofa in the middle of the store and watch Sam Ervin grilling the Nixon gang was welcome, even the bums, and especially the bum who had come with the place.

His name was Mike Ryan. He lived in a rooming house on Munjoy Hill. And he was a waterfront fixture in his battered old conductor's hat and dirty raincoat. He had started showing up at Old Curiosity when the previous owner put out one of those Mr. Coffees for the customers. He read the paper, had his coffee, then headed off to McGafferty's at 11:30, to convert his Social Security check to "a liquid asset."

"Why don't you call the cops on that smelly old bastard?" asked Paul Doherty one day.

"I like him," said Martin.

Doherty sat on the edge of Bloom's desk and swung his leg. He acted like he owned the place because he worked for the landlord, who had hired the thick-necked Vietnam vet to collect his rents. Doherty was not averse to making a little extra money when he could, so he sometimes offered a reduced rent to someone willing to part with a stained-glass lampshade or a shelf of leatherbound books. He brought the lampshades to the antique dealers. The books he brought to Martin Bloom.

At first, Bloom was uninterested. Then Doherty showed up with a signed copy of Joshua Lawrence Chamberlain's memoirs. And month by month, Doherty had gotten better at the book scouting and the antique-talk, too. He said he was a man who preferred self-education to heavy lifting or leg-breaking, so he could soon tell Tiffany from Steuben, Stickley from Morris, a true incunable from a repro or a knockoff.

These two would not ordinarily have had anything to do with one another, but business was business. Doherty was thirty, Bloom ten years older. Doherty had voted twice for Nixon. Bloom had cast his first vote for Adlai Stevenson, and his second, and would have kept voting for him until he won or died.

That was why Bloom talked about his customers instead of politics when he wrote out the rent check. "Mike Ryan's harmless. Besides, he's been watching the hearings all morning. It seems to sober him up."

"So, you're a do-gooder, too? Runnin' a dry-out shelter."

Bloom raised one of those eyebrows. "It's more than that."

"What, then?"

Bloom looked out into the store. Aside from Ryan, the place was empty. "Go out and talk to him. See for yourself. He's an interesting guy."

How interesting, Martin Bloom could not imagine.

But Doherty had a way of saying things . . . a way of needling that forced a guy into revealing himself, even if he didn't want to. "Hiya, Mike," he said.

"Big doin's today," said Mike Ryan. "We got John Dean testifyin'."

"A rat," said Doherty, "rattin' out the best president in my lifetime."

Mike Ryan turned bloodshot eyes on Doherty. "You wasn't alive when FDR was president then?"

"No. I missed that pile of socialist crap."

"Crap? FDR? Why—" Mike Ryan staggered to his feet, as if fixing for a fight.

"Easy, there, big fella." Doherty stepped back. "FDR was president when they got rid of Prohibition, wasn't he?"

"You're goddamn right he was," said Ryan.

"At least he did something good. Bet you were happy about that."

"Fuckin'-A, I was happy." Mike Ryan dropped back onto the sofa, as if he lacked the concentration to stay angry, especially when the talk turned to drink.

Doherty looked at Martin and shrugged. *What was interesting about this guy?*

"Hey, Mike," said Martin. "What do you think of these hearings?"

Before he could answer, Doherty said, "They're unconstitutional."

This brought the response that Martin Bloom was expecting, a kind of drunk's high dudgeon, worth a laugh in the midday:

"Bull*shit*. It's all written right there. Right in the Constitution."

"Which article, Mike?" asked Doherty, taunting.

"Well . . . I . . . er . . . it says advise and consent. And that's what it means."

"So, you've read the Constitution?" asked Doherty.

"I've more than read it," said Mike Ryan. "My mother owned one."

"Oh, yeah?" said Doherty. "Her very own Constitution?"

"Damn right. Worth a fortune if we still had it."

Doherty laughed like what he was, a rent collector hearing another story. "I bet if your mother still had it, you'd be livin' in luxury, instead of in some flophouse."

"Nah," said Mike. "Once my wife died, I was bound for a flophouse and the bottom of a fuckin' bottle." He reached into his pocket and pulled out a pint, then his eye met Bloom's, he restoppered the bottle. "I forgot. No drinkin' in here."

"It's all right," said Martin. "But . . . you said you had a Constitution?" This was something he had not heard. "What did your mother do with it?"

"She give it away. But it was real valuable, with the writin' of the Founding Fathers on it and everything."

"The writing?" Now the rent collector was interested. He had sold enough material to know that *writing* made anything more valuable, if the right people had written it.

"Writin'," said Ryan. "*Handwritin'*. They all left their notes on it, before they changed it in the next version." Then he jumped to his feet. "I gotta go. I need a drink."

"THERE WAS ONLY one version of the Constitution," said Doherty after he had left.

"No," said Martin. "There were three drafts. The first two are very rare."

"Something like that . . . with handwriting . . . worth what?"

"A *substantial* lot of money."

Doherty leaned a little closer. "Who else do you think knows about this?"

Bloom raised an eyebrow. "The question is, who else is paying attention to him?"

"Who else beyond us?"

"Us?" said Bloom.

"We've been workin' together. Right? I've been bringin' stuff to you and you've been sellin' it, no questions asked. Right? And I've been educatin' myself. Right? And I asked that old bum the right questions. Right?"

Right. Right. Right. And *right.*

"So"—Doherty sat again on the edge on Martin's desk—"do you like girls?"

"Do I like girls? You think that because I'm single and dress well and don't leer at every female who comes into the store, I'm a—"

Doherty put up a hand. "If I'm gonna bring you leatherbound books to sell at inflated prices, and if we're gonna keep pumpin' that old drunk . . ."

Martin Bloom made a decision. It would be better to have Paul Doherty with him than against him. "I like girls."

And they joined forces.

After that, one or the other of them bought Mike Ryan lunch almost every day. They bought him beers at McGafferty's, too. They encouraged him to take a shower now and then. They introduced him to a Laundromat where someone would clean and fold his dirtiest trousers.

Mike Ryan responded to their friendship. That didn't mean he sobered up. He liked to drink, and after sixty years of it, he said he had no plans to stop. But he liked to talk, too, and they listened.

To get whatever information they could about this lost Constitution, they had to endure stories of funny passengers on the 5:25 to Boston, of his bar fights, of the Great Influenza Epidemic of 1918, of the Great Flood of 1927, of his McGillis cousins in Millbridge. And one day, he told them about the hoity-toity Perkins family. "They found out they was no better than anyone else when the Depression squashed 'em. The rich die, too."

The guys would listen, buy him another drink, then go home and write it all down.

From time to time, Mike Ryan would disappear, be gone for four days, five, a week . . . and Bloom and Doherty would begin to wonder if they had lost the thread that might lead them to the treasure. Then Mike would show up looking, as Martin said, "bearded, beaten, and bendered again."

He would explain that he had gone to Boston, to visit his mother, sister, and wife, "out to St. Joseph." That was the cemetery. That was his only family.

They would resume their routine, filling him with beer and pumping him for information. But Mike Ryan was wet-brained. He had spent most of his seventy-eight years killing gray cells, so the contours of the story changed from one telling to the next, but the details were too real to ignore.

Eventually, he told them of his arrest in Portland—"the first time I ever got picked up in this town"—and his defense by Gilbert Amory, the man suspected of killing Mike's sister, the son of the man who had given the Constitution to Mike's mother.

"And there's still Amorys livin' here," he said. "I been to visit them. I'm their uncle, I told them, but they didn't believe it."

By *they* Mike meant the children of Aaron Amory.

Tristam had stayed in Portland and followed his father's footsteps into medicine. He and his wife, childless, still lived on Bramhall Hill, and he still walked to rounds every morning at the Portland Hospital.

Daughter Dorothy had married into the Trask family of Bangor. She had one son, a Bangor lawyer named Carter.

Martin Bloom visited both of them, posing as a book scout. He interviewed them and came away with nothing, though he was not certain if they knew nothing or if they knew enough to give him nothing.

Martin and Paul Doherty also viewed all the other first drafts, starting with Samuel Gilman's, at the American Independence Museum in Exeter, New Hampshire. They visited the Massachusetts Historical Society to see Elbridge Gerry's tiny, careful annotations. They went to the National Archives to study George Washington's copy.

They couldn't find evidence of a lost Constitution. But soon, they were New England specialists in the so-called Critical Period between the end of the Revolution and the beginning of Washington's presidency, when the nation was no nation at all but a collection of competing states loosely bound under the Articles of Confederation.

IN THE EARLY seventies, most Americans thought they were living through a critical period of their own. On an August night in 1974, the crisis reached climax.

Paul Doherty and Martin Bloom sat in front of a television in the lounge of the Portland Holiday Inn, chatting up a pair of secretaries from Boston.

The girls were boarding the Nova Scotia ferry the next day, and Paul Doherty had designs on the blonde, but just for the night.

Martin had little interest in the other one, so Paul Doherty had to remind him in the men's room, "Partners help partners get laid. Just keep the ugly one busy while I see if I can get the blonde up to her room. I'll do the same for you sometime."

But the secretaries, like everyone else in the bar, were riveted to the television rather than to the men buying the drinks.

Tricky Dick was on the tube, and for once, said Bloom, he wasn't lying. "I shall resign the presidency, effective at noon tomorrow. . . ."

From one table, a great cheer arose, but from most of the lounge, there was silence. By then, only a few people called themselves Nixon supporters— G. Gordon Liddy, Rabbi Baruch Korff, Paul Doherty, and Pat Nixon . . . maybe. But most people felt that they had just witnessed the climax of a national tragedy.

"This is so terrible," said the blonde. "I'm embarrassed to be an American."

"I know what you mean," said Doherty, "seein' Nixon run out of office like that. A bum rap."

"Bum rap?" said the other girl. "He should have been impeached."

"Yeah," said the blonde.

Paul Doherty, realizing that he was talking his way out of a night in the sack, began to fumble, "Well . . ."

Bloom came to his rescue: "Ladies, we should be proud to be Americans tonight, because we've seen something amazing. If this had happened in any other country in the world, there'd be riots, armies in the streets . . . and we've just witnessed the handover of power without incident. The Constitution works."

The blonde said, "Yeah. I like that."

Doherty looked at Bloom and winked. *Nice work.*

But not nice enough.

The secretaries excused themselves to go to the ladies' and never came back.

So Doherty and Bloom, the Old Curiosities, as they were sometimes called behind their backs, showed up at McGafferty's at the end of the night. Doherty was in a foul mood and getting ready to be a mean drunk. Martin, however, was relieved that he didn't have to make more meaningless conversation with a woman he would never see again.

McGafferty's was no fern bar for secretaries. It was a place for neon Budweiser signs and clear-glass Miller longnecks, for cigarette smoke as thick as the Down East fog and burgers as thick as quahogs. And the ball game was usually on the tube.

But tonight, Nixon's face was looking down, resigning in replay.

Every drinker in the place was talking about Tricky Dick, including a loudmouth at the other end of the bar. *Their loudmouth.*

They had pledged Mike Ryan to secrecy. But what could they expect? He was a drunk. Drunks ran their mouths. And on a night like this, when everyone was talking about the presidency and the Constitution, Mike Ryan had plenty to run on about:

"Yeah . . . yeah . . . I could tell you boys a fuckin' thing or two about the Constitution. I seen it in its original form."

"What's the fuck does that mean?" asked a lobsterman working over a boilermaker and a plate of greasy onion rings.

"What it means is that I had an original in my house when I was a kid."

"And you're drinkin' in here?" asked someone else.

When Doherty started toward the end of the bar, Martin grabbed him and said, "If we go over there, it'll make him talk louder. We get him in private . . . and soon."

An hour later, an ossified Mike Ryan staggered out of McGafferty's and started along the dark waterfront.

Two guys stepped out of the shadows and grabbed him by the arms.

"Hey! What the fuck . . . oh. Hi, fellas."

"Where you headed, Mike?" asked Doherty.

"Up to Bull Feeney's. Get myself a Guinness."

"Don't you think you've had enough, old boy?" said Bloom.

"How about if we walk you home?" added Doherty.

"Wha . . . no . . . I need a drink."

"You know, Mike," said Doherty, "you can't tell everyone about our secret."

"Secret? Fuck you. I tell who I want what I want. And right now, I want a drink."

"Calm down, big boy," said Doherty.

They knew that Mike got more belligerent the more he drank.

"I'm calm," he said. "I'll show you how fuckin' calm I am." He pulled his right hand out of Bloom's grasp and swung at Doherty. He was big and slow, but the move was so surprising that he caught Doherty off the top of the head.

Then he twisted his hand so that he was holding Doherty by the forearm, rather than the other way around. And he hit Doherty again, this time square in the face.

Bloom grabbed Mike as he pulled back his right hand to deliver another blow, and Mike swung around with his left to smash Bloom.

That was when Doherty hit him a cruel, quick shot, delivered with simple instinct and brutal skill. As if he had been shot in the spine, Mike Ryan collapsed, striking his head on the granite curbstone when he landed.

He spasmed two or three times at their feet, then let out a long, wet rasp and was still.

"Holy Christ!" cried Martin Bloom.

A car went by on Commercial Street, its tires rumbling over the ancient cobblestones.

Martin waited until it passed; then he knelt, looked closer, listened for breath. "Holy Christ. He's dead. You killed him."

Doherty was holding his nose, holding back the blood. "Me? You had him by the arm. We both killed him."

"Well . . . should we call someone?"

"Shit no. We should go home."

"But—"

"But *nothing*." Doherty grabbed Martin by the arm and dragged him up the street. "You utter a word of this, it means the end for both of us. So right now . . . a vow of silence."

Bloom's eyebrows rose and fell, and he nodded.

"We never let on that we were here. After we left McGafferty's, we drove out to my place at Cape Elizabeth. You and me, talkin' business through the night. Let's go."

PUBLIC MEMORY OF an old drunk's death did not last. The Portland police investigated for a while. The Portland newspaper did a piece. But there were other crimes, involving people of higher standing. Mike Ryan was soon forgotten.

Some men confronted their guilt, repented of it, and hoped for forgiveness.

Paul Doherty and Martin Bloom, men of very different attitudes and personal style, confronted their guilt by burying it. They had murdered a man and left him on the sidewalk to be discovered by the morning street sweeper. The best way to get on with things was to never speak of the man, his story, or the circumstances of his death again.

They had been brought together by the dream of finding a national treasure. They had been bound together by the darkest secret two men could share.

Sometimes, Bloom admitted to Doherty that he did not sleep well at night.

Only then would Doherty speak of their crime. "We released an old drunk from his pain. What's done is done. So sleep. Or get laid. Or get drunk yourself once in a while. You'll get a chance to make amends some day."

For years, they concentrated on building their business. Bloom developed contacts among other booksellers. Doherty did the scouting across New England, which in the 1970s was a happy hunting ground for the antiquer, the rare book man, the document sleuth. They even found a first public printing of the Constitution from 1787 and bought it for $25,000. A deal.

Along the way, Paul Doherty married three times in thirteen years.

Once for each presidential election, he said. He made the mistake of marrying a Republican the year Carter was elected, so he heard three years of complaints and divorced. He married a Democrat the year Reagan was elected, so he heard three more years of complaints and divorced again. Then, just before the 1984 election, he married a Republican, thinking that this was the one. It lasted less than a year.

Through all of this, Martin Bloom remained a bachelor. He had his lady friends, and people whispered that he had a few boyfriends, too. But his answer, after each Paul Doherty divorce: better to remain single than to marry the wrong woman.

"I've given up women," Doherty announced after the third divorce was finalized in January of 1987. "Given up marrying them, anyway."

"So what will you do with your time now?" Bloom was studying the catalogue called *Antiquaria*, put out by Orson Lunt and his new young partner, Peter Fallon.

"Oh, don't know." Doherty sat in the edge of Bloom's desk and began to swing his leg. "It's the bicentennial year of the United States Constitution, you know."

Bloom kept his head down, his eyes on the catalogue.

Doherty kept talking. "Remember when I used to tell you that you'd get the chance to make amends someday? This is the year, when everyone's interested in the Constitution."

"You mean, you want to interest them in a first draft with annotations?"

"If the owner decides to surface because of all the publicity," said Doherty, "we should be there."

Martin Bloom looked down at an item in *Antiquaria: A handwritten letter from James Madison to Alexander Hamilton regarding Federalist Paper # 13.*

"How in the hell did they get that?" said Bloom. "The young guy, Fallon, he said any time he came across material that related to this area, he'd let me know."

"Don't change the subject," said Doherty. "You've been thinking about this for more than ten years. So have I. Let's see if we can find it. It'll be good for the country. Good for the bottom line."

Good indeed. They'd make a bundle if they commissioned the sale for someone else. They'd make a fortune if they could buy it for short money and sell it outright. The one question they wrestled with: how much to tell? Play it vague or come right out and say what it was?

They had two targets. They decided that one would not be sophisticated enough to know what he had, even if they told him. The other would be too smart to fool.

THEY TRACKED THEIR targets through Maureen Ryan, who had worked for the once-mighty Perkins family, and whose only living relatives had worked at a dying mill in the dying town of Millbridge, Massachusetts.

Martin Bloom went to see Buster McGillis on a brilliant February day, with the snow drifts deep and the temperature in the twenties and everybody wondering if winter would ever end.

But first, Martin could not resist a stop at the mill. He pulled in under a crescent of bare trees. No one else was there. The thunder of the looms, a sound that had rumbled down the valley and deafened workers for over a century, was stilled forever. The mill had closed.

That meant Buster McGillis was out of a job. That might make him an easy mark . . . if it turned out that he or his ancestors were the ones who had the lost Consititution.

Buster was waiting in front of his Greek Revival mansion, a past-its-prime ark that once must have seemed majestic. Four two-story Doric columns supported the temple front, though all of them looked to be rotting. Waterstains dripped down the side, where a drainpipe had come loose. A pair of cheapjack ranch houses flanked the ancient mansion like Warhols flanking a Winslow Homer.

Bloom had been hoping to get inside, but Buster was ready to go.

"You the book guy?" asked Buster.

"Martin Bloom. Nice to meet you." He offered his hand.

Buster had a powerful grip and a big belly beneath a St. Cosmas K. of C. Windbreaker. He lit a cigarette and said, "Let's go down to the diner. Down to my fiancée's place."

"Fiancée?"

Buster laughed. He seemed to laugh easily, and he laughed a lot, a nervous little chuckle that filled the spaces between his words and sentences. Some people said "Right?" a lot, or "Okay?" a lot. Verbal punctuation. Buster had his little laugh. "Yep. Fiancée. Pretty good for an old bastard like me, eh?"

Farrell's Family Diner overlooked the town green. It was busy, loud, and smelled of hot oil frying hand-cut potatoes. Behind the counter a big woman was taking orders, giving orders, and laughing at every lousy joke. When she saw Buster, she gave him a grin and waved him to a booth. "Tommy will be with you in a minute, hon."

"Thanks, hon," said Buster so that everyone heard. Then he turned to Martin. "Best place around to get a hamburger. They can have their Whoppers and Big Macs."

Once they were in a booth, with a view of the town green, the Millbridge Memorial Cannon, and the white steeple of the Congregational Church, a young man with a sullen expression shuffled over to take their order.

Buster introduced his fiancée's nephew, Tommy Farrell.

"Hiya." The kid barely glanced up.

"Once we get married," said Buster, "you'll be *my* nephew, too."

"Yeah." The kid flipped the little order pad. "So what would you and your friend in the bow tie like . . . *Uncle Buster?*"

Buster chuckled and they placed their orders: Cheeseburgers. Coffee. Pie à la mode. American food, cooked live by the American woman at the grill.

"It took me a long time to get up the courage to ask her," said Buster. "But after the mill closed, I had some time for a wife. Once we're married, I'll come to work here."

Martin Bloom said, "How would you like it if you never had to work another day in your life?"

Buster chuckled. "Hell . . . what would I do with myself?"

"Travel. Get away from Millbridge. Get away from the mill."

For the first time, Buster seemed to lose his good nature. "I'd give anything if that mill was still open and the looms were runnin'. My family kept it goin' till the seventies, then we went bankrupt. Along come some guy from New York, took big loans, kept us goin' another ten years, but now he's bankrupt. It's over."

"Well, then"—Martin looked around, lowered his voice—"what if I said that you might have something to bring the mill back to life?"

Buster lit another cigarette and turned up his hearing aid. "What would that be?"

"I knew your cousin, Mike Ryan."

"Only met him once or twice. Sad case."

"Yeah," said Martin. "Sad. He told me about a document that his mother had. He said she gave it away. She never said to whom."

"What is it?"

"It's a lost first draft of the United States Constitution."

Tommy came over and refilled their coffee cups.

Buster leaned back and whistled softly. "That's a big deal."

A big deal? Those words caught Tommy's attention. For the first time, he made eye contact with Martin Bloom.

Martin waited until Tommy had shuffled away, then said, "Damn right. Have you ever seen it? Four folded sheets, lots of different handwriting on it."

Buster shook his head. "I wish I had. But . . . no."

And Martin Bloom believed him.

AT THE SAME time, Paul Doherty was sitting down for lunch at the Pinehurst Country Club in North Carolina.

Outside, players were teeing off on two courses.

Marlon Secourt glanced at his watch, then said. "Welcome to the Vatican of golf."

"I caddied at Poland Springs, Maine, myself."

"A great track, but you can't play golf in Maine in February, not unless you're an Eskimo." Secourt sipped his beer. He was big, brawny through the shoulders, probably a college football player. "So, why did you come all the way down from Maine to see me?"

Doherty explained a bit about their research. Marlon Secourt drank a beer. Doherty explained a bit more. Marlon drank another beer. He sure could drink beer.

Finally Doherty came to the point. "What we're looking for is a first draft of the Constitution that Maureen Ryan might have had. We wondered if she passed it to your grandparents. They would have been the richest people she knew, the kind with enough money to pay her what it was worth."

"Not after 1929," said Secourt. "Lost it all. My grandmother, Florence Perkins, moved to Brookline and raised her two kids. The son died in the war. My mother married a contractor named Sam Secourt of Florida. My grandmother thought he was from the other side of the tracks. But he did well. And I've done even better." Secourt looked around as if he owned the golf course. "The Secourts will never be as rich as those mill-owning Perkinses with their mansion in Newport, but I've done well enough to have a place here, one there, a few others, too."

"Investing?"

"Venture capital. New ideas. Personal computers . . . some day, everybody will have one, home and office. Computers will help you to think, play games, read. Some day, the only people still selling books will be guys like you, guys who sell books as curiosities."

Paul Doherty was not committed to books. He was committed to making money, which he did by selling books. "Which is precisely why we're in this business, and looking for new things to sell, like old drafts of the Constitution."

"Well, if you ever come across one, come to me first." Secourt sipped his beer. "I believe in giving back. And we're blessed in this country, blessed with our freedoms, blessed with our rights, blessed to finally have a president like Reagan."

"The best president of our lifetime," said Doherty. "Stood up to the Russians. Made it safe to do business in this country again."

"Morning in America," cracked Secourt. "I'd like to change the damn Constitution so he could be elected to another term."

"He's getting pretty old. Let him finish this one, first."

Secourt ordered two more beers. "What if we found a draft that said a president could serve as many terms as he wanted? Maybe it would get people to thinking about repealing that amendment they put in after FDR. It could change the world."

"That's why we're lookin' for this draft. To change the world."

Secourt pulled a business card from his pocket and gave it to Doherty. "In case you find it."

Doherty looked at the card: addresses in Florida and Newport. Two phone numbers: One for Aquidneck Capital, the other for the Morning in America Foundation.

"Aquidneck Capital," said Secourt. "Named for the peninsula where Newport is. And Morning in America is my baby. Mission statement: To support and extend the beliefs of traditional Americans."

"Traditional?"

"Pro-prayer, anti-abortion, pro-gun rights, anti–big government, pro-business, anti-recycling, pro-right-to-work, pro-ambition, pro–free enterprise."

"The things that made the country great," said Paul Doherty.

"Damn straight. Newsletters and fund-raising. Mostly money, given to the right groups. Some day, I'll do nothing but play golf and keep America moving in the direction Reagan has set. I couldn't do anything better."

"A noble thought, Mr. Secourt." Though Paul Doherty was willing to say things if he thought he might gain favor by saying them, he meant what he said just then.

The bicentennial of the Constitution passed without the appearance of the first draft, but Marlon Secourt became a regular customer at Old Curiosity.

TWENTY-SIX

ᔥON THE WAY FROM HANOVER, Peter Fallon called the Old Curiosity twice.

The first time, he left a message: He had a few questions and would Martin please call back. Nice, polite, showed nothing. That was how he liked to work.

He clicked off, thought a bit, and decided that he'd had enough. They weren't blowing him off again. To hell with polite. He called back.

"Martin . . . Doherty . . . Guys, I'll be at your store in two hours. If you're not there, I'm coming to your houses to find you. Find you *both*. You owe me a few explanations."

He closed the phone and threw it on the passenger's seat.

AFTER HE'D GONE a few miles, he calmed down and his mind turned back to Evangeline. He was certain he wasn't going to find the Constitution between now and game time. And Kelly Cutter—too honest, too frightened, or too devious—had killed his fallback plan in Vermont. So it was time for him to do some threatening of his own.

He called Evangeline's cell.

"Do you have it?" Jack Batter didn't bother with hello.

"Not yet," said Peter.

"Then what do you want?"

"I'm trying to figure out how in the hell you tracked us to that rotten old ski slope." *Play dumb.* Make them think you haven't discovered the second GPS tracker.

Batter said, "Did you call to tell me something or just shoot the shit?"

"I called to tell you that I'll be outside Fenway Park, at the corner of Brookline Avenue and Yawkey Way, tomorrow night at seven. I'll have the map case."

"Why there?"

"Public place. Evangeline is *your* insurance. Public place is mine."

"You'd better have something in that map case."

"You'd better have Evangeline."

There was a long silence. Peter let it hang. So did Batter.

The sound of the road rumbled; then Batter said, "That all?"

"No." Peter paused. He would enjoy this. They had surprised him that morning. He hadn't thought on his feet. Afterwards, all he could think of were the things he should have said. Now he said them: "If Evangeline is not free—one way or the other—before that ball game, I'll go on Bishop's pre-game show and flat-out lie."

"Lie?"

"About the annotated draft. I'll tell the world that I've seen it. I'll tell them that the Framers wanted us to pay attention to the first clause of Amendment. You know the one: 'A well-regulated militia being necessary to the security of a free state. . . .'"

There was another long pause. Again, Peter let it hang, until—

Jack Batter spat back the second clause: "'. . . the right of the people to keep and bear arms shall *not* be infringed.'"

"Those two clauses have been fighting with each other since they were written," said Peter. "The truth is, I don't really care what happens on TV on Sunday night, or in a Washington committee room on Monday morning—"

"You better care." Batter's voice punched hard in Fallon's eardrum. "Every step that repeal takes is a step closer to ratification. If it gets out of committee, it makes it to the floor. Then maybe it makes it out of Congress. Then it goes to the states, and once the moonbats and do-gooders start calling their state reps, anything can happen."

"Since 1787, there have been thousands of proposed amendments," said Peter, "and only twenty seven have made it all the way to ratification."

"I want to kill this one in its crib. I don't want to gamble."

"Are you willing to gamble that the first draft supports what your side says?"

"If it doesn't, it won't see the light of day. And if you try to play games in front of a national television audience, *you* might not see the light of day."

There. Batter had said it, too. Just like Charles Bishop. Neither of them cared a bit about the truth, unless it was the truth they were looking for.

"Hand Evangeline over tomorrow night," said Peter, "or I tell the television audience: When the Framers said 'a well-regulated militia,' they meant *regulated*, like the National Guard, guys who handle guns regularly because they're regulated. Get it?"

"I get what Madison said in *The Federalist*. 'The Constitution protects the advantage of being armed which Americans possess over the people of almost every other nation.' Period. Full stop." Jack Batter clicked off.

Peter threw the phone on the car seat again. Playing hardball was not his style. But he had no choice.

He was certain that Batter wouldn't hurt her so long as there was a chance that Peter was prepared to lie. And if he could get Batter to divide his forces . . . get some of them to follow the GPS to wherever Walter Stanley ended up and maybe get in his way, Peter might gain an advantage when he faced Batter again.

But where in hell was he going to find that draft? He had followed his protocols, done what he had done so many times before, tracing the document to every location where it had been sighted. And it hadn't worked.

The last autumn color was flaring along Route 89, but he barely noticed. He was running the history of the Pikes and Amorys and Mike Ryan in his mind, because somewhere back there was the last pathway, from a man who dreamed of building a ski slope to an old alcoholic who told his story to a pair of devious Portland booksellers.

A SHORT TIME later, he pushed through Concord and got off on Route 9, which cut across New Hampshire to the Maine Turnpike. He hoped he didn't get behind any slowpokes. When this was over, he was going to get rid of that radar detector and drive at fifty-five miles per hour for the next decade. But for now, he was driving fast. He had to.

The phone rang. He glanced at the screen: Caller: *Unidentified*. Location: *Walpole, Ma*.

He pressed the TALK button. "Bingo?"

"Still a good American?"

"I'm trying."

"It's hard, bein' a good American," said Bingo. "Gettin' dangerous, too."

"How dangerous?"

"You ever hear of a guy named Shiny, out of New York? Big bastard, about six-four. Come up here this week for a special job, but he disappeared off the street in Portland day before yesterday."

"I think I know who you're talking about."

"They call him Shiny because he always wears a shiny black leather coat, a long one in winter, a bomber in fall, even has a black leather sport coat for the summer. Which one was he wearin' when he went after you?"

Peter wasn't surprised. "Sport coat. Who is he?

"It's not who is he. It's who is he workin' for," said Bingo.

"Who's that?"

"Here's the story: one of the boys in here, by the name Bobby Cobb—they all call him Corny—"

"Real comedians. "

"Yeah, well they don't call him that 'cause he likes corn on the cob, if you know what I mean—"

"Get to the point, Bingo."

"Bobby Cobb comes to *me* and asks me about this guy, name of Walter Stanley or Stanley Walters or somethin' like that. Bobby's friends with Shiny, who says that Stanley heard about him and called him in for a little backup muscle."

"Muscle. Is that what they call it?"

"Muscle. Strong-arm stuff. But before Shiny takes the job, he wants to know a little more about Walter Stanley. So Bobby Cobb asks me. I don't know anything, but I know a guy. Vietnamese guy. Doin' time for horsin' drugs. Slant-eyed little bastard, looks at you like a snake, a fuckin' mongoose or somethin'—"

"I swear you're getting old, Bingo," said Peter. "Get to the point."

"We like to talk in here. Talk's all we got. Except for the ones who like to cornhole, like Bobby Cobb—"

"Walter Stanley. What about him?"

"I said his name to the Vietnamese guy and . . . you ever see a Gook go white? Like puttin' cream in your coffee."

"Walter Stanley was in Vietnam?"

"No. Too young. The Gook said he'd been CIA, black ops, maybe, torturin' do-bads in other countries. Then he went into private security."

"In the U.S.?"

"Not at first. He started in the Wild West."

"Where's that?"

"Anyplace not the U.S. He protected businessmen when they go to some fucked-up place to spread the cause of capitalism in the global economy."

"So he's muscle, too, not brains."

"He's both. He started his own company. Called it Comtect. A cross between *computer* and *protect,* I think."

"How did the Vietnamese guy know all about this?"

"He worked with Stanley. Security jobs in Southeast Asia. That's where he learned how dangerous this guy was."

"How dangerous is that?"

"The Gook told me about this businessman they were guarding, got snatched by Muslims in Indonesia. The businessman's wife made the mistake of goin' to the Indonesian government instead of lettin' Comtect handle it. The government pushed Comtect out of the picture and went after the guy themselves. All they found was his corpse, headless and dickless."

"And then?" Peter wasn't sure he wanted to know.

"Stanley says, 'No one gives my company a bad name and gets away with it.' So he gets himself back into Indonesia. Starts trackin' down the kidnappers. Every time he catches one, he cuts off his head and his dick. He sends the dick to the wife, sends the head to the government. Kills ten of them, then gets out."

"Guess he never did business in Indonesia again."

"No, but word got out that he was not to be fucked with. He came back here, became a small but very valuable contractor. Pure mercenary. Known for finishing what he starts. Once you hire him, you do it his way."

"Do you know who's hired him this time?" asked Peter.

"No, but one part I didn't tell you. About that businessman?"

"Yeah?"

"He worked for an American TV network." Bingo paused.

"Yeah?" Peter was getting tired of Bingo Theater.

"Bishop Media."

"You're joking," said Peter.

"I joke more than I used to, but Stanley's no joke. If he's after you, be careful. You don't want to end up dickless, not with that pretty girlfriend."

"Don't want to end up headless, either."

"Not as important. When you got a girlfriend as pretty as her, your brain's just a third testicle anyways."

"Thanks, Bingo. I owe you."

"You get somethin' from me, you give me somethin' down the line. Be at my parole hearing in five years."

"Delayed gratification?"

"The only kind I got. But I look at it this way: If there's no Second Amendment, think of all the money I'll make runnin' guns when I get outta here."

IT WAS AROUND three o'clock when Peter arrived again in Portland.

The town was crowded with Saturday shoppers. He found a parking spot at the east end, near the statue of movie director John Ford, the Portlander who made John Wayne a star. Peter could have used a little of the Duke just about then, somebody to punch through all the complications and straighten everything out in one big burst of action.

Instead, he called the Old Curiosity.

Again, there was no answer. Strange. Saturday was the best business day of the week, especially in a strolling town like Portland.

Peter hurried through the afternoon shadows to the bookstore. The shades were drawn. The CLOSED sign was hanging in the door. Where were they? Paul Doherty was a baseball fan, so they had seen the Bishop Sports ads. They knew that something was going to happen on national TV before the first game of the World Series. Maybe they were out looking for the thing themselves.

Peter tried the door. Locked. So he went up the block, along Market Street, down an alley to the back door. It was the same door that Martin had dumped them out of a few days before. It was steel, with heavy internal locks. Good security for a bookstore that carried a lot more than the latest trade paperbacks.

He put his ear to the door. He thought he heard something. A moan?

He pounded on the door. No answer.

He put his ear to the door and heard it again. Yes. Another moan.

He tried the door. *Unlocked.* He opened it and stepped into the little stockroom.

He stood for a moment to let his eyes adjust, then peered through the half-open door that led to the store. The shades were drawn, so he couldn't see much. The sofa was to the right, the light was on in Martin's office on the left.

Peter waited a moment more, listening for that moan again.

Then he realized that the floor was wet, sticky wet. Something dark.

He felt his balls constrict in the involuntary fear response because he was standing in blood.

Then he heard the moan again . . . on the floor to his right.

Martin lay wedged between two cartons of books.

Peter flipped on the light, crouched, put his hand on his friend's forehead.

Martin's eyes fluttered. He was alive.

Peter turned him over and realized that his intestines were still on the floor.

"Oh, Jesus. Martin. Who—?"

Martin whispered something. "Sh . . . sh . . . Shiny."

"Shiny? Shit."

Martin's eyes moved, as if directing Peter. To what? To turn? Too late.

Peter heard a whizzing sound, right past his ears. Something cut into his neck and closed with crushing force onto his windpipe.

He grabbed at the elbows framing his head, tried to dig in his nails, but all he got was black leather, and his hands skittered off.

He gasped and gagged for air. He shook himself furiously, but . . .

Advantage: Shiny. He was bigger. He was standing while Peter was crouched. And he had the garrote.

Over in minutes. Peter shook himself again.

What a way to die . . . in the blood-soaked back room of a bookstore in Portland.

But . . . grab . . . claw . . . do anything.

He managed to twist . . . got a hand behind him . . . right hand . . . across his body . . . around his back . . . hit the guy's leg . . . quad muscle flexed like steel cable . . . but light fabric trousers . . . maybe . . . higher . . . yes . . . through the fabric . . . his nuts . . . yes. . . .

Grab . . . and . . . rip. . . .

Shiny cried out and tried to twist away without losing his leverage, but they didn't call it a death grip for nothing, and Peter was dying, so he was gripping.

He saw a black spot floating in front of his eyes . . . going under . . . squeeze harder. . . .

He squeezed with all the life left in him, which wasn't much.

Who could hold longer, harder, and force the other to let go?

Peter had no choice. Unconsciousness was coming. So he squeezed . . . squeezed . . .

"Let go, you motherfucker." Shiny was in charge. He was going to win, so, for a second, he took a hand from the garrote to grab Peter's wrist.

Just enough.

Peter pulled and twisted, while he kicked out of his crouch and caught one of Shiny's legs. Peter still had strong legs.

Shiny lost his grip on the garrote, lost his balance, slipped, and hit the floor.

Peter began to slither on all fours through the blood.

The door. The front door.

He had seconds to get out. He almost fainted as he tried to stand. But somehow, he lurched from the stockroom into the store. Sofa to his right . . . office door to his left . . .

"Come back here you fuck—"

It was the universal dream . . . of running but not moving. The last dream. The last nightmare.

The garrote was still around his neck, the wire still cutting the flesh. Hands grabbed the garrote.

Peter jerked back. He was going down . . .

. . . until someone burst out the office and slammed into Shiny: Paul Doherty, covered in his own blood, all but dead, launching himself in a last fit of resistance.

Then Doherty and Shiny were flying through the air, slamming into the sofa.

Peter pulled off the garrote—piano wire with two wooden handles—and stumbled toward the door.

Shiny threw off the dead weight of Paul Doherty and came at Peter again.

Peter's mind was clearer. Oxygen was coursing back. He turned and, with one wooden handle in his hand, he snapped the other and cracked Shiny's nose, then he whipped it back and cracked him again.

Shiny shook off the blows and drove a shoulder into Peter's belly and both of them flew into the display case, shattering the glass.

"Just for that, I'm gonna fuck you up before I kill you," came the cold voice from the black leather.

Peter tried to twist away. He felt his head pulled back.

He swept his hand across the top shelf of the display case—the copy of *Uncle Tom's Cabin*, the picture of the *Portland*, the—

"Fuck you up and cut you up."

Bang!

Shiny slammed Peter's head against the edge of the shelving.

Peter was still reaching. Now he found it. Preble's dirk.

"Fuck you up and cut you up and kill you like these other two."

Bang!

"Your friends should've killed me on the street."

Bang!

"But once we're done, no one will ever know—"

Peter drove the dirk up, through the leather jacket, right into the heart—

"—that the draft at—" Shiny's last words caught in his throat. His eyes opened wide. He grabbed at Peter's hand. Then he fell over.

Peter sat on the floor, on the shattered glass. He did not notice it cutting into his backside and the heels of his hands. He was watching Shiny, expecting him to rise.

All Shiny could manage was a groan, a half turn; then blood gurgled in his throat and he died.

It was some time before Peter could stand and stagger over to the body on the sofa.

Paul Doherty must have fought hard, and he must have been the second victim, because Shiny's knife had been driven down at a furious angle, down behind his collarbone and into an artery, driven down so that it could not be withdrawn. That was why Shiny had come at Peter with the garrote.

But why any of this? Why?

Peter almost fainted again, but he held on to the back of the sofa, then straightened and stumbled into the stockroom.

Martin was still alive. Breathing, just barely. And not for long.

"Who was he?" asked Peter

Martin rasped the word, "Shiny."

"No . . . I mean, why did he do this?"

"Phone."

"I'll call 911."

"No. *Phone.* Ph—" Martin stopped in midsentence. The words caught there. Peter touched his carotid. No pulse.

"Martin! Martin!" Peter leaned forward and tried CPR.

He had never done it before, and he was shocked to feel how scratchy a man's clean-shaven face was.

He ignored the sensation and drove two shots of breath into his friend. Then he ran through the steps as he'd learned them: Find the xiphoid process, the little tail of a bone in the middle of the chest, give thirty compressions.

But Martin did not breathe. And every time Peter compressed the chest, more blood oozed from Martin's abdomen. Before long, Peter gave up. It was hopeless.

He went into the office, grabbed the phone, called 911. He told them there had been a knifing at the Old Curiosity. They needed an ambulance and a cruiser.

He figured he had three minutes to get out, maybe four.

Then he saw the message light flashing on the voice mail.

Was that what Martin meant by "phone"?

He pressed the button. The computerized voice said: "You have three new messages and no old messages."

First message: "Mr. Bloom"—it was the voice of Jennifer Segal—"I'm sorry, but I told Peter Fallon I was working for you. This is all so complicated. I wish you never asked me to help. This Walter Stanley, he's not what I thought." *Beep.*

Second Message: "It's Stanley. Shiny will be there in ten. He has questions. There are still loose ends. We tie them up, our client's document is in the clear." *Beep.*

Our client? Document? In the clear?

Third Message: "It's Peter. I hope you guys are there, I have a few . . ."

Peter pressed the ERASE button.

To delete all messages press twice.

He pressed twice.

He could hear the sirens a block or two away. There was still plenty of evidence of him around the store, but it would take a while for them to find him.

There was a long raincoat hanging in the office. Probably Doherty's. Peter grabbed it and threw it on to cover the blood.

The siren was closer, but . . . one more thing:

He went back to Shiny's body, lifted the flap of the black leather coat and took the cell phone out. Then he left the way he'd come in.

PETER SLIPPED INTO his car, wrapped his hand behind the wheel, put his head on his hands, and began to shake.

He had been doing this work for a long time and had been in a lot of scrapes. But he had never killed a man before. And he had never left the scene of a murder covered in the blood of a friend. This was different. This was the worst.

He opened the car door and lowered his head and let go with a dry heave.

A passerby said, "Hey, buddy, you okay?"

Peter straightened and closed the door. He couldn't let anyone see the bloodstains.

Until he found that Constitution and got Evangeline free, he had to stay alive and out of the hands of the police or anybody else who might detain him.

He put the car in gear and started to drive.

Where was he going?

Out to the turnpike. Out of Portland. Out of Maine.

Then a cell phone rang. It wasn't his ring tone. It was the other phone, Shiny's. He pulled it out. *Caller Unidentified.*

What he remembered of Shiny's voice: a deep growl.

Go ahead and answer. Talk in monosyllables. Lower your voice. Turn on the radio. *Background noise.* Roll down the window. *More noise.*

"Yeah?" He tried to grunt.

"You finished?" The voice was calm, the question routine. *You finished with that soup? You finished with the sports section? You finished with those murders?*

"Yeah."

"Both?"

"Yeah."

"Messy? I told you I wanted it messy. Make it look different from the others."

"Messy as hell."

"That's what they get for dabbling in forgery. Now almost nobody knows it's a forgery. Job's almost done."

Peter just drove, waiting for the voice on the other line to say something.

"You still there?"

Peter croaked, "What's next?"

"For you, nothing. Go back to New York. Watch the World Series tomorrow night. The Yanks won't be in it, but it'll be a hell of a game."

"Why?"

"Just watch." *Click.*

First Buster McGillis, then Professor Stuart Conrad and Morris Bindle, then Jennifer Segal turned into a pillar of fright, and now the Old Curiosities . . .

As Peter drove, he pictured each of them and tried to see how they had all come together, glanced off one another, and run into Walter Stanley.

WHAT A NIGHT TO BE AN AMERICAN. What an ugly night.

In Will Pike's ancient house, Buster McGillis sat with his wife, Esther, and their nephew and watched the president of the United States answer questions that a pimp wouldn't ask a whore.

Buster just shook his head. "What will people tell their kids?"

"A damn shame," said Esther. "A man's private affair is his own."

"Not anymore," said Tommy Farrell. "Besides, Clinton's a hound. Like me."

"Shame on you, Tommy Farrell." Esther laughed. "But we're glad you come to visit, just the same."

"Nobody cooks better meat loaf than Aunt Esther." Tommy patted his stomach.

"Thirty years of cookin' meat loaf every Tuesday and Thursday," she said.

Bill Clinton was saying, "These encounters did not constitute sexual relations as I understood that term to be defined at my January 17, 1998, deposition, but they did involve inappropriate intimate contact."

Buster pulled out a Lucky Strike and put it on his lip. "I can't see how the Constitution lets them do stuff like this to the president."

"High crimes and misdemeanors," said Tommy Farrell.

"Misdemeanors," Buster said. "You ought to know."

Esther slapped old Buster on the shoulder.

"What? Tommy's committed a few," said Buster. "He'll tell you that himself."

"At least he comes to visit us. Not like your relatives. The great Charlie Bishop, and those folks up in Maine."

"The branches on the family tree ain't too close." Buster scratched a match. "But you're right about Tommy here. He's a good boy. If I had any money, I'd help him out."

"Just put me in your will"—Tommy gave Buster a grin—"if you ever find the lost Constitution."

"What that bookseller come askin' about years ago?" Buster held the match a moment too long, then shook it out as it burned his finger. "The guy I brought to the diner?"

"I miss the diner," said Esther.

"He was just lookin' for a quick buck," said Buster. "Not a hard worker like us."

"I don't mind a quick buck," said Tommy.

"No such thing," said Buster. "Work hard. Like my old mother used to say, 'This is America. In America, we get up in the morning, and go to work, and solve our problems.'"

"So, no Constitution?"

"Only thing I have is some scrapbooks from the early days."

"You ought to give them to the historical society," said Esther.

"Yeah," said Buster. "I'll ask Morris Bindle. He'll know what to do."

"Just don't give away anything worth a lot of money," said Tommy.

AT HIS HOME in Newport, Marlon Secourt sat with one of his biggest contributors, Clinton D. Jarvis. He popped a beer and said, "All the energy and money I've devoted to the American cause and this is what we're reduced to."

The president was actually saying, "It depends on what the definition of 'is' is."

Jarvis shot tracers at the screen with his eyes. "That man *has* to be impeached."

"But the Senate will never convict," said Secourt. "Too many Democrats."

"Too many godless men who consider their political interests before their consciences."

Secourt said, "Godless? You sound like Pat Robertson."

Jarvis turned his eyes to Secourt. "God's been good to me. And he's been good to the American people. There's nothing we can do to save them from Clinton. But we have to do something to remind them of what a grand heritage they have."

And Secourt said, "Did you ever hear the legend of the lost Constitution?"

"WHAT A TRAVESTY." Paul Doherty sat in McGafferty's and watched the testimony.

"Who hasn't lied about sex?" said Martin Bloom.

"How would you know? You haven't had sex since Carter was president."

"I know one thing: Clinton's the victim of a witch hunt."

"Clinton lied to a grand jury and suborned perjury." Doherty chomped his hamburger and talked while he chewed. "That's not lying about sex."

Martin shrugged and forked a piece of broiled haddock.

"*That's* why you don't have more sex," said Doherty. "All that fish. Eat more hamburger."

The president was saying, "I think it is clear what 'inappropriately intimate' is. I have said what it did not include. It did not include sexual intercourse, and I do not believe it included conduct which falls within the definition I was given. . . ."

"What a fraud." Doherty dumped ketchup on his french fries.

"The whole thing is a fraud," said Martin. "Let's just hope there's not something going on out there in the big world that he should be paying attention to instead of this."

"DID I WANT this relationship to come out? No. Was I embarrassed about it? Yes . . . Did I ask her to lie about it? No. Did I believe there could be a truthful affidavit? Absolutely. . . ."

On the twenty-eighth floor of the Bishop Media Building, on Sixth Avenue in Manhattan, Charles Bishop watched television: a single camera, poor audio, a sweating president sipping Diet Pepsi from a can between some of the worst answers ever given to some of the worst questions ever asked.

Bishop had ordered up dinner from Il Corso, his favorite Midtown Italian restaurant, and he had gathered with his new Boston girlfriend, Sara Wyeth, and his head of corporate security, Don Cottle.

"Bill is his own worst enemy," said Bishop. "But women love him."

"Not me," said Sarah. "Goober charm. Fool's gold. I like a real man, Charlie."

Don Cottle glanced at her, rolled his eyes, then shifted his gaze back to the flickering glow of seven televisions on the wall, three tuned to the major networks, four tuned to the cable news stations: CNN, Fox, MSNBC, and ANN.

Once it was over, most American televisions clicked back to the sitcoms, the ball games, the VCRs. But the political junkies, the punishment gluttons, and the gleeful Clinton haters stayed with cable for the talking-head analysts.

Rapid Fire was Charles Bishop's brainchild.

The host was a *New York Times* columnist named Harry Hawkins, who needed only to stroke his trademark goatee to send right-wing spear carriers into convulsions about liberal bias in the media. That was why Bishop had picked him.

Hawkins introduced his guests: Constitutional scholar Stuart Conrad of Dartmouth and right-wing radio phenom Kelly Cutter.

"This is what I wanted to see." Bishop picked up the remote, powered up the volume, and rocked back in his chair. "This professor is a scholar, all class."

"Class against Kelly?" said Sara Wyeth. "Class loses."

And they went at it, with Professor Conrad on the New York set and Kelly in a remote studio with a photo of a Vermont village as a backdrop. The professor played the gentleman scholar confronting the queen of conservative sarcasm, a role that Kelly had perfected during a six-year rise to nationwide syndication. But both of them followed the instructions of the show's producer: "On cable, it's about conflict. So argue." Since the producer was Bishop's daughter, the guests complied. If you wanted to be invited back, keep the producer and her father happy.

Harry Hawkins began it: "Professor, can you give a historical perspective?"

"The Framers anticipated disputes like this, and they gave us a process by which to settle them. The Framers were very wise."

"Wise enough to know that we don't need this hound in the White House." Kelly Cutter jumped in.

"I'm not sure I'd characterize the President of the United States in those terms."

"What other terms are there? He's a hound. But of course, the liberal elite will try to get him off the hook by distracting us with talk about the glory of the system."

"I'm hardly elite," said Professor Conrad. "I drive an old Volvo and live in a small house in a cold corner of New England."

"You're a professor at an Ivy League *we're-smarter-than-you-are* college."

"Which must mean I'm right," he responded, "when I say that the system will work, whether Clinton is impeached or not."

"Even when Democrats are a bunch of sheep?" said Kelly.

Hawkins stroked his goatee. "I believe I asked for a little historical perspective, which can always bring some sanity to a debate like this."

"Sanity?" Kelly laughed. "Sanity is seeing a duck and hearing it quack and calling it a duck. So let's be sane about what we've seen: a president who can't tell the truth."

Don Cottle turned to his boss. "You have to admit it. She's good."

"Too good," said Sara.

Bishop brought a finger to his lips: *Listen.*

Stuart Conrad smiled. Professorial? Condescending? "Here's some historical perspective: Under the first draft of the Constitution, Bill Clinton might not have been impeached. 'Treason, Bribery, and other high crimes' was the phrase. They didn't add 'misdemeanors' until the second draft."

"Lying to a grand jury is no misdemeanor," said Kelly.

"Excuse me," said the professor, "but I believe I have the floor."

"You can have the floor, not the high ground." Kelly was a pro. "A president leaving semen stains on blue dresses and encouraging young women to soil good cigars is an affront to the office, to the Constitution, and to cigar smokers everywhere."

Don Cottle laughed out loud.

Charlie Bishop gave him a look. "She's killing him. Who put her on the air?"

"Your own daughter," said Sara.

"I need to talk to her in the morning. But I want to meet that professor tonight."

On the screen, the professor was saying, "Whatever happens to this presidency, that living document guarantees that presidency and nation will both survive."

"PROFESSOR"—BISHOP OFFERED his hand—"you debate as well as you write."

"I meant every word," said Stuart Conrad. "I just hope that Kelly Cutter doesn't."

"I'm afraid she does. It shows you how divided this country has become."

Charles Bishop had chosen to meet the professor alone. The office was dark. The wall of televisions—all with the sound turned down—cast a glow on one side, the wall of glass caught the glow radiating up from Sixth Avenue on the other.

Bishop poured two tumblers of Bushmills Malt 16. "Ice?"

"The nectar of the Gods needs no ice."

"Well spoken." Bishop handed a tumbler to Professor Conrad.

They sat in the corner. Bishop called it his "peaceful power grouping"— relaxed, yes, but the boss took the stressless swivel chair. Guests got the sofas.

"You know what I dream?" said Bishop. "That I can do something to bring this country back together. Do it through television. Sew up the rent in the fabric. But it's difficult to sew if someone's behind you pulling out all the stitches."

The professor swirled the whiskey in his glass. "You mean the Republicans?"

"They want to destroy Clinton. But he'll survive. I worry about the parents who have to explain to their little ones what oral sex is over dinner, because these goddamn Republicans are like dogs worrying a bone. . . . Contentious times."

"The Framers lived in contentious times, too. But they could never have imagined the media weapons we have today," said the professor. "They could never have conferred for three months in total secrecy, either."

"You mentioned a first draft tonight." Charles Bishop took a measured sip of whiskey. "Have you ever heard of one annotated by the New England delegation?"

The professor's glass stopped in midair. "Tell me more."

"As the story goes, they all jotted down their thoughts on a bill of rights."

"My God," Professor Stuart Conrad whispered, "what a find."

"What a find for a divided nation," said Bishop. "Something to remind us that our contentious times have precedent. Every idea we have has been in dispute at one point or another . . . every article of the Constitution . . . even the Bill of Rights."

"Where is this draft?"

"It's a Pike family legend. If you're interested I have a bit of research."

"Well . . . certainly." The professor seemed overwhelmed at such a gift.

"And tell me, what's the title of the book you're writing?"

"*The Magnificent Dreamers.* Something for the general reader, I hope."

"We could use a few magnificent dreamers now. If you keep me posted on your research into a New England draft, I'll give your book the attention it deserves on ANN."

THE NEXT MORNING, Kate Morgan arrived at her father's office, as ordered, at nine o'clock. Sunlight filled the room and turned Manhattan to gold.

She wore a crisp white shirt and tailored black slacks. And she had presence. That was what her father had always told her. Presence and talent. Otherwise, he said, he would never have given her a job.

"Morning, boss," she said. "You wanted to see me?"

"Good show last night."

"Thanks." Kate was a daughter. She liked the approval of her father.

"But answer me this: What did I tell you when you took the job?"

"You told me a lot of things."

"I mean, about which side we're on."

"I thought we were on the side of the truth."

"Sometimes, we need to frame the truth."

Kate sat on the edge of her father's desk. "What are you saying?"

"Kelly Cutter blew that professor out of the water last night."

"You chose the professor. I chose Kelly. I did a better job."

"Is she a friend of yours?" Bishop looked over his reading glasses. "A special friend?"

"I met her in Vermont. I gave her a ride in my plane."

Charles Bishop shook his head. "A daughter who flies planes and shoots guns and spends time with right-wing wacko women."

"I hardly know her, but I'd like to know her better."

"Remember, you produce one of the most influential shows on cable. But it's not an interview show. It's designed to get our political point across."

Two days later, Kate Morgan resigned. "Dear Dad: I wasn't cut out for this. I don't need it. I'm moving to Vermont to shoot my guns and fly my planes and hang out with whoever I want, even if it is a right-wing wacko woman."

THE CLINTON IMPEACHMENT scandal started Paul Doherty and Martin Bloom talking again about the lost Constitution. But they weren't looking for it. Finding something that hadn't been seen in ninety years— if then—would be like hitting the lottery. Only fools played the lottery, especially when business was good. And business was great.

The dot-com boom was making everyone richer. People were looking for ever more exotic investments. And in times of Constitutional crisis, the Founding Fathers paper that they collected only grew more valuable.

The Old Curiosities should have been satisfied with that.

But they had taken a step down a very dark path fourteen years before. Soon they would take another.

ON AN OCTOBER afternoon, Marlon Secourt appeared unannounced at the Old Curiosity. He wore an Arnold Palmer cardigan that billowed on him like a tent because beer had beaten golf in the battle for his belly. His pretty blond wife was with him. She was about half his size, with barely a wrinkle in her pantsuit or on her face.

He had also brought another couple who appeared better matched. The man was smaller than Marlon, fitter, a coiled spring with a crew cut. And the wife had the calm confidence of a first wife who expected to be the only wife: Clinton and Betty Jarvis.

"We're headed for Bar Harbor," said Marlon, "to play Kebo Valley, eighth oldest golf course in America."

Jarvis said, "Marlon's told us you're the best in the business."

That endeared him immediately to Martin, who said, "Is there a period you're particularly interested in, Mr. Jarvis?"

"Please, call me Clint."

"But never Clinton," said Marlon Secourt.

This brought a big laugh from Paul Doherty, something less from Martin Bloom, and a smile from Clint Jarvis. The wives looked at each other and rolled their eyes.

Jarvis said, "I'm interested in documents about the birth of the nation."

"That's how we met," said Marlon. "Over golf and documents at a New England Rarities Convention. Then he started contributing to the Morning in America Foundation. Then along came Bill Clinton. Now we're brothers in arms."

"Our hope is to see a morning in America again soon," said Jarvis.

"A collection like ours proves that there's always another bright morning," said Martin, "no matter which side of the political fence we're on. To mix the metaphor even more, the political pendulum swings, but the center holds."

Jarvis nodded. "It's our greatest strength, that center."

"So," said Doherty, "is there something specific you'd like to see?"

"I'm interested in reading the Founding Fathers' thoughts on their religious faith." Jarvis wandered over to a display case. "But you have a draft of the Constitution?"

"I think you mean the first public printing," said Doherty. "We bought it years ago. We're letting it appreciate in value."

"Is it here?" asked Marlon.

"No. It's in our safety deposit box."

"Mr. Jarvis is interested in all the drafts," said Secourt. "We even stopped in Boston on the way up to see the Gerry draft."

The wives looked at each other again, rolled their eyes again. Fellow travelers, fellow bored-silly sufferers.

"Gentlemen, I won't beat around the bush," said Jarvis. "Marlon brought me here so that I can tell you this: Should you come up with a document like the Gerry draft, with annotations, I'll pay you a million dollars, cash on the barrelhead."

"A million dollars?" Paul Doherty looked at Martin.

"Moreover," he went on, "if you find a draft with annotations that show the thinking of one of the Framers about the relationship of this government to its Christian roots, I'll pay you two million."

When they were gone, Paul Doherty said, "So . . . who was that guy?"

"Someone who doesn't get the part about the separation of church and state."

"Someone with a lot of money, too."

"Maybe we should start looking again."

PROFESSOR CONRAD DID not start looking until the semester was over, which may have indicated how seriously a real scholar took this story. Then he made his annual pre-Christmas pilgrimage to the Old Curiosity to buy rare books, and he brought one of his prized seniors along. Her name was Jennifer Segal.

It was a nasty Portland afternoon with the east wind giving new meaning to the word *raw*. But it was warm in the Old Curiosity. During the holidays, Martin and Paul put up a tree, and in the afternoons they served sherry as well as coffee.

They greeted Conrad and his protégée like major spenders, even though Conrad seldom bought volumes worth more than a hundred dollars and, when he saw a catalogue item he liked but couldn't afford, he came begging for a look before it was sold.

At least his teaching assistants were pretty, said Paul Doherty. This one had long legs, dark hair, and gold-rimmed glasses that seemed like a mask of maturity hiding her innocence.

"I wanted her to see a true time tunnel," said the professor. "A rare-book store."

Martin asked, "What is Miss Segal interested in?"

The professor nodded, as if to give her the freedom to speak.

She said, "I'm doing an independent study for the professor on a legend he's heard about."

"Oh," said Martin. "What legend would that be?"

"That a first draft of the Constitution, annotated by the New England Framers, was spirited out of Philadelphia in 1787."

Martin sat, perhaps because his legs had gone weak.

"We hear—" Paul Doherty cleared his throat, perhaps because it was constricting suddenly. "—we hear legends about a lot of things."

"Indeed," said the professor, oblivious to their reaction. "So if you'd point her in the right direction . . . it could make for an interesting senior thesis."

Martin and Paul looked at each other. *Senior thesis? Is he serious?*

Doherty recovered first and poured glasses of sherry all around. "Where did you hear this wild story?"

The professor took a glass, took a sip, nodded his approval as though he thought they really cared about his opinion of the sherry. "You know Charles Bishop? He owns American News Network. I'm something of a regular now. Have you seen me?"

"You're a star," said Doherty, who usually rooted for Kelly Cutter.

Bloom downed his sherry in a single swallow. "Charles Bishop, you say?"

"It's an old family legend," said the professor. "Bishop descends from Will Pike."

"Of the Pike-Perkins Mill?" Martin refilled his glass.

Whether he knew it or not, Professor Stuart Conrad had just given the Old Curiosities more information than they would ever give him or his student.

THE MILLION DOLLARS that Clinton Jarvis was offering suddenly began to smell stronger, and Martin Bloom decided to follow the scent back to Millbridge.

He called Buster McGillis, who said to come visit, but warned that his wife had died of a stroke at Thanksgiving, so he was feeling pretty gloomy. "I could use the company." And there was that chuckle again, a little softer, a little sadder.

There was snow in the wind on the day that Martin arrived.

This time, he got inside the big house. Buster brought him into the kitchen, the warmest spot in the high-ceilinged gloom. The vinyl tablecloth was stained with coffee splotches, and grains of sugar were scattered from the bowl to Buster's mug. The ashtray was half full and another cigarette sat on the edge, curling smoke into the air.

It looked like a table where a lot of talk had passed over the years, a lot of coffee drunk . . . some beer, too.

On television, Bill Clinton was speaking . . . about something.

"It'll be a terrible thing." Buster filled two coffee mugs. "A terrible thing to convict him. He's for the workin' man. Too bad we got no place to work."

"Too bad the mill's closed," said Martin Bloom.

"Don't even have our own diner in town. We have to go all the way to Route 495 to get one of them Whoppers with Cheese."

"I'm sorry about your wife," said Martin.

Buster took a puff of the cigarette, put it back on the edge of the ash-tray, rubbed his big hands together and crunched the knuckles. "Yeah."

Then the back door opened. "Buster! Hello, Buster!"

A big man with a potbelly let himself in. He wore a New England Pa-triots Windbreaker and a knit cap.

"My only friend, Morris Bindle." Then he said to Bindle, "Here's that bookseller guy. Comes around every ten years or so, lookin' for the same thing."

"What's that?" Bindle gave Martin a suspicious look.

Martin cringed when Buster said it out loud to another total stranger: "A lost first draft of the Constitution. You ever see anything like that layin' around at the historical society?"

"Historical society?" said Martin. "You're in the historical society?"

"I practically *am* the historical society." Morris Bindle poured a mug of coffee. "Tired mill town, you don't get too many people who want to look back. But we try to keep the place open two days a week. The town gave us a nice space in the mill about twelve years ago. We moved all our stuff in there."

"What kind of stuff do you have?" asked Martin.

"Old muskets from the Revolution. The chair from the first town hall, a diorama that someone did of the original Cousins mill. The schoolkids like that."

"Books and papers?" asked Martin. "I'm an expert. I could appraise them."

It was an approach that Martin used often to get in the door. A free appraisal might lead to a nice sale for a society, a nice commission for him. He was a Democrat, but he believed in the mantra of Reaganomics: A rising tide lifts all boats.

"We have printed material. Old diaries, town reports, ledgers, photographs . . ."

A JUMBLE. THAT was Martin's first thought when he stepped into Bindle's little society. But one thing stood out: a large black-and-white photograph: *The Men and Women of the Mill, 1861.*

Bindle said that it had come from the great-granddaughter of one of the men in the picture, a Lebanese immigrant. "He found work in Mill-bridge. His son started a bank, and *his* son watched it fail in the Depres-sion. She gave us the picture. So then I found the picture of her father, standing in front of it in his bank."

Martin Bloom studied the picture, especially the owners of the mill, who were all identified, and he stared at the small and wizened figure of Will Pike. An interesting curiosity, no intrinsic value. Right where it ought to be.

Martin gave a cursory glance to the other things in the museum: mostly junk. He suspected that Bindle knew already, because Bindle had also revealed that he was an antique dealer with a storefront in town.

"Where are the papers?" asked Martin.

Bindle took him up to the second floor. Two big rooms, long tables, bookcases filled with the ledgers of the Pike-Perkins mill, file cabinets stuffed with pay receipts and correspondence and ancient carbon copies, and cardboard boxes everywhere.

"Do you have a card catalogue?" asked Martin.

Bindle laughed. "It's a volunteer society. Nobody volunteers for cataloguing."

Without a catalogue, Martin wouldn't know where to begin. But he knew what he wanted. "Do you have material from the Pikes? Letters to or from famous people? We know Will Pike had a lot of contact with the Framers in Philadelphia. . . ."

Bindle just shook his head. "Nothing like that. But there are some scrapbooks."

"Scrapbooks?"

"From Bartlett Pike. He was the great-grandfather of Buster, grandson of Will. Buster cleaned out his attic after his wife died."

"I'd love to go through the scrapbooks," said Martin.

There was the treasure trove. Martin Bloom sat down and dug in. Two days later, he was still digging, and some of it was pretty tantalizing stuff, like the letter from George Amory to Bartlett Pike, which included this: "I leave you to hunt for a limping Maine timber man and the lost Constitution of our grandfather's fantasies."

Martin Bloom decided not to show that letter to Morris Bindle. Instead, he slipped it into his pocket.

The lost Constitution might still be lost, but that letter proved that in 1874, people knew about it.

What Martin did not know was that Morris Bindle had already gone through scrapbooks, letters, and other memorabilia and taken out almost all the good stuff. And he was smart enough to know what was good. And smart enough to use the Internet to research the values of things like a Henry Knox letter to Rufus King. He didn't need some self-serving bookseller from Portland, Maine, stealing the treasures.

He had put the good letters into a safety deposit box and told no one, not the eight retirees who composed the board of the little society, not Buster

McGillis, not Peter Fallon, the Boston bookseller that Bindle had already chosen to broker the sale of the Henry Knox letter when the time was right.

But Morris wasn't doing it for himself. Morris looked out for his friends, and Buster was his friend.

IN HER PAPER, Jennifer Segal concluded that the New England draft did not exist. This conclusion got her an A from Professor Conrad and a job from the Old Curiosities.

Martin and Paul paid her that summer to research and write the short catalogue descriptions of each item they acquired. Of course, they told her nothing of the lost Constitution. But they liked her. Martin felt paternal in her presence, and Paul Doherty wanted to go to bed with her.

But the Old Curiosites wouldn't be mentors or lovers, because Jennifer headed for Europe that fall. When she returned two years later with a master's in European history, she thought that perhaps Professor Conrad could play both roles.

By then, Conrad had published *The Magnificent Dreamers* and had become the talkingest talking head on cable.

ONE NIGHT IN June of 2005, he appeared on *Rapid Fire* to discuss the latest effort to change the Constitution. He was in Boston for a conference, so he joined the debate from a satellite studio: a camera, a small crew, a live background of the Charles River and the flickering lights of the city.

The issue: Joint House Resolution 10, a proposed amendment to the United States Constitution: *The Congress shall have the power to prohibit the physical desecration of the flag of the United States.*

The professor's opponent: Marlon Secourt of the Morning in America Foundation, which had funded lobbyists supporting the amendment. Secourt argued that all fifty states had proposed amendments, many had passed them, and when the latest Congress voted, they, too, would vote for a flag desecration amendment.

The professor delivered his response in sound bites that showed how much he had learned about television: The Supreme Court had struck down flag desecration laws in 1989 and 1990 as violations of the First Amendment, and among the justices was Antonin Scalia, favorite of the right wing.

"But flag burning is the destruction of our national symbol," Secourt said.

"It's the Constitution that counts, not the symbol."

"Desecration is desecration."

"But who decides what is desecration?" said the professor. "The Ku Klux Klan parading behind the flag is a desecration to me. Should their right be taken away?"

It went on like that for bit longer; then Harry Hawkins told them it was time for new guests, new issues. They didn't call it *Rapid Fire* for nothing.

As the professor was leaving, Congresswoman Harriet Holden was coming onto the set for a segment on the so-called Defense of Marriage Act. She looked perfect, a cool brunette in heels and power suit, so well prepared that she could chat with the professor all the way into camera range.

"I've enjoyed your books, Professor. Loved *The Magnificent Dreamers.*"

"I wrote it as a popular history of the Constitutional Convention. It's been a while since we had a good one."

"*Miracle at Philadelphia*, by Catherine Drinker Bowen. Fine book."

And Stuart Conrad was smitten. A woman who debated great issues in the House of Representatives, looked like Audrey Hepburn with ten extra pounds, and was well read, too. . . . He asked her to have a drink with him after the show.

"How about dinner?" she said.

THE NEXT MORNING, Jennifer Segal let the professor's dog out, poured a cup of coffee, and started her computer.

She loved reading the papers online. *The New York Times. The Wall Street Journal. The Boston Herald.* Electronically, she could get through three papers in the time that it took to read one the old-fashioned way. The *Times* for the news, the *Journal* for its opinions (she was growing more conservative), and the *Herald* because she was from Boston and liked reading "The Inside Track"—who was dating whom among the city's power elite, what local tele-celebrity had been nabbed for DUI, what Red Sox star had been seen chowing after hours with a model who was not his wife. . . .

And "The Track" offered this: "A meeting of minds: Brainiac Dartmouth prof Stuart Conrad and the Back Bay's congress*person*, Harriet Holden, were seen clinking glasses at Davio's last night. Discussing important issues, according to our sources, like Flag Burning, the Gay Marriage Act, and *other* marriage acts, too."

If Jennifer Segal had been reading the old-fashioned way, she would have thrown the paper across the room, the old-fashioned way. As it was, she had all she could do to keep from throwing the laptop, because not only had she been living in Hanover and working at the college. She had been sleeping with the professor.

Once she calmed down, she fed the professor's yellow Lab, took her clothes and her computer, and walked into the town. There was an apartment for rent above a restaurant.

AT THE SAME time, a conversation took place in a bed with a foam core and a pillow top.

Harriet Holden straddled the professor's hips and went for a morning ride before she left for D.C.

Since it was the second time in less than eight hours, it lasted a while. When it was done, and she lay across his chest, and his hands were stroking the soft flesh of her ass, she said, "What would happen if I tried to repeal the Second Amendment?"

"You can't be serious. The NRA would fight you . . . crazies with guns would try to shoot you."

"Somebody has to confront the issue."

"But 'the right to keep and bear arms shall not be infringed.' Powerful words."

She gave him a playful slap and slid off him. "I need to shower."

He grabbed her hand. "Harriet, this has been wonderful. I want it to continue, so . . . if you try, I'll help you."

IN NEWPORT, RHODE Island, Marlon Secourt took a call from Clinton D. Jarvis.

"I saw you on television last night," said Jarvis.

"How did I do?"

"Leave television to Kelly Cutter. Why do you think I invested in her the first time I ever heard her?"

"But they asked me," said Secourt. "I go where I'm asked."

"Even when it's ANN?" asked Jarvis. "Even when it's the enemy?"

"Remember what Kennedy said: 'Let us never negotiate out of fear, but let us never fear to negotiate.'"

"Leave Kennedy out of it. We're talking about flag burning, gay marriage, terrorism overseas, and a culture war right here. It's time to do something."

"Do what?"

"Show the American people an annotated version of the Constitution."

"But we've had the Old Curiosities hunting for years."

"To hell with hunting. I want to see them and their September 1787 printing."

Two days later, a private plane brought the Old Curiosities to Newport, and a limo carried them through the old town to the condo owned by Clinton Jarvis.

Marlon Secourt was waiting with Jarvis. Marlon was drinking beer, Jarvis coffee.

A young man stood in the corner: Walter Stanley, new Jarvis head of security.

Formalities were dispensed, and Jarvis said, "I have something to show you." Then he handed them a sheet of paper. "It's something I want you to sell for me."

Martin Bloom looked at it, and his eyebrows came to life. "A letter from Rufus King, telling John Langdon that he has destroyed the annotated first draft."

Jarvis said, "I'll give you a hundred thousand dollars for it."

Martin Bloom and Paul Doherty looked at each other, then at Secourt. "I don't understand," said Martin. "What's going on here?"

Jarvis pulled out a checkbook. "Do I make it to Old Curiosity?"

"Where did you get this?" asked Paul Doherty.

"Never mind that." Jarvis wrote the check, handed it to Doherty, and said, "Show us what you've brought."

Martin hesitated and Jarvis jerked his head toward Stanley, who slipped the map case from Martin's arm.

The final draft of the Constitution, as printed in the *Pennsylvania Packet and Daily Advertiser*, on September 19, 1787, was spread out on the glass coffee table. It was single sheet, beautifully typeset, with plenty of margin for comment.

"What are you planning?" asked Paul Doherty.

Jarvis ignored him and looked at Walter Stanley. "Do you need to show this to the forger?"

Stanley shook his head.

"What is going on?" said Martin Bloom.

Jarvis looked at Martin and Doherty. "I once promised that I would pay two million dollars if you could come up with a draft that showed us what the Founding Fathers thought about the relationship of church and state."

"We've looked. But we can't find anything."

"So you've never found anything annotated by Langdon of New Hampshire?"

As Jarvis spoke, Paul Doherty was studying the Rufus King letter, holding it up to the light, turning it over.

"A perfect forgery." Jarvis took the letter from Doherty's hands. "And the man who did that assures us that he can do a fine forgery in the hand of John Langdon. We'll invent the annotations, Langdon's thoughts on church and state, have our man set them down, and then we'll buy it from you, because you have found it . . . where?"

Martin said, "I'm not sure that I want to do this."

"Not for two million dollars?" said Jarvis.

Martin and Paul looked at each other.

"Be smart. Take the money." Walter Stanley's voice snapped from the corner. It did not carry the tone of subservience that most employees assumed in a roomful of wealthy men. Instead, it sucked all the authority out of the air. "Twenty-one years ago, a drunk died on the streets of Portland. Somebody killed him but didn't bother to rob him. He was the son of a woman who worked for Mr. Secourt's family. Ten years later you showed up on Secourt's front step, asking about that drunk's mother."

"Take this deal," said Jarvis, "or see what happens when the Portland police reopen the investigation."

Marlon Secourt, who had stood silent through all this, perhaps because this kind of intimidation had never been part of his game, said in his jocular old-buddy-old-pal style, "Come on fellas. You're our booksellers. We're countin' on you."

"But what if the other draft really is out there?" asked Martin. "What if it comes on the market?"

"We'll deal with that when it happens," said Jarvis.

TWO YEARS LATER, it was done. The Old Curiosities had invented a story about finding this draft wrapped inside a cheapjack print of a George Washington portrait, rolled into a paper tube, at a Pawtucket garage sale. Once the news broke, it would be huge for a day or so, then the cycle would spin on.

Meanwhile, Clinton D. Jarvis had written a book that built upon the imaginary notations of John Langdon and prepared to publish it.

When the Second Amendment repeal caught fire, Walter Stanley told the Old Curiosities that he needed to know about people who might be inspired to start looking for the lost Constitution.

"We need to know about our competition," he said, "so that we can deal with them."

Martin didn't like the sound of that and didn't trust Walter Stanley. But Doherty reminded him that they had cashed the check for the forged draft. Better to be millionaires in business than convicted murderers in jail.

Martin had to agree, but he insisted that it was still their responsibility to keep looking for the New England draft. It was the right thing to do. "And it's what *we* do."

"Well, if it is," said Doherty, "we should be watching the competition, too, so that we can beat them to it."

THOUGH THE PROFESSOR insisted he wasn't seeing Harriet Holden, Jennifer Segal's jealousy still burned. She had given herself to an older man, and he had betrayed her. He had tried to apologize his way back into her good graces, but the more time he spent in Washington and New York, the less she trusted him. And on the rare occasions that she let him into her bed, she was always angry with herself in the morning.

When Paul Doherty asked her if she would keep them apprised of the professor's research on the lost Constitution—for a price of course—she agreed. And they promised that if they found it first, they would reward her handsomely.

They made this promise over lobster in Portland and introduced Jennifer to their "associate," a young man named Walter Stanley. Soon he was visiting her in Hanover, sending her flowers, and mixing political opinions with small talk in long phone calls.

He told her he believed that they had to find the first draft to preserve an essential right in American life, one that Harriet Holden would take away. "Just like she took away your boyfriend."

And Jennifer Segal—the serious, would-be historian, who seldom smiled because she knew that men were always looking at her—was taken by Walter Stanley, by his good looks and his charm and his ability to say the right thing. He understood her. She never wondered if what he really understood was how to find her buttons and push them.

"You have to help us," he told her. "It's the right thing to do. Help us preserve the truth, no matter what you believe."

The right thing to do. That made it easier for her. Better that than betrayed love as a motivation.

On a day in October, with the gun debate more ferocious than the fights over flag burning and marriage amendments combined, Jennifer made a call to Old Curiosity. She told them that Professor Conrad had gone to Millbridge to see someone called Buster McGillis. "He's a relative of Charles Bishop. Very distant."

But they already knew that.

THE NEXT DAY Buster McGillis let Walter Stanley into his house.

"So, you played for the Pawsox?"

"Yeah, sure."

Buster shuffled back to his chair and dropped into it, breathing hard from the effort. Then he began to cough, but between coughs, he waved his hand to the chair and told Walter to take a seat.

Instead, Walter Stanley reached over and closed the oxygen valve.

Buster gasped and his eyes opened wide. "Wha—"

"Where is it?" He turned his hand, gave the old man another shot of oxygen. "Where's the lost Constitution. You know where it is, don't you?'

"What the fuck?"

A turn of the hand, closing the valve. A gasp from Buster.

"Where is it?"

Buster shook his head.

"Where is it, old man?"

"I don't fuckin' know, I tell ya. What the hell—"

"If I have to look around myself, I'll be mad. I might leave this thing off till I'm done tearin' your house apart. You want that?"

"I . . . I don't know nothin' about this."

"What did you tell that Dartmouth professor?"

"I didn't tell him nothin'!"

Walter Stanley gave the oxygen valve one more turn, so tight that the old man would not be able to turn it back on. He took the telephone receiver with him. Then he went through the house, lifting pictures, opening drawers but disturbing nothing. When he got back to the living room, the old man was still gasping.

Stanley brought his face close to Buster's. "No oxygen till you tell me where that Constitution is."

"I don't fuckin' know!" The old man tried to stand.

Stanley put a hand on his shoulder and pushed him back into his chair.

"Get your fuckin' hand off me." Buster tried to push the hand away.

Stanley laughed and let go.

Now Buster was gasping, groaning, rasping for breath. He didn't have much strength, but he still had plenty of fight, so he reached for an ashtray to throw.

Stanley grabbed his arm, but lightly. *No bruises.*

Finally he turned on the oxygen. "I guess you don't know, after all this."

Buster sucked down the oxygen. "I told ya—"

"But I can't let you stick around." So he turned the valve again, then took a pillow and put it over Buster's face.

He could have waited, but he had evening plans and a long drive.

THAT NIGHT, WALTER Stanley took Jennifer to dinner at the Hanover Inn.

Over wine, he told her that he thought she was special and he was thrilled that she was helping them. And he told her again that she was doing the right thing.

Then they headed back to her little apartment. On the stairs, they kissed. On the landing, he slipped a hand under her skirt and stroked her through her pantyhose. In the kitchen, he pulled down the pantyhose and panties.

He had performed his romantic rituals in the restaurant. Now he turned her and bent her over a kitchen chair. And he fucked her like that, in the kitchen, both of them looking out at the people passing on the streets of Hanover.

And she liked it. She liked the roughness and the danger. She had had enough of academics twenty years older. There was no foreplay chitchat about the latest historical monograph, no professor behind her, no softening dick. This was something different, something raw and elemental.

He took her with rage that she mistook for passion. When they were done in the kitchen, he picked her up and carried her into the bed. And he fucked her there, too.

THE NEXT MORNING, Walter Stanley whispered to her that he had to get back to Boston. He kissed her and went out into the cool morning air and hurried to his car.

Even he could be touched by the beauty of the Dartmouth green at dawn, with a cloudlike mist hovering a few feet above the grass.

But it was only for a moment.

Once the killing started, Walter Stanley saw no reason for it to stop until the job was done. He was going to make it as clean as possible for his client. Anyone who knew anything about the lost Constitution, the draft that would call into question the annotations on the Jarvis forgery, would be out of the way.

He didn't do this because he had any commitment to the politics of one side or another. He did it because he was a professional. He admired a job well done. And he had a plan of his own.

The Volvo went by a few minutes later.

He pulled out and followed it.

TWENTY-EIGHT

Now they were all dead—Buster, the professor, Bindle, Martin and Paul, all except for the girl.

Peter rolled slowly through the EZ Pass lane at the tolls, because he could see a police cruiser just beyond, waiting to nab the car that went through at twenty-five instead of fifteen. And good that he didn't have to stop and dig for change because if they saw the bloodstains on his trousers, it was over.

A forgery. Something was forged. The Old Curiosities had sold a forgery.

It could have been anything, but . . .

. . . it had to be the John Langdon version. The one that Jarvis had shown them, the one that Kelly Cutter said was the real thing.

Consider the timing. Jarvis was publishing a book, a call to arms for the fundamentalists, the *we-know-better-than-you* crowd who feared that American society was going straight to hell.

Sometimes, Peter agreed with them. But. . . .

Had Clinton D. Jarvis set out to kill anyone who knew anything about the *real* annotated draft? And why? So that *his* draft would get all the attention and none of the scrutiny that a competing draft would bring to both of them?

Was that any way for a good Christian to act?

But people sometimes did strange things in the name of the greater good, and from what Peter had gathered, Jarvis was definitely a "greater good" type of guy.

As for Marlon Secourt . . . he seemed more realistic, a guy with strong opinions and some money to back them up. But murder?

Did Secourt and Jarvis even know what was being done in their name?

Peter could not imagine Jarvis issuing the order to Walter Stanley: *Kill them all.*

He might have given Stanley free rein to protect the interests of the Morning in America Foundation. And Stanley had started so subtly that not even Jarvis had noticed.

Natural causes for Buster. Tragic accident for the professor. Then the "suicide" of Morris Bindle. The almost plane crash. Then "make it messy" in Portland.

And . . . the phone rang. His own phone.

Peter didn't recognize the number. He answered anyway.

"It's Jennifer Segal."

"Where are you?"

"In my car. I'm driving."

"Where to?"

"I can't say. I won't say. I'm out of this, but—"

"Martin Bloom and Paul Doherty are dead."

"Oh, God."

"Jennifer, why did you come to my office last Friday?"

"Paul Doherty sent me."

"You said you were a student of Professor Conrad."

"Paul Doherty and Martin Bloom were paying me."

"Why me? Why did you come to me? What bait did I take?"

"Doherty said he had to find out what you knew. Once you sold the Henry Knox letter, they figured out that you had a relationship with Morris Bindle, and they knew that he had a relationship with Buster McGillis. So he set you up by giving you your own catalogue with Buster's obituary inside it. If you were in the hunt, Doherty wanted to beat you. Martin just wanted the draft found, so he told you what he could. But both wanted to protect you, too, I think."

"Protect me?"

"From Walter Stanley. I thought Stanley worked for Doherty. Then I thought it was the other way around. Then I thought they were both working for Morning in America. But Walter Stanley works for himself."

"Where is he now?"

"In my apartment, taking a nap. He always takes a nap after we . . . stay away from him." The fear in her voice seemed to rise an octave over the rumble of the cars. "He's dangerous."

"He's the one who's been doing the killing."

"I don't care. I just want to get away from here. So I'm gone."

"Where to?"

"Somewhere that's not New England. But there's one thing you should know."

"What?"

"He used my computer last night. He didn't delete his Internet files. He was visiting scalping sights, looking for game tickets. He's going to be at Fenway Park tomorrow night."

EVANGELINE CARRINGTON SAT in a double-wide, somewhere in the woods. She sensed that they were closer to Boston now. Southern Maine, maybe, near Kezar Lake.

There was a television playing. A little kid was crying at the other end of the trailer. Acorns were dropping on the aluminum roof.

One of the guys lived here with his family. She guessed it was Hotshot, since there was a techno thriller beside the bed. She couldn't tell how many were in the house. From the window, she could see a trailer with two ATVs. So . . . two at least.

Make that three. A car was pulling up, a door slamming.

She heard voices in the front room. Men talking. Arguing? Footfalls coming. The door to her room opened. She jumped up, and in walked Judge Carter A. Trask.

"Is this what you guys do to liberals?" she said.

"I'm so sorry, Miss Carrington. I hope you haven't been too inconvenienced."

"Inconvenienced?" She looked around the tiny bedroom. "Hell, no."

The judge perched on the edge of the bed. "Please. I'm sorry."

"I've been having a great time . . . the blindfolded rides around New England, the open-air bathrooms, the marvelous things your boys do with squirrel . . . a vacation."

The judge patted the bed and asked her to sit.

Since there was nowhere else, she did.

He asked, "Do you think Peter Fallon has the document yet?"

"I don't think he's ever going to have it. I don't think it exists anymore."

The judge opened his brief case. "I know where it was in 1935."

"Where? The ski slope? Don't tell me the ski slope, because we've been to the ski slope." She got up and began to pace in little circles. "And don't tell me Livermore, because we went there, too. Peter goes to places where—"

"Miss Carrington—"

"—he thinks the document used to be, as if somebody might have forgotten where they left it, for Chrissakes, then he says if it's not here, it's moved down the timeline—"

"Miss Carrington." He pulled a sheet of paper from his briefcase.

"—because he treats time like a river, and if it isn't near the source, it'll be down near the rapids or out at the mouth or some damn thing—" She brought her hand to her forehead. She had resolved in the car on the afternoon they snatched her that she wasn't going to let them see any emotion out of her.

"There's something I'd like you to look at." The judge held out the paper. "Documentary evidence."

She blinked back tears, straightened, took the sheet of paper: a filing at the Hampshire County Registry of Deeds, dated November 15, 1927.

"It's a loan agreement between the American Immigrant Bank of Millbridge and Bill and Sarah McGillis, who took control of Pike-Perkins after the flood and the Manchaug bankruptcy. It lists the assets put up as collateral for a loan to purchase the mill. Page one lists real property: looms, dyeing tubs, raw material, the building itself. But on the second page, you'll see a listing of personal property that the owners have put up."

She read:

1. House at 65 Blackstone St., Millbridge, Mass . . . 12,000
2. All contents thereof, including mahogany dining room set, silverware, oriental carpets (two at 6×9, one at 9×12, one at 11×18), paintings, and miscellaneous . . . 2,190
3. Various papers, family letters, and historical documents . . . 500

Then she looked at the judge. "Five hundred dollars for historical documents? Then it can't include the Constitution. That would have been worth a lot more."

"Bear with me," he said. "I got to thinking about Bartlett Pike, who lost control to the people from Perkins Holdings. So I looked him up. I found an article on his burial service in *The Blackstone Valley Weekly*. I went from there."

"To what?"

"To considering his descendants. Charlie Bishop has been looking for it now since the Clinton impeachment. And we know that none of the Amorys got it, because then I'd have it. So what's logical? Perhaps it went to the descendants who stayed at the mill and fought the good fight, and most likely it went to them between the date of the 1927 loan and the end of the Depression."

More acorns splattered on the roof of the trailer.

The judge chuckled. "I had to spend Thursday in the registry in

Northampton, Massachusetts, to find this material. And Friday at the *Blackstone Valley Weekly*."

"All this tells me is that there was a relationship between a bank and the McGillises." Evangeline studied the document, stamped, *Paid in full, November 20, 1932*. "It was a five-year note. They paid it."

"Then there's this, from the *Blackstone Valley Weekly*, just a year later: 'Bad news at the Pike-Perkins Mill. Twenty workers were laid off this week.'" The judge thumbed through a few more sheets. "Two weeks later, twenty more laid off. Ten more the following week."

"Bad times," she said.

"The worst," said the judge. "Then, there's this: 'The employees of the Pike Mill got an early Christmas present, when the McGillises announced that they were rehiring all the workers laid off in the last month.'"

"So?" said Evangeline. "They got another bank loan."

"But they didn't. It would have been recorded at the registry. Unless—"

"Unless what?"

"Unless they put up personal property for collateral with a single lien holder. Then there would be no requirement for a filing under existing statutes, which predated the UCC. That's Uniform Commercial Code."

"Stop with the alphabet soup, Judge. Cut to the chase."

"What did they have that would be valuable enough to enable them to pay their bills, rehire, and keep going? They didn't take another loan until the recession of 1938, a commercial loan, duly registered. That got them to World War II, when everyone did well, and they hung on until the seventies."

"Would a local bank have records of another transaction?"

"Possibly. The problem is that American Immigrant Bank failed in early 1934."

"What about the FDIC?"

"It was just coming in. Didn't help the owner. Third generation Lebanese named Chory, loved America, loved American memorabilia, decorated his bank with it."

"How do you know that?"

The judge waved another piece of paper. "Obituary, January 15, 1934."

"He died suddenly?'

"Very suddenly. When the rope snapped. He hanged himself."

"So . . . just a theory with a dead end . . . so to speak."

"No," said the judge. "I think there's another synapse to jump."

Evangeline sat on the edge of the bed. "The mill, the money, the dead bank president. . . . If the bank failed, what would happen to the collateral?"

"The state banking commissioner would auction it. I found the auction records at Northampton, too. But there was no draft of the Constitution put up when the bank's assets went on the block."

"Like I said, a dead end."

"But what if the bank president knew his bank was going down? Say that he decided to put a wad of cash into something that was portable and easily hidden, something the bank examiners might never find."

"A form of money laundering?" said Evangeline.

"Maybe. But his conscience got the best of him. It happened a lot in those days."

Another splattering of acorns rattled on the roof.

"So," she said, "where does that leave us?"

"I'm not sure," said the judge. "But we're close. So we just have to keep thinking. This is America, don't forget. In America, we get up in the morning and go to work and solve our problems."

"What did you just say?"

"It's something Grandpa Aaron used to say. It's like the family motto."

"I think you should call Peter."

"As soon as I get cell coverage."

"If you've figured this much out," said Peter to the judge, "why are you telling me about this bank president named Chory? Why don't you and your boys just go and find the thing?"

"They're not 'my boys.' If they were, your girlfriend would be free. I don't trust them any more than you do."

Peter was back in his brother's warehouse, talking on the speaker phone. "I want Evangeline."

"I'll do my best." The judge's voice echoed, all tinny and distorted. "But Jack Batter will do anything to stop this repeal amendment. He sees it as his duty. His duty as an American. He wouldn't have snatched her if he wasn't prepared for the consequences."

"Did she have any messages for me?" Peter wasn't looking for words of undying love. He knew her better than that. He expected that right now she was scheming as hard as he was.

"She said to tell you that in America we get up in the morning and go to work and solve our problems, especially in Millbridge. She said she didn't want to say more because she doesn't trust me."

"That's why I love her," said Peter. "She's honest."

"She said she has a hunch you should follow to Millbridge. She said you'd know what she means."

"So," said Antoine after they hung up, "do you?"

"Do I what?"

"Do you know what she means?"

Peter had showered, put on clean jeans, combed his hair, gotten the blood off his hands but not out of his head.

"Maybe she's just telling us she's safe," said Orson.

"If this Walter Stanley is as bad as advertised," said Antoine, "she's probably safer than we are right about now."

News of the bloody scene at the Old Curiosity had already made it onto Boston television, and it was a leading story on the Internet home pages: Murder in the Bookstore. There were photographs, none too graphic . . . yet. They were blaming "unknown assailant or assailants."

"Just so long as they're not blaming me," said Peter, "because I think I know what Evangeline was telling me."

"What?" asked Danny.

"That I need to go back to Millbridge."

"What's in Millbridge?" asked Antoine.

"The lost Constitution. We're going to get it, because boys, this is America. In America, we get up in the morning, we go to work, and we solve our problems. Tomorrow, we'll solve ours."

THEY DISPERSED THAT night.

Danny and his son went back to their house in Southie.

"Be careful," said Peter. "This Walter Stanley is unpredictable. But I think he's more concerned about the ball game than he is about us."

"I have a good alarm system," said Danny.

"Yeah," said Bobby. "Rex the Rottweiler. And Mom's a light sleeper."

"And I have my home*bodies*," said Antoine.

"I have a credit card," said Orson.

Peter and Orson checked into the Seaport Hotel. They used Orson's credit card, in case the police had gotten onto Peter's trail.

"One bed or two?" asked the expressionless young woman behind the counter.

"Two," snapped Peter.

Orson covered his mouth and stifled a laugh.

After they ordered room service, Peter called Josh Sutherland in Washington.

"Do you have the draft?" asked Sutherland.

"If I don't, I will have seen it by tomorrow night. That will be enough. Is the Congresswoman still planning to be in the Bishop Media luxury box?"

"Charlie Bishop is going to give her air time . . . one of those remotes before the game, with the reporter asking her about big doings in Washington. She has her sound bites all rehearsed. It's nice when the liberal media bias works for you."

"Has she considered not going?"

"Why?"

"I think she may be in danger."

Sutherland laughed. "You're an expert document-hunter, Fallon. Bring the document. Leave security to the security experts."

Peter then put a call in to a cell phone number that he had held onto for four months: FBI Agent George Hause. He warned Hause about Walter Stanley. And he added, "Once they've dusted the Old Curiosity in Portland, the police may want to talk to me. I'll have answers tomorrow."

"What else am I supposed to do with this information?" asked Hause.

"Have people at Fenway. Something is going to happen there tomorrow night."

At DAWN THE next morning, Peter picked up Danny in South Boston. He wanted this to be a small operation. He didn't think he'd need a lot of muscle, and if Danny was with him, he could tell people they were contractors working for Tommy Farrell.

The last call he made before he left the hotel was to Farrell.

The day came up clear and cool. The reds and golds were still flaring, though the foliage was already fading. Things had changed a lot in a week, and not just the leaves.

It took them an hour. They passed through all those old towns like Milford and Hopedale. They went by the famous old Stanley Woolen Mill in Uxbridge. Then they came into Millbridge.

They cruised past the mill once, to make sure that it was not being staked out. No cops, at least none that were obvious. Just some yellow police tape covering the plywood that now covered the entrance. This had been a murder scene just few days before.

It was more likely that the police were watching Peter's apartment in Boston, considering the phone messages he had gotten that morning. Detectives from the Boston Police, responding to requests from the Portland Police, wanted to talk to him. ASAP.

If the cops were watching the mill from some hidden location, well, that was a chance they had to take. If they swooped in, he'd call George Hause right away.

In the turnaround under the sugar maples, a car was waiting for them. Tommy Farrell was leaning against it. "I don't know what you want to see me for."

"Bindle told me you always came on Sundays." Peter pulled out a cylindrical leather map case and gave it a pat. "Just pretend that we've brought some architectural plans for you to look over."

"Yeah? Why?"

"You're the guy who has the key to the building. Right?"

"Is that why you dragged me all the way up here?" asked Farrell.

"Well, I think you should see what we we're going to do."

"What's that?"

"Make this historical society rich."

"Rich? Hey, I own the fuckin' building."

"You can fight it out with them. Just let us in."

Tommy Farrell gave them both a dog-tooth smile, as if to say that he was smarter than these two, and he'd go along until he swooped in and took what he wanted.

Peter had seen that look before, from guys a lot smarter than Tommy Farrell.

It was cold inside.

Tommy flipped on the lights, which did nothing to warm it up.

The room still smelled of must, moisture, and a past just barely breathing in the present.

But the future was there, too. The past pointed the way. That's what Peter had always believed.

And he was looking right at it: the huge photograph above the book case: *The Men and Women of the Mill, 1861* with the caption, "This is America. In America we get up in the morning, we go to work, and we solve our problems."

Beneath the photograph was a picture of Mr. Chory, standing in his bank, with the larger photograph on the wall behind him.

If Evangeline had been there, Peter would have told her he was proud of her. She was learning how to do this work in spite of herself.

She had remembered every detail of their first Millbridge trip, including the identity of the man in the small photograph that Bindle displayed beneath the big one. When she heard the motto, handed down through the generations, and coupled it with the judge's story of the failed bank, she remembered the picture that once had filled the bank president with such pride. It gave her the hunch that Peter just had to play.

Now to find out if the hunch paid off. . . .

"What are you guys looking for?" asked Farrell. "I don't have all day."

"We're looking for a lost first draft of the United States Constitution," said Peter.

"No shit." Farrell dropped his tough-guy act. "I've been trying to find that thing forever."

Peter noticed Danny slip his hand into his jacket pocket.

Farrell kept talking, as though the guy behind him wasn't even worth looking at. "If you guys think it's in here, I'm layin' claim to it right now. Because this building is mine, and possession is—"

Tommy Farrell stopped in midsentence when Danny's sap took him square in the back of the head and dropped him like a sandbag.

"Fuckin' guy talks too much," said Danny.

Peter turned again to the photograph; then he looked at his brother.

"Let's do it," said Danny.

They lifted the picture off the wall and laid it out on the table.

There was a little label on the back that said, "Gift of Hannah Chory, 1988, at the opening of the Millbridge Historical Society Museum at the Pike-Perkins Mill."

"That was the banker's daughter," said Peter.

It looked as if the picture had been reframed at some point. Though the original matte remained, the paper backing was new.

With a penknife, Peter cut the backing and lifted it off.

Nothing.

There was cardboard beneath the paper, fit neatly into the frame and held in place with little metal grommets.

Peter had a small scissors on his knife. He used it to flip out each grommet. Then he pulled out the sharpest blade and slid it into the corner of the frame.

"Be careful," said Danny.

Peter gave his brother a look. "Do I tell you to be careful with your trowel?"

"C'mon, lift it up."

"I will . . . carefully," said Peter. The cardboard came up, came off. Beneath it should have been matte board, protecting the backing of the photograph.

Instead, there was a sheet of yellowed paper.

"Is this it?" asked Danny.

Peter looked at his brother. In this last moment of anticipation, he forgot everything he had been through, everything he expected to go through, and said, "Danny, I love this job."

"Try bricklayin' sometime and you'll love it even more. Is this it?"

Peter pointed out the impression of the print on the back of the paper. "Do you see that? And that?" There was a splotch where ink had leeched through.

"Is this it? Because if it is, let's grab it and go before this big bastard wakes up."

Peter wiped his hands down the front of his shirt. He wished he had curator's cotton gloves with him. But he couldn't think of everything. Then he gently lifted a sheet out of the frame and turned it over.

"Yes, Danny. This is it."

It looked exactly like the Gerry draft, a folio sheet with large type off-set right, leaving an ample left margin for annotations.

"Holy shit," said Danny.

"Holy indeed."

Sometimes, things went just that easily.

Sometimes, you found what you were looking for.

Of course, before you found it, you had to factor human frailty into the equation. In this case, the president of a failing bank, trying to save something of what his father had built before the tide took it all. Jack Chory had hidden a national treasure behind a photograph. Not a photograph of enormous value because the sheriff might have confiscated it when the bank failed, but an image that had significance for the banker and his family and for the people of the town of Millbridge, too.

Peter carefully slid the four sheets out and laid them on the table.

The preamble lacked poetry; the articles were far different in their arrangement.

But he could feel those men of New England, thinking and arguing and imagining America into existence.

He read: "No law regarding religion; freedoms of press, speech protected; peaceable assembly respected. . . ."

And there, beneath the initials "E.G.": "A well regulated militia being necessary to the Security of a Free State, the right of the people to keep and bear arms shall not be infringed."

A smoking gun? So to speak.

And there, the thoughts of Rufus King: "The right to keep and bear arms must be discussed and defined."

And there, another hand, initialed J.L. for John Langdon, a few scrawled thoughts: "Separation of Church and State paramount. Right to keep and bear arms important. . . ."

Clinton Jarvis was not going to like that. It put the lie to everything in his forged first printing.

Charles Bishop wouldn't be too happy either. Neither would the boys from Maine, because while Gerry laid out the amendment as it was adopted, Rufus King had done some thinking out loud on the draft.

"Now what?" said Danny.

Peter gathered up the sheets, rolled them together, and slid them into the map case. "Let's go to the World Series."

TWENTY-NINE

AT A QUARTER TO EIGHT, Peter Fallon stood on the corner of Brookline Avenue and Yawkey Way, in front of the Red Sox ticket office.

If he wanted a public place for insurance, this was the corner, because at the moment, this was the center of Boston and the hub of the baseball universe.

The Red Sox had made it into the World Series for the second time in the same decade, a feat they hadn't accomplished since they shipped Babe Ruth to New York. So there was a current in the air, a static charge so strong it could have run the huge lights that made Fenway Park an island of daylight in the dark streets around it.

Peter had his cell phone in his pocket. He had his brother stationed across the street, beside the Red Sox Parking Lot on Brookline Avenue. And he had Antoine, in a Red Sox hoodie, scanning the crowd from the opposite corner.

Yawkey Way ran roughly parallel to the third baseline. Turnstiles at both ends street made it a pedestrian mall on game nights. Once inside the turnstiles, fans could visit the souvenir shops and buy the Red Sox hat with the World Series insignia on it. Or they could buy a sausage or a program. Or they could push through Gate A, into the Escher maze of ancient concrete ramps, platforms, and tunnels that led to the inner sanctum itself.

At the Boylston Street end of the mall, television lights illuminated the platform where the guys from American Sports Network were doing their pre-game broadcast.

At Peter's end, the crowd was piling up around the turnstiles as the trains and trolleys disgorged fans at Fenway and Yawkey Station and Kenmore Square. A line snaked out of the main ticket office and around the corner onto Brookline Avenue. Another knot of people jumbled up in front of 4 Yawkey Way, the VIP entrance. Even people who were connected had to push and shove.

There was a brass band playing, and big-screen televisions, brought in for the Series, were showing the ASN feed to all the fans. People were laughing and shouting and shuffling toward the turnstiles or standing on the curbs beneath the street lamps, scanning the crowd for familiar faces, like the brother-in-law who had the tickets or the date who was about to have the night of her life. Cops stood on stoops and sat on horses that looked like big placid rocks in the middle of the crowd. And there were young men moving faceless and hooded through the mob, muttering as they went, "Tickets, anyone need tickets?" or "Anyone sellin'? Who's sellin'?"

Whenever a scalper came near, Peter held his map case even tighter.

He had been waiting forty-five minutes. If he hadn't been so nervous, he'd be getting bored. So he was watching one of the big screens and listening to the baseball analysts discuss the game. Then they threw it to their correspondent on their sister station, ANN.

Cut to the host of *Rapid Fire*, Harry Hawkins, in the Bishop Media Box:

"The first pitch is about forty-five minutes away, Steve, and the excitement is building. We have a fascinating crowd here in the box, so let's meet a few."

Hawkins gestured for the camera to follow him. It went past a big-screen TV that, for a moment, showed an image of the same big screen within another big screen, like a barber's mirror showing the same image to infinity. Then the camera went past the sofas, the bar, past knots of people already in the box having pre-game cocktails and—was that Kate Morgan and Kelly Cutter talking to Tommy Farrell?

All day long, Farrell had been leaving threatening phone messages.

Then the camera was moving toward a wall of glass, then through the sliders, out to where two rows of red and blue seats seemed to be floating above the grandstand. The best seats in baseball. Ten seats to every box.

Charles Bishop was waiting for his interview. It was plain that he had been in the television business a long time, because he knew how to stage a scene: himself in the foreground, and behind him the ballpark—the grass, the shadowed walls, the ancient crannies that outfielders cursed—glimmering in hues of green like a multifaceted emerald.

"Mr. Bishop, it's a great night," said Hawkins.

"Opening night of the World Series. One of the great nights in American life."

"And you say that you're going to have an announcement tonight?"

"That's right, Harry. On a night that should be a national holiday, I'm hoping to reveal a national treasure. My gift to the nation after a blessed life."

Peter had already called and told Don Cottle that the Constitution was in hand.

On the screen, Peter noticed a young man behind Bishop: Josh Sutherland, dialing a telephone. As it if it had been cued, Peter's phone rang. It was Sutherland.

"I can see you on TV," said Peter.

Sutherland glanced at the camera, then turned his back like a good political operative, a man behind the scenes. "Bishop keeps asking about you. You'd better be here before eight ten."

"Why? What happens at eight ten?"

"The National Anthem. Stephen Tyler's singing. When he screams, 'and the home of the brave!' the F-18s will do their flyover. They're coming in from the north, low and loud, right over the left field wall."

"Scripted to the second," said Peter.

"We cut from Stephen Tyler to Harriet Holden with her hand over her heart in the front row of the upper deck, framed so that you can see her and the F-18s, too."

"Does she know that those planes carry weapons?"

Josh Sutherland kept talking as if he didn't notice the sarcasm. "She knows she'll be linked with Boston's rock 'n' roll prince *and* with symbols of American power, in the same visual sentence. A sister in the family of cool and a gun-control Democrat who wells up when she sees some good military hardware."

"Is she going to well up on cue, too?"

"She's in the ladies room now, practicing."

"The female Ronald Reagan."

"It's images, Fallon. That first draft completes the picture. Get it up here."

"I guess this is what Kelly Cutter means about the liberal bias in the media."

"Fuck Kelly Cutter," said Josh. "I can't believe she's in this box."

"It's the Bishop philosophy," answered Peter. " 'Come, let us reason together.' It's what America is all about, in case you've forgotten."

"Kelly doesn't reason with anybody. I don't know why she showed up with that lesbian daughter of Bishop's, unless . . ." Sutherland paused. "*Jesus.* Kelly Cutter and Kate Morgan?"

Peter could see the stories a smart political operator might leak to the press. He said, "If I were you, I wouldn't be worrying about Kelly Cutter. I'd be worrying about putting Harriet Holden out there in the front row."

"Why?"

"You're just making her a target."

"She's been a target since this fight began. There couldn't be anyplace safer than in the middle of this crowd." *Click.*

PETER PUT THE phone back into his jacket pocket and looked around.

More people, more pushing. He moved to a lamppost and leaned against it, as though he were holding onto a tree in the wind.

"Nice colors." Judge Trask materialized from somewhere. "I like the blue blazer with the red turtleneck."

"I picked the team colors," said Peter. "I'm also wearing black running shoes. In case I have to chase anybody, or run from anybody."

"Batter and his boys are coming."

Peter looked around. "Which direction?"

"From Kenmore Square, from the parking lot—"

Peter looked across Brookline Avenue.

"Don't worry. They'll find you." The judge tapped the cylindrical map case. "Is it in there?"

"It's in here," said Peter. "While the rest of us were running around, you dug in the right hole, in the right archive. And Evangeline had the right hunch. Nice work."

"Can I see it?"

"In a few minutes, if all goes well."

"You mean you're not going to swap it for Evangeline?"

"Jack Batter will want it on television."

"Jack Batter will want it. Period. So will the other boys. Good luck."

Before Peter could ask him what that meant, the judge was through the door and into the VIP entrance.

AS PETER SAW it, his job was simple:

Get Evangeline. Get her to safety. Convince the boys who'd grabbed her that it was to their benefit to put the Constitution on television.

If they disagreed, he might never see the draft again, because he was beginning to think that those boys from Maine weren't quite so committed to politics. Snatch the Constitution. Sell it for a fortune. Go to some island country with no extradition. Live large. Why else would they have been so brazen?

Then there was Walter Stanley. Who could be sure what he was up to?

Peter caught his brother's eye, pointed to his own eyes, then pointed into the parking lot. *Keep watching.*

That was when Jack Batter came out of nowhere, put a shoulder into Peter's back to get him to turn, and said, "Do you have it?"

"You're late," snapped Peter. "I've been standing here for forty-five minutes."

"Because—" Batter took Fallon by the elbow and pulled him back, against the building. "—of this." He held the GPS tracker in front of Peter's nose.

Peter laughed. "You followed the tracking device?"

"Whose car is that?"

"His name is Walter Stanley."

"Shit," said Batter. "There's one very nasty guy."

"You *know* him?" said Peter.

"By reputation." Batter gestured to the scar on his face. "Used to be in the same line of work. Overseas security contracting."

While Peter was trying to process that, Batter looked toward the turnstiles. "They're using wands on people at every entrance. Big time security. Checking for weapons. That's good."

"I warned the FBI."

Batter whipped his head around, glared at Peter, pulled up the hood of his camo sweatshirt.

"Not on you," said Peter. "On Stanley."

"Well, if he has a contract on someone at the game, he might have something hidden inside already. Could have sneaked it in on a ballpark tour or as part of a delivery. He might even be dressed as the popcorn guy."

"But why?"

"You could be the target." Batter scanned the crowd again. "He could be watching us right now. I see your brother across the street. I see the black kid under the souvenir sign. But—"

"One thing Stanley said to me—"

"You *talked* to him?"

On the television screen, Harry Hawkins was interviewing someone else in the Bishop Media Box: Marlon Secourt.

"Secourt? On Bishop Media?" said Peter.

Secourt was saying, "Charles Bishop understands that we're all believers in this country. We may argue over the truth, but we all come together on a night like this. That's why we're here. I'm just glad he sent me a ticket."

Batter growled, "Forget that windbag. You talked to Walter Stanley? When?"

Peter pulled Shiny's cell phone from his pocket, punched a few buttons. "That's Stanley's number. Want to give him a call?"

Batter looked at the phone for a moment, then said, "Fuck it. We're here to make an exchange. Let the FBI worry about him." Then Batter pulled out a cigarette and lit it. A signal. "Look across the street, at the entrance to the parking lot."

SUVs and limos were pouring in, people were pouring out. Another crowd of fans had disgorged from the train. And Mercer and Scrawny were appearing at the gate. They had Evangeline between them.

"Let's go," said Batter. "And tell your brother and the black kid to stay put."

"No," said Peter. "We make this switch right here."

"Mercer's already going back. He gave you a look. She's there. Now let's go."

Batter started across the street, against the flow of the crowd.

"Batter!" cried Peter. "This Constitution. You *want* it on television. You want the world to hear this. None of the New England Framers say anything about banning weapons. They barely wonder about it."

Batter looked over his shoulder. "Come on."

Peter gave Antoine a jerk of the head. *Come on.* And Danny, in front of Boston Beer Works. *Come on.*

"They won't do you much good," said Batter. "They'll just get in the way."

The driveway sloped down into a huge lot bounded by buildings on two sides, the commuter rail line and Yawkey Station at the back.

Batter kept walking until he'd led them to a corner of the lot near the tracks. The Maine militia had come in early and parked in a section that filled first, so there were few people there now. The latecomers were all driving into the far side of the lot. So this was the perfect spot for whatever was about to go down.

Batter stopped at the back bumper of a black SUV. Mercer was leaning against the passenger door. Scrawny had gotten back into the car with Evangeline.

Mercer opened the back door.

At first Peter thought it was to let Evangeline out.

Instead, Batter said, "Get in."

"No way," said Peter.

"I want to look the document over," said Batter. "Out of sight."

"Do it out here. The light's better. Besides, you wouldn't know an authentic document if it jumped up and bit you in the ass." Then Peter shouted. "Evangeline. Get out of the car."

Mercer slammed the door. "Fuck that. Let's just take it and get out of here, boss."

Batter looked back at the entrance to the parking lot. "Only one-way traffic, and it's all comin' in. We aren't goin' anywhere for a while." Then he turned to Fallon. "You say the words on the draft favor our side?"

"Yes." That wasn't entirely true, but Peter told him what truth he could: "Elbridge Gerry writes the amendment word for word. It's something the world ought to see."

"Fuck that," said Mercer.

"Maybe he's right," said Jack Batter.

"Maybe, my ass," said Mercer. "We have a plan."

And there they were.

Batter and Mercer on one side.

Peter Fallon, Danny Fallon, and Antoine Scarborough on the other, all in the semidarkness of the big parking lot across from Fenway.

Batter said to Peter Fallon, "I want to see it."

"Let me show it to you on TV," said Peter. "When Harriet Holden sees it, she'll shit."

"Come on," said Mercer. "Let's get out of here."

"I don't know," said Batter. "Maybe he's right."

"You *know* I'm right." Peter waved the map case. "Let's do what we came here to do. Which is to get the truth out."

"We came here to get rich," said Mercer.

Batter ignored him and kept his eyes on Fallon. "If we go back inside, I'm not letting that thing out of my sight."

"I'll give you Evangeline's ticket," said Peter. "But she comes with us. I'm not letting her out of mine."

"How do we all get in?" said Batter.

"I'll buy a scalped ticket," said Peter.

"Good," said Danny. "Get a couple."

"Shut up," said Peter. Then he looked at Batter again. "What are we doing here? Just stealing something to run off with it, or have we gone through all this because of a principle?"

And in a flash, Peter found out.

Mercer took three quick steps and drove the heel of his hand into the back of Batter's head.

Batter dropped to his knees and Mercer bowled over him and came straight at Peter and Danny.

With a quick kick, he drove Danny to the ground, then delivered an elbow right to Peter's face. Peter heard the sound of his nose crunching, and he landed on the tarmac.

Antoine started to come toward him and Scrawny took him down with a well-placed foot and a quick flip.

Mercer tore the map case from Peter's neck.

"We'll never drive out," said Scrawny. "All the traffic is still coming in."

"We ain't drivin'," said Mercer. "Come on." And he started to run toward the commuter train that had just pulled in on the platform.

"We don't even know where that's goin'," said Scrawny.

"It don't matter."

And the two of them headed for the train.

"That son of a bitch." Batter was on his feet again. "Mercer!"

"Sorry, boss. It's worth too much. We dreamed of this from the start."

"Mercer."

"You be a good American. I'm lookin' out for me and Scrawny and our families." And Mercer kept running.

"Son of a bitch," said Batter again. Then he reached down to his ankle and pulled out a pistol with a silencer.

He fired twice. One shot hit Mercer in the back of the head, right at the neck, and dropped him into a heap between two parked cars. The other hit Scrawny in the knee and sent him yelping and limping in a big circle.

But nobody streaming up from the train or from the distant reaches of the lot seemed to notice. All the fans were focused on the building excitement and on the brilliant lights illuminating the night ahead of them.

From thirty or forty feet away, this looked like no more than a dust-up among drunks.

Peter tore open the door of the SUV and pulled Evangeline out.

"Jesus!" she said to Batter. "You killed him."

"He was stealin' the truth . . . just to sell it. Fallon is right"—Batter flipped him the map case—"this is about a principle."

"Shouldn't we call 911?" asked Evangeline.

"Someone'll do that soon enough." Batter shoved the pistol under the car seat. "They won't let me in the ballpark with that. So now, Miss Carrington, tell your boyfriend how much you love him and how much you missed him, and then let's go tell America the truth . . . whatever it is."

Evangeline looked at Peter. "He's right. I love you. I missed you. And you look terrible in red."

"It's the team color," he said. "Let's go."

IT WAS AFTER eight o'clock. By then, the scalpers were getting pan-
icked. No one wanted to be holding when Stephen Tyler started to sing.

So Peter bought a ticket for four hundred dollars. Half an hour earlier,
the going rate had been one thousand dollars.

Danny said, "I guess me and Antoine don't get to go?"

"I don't have the cash," said Peter. "Wait here. Tomorrow night, I'll
scalp you two nice seats."

Then Peter's phone rang.

"It's Sutherland. Where the fuck are you?"

"I'm coming."

They hurried past the big screens at the turnstiles.

On one of them, Charles Bishop was standing inside, introducing
Congresswoman Harriet Holden.

She said, "Thank you, Charles. This is a wonderful opportunity for
me to see the big game."

"You have a big game in Washington tomorrow, don't you?" asked
Bishop.

"Well, I'm not here to mix business and pleasure," she said. "But there
will be a national contest beginning tomorrow in Washington, as we begin
hearings on the repeal of the Second Amendment, to clear the way for
more rational gun laws."

"Something that we need, in my humble opinion." Bishop looked at
the camera.

Peter's phone rang again: Kelly Cutter.

Peter said, "You feel like a stranger in a strange land right about now?"

"Something funny is going on," she said. "Kate and I went for a walk.
I was starting to gag in that roomful of liberals."

"They might have been wrinkling their noses, too."

"Yeah, well, we went from the corporate boxes down into the grandstand. We noticed a guy. We thought he was one of Cottle's guys."

"One of Cottle's guys?"

The name caught Jack Batter's attention. He mouthed the word to
Peter: "Cottle?"

"Yeah," said Kelly. "One of the security guys for the TV people. He
was walking along with a briefcase."

"A briefcase at a ball game?" said Peter.

"He went past this young guy, bland looks, dirty blond hair, good build.
And he gave him the briefcase. I don't know what was in it, but when they
saw us, they looked like they'd been caught fucking a teenage boy."

Peter closed the phone. "One of Cottle's guys is working with Walter Stanley."

"Cottle?" said Batter. "Don Cottle? Bishop Security?"

"You know *him*, too?" asked Peter.

"Not personally, but I wouldn't be surprised if Stanley did."

Two security men had stationed themselves on the step of Gate A and were scanning the crowd.

Evengeline noticed them and tugged on Peter's hand, which she was holding tight so that they didn't get separated in the crowd.

"Yeah," he said. "I see them. Maybe they're looking for Stanley, too."

"If they are, they missed," said Batter. "Stanley's inside with a brief-case. It probably contains a gun, broken down. A sniper's rifle. Good scope. Silencer. High muzzle velocity."

"But Cottle and Jarvis, working together? I don't get it." Peter leaned close, all but shouting in Batter's ear to be heard over the din of the crowd.

"Security firms, private muscle, they do each other favors," said Batter. "Cottle's guy smuggles in a briefcase for Stanley, no questions asked, and someday, Stanley runs a play for Cottle."

"Does Cottle know that you have the Constitution?" asked Evangeline.

"I called him and told him this morning."

"Then you better get up and show it," said Batter. "But keep your eye on it. You just found out that some guys are only in it for the money."

Peter grabbed Evangeline by the elbow and said, "We go in by the VIP door. Smaller crowd. Less security."

"Give me Shiny's telephone," said Batter. "Keep in touch. I'll try to find Walter Stanley for you."

It took Peter five minutes to get past the jam of people around the will-call window. He recognized newscasters, writers, Harvard professors famous for their love of baseball: a who's who of Boston bigwigs, all in line for their tickets, then in line to get up the stairs that led to the luxury boxes and the big pre-game spread in the Red Sox pavilion.

As he worked his way through the crowd, people angled themselves so that he couldn't get by, no matter how many "'scuse me's" he gave them. Bostonians held places in line they way they drove. Passive aggressive. *I'm not going to look at you, but I'm going to screw you.* So he pushed Evangeline ahead of him, and she was so scrofulous after three days in the woods that people made room just so they didn't catch anything.

"Nice work, babe."

"I need a shower."

"After rubbing past you, so do they."

He slid along the hall, then up the stairs that led to the club areas. Then up another ramp on the outside of the ballpark, then they were running along the promenade past the corporate boxes, with the names of the "sponsors" on the doors.

They were stopped twice by polite young men in windbreakers, team "ambassadors," game security. One of them wanted a look inside the map case and seemed puzzled that there was nothing there but paper.

Two security guys—older, bigger, more professional—stood outside the door with the Bishop Media logo. Another flash of the tickets and they were in.

It was 8:05.

It took a moment for their eyes to adjust. Bright television lights were playing on three people over by the sofas, Charles Bishop, Harry Hawkins, and Harriet Holden, who had moved inside for the serious part of the interview. Josh Sutherland was standing just out of camera range on one side and Kelly Cutter, Kate Morgan, and Sarah Wyeth were on the other side. Marlon Secourt and his wife, the judge, and Tommy Farrell were already outside, watching the Dodger introductions.

No other World Series broadcast in history had skipped player introductions, but Charles Bishop owned the network. This announcement, he had already told his director, was more important than watching third-string catchers line up on the baselines to applaud for each other.

Evangeline looked at the blonde with the big jaw and said, "Kelly Cutter?"

Kelly looked her up and down, then offered her hand.

Evangeline took it. "Does lightning strike now?"

"Either that or the earth moves," said Kate.

Charles Bishop saw Fallon, saw the map case, and stuck out his hand. "And now, ladies, and gentlemen, the moment we've been waiting for. Come in here, Mr. Fallon."

But Peter's eyes had been drawn to something else. Over by the plate glass window, Don Cottle had trained binoculars toward the right field grandstand.

WALTER STANLEY PULLED the Red Sox hat low and pushed through the crowd on roof promenade. He was heading for the Sports Pavilion, a big open-air party barn which had been plunked on the right field roof in a recent renovation. It had turned one of the worst spots in the ballpark into one of the popular. The word Budweiser, written against the night sky in giant neon letters, sat on the flat pavilion roof and cast a red glow over the whole scene. A giant bar was crowded with fans ordering—what else?—Budweiser, the only brew on tap.

Walter Stanley had planned every move. He had gotten in dressed as part of the concession crew. He had ditched the uniform in the men's room. Then he had made the pickup in the grandstand from one of Cottle's men. Now watching for security as he went, he worked his way to the rear of the pavilion building. There was a little walkway behind it, in semidarkness. A few fans were leaning against the railing, looking off toward the Back Bay.

He went past them, made sure they weren't looking, and flipped the briefcase up onto the roof. Then, in three quick moves, he lifted himself to the railing, to the sill of the window on the back of the pavilion, to the lintel above the window, up ten feet onto the flat roof.

He lay on his belly a moment, let his eyes adjust to the red neon of the beer sign. Then, keeping low, he opened the briefcase. The sniper's rifle was in three pieces. He pulled out the scope and pointed it across the field, toward the corporate box where the bright television lights were burning.

He could see Don Cottle looking back at him with binoculars.

"Mr. Fallon," Bishop was saying. "Come and show America a national treasure."

Peter shoved the Constitution into Evangeline's hands. "Give me thirty seconds."

"My hair's a mess. I look like shit."

"You look beautiful." He pushed her into camera range.

"Miss Carrington," said Bishop, a bit confused. "Ladies and gentlemen, one of America's great document hunters, Evangeline Carrington. And you are carrying a map case that contains . . . what?"

Evangeline gave the case to Bishop and told him to hold it while she slipped out one of the sheets.

"My God," said Bishop as the paper appeared.

"What's this?" asked Harry Hawkins, who seemed to have lost his job to Bishop.

"This," said Evangeline, "is a first draft of the United States Constitution. The document that holds us together and keeps us arguing, too."

Peter considered trying to get out to right field himself. But he decided he could have more impact right there. So he called Shiny's cell.

"Yeah?" said Batter.

"If he's out there, he's on top of the Sports Pavilion on the right field roof. My bet is that he's right under the giant Budweiser sign."

Peter saw Cottle looking at him, so he punched speed dial, and the voice on the other end of the line answered. "Hause."

"It's Fallon, where are you?"

"Behind third base. Where are you?"

"With Bishop. Get your people to the top of the right field Sports Pavilion."

"Why?"

"Gun."

Now Cottle was coming toward Fallon, so Peter clicked off and stepped in front of the camera, which stopped Cottle in his tracks.

Bishop announced, "And here, ladies and gentlemen, is Miss Carrington's partner, Peter Fallon. Together, they found this remarkable document, which shows so much about the thinking of the men who invented America."

"Mr. Fallon," said Harriet Holden. "It would be interesting to know what the Framers thought about the right to keep and bear arms."

Evangeline heard Kelly whisper to Kate. "Do these people have any idea of how many ratings points they're killing?"

Outside, the crowd roared as the first of the Red Sox were introduced.

"What it says," Peter began, "is what it said two hundred years ago." He held the sheet in front of the camera. "It shows the handwriting of the New England delegates, who set down their thoughts on a bill of rights."

"Amazing," said Harriet Holden.

"And what does it say about the Second Amendment?" asked Bishop.

Peter had told them all what they wanted to hear: that the draft favored them. He had been lying. But he didn't care. He was trying to save the Constitution. Once it was on television and the world had seen it, the truth of it was safe.

He pointed to the document. "Elbridge Gerry tells us, 'The right to keep and bear arms shall not be infringed.' Period. Rufus King offers a statement open to endless interpretation: 'The right to keep and bear arms must be discussed and defined.'"

Charles Bishop looked over Fallon's shoulder.

Harriet Holden did what politicians always did, she reflexively started to talk. "Well, I think—"

Peter Fallon said, "*I* think that the men who set their thoughts down here were men who cared about America. Some of them believed in a strong central government, some of them believed that government governs best which governs least, but all of them believed in the ability of thinking Americans to get up in the morning and resolve their differences and solve their problems. And we've lost that in this country. There are people in this room who've lost it. People on camera who've lost it." Peter glanced to his left, at Harriet.

Outside, a tremendous roar rose from the crowd as the name David Ortiz echoed across the field and the big slugger lumbered to the first base line.

Peter went on, "The Framers created a means of changing this document because they understood that the world would change. But they didn't want to make it easy. So, it's up to you, you baseball fans wondering when we'll stop yapping and get on with the game. Pick up your newspapers, and read them, and think about what you read, and don't always believe what you hear, just because it's what you *want* to hear. And don't just listen to what you want to hear because you hear it from somebody who shouts it loud or makes you laugh. This document deserves more respect than that. It *demands* more. Don't believe the Harriet Holdens who vote straight Democratic, anymore than you believe the Kelly Cutters, who befoul the air waves with rightist rhetoric every day."

Evangeline heard Kelly say, "After all I've done for you."

There was another roar from the crowd. The introductions were finished.

So was Peter. "The theme, on the night when we gather in the oldest ballpark in America, to celebrate America's game and national unity, is that we're all American. And—"

"*Oh say can you see . . .*" Down on the field, Stephen Tyler sang the first line.

"And with that, ladies, and gentlemen, we should go out to our seats," said Charles Bishop.

"And we're clear," said the cameraman.

The television lights went out.

Charles Bishop made a broad wave. "Come on, everybody. We don't want to miss this."

Peter Fallon said, "Maybe we should watch from inside."

But Don Cottle was herding everyone out to the seats overlooking the field, and Josh Sutherland was already down at the railing, giving directions to the cameraman on how to frame the congresswoman.

"*What so proudly we hailed at the twilight's last gleaming . . .*"

Peter grabbed Evangeline and held her back.

Kelly said, "I may have been wrong. It may not have been Cottle's guy.

with the briefcase. Let's go out and hear Stephen Tyler. I love Aerosmith."

Cottle came over and offered a smile that was supposed to look comforting. "Relax. The FBI is all over the place. I've been watching them through my binocs."

Then he reached for the sheet of the Constitution in Peter's hands. "I believe Mr. Bishop and you had an agreement."

"No way," said Peter. "You aren't cutting out Harriet Holden and the judge and the boys from the Old Curiosity Book Shop. And Tommy Farrell out there, he might lay claim, too."

Don Cottle's face looked as if it might spontaneously combust. But then, as if gripped by a fit of good sense, he handed the sheet back to Peter, then gave him the map case. "We'll discuss ownership later."

As this was going on, Sutherland was arranging people in the two banks of seats. When Peter turned back from Cottle, Evangeline was already in her seat outside, right behind Harriet Holden. So Peter had no choice but to go out there.

"Whose broad stripes and bright stars, through the perilous fight . . ."

The giant lights turned the cool October night into uber-day, and the colors were more brilliant beneath those lights than they were at high noon, a swirl of multitoned greens on the grass and the walls, of the reds, whites, and blues of the bunting and the uniforms and the stands where everyone wore Red Sox colors.

And that rock star's voice was stirring it all: *"O'er the ramparts we watched . . ."*

Harriet Holden was right where she was supposed to be, next to the camera. But how did Kelly Cutter end up beside her, and Marlon Secourt beside Kelly, and Tommy Farrell beside Secourt?

Secourt caught Peter's eye and raised his mug of beer. "Fine speech."

Not such a bad guy after all, thought Peter.

Then Tommy Farrell made a clenched fist in Peter's direction.

And Bishop leaned around Evangeline and whispered to Peter, "You'll pay for that fuckin' stunt, reading that Elbridge Gerry stuff out loud."

Judge Trask shook his head and told Bishop to behave, then gave Peter a wink.

". . . were so gallantly streaming."

Peter sensed Cottle behind him, alert to whatever might happen next. If Cottle was out here, maybe nothing was going to happen. Maybe it was all circumstantial fear.

Then Peter looked toward the roof of the Sports Pavilion, some five hundred feet away.

"Oh, say, does that star-spangled banner yet wave . . ."

And here came Stephen Tyler's big moment . . . *"O'er the land of the freeeeeeeee . . ."*

The fans began to cheer Tyler toward one of those screaming high notes.

On the pavilion roof, Walter Stanley lay on his stomach and pressed his eye to the telescopic sight.

". . . and the home of the—"

The ovation began to rise, but like a beast emerging from a sea of sound, something new rose beneath it and grew so suddenly and powerfully that the ovation was drowned out and Stephen Tyler's high note disappeared.

It came from over the left field wall, a distant rumble that in an instant turned into a screaming roar.

The flyover!

Three F-18s came rocketing low, so low that you could see the markings on their undersides, so loud that the plate glass in the windows of the luxury boxes rattled.

Peter felt the hair rise on the back of his neck. Every sense was heightened, then overwhelmed.

He looked up. Evangeline looked up. Everyone in Fenway looked up.

Except for one. Walter Stanley picked his target.

The planes streaked over.

As Peter turned to Evangeline to say something, Marlon Secourt's head exploded.

Blood and brain matter sprayed into the air.

Peter pushed Evangeline to the deck. In front of them, Kelly threw herself onto Harriet Holden. At the same moment, a bullet shattered the seat back behind Harriet Holden and broke Peter Fallon's shinbone.

He landed on his side and screamed at Evangeline, "Stay down."

On the roof of the Pavilion, Walter Stanley swept the scope across the seats. He had gotten Secourt. That was part of his contract. But he had also been hired by the other side, to kill the congresswoman. The second shot had been for her. The third? For Fallon. Could he get a third?

Then his cell phone rang. Cell phone? Who was calling him now?

In the box, Sarah Wyeth, covered in Secourt's blood, was recoiling and screaming, while Mrs. Secourt was wailing, "Oh God, Oh Lord, Oh no."

And Don Cottle was jumping into action. Not to throw his body over Bishop, but to snatch the map case from Peter Fallon. Then he ran.

Evangeline grabbed his leg, but Cottle kicked her away.

Peter opened his cell phone and called his brother. "Tall guy, crew cut, he's coming out at 4 Yawkey Way. He has the map case under his arm. Stop him."

There was no more gunfire.

Walter Stanley could see people in the surrounding boxes, pointing in his direction. Besides, he knew the FBI was in the house. And someone else was coming, too. Someone who had just called him on the telephone.

He left the weapon. *Always leave the weapon.* He scuttled between the "e" and the "r" in the giant Budweiser sign. He got to the back of the pavilion. He used the mullions of the window as footholds, dropped quickly into the space behind the building.

He had a rope right there. Tied to the railing. It dropped straight down to the street. He unfurled it and tugged at his gloves.

But suddenly, there was a big guy with a scar coming straight at him.

The fans on the right field roof had no idea what had just happened on the far side of the park. But now they were witnessing something they would never forget. And it wasn't baseball.

Jack Batter and Walter Stanley burst from behind the pavilion and went at each other, right there amidst the tables on the right field roof. Both were professionals trained in hand-to-hand combat, but Stanley was younger, faster, more lethal. He drove a hand under Jack Batter's chin, lifted him, slammed him against the railing that ran around the roof, grabbed him by the crotch with the other hand and threw him off. Just like that.

A terrified college kid in a SECURITY Windbreaker was the first one to react. He shouted into his walkie-talkie "Backup. Backup. Stay right there, sir. You—"

Walter Stanley swung a leg over the railing, wrapped his hands around the rope, and stepped off just as the first FBI man made it through the crowd.

Down in the street, people were looking at the blood leaking out of Jack Batter's head. Then they saw a man drop out of the sky. But Walter Stanley did not look at them. He calmly crossed the street, started the motorcycle he had parked at a meter on Van Ness Street, and sped off around the back of the bleachers.

At about the same time, Don Cottle came out the door at 4 Yawkey Way.

Danny and Antoine were waiting on either side. They tripped him.

"Hey!" shouted a policeman, and he hurried toward them.

At moment later, a motorcycle roared around the corner and stopped right in front of the ticket office.

Don Cottle shook Danny off and threw him into the policeman. He elbowed Antoine in the belly, and ran for the motorcycle.

A mounted officer swung his horse toward the motorcycle.

Cottle jumped onto the seat behind Stanley, who drove straight at the horses's legs. The horse screamed and reared above the crowd still streaming into the park.

The motorcycle shot down Brookline Avenue, up onto the sidewalk in front of the Landmark Center. Sirens were already chasing them. But Stanley had a plan. He dropped down into the dark, tree-lined park called the Riverway. He ran the bike into the Muddy River. Then he and Cottle crossed a little footbridge to the Longwood trolley stop, where they had left another car in the parking lot. They got in and headed for Route 9.

IN THE BOX, Peter Fallon was trying not to give in to the pain of the gunshot.

Sara Wyeth was still screaming. Mrs. Secourt had gone silent.

And Kelly Cutter was lifting herself off Harriet Holden.

"Thank you," said Harriet Holden.

"I'll save your life, but don't expect me to vote for you."

THIRTY

SARA WYETH BROKE under FBI questioning about an hour after the first game of the World Series had been cancelled.

"They had a plan," said Sara.

"Who?" demanded George Hause. "Who had a plan?"

"Josh Sutherland. He came to Don Cottle and asked him to engineer an event so dramatic that it would put the danger of gun violence in every living room. Cottle told me later that he understood what Sutherland was getting at and asked, 'So who do you want to shoot?' And Sutherland said, 'Harriet Holden.'"

"Cottle agreed to plan that?" asked Agent Hause.

"For a price. Sutherland said that the congresswoman had a big campaign chest, and she'd never tap it because this repeal amendment had brought an end to her national ambitions. A quick wire transfer into a numbered Swiss bank account. No one would ever know. Cottle could live large. And so could I."

"You were lovers?" asked Hause.

"You don't think I was getting it from that old man, do you?"

MOST OF THE story was in the papers the next day, after George Hause went before the cameras.

Peter Fallon watched it from a bed in Brigham and Women's Hospital. His leg was in a soft cast. He was hooked to IVs. He was doped with Demerol. He had a broken nose where Mercer had hit him. He had lacerations around his neck where Shiny had tried to strangle him. And there was no way around it. Gunshots *hurt*.

He lay there and watched, and watched himself, too, because his impromptu speech in front of the TV cameras was now being called a classic by people on both sides of the eternal national debate.

When Evangeline came in, he was pointing the remote at the television and spinning the dial to see how many times he could see his face.

"Good morning, television star."

"This is fun when you're stoned."

She kissed him on the forehead.

"I won't break," he said. "Kiss me again."

And she kissed him like she meant it. Then she pulled up a chair and sat beside him. "Well, we lived through it."

"I told you we would."

A picture of Josh Sutherland, under arrest, flashed on the screen.

"The ultimate ideologue," said Peter, "or the ultimate operator. One sees no gray, the other has no conscience."

"Better than a hired gun," said Evangeline. "Stanley or Cottle . . . I guess it's easier to admire ideologues like Kelly. Or Charles Bishop. At least they stand for something."

"Jack Batter, too. He stood for something in the end."

Now the pictures of Marlon Secourt were playing on the screen, and Clinton Jarvis was speaking on behalf of the Morning in America Foundation.

Matt Lauer was interviewing him. "Do you have any idea why the same assassin who was aiming for one of the most liberal congresswomen in America would also shoot the founder of a conservative political action committee like Marlon Secourt?"

Jarvis said, "I don't know. Bad aim?"

"That's hardly an answer," said Lauer.

"I'm not trying to be funny. I don't understand it myself."

"He knows the answer," said Peter. "He must realize by now that his 'security' man was eliminating everyone who knew the story of his draft, or was close to finding the real one."

"You mean, like us?" she asked.

"If there had been a third shot, it was aimed at me. I'd read the original."

"Why didn't he kill us when he had the chance?"

"In Newport? When he flattened our tires? When he took you for a ride? I think he was trying to gauge what we knew. Maybe he didn't because he liked your ass." Peter gave her a silly grin. "I can say that because I'm on Demerol."

"I told him I liked his photographs. I said I'd send a few to my publisher if he was interested. . . . Funny, but he had a certain charm about him."

"Yeah," said Peter. "So did Ted Bundy."

"Do you think we have to worry about him?"

"FBI doesn't. They expect that he's split with Cottle for parts unknown."

"Are you going to blow Jarvis's cover?"

"I'm going to tell the world that John Langdon was adamant about a 'separation of church and state' clause in his notes. Even if we never recover the first draft, people will believe that I know what I'm talking about."

"After that speech, they'll want you to run for Congress."

"No thanks."

Now Harriet Holden was in front of the cameras in Washington. "Today, we begin our hearings, as scheduled. I have no intention of allowing the actions of a few thugs to keep me from America's work, and I think that last night we all saw what firearms can do."

"You go, girl," said Evangeline.

"Yeah," said Peter. "Go and read the Constitution."

"My bet," said Evangeline. "The repeal is ratified. She's earned her stripes. The public will get behind her."

Peter put out his hand. "I bet that the repeal doesn't make it out of committee."

"How much?" she asked.

"How about . . . if I win, you marry me. If you win, I marry you."

Evangeline brought her face close to his ear and whispered. "You know, we tried living together."

"So let's try it again. The righties are always bragging about family values. How about showin' them a few?"

"That better not be the Demerol talking."

He insisted it wasn't, but it put him to sleep when the nurse delivered another shot around ten o'clock. So Evangeline slipped out. She had an article to write.

At lunch time, Orson, Bernice, Danny, and Antoine visited.

Danny told him that he did a fine job on television.

"Yes," said Orson, "but he looks terrible in red turtlenecks."

Antoine said that he had to work on his hand-to-hand skills if they were going to get into any more action like that, because Don Cottle was tough.

Bernice said, "I wish you'd called on me, boss. You could have used my Beretta. You might still need it if that assassin guy comes back."

"He blew his cover last night," said Peter. "It was his last move."

"Yeah," said Danny. "He probably killed Cottle, or Cottle killed him."

THAT WAS NOT TRUE.

By morning, Stanley and Cottle had driven to Cleveland, where they bought two round-trip tickets for Vancouver, using false IDs.

Two days later, they would sell the priceless document for ten million dollars to an oil-rich collector in Indonesia.

Don Cottle would never be heard from again, though several wire transfers would be made from a numbered Swiss bank account over the next few years.

Walter Stanley's name would disppear. But those who needed his services would know how to get in touch with him. And his services were valued because he always completed a job, except for one. His contract with Clinton Jarvis had been to eliminate everyone who might bring the Jarvis forgery into question. So he had started with the forger. Then he had worked his way along the chain. The last two threats had been Marlon Secourt himself, who talked too much because he drank too much, and Peter Fallon.

FALLON'S FRIENDS STAYED for an hour, and his son called from school at Berkely, too.

Twice Danny commented on the good care. "That doctor comes by and checks your chart every twenty minutes or so."

"Yeah," said Peter. "Doctors, nurses. It's constant. Didn't get any sleep last night. Once the swelling goes down, they'll put a rod in my leg. Then I'll be back to work."

His "family" left when Agents Hause and Luzier came to take his statement, stayed briefly, and left.

Then he needed another Demerol shot, which was followed by that pleasant floating feeling, then a burning in his eyes, then he felt like he was tipping back, then he forgot all the pain and, yes, took a little nap.

He didn't notice when the doctor came back to check the chart on the door again. This time, the doctor came into the room.

Peter woke when he felt a hand take his arm, a finger tap on the vein, then tap again. "Wha . . . I just got my shot."

"Relax. I'm the doctor."

"Doctor Who?"

"Yes."

"Doctor Who?" Peter laughed. He felt drunk. "Who's on first?"

There was a gentle tap on the door.

"Wait just a moment," said the doctor.

"Yeah," slurred Peter. "I need another shot."

The doctor brought the syringe toward his arm.

"Hey," said Peter. "That thing's huge. You givin' me a shot or bastin' me?"

"Lie still."

Then Peter pulled his arm away. "Where's my alcohol rub? You're sub-bose to rub my skin with alcohol. Hey . . . do I know you? Doctor Who? Who's on first? What's on second?"

"No."

"I don't give a damn's on third." Peter squinted through those burning eyes. The doctor was small, compact, like a coiled spring, short gray crew cut. Familiar . . . but a mustache. Peter said, "Doctor Who? Doctor Jarvis?"

He tried to shout it, but Jarvis put a hand over his mouth. Then the big syringe was coming straight at him . . . straight for his neck. . . .

He flailed with his left hand, but he was weak, and drugged. He pounded the side of Jarvis's face and screamed against Jarvis's hand and didn't think anybody heard him.

He pushed the syringe away, and Jarvis jammed his knee into Fallon's chest.

Then the door banged open.

And a flower vase—filled with flowers—flew across the room, hitting Jarvis off the side of the head.

This was followed by two hurtling bodies.

Kelly Cutter and Kate Morgan vaulted into the room.

One hit him high, one hit him low, and both of them landed on Peter's leg.

He screamed.

Jarvis slammed Kelly against the wall and flung Kate toward the window.

Kate cried, "The buzzer! Peter, press the buzzer!"

Peter fumbled drunkenly in the bedclothes.

Kelly called for help.

And help was coming—an orderly first, followed by a nurse, then another orderly.

As they poured into the room, knees flew, and orderlies, too. Jarvis was fighting his way out, until Kate Morgan came up with Peter's bedpan and slammed him on the back of the head.

Before he came to, they had strapped him to a gurney.

"Clinton D. Jarvis," said Kelly, "might just turn me into an independent."

"That'll be the day." Kate picked up the syringe, squirted a little into a cup, smelled. "Drāno."

"Use it to clear the pipes," said Peter, who was already going loopy after another shot. "Go to the Republican National Committee and the DNC and dump it down all the drains."

THE RED SOX won the Series.

And the repeal amendment died in committee.

So Peter won his bet.

On a sleeting Saturday in early December, he and Evangeline spent the afternoon in his condo, before a fire, and made wedding plans.

Marriage in Boston . . . honeymoon . . . where?

"Some place in the States," said Peter.

"Why?"

"Because we're good Americans. We've listened to all the opinions on both sides. And we've done our best to find the truth. That makes us good Americans."

"Good Americans . . . like all those Pikes back there?"

"Most of them," said Peter. "A family of dreamers. Maybe even magnificent dreamers. Good Americans, too, like us."

"But from now on, these good Americans"—she pointed to him and then to herself—"don't go looking for trouble. No more dangerous stuff."

"From now on, we follow the Will Pike recipe," said Peter. "We might be dreamers, but we have to be doers, too. So we get up in the morning, we go to work, and we solve our problems."

Later, while Evangeline read *Entertainment Weekly* about the movies they would go to once Peter could walk out in a crowd, he checked his e-mails.

Something had arrived from a friend in Paris. And before long, he was reading snippets aloud. . . . "You see, there is a fabulously illuminated thirteenth-century manuscript. . . ." He scanned ahead to the words jumping out: "French Revolution . . . the monastery at Mont St. Michel . . . the American invasion of Normandy and the ferocious 1944 battle of St. Lô . . . a book that may hold the key to . . . What?"

"Peter," she said, "I don't like that look in your eye."

"How about a honeymoon in France?"